The Wild Cards Universe

The Original Triad
Wild Cards
Aces High
Joker's Wild

The Puppetman Quartet
Aces Abroad
Down and Dirty
Ace in the Hole
Dead Man's Hand

The Rox Triad
One-Eyed Jacks
Jokertown Shuffle
Dealer's Choice
Double Solitaire
Turn of the Cards

The Card Shark Triad
Card Sharks
Marked Cards
Showdown
(formerly *Black Trump*)
Deuces Down
Death Draws Five

The Committee Triad
Inside Straight
Busted Flush
Suicide Kings

The Mean Streets Triad
Fort Freak
Lowball
High Stakes

The American Triad
Mississippi Roll
Low Chicago
Texas Hold'em

The British Arc
Knaves Over Queens
Three Kings
Full House
Joker Moon
Pairing Up
Sleeper Straddle

The Original Graphic Novels
Now and Then
Sins of the Father

Showdown

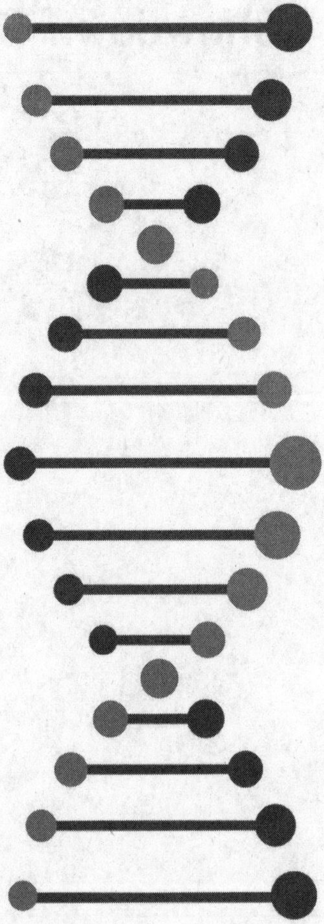

GEORGE R. R. MARTIN

Presents

Wild Cards: Showdown

A Wild Cards Mosaic Novel

Previously published as *Black Trump*

EDITED BY GEORGE R. R. MARTIN

Assisted by Melinda M. Snodgrass

and written by

Stephen Leigh	John J. Miller
George R. R. Martin	Sage Walker
Victor Milan	

Random House Worlds

New York

Published in the United States by Random House Worlds,
an imprint of Random House,
a division of Penguin Random House LLC, New York.

RANDOM HOUSE is a registered trademark, and
RANDOM HOUSE WORLDS and colophon
are trademarks of Penguin Random House LLC.

Originally published as *Black Trump* by Baen Books,
Wake Forest, NC, in 1995.

ISBN 978-0-593-35793-4
Ebook ISBN 978-0-593-35794-1

Printed in the United States of America on acid-free paper

randomhousebooks.com

1st Printing

Book design by Virginia Norey
Helix art: Graficriver/stock.adobe.com

to Dr. Michael Engelberg
with the hopes that it will be coming soon
to a theater near us all

Wild Cards

The virus was created on TAKIS, hundreds of light-years from Earth. The ruling mentats of the great Takisian Houses were looking for a way to enhance their formidable psionic abilities, and augment them with physical powers. The retrovirus they devised showed enough promise that the psi lords decided to field test it on Earth, whose inhabitants were genetically identical to Takisians.

Prince Tisianne of House Ilkazam opposed the experiment and raced to Earth in his own living starship to stop it. The alien ships fought high above the atmosphere. The ship carrying the virus was torn apart, the virus itself lost. Prince Tisianne landed his own damaged ship at White Sands, where his talk of tachyon drives prompted the military to dub him **DR. TACHYON**.

Across the continent, the virus fell into the hands of **DR. TOD,** a crime boss and war criminal, who resolved to use it to extort wealth and power from the cities of America. He lashed five blimps together and set out for New York City. President Harry S Truman reached out to Robert Tomlin, **JETBOY,** the teenaged fighter ace of World War II, to stop him. Flying his experimental jet, the JB-1, Jetboy reached Tod's blimps and crashed into the gondola. The young hero and his old foe met for the last time as the bomb containing the virus fell to Earth. *"Die, Jetboy, die,"* Tod shouted as he shot Tomlin again and again. "I can't die yet, I haven't seen *The Jolson Story*," Jetboy replied, as the bomb exploded.

Thousands of microscopic spores rained down upon Manhattan. Thousands more were dispersed into the atmosphere and swept up by the jet stream, to spread all over the Earth. But New York City got the worst of it.

It was **September 15, 1946**. The first Wild Card Day.

Ten thousand died that first day in Manhattan alone. Thousands more were transformed, their DNA rewritten in terrible and unpredictable ways. Every case was unique. No two victims were affected in the same way. For that reason, the press dubbed xenovirus *Takis-A* (its scientific name) the ***wild card.***

Ninety percent of those infected died, unable to withstand the violent bodily changes the virus unleashed upon them. Those victims were said to have drawn the ***black queen.***

Of those who survived, nine of every ten were twisted and mutated in ways great and small. They were called *jokers* (or *jacks, knaves,* or *joker-aces* if they also gained powers). Shunned, outcast, and feared, they began to gather in along the Bowery, in a neighborhood that soon became known as **Jokertown**.

Only one in a hundred of those infected emerged with superhuman powers: telepathy, telekinesis, enhanced strength, superspeed, invulnerability, flight, and a thousand other strange and wondrous abilities. These were the *aces,* the celebrities of the dawning new age. Unlike the heroes of the comic book, very few of them chose to don spandex costumes and fight crime, but they would soon begin to rewrite history all the same.

These are their stories.

Showdown

Eight

The smell of blood twisted around the muezzin's ululating predawn call to the faithful. A red, slick, looping skein snaked through the night and intertwined with the yodeled vowels; a dream—not a dream. In the silence that followed, Zoe opened her eyes and lay still as Needles walked by her. Inches from her cot, his clawed hand swung past her face. His hand carried the musky stink of fresh blood.

Needles opened the door to the tiny bathroom and slipped inside. Metered water gurgled in the sink. Moonlight marked out the narrow rectangle of the archer's window near the door and outlined the low mounds of sleepers in the high-ceilinged room.

Angelfish, Owl, and Jellyhead lay on their benches on the far wall. They looked so peaceful, her "Escorts," New York street kids who could at least sleep under a roof now, under Zoe's fragile protection. Anne, Zoe's mother, was quiet on her cot. Jan, the littlest of the kids, slept with her feet sticking out from beneath the sheet that she had, as usual, pulled over her head like a tent.

Croyd slept in the alcove, screened off from the rest of the room by a curtain. Croyd had been asleep for weeks. He'd signed on as a boarder, vanished, and then staggered through the door three weeks ago, red-eyed and angry. Needles had listened to Croyd rant for hours until the Sleeper just stopped in midsentence and went limp. Zoe had helped carry him to the alcove and shove him into the narrow bed. He didn't seem to be changing much, not yet, anyway.

In the bathroom, the water kept on running.

Needles patrolled with the Twisted Fists. He was a child. The Fists had sent him home with blood on his hands. Anger made Zoe want to shout out obscenities to the rooftops; the need for silence made her tremble. She jerked the thin cotton sheet from her cot, wrapped it around her, and tiptoed across the room, her bare feet welcoming the feel of smooth, cool concrete.

She leaned close to the bathroom door and hissed.

The light inside clicked off and Needles opened the door. Zoe slipped inside with him. Shower stall, commode, sink, the little closet was small enough that you could brush your teeth while sitting on the pot.

Needles turned off the tap and dried his hands, working a thin terry rag over each claw, polishing them in the yellow glow of the night-light plugged into the single outlet over the sink.

"What happened?" Zoe whispered.

"It's nothing," Needles said. He had been in a major growth spurt since they had reached Jerusalem. He was as tall as Zoe, and he shaved, every single day.

Zoe reached out and touched his cheek. "You missed a spot."

Needles jerked his face away and looked in the mirror. He scrubbed at the sticky black mark with the damp cloth in his hand. "Shit," he whispered. "Oh, shit. Zoe, it's . . ."

"Did you kill someone?" Zoe asked.

Needles sucked a deep breath between his baleen teeth and turned his head away.

"Come outside. We'll talk about it." Zoe held out her hands for the towel. Needles passed it over and slipped out of the room. Zoe washed her hands, rinsed out the cloth, and watched the rusty water drain away, more blood to enrich the fertile sewers of the City of Peace.

Whose blood? Had Needles killed a nat? Had the Fists put the boy through some impossible initiation ceremony? Or had he just helped with the cleanup?

Whose blood? Nat, joker, one of Needles's new friends?

In the Divided City, so many died. The Divided City, Jerusalem, partitioned in those strange days of Britain's withdrawal from Palestine, a war zone for more than fifty years, a walled town swelled to bursting with refugees and warriors. The boundaries of its ghettos were forever in flux. The Muslims gained a few streets from the Christians, who crowded against the Jewish Quarter, and then someone would cut off a water supply or a tourist route in retaliation and the boundaries would shift back again.

The Joker Quarter stayed peaceful. Women and children walked unescorted, shopkeepers hawked their wares under awnings that shaded the narrow streets, and a joker could profess any religion at all, or none.

Weird but true, this was a safer place than New York; jokers and joker children went to school without getting mugged.

The Escorts *liked* school. They came home babbling about how way cool it all was. Arabic and Hebrew and the Koran and the Talmud. But they learned other things, too, crowd management, that was def. First aid was really to hurl, but it feels good to know what to do, right? Jellyhead could break down an Uzi at FTL speeds, they said, and nobody could *touch*

Needles on banking transactions. A school for literate terrorists could only be a Fists setup. Zoe had tried not to think about it.

She didn't question peace for her kids, and good schooling, even though each of the Escorts had some job to do in the quarter, every building had its designated guards—

The Twisted Fists killed five for one. Always. If a joker died, five nats died. If the Fists knew who had killed, they killed the killer and four compatriots. If they didn't know, they took their best guess.

It was horrid justice. It was no justice. It had to be done—maybe. But not by the Escorts, damn it. The Fists by God shouldn't be sending *children* to do their killings. She'd hidden from the truth too long, blocked away the ugly reality of what was going on with the kids because she needed a semblance of normality, a salaried job, help for Anne, a little time to forget those last horrid days in New York, a dose of reality.

Right. Reality was the Sleeper in his alcove, locked in a process of transformation that might mean he'd wake up as a walking nightmare. Reality was five adolescents searching for role models and finding them in trained killers. Reality sucked.

The air in the tiny bathroom was stifling. Zoe turned the tap back on and filled her cupped hand with tepid water. She splashed it on the back of her sweaty neck, slipped out into the room, and eased the bathroom door closed behind her. Needles was awake, his eyes wide and watchful. He looked dazed and numb. He looked hollow, as if something had been drained from him, and she wondered how she had looked in those first hours after she had willed a mannequin to kill for her. But she hadn't had to come home and wash blood from her hands. Poor Needles.

Zoe sat on the edge of her cot and pulled jeans and a maroon silk crop-top from the stack of clothes in the corner. In this crowded space, she had learned the art of dressing under a sheet. Underwire bra, scoop-necked blouse that would show cleavage, one button left undone under the length of blue silk cord that held up her hip-hugger jeans. She shrugged out of the sheet to pull on her sneakers. The clothes would offend the sensibilities of most of the religious groups that crowded Jerusalem's narrow streets, but she was *so* tired of long sleeves and skirts.

Needles stood with his hands in his pockets, rocking back and forth. Fifteen-year-old boys never stopped moving, Zoe had noticed, unless they were deeply asleep.

Zoe grabbed a Little Red Riding cloak of thin cotton gauze, the color of copper, its hood trimmed in thin dangling gold coins. She rolled it into a bundle and tucked it under her arm. Dead bolt, chain lock, and lock, she opened them as quietly as she could. Needles followed her to the tiny landing that led downstairs to the street.

"Zoe?" he whispered.

She felt his fingers, tentative, brush her elbow.

"What happened?"

"I can't talk about it. Orders, Zoe."

"From the Fists?"

"From the Fists, yes. We had a job to do, a retaliation. We did it."

Gods. He was horrified by what he'd done, but he was proud, too.

"You killed someone for revenge? *You?*"

"I had help."

"My God, Needles! Why have they done this to you?"

"This is Jerusalem, Zoe." He lifted his hand as if to grab something from the air. His razor-sharp claws caught the faint light, and he stared at them as if they belonged to someone else.

"This is hell," Zoe said. Enough of this. Refuge or no refuge, this use of "her" kids had to stop.

"It's hell. I'm okay, Zoe. Don't worry about me. I gotta get some sleep, okay?" Needles leaned against the wall and gave a theatrical yawn.

Like hell he would sleep. But Zoe could understand that he didn't want to talk out the night's horrors.

"Go to bed, then. Rest, Needles. You did what you had to do. I'm going somewhere for a while. Lock up after me, would you?"

She could see Needles clench his jaw, could see him gather his defenses to protest. "Let me go with you," Needles said.

"No." She stared down the stairs.

"You're going to the Fists."

Zoe didn't answer.

"You won't find them. Don't get me in trouble, Zoe."

"That's not my plan." So what was her plan? Set up an interview with the Black Dog? Great plan. She ran down the narrow stairs, leaving Needles to fasten the three locks on the door. The task wouldn't keep him from following her, but it might slow him down a little.

"I can't believe you told the goddamn Black Dog about the Trump, Dutton." Fury rouged the skin of Hannah's high cheekbones and penciled fine lines around her eyes. Gregg could nearly see the anger sparking electric blue in her eyes.

Spotlights illuminated a trio of Turtle shells suspended from the gallery ceiling, painting cavernous hollows in Dutton's death's-head face. Back in the darkness, there was the moist gleam of eyes. Gregg sniffed: Dutton smelled like the museum itself—dusty, ancient, a perfume of mold and rust. In the shadows to Gregg's left, there was a rustling of cloth and a soft, polite moan: Oddity, writhing in the pain of their endless transformations.

"We need help," Dutton answered, aggravation riding in his sepulchral tones. "It seems to me that the Twisted Fists are one of the few allies we have."

"They're thugs and murderers. Their idea of a solution is to kill something, five for fucking one. That's asinine and stupid, Charles. I won't have it."

"*You* won't have it?" Dutton snapped. "When were you elected the head of our little cabal, Hannah?"

"I'm not the only one who feels that way. Father Squid—"

"Father Squid was *one* of them for a time."

"And he left them, didn't he? Damn it, we all want Rudo caught and the virus destroyed, but . . ."

"But what, Hannah? You don't think that end justifies *any* means? You don't think that associating with thugs and murderers is worth saving countless joker lives? I'd rather see jokers live than worry about whether I'm associating with the right kind of people."

"Charles," Gregg interrupted, seeing the color deepen in Hannah's face. He tried to speak as soothingly as his high-pitched, whining joker's voice could manage, regretting once more the loss of his old voice and body. *How can you be imposing when you're a four-foot-long yellow caterpillar who sounds like a 33⅓ rpm record played at 45?* "I agree with Hannah. I've had dealings with the Fists; I'm not convinced that bringing them into this is going to help." Gregg glanced at Hannah, who was standing with her hands fisted, glaring at Dutton. "And we have another problem. This press conference you've scheduled for tomorrow afternoon—"

"*My* people"—Dutton accented the possessive heavily, with a significant empty-eyed stare at Hannah. His voice woke sluggish echoes in the dead recesses and far galleries of the

Dime Museum—"have a right to know the danger they're in. It's irresponsible of us not to warn them."

"It's going to cause panic and riots," Hannah insisted, cutting off Gregg's response. He wondered whether she'd even noticed he'd been about to speak. "If you tell them about the Black Trump, if you tell them that the Sharks are going to loose a plague that will only kill those infected by the wild card, then you'll have half the population of Jokertown looking to take some nats down with them. That's a *great* solution, Charles. That way, the jokers just manage to convince the few nats who can help that jokers don't *deserve* help. If getting the Fists involved isn't enough, *that* should just about finish it."

Dutton exhaled: a serpent's hiss. "I take it that you feel we should keep them in the dark so they die quietly."

"That's not what I'm saying . . . *Damn!*" Exasperation made Hannah's last word throaty and ragged. "I just know how important it is to find the vials quickly."

"You're a nat. It won't matter to *you* either way."

"*Damn* it, Dutton, that's not fair—"

"Listen, all of you. The first priority—the *only* priority—is finding the vials. Hannah's right about that." That was the Oddity—John. "Fuck anything else. We heard what Clara van Rensselaer and Dr. Finn have told us: The Sharks will try to cultivate enough of the Trump virus to guarantee a worldwide release. If that happens, we're dead. All of us. Hannah, Gregg, you two have been our spokespersons since we went public with this. What Charles is asking is for you to go into those roles again. As for the Fists, we're going to need all the help we can get to find the vials, and if the Black Dog can help . . ." Oddity shrugged. "Seems like a plan to me."

"A plan, yes," Hannah said. "A smart one, no."

Dutton sniffed. "We can do without the sarcasm."

Hannah turned on the man, hands fisted on hips. "Look,

Charles, I got involved in this involuntarily, but I *am* involved. Totally. Don't tell me that I have to behave nicely because I'm a nat. Don't you *dare* tell me that I don't care enough."

"Hannah—" Gregg began, but Dutton interrupted him, riding over Gregg's weak, thin voice.

"My sources tell me that Barnett's ordered another crackdown," Dutton said. "SCARE aces are involved, the FBI, the Justice Department, anyone who can be enlisted. I don't know what's going to happen, but I suspect that we need to make our moves soon, or we won't be able to move at all."

"We can find Rudo *without* the Fists," Hannah said.

"Considering that the authorities want everyone involved in the kidnapping of Dr. van Renssaeler and Dr. Finn, I doubt that Rudo is even in the country anymore. That's another reason to bring in the Fists. We already know some of the Sharks overseas—" Dutton stopped. "Listen," he said.

Gregg heard it then: muffled shouting from the front of the museum, a few rooms away. *"Break 'em down! C'mon, c'mon, let's GO!"* Then, more clearly, strident and treble through a bullhorn: *"This is Special Agent April Harvest! We have a warrant!"* At the same time, there was a splintering *ka-CHUNK* as something heavy slammed against locked doors.

Quasiman was *there* in that moment, popping into existence in the middle of the gallery with his mouth open and panic in his eyes, words tumbling from his lips wrapped in a spray of spittle. "The clinic," he said breathlessly. "Dr. Finn, the other doctor woman—all under arrest. The parsonage: Father Squid, Troll . . . Got to get—" Quasiman stopped. His right arm had vanished. He looked like a marionette whose strings had just been cut, frozen in mid-speech.

The doors must have held under the battering ram. Faintly, Harvest's voice shouted through the bullhorn: *"Get back. BACK! Let* him *do it . . ."* There was a sustained, crashing thunder of falling brick, punctuated by beams splintering like twigs. Someone shouted in glee in the midst of the clamor, and Gregg recognized the voice with a cold shudder.

"Snotman . . ." he breathed. "Oh, shit."

Loud footsteps sounded in the museum. Flashlights wove mad patterns through the dark galleries. *"Federal agents! Everybody down!"* Harvest's voice shouted again, clearer this time. A dark form filled the door.

"Don't call me Snotman, caterpillar," said someone from the darkness. "Well, look what we got here: the fucking jackpot." The ace sometimes known as Reflector was a handsome, dark-haired man bulging with muscles and fairly glowing with energy. He could take the energy of a blow directed against him, store it, and use it for himself; the people outside had obviously been beating on him to charge up his ace batteries. Gregg remembered the destruction Snotman had caused at the Rox and shuddered. "I never did like you, Battle, but it looks like you got pretty much what you deserve," Snotman said. "Now, who's surrendering quietly and who wants to fight?"

It was night, but the pure white sand still radiated heat from the warm Caribbean day. The breeze was cool and tinged with salt. The stars were a glorious spectacle strewn across a clear, pollution-free sky, but Billy Ray had no time for an astronomy lesson.

The beach was empty but for a clump of gnarled, sunbleached driftwood that sat perched on a hummock of sand like a bizarre terrestrial octopus guarding its territory. Ray came out of the water and crawled to the driftwood. He took off his wet suit and scuba gear and lay on the warm sand for a moment, catching his breath. It had been a long swim in from the government cutter now hidden behind another flyspeck of an island.

Sufficiently rested, Ray dashed across the strip of beach, heading inland. Crossing the pristine beach offended his innate sense of neatness. Leaving footprints behind on sand smoothed clean by the wind and water seemed so messy. Messy—and if the Card Sharks had decent security—dangerous as well.

Ray didn't mind danger, but he disliked sneaking. He was not a sneaking kind of guy. He was more of an in-your-face-right-down-the-gut kind of guy, but sometimes the situation called for sneaking, and this was absolutely one of those situations.

Ray was Shark hunting.

The Card Shark conspiracy had been exposed and broken, though some of the conspirators were still at large. Others were in government custody. Some of them, like Peggy Durand, were singing like the fat lady at the opera. Among other things, Durand had squealed about an island between the Keys and Cuba. It was isolated and inconspicuous, but large enough for a romantic hideaway or a secret headquarters, depending on your exact need. Since it was owned by a dummy corporation that was itself ultimately owned by head Shark Pan Rudo, Ray was inclined to think that it was more of a secret HQ, a sort of Club Med for amoral old farts like Rudo and other Sharks still at large. At least that's what he was here to check on.

The beach quickly gave way to dunes covered with patches of tough, scraggly grass. The dunes dipped and peaked, providing Ray with cover as he made his way to the manor at the heart of the island. He was happy to get off the beach. Because it was night, he'd opted for his black fighting suit, but the pure white sand made for a high degree of contrast with his supposed camouflage. Hunkering down in the dunes made him less of a target, and when he broke into the shrubs and palm trees of the island's interior, he had plenty of shadows to skulk among.

It was a good thing, too, because that's where he ran into the first sign of Shark security: a lone sentry armed with an assault rifle. As Ray watched, the Shark wandered around the shrubbery, stopped, leaned his rifle against a convenient palm tree, and lit a cigarette. After a moment the sweet smell of marijuana wafted to Ray as he crouched in the shadows.

Ray smiled. Sneered, really. "Moron," he said to himself, and he moved. He didn't bother to move quietly.

He caught the sentry in the middle of a long toke. The guard looked up as Ray's shadow engulfed him, more astonishment than fear in his eyes. Ray took him out with a single blow to the jaw. He could have gone for a soft body part, but tonight he felt mean. He wanted the shock of hitting bone to jolt his fist and run tingling up his arm like an electric current. The pain sent an extra surge of adrenaline flowing through Ray's body. As if he needed it.

Ray stood over the unconscious guard, flexing his fingers. It was hard to tell if the sentry was local talent or a Shark import. He was Black. He could have been a local thug. But he was big, well-nourished, and certainly well-armed (*For all the good it did him,* Ray thought as he ground the barrel of the assault rifle into the sand). He even wore a uniform—a khaki paramilitary outfit complete with shiny boots and a fruity-looking maroon-colored beret. Peggy Durand had said that the Sharks had their own security units. Ray's smile fixed and widened. He hoped so.

He considered calling in to the cutter that waited offshore but decided to maintain radio silence. There was no telling how sophisticated Shark security was—though if the bozo snoozing at Ray's feet was any indication, even if they had a state-of-the-art listening post, they'd probably be using it to catch a Peaches game on WTBS.

Ray stopped to put plastic restraints on the sentry's wrists and ankles, stuff the man's beret in his mouth, then wind duct tape over it. He pushed him under some bushes and moved on.

The manor house was a couple of hundred yards away. At first Ray flitted from tree to bush, but he tired of skulking before he'd gotten halfway to his target.

"Screw it," he said aloud. The adrenaline was dancing through his system, and he ached to hit someone, to smash the bastards who wanted to eliminate Ray and the rest of the wild carders from the face of the earth.

Luck was with him—or not, from Ray's point of view. No one saw him as he strode up to the house. He paused for a moment to look around. There was a moving silhouette on the roof, man and rifle held at rest. But the guard was looking the other way, and he never saw Ray as he walked through the back door.

It opened into a dark hallway. Ahead was a closed door with light spilling from the cracks at the floor and ceiling. Ray went to the door and turned the knob, then entered the room.

It was a well-lit, well-appointed kitchen. There was a large electric range, a huge refrigerator, and nice wooden cabinets. A counter ran down the center of the room. Cold cuts, bread, cheese, and condiments were spread over it. One man stood in front of the counter, making a sandwich. Two others sat on stools, eating. Another was perched on the counter near the sink drinking Red Stripe beer from an amber bottle. They all wore the same outfit that the sentry had. Their rifles were piled on the counter among the cold cuts and cheese.

"Who the hell are you?" the man making the sandwich asked, roll in one hand, mustard bottle in the other. He spoke with a Brooklyn accent. He wasn't a local.

Ray shook his head. "Doesn't matter," he said. "But this does: You guys Card Sharks or what?"

"You expect me to answer that?" the other asked incredulously.

Ray smiled happily. "You just did."

The two men sitting at the counter eyed each other. Slowly they started to put down their hoagies and reach for their rifles, and then Ray was among them. He crossed the room before they knew it. He gave one the back of his right hand, the other the edge of his left. He reached across the counter for the third before the first two hit the linoleum. The third waved the mustard bottle at him as Ray dragged him across the rifles and cold cuts. The Shark squeezed the bottle and a stream of brown mustard shot out and splattered the front of Ray's fighting suit. Ray's eyes burned with a sudden cold fury.

"Son of a bitch," he snapped, then headbutted the sentry and left him unconscious among the rolls. The fourth had time to say, "Oh, shit," as Ray turned to him. He swung the beer bottle. Ray blocked it with his left forearm. It shattered, spraying amber slivers of glass. Ray's smile widened.

"Let's talk," he suggested.

Gregg knew it was over. If he had Puppetman again, maybe he could have done something—if nothing else, he could have reached inside Oddity and taken the anger he knew constantly boiled there and turned up the fire until the formidable joker hurled himself at Snotman. Maybe the rest of them could flee in the confusion. But without the old power, in this body . . . Gregg raised himself up and started to lift the tiny hands on his front two limbs in surrender when he caught a glimpse of motion at his side.

Oddity was charging forward like a bull driving toward a matador.

Two of the most powerful forms created by the wild card—joker or ace—collided. Oddity hit like a truck . . . and caromed off, scattering Kevlar-jacketed SWAT-team members like tenpins and crashing into a diorama of the Crystal Palace. Snotman laughed. He hadn't budged an inch. "That felt fucking *wonderful*," he said, and raised his hand toward Oddity, crouching in the center of the gallery.

"Gregg . . ."

A beam of brilliant blue light arced from Snotman, striking Oddity full in the chest. The joker howled with their ruined voice as the bolt of raw energy lifted them and threw them ten feet back like a rag doll. Oddity hit the wall by the archway, crumpling plasterboard, their dented fencing mask flying off. The Turtle shells above Gregg swayed, two of them striking together and ringing like bells. The face underneath the mask—piebald, knobby, a horrible fusion of the three people inside—cried out once and Oddity sagged into a heap on the floor. They tried to stand again, leaning heavily against the broken wall, then sank back.

"*Gregg!*" Gregg couldn't move, even though Hannah called him. He thought for an instant that he could feel Oddity's pain, and it felt . . . *good*. The sensation stunned him, left him rooted to the floor as Snotman chuckled, as Oddity groaned. Gregg could *feel* the shifting of personalities inside Oddity, could sense John—injured and shaken—allowing Evan to take control of their shared body.

Snotman waved back the agents who crowded the gallery as he strode toward Oddity; they seemed happy enough to obey him. Snotman swaggered over, lifting his fist as Oddity raised their hands in weak self-defense. Gregg did nothing, said nothing, felt nothing. The sensation was gone as quickly as it had come. He watched, helpless, feeling acid gnawing at his stomach.

Oddity suddenly kicked upward, striking Snotman square in the groin. Snotman sneered. "You son of a bitch," he said. He looked stronger and more dangerous than ever. Oddity charged again, like a groggy linebacker determined to take down a receiver, but Snotman slapped him aside contemptuously.

Oddity fell, unconscious. Snotman, laughing, lifted a booted foot to smash the tri-featured head below. *"No!"* Hannah shouted, running forward.

Snotman chuckled. "Ahh, you're no challenge at all," he said, and pointed at her.

Hannah screamed in pain as Snotman's lightning sent her tumbling backward. Gregg screamed with her, but another voice sounded louder than Gregg's. *"Hannah!"* The word was a shriek, primal and shrill, and it came from Quasiman.

Snotman grinned. "C'mon, hunchback. Let's see what you can do."

"Quasi, no!" Gregg said. He had scuttled over to Hannah, who was shaking her head groggily. "Hit him and you just make him stronger. We're done here. We've lost. Give it up."

"Snotman hurt Hannah," Quasiman said slowly, without looking at Gregg.

"Don't. Call. Me. SNOTMAN!" The last word was a shriek of fury.

Quasiman hurled himself at Snotman. The ace spread his hands wide, as if in embrace. "Come on, asshole," he said.

Quasiman struck the ace square on the chest. The joker's stubby arms locked around the ace. "Run, Hannah!" he shouted.

And Quasiman vanished, taking Snotman with him.

For a moment, an awed silence reigned. Then Gregg saw the agents gathering themselves, the blond-haired woman who must be Harvest motioning them forward. "Get to the back of the gallery," Gregg hissed at Hannah and Dutton. "Pretend you're surrendering." He skittered to the side, clambering up the wall. He made the short leap to the nearest of the Turtle shells. He concentrated on the delicious smell of the metal, of the way it might taste, and felt his gorge rising. Gregg let it come, let the noxious stuff hurl from his mouth onto the cables holding the shell to the ceiling. He leapt to the next shell and did the same, then to the next. Already he heard behind him the groan of overstressed steel. "Run!" he shouted to Dutton and Hannah. They were standing with hands raised over their heads as the agents entered the room.

Cables *twanged* and separated. The shell tilted, dangled on one cable for an instant, and fell.

The din was incredible, as if all the church bells of New York had fallen at once, and the building shook and swayed. Someone screamed; a gun went off and a ricochet whined from the plate metal of the shell. Another shell fell, striking the first and bouncing dangerously end over end like a giant metal football, smashing exhibits. The shell on which Gregg stood suddenly tilted. Gregg leapt for the wall as it came down. He let himself half-fall, half-run to the rear of the gallery. "Go! Go!" he shouted into the echoes of clangorous metal. Dutton and Hannah ran with him, farther into the depths of the museum.

They could hear Harvest shouting orders, and running steps as the agents moved through the museum. Gregg turned left into the next gallery, Hannah following. "Where's Dutton?" he asked suddenly, standing on his rear two legs.

"I don't know."

Someone appeared in the doorway to their right. Hannah

shoved Gregg and then leapt and rolled as a gunshot cracked, taking off the wax snout of Xavier Desmond, the old "Mayor of Jokertown." They tumbled into the next room, lit dimly by the exit signs over the archways.

Across from the Syrian diorama, Jetboy and Dr. Tod were locked in their final confrontation. "There!" Gregg whispered. He wriggled between Jetboy's feet as Hannah slipped between the wax figures.

Gregg pointed to the door of the gondola, set against the wall of the display. "Hurry!" Gregg said.

"Gregg, this is a dead end."

"Trust me. Just open it!"

Shaking her head, Hannah turned the wheel and pulled; the door hung open a bare inch. Behind, they could hear renewed shouting: "Harvest! Battle's back here!" From somewhere nearby, Dutton's voice rang out, protesting loudly. "I want to see your warrant *and* your ID—"

Hannah braced her foot against the wall and pulled harder. The door hinges gave with a soft groan, and Gregg slithered into musty darkness. Hannah quickly followed him. She pulled the door closed, and all sounds from outside were abruptly cut off. "Gregg?" she whispered.

"I'm here." Gregg found that the darkness was no longer quite solid. He could *see* Hannah—her form shimmered ruddily, the face nearly as skull-like as Dutton's. Another new quirk of his joker body: He might not be able to see very well, but he could see into the infrared. Gregg sniffed; there was a faint scent, a feeble movement of the air, telling him that the gondola room continued farther back. "Dutton always hinted that there were hidden ways out of the museum," he said to Hannah. "I found this when . . ." Gregg stopped. *When I was sneaking around here spying on Dutton, when I was trying to find you to give you to the Sharks. That's the truth, but I don't want to say it.* "Well, how I found it doesn't matter now, I guess." Gregg moved farther away from the door, carefully. As he remembered, there was a narrow corridor, moving to the left.

"I wish Dutton would put lights in his hidey-holes," Gregg said. "Stay there . . . Yeah, there's stairs here, a little farther along. This must lead between the walls. Careful now. I'll go first; just keep your hand on the wall . . ."

Slowly, Gregg led Hannah through the blackness. The stairs continued down, turning once ninety degrees to the right, then opening into a long corridor that jogged three or four times. Gregg quickly found himself losing track of time as they moved through the blackness: They might have walked ten minutes or twenty before the corridor ended and they headed up another flight of stairs. At the top, another door blocked their way. Gregg could smell oil, old garbage, auto exhaust: outside. Gregg pressed one of his clown ears against the wood, listening. "I don't hear anything. Can you open the door, Hannah? I'm not real good at knobs . . ."

The door opened onto an alley and they stepped out into the Jokertown night. The lights of police cruisers bounced blue and red strobes across the brick walls. Gregg scurried to the mouth of the alley and peered out. They'd emerged from a building south of the Dime Museum. The street in front of the museum was strewn with bright police vehicles illuminating the neighborhood. More sirens wailed in the distance. "They're scared," Hannah said behind Gregg. "They know we're right, but they don't want the word getting out. The bastards . . ."

"They can't hold most of them for long," Gregg told her. "Even jokers still have some rights. I've known Dutton for years—he'll have his lawyers on the phone in an hour and he'll be free before morning. There's nothing on Father Squid, Dr. Finn, or the others." A shudder ran along the length of

Gregg's body. He could feel himself shivering, on the edge of panic. He wanted nothing more than to find a dark corner somewhere and hide. "Let's get out of here while their attention's still on the museum."

"We can't go wandering the streets, Gregg. They'll find us."

Gregg looked at her. Hannah was dressed in beige Dockers, a Rox T-shirt, and sneakers. She looked normal, if a bit yuppie-casual. As he had a few thousand times in the past few days, he found himself wondering how she could still claim that she cared for him. He wondered what she saw in him now that he was a joker. *I'm a sham,* he wanted to tell her. *I killed people; I hurt them, and I reveled in their pain. I still can feel that pleasure . . .* "Hannah, you have to hide, and your best chance is without me. Dye your hair, cut it short. This is your chance, Hannah."

A faint smile played with the edges of her lips. "Are you saying you want to get rid of me, Gregg? You're *dumping* me?"

"Hannah . . ." He could not answer that smile. "I'm saying that I'm a big liability to you. You stand a much better chance without me. That's just the truth. I think you should take the opportunity."

"Gregg . . ." Hannah crouched down beside him. "When are you going to understand? I don't give my friendship lightly or casually. I lost you once and the pain . . ." Her voice faltered for a moment, and she looked away. "I don't intend to have that happen again," she said at last.

"I'm a goddamn *joker,* Hannah." *I've laughed and taken pleasure in innocent people's deaths. I've done more horrible things in my life than you can imagine.* He thought it; he said nothing. "That changes things, I understand that. I really do."

"Yes," she said, and the word hurt. "I know that. But you're still Gregg Hartmann. You're someone I . . ." She stopped. Gregg wondered what she was about to say. *Love?*

". . . care about. That hasn't changed."

"Hannah, I—" Gregg didn't know what to say. *I don't deserve this, not after all I've done . . .* He could only look at Hannah in wonder. "Hannah—"

"Look, you can't even open doors by yourself. You *need* me. We both need each other." She nodded her head toward the museum, where they could see the Oddity being escorted out under guard. Gregg watched, remembering that odd feeling of momentary connection he'd felt during Oddity's fight with Snotman.

Khaki-uniformed men were beginning to scatter through the streets, and more NYPD squad cars wailed their arrival. "We don't have time for this," Hannah said abruptly. "We stay together, Gregg, whatever happens." Her hand cupped his head, and he felt the delicious warmth through his wrinkled skin. Still thinking about the Oddity, Gregg tried to do what he'd once been able to do with a touch—to insinuate himself inside her mind, to establish the mental link that would allow him to ride with her emotions and control them.

But he couldn't, and Hannah took her hand away too quickly. He tried not to notice that she unconsciously rubbed the hand on her pant leg afterward.

"How's your sense of smell?" Gregg asked.

"Pretty good. Why?"

"That's a pity. Because where we're going, that's not exactly an asset. Now—before someone up there starts looking around . . ."

Gregg went to the rear of the alleyway and bolted across the street behind the Dime Museum. They hurried away, keeping to shadows, ducking into entranceways and between buildings when cars passed. Finally Gregg led Hannah into another narrow alley near where the Crystal Palace had once stood. He jabbed a truncated arm at a sewer lid.

"Our path out of here," he said. "And my home for the last few months. I hope you like it."

Ray chugged the last of the Red Stripe, popped the rest of his sandwich into his mouth, and chewed. It was well-aged Swiss cheese and an excellent honey-cured ham with a dab of spicy brown mustard. He adjusted his beret and winked at the Shark lying trussed up in his underwear among his still unconscious comrades. Ray didn't much care for the beret, but it was part of the costume. He left the kitchen whistling tunelessly, proud of the subtlety he was showing, anxious for more action.

The Shark security man had told him some disturbing things. The guy was only low-level muscle, so he wasn't exactly sitting in on policy meetings, but he was with the detachment that had come to the island with General MacArthur Johnson, the head of Shark security. They'd brought half a dozen jokers to the island with them. The jokers had been dumped at the entrance to the manor's mysterious east wing, which was off-limits to most of the staff. That was the last he'd seen of them. A few days later a young blond guy had shown up and taken residence in the living quarters in the complex's west wing. The security man had never seen him before. Rumors spread quickly among the staff that it was Pan Rudo, leader of the Sharks, in a brand-new body.

Ray didn't like the sound of any of this. The body-switching was entirely possible. All the jumpers were supposed to be dead, but "supposed" isn't "certain." Ray also didn't know exactly why the Sharks needed jokers from the streets of New York City, but he knew they weren't going to treat them to two weeks of fun in the Caribbean sun. The rumors had to be true. There must really be a Black Trump, the Sharks' final solution

to the wild card problem. Maybe Rudo or one of the other escaped Sharks had some of the virus, and they were going to
test it on the jokers. Maybe.

In any case, the answers seemed to be in the east wing. Ray
would worry about tracking down the rejuvenated Pan Rudo
later. He had to discover what the Sharks were doing to the
jokers. And he had to be damn careful doing it. The Black
Trump could bring him down as easily as the scrawniest,
weakest joker.

Ray sauntered off toward the east wing. He didn't know
how he was going to get in if it was off-limits to most Sharks,
but that was something he'd worry about when he came to it.
He was quite pleased to see his simple disguise working as he
passed a couple of security men hurrying down the hall. They
didn't even glance at him as they hustled by.

Sometimes it pays to be subtle, he told himself as he passed
from the central part of the manor where the kitchen and service areas were located, to the mysterious east wing. He knew
he had reached his goal when he came to a guarded checkpoint. There were two uniformed Sharks at the double doors
leading into unknown territory. One wore sunglasses even
though the lighting was soft fluorescent.

"What's up?" Ray asked as he approached.

"You haven't heard?" the one without sunglasses asked.

"Heard what?"

"There's an intruder in the perimeter," the Shark said. "One
of the sentries patrolling outside was cold-cocked."

"That right?" Ray asked. He smiled at the one in the sunglasses, who looked back stonily.

"Who are you, anyway?" the talkative Shark asked. "Did
you come in with the new detachment last night?"

Ray shook his head "Nope. Got here later than that."

Ray waited. The one in the sunglasses caught on first. He

tried to bring his rifle up, but Ray grabbed it by the barrel and ripped it out of his hands. He swung the butt hard, catching the Shark flush on the chin. The guard shot backward, banged his head on the wall, and slid down to the floor.

Ray pointed the rifle casually at the other sentry. "You going to open that," he said, gesturing at the door with the gun barrel, "or do I blast it down through you?"

The sentry looked as if he didn't know if he wanted to be afraid or pissed.

"You wouldn't."

Ray took a step forward and jabbed the rifle barrel into the sentry's stomach. "Don't bet your life on it, moron. My name is Billy Ray. They call me Carnifex. And I'm a wild carder, motherfucker."

"All right," the guard said, his voice quavering. Slowly he reached for the key chain at his side, selected a key, and put it in the lock. "This okay, huh?"

"Yup," Ray said, and clipped him on the back of the head with the rifle barrel. This was getting monotonous, Ray thought. The Sharks really needed to hire a better class of goon. He slung the rifle, then reached down and grabbed one of the sentries by the collar, the other by the pants leg, and dragged them inside. He tossed the rifle and closed the door behind him. He looked around.

"What the hell is this?" he asked aloud.

It was a laboratory—something Ray wasn't all that familiar with. He recognized glass flasks and test tubes, stainless-steel sinks and scarred wooden workbenches, but that was about it. He had no idea about the autoclaves, incubators, freezers, and the electron microscope. The room was clean, orderly, very white, and antiseptic-looking. Ray approved. But there was no sign of the jokers.

As Ray looked around with a frown on his face, the door in

the back wall opened and a woman wearing a white lab coat entered the room. She was intent on reading her notebook and almost bumped into Ray.

She looked up, startled. "You shouldn't be here."

Ray smiled. "Should you?"

"What? What are you talking about?"

Ray pointed at the door through which she just came. "What's in there?"

"Are you insane?" She tried to go by Ray. "I'm getting Mr. Johnson."

Ray grabbed her arm, swung her around. "I'm sure we'll meet soon. In the meantime I want you to tell me about the jokers you brought here last week."

She looked indignant and tried to pull away but quickly realized the futility of that. Her indignation turned to fear. "Who are you? You're not one of the regular—" She noticed the unconscious sentries lying on the floor. "Oh."

"Very observant," Ray said. "You must be a real rocket scientist." His grip tightened. "Who are you?"

"I'm not—" For an instant she seemed defiant, then Ray squeezed hard enough to bruise her arm. She winced and made an instinctive, abortive move to pull away.

"You are?" Ray said. He put his face close to hers. "I've had it with this pussy-footing shit. I'm going to get some answers soon or I'm going to start breaking things. And you're right at hand, babe."

"My name is Michelle," she said quickly. "Michelle Poynter."

"Poynter." Ray thought for a second. "Oh. You're Faneuil's assistant."

"Yes. How did you know?"

"Your boss is in a cell singing like a fucking canary."

"You're from the government?"

"Yeah. And you're under arrest. Now where're those jokers? In there?"

He dragged her with him as he went through the door and into another room that was as big as the lab, or would have been if it wasn't partitioned off into half a dozen small cells, furnished only with rack-like beds, stainless-steel sinks, and lidless toilets. They were separated from the main room by a glass wall rather than metal bars. There was nothing in the main room besides a desk and matching swivel chair.

Some of the cells were empty. Some weren't.

Ray looked angrily at Poynter. Subconsciously his grip tightened so hard that she went limp from pain. "What is this shit?" Ray hissed in a low, shocked voice.

Four of the cells had occupants. It was hard to say if most of the prisoners were alive. One was sprawled in a heap between his bed and the glass wall that separated his cell from the rest of the room. He lay in a pool of black, coagulated blood. He wasn't moving. Two lay in their narrow beds. One was covered to his chin—Ray thought he was male, though he couldn't be sure—by a sheet stained with blotches of blood and other, less identifiable fluids. The man's eyes were open, but he stared at the ceiling as if he were sightless. He seemed to be crying tears of blood. The other joker lay on her side, naked, her sheet twisted into a stained lump around her feet. Her skin was covered with pulpy, purple bruises; her eyes were fixed with the classic thousand-year stare, looking off into eternity. The fourth stood in front of her cell's glass wall. She was just a kid, maybe twelve years old. Her face was that of a zombie with a fixed expression and sunken, staring eyes. Suddenly, though, she focused on Ray. She put the palms of her hands flat against the wall of glass. As Ray watched, the skin on both palms broke and blood oozed from the tears. She slowly sank to the floor, leaving two smears like bloody snail-ooze on the glass. Ray couldn't hear her because of the wall between them, but he could read her bruised and pulpy lips.

"Help me," he thought he saw her say. Or perhaps it was, "Kill me."

Jay Ackroyd was making love to his wife when the hunchback appeared in his bedroom.

Hastet was on top, rocking faster and faster as she built toward her climax; Jay was underneath, lost in her and the moment, watching her face, the way her breasts moved as she rode him, listening to the sounds she made, feeling her wetness as she slid up and down on him.

Then her eyes opened wide, and she screamed, and for a moment Jay thought she was coming, until she scrambled off him, clutching up a tangled sheet to hide herself. *"Jay,"* she said in a choked voice, staring past him.

Jay had been pretty close to coming himself; the sudden disengagement left him a little unsteady. It took him a moment to get his breath back and look over to where his wife was staring, and even then he couldn't believe what he was seeing. Street light filtered through the shades, but otherwise the room was dark, all shapes and shadows, and in that dimness it looked for all the world as if a headless hunchback was standing in the corner.

Jay leaned over and turned on the bedside lamp.

A headless hunchback was standing in the corner.

"Oh, great," Jay said, disgusted. His erection was gone by then, and his balls hurt. "This is going to be one of those nights, isn't it?" he said to no one in particular.

Hastet held the sheet against her breasts and looked at Jay

suspiciously. "Another one of your friends?" She'd been on Earth long enough to realize that her husband knew some peculiar people.

"Quasiman," Jay said. "Not exactly a friend, but I know him. He lives down at Our Lady of Perpetual Misery."

"What's he doing in my bedroom?" Hastet hissed in annoyance.

Jay shrugged. "Nothing much, at the moment." The hunchback was standing by the wall, his hands clenching and unclenching slowly with the rhythm of his breath. He didn't seem to have noticed that his head was gone. Or maybe he had—it was hard to tell.

Jay got out of bed and pulled on his pants. Whatever the hell this was about, he didn't want to deal with it naked.

Hastet took it all in stride, more or less. That was one of the things Jay loved about her. "Where's his head?" she asked.

"It'll be along shortly," Jay assured her. "Parts of him drift off to other dimensions from time to time, but they usually drift back before too long." Hastet got to her feet with all the dignity she could muster and started gathering up her underwear. "Next time, tell him to knock," she said as she padded off to the bathroom. A moment later, he heard the shower running.

Jay pulled on an undershirt and sat on the bed to wait for Quasiman's head to show up and explain. He wondered how the hunchback had managed to teleport himself here. Jay Ackroyd was a projecting teleport himself, but he could only pop things off to places he knew and could picture in his mind. So far as he could remember, Quasiman had never been up to his bedroom before. How did he even know where Jay lived? Hell, he barely knew where *Quasiman* lived. The hunchback's teleportation must work differently from his own. That was half the fun of the wild card, Jay reflected sourly; everybody got to make up their own rules.

Quasiman's head appeared suddenly and blinked. His eyes were glazed and a thin line of drool ran from one corner of his mouth. "Jay Ackroyd?" he said uncertainly.

"Real good." Jay stood up. "What can I do for you?"

"Father sent me to find you," Quasiman said. "To tell you." His voice trailed off into silence.

Jay nodded. So far so good. Father Squid was the joker pastor of Our Lady of Perpetual Misery. Quasiman worked for him, kind of a part-time handyman and part-time gargoyle. When he wasn't sweeping out the vestry he was crouched up on the steeple, staring off at nothing. "To tell me . . ." Jay prompted.

"To tell you," Quasiman echoed, nodding.

"To tell me *what*?" Jay asked.

Quasiman frowned, his brow beetling with concentration. "Hannah," he said. "Hannah got away."

"Real good," Jay said. He didn't have to ask who Hannah was. Hannah Davis: the arson investigator who had exposed the Card Shark conspiracy. She'd taken her evidence to Gregg Hartmann, the former senator, and Hartmann had hired Ackroyd and Creighton Investigations to check out her allegations. They'd managed to confirm enough of it to give Jay a lot of sleepless nights. Then Hartmann got himself killed and stiffed them on the bill.

"The other one got away, too," Quasiman said. "The yellow man with the legs. Hartmann."

"Hartmann is dead," Jay told him. Quasiman shook his head. Jay made it a point never to argue with a hunchback. "Does Father Squid need to see me about something?"

"They took him," Quasiman blurted. You could almost see the memory come flooding back into him. His eyes seemed brighter, his manner suddenly animated, even agitated. "They took them all." He vanished suddenly with a *pop* of inrushing air, the same noise Jay made when he teleported something with his finger, and reappeared just as suddenly across the room. "Mr. Dutton, Dr. Finn, Dr. Clara, Oddity, Troll, everyone who knew. They would have taken me, too, but I carried him *away* and went home. Sometimes I forget but not this time. Only the church was empty. I waited and waited up on the steeple but no one came so finally I went to Father and he said to find Jay Ackroyd so I went to your place but you weren't there and the looking-at-you man said that you were home so I came here."

"The looking-at-you man?" Jay said.

"The stinking badges man," Quasiman said. "The play-it-Sam man. You played it for her, you can play it for me."

"Humphrey Bogart," Jay said. He was astonished. Not that Bogie had told Quasiman to look for him at home, that part he'd figured out at once, but Quas knowing all those movie lines, *that* blew him away. He wondered who or what the hunchback had been before the wild card had changed him.

"Who took Father Squid and the others?" he asked.

That was evidently a stumper. Quasiman groped for words, his mouth opening and closing soundlessly. Distantly, Jay heard the sound of the shower cut off.

"Was it the Card Sharks?" Jay asked.

"Card Sharks," Quas agreed.

"Or was it the police?"

"Police," Quas agreed.

Jay sighed. "Try to remember. Were they wearing uniforms? Did they tell the Father that he was under arrest? Did anyone show you a badge or a warrant?"

"We don't need no stinking badges," Quasiman said, smiling, his memory stuck on Humphrey Bogart. For a moment,

Jay wished his junior partner was there, so he could give him a good slap.

"Were any of them aces?" Jay asked, groping.

"Aces," Quasiman agreed. He pointed an angry finger at Jay. *"Don't call me Snotman!"* he warned.

"Ah," Jay said. Snotman. Well, that was something, anyway. A place to start.

"Card Sharks, police, aces," Quasiman chanted. "Ring around the rosie, pocket full of posies, ashes, ashes, we all fall down."

"Eenie meenie minie moe," Jay replied, "catch a hunchback by the toe. No offense, Quas, but the next time Father Squid wants to send me an urgent message, maybe he could consider Western Union."

Quasiman wasn't listening. The hunchback's left hand had disappeared. Quas stared curiously at the end of the arm where it had been just a moment ago. Then he looked up at Jay, his eyes wide and bright and curiously innocent. *"Save us,"* he whispered urgently. *"The Black Trump."* Then he vanished.

When Hastet returned from the bathroom, wrapped in a terry cloth bathrobe with her hair up in a towel, Jay was pulling on his socks. "Your friend leave?" she asked.

Jay nodded. "Think of all the money he saves on doors," he said. "Where's the mate for this sock?"

"Why? You're not actually going to wear matching socks, are you? Is this some sort of disguise?"

"The whole Ilkazam harem falls madly in love with me and I have to marry the Henny Youngman of Takis," Jay said. He found the matching sock, pulled it on, and looked around for his shoes.

"Where are you going?" Hastet asked him.

"Down to the office," Jay told her. "I have a bone to pick with Humphrey Bogart. Don't wait up."

— — —

Ray turned to Poynter in sudden fury. He shook her, snapping her head back and forth like a tree branch in a hurricane.

"How can we help them?" he said between gritted teeth.

"St-st-st-stop," Poynter stuttered. Blood dripped from her mouth as she bit her tongue.

Ray somehow controlled himself. "How can we help them?" he repeated.

Poynter shook her head dazedly. She put her hand to her mouth and looked in stupefied fascination at the blood on it. "We can't," she said. "They're in the final stage. They won't last long."

"Is it the Black Trump?" Ray asked.

Poynter looked at him as if afraid to answer. He let some of his strength flow from his hands as he squeezed her arms again, not caring if he broke them. *"IS IT?"*

"Yes," Poynter admitted.

He dragged her to the glass cage that held the girl. She lay huddled in a miserable pile. She focused on Ray as he approached. There was no hope in her eyes, only pain and knowledge of imminent death.

Ray had never felt so helpless in all his life. There was nothing his speed or strength could do. He grabbed Poynter by the back of the neck and shoved her face against the glass wall.

"You did this, didn't you? I should break your fucking neck."

She was crying, whether from pain or fear Ray didn't know, or care. He felt his fingers tightening on Poynter's neck.

"Wa-wa-wait," she stuttered. "Don't. I can tell you—I can help—"

"Tell me what?" Ray asked.

"Rudo's journal. About the Black Trump—"

"Where?"

She pointed a trembling hand at the desk.

Ray let her go. She moaned and slipped down against the glass until she, too, was huddled on the floor, a mirror image of the dying girl on the other side of the wall.

"Stay put," Ray ordered as he went to the desk. An orderly stack of papers sat in the center of a dark green blotter. Some were memos, some were letters addressed to Dr. Rudo.

Ray scanned them quickly, but they said nothing about the Black Trump. He tried the desk's center drawer. Locked. He pulled at the drawer, and it came loose with a screech of tearing metal. Among the miscellaneous crap that you find in most desk drawers, locked or not, Ray found a journal. He smiled.

He opened to the last page. "Last vial to Casaday," the note read. "Johnson and I will divide the remaining culture and head for our targets tonight. God help them then!"

Ray looked up, frowning at the sound of the door swooshing shut. Poynter had snuck out of the room. He tucked the journal into the deep thigh pocket of his appropriated fatigues and went after her.

She was in the lab ahead of him, but she'd stopped and turned to look back as he skidded to a halt. There were a dozen well-armed Sharks in the room with her.

"Shoot him!" she screeched, pointing at Ray. "Shoot him!"

"We will, but not just yet." The man who spoke stood behind the security men. He was tall, muscular, and Black. He wore the fatigues of the Shark security forces. He was their leader, General MacArthur Johnson. "Billy Ray, isn't it?"

Ray's fury had burnt so deep that he appeared relaxed, almost casual as he leaned against a lab bench that had a mess of glassware on it. There was no hint of anger in his voice as he calmly answered. "That's right."

Johnson shook his head. "How'd you find us?"

"Your comrades are singing their butts off," Ray said, "hoping to avoid serious time in the federal pen—though that's not too likely."

"We should have killed those motherfuckers," Johnson said. His voice was an angry bass growl. "We can still have it done."

"Too late." Ray was almost smiling. "You're under arrest. All of you."

"You're nuts," Johnson said. "You know, it'd be a real pleasure to see if you're as tough as they say, Ray." He flexed his hands, his smile feral.

"I'm tougher, Johnson. You're just a fucking nat. I'm an ace. Take me about a second to rip your head off and stuff it up your ass."

Johnson twitched, took half a step forward, then controlled himself. "No . . . no. Much as I want to, I'm not going to dick around with you, you mutant diseased scum." He stepped back behind his men. "Hose him down."

Fingers twitched on triggers. Poynter was standing out of the line of fire, but the Sharks had released a firestorm of death. Bullets whanged off the stainless-steel benches and sinks, caromed off the white-painted walls. Ricochets buzzed like angry bees and Poynter gasped as a couple of rounds cut through her. She went down.

Ray had moved before Johnson gave the command to fire. His head was full of white noise. The only thing he knew was that this was payback time for those poor fucking jokers. He vaulted over the lab bench as the fusillade began. One bullet punched through his left calf, but it missed the bone and the wound was already starting to close when his feet hit the ground. Not that it didn't hurt. It hurt like a motherfucker.

Ray grunted with pain. He squatted behind the bench as the fusillade continued, ignoring the ricochets that whined around him. For once Ray was lucky. None hit him. He put his arms out, against the bench. He pushed, and it scraped along the floor.

"Yaaaaahhhhh!"

He pushed harder, screaming, and he and the bench picked up speed.

"Holy shit!" he heard, then he felt the shock of impact as the lab bench slammed into the gunmen crowded around the door. There were screams and groans. The bench bucked like it was going over a speed bump, then the shooting mostly stopped, and Ray was in the middle of the gunmen.

Only half of them were standing. The others were under the bench or smashed like flies swatted against the wall. Johnson was standing in the doorway, undecided.

"Come on!" Ray shouted.

Johnson and Ray locked eyes.

"I'll eat you up," Johnson promised, "and spit you out!"

"Eat this," Ray said as he grabbed one of Johnson's men by collar and crotch, heaved him off the ground, and threw him.

Johnson ducked. The Shark slammed against the wall. There was a loud cracking as bones snapped, and the man slumped to the floor.

"Hold as long as you can," Johnson ordered the remaining Sharks and ducked into the hall.

The two standing security men looked at each other. One shook his head and dropped his rifle. He put his hands up. The other did the same. Then they saw the look on Ray's face and they ran, too.

Ray hurtled down the hall after them, grinning like a madman. He had them on the run. It was only a matter of time— What *was* that smell? he thought as he blundered around a corner and ran into a man-sized heap of stuff that smelled like shit and garbage.

Ray had momentum on his side, but it didn't help any. He

hit and bounced, sputtering and spitting unmentionable filth. He was back on his feet almost before he hit the floor, but he stopped, stunned, when he realized whom he was facing.

It was a shambling mockery of a man, and it smelled like it was long dead—which it was. Its stench was awful, its appearance hardly less so. It wore a sagging uniform that once fit tautly across its broad chest and wide shoulders. Now the cloth hung loose on a battered body that was sunken, twisted, broken, and charred. It couldn't possibly look that bad and still be alive—and it wasn't—but the one eye that was exposed by its full hood was open and tracking blearily on Ray as it stood and blocked his path.

"Bobby Joe?" Ray said unbelievingly. "How the hell are you still getting around?"

The dead ace called Crypt Kicker wasn't fast in his best moments. The accumulated wear and tear of his previous few adventures, some of which he'd shared with Ray, had taken even more of a toll. When he spoke, it was in an agonizingly slow, barely understandable drawl.

"The Lord isn't ready to receive me yet. There's still more for me to do here on Earth."

Ray felt like screaming in what was left of Crypt Kicker's face (thankfully hidden by the hood he wore) but restrained himself.

"Well, Jesus, Bobby Joe, get the hell out of my way and let me do what I'm supposed to do."

Ray went to step around Crypt Kicker, but the huge ace snaked out a hand and grabbed Ray around the upper arm in a grip that even Ray's strength couldn't break. "I can't let you do that, Billy."

"You fucking moron," Ray blazed. "You're working with the Sharks?"

Crypt Kicker nodded ponderously. "Yes. They have a serum to cure the wild card. It's the Lord's work, to bring an end to the pain and suffering."

Jesus, Ray thought. "Let me go, Bobby Joe," he said in a low, tight voice.

"Can't . . ." Bobby Joe Puckett said, and Ray struck him in the forearm hard enough to snap the bones of most men.

But Crypt Kicker clung on doggedly. Ray swung again and again as the massive ace wound up to retaliate. Puckett's blow came with all the force of a diesel locomotive and all the speed of a sleeping sloth. Ray ducked and Puckett's fist slammed into the wall. The wall buckled, Puckett turned his attention to pulling his fist out of the hole it'd made in the wall, and Ray yanked free. He turned, grabbed the back of Puckett's hood, and slammed his head as hard as he could into the wall.

The wall gave before the onslaught of Puckett's head. Ray took a deep breath of thanks, but before he could get away Puckett bellowed like a wounded elephant and tore out a huge chunk of plasterboard as he pulled himself free of the wall.

"Shit," Ray said, and Crypt Kicker, flailing around blindly, caught Ray across the chest with a blow powerful enough to knock him off his feet and send him skidding down the hall on his backside. By the time Ray got up, Puckett had managed to extricate himself from the piece of wall framing him like an especially ugly Picasso.

Ray charged and Puckett lifted his hands and let fly with the toxic wastes and poisons that had accumulated in his body. Ray tried to twist away from the streams of venomous chemicals, but some splashed against his side, sizzling through his borrowed fatigues and eating skin and flesh.

Ray didn't even try to suppress his scream. Yelling like a maniac, he hurled himself at Puckett. The dead ace waited with open arms, wanting, no doubt, to enfold Ray to his massive bosom where he could alternately crush him with his inhuman strength and fry him with the toxicity of his flesh.

Ray knew that he couldn't out-strength Puckett. He had to out-think and out-quick him.

At the last second he went down, hitting the floor and kicking out with a leg-whip that smashed Crypt Kicker's knees. Puckett toppled like a falling redwood. Ray leapt to his feet and stomped hard on Puckett's throat. Puckett clutched at his legs, but Ray pulled away. He stomped again, then again, and he heard a sickening crunching sound as cartilage and flesh collapsed. Puckett clutched at his throat, wheezing like an organ with a broken bellows.

Ray stepped away from him, shaking his head. "Stupid fucking redneck," he said. Then he turned and ran down the hall after Johnson.

He activated his throat mike as he ran and screamed, "Come in, come on in! They're bolting like fucking rats! Don't let anyone get away!"

He saw no one as he ran through the manor and burst outside. The government cutter he'd called was bearing down on the island at full speed, lights flashing and clarions blaring. Amphibious helicopters were swooping in like birds of prey, guarding the sky in case the Sharks tried an aerial escape.

Ray went around the back of the manor to the small airstrip where something was taxiing out of a hangar. He put on a burst of speed. He wanted to reach it before the choppers did. He wanted to tear Johnson and whoever was with him to pieces.

But Johnson's aircraft suddenly rose straight up. It hung there insouciantly for a moment, as if daring the choppers to try to tag it. Then it was gone with a scream of jet turbines, leaving the choppers far behind like the fat, clumsy children they were. Ray's sprint stumbled to a halt, and he stared in disbelief.

"A Harrier," Ray swore under his breath. "A fucking vertical takeoff fucking jet." He sat down on the edge of the runway, suddenly very tired. "Where the fuck did Johnson get a fucking *Harrier*?"

He sat with his head in his hands for a long moment, a pose very uncharacteristic for Billy Ray. Then he stood and strode around the manor to where the assault team had gathered on the beach. The choppers bumbled around like angry, uncertain bees. They knew they had missed their target, but they had no idea what their target was.

Ray knew. He knew it was the Black Trump, death to all things born from the wild card.

By tradition, the muezzin called when he could distinguish a black thread from a white. In the dim dawn light, the faithful hurried to prayers, dodging their way past vendors who brought polished vegetables down from rooftop gardens. Silent jokers carried plastic coolers on their shoulders, hurrying toward the City Gate where traders would fill them with crushed ice and eggs and farm-raised fish from pens in the Sea of Galilee. Soon, boys would begin their morning rounds, carrying brass trays hung from swinging chains. The trays would be loaded with cups of thick coffee and steaming tea and cans of trademarked, guaranteed genuine Coca-Cola. It never tasted right to Zoe, in spite of the logo.

The air smelled of cucumbers and orange blossoms, of compost and last night's cooking. Zoe followed the vendors toward the souk, the area outside the City Gate where an uneasy truce held, the city's denizens usually kept at peace by the necessities of trade. She stayed in the shadows and walked as quietly as she could. If she found Needles following her, she planned to send him right back home. He would follow, she was sure of it, thinking to protect her, or to protect himself. She watched and listened, but she couldn't see him.

She hadn't gone half a block before she picked up a tail, a hunched figure in a black cloak. Needles? The figure vanished behind her.

The street angled sharply. Upper stories overhung the cobblestones in this section, so close that neighbors could borrow a cup of sugar through the opened windows. Or, more likely, exchange insults. The night's shadows lingered here and made the street seem even narrower than it was. Zoe heard heavy breathing behind her and caught a glimpse of the figure in the black cloak. She forced herself not to run. The black cloak brushed against the wall beside her in a passageway narrow enough that Zoe's hand touched a doorway on the opposite side of the street.

"You look nat." Not Needles. The joker's voice came from the folds of his hood, a cultured British accent, a fine tenor. He spoke in quiet, conversational cadence. A giant snail's foot showed beneath swirling folds of black cotton. The joker's cowled head bobbed at the level of her elbow and something was wrong with the shape of his back and shoulders. "Are you a whore?"

This man wouldn't kill a joker, not in the quarter. But a nat might die here and vanish from the street in some narrow doorway. "No," Zoe said.

"Are you, perhaps, a customer? My equipment is both adequate and unique."

"Not a customer," Zoe said.

"Pity," the joker said. "It is my duty, then, to escort you out of the quarter."

"I'm going to the City Gate," Zoe said.

"That is fortunate," the joker said.

They walked in silence for a while.

"I'm going to the City Gate because I know it's guarded—by the Twisted Fists."

She heard his indrawn breath. "A shadow organization. A myth," the joker said.

His dismissal was too casual, too offhand. He was a Fist, or he knew them. "Bullshit," Zoe said. "They've enlisted five of my kids."

"Five? You look rather less maternal than that. My compliments."

"Wards. Foster kids. Whatever. You're a Fist, aren't you? Isn't everyone around here?"

"You are a fool," the joker said. "Go home."

"No," Zoe said. What could she do to get shuttled up the chain of command? Offer to screw someone? Use her ace? She hated to do that, wouldn't unless she was forced; she didn't want to be known in the streets as an ace, for aces were feared here almost as much as nats. Maybe more so.

Zoe and her one-footed companion turned a corner into a wider street where small signs printed in three or more languages hung above barricaded doorways. Above them, the massive bulk of the gate loomed black against a cloudless violet sky.

Jokers came from the night's shadows to set up their wares in the little square, some yawning, most silent. One looked at her and hissed. Another spat in her direction and made a sign to ward off the evil eye. A breeze brought a scent of hot fat and charcoal, of garlic and coriander and frying dough.

Zoe clenched her folded robe in her left hand and walked to the center of the souk. The stone ramparts of the gate looked empty, but there were men with rifles hiding in shadows. She knew it.

The snail-footed joker accompanied her to the middle of the square. "You can't leave yet," he said. "The gates won't open for another half hour."

"I know," Zoe said.

The joker backed away from her. In a moment, he had vanished.

Zoe picked out an area of the wall where the shadows were deepest, where a cul-de-sac cut into the stone bulk of the gate. She walked toward it with all the bravado she could muster, her ears listening for the click of a safety. The cul-de-sac hid a passageway that seemed to end in a blank stone wall. A hooded figure waited there, his rifle pointed at her belly.

"Good morning!" Zoe said.

The swathed black figure wore a veil. She looked like a Halloween depiction of death.

"Are you in charge here?" Zoe asked. She smiled brightly and tried to look innocent and confused.

Eyes don't have much expression, Zoe knew. The mouth does. She couldn't see this joker's mouth or gauge her facial language. The guard's rifle barrel drew a small circle in the air, still pointed at Zoe's belly.

"The gate opens at six," the guard said. A man, not a woman. "You go home then, nat."

He had a local accent, the melodic lilt of the Mideast. The man was tall, almost skeletal, beneath that swirling robe.

"But I don't want to leave," Zoe said. "I want to talk to you." To *you*, Fist, and I don't want formal speeches that you've memorized from the how-to-deal-with-stray-nats handbook. Zoe took a step forward in spite of the objections of her belly button. It was trying to retreat toward her backbone. Terror was one hell of an ab exercise, it seemed.

"Stop!"

Zoe stopped. "But I only want to *talk* . . ." The quaver in her voice was not faked.

Someone laughed, high above them on the gate, a terrible laugh.

"I want to see the Black Dog," Zoe said. "I—I have information for him."

She felt the jokers behind her before she saw them. Two of them, silent and fast. She saw an outstretched arm. A solid blow to the back of her knees knocked her flat, sprawled on the caftan she'd dropped. One of its bangles cut into her cheek. Someone twisted her arms behind her and ground his knee into the small of her back. Hot pain drew diagrams of the joints in her shoulders.

"Nat," one of her attackers hissed. "Nat whore. Don't yell, pretty thing."

"Why are you looking for trouble, nat?" the tall joker said. "Tired of living?"

"Let me have her." The joker behind her twisted her arms a fraction more. "She'll talk. She'll scream. I like screams."

"Take her inside," the tall joker said. "She'll last long enough for all three of us."

Terror or sexual arousal—either of those activated Zoe's ace, her anima, her gift of the breath of life. Sometimes she had to force its appearance. Not now. She drew in a single breath and sighed into the caftan—a desperate breath that included memories of Needles's desolate face as he scrubbed blood from his hands, Turtle's gentle touch in a dark hotel room, the long black fingers of an animated mannequin locked into the flesh of a skinhead's throat.

The cloak twisted out from beneath her. It rose like a dervish, its gold coins razor-edged, a spinning terror of writhing fabric with a woman's shape and the speed of a whirlwind.

The dervish whipped an arm toward the tall joker's eyes. He dropped his rifle and fell backward, screaming, his hands clutching at his torn eyelids. The dervish scattered drops of blood and spread into a whirling net. It dropped over the joker on Zoe's back and cocooned him in windings of steel-strong mesh. The cocoon flung itself against the third joker, slamming him against the wall. A pseudopod of twisted copper snaked around the third joker's thick neck and squeezed.

Zoe belly-flopped toward the rifle and grabbed it. She got to her feet, turned toward the faint light of the souk, and collided full tilt with the solid bulk of a man in a black cloak. He twisted the rifle from her grip and immobilized Zoe in a bear hug. A joker in a black robe took the rifle from him and aimed it toward Zoe. The barrel of the thing looked as big as a cannon. Zoe kicked at her captor's legs, but she couldn't get any leverage.

"Whoa, there! What the hell is going on?" The man who held her had a southern drawl. His eyes were huge and yellow, a devil's eyes.

"Those pricks tried to rape me!" Zoe yelled. "Let me go!"

The vendors in the souk continued to set up their wares for morning, pretending not to notice the commotion near the gate.

The joker with the captured rifle looked in at the mess in the cul-de-sac and whistled. "She tore 'em up good," he said.

"Deal with it," the yellow-eyed man said. He turned Zoe around so that she stood beside him. His fingers found a nerve just above her elbow and squeezed it.

"Ouch!"

"Hush," the man said. "Come over here."

He marched her to an enclosed space between the wall and the back of a striped booth that sold tea. He didn't let go of her arm.

"What happened?"

"I'm looking for the Fists. I need to talk to the Black Dog. Those bastards tried to kill me."

"All you wanted was to talk?"

"That's all."

"What's the message? If it has to do with danger for the quarter, you'd better tell me."

"No. I'll talk to the Black Dog, but not to anyone else."

"You just took out three good men," the joker said. "Who are you?"

"Zoe. Zoe Harris." That wasn't the name on her paycheck, that wasn't the name on the checks she gave her landlord. "Uh, Sara Smith."

"Yeah. Sure."

"I want to speak to the Black Dog."

"He doesn't like aces. Neither do I."

"I'm not—" But she was. The evidence of her powers was smeared all over the walls of that cul-de-sac. "I don't—"

"Balthazar!" Needles bellowed as he skidded around the corner of the booth. "Let her go, man!"

Balthazar turned Zoe so that she was held tight against him, a human shield. She felt a cold circle of metal push against her ribs. Needles braked to a stop, his claws flashing, and dropped his hands to his sides.

"She's mine. She won't mess up again, I promise. Please, Balthazar?"

"Jesus, kid. You almost got her killed." Balthazar pushed Zoe toward Needles. "Take her home. Get her out of here."

Needles grabbed her waist. "We're going. We're going, okay?"

"Tell him!" Zoe yelled over her shoulder as Needles turned her toward the souk.

"Shut up," Needles hissed in her ear. "Please, Zoe."

There were tears in his eyes. He would die of embarrassment if she noticed them. She let the boy lead her home.

Forty-Second Street wasn't what it used to be. A couple of years back, the Deuce was solid porno theaters, adult bookstores, and sleazeball hotels, teeming with hustlers, junkies, and midnight cowboys. These days . . . well, you wouldn't call it respectable, but so much of the XXX action had moved over to video that half the porno theaters had been forced to convert to real films or go dark.

The Wet Pussycat used to be half a block down from Jay's office, a lifetime ago. Now Ackroyd and Creighton Investigations owned a whole building in the West Village, Jay's old office had been taken over by a Korean psychic, and the Wet Pussycat was the Cinefan, screening black-and-white classics twenty-four hours a day. It cost nine bucks to get in, which made the Cinefan either the most expensive movie house on the Deuce or the cheapest hotel, judging from the number of bag ladies, junkies, and teenage runaways nodded out in the sagging seats. Jay figured it was the latter.

It was still very dark, though.

Jay waited until his eyes had adjusted and strolled slowly down the aisle, scanning the faces of his fellow cinefans. Only a few were paying any attention to the screen, where people in evening dress were throwing huge coins at a very large monkey with a piano on his head. The man Jay wanted wasn't hard to pick out. There he was in the sixth row, center, engrossed in the drama—a huge man, ugly as sin, eating popcorn with both hands. Jay sat down beside him. "Rondo Hatten, right?" he said.

Rondo looked at him, startled. He was uglier than half the people in Jokertown. "Jay? What are you doing here?"

"I got a sudden urge to see *King Kong* at two in the morning, what else?" Jay said, helping himself to some popcorn. It was stale and tasted of hot grease. *Golden Flavor*, they called it at the concession stand. Some things never change.

"It's *Mighty Joe Young*," Rondo corrected him.

"Just so long as it isn't giving you any ideas," Jay said.

"How did you know I was here?"

"You weren't at home, you weren't at the office, and you weren't at Ezili's. Where else would you be?" Onscreen, the big monkey was tearing up the nightclub now, and lots of people in evening dress were running and screaming. "Don't you have this on tape?"

"On laser disc," Rondo corrected, "but there's nothing like seeing it on the big screen, the way it was meant to be seen."

"Right," Jay said. "I forgot, you're a purist, you want the whole filmic experience, the sticky floors, the rancid grease on the popcorn, the audience all around you . . ."

"*Hey, shut the fuck up,*" someone behind them shouted.

"Let's go over to Port Authority and grab a cup," Jay told his partner. "We need to talk."

"You don't want to miss the part where Joe saves the orphans from the fire," Rondo Hatten said.

"Yes, I do," Jay told him. "Besides, I think we got some orphans of our own that need saving."

"*I told you guys to shut the fuck up!*" the angry voice said. A hand the size of Rhode Island grabbed Jay by the shoulder.

Jay glanced back. The face behind him was prettier than Rondo Hatten's, but not by much, and the breath that came with it was a lot worse. "Don't you know it's rude to talk in a movie theater?" Jay asked. He shaped his right hand into a gun and pointed it between the close-set eyes. "Let go of me, please."

"You want that finger shoved up your asshole, you just keep pointing it at me," the angry man said.

"Wrong answer," Jay said, squeezing his trigger. There was the familiar soft *pop* and the angry man was gone. He turned back to his partner. "Let's go."

The junior partner in Ackroyd and Creighton Investigations, who sometimes called himself Mr. Creighton and sometimes Jeremiah Strauss and sometimes Mr. Nobody, cleaned the Golden Flavor off his fingers with a napkin and followed Jay up the aisle and out onto Forty-Second Street.

"Where'd you send him?" he asked when they were outside the theater.

"Our Lady of Perpetual Misery," Jay said.

"The church?"

"The steeple," Jay said. "He didn't look real religious to me, but you never know. Besides, if Quasiman is going to pop into my bedroom, I figured turnabout was fair play."

"Oh," Jerry said. "He found you, then." He scowled. A scowl on Rondo Hatten's face was quite a sight to see.

"He found me," Jay admitted.

Jerry brooded on that as he ambled along, hands in his pockets. Finally he got the complaint out. "How come he wanted *you?*" he said querulously.

"What am I, a potted plant?"

Jay sighed. As much as he liked his junior partner, Jerry's insecurities sometimes wore him out. "I've been working Jokertown a long time. Father Squid and Dutton and the rest trust me. They don't know who you are."

"My name is right there on the door with yours. Ackroyd and Creighton Investigations."

"So you're a name on a frosted glass door. Jokers don't trust anyone, not without good reason. What's Creighton to them? They don't even know his first name. For that matter, *I* don't know his first name. Does Creighton *have* a first name?"

"I haven't made up my mind yet."

"Real helpful," Jay opined, deadpan.

"Even so," Jerry said, "it was rude. I was the one on duty. He could have told me what the case was about. All he said was, *'The Black Trump,'* and *'Where is Jay Ackroyd?,'* and I was so startled I told him. Then he vanished, just like that, without so much as a by-your-leave. He treated me like I was nobody."

"You *are* Nobody," Jay put in.

"Yes, but *he* doesn't know that."

Jay was losing his patience. "Father Squid didn't give him any messages for Humphrey Bogart."

Jerry looked startled. "How did you know that I was—"

"I'm a trained detective," Jay said. "You know, Jerry, if you keep turning into movie stars around the office, people are going to figure out that Creighton's not what he seems."

"It wasn't Bogart, it was Sam Spade," Jerry said, his tone defensive. "I forgot I had it on. The office was closed, the door was locked, I was finishing up the report on the Wedaa surveillance, and all of a sudden Quasiman pops out of nowhere. There was no time to work on my face." He put on a peevish tone and tried to change the subject. "What's a Black Trump, anyway?"

"No idea," Jay told him, "but I don't like the sound of it."

The Port Authority Bus Terminal was a hop, skip, and a couple of junkies down the street. They found an all-night doughnut stand. Jay ordered coffee, black and very strong, served in a cardboard cup. Jerry got a cruller sprinkled with powdered sugar. The muggers and the chicken hawks were giving them a wide berth, and no wonder. Rondo was almost as big as the monkey in the movie, only meaner. "I can see why you picked this look," Jay said.

Jerry smiled. It looked odd on that huge misshapen face,

shy and tentative and strangely gentle. "Rondo's great for walking around bad neighborhoods late at night," he said proudly, "but you wouldn't want to wear him on a date."

"No," Jay said. "Listen. We got trouble. A whole bunch of Jokertown's leading citizens were picked up earlier this evening. Father Squid, Charles Dutton, Finn and another doctor down at the Jokertown Clinic, Oddity, Troll, God knows who else."

"Picked up?" Jerry asked. "By the police?"

"Feds, I think. The NYPD knew nothing about any of this until it went down. They were howling bloody murder for an hour or two, then someone got a phone call and now they won't say a word. Quas said Snotman was involved, so I had Melissa do some digging."

"You went to her first?" Jerry said, miffed again.

"She was with Justice for years, she still has contacts. I figured she could find out the score if anyone could. I was right. The operation was Special Executive Task Force, start to finish. The strikes were well coordinated, simultaneous, and there was a SCARE ace with each team. Snots at the Dime Museum, Lady Black at the Jokertown Clinic, Jim Dandy at the church. Slamdancer, Bloodhound, and a couple of others are in town, too, so it could be there were more arrests we don't know about."

"Hoo boy," Jerry said. "Sounds serious. Was anyone hurt?"

"The Oddity tried to fight back and Snotman pounded them into guano. Then Quas gave Snots a bear hug and both of them vanished. That's the last time anyone has seen Snotman."

"Where did they take the people they arrested?"

"That's the sixty-four-thousand-dollar question. Problem is, the answer is classified. No one has been charged with a crime, you understand. According to my sources in the cop-house, Father Squid and Dutton and the others are just being held in protective custody."

"Can they do that?" Jerry asked, surprised.

"Not legally," Jay said. "Melissa is going to hunt up Dr. Praetorius. He'll file a habeas corpus and wave some papers at them, but I wouldn't hold my breath on it doing a whole lot of good. You know what this smells like to me?"

"Card Sharks," Jerry blurted suddenly.

"Bingo," Jay said, smiling.

"But why?" Jerry asked. "What's this all about?"

"I don't know," Jay admitted. "What's worse, I think the feds just scooped up everyone who *does* know." He leaned across the table and brushed powdered sugar off his junior partner's lapel. "Now here's the interesting part. Quasiman isn't the only one on the loose. He said that Hannah Davis escaped them at the museum, along with a joker who may or may not be Gregg Hartmann."

"Hartmann?" Jerry said. "Hartmann's dead."

"Is he?" Jay asked. The last few years, with the jumper gangs running around stealing people's bodies, you could never be sure who was dead and who wasn't. Dr. Tachyon, the Turtle, Elvis, even Jerry and Jay themselves, at certain points all of them had been presumed dead. "Maybe he is and maybe he isn't; I don't care. The point is, somewhere out there is a loose end. Two loose ends, actually. Hannah Davis and a joker who looks like a yellow caterpillar."

Jay had a good view of the escalators that led down to the subway. A boy got off the Up while Jerry was pondering the case. He stood there a moment, a file folder tucked under his arm while his eyes searched the terminal. A firefly was buzzing around him.

He was well dressed for a kid who looked no older than

eleven. His suit was Italian, charcoal gray, and he wore it with black wingtips, a white shirt, and a red silk tie, but there was still something about him that made you think of *Hee Haw*. Maybe it was the mop of blond hair that fell across those deep blue eyes, or maybe it was the freckles. He had freckles on freckles on freckles.

His firefly was a point of light, bright and quick, tireless. It darted and circled around him like an electric mosquito.

"Him too?" Jerry said when he saw the kid. "Why am I always the last one on the big cases? If you called Sascha back from Maui, I'm going to be really annoyed."

"I wouldn't dare," Jay said. "Sascha knows where all the bodies are buried. Never mess with a telepath's vacation."

A teenaged hooker sauntered up to the freckle-faced boy. "So who are you, Peter Pan?" she asked, to general laughter.

"That's *Pann*, you douchebag," the boy snapped at her. He pronounced it *Pahn*. "It's Dutch."

"*Peter*," Jay called out. "Over here."

Pann turned and spotted them. He walked over briskly. "I want double time for this," he said as he sat down. "Do you know what time it is, Ackroyd? Pinkerton's never woke me up at three in the morning." His tink darted around his head, buzzing. Peter swatted at it irritably.

"Let's see the picture," Jay said. He didn't bother asking if he'd gotten it. Pann had been with Pinkerton's in Chicago for nine years before Jay hired him away. He was as good as they came. Not to mention being a wild card.

Peter handed him the file folder. Jay opened it and took out a mug shot, a glossy enlargement of the face of a young woman. It was a terrible picture, but she was still beautiful. He showed it to Jerry Strauss. "Hannah Davis," he said. "This is a blowup of her fire department ID photo."

"I remember seeing her on *Peregrine's Perch*," Jerry said. His

Rondo Hatten face suddenly brightened. "I get it," he said eagerly. "We're going to find her."

Jay shook his head. "Nah," he said. "The feds are."

Ray was not a happy camper on the flight back to D.C. He and Crypt Kicker sat across the aisle from each other, the only passengers in the small courier jet winging back home at supersonic speeds.

"Jesus, Bobby Joe," Ray said, "how could you work for that scum?"

Puckett shrugged ponderously. When he spoke, it was even more difficult to understand him. Since Ray had crushed his windpipe, his every breath was accompanied by a gasping wheeze that sounded just awful. Ray often wondered what incredible spark of vitality kept the dead ace going and going after suffering such tremendous physical damage. Maybe it was as Puckett himself believed, a touch of the divine.

"Well, I'm sorry, Billy, but they told me they was doing the Lord's work."

"I don't pretend to know God's mind," Ray said, "but somehow I doubt that he wants all jokers and aces wiped from the face of the earth."

Puckett shook his head ponderously. "That's not what their serum does," he said. "It helps people, not kills them. Why, I feel better already."

"WHAT?" Ray jumped up in his seat and backed away from Puckett as far as he could get. "You let them inject you with the Black Trump?"

"Sure," Puckett wheezed. "And I don't feel bad at all."

"You stupid son of a bitch," Ray groaned. "You just stay over there. Keep your distance."

Jesus! If Crypt Kicker was infected, maybe he'd caught it,

too. He'd fought the dead ace, *touched* him, for Christ's sake. Ray suddenly ran to the plane's tiny bathroom and locked himself in. He scrubbed his hands furiously, part of himself saying that this was foolish, that it was probably already too late. Another part of his mind said well, maybe not.

Puckett was an unusual case. He was an ace, for one thing. For another, he was already dead. How the Black Trump would affect him would be anybody's guess. Maybe it wouldn't affect him at all.

Ray went back into the cabin and sat as far away from Puckett as possible.

"I'm sorry, Billy," the dead ace said in an apologetic voice. "I didn't mean to hurt you when we was fighting. I just want to do the Lord's work and avert suffering and all."

"That's fine," Ray said. "You just do it over there while I stay here."

An hour passed and Ray began to think that maybe he was worrying for nothing. Puckett, after all, was the most indestructible being he had ever run across. Nothing could do the motherfucker in. Nothing could—

Puckett suddenly turned from his seat in the front row to face Ray sitting in the back.

"I feel strange, Billy. Did it get hot in here?"

Ray stood slowly, staring at Puckett. "No, Bobby Joe, I don't think so."

Puckett pawed at the hood that covered his face, finally pulling it off to reveal his grotesque features. Puckett had killed himself before his ace had turned so strangely. He'd put a gun in his mouth and blown away most of his right cheek and his eye. That part of his face was a hideous ruin. The other part was even uglier. It was speckled with dozens of tiny hemorrhages. His remaining eyeball was filled with blood and was a sickly purple color. As Ray watched, Crypt Kicker's eyelid started to leak blood and a black fluid ran from his nose down over his mouth and chin.

The hulking ace stood, clutching at the cabin wall for support. He tried to shuffle toward Ray.

"I . . . can't . . . move . . . my . . . left . . . side . . ."

He toppled and hit the cabin floor without even trying to break his fall. In moments he lay in a pool of blood that ran from his nose, eyes, mouth, and the horrible gunshot wound in his head, as well as the hundreds of tiny ruptures that had opened in the skin all over his body.

"Help . . . me . . . Billlll . . ."

Whatever vitality powered the engine of Puckett's body had finally run out. Ray stared as Bobby Joe Puckett continued to leak blood and fluid and unidentifiable slime. He seemed to melt, liquefying before Ray's horrified eyes.

Ray stifled a scream. He had never felt such fear in his life. The Black Trump wasn't a foe he could fight. It was an insidious, cowardly force that tore invisibly at your body, breaking it down until you were nothing more than a nauseating pool of puke.

Without thinking, he went to the center of the cabin and kicked at the emergency escape hatch. The door popped open and air went screaming from the cabin as it suddenly depressurized. Oxygen masks fell down from the ceiling. Ray went past them. The pilot came on the intercom, asking, "What's going on in there!"

"Don't come in here!" Ray screamed. "Stay out!"

He snatched one of the oxygen masks and took a couple of deep breaths. He let go of the mask and grabbed a seat cushion. He approached what was left of Puckett's body and used the cushion to push it to the cabin door where it was sucked out and away, falling down to the ocean below. Ray mopped up what fluid he could with the cushion and a couple of pillows, letting them fly out the door when they got soaked.

When he could clean up no more of the goop that had been Bobby Joe Puckett, he just stood and stared at the dark stain on the cabin carpet where Puckett had lain. He kept the emergency exit open a long time, breathing from the oxygen masks dangling from the ceiling.

After twenty minutes or so, he shut the door. He stayed on the canned oxygen for the rest of the trip to D.C.

But he wondered if it wasn't already too late. The Black Trump had killed an ace who was already dead, an ace whom neither flood for fire nor God himself could kill.

And he'd been exposed to it. He put his hand on his forehead. Was he already feeling a little warm?

Seven

"Colonel Sucharayan," the president of the Republic of Free Vietnam said, "you've been trying to divert the Mekong River again. That's got to stop. *Now*."

As if for emphasis, she swung her legs around and draped them over the arm of her heavy French Colonial chair of carved teak and green velvet upholstery. She wore what appeared to be tight-fitting black Danskins, and a black half-mask, figured to turn her face into a living yin-yang. Her hair was black, heavy, and unbound.

Despite the bat-wing swish of the fan suspended on a brass stalk from the ceiling high overhead, which at least kept the lethal Saigon afternoon air circulating, a trickle of sweat ran down one side of the Michoacán clay mask that served the Thai ambassador for a face. He was not used to being addressed in that tone of voice by a mere woman. Not to mention one whose dress and behavior were nothing less than scandalous.

On the other hand, Royal Thai Army intelligence had it on good authority that she could rip the colonel's arm off as casually as he might pull the wings from a fly. That she was an ace stacked insult atop injury. Still, the situation called for circumspection.

"Madame President," the ambassador said, bowing his head. His English was excellent. He had received training at Fort Bliss. "*Muang Thai* requires much water to supply the rice-growing lands of the Khorat Plateau. We must feed our people. Surely the Mekong belongs to all the peoples along its banks."

The president's audience hall had once been the great room of the grand French Colonial villa in the heart of Saigon—the unwieldy name "Ho Chi Minh City" was scarcely a memory anymore—which had been co-opted as the seat of government for Free Vietnam. It was as unorthodox as its occupant, being hung to either side of the chair of state with parachutes tie-dyed into ludicrous fireworks, bursts of color. Both were hard for the colonel to take seriously.

Moonchild wagged a finger at him. "And by both treaty and custom the people downstream from your country are entitled to a share."

"That is a very difficult question," the colonel murmured. "There is great drought in my country."

"Which you brought on your own damned selves," said the person who stood at the president's shoulder. A meter and three quarters tall, with the white-feathered and fiercely beaked head of a bird of prey, and claws to match emerging from the sleeves of his tiger-pattern camouflage battle dress, he twisted the colonel's sensibilities. Southeast Asians, by and large, had a loathing for human deformity, and thus for jokers. "You cut down all the *trees* in your country, for Chrissakes. Fucked up your watershed something fierce. Not *our* fault."

Sucharayan's thin lips drew tighter, giving the impression that his face might be about to implode. "The internal affairs of my country are no concern of yours," he hissed.

"When you interfere with the flow of water to the farmers of the Mekong Delta, you make it our affair," Moonchild said.

She raised her legs and spun on her butt until she faced forward, then placed her black-slippered feet primly on the floor. The colonel's eyes started out of his head.

The joker thrust his yellow break forward so that its hooked tip was inches from Sucharayan's nose. "Keep trying to steal our water," he said, "and you're engraving yourself an invitation to an entire world of hurt."

The colonel puffed up like a frog. "If you are making threats, permit me to assure you that the Royal Thai Army—"

"Can't find its butt with both hands." The joker raised his head and emitted horrid cawing laughter. "Remember those Thai Ranger teams you infiltrated through Cambodia, back when Bush was president? The ones with the Green Beanie advisers? How they like us now, baby?"

The colonel put his finger inside his collar, where pressure from his necktie was chafing him. He did not look happy. It had been necessary to liquidate several of the survivors of the missions the Thai Rangers had undertaken in cooperation with the American DEA and Special Forces, to prevent them from telling demoralizing tales.

"That's right," the joker said. "You keep messing with the Mekong, shit's gonna *happen*. You dig? Your officials are going to start acting weird. River monsters will run off your workers. Your heavy equipment's gonna burn. There will be *problems*."

Moonchild held up a hand and gave a little Queen Elizabeth wave. "Peace, Colonel Inmon." She smiled sweetly. "I'm sure he wants to get along just as much as we do."

She giggled. The colonel stared at her. Sweat streamed down his face.

A woman—a girl really, no more than eighteen—came bouncing into the audience hall. Not just *any* girl, but a tall glorious Western girl with hair like spun gold, wearing a floppy sun hat, a red halter top, and cutoff jeans that showed how impossibly long her legs were. In one hand she held a string bag full of oranges. The other cradled a pink teddy bear to her breasts. She was every tinpot Third World dark-sunglasses-wearing fascist brickhead colonel's ideal vision of what a Western woman *ought to be*.

A pair of jokers so hideous the colonel couldn't bear to look at them followed her in. They spread out to either side, flanking the door with AKM assault rifles held ready. Trying to ignore the scrutiny of five unfriendly eyes, the colonel watched the girl skip to the president, lean forward, and plant a kiss on her unmasked cheek.

"Hi, Isis," she sang in a little-girl voice. "I'm *ba*-ack!"

"So glad to see you, Sprout, dear," the president said. "Run along now, please. I've important business to tend to."

"Sure." The girl turned, flashed a smile dazzling enough for a beer commercial at the colonel, who was making no effort to hide an expression of sheer disgust. Then she went bopping out of the room, all unconcern.

"Sprout," the president said, eyes lingering on the door she'd left by. "My—that is, my chancellor's daughter."

"A most charming creature," Sucharayan said in a voice starched with irony.

"Yes she is, isn't she?" The president grinned at him. "Now, then, Colonel, I'm sure the Kingdom of Thailand is as eager as we are to see relationships between our two countries remain friendly. We can work this out."

"No doubt we can," the colonel said.

"So," the president said, crossing her legs and rubbing her hands together, "now that we've got business out of the way—you wouldn't happen to have a *daughter*, would you, Colonel?"

— — —

Jay Ackroyd shook two aspirin out of the jumbo bottle he kept in his desk drawer and washed them down with a swallow of cold coffee from yesterday's pot. Then he made a face. The stuff tasted like Rondo Hatten's socks.

He wondered how his junior partner was doing. They should have heard something by now.

Peter Pann was asleep on the long leather couch in the corner of Jay's office, snoring a sweet little eleven-year-old snore. His tie was loosened and his shoes were off. "Wake me up when the tink gets back," he'd told Jay before nodding off, hours ago.

"What the hell is *taking* so damn long?" Jay said irritably.

Across his desk, Melissa Blackwood looked up from her little bitty computer. It was the latest experimental prototype, she'd explained to him, a NEC Neuromancer powerdeck with bubble memory and holographic display, wouldn't be on the market for another two years, minimum. "We don't even know if he's been arrested yet," she said. Readout flickered in the air in front of her eyes, phantom letters that Jay found vaguely disconcerting. "And they will probably want to interrogate him before they take him to wherever the others are being held."

"God, I hope not," Jay said. "I don't know how long he can carry this off."

"You worry about him too much," Melissa said. "He'll do okay. You should get some sleep." Her hair was an unruly cascade of red curls spilling out from beneath her hat, her body hard and small. Very small. Beyond petite, maybe five feet on a tall day. If she wore boots. This morning she wore a jogging suit, a pair of old Reeboks, and a shiny, black silk top hat.

The top hat was her trademark. *Aces* magazine had named her Topper back when she was still a teenybopper protégée of Cyclone out in San Francisco. During the years she'd spent with the Justice Department, Melissa had played the part to the hilt, dressing in a distinctive uniform of white shirt, bow tie, long-tailed black tuxedo jacket, black satin short-shorts, black fishnet stockings, and high-heeled black fuck-me pumps.

She'd walked away from the costume, and the feds, soon after the Rox War, for reasons she still refused to discuss. Jay figured that Cyclone's death had something to do with her decision. There was no way to walk away from the top hat, however. Her power didn't work without it, the same way Jay couldn't teleport anything without making his fingers into a gun. Ace crutches were a funny thing.

"You getting anywhere with that thing?" Jay asked, gesturing at the powerdeck. For the past hour, she had been trying to hack into the sealed files of the Special Executive Task Force down in Washington, in the hopes of finding out what the hell was going on.

"Nothing we didn't already know," she said, turning off the machine. The phantom letters vanished. "The feds have three major Sharks in custody: Dr. Etienne Faneuil, Philip Baron von Herzenhagen, and Margaret Durand. Durand's cut a deal and she's snitching out the other two. Pan Rudo, who seems to have been the head of the whole operation, is supposed to be dead, murdered at the UN by this six-legged yellow joker, who's either George G. Battle or Gregg Hartmann, depending on who you believe. On paper, it looks as though the Shark organization has been pretty well smashed up."

"What do you think?"

Melissa closed up her powerdeck. "Faneuil and Durand are in nice young bodies, which has got to mean that the Sharks have a tame jumper, or had one at one time."

Jay groaned. "Jumpers," he said. "Why is it always jumpers? From now on, we charge triple time for any case with jumpers in it."

"I know how you feel," Melissa said. She disconnected her modem, wrapped the line around the computer, took off her top hat, and thrust the whole works inside. "Von Herzenhagen used to run the Special Executive Task Force, until he was exposed as a Shark. Now he's been replaced by Straight Arrow. That ought to be good news for our side. Nephi's an ace, and more important, he's a decent man, honest, loyal, hardworking . . . only . . ." She hesitated.

Jay didn't like the sound of that *only*. "Only what?"

"Only . . . is he *really* Straight Arrow?" Melissa put the top hat back on her head and cocked it at a rakish angle. "With all this body-swapping going on, there's no way we can be sure who's who, or even who's alive or who's dead. We could be dealing with a Shark in Straight Arrow's body. All those SCARE aces could be Sharks by now. That would explain last night's raids. For all we know, Rudo is still alive in a new body, just like Faneuil and Durand."

"Not to mention how many more Sharks are still out there, undercover," Jay said gloomily. "Leo Barnett in the White House, hell, this damn thing may go right to the top." Jay's head was throbbing. He needed hot caffeine. He pressed his intercom. "Ezili, make some fresh coffee, will you?" There was no answer. She probably wasn't in yet. Ezili came to work when she felt like coming to work, usually around ten-thirty or eleven, but sometimes two or three. He looked hopefully at Topper. "I don't suppose—"

"You don't pay me nearly enough to make coffee," Melissa said. "Make it yourself."

"Have you ever tasted my coffee?" Jay said. "Have pity."

Melissa made a face at him. "Just this once," she said. She took off her top hat, reached inside, and pulled out a Styrofoam cup of coffee, black and steaming. She put it on Jay's desk.

He picked it up with both hands, blew on it, took a swallow. Life seemed slightly more tolerable. "Real good," he told her. He looked wistfully at the hat. "I don't suppose you have a cheese Danish in there?"

"Don't press your luck."

Something *pinged* against the office window. Jay looked up. A bright point of light hovered outside, beating against the glass, darting and fluttering back and forth in a frantic aerial dance, trying to get in. He got up and opened the window. The light shot over to Peter, circled around his head, then zipped up to the ceiling, buzzing wildly. "What's she saying?" Melissa said.

"How should I know? I don't speak tink." Jay went to Peter and shook him roughly by the shoulder, until he sat up groggily. The tink zoomed down and hovered in front of his face. Its buzz was frantic, insistent. Peter rubbed sleep from his eyes and listened. "They took him to Governors Island," he said. "They're all there. We going to break them out?"

"Might as well," Jay said. "Can't dance."

When the Thai was gone, Moonchild waved her chief of security away. Inmon nodded his feathered head and left.

After the door shut on him, Moonchild rose from the ornate chair and walked toward another door at the back of the great room. She weaved slightly. As she approached the door, painted in layers of white enamel, her feet sank several inches into the scuffed parquetry floor.

"Whoops," she said, and giggled. "Shit. I'm starting to lose it." Her outline blurred, shifted, and suddenly it was a man, small and blue-skinned, enveloped in a hood and billow of black cape, who stood reaching for the brass doorknob.

"Screw this," he said in a high-pitched and peevish masculine voice. "I'm Cosmic Traveler. What do I need with doorknobs?" And he walked through the door.

On the far side a short hall led to another door. "That fool Meadows needs to quit fretting like a brooding hen," the cowled figure muttered as it walked forward. "I've got all the memories that high-kicking bimbo does. *And* a lot more upstairs. Anything she can do, I can do better." At the door he paused and smirked. "And then some," he said, and stepped through. As he passed through the wood, he felt tearing dislocation. "Oh, shit!" he exclaimed. "It's too soon—"

He fell forward, through the door onto the polished hardwood floor of a small office. What landed on all fours was another male figure, tall and lanky, dressed in jeans and a blue work shirt, with ashy blond hair getting long and the beginnings of a goatee.

"Whoa," Mark Meadows said in a long expulsion of breath. "Almost lost it there."

He shook his head and reached for round wire-rimmed spectacles that had dropped from the aquiline bridge of his nose. "I'm being the Traveler too much. It's giving me a death wish."

Not to mention the fact that at the end of the interview, Trav had broken character to ask if the colonel had a *daughter*, for God's sake. "If you can't maintain better," Mark said aloud, "I'm gonna start leaving you in the bottle and winging it myself."

Down the dim and dusty back corridors of his mind, a dry mocking laugh rebounded. The threat was empty, and no one knew it better than Cosmic. Power in Asia was a personal affair, and the president of Free Vietnam was Isis Moon, also known as Moonchild. Mark was her chancellor, fully authorized to speak for her—but unless she put in fairly regular appearances, people would sense an opening and start to conspire.

And Moonchild wouldn't come out to play anymore. Not since she had broken her vow against taking human life by breaking the neck of the joker-ace Ganesha. Small matter that it was an accident—and that Ganesha had been trying to rape Sprout. Moonchild's powers and very existence were predicated upon observing the Tenets and Student Oath of *tae kwon do;* to her the third portion of the Oath, "I shall never misuse tae kwon do," meant she could not use her ace powers or martial arts skills to kill a human.

Mark had tried. Endless internal monologues elicited no response. When he took the silver-and-black powder that summoned Moonchild, he curled into a fetal ball and went catatonic for an hour. He didn't even know if she still *existed*. Or whether, like Starshine—killed by a Ly'bahr cyborg in orbital combat over Takis—she was simply *gone*.

So he had to rely on Trav, slimy and unreliable as he was. He was taking the blue powder too much; and when he took a single potion too often, bad things happened. Like the one-hour duration of a "friend's" visit became unstable, and you risked translating back into solid with skinny Mark Meadows in the middle of a hardwood door . . .

A knock on the door. It made him shudder. He picked himself up with the sense of assembling scattered pieces.

"Come on in."

It was Osprey, pumping a feathered fist in the air. "Yeah! You'd think that stiff-necked son of a bitch never heard of 'good cop/bad cop.' And you should've seen the boss! She worked him to perfection. *Perfection*."

He blinked his huge, golden eyes. Beetling eagle brows frowned. "But she's starting to act, I don't know, a little *weird*.

She's still an ass-kicking little lady, but man, maybe you better talk to her about taking some time off."

"I'll do that," Mark said, in what he hoped wasn't as much a croak as it felt like.

He folded himself into his swivel chair. "What's eating at you, boss?" Inmon asked, perching on the edge of his desk.

A two-time Joker brigadier, Mark's comrade in arms in the fight to liberate South Vietnam, Osprey had proven himself a shrewd and resourceful warrior. But sometimes Mark thought he had a tendency to let natural optimism get the better of him. It had to be a powerful sense of optimism, after all; it had survived the wild card turning him into a creature fit to frighten children, not to mention Thai colonels playing at diplomat.

Osprey was not as capable as Mark's former spymaster, security chief, military adviser, and friend J. Robert Belew had been. Then again, Mark suspected hardly anybody *was*, outside the movies. Belew was long gone. Ordered into exile by Mark himself.

He gave his head a prissy-tight little shake—and was immediately uncomfortable; that had too much Traveler in it.

I'm not gonna beat myself up over that one anymore, he told himself. Yes, he had allowed himself to be manipulated into unfounded suspicion of his friend and adviser J. Bob; yes, he had flown into a rage in the aftershock of having killed the man he hoped would be the guru he'd been seeking since his belated face-first fall into the hippie subculture. He had tossed his right-hand man out of the whole country—and had only just managed to avoid ordering him shot out of hand, just like any fascist Third World dictator with aviator shades and "gilded" bird crap on the bill of his hat.

But he hadn't *just* been in Ferdinand Marcos–emulating mode. The fact was, he *couldn't* trust J. Bob, not indefinitely. The merc himself had told him not to. J. Bob was a right-winger and a super patriot, and he had his own agenda—which could not be relied on to run parallel with Mark's clear over the horizon into infinity. The break was coming, was needful; and though not for the best reasons, Mark had done the best thing, by making it clean.

He sighed. "I just wonder if it's . . . *worth* it, man." Right or wrong, he missed J. Bob acutely now; J. Bob knew about his "friends." Not being able to share the truth of his masquerade with anyone—even his closest remaining friend—weighted him down like a backpack anvil. "What we're doing here."

Osprey shook his head in disbelief. "Not *worth* it? Listen, man. Think of all we've done. We've given the wild cards a place where they can be free and pretty much safe. We've given the Viets something they wanted for a long, long time, which was mainly to be left alone. There's starting to be an economy here in the south; people are starting to make stuff, and to trade.

"The traffic is flowing south, not north; shit, everybody says it's just a matter of time before the boys in Hanoi throw in the towel and petition to join us. You've kept us on good terms with the Chinks without sellin' us down the river. And with all this shit about the Card Sharks breaking in the news and all, the way you and J.—and the major was the first ones to make a stand against them, it's makin' us all look like heroes. Nothing like a little attempted genocide to rehabilitate us wild cards in the eyes of the world."

Mark found himself nodding. He thought J. Bob was raving when he first told Mark they were up against a branch of a worldwide conspiracy to exterminate the wild cards, way down yonder in Vietnam. But J. Bob had been right. As usual. Now the Sharks were exposed, discredited, and on the run.

"We ain't an 'outlaw state' anymore," Osprey said. "People are startin' to think what we're doing here is pretty right-on.

And old President Leo, he don't like wild cards much—but he don't have a personal hard-on for your skinny white butt like George the Shrub did. When the polls tell him to back off the Nam, he listens up."

He laid a hand on Mark's shoulder. Mark felt the tips of his talons, needle-sharp, gently prodding his flesh through the blue chambray of his shirt. Power under control: That was Osprey.

"Moonchild's the boss," the joker said in a quiet voice. "But not to take nothing away from her, you're our point man. Always been. We'd never have made it this far without you. I hope you stick it out."

"Wherever it takes us?"

"That's affirmative."

Mark reached up to grip the claw briefly. "Thanks," he said. "I'll do my best."

Billy Ray was pissed, absolutely and totally. He'd been quarantined, put under observation twenty-four hours a day by a bunch of white coats who looked at him as if he were some kind of interesting, but ultimately disgusting, bug. When they weren't sticking him with a needle to draw blood, scraping his tongue with a Popsicle stick, or knocking him on the knee with some fucking little rubber hammer, they were asking him to piss in a bottle or do even more disgusting things with other bodily fluids. Worse, the TV set didn't even get cable and by the end of the week Ray was so wound with pent-up energy and frustration, he was ready to explode.

The only positive thing was that so far he'd shown no sign of having the Black Trump. The doctors at first considered this a minor miracle since Ray had been trapped on a plane with Crypt Kicker, breathing the same air for an hour or so before he'd realized the ace was infected. Then it dawned on the dome-heads that Bobby Joe Puckett wasn't your ordinary type of guy. He was already dead, for one thing, and one of the scientists postulated that maybe he didn't breathe, "as we know it," therefore he didn't pass the contagion on to Ray. They were pissed that Ray had kicked the body overboard rather than bringing it in for study.

But that was okay. Ray was pissed, too.

He had way too much time on his hands and, very unlike himself, spent a lot of it brooding. He had always thought of himself as, well, invincible. More than once he'd taken wounds that would've killed most men, from the time the pack of werewolves had gnawed on him to the time Mackie Messer had unzipped him from crotch to sternum. But he'd always come back. He was the toughest bastard on the planet. Nothing could bring him down. Nothing, apparently, but a bunch of microscopic bugs too small for him to see. It bothered him. It bothered him a lot.

It was still bothering him when someone knocked on the door and came in without waiting for him to say anything. That was another thing that bothered him. The fucking doctors were always doing that, knocking and then coming right on in. But this time it wasn't a doctor.

"Hello, Ray," he said as he entered the tiny quarantine chamber. "How're we feeling?"

In Bush's day the Special Executive Task Force had been headed by Dan Quayle, but Quayle (thankfully) had had little to do with day-to-day operations. Department heads had had free rein, but as it turned out that hadn't worked so well, either. Barnett's election had changed things. His VP, ex-general Zappa, had been given other duties, and to show what a swell guy he was, Barnett had turned the SETF over to one of "them." Of course, the "them" he'd turned it over to was the most unwaveringly conservative, boringly white bread of "them" possible.

"Hi, Nehi. We're feeling just fine."

Nephi Callendar, the ace known as Straight Arrow, sighed like Job, only even more put-upon. "That's *Nephi*, Ray. Actually 'sir' would be more appropriate. Even 'Mr. Callendar.'"

"Right," Ray said. "Listen, sir, you'd better get me out of here before I start breaking things. There's a lot that has to be done."

"You think I don't know that? Get dressed. We have an important meeting."

"Oh, a meeting," Ray said as he went to the closet. "You don't know how much I've missed going to meetings the past week. You can't imagine the hours I've spent here pining away, wishing I had a meeting to go to."

"No," Callendar admitted, "I probably can't."

There was a limo waiting for them outside Walter Reed Hospital. Ray whistled when he saw it. "Jeez, you're moving up in the world, Nehi. I remember when you were just one of the guys in the Secret Service. Now you get to be the token wild carder on Barnett's staff with your own chauffeured limo and all."

"Try not to be offensive, Ray, if you can."

"All right," Ray said as the limo pulled out into traffic. "I'll try."

"Fine. As you know, the Task Force's currently operating under a special directive from the president to clear up this Card Shark problem."

"Yeah," Ray grumbled. "I'm sure he's been staying up late nights worrying about it."

"He has, actually." Callendar leaned forward. "Look. I know you don't think much of my decision to take this position in the Barnett government. But it was my decision and I stand by it. I'm not sure what Barnett intends for wild carders, but don't forget that I'm one myself. I'm in a position to . . . well, watch out for things. You may not believe it, but I am. Ray, you did a good job on the island, but according to the journal you recovered, Rudo had already left. And he'd taken a supply of the so-called Trump with him."

"Goddamn it," Ray swore. "You didn't see what that stuff did to Bobby Joe. Christ! I thought nothing could do in that shit-kicker for good, but it turned him into a pile of pus and Jell-O right in front of me."

"I saw the photos of the other victims," Callendar said coldly. "Our scientists are working on Rudo's journal and we'll have some concrete information about the Trump any time now. And there's one thing you should remember. Blasphemy does no one any good."

"I'll jot that down in my thought book. Are you sending me after Rudo and the Trump?"

"You'll find out about your assignment soon enough," Callendar said.

The limo turned off the street. Ray glanced out the window. He'd been a Secret Service agent long enough to recognize the back way into the White House when he saw it.

"So what do I call him?" Ray asked Callendar.

"Who?"

"Barnett. Do I call him Mr. President or Reverend?"

Callendar sighed again. He did that a lot in Ray's company. "You're not going to pray with the man," he said. "You're going in for a very private, very high level briefing. Be courteous, be attentive, be quiet, and you might still be in government service when the meeting's over. Okay?"

"Sure, okay, Nehi. Whatever you say."

Callendar suppressed an urge to roll his eyes. He was learning that the best way to deal with Ray was to ignore half his comments and pretend to ignore the rest. Ray was quiet as they parked the limo, went through the various security checkpoints, and walked down the hallway to the Oval Office. Still, as they stopped before the office door, Callendar felt compelled to issue a final warning. "Just behave yourself with Rev—er, President Barnett. Okay?"

"Of course," Ray said, stepping in front of Callendar. "Think anyone's home?" he asked as he pounded on the door.

It was opened by a Secret Service agent who neither Ray nor Callendar recognized. He was a nat, though. Barnett had weeded all wild carders, ace and joker alike, from those assigned to guard himself and his family. The agent wore mirrorshades. His meticulously pressed suit made Ray envious. He had the omnipresent radio plug in his ear. He looked back inside the office. "Agents Callendar and Ray to see you, sir."

"Show them in, Frank," Barnett said in his soft southern drawl. "You may wait outside."

The agent stepped aside and waved Ray and Callendar in.

"Don't you think the shades are overdoing it a bit?" Ray asked in a low voice as they went by. The agent sneered silently, and Ray put him on his list.

Ray looked around the Oval Office. It hadn't changed much since the last occupant had left, but Barnett had added his own personal touches. All and all it wasn't bad, though the pen and pencil set fashioned as a model of the three crosses on Calvary looked a little out of place on the presidential desk.

Barnett stood as they entered the room. He was a tall, fit man, and handsome in what Ray considered a slightly effete way. His voice was rich and powerful. Ray half-suspected that Barnett had some kind of wild card ability. But he didn't. Barnett was just a salesman and a politician, and he was good at both.

"Sit down, Agent Ray," Barnett said warmly, indicating one

of the chairs in front of the huge desk that dominated the office. "Just sit yourself down right here."

Ray could swear that he almost heard a twinkle in Barnett's voice. Whatever the hell that could be.

"Thanks, Nephi. Sit yourself down," Barnett said as he put his expensively clad butt in the chair behind the desk.

Callendar nodded and took the second of three chairs arranged in front of the president's desk. Barnett turned directly to Ray and smiled long enough to make Ray feel more than a little uncomfortable.

"Well," Barnett said after what seemed to be a long time. "Well, well, well." He looked down at his desktop and gestured vaguely at the thick file that rested there. "It's good to see you again. Let's see. When did we last meet?"

"In Atlanta, Mr. President. When I got gutted by Mackie Messer on the floor of the Democratic National Convention." The memory of the twisted little ace with the buzz-saw hands still gave Ray nightmares, though he wouldn't admit that to anyone.

"Of course," Barnett said. "You know, I've been looking up your record. Extraordinary. Truly extraordinary. You're a fine example of American patriotism. All that you've done for your country over the years . . ."

I just like to kick ass, Ray was about to say, but he remembered what Callendar had said and for once he managed to hold his tongue as Barnett stared at the closed cover of the dossier, seemingly lost in his own thoughts. When he looked up his eyes were large and soulful, his voice dripping with worry and regret.

"I don't have to tell you," he said—and then did—"that our great country stands at the center of a difficult crossroads. The wild card is a curse on this land—oh, I know that might sound harsh to you, but after all you benefited from that hellish virus."

"Yes, sir," Ray said quietly.

"Yes, well, naturally you've seen the suffering and pain caused by the wild card. I have. I see it constantly. I'm doing my best to end the suffering for all citizens, but recent events have made things . . . precarious."

There was another long silence that Ray felt compelled to fill. "You mean the revelations about the Card Sharks?"

"Yes," Barnett said. "Exactly. Their methods in dealing with the wild card problem have been unnecessarily brutal and have led to no end of disquieting publicity."

"That's one way of putting it."

"Worse," Barnett went on as if he hadn't heard Ray, "many of these so-called Sharks had government connections. Some very high level connections. Most have been exposed and, uh, dealt with, but some still remain at large."

Ray nodded. "Pan Rudo. Johnson." Ray suppressed a smile. He thought he knew where this was heading, and he was more than ready to go out and kick more Card Shark ass.

"Yes. Among others. If you hadn't botched the assignment"— Barnett quickly retreated when he saw Ray's sudden coloring— "not that it was totally your fault, of course. Still. Still . . . I know that Agent Callendar has now assigned you to go after one of your own people—"

"My people?" Ray asked, then added, "He what?"

"Well, it's true that Senator Hartmann is apparently a joker—"

"Senator Hartmann?" Ray turned and looked at Callendar. "What's he talking about?"

"Well, Mr. President, I hadn't quite got around to telling Ray about his new assignment."

"Hadn't you better, then?" Barnett said, all the twinkle gone from his voice.

"Yes, well. Hartmann, of course, broke the story on the Card Sharks. Now he's on the loose . . . If only we'd listened to him in the beginning, but, after all, world-spanning conspiracies and all that . . . Well, never mind. We figure he may know something more about this Black Trump. Other agents are looking for him, but you were so close with him for so long that we thought you might have more of a handle on what he'd do, where he'd go."

Callendar was speaking faster and faster as he saw the increasingly hostile expression on Ray's face. When he finished, Ray glared at him and spoke in a voice of glacial coldness.

"Let me get this straight. Rudo and Johnson are running around loose in the world with God knows how much of this Black Trump stuff, just waiting to set it loose and kill every wild carder in existence. And you want me to go chasing after some fucking yellow caterpillar because he might, he just *might* know something about this shit? Well this is the biggest piece of—"

"Ray!"

"—fucked-up—"

"Agent Ray!"

"—government bullshit—"

"Agent Ray!" Barnett bellowed in a voice that easily overwhelmed Ray's. "I will not tolerate such language!"

Ray clamped his mouth shut and looked sulkily at Barnett. "Yes, sir," he said, almost without an edge in his voice.

"That's better," Barnett said. "Now. You're going after Hartmann—that is, if your new partner hasn't captured him already."

"Partner?"

"Yes. For the sake of appearances and, well, fairness and

equal opportunity, I'm going to partner you with another agent." Barnett swiveled and spoke into the intercom set on his desk. "Send in Ms. Harvest." He turned again and looked at Ray. "I'm implementing a new policy, Agent Ray. I think it would be appropriate to have a normal agent, that is, a non–wild carder, teamed with those infected, that is, those with . . ."

Ray's blood pressure started to rise again; then the door to the Oval Office opened and Ms. Harvest entered. She was young, tall, blond, and lean. Her skirt was blue silk; her blazer matched. Her blouse was white with a cute little black string bow tied at the base of her long graceful neck. Her hair was thick and straight. She wore it short, just covering her ears. Her glasses were gold wire rims. Her legs were leanly muscled, like a dancer's. Ray stood automatically as she approached.

". . . Agent April Harvest," he heard Barnett's words again as he took her hand in his. Her handshake was cool and firm. Much, he imagined, as the feel of her body would be, knees to breasts, pressed against his. "She'll be in charge of the operation."

Cool to begin with, but—

"What?" Ray's sudden fantasy was interrupted by harsh reality. He turned to face Barnett. "What?"

"I said that Agent Harvest will be in charge of the operation to find Senator Hartmann."

"Are you serious?" He looked back at her with a frown. "Is she out of high school yet?"

Harvest pulled her hand from Ray's grasp. "I'm twenty-four years old, Mr. Ray, and I've been in government service since I graduated from college. Princeton."

"Well, let's give you a kiss on the cheek and a medal! Twenty-four!"

"Agent Ray," Barnett said, allowing more than a hint of severity to creep into his voice. "Sit down." Ray did, reluctantly.

Harvest took the chair next to his. Ray was so disgruntled that he didn't even glance at her legs as she settled down. "If you'd been successful in your last mission, the urgency of this one wouldn't be so great."

"It wasn't my fault," Ray muttered.

"Hmmmm," Harvest said.

Barnett waved his hand. "Whatever. We're not interested in apportioning blame here."

No, Ray thought. *You've already pinned it all on me.*

"We're concerned about the future." Barnett leaned forward, a concerned look on his face. "We must move quickly to capture those who know about the Black Trump. We can't let knowledge of the virus leak to the populace. Think of the riots that would happen if the unfortunate citizens of Jokertown should learn of the existence of the Black Trump. Think of the damage to property and life alike." Barnett turned his attention to Harvest. "Agent Harvest has already led an operation to that end. In fact, I'm eager to hear her report."

"The dragnet was generally successful," she said crisply. "Most of the targets have been placed in protective custody on Governors Island."

"Including Hartmann?" Callendar asked.

"Well, no." A hint of annoyance crept into Harvest's voice. "He escaped, along with his companion, Hannah Davis. I've just received word that we picked up Davis, but Hartmann remains at large. The joker known as Quasiman also escaped, but he's not too much of a threat to reveal information about the Trump." She hesitated. "We also lost the carder once known as Snotman, now the Reflector. We're not quite sure what happened to him."

Barnett waved his hand. "He's a minor player. The one that concerns me is Hartmann." He turned his full attention to Ray.

"So you see, your mission becomes even more valuable. You must bring in Hartmann and all others he might have told about the Trump. We can't have them running around, spreading wild rumors."

"Certainly not, sir," Harvest said.

"But they're not *rumors*," Ray interjected.

"We know that," Barnett said. "But the effect would be the same, whether this Trump exists or not—"

"It exists," Ray said flatly. "I've seen the results."

"Whatever. The existence of the Trump is to be kept top secret. It is not to be discussed, hinted at, or supposed about. Officially, it does not exist. Understand?"

"Yes, sir," Harvest said.

"Agent Ray?"

Ray looked at the president for a long moment, then he nodded. *You bastard,* he thought. *I'm glad I never bothered to vote.*

"Good." Barnett nodded decisively. He picked up the dossier on the presidential desk, stood, and handed it to Harvest. "You'll need this. It's all the information we've been able to gather about Hartmann and his movements in the past few weeks."

Harvest took the file. "Thank you, sir."

Barnett came around the desk. "One last thing, before you go."

Ray watched in horror as Barnett got down on his knees on the rug in front of his desk. "Pray with me. Pray with me for the success of your mission and the fate of this great country that's been given to my keeping."

Callendar got down on his knees next to the president and Harvest joined him. Barnett looked expectantly at Ray.

"Well—"

Barnett gripped Ray's wrist. He was surprisingly strong,

but Ray could have easily pulled free. Somehow, though, that didn't seem like the thing to do. "Pray with me, son, for your success and the soul of this great nation."

Ray got down on his knees, surreptitiously scanning the rug to make sure it was clean. The last thing he wanted was stains on his trousers.

"All right," he said. He bowed his head but still kept an eye on his commander in chief. *If he starts talking in tongues,* Ray said to himself, *I'm out of here.*

Fridays for mosques, Saturdays shul, Sundays church. Subtle Scents ran twelve hours a day, Monday through Thursday, with optional shifts on the three weekend days. Mondays, everybody worked. Zoe finished a Monday shift and marched home, thinking of a hot shower and an early bedtime. The smell of sizzling butter met her halfway up the stairs.

"Blintzes for dinner, Mama?" she asked and stopped short with the door half open.

A thin Robert Bedford type, blond, mustached, and at ease, sat at the tiny table. He was grinning hugely and scarfing down a stack of blintzes between smiles. The table held a half gallon of orange juice, a pot of coffee, and a nearly empty quart jar of Anne's hoarded Hungarian cherry preserves.

"When you wake up, it's breakfast," Anne said.

"Hello, Zoe," Croyd said.

Zoe dropped her purse on the floor and sat down at the table. She looked him over, unable to stop herself, looked for horns or a tail or feelers, whatever. Needles had told her stories about Croyd that she wasn't sure she wanted to believe. He was thin, yes, and he had a prodigious appetite, but the parts of him she could see looked nat.

"Hi."

"Another batch, Mr. Crenson?" Anne asked.

"No, thank you. This last dozen should be enough to take the edge off."

"Dozen?" Zoe asked.

"He has a good appetite," Anne said.

"Where are the kids?"

"Busy," Anne said. "Busy and fed. They ate early."

If Anne didn't like where they were, Zoe would have heard it in her voice. They were somewhere, and they were okay.

"Some for you, Zoe?" Anne asked.

"Two."

Anne handed over a plate with three blintzes. Zoe scraped the last of the sour cream from a depleted carton on them and tucked in. They were very, very good.

Croyd attacked his plate, and while he ate he went through some funny facial stuff. A sort of tic, Zoe thought, but it might have been facial exercises. She couldn't tell. Anne made suds in the tiny sink and washed the mixing bowl.

Anne looked good. The docs were calling it remission. Her hair was growing back, the thick lovely hair that she had lost with the chemo. And she looked different with a nat-style torso, two breasts, fake but shapely. She wasn't even unhappy about the line of scars where her other five pairs of breasts had been.

Humming a tune. Zoe hadn't seen her this happy—since she cooked for Bjorn. Zoe swallowed coffee and tried to swallow the sudden lump in her throat.

Croyd polished off the late plate of blintzes, drank down the juice, chased it with coffee, and got up. He brought his empty—make that *gleaming*—plate to Anne.

"Excellent blintzes. Wonderful blintzes. The best blintzes I have ever had." He bent and kissed Anne's cheek, as if he were a son, a long-lost member of the family. Anne just glowed.

"I like a little exercise when I wake up," Croyd said. "Is it spring?"

"It's May," Anne said.

"Good. I need to walk. Come with me, Zoe." He twisted his hands in odd circles, stared at his palms, lifted up on his toes as if he were trying to fly. Weird.

"Uh . . ."

"Please?"

Well. She might just be inclined to follow that grin almost anywhere, and she didn't want his twitchy behavior to disturb Anne.

"Sure."

Zoe gave her plate to Anne and hugged her.

Croyd hurried toward the souk at a fast pace, his hands in his pockets, alert, watchful. He sniffed at the air as if to catch every scent.

"So those were blintzes," Croyd said. "I've never had blintzes before."

"Did you like them?" Zoe asked.

"Yeah."

She was glad she had her sneakers on. They were moving at almost a trot.

"What's the hurry?" Zoe asked.

"I'm hungry," Croyd said. He looked up at the rooftops along the narrow street and suddenly swerved to get close to the wall. "We're being watched."

"Yeah. Fist guards." She couldn't see anything, just purple twilight and a clear sky. "They watch everything."

"I don't like it."

"They're on our side, Croyd."

She followed him under a vendor's awning. On our side? Well, yes, maybe. The bastards. She'd been unable to figure out a safe way to contact them again. They weren't exactly in the phone book, and she didn't think another trip to the gate was a good idea.

Needles hadn't said a word to her since her visit to the gate. He was trying to be subtle about it, but he just wasn't around when Zoe was awake. Angelfish had found things to say to her, had been very nice the last few days, had been available to chat, which wasn't like him at all. Guarding Needles from her, her from Needles. But Needles looked okay. Sort of.

Croyd bought three skewers of shashlik: lamb and peppers and tomatoes, richly spiced, dripping and grilled almost black. He dipped the sticks in a paper cup of yogurt sauce and munched them down. "Want one?" he asked.

"No, thanks. Why were you wiggling around at home?"

"Checking to see what powers I've got this time."

"Did you find out?"

"Nope." He turned to the vendor and thanked him effusively in a language Zoe had never heard. The old man bowed, slapped Croyd on the back, and replied at length, smiling a gap-toothed smile.

Croyd did a little bow, one of those maneuvers with gestures toward his forehead, heart, and middle. He handed over the skewers and grabbed Zoe's hand, pulling her toward the back of the stall and through a gloomy doorway.

"Well," Croyd said. "I never spoke Basque before."

"Basque?" Zoe asked, but they were in a dim space filled with brass and carpets, and Croyd was chatting with a very large man dressed in a caftan of a most violent shade of purple. Something went from Croyd's hand to his, and something went in Croyd's pocket.

Out the back door, into an alley, through another door, and then another. Zoe had never known the Joker Quarter to have so many passageways, or so many places to eat.

Croyd tried a piece of baklava and then bought a pan of it.

He ate cucumbers, tomatoes, scallions dressed with oil and coriander at another stall.

"Do you always eat like this?" Zoe asked.

"When I wake up, yeah." He stopped to buy something wrapped in soft, puffy flatbread, something that reeked of garlic and fenugreek. He seemed to like it.

They turned another corner, into a section of the quarter that Zoe didn't know at all. She felt like a tourist. Croyd's sunny enthusiasm put a different light on the sights and smells. He was having fun. So was she, come to think of it, chatting and walking, his hand reaching for hers when she flagged behind him. Croyd wasn't coming on to her; the interaction felt more like teenage buddies touring Disneyland. Nice.

The next doorway opened into a restaurant. Croyd stuck his head in, sniffed, and grinned. The waiter motioned them toward a nest of pillows and a low table and left them. He returned carrying a pitcher in one hand, an atomizer in the other, and a basin, which he held in the curl of his prehensile tail. The arrangement made the process of handwashing and rosewater spritzing a one-step operation.

Zoe nibbled while Croyd demolished platter after platter of wonderful things.

"Bastilla," Croyd said. "Pigeon pie. I love Morocco."

"We're in Jerusalem," Zoe said.

"Yeah. Right."

He talked. He talked a lot. He was full of questions about all of the Escorts, about Anne, about news since he'd gone to sleep. Orient me; that was the gist of what he asked. Tell me about the world. In a corner, three musicians played some sort of drum, a flute, something flat with strings. They finished a song and said a few words, the order of the next set or something. Croyd stopped talking and listened to them.

"Dumbek, but it once was called a naqqua. The naq is the flute, and that thing on the woman's lap is a qanan, sort of a zither. The city is called Al Q'uds, except by the Jews and the Christians . . . I think I know every language on Earth. Now that's strange." Croyd's brown eyes were bright. He popped another square of sweet pastry in his mouth. "It's time to powder my nose. See if that guy will bring us another tray of these while I'm gone."

He unfolded his legs from the pillow and darted away. Zoe sipped sweet mint tea and listened to the players, the sinuous melodies of the desert, ancient, resonant. This land could be a place to love, if it were at peace. If.

She felt full, and amused, and almost happy. A little spaced but maybe that was the relief of a few hours away from— *Don't think about the past,* she told herself.

She saw Croyd threading his way through the tables, circling back toward her. Something was wrong; she sensed it. Croyd crouched beside her pillow and whispered in her ear, danger all too apparent in the relaxed way he moved. "There's some nasty muscle asking for you. Three of them. Here's what we do. You leave. Left, right, left, left, count three doors and you're back to the moneychanger's place, the dude in the purple. Act like you're mad at me and get. I'll follow you and try to pick them off."

"Who are they? Why me?"

"Something about a guy who's cut up pretty bad."

"Oh, shit. Can't we stay here?"

"The waiter's in on it."

She could see him watching, his tail whipping back and forth like a restless cat after a mouse.

"Why are you helping me?" Zoe whispered.

"Because you're cute. Do it," Croyd said.

Believe him? She had to. But Croyd could have turned her in to the guards' friends; he'd talked to so many people while they wandered. Get away.

She slapped him, a good solid whack, and ran from the restaurant. Behind her, Croyd shrugged and poured money on the table.

Left, down the alley. Old stone, garbage smells, the shadows so black. Croyd had spent most of the night eating; it was later than she had thought. Running, her sneakers made *meeping* sounds against the pavement. She concentrated on making no noise. Turn right, then left. This little jog, was that the next left? Damn, she hadn't really been watching. It had seemed that they had walked farther than this coming in, and she couldn't remember this totally incongruous storefront filled with shiny kitchen appliances. Surely she would have noticed.

Croyd had said left. She turned. The alley jogged toward freedom; a block away, there were lights beyond the corner, people, some safety.

Nightmarish, impossible, a man's face and torso appeared beside her. He was a hunchback, pathetic, armless. She flinched away from him, away from his pleading gaze, the silent words his mouth formed. The apparition vanished.

Had the monkey-tailed waiter drugged her tea?

A joker in black swirled into motion dead ahead of her, his cloak darker than the shadows. Not this way. Zoe spun around the corner and ran, trying to dodge the other shadow, the huge hands that reached for her. She fought him, and the next one, but they were big, and things moved too fast, and she didn't know *how* to streetfight.

Croyd was right about the numbers, she thought, as a six-fingered joker tied a black gag around her nose and mouth. There are three of them.

"You'll follow us." Six-fingers held her hand, and someone

dropped a black veil over her eyes. The gag cutting into her lip smelled of stale sweat.

They led her. She could see the black shoulders of the joker in front of her, the steps when they told her to go up, go down. The night was too dark to see anything else. They entered a building, or a cave, some space of corridors and hallways, all square and closed in.

She felt drugged, dazed. It seemed inevitable, it seemed right, that she would be pushed through a door, locked inside, still gagged. This was what she had expected, even hoped for, since that day in Manhattan when the mannequin had killed for her.

Their footsteps echoed down the hall outside. She could hear nothing at all.

Her hands were free. She pulled off the veil and the gag.

Yell? If she did, the men in black might come back in and hit her, hurt her. That thought was too scary to deal with. She tried the lock. Animate it? But they hadn't hurt her yet, and this must be the Fists' stronghold. If the plan was to kill her, they could have done it by now.

"You're safe here," a voice whispered.

The vague outline of a hunchbacked man seemed to hover near the ceiling. Zoe screamed and clung to the door, pounding her fists against it. No one came.

"Don't be afraid. Stay here. Don't run away."

What was it she had heard about hearing voices? Don't talk back to them, that was it. As long as you don't talk back to them, you aren't really crazy.

"You're—*important*." The voice was so kind, so wistful. And it wasn't there, anyway; there was nothing in the room at all.

The minutes crawled by.

What had the waiter given her? Acid? PCP? She hadn't tasted anything in her tea but mint and sugar, and her sense of taste was superb, a part of the ace she'd been dealt. But still, she felt dissociated, distant.

This was the Fists' stronghold. She was in the center of it, as close to the Black Dog as she was ever going to get. Wait, take the opportunity, talk to him or hurt him, make him stop messing with the kids.

They might let her starve, or die of thirst.

As soon as she felt less spaced out, she would animate the lock. If they didn't come for her. Soon.

There was a single wall outlet, no switches anywhere. The room was lighted by a nursery night-light, a plastic model of Turtle's Great and Powerful Shell. It must be a promo toy, a tie-in. Maybe the movie was in production. Zoe hoped so.

She sat down on the floor beside the little light and waited. And waited.

Hannah went aboveground daily to pick up newspapers and buy food. She and Gregg scanned the articles for news, but after a lone mention of a "disturbance" at the Dime Museum (buried on the third page of Metro), there was no follow-up. The *Jokertown Cry* carried an editorial questioning the fact that no one had seen Dutton, Father Squid, or Dr. Finn since the night of the "suspicious raids on several Jokertown locales," and suggesting that "Hannah Davis's well-known Card Sharks conspiracy" may have been ultimately responsible. None of the major papers picked up on the accusation, nor did any of the other news media.

Dutton and the others had simply vanished. Gone.

"We're on our own," Hannah told Gregg. Since the raid she'd dyed her hair; it was now a nondescript medium brown, trimmed short. The hair was too dark for her complexion, but Gregg admitted that she looked very different from the Hannah he'd known. She set the paper down on the pile and looked around the wet, dank vault in which they sat, pierced by the thick veins and arteries of Jokertown's sewer lines. "We can't stay here. I *won't* stay here."

"We're *safe* here. We can't exactly take a cab out of the city right now, can we?"

"*You* aren't safe," she reminded him. "You're not going to hide from a—" Hannah stopped. Her eyes widened as she looked at something behind Gregg. "*Quasi!*" she shouted, a squeal of delight. Hannah was up and running, brushing past Gregg to hug the hunchback who had suddenly appeared in the darkness of their artificial cavern. Gregg felt a sudden stab of jealousy as he watched them, as Hannah kissed Quasiman on the cheek and the two embraced.

Two days here and Hannah hasn't touched you, a voice said inside. *The two of you were lovers when you were normal, but now that you're a lousy yellow worm, you're nasty and awful. She kissed you once, when you first came back, but she hasn't tried it since, has she? She keeps talking about how she still loves you, but you know it's not in that way, is it? Quasi is at least humanoid. She can hug him, she can kiss him. But not you, Gregg. Not ever you.*

Gregg could see Quasiman's face as he hugged Hannah. In Gregg's nearsighted view, his expression was clear enough to see that Quasi was involved with Hannah beyond simple friendship. Gregg *knew.* He could see the infatuation in Quasiman's eyes, in his lopsided smile, in the way he pulled Hannah to him. And when Quasi saw Gregg, Gregg saw reflected there the same strange, angry loathing that Gregg felt when he looked in a mirror.

"Quasi," Hannah was saying, "have you seen Father Squid or Dutton? Any of the others?"

Quasi seemed to shudder. His attention drifted and he appeared to be looking at something not in the room. "Saw them," he said, stuttering. His gaze went back to Hannah. "An island. A you who wasn't you."

"What's that mean, Quasi?" she asked. Her hand brushed the joker's cheek, and Gregg felt his stomach churn acidly at the same moment. "I don't understand."

"You leave," Quasi said suddenly. "Water. Leprechauns. Fists." He looked at Gregg and scowled. "He knows how," Quasi said. "Do it."

"Do what?" Gregg asked him. "If you'd talk in something approaching a complete sentence, we might be able to make some sense of what you're saying."

"Gregg!" Hannah said, whirling around to look at him. "That's cruel. He can't help himself; you know that."

Gregg wrinkled his clown nose, squashing his round face like a hand puppet. The unfocused anger within him burned, and he wasn't sure who he was angry with: Quasi for interrupting their solitude, Hannah for making her affection for the joker so obvious, or himself for allowing it to bother him. "All right, I'm sorry. It's just—"

"You should *leave*," Quasiman said. Each word was an effort, separated by a breath.

"Leave New York?" Gregg asked. "Go to some other city?"

"Farther than that," Quasiman answered. "Other countries. Sentences. You must leave. There's nothing you"—Quasiman's lower jaw disappeared; his tongue waggled helplessly like a gray slug for a moment before the jaw reappeared—"can do here," Quasiman finished. "Complete fucking *sentences*."

Gregg had never heard Quasiman swear before. The word was so surprising that Gregg almost laughed. Quasiman glared at Gregg, defiant. His arms disappeared, first the left, then the right. The glare went slack and empty, and the joker stood there like a wax dummy, empty and cold.

"Poor Quasi," Hannah sighed. She touched his shoulder

above the bloodless wound of the missing arm. Quasiman didn't respond. He was gone to wherever he went in his fugues. "Gregg, you know he can glimpse the future. He's helped me so much before." She crouched down in front of Gregg, but she didn't touch him. Her eyes were full of something that might have been affection, but she didn't touch *him*. "I trust Quasi. He's seen something and he's trying to warn us."

"I can get as much information reading Nostradamus," Gregg muttered, and at her look: "All right. Maybe he's right. We sure aren't getting anything accomplished sitting down here. But what do we do?" There was a soft *pop* that echoed ringingly in the underground quiet. When Gregg looked up, the hunchback was gone. "So much for asking Mr. Complete Sentences."

"He wants us to leave the country," Hannah said. "I understood that much. It makes sense, especially if Rudo's fled the country, too."

"Right. And where do we go?"

Hannah looked at him. "Dutton said it back at the Museum: Rudo and Johnson will go to ground with the people they trust—the influential Sharks overseas. You're the one with the contacts. Let's use them."

Hannah watched him, and he saw his alien face reflected in her eyes. He wondered what she was feeling. He felt that if she touched him then, that he might be able to know, that the contact might spark some connection. Hannah's hand was lifted, as if she might reach out to him, but she drew it back and smiled grimly instead. "I just want to find Rudo and the vials," she said. "Wherever they've gone. I want this done."

So you can leave me then? Gregg wondered. *So you can return to a normal life?* he wondered, but the glimmerings of a plan had formed. "Let me make a call," he said.

— — —

April Harvest looked down the short staircase dubiously.

"Are we going to hit every dive in town?" she asked.

"If we have to," Ray said. "You want to find jokers, you go to places where jokers hang out: Freakers, Club Dead Nicholas, the Twisted Dragon. Now this place is something special. I read all about it in an article by Digger Downs in *Aces* magazine. You'd be surprised how much goes on in a place like Squisher's."

"I think I'd rather not know." She wrinkled her nose in disgust. "I can smell it from *here*."

Ray grinned, the fluttering neon light from the sign for Uncle Chowder's Clam Bar making his face look surprisingly sinister. Squisher's Basement was located below street level under the clam bar. The small metal sign with the bar's name on it was peeling and rusted. The hand that pointed down the stairs had six fingers.

"Don't worry," Ray said. "I'll take care of you."

"You don't have to take care of me, Ray. I do that all by myself. It'd be better if you'd remember that I'm in charge of this investigation. I'm only following your suggestion because all our previous attempts at finding Hartmann have turned up empty."

Ray nodded. "Whatever you say."

Squisher's Basement was a dive, a joint where the locals went for cheap but bad food and serious drinking. It smelled like Jokertown: old and dirty and sad. Inside it was dark and quiet. Most of the light came from the fluorescents hanging above the huge aquarium behind the bar, where Squisher resided. The few muted conversations among the patrons dropped off into silence as Ray and Harvest walked to the bar. Every eye in the place was on the two—even Squisher's, as he floated silently in his aquarium.

"I'm looking for someone," Ray announced.

"You'll be looking for your own ass in a minute," someone rumbled from the bar.

"Yeah, you tell him," a joker standing near Ray said.

"Yeah, tell him," the other head sprouting from the joker's torso said.

Ray smiled. There was genuine amusement in it, as well as anticipation.

"Who the hell are you?" he asked the two-headed joker.

Actually, they had more than two heads. They shared a single massive set of legs and one pelvis but were bifurcated from the waist up: two heads, two sets of shoulders and arms, two massive torsos. They were thickly built and looked strong but unwieldy. Separately they would have outweighed Ray by sixty pounds each. Together, they dwarfed him.

The two heads looked at each other. "My name is Hans," one said with a sudden, strange accent. "This is Franz. Who are you, girly-man?"

Some of the bar patrons tittered. Ray smiled more widely and turned to face the jokers squarely.

"You must be as stupid as you are ugly," he said, "if you think you can get away with that weak shit. You're really . . . uh . . ."

"Rick and Mick Dockstedder," Harvest said crisply. "Cheap muscle. Used to work for the Shadowfists, now freelance."

"Right," Ray said. It seemed she did know her shit.

"Are you heat?" Hans—that is, Rick—asked.

"That's right, moron. The hottest kind. Federal. This is Agent April Harvest. My name is Billy Ray and I can lick every man in this place."

"Oh," Rick said.

"Oh," Mick said.

They sat down.

Ray looked up and down the bar. "We can fight," he said, "or we can drink. Either is fine with me."

There were some mutters, but no challenges.

"Okay," Ray said. "We drink. A round for the house on me. And give me a receipt."

The bartender drew the drinks, and Squisher breathed easier in his aquarium as Ray explained his mission.

"I'm looking for Hartmann, Senator Gregg Hartmann. You may remember him. He's been jumped into the body of a guy named George G. Battle. Battle used to be a government agent, but he went bad. He turned into a joker, then switched bodies with Hartmann. Battle got his ticket punched but Hartmann's still around. He's hiding somewhere in J-town as a yellow caterpillar. Now I know all about joker solidarity and all that shit, but we need to talk to Hartmann about this Card Shark mess. I want his ass, and one of you can probably give it to me. There's bucks in it. You can reach each of us at the Carlington Hotel." He looked around the room. "Got it?"

Some of the jokers looked angry, some indifferent. A few looked thoughtful. "Okay," Ray said. "See you on the funny pages." He turned to Harvest. "Let's go."

"Think it'll work?" she asked as they started toward the stairs.

Ray shrugged. "Maybe. We just have to wait and see."

There was a sudden, unexpected *pop*, and a wide-eyed hunchback was standing in front of them. Ray and Harvest stared. Some of the bar patrons looked up, then went back to their drinks. It was no big deal in Squisher's.

"It's that joker!" Harvest said.

"Quasiman," Ray confirmed.

"Get him!"

"All right, cool down. It doesn't look like he's going anywhere." Ray turned to Quasiman, who was staring sightlessly past the both of them. There was a look of real horror on his face. Ray put his hands on Quasiman's shoulders and looked into his eyes. "What is it? What's the matter?"

Quasiman roused himself from his stupor. He focused slowly on Ray's face. "The mushroom flower," he said distinctly, "blooms where it's sunny."

Ray glanced at Harvest and shrugged. "Sure. Why don't you come with me and we'll talk about it?"

He tried to get Quasiman to fall into step, but the joker was going nowhere. He stood, rooted to the spot, a line of drool dribbling unnoticed on his chin. His eyes suddenly narrowed and his brow furrowed in concentration. It was as if he had to tell Ray something of great importance, but he couldn't force it out. "Duh—don't drink the wine," he finished in a rush.

"Don't drink the wine?" Ray asked, puzzled.

Quasiman nodded, his head bobbing up and down like a puppet's on a string. And then he vanished, popping away to wherever it was that he went to when he popped away. Ray staggered, finally catching his balance as Harvest looked on in disgust.

"You had him," she said, "and you let him get away."

"Well, how the hell was I supposed to stop him?"

She shook her head. "Never mind. Let's go."

Ray followed her up the stairs. "Don't drink the wine," he said, half to himself. "I never drink wine. I hate the stuff."

"Miss Harris?" The voice was diffident, and there was a shy tapping at the locked door.

"Come in," Zoe said, which was the most ridiculous response she could imagine anyone making who was locked in a cell. The words just slipped out. Had it been three hours, four, since they locked her in here?

The door opened. A girl beckoned to her, a joker girl with a pearly unicorn horn in the center of her forehead. The girl wore Fist black and carried an Uzi. "Would you come with me, please?"

Please, and a gesture with the Uzi. Zoe blinked at the light in the corridor and went where the girl pointed.

To a thick metal door, polished and gleaming amber in the reflected light of eye-saver fixtures. A joker with a snail's foot came through it. That guy, yeah, the one from the souk. Faintly, she heard vendors calling out their wares, the morning bustle of the waking city.

Snailfoot looked up and smiled. Unmasked, he was handsome in a rather Peter O'Toole-ish fashion. "We meet again," he said.

Beside Zoe, a black robe rustled. She could have sworn there was no one else in the corridor.

"Zoe Harris," a tall joker said. His baritone voice was slightly muffled behind the black beast mask that covered his face. "You wanted to see the Black Dog. You're seeing him." He offered his arm and Zoe reached out for it, compelled by the man's presence, the aura of power that surrounded him. His forearm was muscular and very warm. "Come with me. Snailfoot, tell Balthazar to get his ass in here."

Snailfoot nodded and slithered away. The Black Dog opened the metal door. Stone steps lighted in amber led down to a landing and continued down into gods-knew-what.

"You've got to learn to control that ace of yours. All you did with that business at the gate was you let a lot of jokers know you've got powers," the Black Dog said. "You can't afford to panic."

Brooklyn? There was some Brooklyn in his voice, under the European sounds that Israelis used when they spoke English.

"Guns make me just a little tense," Zoe said.

"You'll get over it."

He started down the stairs, and Zoe found she was following him. She didn't *want* to go down those stairs. The guy was hypnotic, and scary as hell. She had expected to be brushed aside, dismissed, or challenged, and it seemed she was being *welcomed*. Something was a little skewed here.

"Hurry." The Black Dog's cloak swirled out behind him. *Darth Vader,* Zoe thought, *and this is the Death Star. This should be funny, and it isn't.* Someone was behind her on the steps. Needles. He shook his head at her, pleading for her silence.

"Go *on,* Zoe," Needles whispered.

The bottom of the stairway led into a rough stone corridor. The air was fresh and cool. Zoe heard a faint whine of ventilator fans.

"Why am I here? Why did your goons lock me up?"

"I let them unleash some of their anger. You hurt one of our people. Remember?"

"I was only trying to communicate with you. They played rough."

"Communicate? What important communication did you have for the Twisted Fists?"

Her concern sounded so foolish, but she had to say it anyway. "I don't like what you're teaching my kids." He wouldn't listen to her. Why should he? "I'm royally pissed about the way you're *using* them."

"Are you?" the Black Dog asked. "They're getting the best training in Jerusalem."

"Training for murder?" Zoe asked. "That's supposed to be good?"

"Training for survival," he said. "It's hard to educate corpses."

"They will become inhuman! Monsters!"

She hurried to stay behind him in the narrow space.

"They aren't human now, and 'monster' isn't the worst thing I've heard them called." He sounded amused.

"Please, Zoe, don't," Needles whispered behind her.

"Is life as a murderer worth living?" Zoe asked.

The procession traced its way down a slanted passage cut into rock.

"Is it, Zoe?"

No. No, her knowledge screamed at her. *It's no life at all.* Zoe remembered the spasms of the skinhead she had killed as he shuddered out his life, his arms clutching her father's corpse in an ugly embrace. Dreams, dreams and nightmares, when she dreamt it was her hand on the knife in her father's belly. In her dreams, *she* killed Bjorn, over and over. At night, she wanted to die, to rid herself of dreams. Every night, she forced herself to live one more day, to stay alive as long as Anne needed her. Anne's death had begun to seem a liberation, because then Zoe could stop living, stop sleeping, stop dreaming. A suicide. Was that the message she would leave the Escorts? Give up, die, your life is shameful?

The tall man with the yellow eyes of a goat came from a side corridor and fell into step beside Needles.

"Balthazar was impressed by your talents at the gate. That's why you're alive. Thank him, someday."

The corridor made a sharp turn and widened enough for two people to walk side by side. The walls were honeycombed with rectangular crypts, some occupied by stone sarcophagi, some, high up in the shadows, filled with reclining, placid skeletons.

"Where *are* we?" Zoe asked.

The Black Dog walked beside her in the wider space. He was tall, his masked face immobile and inhuman save for the moist gleam of the whites of his eyes, stained amber by the scattered lights in this quiet maze of catacombs.

"Under the city."

They left the graves and entered another stairway that led down. The air temperature dropped. Zoe pulled her cloak tight around her shoulders. Pipes and conduits mazed along the ceiling. Doorways led into dark, vast rooms, full of canisters and angular crates that could have held anything—guns, portable buildings, tractors, or tanks. The city hid a city beneath its streets.

"Was I drugged? Are you so afraid of aces that you had that monkey-man put drugs in my tea?"

"Monkey? No. No drugs."

He sounded so puzzled that she believed him. Her sense of taste was still okay. She was just crazy. Great.

Side doors led to offices. The corridor ended in another armored door.

"Needles, come in with us," the Black Dog said.

Balthazar clenched his fist in salute and stayed in the corridor. The Black Dog led Zoe and Needles through a doorway screened with a beaded curtain, into a carpeted room scattered with pillows.

Croyd sat cross-legged on the floor next to a stocky woman in full chador. The woman rose as the Black Dog entered.

"Welcome, Hound of Hell," the woman said.

"Good morning, Azma." The Black Dog bent and took the woman's hands in his. He brushed the muzzle of his mask across her fingers. She bowed to Zoe and the newcomers and left the room. Croyd got his legs under him with less grace, but he got up without using his hands, which were wrapped around a tiny coffee cup.

"I think you have to grow up sitting on the floor," Croyd said, "or your knees just don't bend the right way."

"Miss Harris, this is Croyd Crenson."

"We've met," Zoe said. She tried to put enough ice into her voice to freeze his nose off.

"Hello, Zoe," Croyd said. He toasted her with his cup and sipped more coffee. "They got me, too."

"So I see."

The Black Dog seated himself on the floor and pulled a floor cushion up to use as an elbow rest. He poured himself a cup of coffee from an ornate silver urn. The coffee smelled of cinnamon. *Don't sit down*, Zoe told herself. *Keep the tiny advantage you have by standing while he sits, make your speech, and go.*

"I wanted to plead with you the first time I came here," Zoe said. "I still do. I don't want my kids trained as killers. I'll do anything I can do, pay any price that I'm able to pay, to prevent that. I don't mind that they're associated with the Fists. We can't live here otherwise, I know, but surely they can be trained as noncombatants. I beg you, don't do this to them. They are tough kids, but they're good kids. Please. That's all I have to say. I'll go now."

"Thanks for the coffee," Croyd said. "I'll just be running along myself."

A guard, not Balthazar, appeared in the doorway, his rifle at the ready.

"Please," the Black Dog said. "Sit down, both of you. Needles, pour the lady a cup of coffee." He motioned to the floor in front of him. Zoe sat. So did Croyd.

"You're here for a reason. You too, Croyd. You're here because I need you, and because you both look like nats. I don't like nats. I don't like aces. I don't trust them. But trust can be contracted, if the terms are right. I need your help."

Needles handed Zoe a cup of thick black coffee.

She stared at it. Was it drugged, too?

"I need you to go to the Ukraine and buy a nuclear warhead," the Black Dog said.

His words were clear enough. He had just said, "I need you

to go to the Ukraine and buy a nuclear warhead." Right. Zoe had a lot of experience in international arms trade, sure. That's why he had kidnapped her, of course. The man was totally psychotic, she had no business here to begin with, and a rifle was pointed at her back.

"The Card Sharks have a biologic weapon that can kill all of us," he continued. "Jokers, aces, carriers, anyone infected with the wild card. The Sharks have developed a killer virus they call the Black Trump. If it gets loose, we'll die. All of us."

"That's crazy," Zoe said. No one could develop such a weapon and be sure it would work. "The Card Sharks were a delusion of Gregg Hartmann's. He said so." But then Hartmann had always had a tendency to bend the truth, Zoe remembered.

"Needles? The case report, if you would."

Needles handed Zoe a manila folder. She opened it, seeing scattered words: Hemorrhagic shock. Lysis of internal organs including the brain . . . the victims exhibit lethargy and cerebral dysfunction so that they appear to be dead while still alive . . .

Zoe slapped the folder shut. An eight-by-ten glossy slid out, full-color reds and blues of something collapsed and limp that might have once been a joker.

The Black Dog retrieved the photo, slipped it back inside the folder, and handed it to Croyd.

"The virus has been tested. It works. The Card Sharks aren't a delusion. The Sharks are real, and they have the Black Trump. I don't want it turned loose in Jerusalem. I don't want it turned loose *anywhere*."

"Go to the police. Go to Interpol. Go to the UN."

The UN didn't do such a great job in Jerusalem as it was. So many UN "peacekeepers" had died in Jerusalem that their presence was now a carefully calculated sop for tourists. They left the real violence in the city alone. Maybe not the UN. Maybe CNN.

"Your friend Charles Dutton is under arrest. Father Squid is missing. No one can find that little horsy doctor from the Jokertown Clinic."

"Dr. Finn? Missing?"

"Everyone in New York who knows about this virus is missing. Jokertown's most colorful freaks vanish and there's not a whisper, not an arrest, no inquiry."

"That much cover-up couldn't happen."

"It has."

Bjorn had believed Hartmann's stories about a conspiracy. If this were one, it had to go all the way up. All the way.

Impossible.

But there had been all that trouble about getting Anne's records out of the clinic, strange voices on the phone, delays, no way to talk to Finn, and he had liked Anne.

"That's why we need a bomb. If we can blackmail the Sharks with it, we will. If we can't, and there's an outbreak—"

"You'd have to pray that the virus was loosed only in one confined place. You're crazy. Can't you just *tell* the Sharks you've got a bomb?" Zoe asked.

Well, no. The Sharks couldn't be that stupid; the Black Dog couldn't be sure that some of his people didn't report to the other side.

"What do you plan to do with this . . . device . . . when you get it?" Zoe asked.

"Threaten to expose the plot. Bargain for the virus. Turn the warhead over to the UN when we can."

Uh-huh.

"If you're looking for a smuggler, you're looking in the

wrong place," Zoe said. "I've never even shoplifted anything."

Croyd shut the folder, laid it on the floor beside him, and
sipped at his coffee.

"Mr. Crenson has skills in this area," the Black Dog said.

"Your pictures don't scare me and I don't understand some
of the big words in that report. Pictures can be faked. Forget it.
I don't do nukes," Croyd said.

The Black Dog leaned back against his cushion and rested
an elbow on his knee in a storyteller's pose from a bad movie
of the Arabian nights. His masked face seemed to stare at
something above Croyd's head.

"Croyd Crenson has always been afraid to sleep. His fear is
not of sleeping but of waking." The Brooklyn street slang in
the Black Dog's voice vanished, replaced by the sonorous cadence of a storyteller in the souk. "Because he believes that one
day he will wake as a madman, as demented as the mother
whom he scarcely remembers."

"How could you know that? Nobody knows that." Croyd's
face went pale and his eyes locked on the dog mask.

"We spoke of contracted loyalty." The Black Dog sighed as
if he were contemplating human treachery with great sorrow.
"There was a man once who wanted to *help* you. Do you remember?"

Croyd's lean body had looked almost gaunt. It wasn't, Zoe
realized. He was thin in the way bodybuilders called "ripped."
Every muscle in his forearms, in his neck, stood out in tense
definition. She pulled her shoulders in, trying to look smaller
and nonthreatening.

The Fist's leader settled back on his cushion again. "Pan
Rudo. Here's the deal, Croyd. Bring me the bomb. We'll bring
Pan Rudo to you. I promise it."

"Bullshit," Croyd said. "One, the Card Sharks *are* cranks. And two, I finally managed to kill that son of a bitch Rudo. He's dead! I killed him. Count me out of this, okay? I gave at the office."

"Pan Rudo's alive. He was jumped into a strong, young body. We're looking for him now."

"No!" Croyd moved with the speed of a trained athlete, on his feet in an instant with his hand stretched toward the Black Dog's throat. The guard at the door snapped his rifle into position, and Croyd stopped in what seemed to be mid-leap. He had managed to put down his coffee cup before he moved, Zoe noticed. He hadn't spilled a drop.

"Sit down, Croyd. The Twisted Fists are after Rudo now. We'll find him. When we find him, he's all yours."

"He's dead, damn it!"

"He's young. Younger than you, by the calendar. He's a handsome man, so I hear. Not many men get to taste their dearest enemy's death twice, Croyd. Think about it."

"I don't believe you," Croyd said.

"I think you do," the Black Dog said.

Croyd settled back on his cushion. His eyes never left the Black Dog's face. He motioned with his empty coffee cup and Needles filled it for him.

"Zoe Harris, you think you can't be part of this. Nice girls don't play games with horrors. Your moral code would never let you touch a situation like this, even if your refusal meant your death and the death of every joker and ace in the world. Yeah. I might just feel that way myself, if I had the choice.

"I don't. Here's my offer. You get this bomb back to Jerusalem. Once that's done, you'll never hear from us again. We'll send your kids to Vietnam. All of the kids go and they go to school. The Fists pay the bills. Jellyhead wants to be a doc, I hear. She's got real talent in that direction."

She did. The Black Dog was talking security for all of them, more security than a wage earner under threat of extradition could hope for. Vietnam would mean another move, another displacement, another culture for the kids to fit themselves into. The situation might change there, but there were enclaves that might be free of the sound of gunfire for a few more years. A few quiet years to grow and hope.

She couldn't do this. Could not. Would not. In the photo, the half-dissolved sagging body of a joker, blood oozing from eyelids, nostrils, fingernails . . .

"That's my offer, but that won't be enough to convince you. Needles, speak to her," Black Dog said.

"You have to help," Needles said. "I mean, you don't have to. But Jan is in this bomb thing. She's the only one of us who looks nat. Zoe, it has to be nats. There's borders to cross, and jokers don't get past them alive. You haven't seen what they do to jokers in the desert, what they do to the kids if their card turns and we can't get to them in time.

"Jan's already headed for the Black Sea, Zoe. She's with Balthazar."

Jan? Pick the one that's closest to my heart, except all of them are close to my heart. This was vile blackmail. But Jan? What if she panicked and let her joker eyes show at a border crossing?

"I don't know *how* to buy a bomb," Zoe said.

"Most of the arrangements are made. The package is ready. Payment has been discussed. You and Croyd are buying some farm equipment. That's all there is to it. You pick up the package; someone you'll never see hands over a draft on a Swiss bank. You're just mules. It isn't all that cloak-and-dagger stuff. Forget that.

"You, Jan, your husband Croyd, and his brother Balthazar. An innocent, hardworking family transporting an irrigation pump. You'll manage this, Zoe Harris. You will do whatever you can to keep your 'daughter' alive. And in the process, the rest of us may buy time to destroy the fucking Trump. We have to try, anyway."

"I don't get it. Why Croyd? Why me? Why *Jan*?"

"You might get stopped. You might be asked questions. You don't know much about the Fists. If you're caught, you can't say much, any of you, that would hurt us. We deny that we ever heard of you. That's how it has to be."

"You bastard," Zoe said.

"Yes," the Black Dog said. "Oh, yes."

"I don't speak anything but English," Zoe said.

"Croyd does. Needles, take them to Snailfoot. He can brief them." The Black Dog's robes swirled around him as he rose and vanished through the beaded curtain.

"Come on, Zoe," Needles said. "You'll like Azma. She'll do a good job with your hair."

Hair? Nuclear warheads? A trip to Ukraine? But Needles was smiling at her, as calm as if he'd just mentioned a trip to the souk for cucumbers. Croyd Crenson didn't look like a Turk. What if he fell asleep? Irrigation pumps? A disease that dissolved jokers in their own blood?

The room itself seemed a stage set. Zoe felt that if she pushed one of the stone walls, it would break like cardboard. She would see the barren brick wall behind it, and stagehands running back and forth to set the next scene.

She stood, walked to one of the walls, and laid her hand on the solid stone, cool and unyielding. She punched at it.

"Zoe?" Needles asked.

Her knuckles bled from tiny scrapes. She held her fist in her hand feeling the bones. She hadn't broken anything.

"My hair. Black?"

"Yeah, sure. You too, Croyd. Come on."

— — —

Gregg had learned the layout of the sewer lines in the month or so he'd spent hiding there after he'd been jumped. He came up into the subbasement of Squisher's establishment, through a loose grate in the storeroom floor. He pushed open the unlocked door and eased himself out into a dimly lit corridor. Worn concrete stairs led to the bar just below street level. As Gregg remembered, there was a phone booth here, in an alcove between the restrooms.

So far, so good. Squisher's seemed safer than up on the streets where he was being hunted, and this was a call that Gregg had to make, not Hannah. In the early afternoon, Squisher's was mostly empty. Gregg could hear the sounds of someone's heavy tread on the floor above and the insistent bubbling of Squisher's tank behind the bar. The low drone of a TV masked the fragments of conversation that drifted down the stairs. The basement smelled equally of uncleaned urinals and spilled alcohol.

"I think I prefer the sewers," Gregg muttered to himself as he went to the phone booth and heaved his long body up on the seat. He pushed the receiver up with a tiny hand; it fell, dangling from the short cord. He'd been clutching a quarter in one hand, resisting the temptation to pop it into his mouth like a piece of hard candy; now he slid it into the slot. Gregg punched numbers and pressed his ear against the swaying receiver, waiting. One ring. Two. Three. Gregg sighed, thinking the answering machine would kick in, when he heard someone pick up the phone. "Yeah?"

Gregg lifted his body slightly so he could speak into the mouthpiece; his truncated arms couldn't bring the receiver to his head. "Bushorn? Bushorn, don't hang up please. You have to listen, have to hear me out."

Gregg dropped down. "—listening," a faint bass voice answered.

Up again. "Good. You remember your court case a year and a half ago? East Air Freight fired you because you were a wild carder, said you were 'dangerous.' We agreed on half a million in an out-of-court settlement; you said you were going to buy that plane you always wanted. You also said that if I ever needed a favor, to just ask. We were standing in the street outside the offices. You shook my hand, my left hand, and you said it didn't matter what, didn't matter when, just call Gary Bushorn. Well, I need that favor."

He dropped down again. "—artmann? Gregg Hartmann?"

Up. "Yes. I'm Gregg Hartmann. Much changed, I'm afraid. Gary, I need a flight for two out of the country, and I need it now."

Down. "—rumors about you are true, then. With what I've been hearing, that explains a lot, I guess. Look, I . . . I guess owe you one, maybe. But I have to file a flight plan, get the plane ready, make sure things are set here. That's gonna take a day or two. Just where you planning to go?"

"How far can you take us?"

"—outh America. Upper Canada. Europe, if we take it slow and easy."

"Europe," Gregg said. As Hannah had said, the vials would be with the Sharks; if Rudo had indeed fled the country, then he'd have run to one of them—and they knew that the British general in Ulster, Horvath, was a Shark. If that didn't pan out, then England was close, and Gregg knew people there: Captain Flint, Churchill. Suddenly Gregg was feeling less useless. "That sounds good. How soon, Gary?"

"—days. That should do it."

"When? How many days?"

Gregg was suddenly aware of someone watching. He could

feel the pressure of a gaze. His head jerked up to see the large body of the joker known as Mick and Rick staring at him from the stairwell leading to Squisher's. The two-headed joker didn't say anything, and Gregg wondered how long they'd been listening. Bushorn was talking. He thought he heard the word "Thursday."

"We'll be there," he said quickly, and he pressed the hook, disconnecting Bushorn. Gregg slid down from the seat. Mick and Rick watched, the doubled heads swiveling as Gregg scooted across the hall and into the storeroom.

"Where's he going now?" he heard Mick say.

"How the hell should I know?" Rick answered. "I ain't getting near him. I heard his puke can melt metal."

Gregg slithered down the narrow sewer inlet feetfirst. He pulled the lid over him. He hoped Bushorn understood, hoped he had the right day. That left only one small problem—how to get to Tomlin.

The waiting was boring. When Ray got bored, he had too much time to think, and now he had something to think about. He came back from the bathroom where he'd just taken his temperature (normal: one hundred and three degrees) and spent a minute or two staring at his tongue (looked normal, but Ray wasn't sure; he'd never really looked closely at his tongue before). He *seemed* to be all right, but then Crypt Kicker seemed okay until he'd turned into a pile of shit right in front of Ray's eyes. This Black Trump stuff was maddening. And Ray had the feeling that he'd have to go face-to-face with it again. He didn't want to, that was for sure. He didn't know if he could. He'd never run away from anything in his life, but the Black Trump was like nothing he'd ever faced. Maybe he was better off chasing Hartmann than chasing death.

To get his mind off the Black Trump he looked at Harvest, who was sitting at the hotel room's tiny writing desk, reading the dossier Barnett had given them. Her silk-clad legs were crossed at the knee, her blond hair was attractively tousled. She looked good enough to eat.

"Harvest," Ray said as a conversational gambit. "What kind of name is that?"

April Harvest looked up from the dossier. "A last name," she finally said.

"Well, it's an *unusual* last name."

She looked at Ray expressionlessly. "Not to me it isn't."

"Well . . ." This wasn't going very well. Ray didn't know if he should be exasperated or angry. He suspected he'd reach the latter stage soon enough. She continued to look at him. He felt trapped by the gaze of her killer blue eyes. "Well . . ." he said again. He felt like an idiot. This wasn't going well at all.

A knock on the door rescued him.

"Who is it?" he barked, louder and harsher than necessary.

There was a momentary silence, then a voice on the other side of the door said, "No one. No one's here."

Ray frowned. He looked at Harvest. She was frowning, too.

"Yes, there is," another voice said. "It's me."

Ray growled. He got off the bed and glided to the door with his usual effortless grace. He yanked it open. "Oh. It's you." Ray stepped back.

"Come in."

"No, I have to be going," Mick Dockstedder said. "Nice seeing you again." He gave a jaunty little wave and tried to walk away, but his conjoined twin wasn't having it.

"Now just wait a minute, Mick," said Rick. "I want to talk to Ray."

"I don't!" Mick said a bit sharply. "Let's go."

"No!"

"Yes!"

"No!"

Ray silently watched the twins' struggle for control of their single pair of legs. This was it, he told himself. There was no doubt, now. It was anger.

"Get inside," he growled in a low, dangerous voice, "before I knock the crap out of you . . . out of both of you . . . and drag you in."

Mick looked at his brother with hurt in his eyes. "You've done it, now, Rick."

"No I haven't," Rick said as Ray closed the door behind them. "It'll work out just fine. Won't it?"

"You bet," Ray said without enthusiasm.

Rick and Mick stopped when they saw Harvest look at them with disbelief and disgust on her finely chiseled features.

"Who's that?" Mick asked.

"You remember her," Rick answered. "She was at Squisher's."

"I *know* that," Mick said. "I want to know who she is."

"She's on the Special Executive Task Force," Ray said.

"I'm his boss," Harvest added.

"Maybe we can trust Ray," Mick said, "but we don't know anything about her."

"You a wild carder, lady?" Rick asked.

Harvest shook her head.

"That's it," Mick shouted. "I'm out of here."

"No, you're not," Rick shouted back. "You wait right here for me."

"I won't!"

"Oh, yes you will, you dummy!"

"Well, yeah, I'm smarter than you any day of the week!"

"Are not!"

"Are too!"

The two shouted invectives at each other as they moon-walked back and forth across a patch of carpet, heading to the door and back, the door and back. Ray planted himself in front of them, grabbed them, and spun them around.

"What the hell do you guys want?" he roared.

"Nothing!" Mick said. "My mouth is shut."

Ray grabbed his nose and twisted. "Keep it shut," Ray barked. "Or I'll tear your nose off." He looked at Rick. "How about you?"

Rick licked his lips. "You said there'd be money in it if we told you where Hartmann was."

Ray nodded, suppressing a smile. "That's right."

"How much?"

"A thousand."

Rick looked at his brother.

"Tell him to let go of my nose," he said. Ray sighed and did. Mick refused to meet his brother's eyes. Rick nudged him, but Mick shook his head. "Nope. This is your doing. I want no part of it."

"Okay," Rick said. "Suit yourself." He looked at Ray. "I been around, you know. I know a lot of what's coming down."

Ray nodded impatiently. "Sure. But what do you know about Hartmann?"

"He's been seen in the company of some blond nat bimbo—oh." Harvest had cleared her throat and stared at him with her hard blue eyes. "No offense, lady, um, ma'am. He's been hanging with Father Squid, too."

"We know that," Harvest said briefly.

"He's been on his own since Father Squid and the others were picked up by the police. But he wants to get out of the city. I overheard him in Squisher's."

"How's he trying to get out?" Ray asked.

"A plane," Rick said. "He's trying to hire a plane. Ain't that right, Mick?"

Mick shook his head. "*I* ain't saying."

"Where? Tomlin? LaGuardia? Where?" Harvest asked.

Rick shook his head. "I don't know."

Ray frowned thoughtfully. "That's not much to go on."

Rick looked indignant. "It's the skinny. You can trust me."

"Hah!" Mick interjected.

"Sure you can, Mr. Ray. I wouldn't want to screw with you."

Ray nodded judiciously. "Damn right. Okay." He reached into his pocket for his wallet. He counted five hundred-dollar bills and handed them over to Rick.

"You said an even thou."

"Another five hundred when we get Hartmann."

"But—"

Ray looked at him.

"Okay. That's fair." Rick stuffed the bills in his pants pocket.

"Here." Ray handed him a sheaf of printed forms. "Sign this receipt."

"Okay."

Rick's signature was accomplished in a laborious scrawl. As they headed out the door, they began arguing about what to do with the money. Mick was all for a big celebration dinner and maybe a visit to Chickadee's. Rick was firm that this was his money and Mick wasn't going to benefit from it. He remembered that there was a new edition of Star Trek porcelain plates rimmed in real fourteen-carat gold that he'd wanted for his collection. Ray stood at the door, watching them argue as they lurched off down the hall. He shook his head and shut the door.

"Can you believe those two?" he asked Harvest.

"I don't know. You've invested five hundred dollars of the government's money in them."

"Plenty more where that came from. What are you doing?"

She stopped dialing the phone and looked at him with eyes that could melt ice. "Setting up a dragnet to cover all the airports in the metropolitan area. You have a better idea?"

Ray opened his mouth, then shut it and shook his head. Nothing he felt he could go into right this moment.

In New York, it was said the prerequisite for a taxi driver's license was that the recipient must be unable to speak English. Supposedly it was an added bonus to look more like roadkill than anything human.

From what Gregg could gather between the plastic bars of his cage, this cabbie met both requirements. The driver of the cab Hannah flagged down near Roosevelt Park had too many arms, all of them seemingly slathered with green slime, and the parrot's beak set in the middle of the oversized wrinkled prune the joker used for a head looked disturbingly unsuited for normal speech. "Wayryegot?" he squawked at Hannah as she opened the rear door and slung the pet carrier holding Gregg across the cracked vinyl seat.

"It's my dog," Hannah said. "Spot. We—I mean I—need to get to Tomlin. Take the Manhattan Bridge, please."

Something round and saucer-like blinked in the center of the prune as the driver looked back at Hannah. Gregg could see a yellowed copy of the newspaper photo of himself clipped to the passenger seat visor, half obscured by someone's school picture—if it was the driver's daughter, there was no visible sign of the wild card in her. Gregg huddled back in the carrier, hoping the joker wouldn't notice his yellow skin through the vents. A slimy hand punched the meter on the dash, another plucked the microphone from the set; another waved out the window at traffic, while the final one turned the wheel as the cab pulled out onto Chrystie. "Nubberhunneredfurdysebben. Goderfair," the joker garbled into the mike. "HeddbingtoTommin."

The receiver squealed back something equally unintelligible. Thankfully, the driver didn't try to make conversation on the way. The radio blared percussive, bass-distorted hip-hop.

"Spot?" Gregg whispered through the bars to Hannah.

"Hush. It was the only thing I could think of. Now lie down. Good dog."

Hannah placed her hand on the carrier. Nervously, they both watched the buildings of Jokertown pass.

They'd debated how to get to Tomlin and Bushorn's hangar. Neither of them knew how to steal a car, and everyone they knew who they could have trusted to provide transportation had disappeared. That left public transportation. Buses were full of too many people. They'd judged that with Hannah's changed appearance and the animal carrier, their odds were fair to good hailing a cab.

The choice had been a good one, so far. As they went south, Jokertown gave way eventually to Chinatown, where they turned east, then the wharves of the East River appeared, the towers of the Manhattan Bridge appearing over the low roofs. To their right, a little farther south, they could glimpse the broken-toothed ruin of the Brooklyn Bridge, destroyed when the Turtle had smashed Herne's Wild Hunt, the same night Gregg had lost his right hand to one of the hellhounds.

That was your utter nadir: Puppetman gone, the Gift yet to come. You were reviled and weak.

What have I got now? Gregg responded to the voice. *What makes this any better? I'm hunted, reduced to pretending to be a goddamn fluorescent-yellow dachshund. I feel so fucking useless.*

Inside, someone seemed to chuckle.

They were nearing the approach to the bridge when Gregg

felt the cab slow and come to a stop in a miasma of gasoline fumes. Hannah leaned forward. "What's going on?" she asked.

"Rodeblog," the driver said. Assorted arms lifted in what might have been an attempt at a shrug. "Noddineyekundo-abohdit." The meter clicked metallically.

"Shit." Hannah sank back in the seat. Gregg saw muscles tensing in her jawline. He could almost *feel* her quick fear—a taste in his mouth, a tang like steel, as delicious as iron. Hannah leaned over to him; he inhaled the warmth of her breath as she whispered. "Police," she said. "It looks like they're checking cars. They're looking for us, don't want us to get out of the city. I know it. I just *know* it. Damn!"

Hannah lurched forward again before Gregg could say anything. She gestured at the driver. "Turn around," she told him. "I want to go back."

Another multiarmed shrug. "Iztoolade. Candoit." One arm pointed at the car in front, another at the one in the rear. They were jammed in bumper to bumper. Uniformed police were moving down the line, peering into cars and then waving the drivers on, sometimes looking into trunks. The car ahead crawled forward; their cabdriver didn't move, looking to turn around in the open space. The cars behind started to honk their horns, and the cops looked up to see what the disturbance was down the line. Two of them began walking toward them.

It wouldn't be a problem with Puppetman. Cops were always easy, nice, big, fat strings to pull. But now—you're trapped, already nicely packaged for them. "Hannah, let me out!" Gregg said, and the driver jumped wide-eyed at the sound of Gregg's voice even as he started to turn the cab.

At which point he got another surprise.

There was someone else crowding into the front seat: Quasiman. The cabdriver squawked like a distressed parrot at the joker's sudden appearance and jammed on the brakes. Gregg's carrier hit the back of the front seat and rebounded. Hannah yelped, half in distress and half in joy.

"Hannah," Quasi said. "Going wrong way."

"I know, Quasi," she said. "We need your help. Take us to Tomlin."

"Can't," Quasiman said. "Not with *him*." Gregg could see Quasiman's gaze locked on him through the vents of the carrier, and there was no friendliness in the hunchback's eyes at all. They were not the eyes of a fool; rather, they seemed to see too much. "Charon," Quasiman said.

"What?" Hannah asked.

Quasi looked back at Hannah. "Charon. I saw you. The river at night. Charon." Quasiman blinked. "My friend," he said. "I love you."

"I love you, too, Quasi," she answered softly, and glanced up at the approaching officers. "Quasi, you're going to have to help us now. I need you to stop those men. Do you understand? You need to get out of the car and help us get away from here." Quasiman just stared dumbly at her, and Gregg knew the joker was lost in a fugue once more.

"Hannah!" Gregg said again. "Open my goddamn cage!"

She ignored him. "Quasi, please," she crooned softly. Gregg saw her reaching toward him, but Quasiman was gone.

And just as quickly back, just outside the cab. The cops, a few car lengths away now, shouted at him. Quasiman stooped down and grasped the rear bumper of the late-model Toyota Camry in front of them. He grimaced.

The car lifted slowly, the metal creaking. A trio of teenagers scrambled from the tilting vehicle as Quasiman lifted it up and sideways. He grunted and pushed: The Camry went sliding on its side, screeching against pavement. The cops made a judicious retreat.

"I believe there's room for you to turn around now," Hannah told their driver. Several of the cars behind them were doing the same. He nodded. Quasiman had taken the next car and stacked it on top of the Camry. The cops had moved well back and were calling for backup.

"Godcha," their driver said. "No problem."

"This is insane," Peter Pann complained as the sailboat sliced through the cold green waters of New York Bay. He was wearing shorts, sneakers, and a Dodgers T-shirt. "Governors Island is a maximum security installation. I told you what the tink saw. Armed guards, security cameras, computerized cellblocks, titanium bars. We can't just sail in, hop out, and let everybody loose."

"You got a better plan?" Jay asked. The boat was leaning perilously to one side, and Jay was turning green. "Don't worry, whatever happens, you're home free. Nobody's going to shoot a guy that looks just like Opie Taylor."

Peter made a face, took a fat black cigar out of his pocket, and bit off the end. His tink buzzed at him furiously as he lit up. He sucked in a lungful and blew a cloud of smoke at the dancing light. The tink dimmed and fluttered and fell, extinguished.

"You're so *mean* to them," Melissa Blackwood called out from the back of the boat. The aft or the stern or whatever the fuck it was, Jay wasn't nautical enough to be sure. She was holding the tiller or the rudder or whatever with one hand and her top hat with the other. A brisk salt wind kept trying to snatch it off her head.

Peter Pann slammed his foot down on the fallen tink, crunching it under his heel. "They're like flies," he said. "How'd you like to have a glowing housefly buzzing around your head twenty-four hours a day?" He blew a smoke ring. The wind ripped it apart.

Governors Island loomed ahead, dominated by the red brick walls of its Civil War fort. "Here we go," Jay shouted. "Remember, we're just some salty dogs out for a family sail." He adjusted the jaunty white captain's cap he'd bought in Times Square. "Peter, put out the fucking cigar, you're supposed to be eleven years old. And you, Melissa, off with the top hat, you'll give the game away."

Peter Pann sucked in one last lungful of smoke and flicked the cigar out over the side of the boat. It hissed as it hit the water. Melissa grinned at Jay, doffed her hat, and gave a practiced flick of the wrist. The topper folded up neat as a pancake. She sat on it.

A Coast Guard patrol boat appeared from behind the island as they headed for the landing, booming out commands on a loudspeaker. Melissa pretended not to hear. Ahead of them, a dozen uniformed men with semiautomatic rifles were waiting on the pier. Jay wondered if this had been such a terrific plan after all. He hadn't expected such a *large* reception committee.

"SHEAR OFF," the voice from the patrol boat boomed. "YOU ARE ENTERING RESTRICTED WATERS." It was a smallish boat, scarcely bigger than a cabin cruiser, but the machine gun on the roof gave it a certain authority.

"How many crew on that size boat?" Jay asked Peter Pann as they bounced and rolled through the waves.

"Oh, six or eight," Peter said. "This is a felony, you know. We're all going to lose our licenses, at the least."

"Only if we get caught," Jay said.

The patrol boat was coming up fast. "SHEAR OFF IMMEDIATELY."

Melissa shouted out a reply. *"I don't know how to steer this thing,"* she cried, doing her best to look helpless and lost.

"PUT ABOUT AND PREPARE TO BE BOARDED," the patrol boat thundered. It was very close now, racing in toward them. Two guardsmen scrambled over its deck, lowering some kind of padded fenders. There was a third man visible at the wheel, speakerphone in hand, and a fourth taking up position by the machine gun.

Jay cracked his knuckles. "Here goes nothing," he announced to his stalwart crew. He made a gun and pointed over the water at the captain of the patrol boat.

"THIS IS YOUR LAST—" the patrol boat warned. The motor was too loud to hear the *pop* as the speaker vanished in midsentence. The wheel spun and the boat veered wildly off course. Jay moved his finger and teleported off the guy by the machine gun.

The guards on the pier hadn't figured out what was happening yet. Jay swung his hand around and starting popping. *One, two, three,* and someone finally saw his buddy disappear before his eyes. He started to shout, but Jay nailed him before he'd gotten out much more than *"Hey!"* That was four. *Five, six,* and now several of them were shouting. *Seven, eight,* and someone began shooting at them, the bullets kicking up the water around the sailboat. *Nine,* and the shots stopped, but two of the remaining trio dropped flat, and the last guy started running up the hill screaming. Jay got him on the run, *ten,* but the two on their bellies were firing. A bullet ripped the sail behind him, another punched through the plastic hull, Peter Pann was yelling something at him, and the sailboat was coming around hard, lifting him up in the air. Jay tried to keep a bead on the guardsmen as a stream of bullets came ripping out of one muzzle and tore up the water. There! He popped on the bounce, *eleven,* and a shot knocked his jaunty little captain's cap right off his head and reminded him of how much he hated guns. He locked his left hand around his right wrist to steady his arm, took careful aim, and brought down the hammer of his thumb. The last man blinked out with a surprised look on his face. The last bullet whizzed harmlessly over their heads.

They slammed against the pier, hard. Peter Pann jumped across, rope in hand, and tied them up. Jay looked back behind them. The Coast Guard had finally gotten its patrol boat back under control, but it was too far off to pop the new guy at the wheel. *"Move it!"* he shouted to Melissa.

She was right behind him as he clambered onto the dock. Peter offered a hand to help her up, but she ignored him and jumped for it. Her hat was in hand. She popped it out and planted it on her head. "What now?" she asked.

"Phase two," Jay told her. He started to clap. Melissa joined in. All around Peter Pann, tinks winked into existence. Two, six, a dozen tiny lights dancing like fireflies on speed. One by one they scattered, zipping off in all directions, a ring of scouts.

"The prison's this way," Peter said. He led them up the hill at a dead run. They were halfway there when the door opened and more guards came pouring out. Jay started popping them away before they knew what was happening.

One of them lost his rifle as he vanished. Peter Pann bent and scooped it up. *"Put that down!"* Jay yelled. "We win or we lose, but we aren't going to shoot anyone." Peter dropped the gun.

The heavy iron door, a relic of the old fort, had slammed shut behind the guards. Jay pulled at it ineffectually. "Locked, damn it."

A tink came zipping back over the walls, buzzing. "More guards on the way," Peter warned them.

"We have to get inside," Jay said.

"Let me," Topper said. She took off her hat, reached in, pulled out a key, unlocked the door. "After you."

Jay and Peter went in together, left and right, rolling. Gunfire stuttered around them. Jay heard Peter cry out in pain. He got the shooter in his sights and popped him away.

An alarm began to hoot, making an annoying *whoop whoop* sound. Jay did a quick look-see and spotted a guard in a glass security booth over their heads. He pointed a finger, dropped a thumb. The guard vanished. The glass was probably bulletproof, but that meant fuck all to Jay's finger. If he could see it, he could pop it. The alarm went on and on.

So much for stealth. The cellblock was in front of them, behind a wall of titanium bars embedded in bulletproof glass. Jay didn't see any keyholes. Topper's hat was going to be no use here; they were sealed out.

Melissa knelt over Peter, pulling off his T-shirt. His arm was bleeding. "I get triple time for wounds," he said through gritted teeth when Jay came over to look at the gunshot.

"You know, sometimes I think of you as the son I never had," Jay told him. He had to shout to be heard over the *whoop whoop whoop*. "How bad is it?" he asked Topper.

"The bullet went clean through. He'll live."

"Only if you kiss it and make it better, honey," Peter Pann said to her. The alarm *whooped*.

"I'll kiss it all right," Melissa said grimly. She pulled a bottle of iodine out of her hat and splashed some on his arm. Peter let out a remarkably authentic eleven-year-old shriek. Melissa produced a length of sterile gauze and began to dress the wound.

A tink came racing back from somewhere and buzzed in Peter's ear. He made a face. "Trouble," he shouted to Jay. "They've sealed off the whole complex. Electronic locks."

"That's your department," Jay told Melissa. "I'll finish him."

"Don't I get a vote?" Peter Pann asked.

Jay ignored him. Topper pulled her powerdeck out of her hat and nodded at him. Jay studied the empty security booth overhead. There was a bank of monitors, a huge console, a swivel chair. *Whoop whoop whoop* went the alarm. "First thing you do," Jay shouted, "you turn off that fucking alarm." He made a gun of his fingers.

Melissa Blackwood vanished with an inaudible *pop* and re-appeared above them, behind the wall of bulletproof glass. Jay saw her looking around carefully. Then she hit a button, and the alarm died in mid-*whoop*. The sudden silence was a blessed relief.

"Hey, remember me?" Peter nagged. "I'm bleeding over here, boss man. The health plan damn well better cover this."

Through the glass, Jay could see Melissa jacking in with her powerdeck. He turned his attention back to Peter Pann and finished up the dressing. No sooner was that done than he heard a low humming noise behind him. Jay turned just in time to see the cellblock door sliding back smoothly into a wall. Melissa was smiling down from above, giving him a thumbs-up.

Jay ran through the door with Peter right behind him. The cellblock was a three-story affair, metal catwalks fronting the upper levels on both sides. The cell doors were still locked, sealed with heavy titanium bars. Jay went to the closest cell.

Inside was a pony-sized palomino centaur, his blond tail flicking nervously from side to side. "Ackroyd? Is that you?"

"Nah, it's my evil twin," Jay told him.

"What's going on? The alarm—"

"We're getting you out of here. Hold still."

"Never mind me. Get Clara! The women are on the second level, listen, Clara knows—" Before Finn could protest further, Jay pointed and popped.

The centaur vanished.

As he started to the next cell, Jay heard a series of loud metallic *clicks*. All up and down the corridor, the cell doors began to open. Peter Pann whooped with triumph. Prisoners began to wander out into the central corridor. Father Squid naked from the waist up, tentacles twitching beneath his nose, his wet gray flesh obscene in the fluorescent lights. Charles Dutton, looking like the grim reaper's ugly brother. The Oddity, huge and twisted, their mottled flesh moving and shifting with each step they took. There were others, too, jokers that Jay did not recognize.

A woman's voice called down from the catwalk above him, "It's about time you guys got here!" Jay glanced up and saw Hannah Davis in prison grays.

"You know how hard it is to rent a sailboat in Manhattan on short notice?" Jay said, defensively.

On the catwalk beside Hannah, a brown-haired woman in oversized glasses stepped from her cell. "Bradley," she called out anxiously. "Where's Finn?"

"Safe," Jay said. "I popped him out already."

Farther down the second tier, a gigantic iridescent snake with a woman's face was slithering out of a distant cell. The brown-haired woman cried out, *"Maman,"* and ran to embrace her.

Father Squid was looking at Peter Pann, aghast. "My son," he said to Jay, "thank you for your gallant efforts on our behalf, but you ought not to have brought a child to this dreadful place."

"Who's a child?" Peter said angrily. "Watch the mouth, jellybelly, or we'll leave you here."

Everyone was shouting. Jay heard *Black Trump* and *Card Sharks* and *Pan Rudo* from a half dozen different throats. No one was listening to a word anyone else was saying. He put two fingers in his mouth and whistled. They all shut up.

"Better," he said. "Look, there'll be time to fill me in later. First we need to get you all out. If everybody will just stay calm and do as they're told—"

But then suddenly Peter Pann was screaming at him. Jay turned and saw a swarm of tinks buzzing around Peter's head. "*Gas!*" Peter was yelling over and over.

All around him, Jay heard a hissing sound, and sleep gas began pouring out from the air ducts.

He told himself to hold his breath, but it was already too late. His head swam dizzily. Jay took a step, thinking, *I've got to get my people out first.* He found Peter Pann, pointed. The boy vanished, leaving behind a cloud of tinks in the place he had been. Reeling, Jay clutched the bars of a cell for support and looked up. Hannah Davis had begun to slump. He popped her away, let go of the bars, searching for Topper. The cellblock was dark with gas. *Forget Topper,* he told himself, *pop Dutton or Father Squid, anyone you can find.* But they were all down by now, and Jay's chest hurt, and the world was whirling around him.

He felt his legs go out from beneath him, but he was gone before he hit the floor.

From a second-story window Mark glanced out. The late-night grounds were dark and still, though when he looked hard he could see the glow of an ember where a sentry squatted in the rosebushes smoking a cigarette. Like everything else in the ostensible Moonchild regime, security was pretty informal—but it was fanatical, and, at need, ruthless.

J. Bob had seen to that. But while that ruthlessness sometimes appalled Mark, he never tried to change it. Because it was needful when there were people out there who would come to kill you, who would not be dissuaded if you stuck a fucking daisy down the barrel of their Kalashnikov.

It wasn't for himself that he ringed the palace with guns, and jokers and Vietnamese who were only too eager to use them. Not rationalization, but plain fact: He wasn't fanatical about clinging to his own life. Nor did he believe that only he, in his complicated Traveler-as-Moonchild guise, could lead Free Vietnam.

He *was* fanatical about Sprout.

He looked into her bedroom. She lay on her side atop the coverlet, curled up asleep with her teddy bear clutched to her chest and her thumb in her mouth. He went into his own less-than-sumptuous room across the hall, sat down on the brass bed, and kicked off his sneakers.

One advantage of the stress the chemically induced masquerade laid on him was that he was exhausted clear down to the marrow each and every day. He was gone as soon as he was horizontal.

Gregg and Hannah stood on a pier in the midnight fog, looking down at the greasy, black water of the East River lapping at the pilings. Getting here—especially after the fiasco of yesterday—had been a slow, long process, moving through the sewers and subterranean service ways of the city until they surfaced—still in Jokertown—near the East River.

"What now?" Hannah asked Gregg. Their trip had lent Hannah and Gregg a certain miasma. Hannah's hair and Gregg's spiky tufts were wet, and Hannah's clothing was hopelessly soiled. What Gregg could see of his own body told him that he hadn't fared any better.

"I'm not sure," Gregg said. "But this is where Charon used to come. We wait, that's all."

They waited, occasionally ducking back into shadows when security guards came by on their rounds. The hours went by slowly, but the waters of the East River remained unbroken and dark. Charon, the joker who had once ferried others to the Rox, and who—it was whispered in Jokertown—still came here to the edge of Jokertown to pick up passengers, never arrived. A false dawn began to touch the building on the far shore. Gregg sighed. "I guess this was a mistake," he said.

"Let's stay a few minutes more," Hannah said. "Quasi said Charon would come."

The mention of Quasiman sent a shiver through Gregg, and the memory of Hannah hugging the joker. Gregg huffed, irritated. "Seems to me that Quasi could have just zapped us over to Tomlin himself, if he really wanted to help," he said.

Hannah looked at him, and he knew she'd been cut by the edge in his voice. "Quasi can't control what he is or what happens to him, Gregg," she said. "You can't blame him for that. I get the feeling that something else is bothering you."

For several seconds, her gaze held him. He was glad, for once, of his expressionless joker face. *I want you to love me the way you did before*, he thought. *You loved me without my making you love me, and I want you to feel that way again. I want you to act as if I were normal, and if I had Him back, I'd make you do it. I'd twist your emotions and wring them out; I'd bind you to me so tightly you couldn't goddamn breathe without me.*

"Nothing's bothering me," he said blandly. "Nothing at all."

"Gregg—" She crouched down alongside him. Her fingertips brushed his side, tingling like a live circuit, and left quickly. Too quickly. "Have I done something to hurt you? I . . . I never meant—"

"You didn't do anything. I'm fine."

Her eyes searched his face. He wondered what she saw. "Good," she said at last. "Because I *do* lo—"

"I know," he said. He wouldn't let her say the words because he didn't want to hear the falseness in them. *You're a joker. She can't love you, can't even touch you. Not anymore. It's over.* "I don't want to lose you, that's all."

She smiled at the words. "That's not going to happen," she said.

"Good," he answered. "All right. We'll wait a few more minutes, I suppose. Until the sun's up."

Not long after, Gregg heard a soft wave wash over the pilings. He looked down as the waters of the river rippled and parted below them, and a huge, bizarre creature surfaced. As the first light of dawn touched the towers of Manhattan, Charon's bulk broke the dark waters, phosphorescent dots puckering the transparent flesh like cheap Christmas lights. The vestigial head on top peered at them. "To the Rox again, is it, Senator?" he said to Gregg.

"You recognize me?" Gregg said, incredulously.

"I see your mind," Charon said. "And everyone in it." Gregg had no time to wonder what Charon meant by that. "You nostalgic for the Rox, Senator?" it asked again.

"The Rox is gone," Gregg told him.

"Yep, that's what they say. The question's still there, though. Are you going where I'm going or aren't you?" Charon paused. "I heard you calling. I came."

"We need to get across the river," Hannah said, and Charon's head turned slowly atop the massive body bobbing in the water. A streamer of raveled magnetic audiotape was wrapped around the cilia near the waterline.

"*That's* all you want?" it rasped. "Take a cab."

"We tried that," Hannah said dryly.

"Charon," Gregg told the joker. He cursed his weak, ineffective voice. "We—I—need your help. I don't know what you've heard, but They've"—his voice added the capitalization—"arrested Father Squid, Troll, Oddity, Dutton, and God knows who else. Things have broken loose." Gregg gave Charon a brief explanation of the Black Trump virus. Afterward, Charon seemed to shiver, as if the dawn air was cold around its slimy body. "Bloat's war isn't over," Gregg said. "It's just changed tactics and battleground."

"That's news I'll have to relay. I thought something new and nasty was happening. I could feel the pain, every night that I come here, a tide of sadness washing out from Joker-town," Charon said. "I've been feeling it more and more recently. Business lately has been"—he paused again—"brisk," he finished.

"Where do you take them?" Hannah asked.

"To where all outcasts go."

"Then take us where *we* want to go. We're outcasts, too."

Charon seemed to harrumph. Bubbles fluttered to the surface of the water with the sound. "It's that important?" it asked.

"Yes," Gregg answered for both, his high voice piping.

A froth of bubbles erupted around Charon as it rose higher in the water and moved toward the pilings where they stood.

"Then get in," it said. "Your meter's running."

Mark tried his damnedest to be just, but tonight he wasn't sleeping that way. He dreamt a crooked dream.

In that dream a crooked man appeared. He was big and powerfully built, with his shoulders cast at an odd angle and his head held low and to one side. He stood at the foot of Mark's big, colonial four-poster bed, swept his glance over him, then looked at the chintz-covered windows with a distracted air.

"Father Squid and Dutton got taken," he said in a soft, musing voice. "Or did they? Maybe that's going to happen." He shook his head. A vacant look closed like shutters behind his eyes, and a string of drool ran down his chin. "You're somebody," he said, seeming to come back to himself. "Somebody who's important. Or . . . going to be important. It's all jumbled up in my mind."

In his dream Mark sat up in bed. Sweat made his T-shirt cling to his ribs in a clammy intimacy. "You're Quasiman," he said. "I've heard about you."

"I've heard about you, too. If I could only remember when, or what. Or why . . ."

He wandered out from behind his eyes again. Mark sat watching him, propped on his arms, aware that this was a very realistic and immediate dream—so much so that the muscles in his arms began to tremble from unaccustomed exercise.

A furtive sound from the hallway. A dream? Quasiman blinked and raised his head. "That's it, Mark," he said. "It's why I came."

He shrugged uneven shoulders. "It's about your daughter—"

He vanished.

Mark's senses stretched out like a long-parted lover's arms. No mistake: scuffling sounds from somewhere.

At the base of his door, shadows occulted the thin strip of yellow hallway light.

Mark was out of bed in a stork-legged leap for the door before he was aware that this wasn't a dream, any part of it. With a shattering sound the door slammed open, the lock's receiver ripping right out of the jamb with a squeal of tearing wood.

A dark figure in the door, features hidden by a black ski mask, machine pistol held ready. Without thinking, Mark lashed out with his foot. It caught the dark figure smack in the crotch.

With a soft grunt the intruder let his weapon drop to its

sling's extent, clutched himself, and went to his knees. Mark rushed past him into the corridor.

Two more dark figures stood by Sprout's door. One turned as Mark lunged at him.

Befuddlement was transmuting to frightened anger in Mark. Somehow he remembered that on those few occasions when he'd punched people in the face in the past, he had hurt his hand. Or maybe he recalled some of the unarmed self-defense Belew had tried to drill into him; or perhaps even part of Moonchild that was still in him—or part of that in him which had been Moonchild—kicked in. He swung his clenched right hand in a wide arc at a ski-masked temple and struck not with the knuckles but with the fist's bottom.

Impact jarred his arm. The man in the mask fell against the door and slid downward, looking limp.

His companion was trying to swing his own MP5 around. To Mark's inexpert eye, its barrel was unusually stubby.

He jumped on the gunman's back, wrapping his arms with his own long limbs, trying to pin elbows to ribs. The man turned with Mark riding his back like a hundred-dollar-a-day habit, threw himself backward against the wall.

"Oof!" Mark said.

"What the fuck's going on here?" It was Mason, a joker whose skin had the appearance of brick, down to the mortar seams. He stood at the end of the corridor by the stairs, raising a Kalashnikov.

Unfortunately, his skin didn't have the *consistency* of brick. The man whose back Mark rode raised his MP5 one-handed, fired a short burst. The noise was loud in the confines of the hall, but nowhere near as loud as a raw nine-millimeter going off; the weapon had a built-in suppressor.

Mason reeled and fell. His body convulsed as he died, but he didn't have his finger on the trigger.

This was getting serious. Mark thought about his hand-to-hand combat repertoire, which he'd just about exhausted, and *look* where he was. He thought about the vials of potion—all safely tucked away in the nightstand by his bed, and a few more covert locations, all equally remote—that would turn him into somebody *much* more useful in situations like this, such as JJ Flash, Esquire. He thought about Sprout, asleep and helpless in her room.

Screw pride; I'm useless. He opened his mouth to holler for help. From the corner of his eye he saw the man he'd nut-kicked leap at him. Before Mark could force sound from his mouth, the man slapped a wad of gauze soaked in something cold over it.

Mark's head filled with astringent fumes. Instantly it swelled like a balloon and began to float away from his shoulders. *Great,* the biochemist in him thought. *Chloroform. That's*—

Jay awoke in darkness, his face a mask of hurt. A bolt of pain went through him when he moved, hitting him right between the eyes. His mouth tasted of blood. Gingerly, he felt his nose. When he touched it, it moved. Jay let out a muffled gasp.

"You broke your nose," a vaguely familiar voice said from the darkness.

"Someone broke my nose once. It was a long time ago. I remember it hurt." Jay moaned. It was black in here. He couldn't see a thing. Memories of his disastrous raid on Governors Island came back to him. He must have landed on his face when the gas hit him. "Where am I?" he said aloud, although he figured he knew. "Doesn't this fucking prison have a hospital? Damn it, I need medical care, I want to see the warden."

A match flared in the darkness. Quasiman peered at Jay with concern, his broad homely features twisted in concentration. "I don't know the warden," he said uncertainly. "Who is he? I can go tell him you want to see him if you like."

Jay struggled to sit up. "No," he said, "no, forget the warden." He groped at Quasiman's face. The hunchback felt real enough. He wasn't dreaming. Was he? "What is this place?"

Quasiman looked around the gloom. "This is the house of the wax people. I like to come here when it's dark and quiet. Sometimes I look at the wax people and I remember things."

"The Famous Bowery Wild Card Dime Museum," Jay said. Dutton's museum. He knew the place. It gave him the creeps. Some unfortunate things had happened to him over the years in the Famous Bowery Wild Card Dime Museum. On the other hand, it beat the hell out of the prison on Governors Island . . .

Quasiman was watching. The match had burned down to his fingers. He studied it, his face blank, as his flesh began to burn. Then he blew it out, and the dark swallowed them.

"How did I get here?" Jay said. "Did you carry me out?"

"I saw you," Quasiman told him, his voice strange and low in the darkness.

"You . . . saw me?" Jay said, baffled. "Where? In the prison?"

"I saw you at the end," Quasiman said. "You were up in a big balloon fighting a man with half a face."

"I think you're confusing me with Jetboy," Jay said. This was fucking useless. He needed to reach Finn if he was going to make sense of this, the sooner the better. At least he'd gotten one of them out. How long had he been asleep, anyway? "I've got to get to a phone," Jay said, struggling to his feet. His broken nose sent a bolt of pain through him when he rose. He ignored it, stumbling through the dark and groping for a wall. He walked into a wax figure. It fell with a crash. "Where are the lights?" Jay bitched loudly. "I can't see a goddamn thing."

Light flooded the room. The sudden glare made Jay throw up his hand in front of his eyes. He hit his nose and moaned. He found himself in the middle of the Aces High diorama, face-to-face with a wax Astronomer. The figure he'd knocked over was Modular Man, Jay saw. The android had lost his head in the fall.

Quasiman was outside the glass, standing by the light switch. "Is that better?" the hunchback asked.

Jay started to nod. His nose reminded him that nodding was a bad idea. "Yes, thank you," he called out instead. He could see his reflection in the glass wall of the diorama. Under the dried, caked blood, his nose was starting to resemble Rondo Hatten's. His eyes weren't black yet, but they would be soon, both of them. He'd look like a raccoon. *This is just fucking great,* he thought.

He found a hidden door in the back and exited the diorama. A narrow access corridor led him out to where Quasiman was waiting patiently. Or maybe it wasn't patience . . . Jay looked closely and saw that the hunchback was in some kind of fugue, his eyes glazed and cloudy, his hand frozen on the light panel. He sighed and left Quas where he was as he searched for a phone.

The Dime Museum was closed and deserted. There was a bank of pay phones outside the men's room. Jay dropped a quarter, started to punch in a number, and then froze. He'd been about to call Hastet, but maybe that wasn't such a good idea. The feds had to be looking for him by now. If a platoon of Coast Guardsmen showing up in the middle of White Sands Missile Range hadn't been enough of a clue for them, they had Topper. His home phone could be tapped. Ditto for Starfields and the office lines at Ackroyd and Creighton.

Well, okay, he thought. *They'd prepared for that possibility.* He punched in the number for Jerry Strauss on Staten Island and for once felt thankful for his junior partner's stupid secret identity. With luck, the feds didn't know that Creighton was really Strauss.

"Hello?"

"Jerry, it's me."

"Where are you?" Jerry said, astonished. "I thought they had you for sure. How'd you get off the island?"

"A trained detective is always resourceful, even when he's unconscious."

"Is Topper with you?"

"She didn't get out," Jay said. "Don't worry, Topper can take care of herself. Do you have Finn?"

"He's down in my wine cellar," Jerry said, and Jay breathed a sigh of relief. "Peter's with him. We were having a strategy session when the phone rang. Jay, you better get here as soon as you can. This Black Trump thing—"

"Did Finn tell you what the fuck it is?" Jay interrupted.

"A virus," said Jerry, his voice gone grave. "A virus designed to kill every ace, joker, and wild card carrier in the world."

For a moment, words failed Jay Ackroyd. A wisecrack curdled and died unborn on his tongue. What do you say to something like that? Finally he managed weakly, "This thing exists?"

"Finn says so," Jerry replied.

Jay could tell there was a second shoe waiting to be dropped, so he reached out and shook the shoe tree. "And the *Card Sharks* have this virus, is that it?"

"I'm afraid so."

There was a sudden throbbing behind Jay's eyes. It was hard enough to get a taxi to go to Staten Island at the best of times, he thought, never mind trying to get one in Jokertown at night with your nose mashed in and your face covered with dried blood. "I'm on my way," he said wearily, and hung up the phone.

— — —

Hangar Fourteen—thankfully—lay out in the low-rent district of Tomlin facing the East River, well away from the distant busy terminals of TWA, American, and Pan Am. The steel frame of the building may well have been of World War II vintage, decades of use half-hidden under the cosmetics of paint. Unlike many of the hangars lined up in the area, Fourteen had no corporate logos or names painted above the main doors. A small sign was mounted alongside the side door, but neither of them could read the letters from their hiding place—for that matter, Gregg could barely make out the sign itself.

Gregg and Hannah watched the hangar from the cover of tall weeds along the river. The big hangar doors had been opened to the stained and cracked concrete apron leading out to Tomlin's maze of runways; inside, the rising sun touched the red-and-white sleek fiberglass lines of a five-seat Learjet. A Black man in blue overalls was inspecting the undercarriage of the craft. Twice while they watched, the man straightened and looked out across the field, shading his eyes against the rising sun. "Bushorn?" Hannah asked Gregg.

"Yes. I hope he's still expecting us."

"I know one way to find out."

Fright shivered down Gregg's body. He was afraid to stand up, afraid to move at all. "Hannah—"

She ignored him, rising from a crouch and vainly brushing at the stains on her clothing. She ran fingers through her cropped newly dark hair and began walking toward the hangar while Gregg watched as Hannah's figure blurred with distance. Bushorn noticed her about halfway there. He straightened, silently watching her approach. Gregg wished he could see the expression on the man's face. They talked for a moment, then Bushorn disappeared into the interior shadows of the hangar. Gregg heard the whine of jets warming up. A few minutes later, Bushorn came out again with a large cardboard box. Leaving Hannah by the hangar and the idling aircraft, he walked out across the concrete and into the high grass, whistling tunelessly as he approached Gregg. Gregg huddled down in a crouch, poised to run at need.

"I see you," the man said softly. "Don't be running away, my man. That body's damn near neon."

"Gary, it's good to see you."

"You want me to say 'me, too' or would you prefer the truth?" A quick grin pulled at the edges of his mouth and vanished as he set the box down, its open end facing Gregg. "Get in," Bushorn said. "Can't have anyone spotting you."

Gregg crawled into the box. The carton smelled of Styrofoam—a few peanuts clung stubbornly to the sides—old tape, and delicious metal. The smell reminded him how long it had been since he'd eaten. *A nice stainless-steel tire rim, with a side of pot metal . . .* Bushorn tipped up the box and lifted, grunting. "Damn, you sure didn't lose weight when the virus shrunk you down."

"It's my diet," Gregg said. "It's on the heavy side."

"I believe that." Bushorn grunted again, adjusting his grip, then began walking back toward the hangar. He didn't look down at Gregg, he didn't smile. He smelled of soap, grease, and jet fuel, all overlaid with sweat—now that the man was close, Gregg could see beads of perspiration clinging to the man's skin like dew, even though the morning was cool. He remembered that Bushorn always sweated profusely, even on the coldest days—the wild card had reset his core temperature. "You sure you two weren't followed?"

"Not unless they used a submarine."

Bushorn snorted at that. His footsteps jarred Gregg rhythmically; perspiration rained from his forehead and into the box. Gregg would have sworn that he could feel the heat of the man's skin through the barrier of cardboard. They were nearly at the hangar. Gregg could see the roof of the building; then the sky was replaced by high girders and a corrugated steel roof. Bushorn set the box down, pulling a handkerchief from his back pocket and mopping his face with it. "Europe still on the itinerary?" he asked, half-shouting over the rumble of the jets.

"We're not in a position to be real picky," Hannah told him. "But that's our thought."

"Mmmm." Bushorn shrugged. Sweat darkened the spine of his uniform shirt; when he wiped his hands on the overall pants, he left behind streaks. "Well, let's—"

Bushorn stopped. He looked out toward the tarmac and covered his eyes against the sun's glare. Gregg looked that way and could see nothing but a vague blur of grass and concrete. "Why don't you two get into the plane? Now."

"What's going on?" Gregg asked.

"There's a car heading this way."

"Police?" Hannah asked.

"Uh-uh. A black panel van." Bushorn shook his head; droplets of sweat scattered like silver rain. "They're accelerating. Damn, what've you got me into, Hartmann? Shit . . ."

Hannah put her hand on his arm. She looked at Gregg, then back at Bushorn. "Look, Mr. Bushorn—Gary—you don't have to do anything. Not now. We understand. You didn't ask for this trouble."

He looked at her with his solemn face. "You understand, huh? Yeah, well, I know you, too, even with the new hair. I know what you've done. Just stay ready to head for the damn plane."

As Gregg and Hannah watched, Bushorn jogged over to a large metal barrel just outside and began pumping liquid through the nozzle of a hose attached to it. The smell of petroleum wrinkled Gregg's round Rudolph nose as the stream spread over the concrete in front of the hangar. He stood waiting, holding the still-trickling hose, as the van approached.

The side doors of the van crashed open as it squealed to a churning stop in front of them. An athletic man in a white suit leapt out, followed by a lithe blond woman Gregg recognized as April Harvest, who had led the raid on the Dime Museum, and a quartet of gray suits in sunglasses. A lopsided grin hung on Carnifex's face as he stepped forward. He stood at the edge of the growing puddle on the concrete; if he noticed any smell, he gave no indication. "Surprise! Seems we're just in time," he said. He glanced at Bushorn and obviously dismissed the man. His gaze lingered appreciatively on Hannah for a second, then the grin widened as he looked at Gregg. "Hey, I *like* that look, Gregg," he said. The grin vanished. "You never even fucking came to the hospital after I saved your lousy life at the Atlanta convention. You never even called and said thanks."

"Ray, you talk too much. Just do it," Harvest said, and Ray gave her a lopsided scowl before motioning toward the van.

"Hartmann, nothing would make me happier than having you resist arrest," he said, "but let's just make it easy and get into the van. You too, Ms. Davis." He glanced again at Bushorn. "And you, mister. Surprised there's still nats willing to stick their necks out for jokers."

"I'm not a nat," Bushorn said.

Carnifex narrowed his eyes. A look of pleasure and anticipation crossed his torn face. "Oh? You're no ace I've ever heard of," he said.

"I'm not an ace, either," Bushorn said slowly, his voice barely audible over the screech of the jets in the hangar. "I'm just a deuce." His eyes on Carnifex and the silent men behind him, Bushorn crouched down. His fingertip touched the pool, dimpling the liquid. A faint smoke whirled in the breeze around the finger.

And then flame, louder than the jets, roared across the small lake, leaping and curling ten feet in the air with a concussive blast. Gregg heard Carnifex swear and Harvest yelp, heard the other men shouting. Then they were lost behind the screen of flame and heat. Gunshots punctuated the din; bullets whined and pinged on the back wall of the hangar. Bushorn was running past them toward the plane, cradling his right arm to his body. "Inside! Now!"

Hannah ran; Gregg scuttled with them, all six legs pumping. Bushorn picked Gregg up, heaving him over the wing and into the small cabin. Hannah, breathless, followed, and then Bushorn swung in, taking the pilot's seat. "Buckle in. This could get rough," he said over his shoulder.

"You're hurt," Hannah said, grabbing at Bushorn's hand. Gregg saw that the skin of Bushorn's right hand was a seared, white ruin to the wrist. Even Gregg's unskilled eyes could tell that Bushorn's hand would be a scarred, stiff horror, if he managed to save it at all. He hated the concern he saw in Hannah's eyes.

"It happens," Bushorn answered. Sweat was running down his arms, over his brow. He wiped at his eyes with his sleeve. "I heal quick. Anyway, we ain't got time to worry about it now. Hang on." Bushorn pulled back on the throttles left-handed; the jets screamed like twin banshees and the craft shuddered. Bushorn released the brakes, feathered the pedals, and the plane began rolling, picking up speed. Through the windows, Gregg could see the flames rushing toward them, filling the windows with orange fire and black, greasy smoke. Then they were through.

All of the suits were down; Harvest was on her knees, firing at them with a handgun. Gregg caught a glimpse of Carnifex, shouting wordlessly and rolling as the plane's wing nearly decapitated him, and then doing an impossible leap up onto the plane's wing. The ace began running along the wing toward the cabin. "Damn!" Bushorn grunted, and turned sharply left.

Carnifex made a desperate leap and grab as the motion took his balance. His fingers caught the plane's antenna; muscles corded in the ace's arms as he pulled himself upright. They could see Ray's face pressed against the cockpit window, grimacing with effort and flushed with anger. "He's a persistent little fuck," Bushorn said and gunned the engines, at the same time turning sharply right. The antenna snapped off, still gripped in Ray's fingers, and the white-uniformed man went tumbling over the back of the wing and disappeared. Bushorn played the brakes and turned the aircraft left again, the tip of the wing screeching as it left a long graze on the side of the van, and then they were rolling freely down the concrete, picking up speed. Bushorn pulled a headset from its holder and pulled it down over his head.

"Tower, this is Alpha Delta Rio One Niner Six Four Oh. I need runway Five NW cleared immediately." A thin voice answered back through the headset; Gregg could hear none of the words. "Look, I know all about regulations and my damn license, and I don't fucking much care, Tower. They've got a gun on me"—Bushorn grinned at Hannah and Gregg—"and I'm taking off on Five NW in about thirty seconds. If you *don't* clear it, there's going to be one hell of a mess, and you'll be responsible. Is that clear enough for you?" The voice sputtered in the earphones again. "Good."

Bushorn sighed. He looked back at his two passengers. "I sure as hell hope this is worth it," he said.

"It is," Hannah said.

"That's all I need to know, then."

Bushorn steered them down the complex of concrete, turning at last at the end of a runway where a queue of 727s waited, the heat of their jets shimmering the air. There, Bushorn took a long breath before pulling back all the way on the throttles. The aircraft leapt forward, pressing Gregg and Hannah back against their seats as the jets roared their power. As they began to race down the runway, the black van pulled in front of them a few hundred yards ahead, blocking their path. "Bushorn!" Hannah shouted, but the man paid no attention to her. They continued to race toward the van. Carnifex, in soot-stained white, opened the driver's door and ran, diving into the grass alongside the runway.

Gregg wondered what it would feel like when they crashed. He wondered if he'd feel the pain. Hannah hugged him; he folded his tiny arms around hers, glad for her closeness at the end.

Bushorn yanked back on the controls. With agonizing slowness, the nose of the plane lifted and the rumble of the wheels stopped. Gregg felt a distinct bump as the tires grazed the top of the van, and he was certain they'd pinwheel back onto the runway. Bushorn cursed and fought the controls. The wings waggled, the nose dropped, and the engines wailed, but the plane steadied a few seconds later, and Bushorn took them in a long, climbing turn.

Tomlin, New York, and Billy Ray receded behind them.

"That feel any better?" Dr. Bradley Finn asked.

Jay Ackroyd felt his nose. It was numb from the anesthetic, his nostrils packed solid with dressing, the whole thing covered with a bandage the size of Jetboy's Tomb. "I can't wait to do some undercover work, I ought to blend right in," he said gloomily. "I must look like Jack Nicholson in *Jokertown*."

"Oh, no," Jerry Strauss put in, never the one to let a movie reference go unchallenged. "Jack Nicholson didn't have two black eyes, and his bandage was much smaller."

Jerry was wearing a smoking jacket today, to go with Errol Flynn's face. He was incognito. Finn knew Jerry Strauss by sight, as a patron of the Jokertown Clinic, and Jerry didn't want the Strauss identity compromised, so he was being Creighton. "Fred," he'd whispered to Jay as he'd escorted him through the huge old house, past walls covered with rare mint-condition movie posters. "It's Fred Creighton, short for Frederick."

"Personally, I think he looks more like the star of *Bandit, the Wacky Raccoon*," Peter Pann said. He was perched up on top of a huge wooden cask of amontillado, his arm in a sling and a pair of tinks orbiting his head.

"Enough," Jay said. He was in no mood for extended discussions of his nose, not with global genocide staring them in the face. "We've got more serious problems."

Bradley Finn sat on his haunches. "You have a plan?" he said. Finn was smallish as centaurs go, but he still filled up most of the Strauss wine cellar. His back half was a palomino pony, complete with blond tail and mane. His front half looked like a surfer, especially in the oversized Hawaiian shirt he'd borrowed from Jerry.

"Face it, Ackroyd," Peter said, swatting lazily at a tink, "this is too big for us, *way* too big. We've got no choice but to go to the authorities."

"The authorities know," Finn said sharply. "Clara and I went straight to the police after we escaped from the Sharks. The police called in the FBI. We were questioned for days. Then they classified the whole thing and rounded up all of us who knew the score and shipped us off to Governors Island." His voice turned bitter and sarcastic. "Temporarily, of course. Strictly for our own protection."

"Who questioned you?" Jay wanted to know.

Finn shook his head. "Who didn't? The FBI, the CIA, lawyers from the Justice Department, some guy from Treasury, a couple of doctors from the Centers for Disease Control in Atlanta . . ."

"Anyone from the Special Executive Task Force?" Jay asked.

Finn looked surprised. "As a matter of fact, yes. A pair of them. Straight Arrow, you know, that Mormon ace, and a woman named April Harvest. You don't forget a name like that. She asked most of the questions. Why?"

"The Task Force was a Card Shark front when it was headed by Herzenhagen," Jay told him, frowning. "It could be legit now, I don't know . . . Hannah Davis exposed Herzenhagen and Battle and a few other Sharks, but who knows how many more are still hidden?"

"Leo Barnett," Jerry said in a glum voice.

"You guys are all paranoid," Peter Pann insisted. "The whole federal government can't be made up of Card Sharks."

"Paranoids have enemies, too," Jerry warned, sounding ominously like Richard Nixon.

"I delivered that son of a bitch Faneuil to the police personally. They ought to be way ahead. They ought to have arrested Rudo and Johnson by now. Instead they're arresting us."

Jay thought about that for a moment. "It's not hard to figure why they don't want news of the Black Trump getting out. You tell a couple hundred thousand jokers that they're under a death sentence, and you'll have a riot that'll make that Rodney King thing look like a block party. And I don't even want to think about what some of our more unstable aces might do."

"Are you saying that's why they brought in Finn and the others?" Jerry asked.

"Sure," Peter said. "A public safety thing, misguided, even illegal, but you can understand why they did it."

"Or maybe they're all Sharks and they wanted to silence us," Finn said. He stood up, his tail lashing angrily, flicking thick clouds of dust off rare vintages in the racks behind him. "We have to go back out there and get Clara!"

"No way, Flicka," Peter said. "Once is enough for Mrs. Pann's little boy."

"He's right," Jay said. "I'm sorry, Finn. Last time was a disaster. Peter got shot, and we had to leave Topper behind. I was lucky to get out of there."

"*Clara's* the one you should have gotten out of there!" Finn said angrily. "I *told* you, damn it! Clara *designed* the Black Trump, she was part of the Shark inner circles, she can give you chapter and verse on who they are and where they are . . . facts and figures, names and numbers . . . *She's* the one you need!"

"Yeah, well, you're the one we've got," Jay said.

"How much time do we have?" Jerry asked worriedly. "You know, before . . . well, before the end . . ."

Finn sighed heavily. "A month. If we're lucky. They'll need at least that long to culture the amounts they need."

"Explain," Jay said. "In small words. I flunked high school chemistry. Angela LaBruno was my lab partner, and I couldn't take my eyes off her chest long enough to follow the experiments."

"All right," Finn said. "The Card Sharks have the Black Trump, but right now they don't have *enough* of it. Clara managed to destroy most of the cultures. The strain they have is only lethal through three or four generations, so—"

"Wait a minute," Jay interrupted. "What does that mean? That generation business?"

"I get the virus," Finn said. "First generation. Before I die, I pass it to you. Second generation. You die, too, but first you give a dose to Peter Pan here."

"*Pahn*," Peter said sharply. "It's Dutch."

"Third generation," said Jay.

"Right, and Peter Pan dies, too, after he infects Mr. Creighton, and Creighton maybe gets real sick, but he *doesn't* die. It's fourth generation, and the Black Trump isn't lethal anymore. What's more, Creighton continues to spread the virus, only now it's just a bad flu, and anyone who comes down with it is immunized against the fatal, first-generation strain of the disease."

Jay was starting to see the big picture. "So the Sharks can't just release this bug and wait for it to spread . . ."

"Not in the small quantities they have, no," Finn said, "not unless their goal is to kill a few hundred jokers and give the rest of the wild cards around the world a nasty flu. To get the kind of pandemic they want, first they need to culture a larger supply of the deadly first-generation strain. For maximum spread, they'd want a simultaneous release in several major cities, preferably ones with large wild card populations and major international airports."

"Airports?" Jerry said, puzzled. "Why airports?"

"Airplanes spread epidemics faster than anything I know," Finn said. "One guy coughs at O'Hare, and in twenty-four hours strangers in nineteen time zones and five continents have got his cold."

"Hoo boy," Jerry said. It sounded strange, coming out of Errol Flynn's mouth. Errol didn't look like the kind of guy who said "Hoo boy" a whole lot.

"*Jesus,*" Peter Pann swore, "you're talking *global* here! This is a job for Interpol or the World Health Organization or somebody."

"Pan Rudo was practically the *head* of the World Health Organization," Finn pointed out. "Etienne Faneuil was working for WHO when he was giving AIDS to jokers in Africa."

"I'd like to pass this buck, too," Jay said to Peter, "but I don't think we dare. Maybe the feds and Interpol and the Mormon Tabernacle Choir are all hot on the trail of Pan Rudo at this very moment, but if they're *not* . . . if they're not . . ."

"Ring around the rosie, pockets full of posies, ashes, ashes, we all fall down," Bradley Finn said slowly, his voice grim.

Jay threw him a sharp look. "What is this, national nursery rhyme week? I got the same thing from Quasiman. I thought he wanted to skip rope."

Finn said, "No, Jay. That little song dates from the Middle Ages. It's about the bubonic plague. The Black Death." His voice softened. "They used to burn the bodies."

"Ashes, ashes," Jerry Strauss whispered. *"We all fall down.* It killed half the population of Europe."

"Well, fuck it," Jay said, angrily. "Not this time."

His junior partner nodded. "Not if we can help it."

Jay looked around the wine cellar. A faux swashbuckler, a centaur, an eleven-year-old kid, and a guy who looked like a raccoon with a broken nose. What a team. The Card Sharks were probably shaking in their boots right now. He took a deep, deep breath.

"So where do we start?" Jerry asked.

Everyone looked at Dr. Bradley Finn. The centaur gave a hopeless shrug. "Clara is the one to ask, she . . ." He stopped in midsentence, running his fingers through his thick, blond hair. "Her father," he said. "Clara's father, Brandon van Rens-saeler. He was a Card Shark for years and years, but he was opposed to the Black Trump project; he thought it went too far. Clara warned him before she went to the police, to give him time to run."

"And did he?"

Finn nodded. "She figured he'd go to Australia. He had a friend down there, another Shark. What was his name now?"

He snapped his fingers impatiently, frowning with concentration. "Farmer or Fielding or . . . No . . . He had the same name as the guy who wrote the James Bond novels."

"Ian Fleming," Jerry provided helpfully.

"*Eric* Fleming," Finn said.

Peter knew the name. "Eric Fleming owns half the newspapers in Australia, along with a couple in England and one or two over here."

"Then he shouldn't be that hard to find," Jay said. "All we have to do is get to Australia." There was a problem with that, he realized. "I suppose it would help if I had a passport."

"Usually," Peter Pann said.

"I have a passport," Jerry Strauss said quickly. "I'll go." Errol Flynn had never sounded so puppy-dog eager. "Just give me time to pack a suitcase, I'll get the first flight out. I can be in Sydney tomorrow morning."

"Australia requires an entry visa, too," Peter said. "Six weeks, minimum."

Jerry looked stricken, but he was fast on his feet, Jay had to give him that. "I'll change into Paul Hogan and say my passport was stolen by a fan," he said. "They wouldn't turn away Paul Hogan."

Jay had actually been thinking about sending Jerry to find Fleming all by himself. His junior partner had been doing some good work lately, and there was no doubt that he'd drawn a versatile ace. That way Jay and Peter Pann would be free to follow up other leads. On the other hand, they *had* no other leads, and he wasn't sure Australia was big enough for two Paul Hogans. "Maybe we should both go," Jay said. "There are a dozen places in Jokertown where we can get fake papers that look better than the real thing."

"I'm going with you," Dr. Finn announced.

Jay looked at him, surprised. "That's not a real good idea."

"I'm going," Finn repeated, in a voice full of resolve. "I have a personal stake in all this. Those Shark bastards made me an accomplice to murder in Kenya, and then they used me as a hostage to force Clara to re-create the Black Trump. I owe them."

Peter Pann laughed. "Great speech, Flicka, but you just escaped from federal detention. How the fuck do you think you're going to get to Australia? Creighton can change into anyone he wants, and Jay's got this swell raccoon disguise, but you . . . Well, no offense, Doctor, but you're a horse."

"I wasn't planning on flying Quantas," Finn put in. "My father has a Learjet. I'm sure he'd let me borrow it."

Peter made a face. "Who's your father, Secretariat?"

"One more horse joke and I'll make *sure* you never grow up," Finn said, giving Peter a hard look. He turned to Jay. "Well?"

"A private jet would be handy, but last time I looked, you were a doctor, not a detective. The only thing worse than an amateur is an amateur with something to prove."

"I'll keep my head down and do what you tell me," Finn said. "And if you don't take me, I'll go anyway."

"All right," Jay said, dubiously. He was remembering the last time he let someone go with him to play detective. He still had nightmares about that night. "I'll arrange for our passports. Finn, get on the horn and see about that plane. Jerry, make sure you pack lots of money. We may need to bribe people."

Finn was confused. "Jerry? I thought his name was Fred."

"It's, ah, Jeremiah Frederick," Jay said glibly.

"What am I going to be doing while you guys are throwing a shrimp on the barbie?" Peter Pann wanted to know.

"Holding down the fort," Jay said. "There's nothing to connect this house to anyone at the agency, so you should be fine so long as you stay here. We can use the phone as a message drop, check in every few days in case anything breaks. I want you to smother this city with tinks. Maybe they'll pick up something. And get a hold of Sascha. We'll stop on Maui and pick him up."

Peter grinned wickedly. "He'll be *so* happy."

"I guess they're going to let us live," Bushorn said. "If they were going to shoot us out of the sky, they'd've done it already. They'll be tracking us with radar, though."

They'd been heading steadily eastward for the last several hours. Bushorn had throttled them back not long after their takeoff—*"We aren't going to outrun an F-14, and if we try, we're just going to run out of fuel in the mid-Atlantic."*—and set the plane on autopilot.

"They want to know where we're going," Hannah said. "They can wait."

"Which means we're going to have a reception waiting for us when we land, wherever we go. You got any other tricks you can do, Bushorn?" Even in the chilly cabin, Bushorn was still perspiring heavily.

"I'll admit I'd hate to have your laundry bill," Hannah said to him. "You always sweat like that?"

Bushorn chuckled softly in the pilot's seat, turning around to them. "It's the wild card's fault. Hit me late, while I was in the service in South Carolina, flying transports. Started out running a fever, and just got hotter and hotter. Literally burned off my robe, set the bed on fire, too, but it didn't do much to me. About like this. Remember what this looked like?"

He held up his hand; his palm was now a mass of fluid-filled blisters, like a handful of gelatin capsules. Hannah reached out and cradled Bushorn's hand in her own. *She'll touch him. You see; he's normal* . . . Gregg forced the voice down, but he watched. "You had third-degree burns there before," Hannah said wonderingly. "Now . . . Well, I've had worse burns myself."

"Cooking?"

She gave him a look. "Firefighting. I'm—I mean, I *was*—an arson investigator."

"Then you know about how flammable jet fuel is."

"Yeah," Hannah said softly. "I know."

"Guess Mr. White Suit does now, too." Bushorn smiled at Hannah.

"Probably. Nothing like firsthand experience to teach you lessons you'll never forget."

She was still holding his hand. Gregg could almost feel the touch, as searingly hot as the fire Bushorn had set. *I could have made you leap into the fire yourself,* Gregg heard himself growling inside. *You were angry; I could have made you furious, enraged* . . .

"You need some ointment on this? Some bandages?" Hannah was saying.

"Nah. By tomorrow it'll be gone." Bushorn took his hand from Hannah. "Took a long time, but I finally managed to get all this under some control. Now I can light a cigarette without a lighter. Big deal—a damn parlor trick. The government was interested until they decided that it was a pretty useless talent, then they discharged me fast. I ain't no friggin' Jumpin' Jack Flash, throwing fireballs and flying through the air. And I pay for it with having to pay attention to how hot I'm running all the time. Nights, I sleep in asbestos sheets just in case, and I run my damn air conditioner in the middle of winter. You ask me, I ain't much better off than a joker."

"So what happens to us now? Where we heading?"

"I'm following Gregg's instructions." He gestured toward

the array of instruments and nodded to Gregg. "You said Europe; I've got us headed for England."

"And they'll be waiting for us when we land," Hannah interjected.

"You can bet on it," Bushorn said. "Unless you've got a better idea."

"I do," Gregg said.

Six

For a time Mark was in Limbo. Or maybe
it was Hell.

It was a lot like Hell, certainly. But he could never really believe
it was. Because Sprout was there with him, and he couldn't believe
that even the hating vengeful god of the fundamentalists—name
your flavor, Jewish, Christian, Muslim: all one, all one, all one—
could damn such innocence. Only men were that bad.

Mark hoped.

He came partway back to himself lying on his back in the
bottom of a sampan stinking of spoiled fish and rubber tires,
staring up at daylight that oozed like acid between slats of the
bowed wood roof. From somewhere past his head an outboard
engine sang its whiny, thumping song. Beneath nuoc mam and
Ho Chi Minh slipper-soles, he could smell mud-rich river
water, hear it slogging against the thin hull, heavy and slow.

Discomfort had roused him. He lay on his arms. His wrists
chafed his coccyx while the boards of the hull rubbed them
raw in turn. He tried to pull them out from under. He couldn't.
Something like a big plastic twist-tie secured his wrists and bit
in when he struggled.

He raised his head. The slight rise in blood pressure made it
throb counterpoint to the engine. A small brown man in black

pajamas squatted by Mark's feet. He held a rifle across his knees—a new AK-74, he could tell by the bright-orange plastic banana magazine. It was amazing what bits of information you picked up in Southeast Asia.

"Daddy!" Sprout knelt beside him and cradled his head on her lap. His first reaction was pleasure that she was near. Guilt at his own selfishness followed at once, then despair that hit like a sledgehammer and numbed like a shot of Novocain.

Because wherever he was, he was in trouble, and his daughter was in it with him.

"Oh, Daddy," Sprout said, shaking her head so that tears fell on his face like hot monsoon rain, "what's happening? Where are they taking us?"

"I don't know, honey," he said. "But it's okay; everything's going to be all right."

Then he got to hate himself for lying to her.

The boat carried them north along what Mark was sure was the Mekong. That meant that within a day or two—Mark had no way of knowing how long he'd been under; from the way he felt, he suspected they'd given him a needle to keep him down after knocking him out with chloroform—they crossed the border into Cambodia.

That wasn't something a sane person would be eager to do. Cambodia was undergoing a civil war in which history's champion genocides, the Khmer Rouge, blithely ignored UN efforts to make them play nice and accept a civilian government and promise not to try to finish off the two-thirds of the country's population they hadn't gotten to murder in the seventies.

It was especially uncomfortable for Mark. The Red Khmers had tried to use Vietnam for an operating base. Though they

had been J. Bob's playmates once upon a time, his advice mir-
rored Mistah Kurtz: "Exterminate them—exterminate all the
brutes!"

After Free Viet patrols found a couple of villages depopu-
lated by KR "People's Tribunals," with the usual atrocities,
Mark had swallowed his Summer-of-Love scruples and ordered it done. If the chancellor of Free Vietnam, not to mention
his beautiful blond daughter, fell into their hands, they could
expect to be treated . . . well, the way the Khmer Rouge treated
everybody, which was basically as if a race of giant alien insects
had come to Earth and decided to take vengeance for the way
generations of small boys had treated their tiny cousins.

In fact, after their first night on the river Mark feared their
captors *were* Khmer Rouge. He couldn't tell. Little brown men
in black pajamas were pretty much the population of main-
land Southeast Asia, along with similarly clad little brown
women. All he knew was that they weren't speaking Vietnamese. That told him nothing; lots of people in Vietnam didn't
speak Vietnamese, either.

The kidnappers never spoke English. They communicated
their requirements with grunts and jabs of their gun barrels.
That truly *was* the universal language; it worked on Takis, too.

Whoever they were, the kidnappers wanted no more to do
with the Khmer Rouge than Mark did. After Mark's second
day back among the living they moved exclusively by night,
lying up in the weeds by day. Mark and Sprout stayed tied up
in the boat, hanging over the edge of suffocation in the dry-
season heat.

At least under way they untied Mark's hands. Sprout stayed
handcuffed to a stanchion by one ankle, except when the captives were prodded ashore at gunpoint to answer the call of
nature. The small brown men understood too clearly that if
Mark couldn't take his daughter, he'd never run.

They seemed curiously untroubled by the prospect that Mark might pull a Rambo, overpower them all, and escape with the girl. To his great shame, they were right—dead right, the way those defensive-driving TV commercials put it when Mark was a kid. He had his *friends,* of course, next to whom Rambo was a quadriplegic Girl Scout. But those friends—Aquarius, the were-dolphin; JJ Flash, the flamboyant fire-shooter; Cosmic Traveler; and, if she even still existed, Moonchild—came in vials of brightly colored powder. The kidnappers had thoughtlessly neglected to bring any of them along.

Without them Mark was helpless. He towered a foot and a half above his tallest captor, outweighed them by God knew what. But without his drug- and wild card–induced friends he was a tall, weak, skinny middle-aged man who had no more idea of how to fight than he did of how to fly flapping his arms, as his futile Palace-hallway efforts showed with painful clarity. It was chemical dependency of a kind the drug warriors never even *thought* of.

Helplessness tormented him. His alter egos were superhuman. He was useless. *Am I anything without them?*

And if he *were* something . . . shouldn't he be able to protect Sprout? In all his life, she was what mattered the most.

He felt his impotence most keenly the first time muzzle blasts flared from the darkened riverbank with head-busting racket. One of his captors shoved him down to the bottom of the boat and sat on him. Someone else pushed Sprout, wild-eyed and clutching her pink Gund bear, down beside him. The engine roared flat out while the four men in black pajamas shot back in deafening hiccups of fire. Mark could do nothing but murmur encouragements to Sprout—protestations even her perpetually four-year-old mind must know were false.

Miraculously, or so it seemed to be by the sheer quantity of noise and muzzle flash, they escaped the ambush unscathed. Two nights later a single burst of gunfire erupted out of blackness. One of their captors grunted softly and went over the gunwale with a splash. His comrades never even glanced aside. They just fired back and kept the prop churning thick water until they were beyond the reach of their unseen enemy's bullets.

"Everyone ready?"

Hannah glanced at Gregg with Bushorn's question. Despite—or maybe because of—the situation, she chuckled at the sight. Her amusement made Gregg scowl, but he forced the irritation down.

"Go ahead and laugh," Gregg told her. "I think I can imagine . . ." Gregg wriggled in the odd assortment of straps and buckles that Bushorn had rigged around his body. If the glimpses of himself he'd caught in the windows were any indication, he looked like a dominatrix in a porn film for caterpillars. Gregg regarded Hannah in the jumpsuit, helmet, and goggles Bushorn had provided. "You're rather attractive, actually, in a military sort of way," he told her.

"Thanks. You look . . . uh . . ."

"Never mind. I can guess." He wondered if she could guess how scared he was. If anyone bumped him, he was liable to go skittering around the plane like a banshee on speed.

Hannah smiled at him. Bushorn tugged at Gregg's parachute harness, then tightened a strap on Hannah's. "Either of you done this before?" the man asked.

Hannah just chuckled again, nervously. Gregg gave Bushorn what he hoped was a sarcastic tilt of the head—it was hard to tell what his body language communicated anymore. "No, huh?" Bushorn answered. "Well, we're a bit south of Belfast in

Northern Ireland. We're on a heading that will take us into Glasgow; I imagine the reception committee will be waiting for me there. My story is that you hijacked me and that you jumped out over the Wicklow Hills near Dublin; that should buy you some extra time while they look for you in the south."

"Are you going to be all right?" Hannah asked Bushorn.

The man shrugged. "I hope so. If not, I'm sure Gregg can recommend a good lawyer."

"Bushorn, thanks," Gregg told him. "You didn't have to do this."

"Yes, I did. I followed all that stuff about the Card Sharks in the papers; I saw you two on *Peregrine's Perch*. I know what you're running from, and I figure it's my little contribution. Looks to me like you two got the hard job." Hannah hugged Bushorn tightly at that, causing another stab of jealousy to prick Gregg's soul. He thought she held the embrace just a little too long. "I hope we'll see you soon," she told Bushorn.

Yeah. I'll bet you do. He looks normal. He's not a damn worm. Then: *You're not being fair, Greggie. She's acting the way Hannah has always acted—friendly, open, trusting. It's your vision that's screwed up.*

Fuck you, Gregg told the voice.

Bushorn was scanning the instruments. "All right. This is as good a place as any. Let's get you two on your way." Bushorn led the way to the back of the plane. Gregg followed Hannah, the bulky pack of the parachute dragging behind him like a soft anchor. His body kept threatening to go into overdrive just from fear. He tried to calm himself: *People jump out of airplanes all the time. Really. Most of them even live through it . . .*

"This is going to be a lot worse than a normal jump," Bushorn was saying.

"Great. That's a real comfort," Gregg said.

Bushorn almost grinned. "You want me to lie to you?"

"Yes."

"I won't. We aren't in some poky Cessna trainer. When I pop this door, the wind's going to try to tear you right out of here. It's going to be cold and very dark. I'll give you two a push, Gregg first, then you, Hannah. Let yourself fall for a count of ten, then pull the cord. If your main chute doesn't open, don't wait—go for your backup chute. If you can, try to stay together as much as possible. The landing's going to be the real problem, though. There's a moon tonight, at least, so you'll be able to see somewhat, but we're over rural and hilly country—use the lines to control your flight down. See if you can find a flat meadow somewhere. There should be farms around here—plowed fields should be pretty soft. As soon as you're down, cut loose and head for cover. If we're lucky, you'll be able to see each other and make a connection. If not . . . well . . ."

Gregg looked at Hannah. His stomach was already doing somersaults, and he struggled to keep whatever was in there down. Hannah crouched down alongside him. "I'll see you on the ground, love."

Gregg grimaced at the word. *I don't believe you. You say it, but you don't mean it.* "Sure. What's left of me, anyway."

Hannah's smile was wan and a little unsteady. Oddly, that gave Gregg a spasm of pleasure. Back in the cockpit, an alarm shrilled. "Okay, now!" Bushorn said. "Here you go—"

Gregg wasn't prepared for the noise and the violence as the hatch blew open and went pinwheeling away. He didn't have much time to contemplate the situation as Bushorn— *"Remember! Count to ten!"*—pushed him out of the plane. The wind hit him like a steel wall; the blurred bulk of the plane streaked past him as he tumbled. The frigid wind rushing over him thrummed the strap around his body and took his breath away; the goggles Bushorn had tried to wrap around his head went flying away. His *eyes* teared up uncontrollably, not that it mattered.

Gregg's joker body went into its instinctive overdrive, the legs kicking and pinwheeling uselessly. The world roared around him in a giant's bass voice, and Gregg fought to exert his will over the body's flailing.

He found that he was still grasping the iron ring of the cord, but it seemed like he'd been falling for ages already and he'd forgotten to count. *To hell with it*—Gregg pulled the cord and the chute blossomed above him in the darkness; he grunted as the nylon grabbed air and halted his headlong rush to the ground. He couldn't see: Between his myopia and the darkness he might as well have been falling from the top shelf of the world's largest refrigerator.

"Hannah!" he called into the night. He thought he heard a faint answer, but when he called again, he didn't hear anything.

At least his panic seemed to be subsiding. Gregg experimented with tugging on the lines, as Bushorn had told them—he could tell that he was turning as he swayed in the straps, but without being able to see the ground or have some stable reference point, it was a pointless exercise. Gregg hung there for long minutes, waiting for the world to come up and swat him back to reality.

He wondered how fast his legs would be able to go after *that*.

He wondered if he'd survive the experience.

Gregg squinted into the night, wriggling his long body in the straps to peer down. Suddenly something—*trees? a hillside?*—was rushing by him, and a blur of green came up like a fist and slammed into him. His body kicked into a useless overdrive that the straps contained, and his legs were pummeling only air. He realized that he was swaying back and forth a good thirty feet above the ground, the parachute draped over the branches of a huge oak on the border of a wide field. A strong, chill, wet wind blew in his face; the moon was obscured by clouds. From where he dangled, through the branches of the trees shielding him, he could see the spectral blue-and-white blur of Hannah's chute coming in across the field. She missed the woods lining the far side of the field, hitting the tall grass and falling to be dragged several yards by the chute. "Hannah!" Gregg called into the wind. She didn't turn, didn't look. She stood, dropping the straps from her and stepping out of the harness, her back to him.

A voice chattered softly, a whisper he could just barely hear.

She isn't going to help you. She's going to leave you because you're an ugly joker and she really doesn't care about you. You could have betrayed her, could have given her to Brandon van Renssaeler and the Sharks, but you chose not to. You helped her; you gave them the information they needed about the Black Trump. So here's your payback—left to the Irish authorities to arrest; a joker caught in a tree, helpless . . .

"Hannah!" he called again. She had pulled the chute in, crumpling the nylon. She looked around her once—*how could she miss seeing you, even in this darkness?*—and ran toward the trees, chute and all. In a moment she'd disappeared into the dense shadows underneath the branches. Gregg fumed in his straps, the wind tossing him, the cold beginning to seep into his bones. He could smell the fragrance of moss, of humus, of the cow droppings in the field. The tree limbs creaked and groaned in the wind; the clouds played hide-and-seek with the moon.

"You planning to stay up there all night?"

Gregg looked down. Hannah was below, her head back as she stared up at him.

"Hannah! You went into the woods . . ."

"I thought that'd be better than going across the field in case someone was watching."

"I thought . . ."

Hannah smiled up at him. "You think I'd leave you? No chance. You're the one with the contacts, remember?" As Hannah started to climb the tree, the voices warred inside Gregg.

Don't flatter yourself, Greggie. She isn't doing this for you. She doesn't want to be alone here. Not yet. She'll wait until she's found a better time. And then . . .

It's not true, he answered. *I know it's not.*

Think about it. "You're the one with the contacts." She's using you, and when you're more a liability than an asset . . .

Hannah had scrambled up the tree and was sitting on the limb above him, hugging it with a wan grin. "Haven't done this since I was a kid," she said. "What do you think, Gregg? Should we take up skydiving for a hobby?"

Gregg forced his tiny mouth to smile back at her.

Let her laugh at you. One day you'll be doing the laughing, if you're smart. If you listen to me. Just listen to me . . .

"**. . . has been no** word from President Moonchild since the devastating explosion that leveled Saigon's Presidential Palace," Bernard Shaw was saying. Behind him was the smoking ruin of a French colonial villa. "Among the half dozen bodies pulled from the rubble this morning were those of her chancellor, Marcus Aurelius Meadows, and his daughter, ah, Sprout."

The director cut to the image of a stuffed toy, a plush pink fish burned almost beyond recognition.

Jay stood by the bar, staring up at the television, the beer in his hand forgotten. The lounge at Kapalua Airport was crowded with tourists coming and going, grabbing a quick one between planes; sleek tanned women and smiling men with suitcases, lugging their swimsuits and leftover sunblock and jars of macadamia nuts back home from Maui. Mark Meadows was never going home now, but none of them cared or paid the slightest attention.

CNN filled the screen with old footage of Mark in his purple Uncle Sam suit as Shaw droned on. "Meadows, the notorious ace known as Captain Trips, was wanted in the United States for kidnapping and drug trafficking when he led a joker revolution that established the outlaw nation he called Free Vietnam. In the wake of his death, three members of the cabinet have proclaimed themselves his successor, and there are reports of joker rioting all over Saigon."

"That's a fucking shitty epitaph," Jay said sourly. The Mark Meadows he had known deserved better. He remembered how thrilled Mark had been when their starship lifted off Earth. Space travel had been one of the most relentlessly boring experiences of Jay Ackroyd's life, but Mark had been beside himself at the wonder of it all. What a goddamned dreamer he'd been, still full of romantic notions despite everything he'd gone through.

Not Jay. Jay considered himself hardheaded and practical. Takis had been just another job to him; for Meadows, it had been a childhood fantasy come true. Yet it had been Jay who found love on Takis and brought home a wife. Mark found only death. Starshine, one of his "friends," had perished in a space battle, and Meadows had come back to Earth having lost part of himself.

And now it seemed he'd lost the rest as well. Jay wondered if Meadows and his other friends had found Starshine again. He hoped so. If ever a man deserved his peace . . .

He left his beer on the bar, untouched, and strode out into the terminal. Dr. Finn was off with the pilot, getting their plane refueled, but Jay found Jerry Strauss at a pay phone, taking notes on a yellow legal pad as he talked to Peter back in New York. "Okay," he kept saying. "Right, right, got it. Okay, right." Sascha Starfin stood beside him, wearing a black Hawaiian shirt and a wide-brimmed hat that shadowed his face where his eyes weren't. The skin over his empty sockets was as tan as the rest of him.

Jerry hung up. "Peter's trying to hack into some of Fleming's corporate records, but he hasn't been able to get access. He got us some basic biographical stuff." He noticed Jay's face. "Is something wrong? You look terrible."

"The commies blew up Mark Meadows," Sascha told him, plucking the thought off the top of Jay's mind. Jerry's mouth fell open and he gaped like a fish, his eyes blinking.

"Stay the fuck out of my head, Sascha," Jay snapped at the joker telepath.

"Give me what you've got," he said to Jerry.

Jerry shut his mouth and read from the legal pad. "Eric Fleming, born 1948 in Queensland, second son of a millionaire rancher named Thomas Fleming. His older brother was killed in the Vietnam War and Eric inherited the entire estate when his father died of a heart attack in 1974. He's multiplied the fortune many times over, buying and selling ranches, luxury resorts, cruise ships, television stations, and especially newspapers. His first paper was *The Townsville Drover*, a weekly he acquired in 1975. Today he owns nine papers in Australia, four in England, and two in the United States, plus six magazines and a paperback book company."

"Where does he live?"

"Well, he owns houses in Townsville, Brisbane, Melbourne, London, and New York, but Peter says he spends most of his time at a private island off the Great Barrier Reef."

Jay groaned. "Another island. Real good. Topper was the

only one we had who knew a rudder from a rutabaga. Five'll get you ten that's where he's stashed van Renssaeler, too."

Jerry fingered his chin thoughtfully. "Well, I could—"

"If you say one word about the Creature from the Black Lagoon, I'll leave you here," Jay warned him. "What else do we have? Any personal stuff?"

Jerry looked back at his notes. "Nothing good. Just the usual *Who's Who* junk on his marriages. Let's see, he's been married four, no, five times." His finger moved down the page as he read the names. "Married Lucy Taylor 1971, divorced 1973. Married Jane Carson 1973, divorced 1974. Married Jennifer Simms 1977, divorced 1984, two children, Thomas and Stephen. Married Cassandra Webb, an American actress, 1985. She died in a boating accident in 1988. Remember her? I was an ape when most of her movies came out, but I caught some of them on tape. Hoo boy, there was a girl with a figure. She was in *Black Roses*. And *Doc Holliday*, remember, with Donald Sutherland? She was the dancehall girl who gets killed in the cross fire. Peckinpah directed that one . . ."

"Did I ask for a filmography?" Jay said. "You said five wives. Who was the last one?"

Jerry flushed. "Sheila McCaffery," he muttered, glancing back down at his notes. "She was a model. She married Fleming in 1990, divorced 1992. One child, a daughter named Joan.

"A model and an actress," Jay said. He rubbed at the bandage over his nose. The pain was creeping back, a dull ache now, but soon it would be a throbbing. "He liked a good-looking woman."

"You have an idea?"

"Maybe the beginnings of one," Jay admitted.

— — —

Ray watched the night go by through the ripples of rain sliding down the plane's window. There was little enough to see. It was dark, they were flying through masses of clouds, and they were over the ocean. Infrequent flashes of lightning tore the darkness, illuminating nothing.

Ray was in a bad mood. In the best of times he hated transatlantic flights. They were dead boring. He had nothing to do but squirm in his seat for hours and hours, and think. But this was not even the best of times. His burns were healing, but they still hurt like a motherfucker. And his throat was raw. It often was when he had to breathe stale, recycled airplane air. But now he had to worry about whether the rawness was caused by bad air or the Black Trump. Maybe a colony of the vicious little viral bastards were sitting in his lungs, enjoying the steamy wetness, laughing and partying and having a jolly old time as they replicated like maniacs, sending out fine tendrils to clog and choke his system, spreading like some damn killer fungus from his head to his toes.

Life had been so much simpler, Ray thought, when he'd believed himself invincible. He sighed, glancing at April Harvest in the seat next to him. She was sleeping. Some women looked goofy when they slept, mouth open, hair mussed, makeup tracked all over the sheet or pillowcase. Harvest lost none of her beauty. It became softer, lost a little of its edge. It made Ray feel more confident when he looked at her while she slept. It made her look like maybe she wasn't too quick for him, too fast and sharp.

It was hard to say what made him more uncomfortable, thoughts of April Harvest or the Black Trump. He'd have to deal with both when they arrived in Scotland, where radar had traced Bushorn's plane. Right now, he just wanted to turn off his brain and rest, but he couldn't.

Somehow the hours passed. Harvest woke up after a while

and buried her nose in one of the thick dossiers she was always reading. When they finally disembarked at the Glasgow airport, Ray had that unfortunate mixture of wiredness and tiredness common at the end of transatlantic flights. And the greeting committee did little to improve Ray's mood.

"What'd you say?" he asked with an irritated frown, leaning closer to the giant of living stone who loomed before him and Harvest in the mouth of the disembarkation gateway.

The giant sighed. The sigh, like his voice, was a soft whispering that contrasted weirdly with his immense, sharp-edged appearance.

"I said, welcome to Scotland. Miss Harvest. Mr. Ray." The giant nodded at them as he spoke in barely audible tones. His ghostly voice gave Ray the creeps, and Ray didn't care much for the way the guy looked, either. He towered over Ray like a cliff face. His body, hard-edged and unyielding, looked like living rock, not human flesh. His eyes were twin flames dancing in the recesses of his roughly hewn face. *"I'm Kenneth Foxworthy."*

"Of course." April Harvest pushed past Ray. "Brigadier Foxworthy. Grand Marshal of the Most Puissant Order of the Silver Helix. I've read a lot about you and your career."

"Oh," Ray said, the light dawning. "You're the guy they call Captain Flint."

"Indeed." Flint glanced at the hand Ray offered and shook his head ponderously. *"Please take no insult."* He held out his own massive hands. *"My fingers are razor-sharp and rock hard. They would cut your flesh to ribbons."*

"You must be a holy terror on the handball court," Ray said.

"Yes," Flint said without a trace of a smile. *"I have news about your quarry. Good and bad news, I'm afraid."*

Ray and Harvest glanced at each other.

"Well," Harvest said, "let's hear the good news first."

"*This way, please,*" he whispered, starting off slowly down the corridor. "*More privacy.*"

They made their way to an empty, glassed-in debarkation lounge that was guarded by a pair of agents. British, American, whatever, Ray could spot them instantly. Flint moved about as quickly as a glacier and it took all the patience Ray possessed to slow down to match his pace.

"*My men picked up Bushorn when he landed,*" Flint whispered once they were behind the glass walls.

"Great," Ray said. "Let's go talk to him."

Flint shook his head ponderously. "*Now comes the bad news. You won't get much out of him. He was the plane's only occupant. He claims that he'd been hijacked and forced to fly across the Atlantic.*"

"What happened to the hijackers?" Harvest asked.

"*He says they bailed out when they were passing over Dublin.*"

"I see," Harvest said. She looked thoughtful. "That's all we have to go on?"

"*Yes.*" It was positively creepy the way Flint said that word in a sort of whispery hiss.

"Then," Harvest said, "I guess we'd better go to Ireland."

Flint nodded, his head teetering like a boulder on the edge of a cliff, trying to decide whether or not it wanted to roll down the slope of his chest. "*I have a plane waiting.*"

The sign pointing south said CARRYDUFF 2; below, another plank pointed north with the legend BELFAST 10. The road was cracked blacktop barely two lanes wide, but it was a highway compared to the rutted dirt track they'd been following. A dry goods store with a petrol pump sat at the intersection. Since the sun had just risen, they'd decided to hole up in a dense growth of trees and brush on the top of a small hill not far off the road. They watched the occasional lorry and car pass, most of them traveling north to Belfast. A woman came and opened the store. Gregg breakfasted on a hubcap they'd found in the gulley alongside the road. Hannah had contented herself with raiding a cottage garden they'd passed before dawn.

"What do we do now?" Hannah asked Gregg. Below them, a small pickup truck had stopped. An older man got out and went into the establishment.

"I don't know," Gregg said. "We need to get to Belfast. There's a small Jokertown there—I've toured it a few times. We should be able to lose ourselves in the city—Peter Horvath's here; he might be able to lead us to Rudo."

"If we can get to Belfast before someone finds us," Hannah said.

She was grinning at him. "Yeah. If," Gregg answered.

"Then I think I can do something about it. Just make sure you pick up on your cue." With that, Hannah got up, brushed the dirt from her jeans, and started down the hill toward the grocery.

"Hey!" Gregg called. "What are you doing?"

"I'm just a poor American girl from Belfast whose boyfriend took her on a ride out this way. We had a terrible argument, and he left me here. I'm lost and a little scared. I just need a ride back to town." She smiled at him. "You'd give me a ride, wouldn't you?"

"That's not going to work," Gregg told her.

Hannah stopped. "You have a better idea?" she asked.

Something in her tone put wrinkles around the round balls that served Gregg for eyes. *You're just a joker, after all* . . . "No," Gregg admitted.

"Then get ready to hop on. Our bus is leaving in a few minutes."

Gregg watched Hannah jog down the hill and go into the

store. Gregg followed her reluctantly, crouching behind a heap of empty boxes at the side of the building. A few minutes later, Hannah came out with the driver of the truck. As she climbed into the passenger seat, she looked around, saw Gregg, and nodded slightly. "I really appreciate this," she was saying as she closed the door. "Michael just left me . . ." Gregg leapt up onto the bed of the pickup and wriggled his way behind a tool-box there. The truck engine coughed, the transmission whined, and they were off. Gregg contented himself by opening the box and eating a socket wrench.

An hour later, after a slow and leisurely drive, they were in Belfast. The Jokertown district lay along Belfast Lough in the western part of the city. They were passing through the area when Gregg heard the truck door open as they waited at a light. "You don't want to get out *here*," the driver said.

"You're probably right, but I'm doing it anyway," Hannah answered as Gregg wriggled out from behind the toolbox and quickly leapt over the side of the cab. "Thanks for the ride." The driver was shaking his head at Hannah, who waved at him and smiled. Still shaking his head, the man threw the truck into gear and drove off. Hannah looked at Gregg, then surveyed the close-ranked buildings around them and the jokers walking the streets. "Welcome to Belfast," she said to Gregg. "I got us here. Now it's your turn."

Not much had changed since Gregg had last been in the city a decade ago. Belfast's Jokertown was a smaller, dingier, and poorer version of the original. Most of New York's Jokertown looked affluent by comparison. The buildings here were ancient, and as dark as if they'd inhaled the patina of violence and struggle that had washed over Belfast through the centuries. The briny smell of the harbor mingled with the odors of factories and fireplaces and automobile exhaust. The lowering gray sky pressed down uncomfortably, and the occasional drizzle that passed did nothing to wash away the dirt.

As for the jokers, they were no different than those prowling Jokertown streets back home. Twisted and changed by the wild card virus, they came in the same infinite variety of shape and form, the same infinite variety of pain.

The wild card virus had first been labeled the "Protestant Disease" here—perhaps aptly, since the initial and largest outbreak of the disease had been in Belfast. Until the early sixties, the virus had capriciously spared the island; then it had struck with a vengeance: The 1962 Belfast infection had rivaled in virulence and suddenness the original New York City outbreak. The IRA had originally claimed credit, a claim that many still believed. It may even have been true. The wild card indeed struck the Protestant areas hardest—at first, anyway. It was not to remain that way for long.

The outbreak had fueled some of the most vicious fighting in decades. Belfast had burned; the British had brought in troopships and a cadre of diplomats to handle the violence, but—perhaps from fear of the virus—the tendency was to shoot rather than negotiate, and the level of violence simply escalated. There were reprisal bombings nearly every week in Belfast, and across the Irish Sea in Manchester, Liverpool, and London. Two hundred of the British troops were killed, along with untold numbers of Catholic and Protestant partisans, before some semblance of order was imposed on the north.

And the virus, uncaring about such political niceties, had traveled south. The "Protestant Disease" proved to be all too catholic. It didn't care what faith its victims professed to believe. It prowled from Ulster to Connacht, Leinster, and Munster, capricious and unpredictable, and always, always deadly. Over the last thirty years, the Protestant/Catholic problems had sometimes been overshadowed by those of wild carder and nat. The events had colored the treatment of the wild card victims in all of Ireland. Three decades later, Irish jokers had reason to hate the nats who controlled them. Being Irish, they had long memories for wrongs.

Hannah was looking at Gregg expectantly. They were drawing stares from the jokers passing them, Hannah getting most of them. Gregg noticed that she was the only nat visible other than those passing in cars. "First, let's get off the street. By now, Bushorn's told them that we bailed out over Ireland. They may already be looking for us. There's got to be a pub around here somewhere . . ."

A few minutes later they entered Joseph Coan's, a small, dim pub on the next corner. The patrons were jokers; there didn't seem to be a bartender. As they entered, the buzz of conversation stopped as if cut off by a switch; everyone glared at them suspiciously. "I thought that only happened in movies," Hannah muttered to Gregg. Gregg heard her inhale, and she pushed the door wide and went to the bar. She put her hands on the polished wooden surface . . .

. . . and pulled them abruptly away. "Jesus!" she said loudly. "It *moved*."

That brought laughter from around the pub. "Did'ja hear that, Joseph?" one of the jokers called.

"Indeed I did," a bass voice answered from somewhere in front of Hannah, and she took another step back from the bar.

"It talks, too," Hannah said to Gregg.

"And it has a name," the bar said. "I'm Joseph Coan, and I own this establishment, or rather, I suppose you might say, I *am* the establishment. Now, are you thirsty or did you come in looking for some local color, lass?" Hannah looked at Gregg and stepped forward again.

"Two pints of Guinness," she said.

"That'll be one pound five," Joseph said. The voice seemed to emanate from directly in front of Hannah.

Hannah pulled a few notes from her pocket—Irish currency purchased in New York—and peeled off a five-pound note. "Umm, where do I put it?" she said.

"On me," Joseph answered. Another wave of laughter rippled through the bar. Hannah smiled into the laughter and stepped forward. "All right," she said. "Here you are." She laid the bill on the table.

The wooden surface seemed to melt under the paper, and the note disappeared under the varnished surface as if drifting through thick water. A moment later, more bills and some coins wafted upward, the bar solidifying under them. "Your change," Joseph said. A glass mug slid by itself along the rear shelf, and a bar tap dunked forward as the mug filled with dark brew. The tap clicked back, and the glass glided toward Hannah, as if pushed by an invisible hand, as another mug slid under the tap. "There you go. Looks like all the booths are empty; have a seat by me."

"Are you part of the seats, too?" Hannah glanced at the barstools cautiously.

More laughter cascaded from the booths and tables. "What's the matter, lassie? Don't want old Joseph touching your bum?"

"At least I'm warm," Joseph said.

"If I get splinters, I'm holding you personally responsible," Hannah said. A barstool slid in place behind her. Hannah sat. Another one slid into place as the second glass of Guinness eased into place alongside. "For your friend," Joseph said. Gregg grimaced and scuttled across the floor to the stool. He jumped up, sitting with his rear two feet tucked underneath. He looked at the Guinness and the thin brown foam atop the black liquid. The brew didn't look or smell anywhere near as appealing as it had when he'd been normal. He wondered how accommodating Joseph would be if he asked for a side order of wing nuts.

"Don't often get Americans in here," Joseph said conversationally while Hannah took a sip of the Guinness. Gregg noticed that he could see a faint pair of lips moving below the surface of the oak, like something glimpsed in murky water. The rest of the jokers in the pub had gone back to their private conversations now that they were sitting at the bar. Gregg peered myopically into the haze of pipe smoke. He had a sense that someone was watching, but he found it impossible to find the source. Near the back, a joker with three legs got up and left the pub by a rear door. "And one of you a nat, no less," Joseph was saying. "Very unusual. Very noteworthy."

"Is someone taking notes like that?" Hannah asked. She gave a small, forced chuckle that took some of the edge from the question. Gregg's unease increased. He could feel something—someone—approaching, a malevolence that almost felt familiar. His body tingled with the feeling, a buzz of adrenaline that made his legs twitch.

"I did not say that, lass. I was only making conversation. Being friendly, don't you know. No need to take offense."

"No offense taken," Hannah told him. She seemed to jump slightly, squirming in the seat. Gregg noticed that she was careful not to touch the bar. For that matter, he didn't, either. "But if you squeeze my ass again like that, I will."

The bar chuckled, the surface jiggling with the sound and rippling the stout. "Ahh, sorry. Old habits, you know."

"How much of this place is, well, *you*?" Hannah asked. Gregg was content to let her do the talking. All the hairs on his body were standing erect. The three-legged joker had come back in, and Gregg thought he saw a small shape move in the shadows behind the man as the door closed.

"More than you'd think," Joseph was saying. "I can get feeling from most of the surfaces—the tables, the booths, but I can't manipulate them. Most of *me* is here in the bar, if that's what you mean. You haven't touched your Guinness," he said, and Gregg realized that Coan was talking to him.

"Sorry," he told the bar. "I guess I don't drink anymore."

"Then I'll drink it for him, Joseph." A voice spoke behind Gregg, and the deep timbre of it made Gregg spin around in his seat, almost losing his balance, as his mind sensed a darkness, a blackness shot through with red like fire. The feeling was familiar. *No, it can't be* . . . "Gimli?" Gregg cried, squinting.

A short, green man was peering up at him, his head cocked expectantly at Gregg, his eyes as bright an emerald as his skin. He held a gun, pointed at Gregg's red clown nose.

"Jesus! A *leprechaun*!" Gregg cried.

The doors to the warehouse stood open to Odessa's docks. Zoe watched the numbers blink on the cheap watch she wore. Eight minutes since Croyd had gone in to set up the buy; four more and she would walk in, find the office door somewhere in there in the murk, and hand over the sack of Israeli multivitamins that were part of the deal. The Russians were entranced with vitamins, Snailfoot had said. They thought they protected them against the fallout from Chernobyl, maybe.

The ship that was to take Croyd and Zoe across the Black Sea waited at the pier. Zoe stood as close to the gangplank as she could, as far away from the warehouse doors as she dared. The ship was the most beautiful ship Zoe had ever seen, a stubby freighter with rust stains oozing down its sides from every porthole, beautiful because she promised shelter and escape, if only for a while.

Nine minutes. Zoe stood on the docks because that's where the plan told her to stand. The plan was all she had.

She felt numb all over, a forced numbness that had begun in the catacombs of Jerusalem. Follow the plan. Do what you're told. Go here, do this, wait for that. Her head was reeling with things she had never wanted to know and desperately needed to know; Snailfoot's dry discussions on the potential radiation hazards of something she could now think of only as The Device; Azma's quick, sharp lessons on proper decorum for a Muslim wife. Behave this way in Turkey, but this way in the desert. Keep your eyes down; don't stare at anyone; don't, for the love of Allah, stare at a *man's* face. Snailfoot's dry British voice saying, Croyd you will go to *this* café, you will discuss this year's crops with a man fitting *this* description, you will remark on *this* amount of rainfall. Zoe, you don't need to know this part, try not to listen, and that was when she'd gone numb, had begun to concentrate only on her role in this charade.

No cloak-and-dagger stuff, no. This was simply a business deal. Meet the seller. Hand over the cash and pick up the merchandise. Don't even think about the complicated politics and the feuds over a collapsed empire that left holes in the Russian system big enough for a nuclear warhead to slip through. It's not cloak-and-dagger anymore. It's just business. Smile.

Odessa went about its bustling business on a hazy day, a port city testing the rituals of capitalism, and smiling.

There were so many smiles here, smiles that flashed on acres of cheap dentures and dull metal fillings. The clerk at the hotel had smiled last night, and carried their luggage with a smile, and held out his hand for a tip with a smile.

Zoe's face ached from a forced smile that she had plastered on her face, for anyone who didn't smile must not have anything to sell, and therefore was a potential customer for any newly fledged entrepreneur who had a string of sausages to sell, or lettuces to spread on a cloth on the sidewalk.

Smiling last night while she and Croyd climbed the Potem-

kin Steps up from the water to the promenade and found seats
in the little café at its edge. She had sipped sweet hot tea from
a glass and toyed with some sort of salt fish canapé that she
couldn't force herself to swallow. In the dark café, she'd kept
smiling while Croyd made his speech in what he'd said later
was Ukrainian peppered with Russian peppered with Arabic.
Smiling while the short, bouncy boy with swarthy skin and
curly chestnut hair had talked about rain. Crops and rain. No
cloak-and-dagger stuff.

Smiling when Croyd tensed beside her, those scary knots of
his muscles rising in his jaw, for the boy had gone on to offer
Croyd a sheaf of stock in some bedamned company or other,
all printed on thin cheap paper in Cyrillic with huge red and
black capitals, and *that wasn't in the script.* But Croyd had said
something that made the boy laugh, and nothing bad had happened.

Zoe smiled in no one's direction and watched a pair of pale,
bulky, smiling tourists in flowered short-sleeved shirts, maybe
recovering from black-mud baths at one of the spas. They
walked away, their buttocks fighting rhythmic battles beneath
their baggy khaki shorts. It was two in the afternoon on a hazy
day, and all was calm, busy and calm. The port city rumbled
with commerce and smelled of coal smoke.

From the opened sliding doors of the warehouse, long-
shoremen trundled out with crates of powdered milk and
sacks of grain stacked on clumsy-looking hand trucks. They
roped their loads to the hook of a winch and yelled at each
other in a bored sort of way as the cargo lifted over the side of
the ship and vanished, swaying, into the hold.

Zoe lifted her head to look up at the ship again, and the silk
scarf slipped backward on her hair. Anne hated her black hair.

"Why that color?" she had asked.

"Just a whim, Momma." They had kept Croyd away from

the apartment once his hair was dyed black. Two "whims" at once might have clued Anne that this "business trip" wasn't quite what it seemed.

Zoe tightened the knot under her chin, settled the strap of her canvas tote on her shoulder, and walked into the warehouse.

Follow the plan. The office won't be at the front; go to the back right corner. Follow the plan. The aisles changed every day as goods got loaded in and out, no one knew which path led back there, just go. Keep your eyes down.

Beside her, lined up in a row, one of these machines contained The Device. Green enamel, thick cast iron, the pumps were the size of a Maytag washer and dryer bolted together. A dozen, twenty, all alike, they looked efficient and innocent. But not this one. Zoe stopped, unable to take the next step, sensing the heavy package behind the bland metal, a casing of thin lead and thick steel that hid a heart of darkness, a limitless black universe where tiny particles flashed blue-white like falling meteors in a dark night, a chattering of brutal entropic decay never meant to be confined.

"*Bos?*" the man asked. "*Bos?*"

The voice startled her into motion. She looked up at the man, stubbled, gray hair and a grin that gapped over some missing teeth. "*Ya nyeh gavaryu pa Russkie,*" Zoe said. Croyd had taught her that much.

"*Von!*" The man gestured toward the rear of the warehouse.

"*Spasebo,*" Zoe whispered. She went where he pointed.

A square of frosted, ornately leaded glass, thick and dusty with age, filtered gray light through the carved mahogany door. The door was a relic of a gaslit past, incongruous in this dank, musty warehouse. It looked like Sam Spade's door strained through a samovar. Zoe could see the warehouse manager in his place behind a desk and the back of Croyd's head, black hair, a black pilot's cap, leaning back in the visitor's chair.

Zoe opened the door. The man in the cap wasn't Croyd. Croyd slipped in beside her, quick and silent, and before she could take a breath they stood in the office with the door closed and Zoe had moved sideways to get her back against the wall. Beneath her palms, its texture was slick, greasy, gritty.

The manager had a pair of heavy chins and a belly that he rested against the front of the desk. The man in the visitor's chair turned toward them, black eyebrows raised over wary Mideastern eyes, narrow eyes, the pupils dilated with fear. The smile faded from the face of the man behind the desk. His thick fingers splayed out across a bearer draft, covering some of the printed zeroes marching across its face. A lot of zeroes.

Croyd moved in what seemed like slow motion. He reached a hand toward the swivel chair and tipped its back toward him. The knife against the Mideasterner's throat hadn't been there before but now it was, the man's head tilted back and cradled against Croyd's belly. A single drop of blood formed in the dimple the point of the knife made in the Mideastener's skin, right over the Adam's apple.

Croyd asked something in Russian. The manager replied in a spate of rapid words. His silver front teeth were separated by a large gap. He gestured with the hand that wasn't holding down the bearer draft, indicating Croyd, the man in the chair. Then he rubbed his fingers against his thumb as if they held cash. Croyd spoke again.

"*Oh-kay,*" the manager said.

"Zoe, give him the package," Croyd said.

She pulled the white, crackling paper sack, filled with vials of multivitamins, out of her canvas tote and reached forward to lay it down on the scarred wood.

The manager grabbed it and tipped the contents onto his

desk. Bottles rolled in all directions. Bright candy-colored pills scattered from an opened container and fell to the concrete floor with a sound like popping corn. The manager's thick fingers teased at the fold in the bottom of the sack. He tugged at a paper folded in the bottom and eased out a bearer draft. He laid it next to the other one.

Snailfoot hadn't told her she was the courier for the bank draft. The bastard.

"Sure," Croyd said. "Cash 'em both. Why not?"

The manager smiled.

Croyd's forearm tensed, the cords of the tendons leaping under his dyed brown skin. The Mideasterner's torso jumped. Both his arms reached skyward with a jerk. The gun in his hand made a soft popping sound.

The manager's eyes went vacant and his lower jaw sagged. A tiny amber fishing fly—a dart—quivered in his upper lip, just above the gap between his front teeth. The dart gun fell from the Mideasterner's hand. The manager's belly held him in his chair as he sagged forward against the desk, and Zoe thought, *There's only one door in here. Only one fucking door. We've got to hide the bodies somewhere.*

"Shit," Croyd said.

"Yessss." Zoe couldn't get her jaw open enough to stop hissing.

"We just leave 'em, I guess," Croyd said.

"The knife."

"Yeah." He tossed it onto the desk. "They killed each other. That's cool. But we've got to keep anybody from coming in here until the pump is on board. Any ideas?"

"No. This man. Whose is he?"

"Shit, Zoe. I don't know. Ivan, over there, didn't know. Ivan thought he was *me*."

Someone knew about the Fists, someone was trying to stop

them, and it wasn't any legitimate power, not the UN, not the FBI. The Sharks? Or had the fucking Black Dog set this up for overkill? A failsafe in case Croyd or Zoe chickened out?

Zoe wanted out of here. And if she left now with Croyd, ran for it, they wouldn't have a clue on where to go for safety. If they left without the bomb, the Black Dog would hurt Jan somehow. Zoe *knew* it.

Three men, a woman, a deal being cut. A need for privacy. "Croyd, you're a pimp."

"Huh?"

"Just get your skinny ass outside and guard the door. I'm adding a little something to sweeten the deal, right? A little extra service. Deals get cut in here; we have to figure this isn't the only business that goes down on the docks, or at least we have to hope so. Just thump on the door twice if I need to do some heavy breathing, okay? And for God's sake, let me out of here once that pump is on board!"

"Right," Croyd said.

He opened the door and closed it behind him. She could see his blurred outline, his back against the door.

Neither of the corpses was bleeding much. The little wound in the center of the Mideasterner's throat looked so tiny. The Russian—no, the Ukrainian—the manager wasn't messy at all.

The Mideastener's head lolled back against the chair. His cap hadn't fallen off. From the window, maybe he'd just look relaxed. Zoe tiptoed around him and sat on the desk, her back to the window, her legs on either side of the manager's fat belly. She tore off her headscarf and tossed her hair loose. The manager was close enough that she could kiss him if she leaned forward.

The tiny dart hung limp in his upper lip. He had cut himself shaving this morning; there was a little scrape on one of his chins. What had been on the dart? Shellfish toxin was the only thing she'd ever read about that could work that fast, and even then there should have been a breath, a gasp, a struggle of some sort. This man had gone as still as a stop-motion sequence in a bad movie.

She had heard that dead men smelled of shit, but these two didn't. The air in the office smelled of dust, paper, and cheap ink. The Mideastener reeked of stale sweat. And that was all.

A cart rumbled by outside. She heard it, but the office was dead silent.

Dead.

Silent.

Don't think. Follow the plan, even if this was never the plan. Why didn't they load the fucking pump? How would the Ukrainians ever manage a free market if they couldn't learn to load freight? Didn't anybody ever work around here?

The dead manager stared at her. He was just someone trying to get along. He looked like a family man, a guy with kids. She imagined him at home in one of those baby-blue apartment buildings with the rococo balconies, eating sausages stewed with cabbage. There were no rings on his fingers. Zoe had noticed that when he caressed the bank drafts.

She reached out a tentative finger and closed the dead man's eyes, one, the other.

A voice called out some sort of query in Russian.

"Nyet! Minutku!" Croyd said.

He said something else. Zoe turned her head just enough to see his shadow at the door. She couldn't see anyone beside him.

Just get the pump loaded, okay? Come on, Ukrainians. Load that ship and we'll leave. We'll never come back here, honest.

Croyd said something tersely. Zoe heard a clang, metal falling on concrete. Croyd didn't thump on the door, but what if he were afraid to? What if someone stood watching, some eagle-eyed employee who wondered what was going on?

Zoe grasped the manager's neck in her hands and pulled. It didn't want to move. She tugged. His neck sagged forward. The dead weight of the corpse's head fell against her lap, his forehead pushed against her belly, the lethal dart dangling free and not in contact with her cringing skin. She held him there, aware of the rough, light-brown stubble on the back of his neck, the thick texture of his skin. His skin was warm, but it was doughy. She closed her eyes and felt hot, silent tears run down her cheeks.

How much longer? How long?

She whimpered.

The whimper threatened to change into sobs. No. The plan. She had to remember the plan, and she heard someone coming toward the door, and Croyd's voice.

Croyd's heel tapped the door, twice.

Zoe panted. She arched her back and let her neck tilt, and she twisted back and forth a little. She panted again. She moaned. She heard Croyd say something, a sharp comment, and then she heard a different voice, a chuckle.

Boots scuffled on the concrete, someone walking away.

And nothing happened. Zoe sat there, the manager's head in her lap, afraid to move. A muscle in her lower back began to ache.

"Zoe!" Croyd hissed. He opened the door just wide enough to peer inside. "Come on!"

She scooted backward across the desk, leaving the manager where he sat. Croyd held the door ajar.

"What about the bank drafts?" she asked.

"Leave them," Croyd said. "They're trouble for somebody. You look—well, never mind." He brushed a hand across her cheek, wiping away tears. "Keep calm."

Her scarf. She picked up her headscarf from the desk and twisted it around her hand. The door closed on the hell behind them.

Follow the plan. Croyd waited for her to come to his side, visibly at ease if you didn't look at how controlled his motions really were. They strolled between crates and boxes toward the hazy sunlight. The man who had yelled *"Bos!"* put down a crate and watched them. Croyd stared past him and maybe he didn't see the man's spit hit the floor behind his heel.

Stroll, don't run. Zoe didn't see the pump. Maybe it wasn't on board. Maybe the warehouse had loaded the wrong one. It didn't matter. Follow the plan.

Someone had backed the crane away from the side of the ship. She could hear the ship's diesels rumbling. A sailor leaned over the rail above her, looking down. He was smoking a thick cigarette rolled in tea-colored paper.

She walked up the gangplank beside Croyd. Cloak-and-dagger stuff was for the middle of the night, not for a spring afternoon.

The sailor tossed his cigarette over the side. He ambled over to a set of chains and pulled the gangplank up into its slot on the ship's side.

Croyd led her into a small passageway, metal and smelling of mechanic's grease. Outside the porthole, the warehouse doors stood open.

Croyd paced back and forth, watching the open doors. Slowly, as if in a dream, the ship eased away from the pier, out into the Black Sea.

They entered a hilly region that Mark took to be northern Cambodia, where the land started to rise toward Laos's

Bolaven Plateau. The river spread out to accommodate numerous tree-crowded islands. On one of these the boat put ashore.

Mark and Sprout were allowed to spend the day hidden beneath the trees. After dark came the drumbeat of rotors from the west, and with its distinctive *thud-thud-thud* an ancient American Huey utility helicopter—showing more rusty, dented metal than olive-drab paint faded gray by the terrible Southeast Asian sun—settled down on a sandbar. The kidnappers chivvied Mark and Sprout on board with their muzzle brakes and stood back to watch, expressionless to the last, as the chopper jumped into the air and flew west.

The helicopter churned between low tree-furred mountains and out over drowned paddy land glittering like mercury pools in moonlight. Mark reckoned they were over eastern Thailand. The pilot was a heavyset, balding white guy in a polo shirt and khaki pants. He might have been American, but then he also might have been French, German, Russian, or God knew what. He said nothing in Mark's hearing, either to captives or to the quartet of black-pajamaed brown men who rode with him. This set showed subtle differences from the last to Mark, in details of dress and body language, and the singsong inflections of their language. He still couldn't identify them.

Near dawn the helicopter set down among barren red hills. Men in Royal Thai Army cammies refueled the craft. The black pajamas ushered Mark and Sprout outside and into the brush to tend to this and that while the pilot went out of earshot to confer with the soldiers. Then the little ship rose into a sky so hot its blue was nearly white, and flew on.

They crossed a mountain range, stopped for the night in another armed camp. This one was occupied by more little brown men, wearing military castoffs from half a dozen nations, carrying an equally eclectic assortment of weapons. Some wore skirts of striped dark-green cloth to augment their uniform bits and pieces. They were obviously bandits or guerrillas, and their appearance and language struck Mark as similar to that of his current escorts. But the four in black kept themselves and their captives apart from the others. The pilot went away with some locals and did not put in an appearance until daylight, by which point he smelled alarmingly of gin.

They flew over more mountains, and then a deep river gorge, a stroke of beauty to clog the throat, if you weren't too preoccupied worrying whether the pilot was sober enough to *drive* this thing. Sprout, who adapted more readily than her father, looked out the open side doors and clapped her hands in delight. Despite their predicament, the spectacle moved Mark as well—though he kept an eye on her, to make sure she stayed securely strapped in, and kept a firm grip on her bear.

Beyond the gorge rose dense, forested hills. As the sun began to roll down a cloudless sky, a broad clearing came into view, filled with huts clustered around an open square. The helicopter settled down in the midst of the open area. Mark and Sprout were prodded forth, blinking and wobbling to meet a trim brown man on a big white horse.

A tall Westerner stood by the horse, studiously clear of the hooves it flashed as it pranced and snorted at the helicopter's red dust whirlwind. He wore a white linen suit with an open collar. One hand clamped a white straw hat to an immense round head against the rotor downblast.

The black pajamas prodded Mark in the kidneys with their AKMs. He dropped to his knees. The man on horseback gazed down on him impassively. He had that handsome, ageless, Southeast Asian look. He wore tiger-stripe camouflage fatigues with the creases pressed to razor edges and an American .45 holstered on a webbing belt. He smoothed his mustache with a thumb and nodded.

"Is this the man you wanted, Mr. Casaday?" he asked in clear English.

The tall man's face split into a jack-o'-lantern grin. "The very one. Marshal Hti. My main man from here on in. *And* his lovely daughter, too, I see."

He laughed. "Your people have done me proud, Hti. You'll be well rewarded."

"Anything that hurts Yangon rewards us," the marshal said, "but money is always appreciated." He wheeled the horse and rode off at a crisp trot toward a beaten-earth practice field where ranks of sweating men charged one another head-down like boars.

Kalashnikov barrels gouged Mark to his feet. "Bring them both," Casaday said, turning away.

". . . and so he hollers 'Jesus! A *leprechaun!*' in a little scratchy voice that could cut glass, like *he's* as normal as the bloody Prince of Wales. I thought he was going to ask me to give him the pot of gold, I did."

Gregg winced as the laughter rolled around the back room of Joseph Coan's. Around Hannah and him were a quintet of jokers: the "leprechaun" who so eerily reminded him of Gimli; a woman who looked normal until she lowered the scarf around her lower head, revealing unbroken skin below the nose; a man with arms and legs that looked like they'd come from four radically different people; a joker who huffed asthmatically as far away from the fire as possible, his skin as impossibly bright a red as his hair, dry and papery—he looked like a match could reduce him to quick ashes; and the three-legged joker who had first spotted Gregg and Hannah. All of them were well armed. The others had arrived not long after the leprechaun had gestured with his weapon, herding Hannah and Gregg into the room.

("I don't want no trouble here," Joseph had called to the small joker as Gregg and Hannah moved reluctantly ahead of him into the back room. "There may be trouble, but it won't be here, Joseph," the joker said. "I promise you that.")

"You can call me King Brian, since you think I'm one of the Little People," the leprechaun said now. "That's Cara, Stand-in, Scarlet Will, and Trio." Brian pointed at each of the jokers in turn. "You've given us a bit of problem, you have."

"What do you mean?" Hannah asked. She glared down at Brian, hands on hips, defiant. "We haven't done anything to you."

"No? Then why'd you send the hunchback to us? How'd you know how to tell him to find us?"

"Quasi?" Hannah asked. "He came here?" Hannah laughed, looking at Gregg. "What did he say?"

«We didn't understand most of it.» A feminine "voice"—Cara's, since she was looking directly at them—seemed to emanate from within Gregg's head, muffled as if he were listening to a conversation behind a wall. The others were hearing it, too, nodding with Cara's statement. «He said something about a virus, that you would need to go to the Black Dog, that we were to help you . . . »

"You're Twisted Fists," Gregg burst out suddenly.

"Ahh, *now* he gets it," Brian said. "A better guess than leprechauns, after all." The others laughed, grimly. "So you see, we've been waiting for you. 'They'll come to the place where the wood speaks,' the hunchback said. That's as good a description of Coan's as any I've heard."

"The hunchback mentioned Father Squid, too, and a few of

us here remember the man," Scarlet Will said. His voice was as papery as his body. "But Squidface is no longer one of us. He follows his own way now. But I'll at least listen to someone who knows the Father. If you have information about this Black Trump, tell us your tale."

"Not here," Gregg said. "Not yet." The glimmering of a new plan began to form. He looked at Hannah. *She may be a problem. She was against dealing with the Fists. But maybe, maybe . . .*

Forget her, came an answer from somewhere. *Worry about yourself.* "How do we know you're who you say *you* are? If you're Fists, prove it. Put us in contact with the Black Dog. I'll speak to the Hound of Hell," he said. "No one else."

They laughed. "By the blood of Christ, man, you're in the wrong country for that," Brian said, and guffawed. "Now, maybe we can send you to the Dog, and maybe we can't. You're just going to have to trust us, aren't you?" Brian slapped his thigh, then the amusement left him suddenly. His eyes went expressionless. "So you will tell us, will you not?"

"We didn't come here to find the Fists," Hannah said suddenly. She was looking at Gregg. "I'm sorry, but I won't deal with terrorists."

Brian glared at her with a lopsided grin on his face. "It doesn't appear you have a choice."

Hannah shook her head. "Damned if I don't," she said. "I'm outta here. Gregg? You coming?" Hannah started to walk toward the door. Gregg didn't follow, but Brian moved quickly to block her path, his weapon snapping up, a semiautomatic that looked huge in his tiny hands.

Hannah looked down at the joker. "Damn it, get out of my fucking way or I'll shove that goddamn penis substitute up your little green ass."

Brian clucked. "Oooh, such language from a lady. You're an ace, then, since guns don't scare you."

"No," Hannah said angrily.

"A nat?" Brian cooed. "I *hate* nats. I'm thinking that you owe us all an apology." Deliberately, he brought the notched muzzle of the weapon up, so that it prodded Hannah in the breast. A delicious fright rippled along Gregg's spine, frightening and yet at the same time tantalizing. *Gregg, you can't let this happen . . .* someone was saying, but another, darker voice answered. *Why not? Isn't it what she deserves?*

Shut up! he told the voice. *Leave me alone!*

Hannah faced Brian without flinching. "Then you're a fucking stupid man along with being a small one," she told Brian. "I've spent the last year of my life and lost everything I once had dealing with the wild card virus and the Sharks, and if it *still* matters more to you that I'm a nat and not a joker, then you deserve the fate you're going to get when the Sharks release the Trump."

Someone—Gregg thought it was Stand-in—chuckled in the background, but Brian became apoplectic, his face flushed and tight. Gregg saw muscles bunching along the man's arm, and he was certain that Brian was going to pull the trigger.

Gregg, you can't let this happen . . .

And Gregg did something that utterly surprised even himself.

Puppetman would have eagerly licked at Brian's rage. He (with Gregg riding him) would have enjoyed the terror, would have escalated it for the sheer pleasure. If Hannah happened to die, then, well, too bad. There were always other puppets to be had—what was the loss of one compared to the pleasure of her death?

Gregg—after the death of Puppetman, his ace gone—would have cowered in terror, too frightened to do anything. He would have been pleading for his own life. He would have regretted Hannah's death, but his own survival would have been far more important.

Since he'd become a joker, Gregg had never responded to a crisis with any reaction but flight. But Gregg—the joker—the coward—leapt in front of Hannah. He could feel the adrenaline pumping, just on the edge of kicking him into overdrive yet again. "Out o' the way," Brian snarled. "I don't wish to harm jokers, but if I must . . ."

Gregg almost obeyed. He wanted to run, and the welter of emotions confused him. *Get out of his way!* the voice screamed inside, but Gregg shook his head. *I'm not listening to you. Not again!* Suddenly it didn't matter. The churning in his stomach could not be denied. Gregg opened his mouth and heaved.

A viscous jet of vomit slathered Brian's hands and chest and dripped from the gun muzzle as Brian looked down at himself in horrified disgust. Gray-green effluvium sizzled on metal. The vented barrel of the automatic weapon suddenly sagged and drooped, and Brian let the thing drop with a scream and then—abruptly—upchucked himself, on top of the whole mess.

The smell was overpowering, horrendous, and—to Gregg— utterly delicious. It made him want to lap at the sweet, puckered metal.

Behind him, Gregg heard Hannah struggling to control her own stomach. "Sorry," he said to the company in general. "But I couldn't let you do that. If you hurt Hannah, you hurt yourselves far more. You don't know how much she's done for—" . . . *me,* he was going to say, but the bitter voice, the one in the shadows of his mind, laughed. *She's done nothing for you, Greggie. You were a convenient fuck when you were a nat, and now that you're a joker, you're nothing at all.* Gregg swallowed. "Us," he finished shakily. He forced that voice down.

«I believe she mentioned that somewhere in the tirade,» Cara said, amused and speaking in their heads.

"Hannah uncovered the entire Card Sharks conspiracy," Gregg continued, looking at Brian, who appeared to be a little greener than usual. "Goddamn it, kill her and you might as well blow your own fucking brains out. Kill her, and the Black Trump might just get released—and if *that* happens, you've signed the death warrant for every damn joker in the world. The Sharks and the nats will have gotten exactly what they've always wanted."

I couldn't let you do it because I care for her. That, somehow, he didn't—couldn't—say. He was confused. Voices warred inside him, and he didn't know who to listen to. He wasn't certain where the sudden bravery had come from or why he'd put himself between Hannah and Brian's threat, especially since he was no longer sure what Hannah felt for him. All he knew was that thinking she was going to die had forced him out of inaction.

The realization, after all the doubt of the last several days, startled him. Maybe for the first time in his life, Gregg had done something because he cared more about someone else's life than his own.

He marveled.

Gregg stopped breathing heavily. Behind him, he could feel the warmth of Hannah's body and hear her own quick breath. Brian was glaring at them, his hands still dripping with Gregg's vomit. The other jokers waited.

Finally Brian nodded, and he smiled, but there was nothing friendly or sympathetic in his smile. It was merely a random movement of the dark green lips. "All right. But you *will* tell us all about the Trump, if you expect any help at all." Brian nudged the misshapen mass of his half-melted weapon on the floor with a careful boot. "That be a useful trick you have there, but it's not enough. Tell me what you plan to do here, and then we'll see about letting you talk to the Black Dog, eh?"

"You're wasting time," Gregg said. "Time that we don't have. God knows where the Trump is now, or how long before they'll release it. The longer we delay, the harder the three vials are going to be to find."

Brian shook clinging goo from his hands. "You act like you could go to fucking Churchill and ask him for help."

That brought bristles erect on the folds of Gregg's skin. "Churchill? *He's* here? In Belfast?" Gregg asked. Brian guffawed.

"Aye, he is—on another one of his useless quests to pacify the poor, wayward colonials, meeting with Sinn Fein, the DUP and the UUP, even though it's all a useless bother. Why don't we send him a calling card? Who should I say requests the presence of his Lordship's company?"

"Somebody he's met before," Gregg said, ignoring Brian's sarcasm. "Somebody he'll listen to."

When the door opened, a frigid blast of conditioned air almost blew them back up the stairs. Mark blinked eyes from which the moisture had abruptly been sucked into the Arctic wind.

It was a laboratory, crammed with modern equipment, chrome and plastic and Formica, all agleam in the nervous light of fluorescents hanging from a dropped white acoustic-tile ceiling. The scene contrasted so violently with the grubby, hot guerrilla camp hacked out of oak forest aboveground that it seemed to lie in an alternate dimension, as if Mark Meadows had been thrust down the White Rabbit's hole instead of down the steps of a bunker blasted into the thin, red dirt and limestone of Burma's Shan Plateau.

"What the hell is this?" he asked the man in the white linen suit. The AC was raising goosebumps on his bare, sunburned forearms.

O. K. Casaday smiled smugly. Mark was already learning to hate that expression. He knew a lot about the CIA man already—Casaday had been one of his major antagonists during the fight for Vietnam, and was by way of being J. Bob Belew's pet hate—but Mark had never laid eyes on the man before.

"This is where you'll be working, Dr. Meadows. Like it? Most modern facility opium money can buy."

"You kidnapped me from Saigon so I could make *drugs* for you?" The precariousness of his position did not inspire Mark to try to play things cool. It wasn't that he was too naïve to realize how deep the shit he was in; the events of the last five or six years had scoured a lot of the innocence from him, at least of the wide-eyed, "oh, wow" flower-child sort. He knew he was screwed; yet after all he had been through—fugitive from the law; flying saucer passenger, household warrior on Takis; corpse floating in orbit; fugitive again hunted across damned near the length of the Eurasian landmass; president, chancellor, and (literally) pretender of Free Vietnam—he found it hard to get all worked up anymore. It was a pissoff, sure; but nothing *cosmic*.

Besides, they weren't going to kill him. They needed him.

"Get real," he said.

Casaday nodded his big, round balding head. Lank blond hair bobbed above his collar. "So it's reality you want, Doctor?"

He glanced at the man who stood by Mark's left shoulder. He was shorter than Mark by about two inches. That still left him fairly tall, six two or so, and unlike the erstwhile chancellor of Free Vietnam he was young and in excellent shape.

"Layton," Casaday said. With a smile and his right hand, the young jock grabbed Mark's arm above the left elbow and squeezed.

Mark gasped. His blue eyes watered behind his Lennon glasses, and his knees got weak. But he didn't go down. Nor did he turn his head to look at his tormentor. He just kept glaring at Casaday.

"This is really making me feel *cooperative*," he said, choking only slightly. "You CIA boys sure learned a lot about winning hearts and minds back when you were losing the Vietnam War."

"Tough guy," a voice said in his ear. Like Mark's, it was American, Southern California–accented. Its owner had narrow cover-boy features and a blond ponytail, and lots of big muscles he liked to show off. Right now he was wearing a muscle shirt with a skull in a green beret on the front, above the legend GRAB 'EM BY THE BALLS, AND THEIR HEARTS & MINDS WILL FOLLOW.

The hard boy in the ponytail had never been in the US Army Special Forces. If he *had* been, he wouldn't have been caught dead in that shirt. Mark found himself wishing J. Robert "A Green Beret is just a hat" Belew was on hand to rip it off his back. Then he thought dismal thoughts of lying in the bed one has prepared oneself.

"Want me to adjust his attitude a little, boss?" asked the muscle boy, keeping the pain grip on Mark's elbow.

Casaday chuckled, a sound like pebbles shaken in a tin pail. "You really think you can beat him up until he helps us, Layton?"

He reached out and grabbed a pinch of the pretty boy's cheek. "Sometimes I think you're as dumb as the Last Hippie here thinks *I* am." He let go of Layton's face, slapped it lightly, and walked into the lab.

"I'm *not* dumb," Layton said in a petulant whine. He relaxed his grip. "I'm a warrior. I don't see any point in coddling this son of a bitch just because he's some kind of hot shit *scientist.*"

"Bring him." Acoustic tiles muffled Casaday's words. The muting of sound added to Mark's sense of dreamlike irreality, as if his brain was wrapped in cotton batting.

Sprout sniffled. *That* snapped him back. He reached out to squeeze her hand.

Layton pushed him hard between the shoulder blades. "Get going, you," he said. Then, to himself, "I'm not dumb."

Casaday was talking. Mark tried to make himself pay attention. In the last few years he had discovered in himself far more physical fortitude than he had ever imagined. What had actually happened, he realized, was that he had achieved a state of apathy about himself that amounted to near-perfect insulation from threats years before. Many years ago, back in the mid-seventies, when it was becoming painfully clear that his storybook romance with Sunflower was going to have an all-too-mundane and sordid ending, and that he was never going to recover his one moment of glory as the Radical, golden ace hero of the Movement who had battled the forces of repression, back-to-back with the Lizard King in People's Park.

But Sprout—she had been what he lived for, what he fought for, every minute since she was born. He had sacrificed more than he ever imagined he *had* for her.

These bastards had her. That meant he would do what they asked. Period.

Or at least until I figure out a way to call my friends.

Something the CIA spook said snagged his preconscious mind and snapped his attention back like an elastic band.

"*What* are you saying, man?"

"That the Black Trump virus has a flaw," Casaday replied, "which you are going to help us correct."

Mark stopped dead. Layton grabbed his arm, applied his pain grip again.

"No way."

Casaday laughed as if that was the funniest thing he'd heard all month. "Yes, way," he said. "Dr. Meadows, permit me to introduce your research associates, Dr. Carter Jarnavon and *Oberstleutnant* Gunther Ditmar."

They had reached the underground lab's far end, where desks and computer workstations formed a U-shaped niche. Two men stood waiting. Both were evident Westerners of medium height. That summed up their similarities.

The first wore a lab coat, horn-rimmed glasses, and an expression of earnestness that elsewhere and elsewhen might have been comical. "I'm Jarnavon," he said, thrusting out a pale hand. "I can't tell you how honored I am to meet you, Dr. Meadows. I've read everything you ever published. You were something of an idol of mine, growing up. A pioneer in my field in genetic engineering."

Mark looked down at the hand as if it had died some time ago and begun to smell. Jarnavon's face fell. It was a square, near-handsome face, clean-cut, and could not possibly be as young as it looked.

"My friends call me Carter," the young man said in words that stumbled out. "I, uh, I hope you'll call me that, too."

Mark looked at the other man, who nodded crisply to him. He was a heavyset specimen in a blotched and crumpled linen suit, who stank impressively of tobacco, alcohol, sweat, and mildew. He had a moon face, protuberant Baby Huey lips, and one black eyebrow that stretched right across his forehead. He wore a horrible little green fedora, with a brief feather stuck in the band, like something a Bavarian tourist might wear on a jaunt up to *Schloß Neuschwanstein*.

"*Herr Doktor Professor* Meadows," he said. From his academic German, Mark recalled that *Oberstleutnant* meant "lieutenant colonel." He wondered what a lieutenant colonel of anything might find to do in this lab.

"It's just *Herr Doctor*," Mark said reflectively. "I don't, like, have a chair anywhere."

"That's a terrible injustice," Jarnavon piped up. "If you help us here, maybe we'll be able to do something about that in the future."

"As if *I* have any future, if you nutcases kill off all the wild cards," Mark said. Jarnavon jerked his head back as if Mark had slapped him. "I can commit suicide a lot easier *without* helping you, Casaday."

"We're not asking you to commit suicide, Dr. Meadows," Casaday said briskly. "Obviously, we can protect you from the Trump when it's released. And then a simple vasectomy to make sure you don't do any more pissing in the gene pool, and we all go our separate ways."

"Yeah. Right."

Casaday chuckled. "That's why we have the colonel, here, on the team. You might call him your *incentive*."

"What are you talking about?"

"Well, see, not all mercenaries of the Cold War era got their jobs through *Soldier of Fortune*. Quite a lot were working the other side, if you catch my drift. For example, the colonel here belonged to an elite cadre dispatched by the former East German *Stasi* to the far corners of the Earth. They specialized in teaching the fine points of physical interrogation to Third World counterintelligence agencies."

Ditmar smiled a greasy smile. "Heart *and* minds," he said.

"The colonel is a second-generation torturer," Casaday said.

"His father worked for the Gestapo before the Soviets caught him. Then he worked for *them.* Gunther here was raised in the business, so to speak."

He nodded. The two men in black pajamas thrust Sprout at the German. Mark tried to intercept her, but Layton held him back. Ditmar grabbed the girl, held her. His hands were unusually large, with long fingers. Despite his flabbiness, he held the writhing Sprout without apparent effort.

"So," Casaday said. "The problem with our Black Trump is that it only remains viable for three to four generations. What we need you to do is fiddle with this bug until it gets more staying power."

He looked significantly at Ditmar. The former East German stroked Sprout's long blond hair with the back of one stranglers hand and smiled wetly at Mark.

"If you actually do the work for us, and don't jack us around, not only will we make sure you get to live, but I won't let Gunther here play with your baby girl. Am I generous, or what?"

"Please prove obstreperous, Dr. Meadows," Ditmar said. Along with his Katzenjammer Kids accent, he had trouble pronouncing his *r*'s, which made him sound like a Nazi Elmer Fudd. The threat's cartoonish quality, combined with the sick certainty that this *wasn't a fucking game,* pierced Mark like a stainless-steel probe to the medulla.

The torturer smiled. His upper right canine was steel.

"I *like* little blond girls," he said.

"How do I look?" Jerry Strauss asked as he inspected himself in the mirror. Her voice was low, throaty, seductive.

"You look more like Peregrine than Peregrine does," Jay reassured him.

"Just so no one expects me to fly." Jerry fluttered his huge white wings nervously and tugged down on the hem of the short black dress so it revealed a shade more cleavage.

"That's too much, Jay," Bradley Finn said. "You can see the top of his nipples."

"Her nipples," Jay corrected. Pronouns were confusing when dealing with his junior partner.

"Whatever," Finn said irritably. He shifted the cumbersome minicam from one shoulder to the other. "Peregrine never wears anything that revealing."

"Oh, I don't know," Jay said. "You ever see her *Playboy* layout? Anyway, at the moment we're more concerned about Eric Fleming's dick than Peri's TVQ."

"If his dick works anything like mine, we're on the right track," Sascha Starfin put in. "I believe I'm in love."

Jay couldn't resist a glance down at the front of Sascha's trousers. There was an impressive tenting effect going on. "Looks like love to me," he admitted.

Jerry turned around to see for himself. "Sorry, Sascha, I'm saving myself for Mr. Fleming." He gave his wings a coquettish flutter.

"Your lips are saying no, but your mind is shouting *yes, yes, yes!*" Sascha replied, smoothing his pencil-thin mustache with the back of his hand. With mirrorshades in place to cover the smooth skin where most people kept their eyes, Sascha could pass as a nat, and his telepathy—though limited to surface thoughts—was a real plus in any interrogation.

Bradley Finn was getting annoyed. "This goddamned camera is *heavy*. Are we going to do this or not?"

"Might as well," Jay said. "Can't dance."

The rental company had delivered the minivan to the hotel parking lot. Jay got in on the driver's side, realized that the steering wheel was missing, and slid over. Jerry-Peri started to get in beside him, until her wings got tangled up in the door frame. "How the hell does she ever sit down with these things sticking out of her back?" he complained.

"I think they fold up somehow," Finn put in from the back of the van, where he and Sascha were loading the minicam and the sound equipment.

"Maybe *hers* fold up," Jerry-Peri said. "Mine don't seem to." She/he gave an annoyed flap, and feathers went flying everywhere. Somehow he/she managed to get inside the van, hunched over and wedged around sideways in the passenger seat. The little black dress had hiked up over her crotch, and the dark shadow of her pubic hair was visible through her white silk panties. Glancing over, Jay had to admit that the view looked just like he remembered from *Playboy*. When Jerry did an impersonation, he went all the way.

"It's a short drive," Jay said, turning the ignition. He flicked the lever to signal that he was pulling out, and his wiper blades started up. This driving-on-the-wrong-side business wasn't going to be as simple as it looked.

On the way there, Finn started getting anxious. "Do you really think this harebrained scheme is going to work? Fleming is a Card Shark, he hates wild cards, so why would he consent to an interview with Peregrine?"

"He hates wild cards but he loves actresses, models, and sexy babes," Jay said. "When a man's good sense says one thing and his dick says something else, bet on his dick every time. Trust me, I went to detective school."

"What if he decides to check our credentials?" Finn asked. "What if he phones New York and finds out the real Peregrine is right there taping her show, half a world away from Australia?"

"Now why would he do something like that?" Jay asked.

"I don't know why," Finn said. Jay could see his long blond tail flicking nervously in the rearview mirror. "Maybe he's paranoid. Maybe he's cautious. Maybe he's a member of a secret conspiracy and he's used to checking out everything, just in case. Just assume for a moment that he *does* check, and he finds out that Creighton isn't really Peregrine. What then?"

"Then we're fucked," Jay said, as he pulled up in front of the offices of the *Townsville Drover*.

There were bars on the hut window through which Mark watched his daughter. Beyond that, he had to admit her quarters weren't bad. Though the one-room structure looked like an ordinary bamboo hut, it was sealed, with air-conditioning inside, as the chill beating off the glass windowpane demonstrated. There was a bed and a dresser, and a pile of colorful stuffed toys including Sprout's favorite pink bear. Sprout herself sat on a stool with her back to the window, while two Black Karen women in black pajamas fussed over her hair.

"These dinks think we're funny-looking," O. K. Casaday remarked, "but they can't get enough of that long blond hair."

"Huh," Mark grunted. He turned away. The movement apparently tweaked the peripheral vision of one of the local women, eliciting a reaction Sprout caught—because suddenly her face was pressed against the window, muffled voice screaming, "Daddy! Daddy!"

Mark turned back, pressed his lips to the glass over hers for a kiss. Then he tore himself free and went loping across the compound with great-legged strides, tears pouring down his face. Big black crows picking over the hardpacked earth jumped up out of his path with caws of complaint and wheeled into the red explosion of sunset over the evergreen-oak woods.

"You see, Meadows?" asked Casaday, matching Mark stride for stride. "We're not total monsters. We believe in the carrot as well as the stick. Wait'll you see your quarters; they're even plusher."

Mark moistened his lips with his tongue, forced himself to think about something other than Sprout and the danger he had placed her in by being—what? Too smart? Too weak? He had no idea what he might have done differently, but he could not shake the conviction that he was to blame.

"Quite an operation you got here," he said huskily. "I saw the poppy fields on the flight in. Aren't you afraid a KH-12 will spot them?"

Casaday's face creased in a frown. "Where in hell does a hippie burnout hear about the Keyhole bird?"

Mark just looked at him. Casaday laughed and slapped his substantial forehead. "Of course. Where did I leave my brain today? Your dad used to be head of the Space Command."

"And I used to be chancellor of Free Vietnam," Mark said. "I know a little bit about American spy satellites."

"Well, think about who actually owns and operates the birds. That's why we have such good leverage on Marshal Hti, here. If it weren't for our goodwill, the DEA could feed the Myanmar government the serial numbers on the guards' fucking rifles. Rangoon goons would hit this camp like a plague of fucking locusts."

"I thought the US had repudiated you bastards."

"You mean us Sharks?" Casaday snorted. "Well, officially— too bad that Jesus-freak asshole Barnett turned out to be such a wimp, but fuck, what do you expect from politicians? They have no balls, by definition. No, we're outside the law now, just like your favorite Mel Gibson character. And just like your favorite Mel Gibson character, we still have some friends on the *inside*, if you know what I mean."

"I don't *have* a favorite Mel Gibson character," Mark said.

His quarters were fairly nice as trailers went. Mark always had a sort of prejudice against them, which he vaguely suspected was class-based. It was one of the old metal rounded hunchbacked ones, maybe thirty feet long and about twelve wide, with a living room, kitchen, bedroom, and bath. There was even a TV with a remote control and VCR, hooked into the compound's satellite dish. Though the consumer electronics were reasonably up-to-date, Mark suspected the trailer itself dated from the Vietnam War. The furnishings were comfortable enough, smelling only slightly of wet rot, and the air-conditioning was sufficient to keep the awful daytime heat at bay.

Not bad. For Hell.

Ireland, as Ray watched it unroll outside the limo's window, was the greenest country he'd ever seen. The blush of early summer was on the land. Cottages gleamed whitely among the emerald lawns and fields. Roses were scattered about like unburning red stars. It gave Ray the creeps. Made him feel like he'd fallen onto a postcard.

They drove from the airport to a hotel on the outskirts of Dublin where Flint dropped them off.

"You're sure we can't help in the search, Brigadier?" Harvest asked.

The British ace shook his head ponderously. "I doubt anyone would open up to strangers. We have local men canvassing the villages and farms, looking for witnesses to the parachuting. Besides, you should rest after your long flight. With any luck we'll turn something up by tomorrow."

They got adjoining rooms. Ray was still restless and edgy, despite or maybe because he hadn't slept during the crossing. He tried watching television but there was nothing interesting on the few available channels. For a while he watched a sport that seemed to be a cross between football, soccer, and freelance mayhem, but he couldn't figure out the rules and the thick accents of the announcers annoyed him. He shut off the TV, paced the room for a while, then stopped before the connecting door between his room and Harvest's. He knocked and heard a faint "Come in" from the other side of the door.

Harvest was sitting up in bed, poring over one of her everpresent dossiers. She still wore her skirt but had taken off her blouse to reveal a blue-satin and lace teddy.

"I thought," Ray said, "we should talk or something. Make some plans."

Harvest smiled. "Or something?" she said.

Why the hell not? Ray thought. He crossed the room, leaned over, and braced himself with his arms against the headboard. He kissed Harvest hard. He pulled back after a moment, and looked down at her and smiled.

She slugged him. It wasn't a slap or a gentle tap. It was a shot to the jaw that rocked his head back.

"Hey!" he protested.

"Nobody kisses me without my permission," she said, staring hard at him.

Ray rubbed his jaw. "Well, excuse me for not asking—"

"All right," Harvest said. She grabbed his tie and yanked. He wasn't expecting it. He fell down on top of her. She held his tie as she pulled his face to hers and kissed him fiercely. Her tongue went into his mouth and fought with his.

"Hummpphh."

Ray wanted to say something but her mouth swallowed his words, and then he quickly forgot what he was going to say anyway. She released his tie and rolled him over so that she was on top, straddling him. She unzipped and shimmied out of her skirt. Underneath she wore silk stockings and a garter belt that matched her teddy. She looked down at him, still smiling.

"You're a big talker, Ray. How are you for action?"

"I think you'll find that I'm big enough."

"We'll see," she said, and tore his shirt open, sending buttons flying all over the room.

Sometime later, the phone rang. Ray reached over her and picked it up.

"*Hello,*" said Flint's whispery voice. It sounded even more ghostlike over the phone. "*I trust I'm not interrupting anything.*"

"Nope," Ray said. "Close, though."

"*We found two parachutes abandoned near a field. Only the field was outside Belfast, not Dublin.*"

"Damn Bushorn," Ray said. "We've lost another day to his lies."

"*It's too late to do anything tonight. Tomorrow we'll motor to Belfast. I'll ring you up first thing in the morning.*"

"First thing," Ray said. He hung up the phone and leaned back on his side.

Harvest was looking at him. During their lovemaking she had shed her teddy. She lay against the sheets, exposing her lithe, athletic body to Ray's appreciative gaze.

"You hear what the whispering rock had to say?"

She nodded. "Enough. We'd better get some sleep." She swiveled onto her side and slung a silk-clad thigh over Ray's hip. "Take my stockings off."

Ray grinned. "It'll be a pleasure."

Five

"Gregg, is meeting Churchill really going to do any good?"

Hannah asked the question in the dark of the room. Brian and the Fists had taken them to a run-down apartment building deep in the warrens of the Belfast Jokertown while the message to Churchill was sent. *It will take a few days,* Brian had said. *But he'll get it.* Scarlet Will was just outside the door, and Gregg knew the man was there as much to guard against them leaving as to protect them.

Hannah sat on the sagging mattress of the bed; Gregg hopped up alongside her. The only light in the room was what managed to get through the grimy window shade that looked out onto an alley and the building across from them.

"I know Churchill," Gregg told her. "I've met Winston several times, and he's solidly on the side of the wild carders. He's publicly admitted he's infected by the virus himself—and I'd say the wild card gave him extended life, since the man was born in 1874. He'll help us."

"If we can get to him."

"There's that, yes."

Hannah laughed in the twilight. "Well, I'll give you credit

for trying. And Gregg, thanks for what you did before. I think you probably saved my life."

"Don't worry about it."

"I do." Hannah stroked him, her hand moving from his head down the rolled, bristly flank. Gregg watched her face, watched the way the smile wavered as she touched him. Gregg found himself pushing up, trying to prolong the touch. The reaction was instinctive, automatic. Hannah pulled away, just slightly. Her eyes questioned. "Gregg?"

"Hannah, I—" Gregg didn't know how to answer. He didn't know what he wanted; didn't know what his body wanted. He wasn't sure how this body responded sexually; he wasn't even sure it *had* a sexual response. He could feel odd sensations along his lower flank, sensual. Hannah's hand, brushing the wiry clumps of hair, was a delicious agony, and something bright neon orange and bifurcated like a divining rod was protruding low down on his body.

"Oh," Hannah said. Her hand came away. She moved away from him—just a few inches, but they both noticed the instinctive retreat. "Gregg, I'm . . ." There were tears in her eyes now, and she bit her lower lip, her breath trembling. Her gaze went to her hands, on her lap.

He could have deflected her apology. He could have made a joke, could have dropped down on all sixes again so that the embarrassing, unbidden erection couldn't be seen. He didn't. *You see? She's disgusted by you. She can't even look at you.*

"Gregg, I don't know . . . I don't know if I *can.*" A breath. Her blue eyes found him again, but she would not look down the length of his body. "I'm sorry. Look, give me some time, and maybe . . . I didn't mean to . . ."

"Didn't mean to arouse me?" Gregg seemed to say it in concert with an inner voice. A bitter laugh followed the words.

The tears were tracking down the sides of her face. Part of

Gregg felt pity for her obvious emotional torment. *I understand,* he wanted to say. *I'm sorry, too.* But he didn't. "No," she said. "Gregg, look . . . Shit . . . I'm the one who's failing here. Can you understand? It shouldn't make any difference, not after all you've meant to me . . ." Her voice trailed off.

"But it does?"

Hannah nodded.

Bitch . . . The erection was fading, withdrawing back into his body. Gregg dropped until only his first two segments were up. Hannah watched him. Her hands were on her lap again, her eyes were rimmed with tears. *Nat bitch . . .*

"It's okay," he said. "I know what I look like."

"Gregg—"

"Like you said," Gregg told her, and he knew that the very understanding of his tone was cutting at her soul, tearing at her. He liked knowing that. "Give it some time. We have more pressing problems." Hannah was looking at him bleakly, and he continued, enjoying the hurt in her face. "I figure that our message will get to Churchill sometime tomorrow—the details I put in there should convince him that I am who I am. I know Churchill; he's not going to be able to resist the invitation to meet. Brian should hear from him soon. So—"

"Gregg, I'm so sorry."

"Don't worry. It's not that important," he told her, and he saw the way she grasped at that, the way she gave him a weak, uncertain smile. She clutched at the lie, wanting to believe it: "It's not important at all."

But it really is, isn't it, Greggie? It really is . . .

"Nanotechnology," Carter Jarnavon said, with the air of a benediction. "That's where the promise for the future lies."

Mark sat in one of those terrible spring-loaded office chairs that tempts you to lean far back and dumps you on your cranium if you do, leafing through a printout of the lab journal of an anonymous researcher. He wondered idly what parts beside the name had been cut out.

The researcher had modified a comparatively mild droplet-carried human-virulent flu virus—affecting both nats and wild cards—by hanging a Black Trump gene on its DNA.

> For the control cultures, in which the wild card initiator sequence isn't present in the DNA, the Black Trump has nowhere to attach on the genome, so it and the transposon remain as junk floating around in the cell. The carrier—a much less dangerous virus—proliferates instead.
>
> In the wild card cell cultures, the Black Trump attaches at the initiator site on the DNA. The linked transposon element wildly recombines and reproduces the Black Trump, causing random genetic insertion and throwing the cell immediately into lytic phase. The cells burst, dispersing the Black Trump virus to other cells.
>
> In theory this should be deadly. But the 94-15-04-24LQ virus got progressively weaker as it was transmitted from cell to cell . . .

"I was working in nanotech," Jarnavon said almost dreamily, sitting on the stool with hands clasped between his knees. "Pioneering work. Vital work. Work that could have transformed the world."

Mark almost smiled. The nameless researcher had succeeded *too well*. Virus 94-15-04-24LQ, dubbed necrovirus Takis I, was so mutable that, in reproducing, it created versions of itself that, while less lethal, managed to outcompete the original. As it was, it was nasty enough to kill up to four generations of hosts.

But it would hardly suffice to rid the world of aces, jokers, and ever-elusive dormant carriers.

"I had a grant from the DEA. It was written to research a self-replicating assembler, that's something like a robot virus you can program to perform tasks"—a chuckle, accompanied by a quick thumb-stab to slide heavy-rimmed glasses back up the bridge of his nose—"not that I need to tell *you* that, Doctor. This assembler was designed to wipe out the world's supply of coca plants and end the cocaine plague once and for all."

The uncontrollable self-mutation of the Black Trump, Strain I, added another joker to the deck, so to speak. It could conceivably mutate into something that would burst cell walls *without* being triggered by attachment to the original wild card sequence. That would make the virus as deadly to nats as wild cards—the deadliest plague in human history.

"Worthy as that goal was—and achievable, too, I'm sure you understand—that wasn't the project I was *really* working on. I was actually put to work on a project to achieve control of the human mind through nanotechnology. Programmed happiness—no more disobedience to authority, no more self-destructive behavior. Utopia. And that led me to you, Dr. Meadows."

The journal promised results on a Black Trump II, 94-04-28-24LQ, "by Sunday." And that was all she wrote. Sunday never came, the old song had it, and evidently it hadn't.

Jarnavon's words infiltrated Mark's forebrain. He glanced up and blinked through the round lenses. "Huh?"

The younger man nodded, smiling a smug toad's smile. "To you. To the journals describing your own hegira through the labyrinth of human consciousness. We have them, you know—Drug Enforcement, that is."

Mark struggled to shift the gears of his mind. *Hegira?* It was as if he had fallen into a recursive looking-glass world, defined by laboratory journals.

"You looked through my notebooks?" Suddenly rising outrage burned his cheeks. He felt violated—that this hackwork Frankenstein wannabe had raped his personal diaries with his eyes, in the service of his ancient nemesis, the DEA.

The young man bobbed his head. "Yes, yes, and a treasure they were. You truly could not grasp the vistas you would help to unfold, Doctor."

No, Mark thought, *I damned well didn't.* "I helped you design a mind-control nanodevice?" he asked in horror.

"No," Jarnavon said sadly. "Someone blabbed. A reporter caught wind of it, started asking questions. Oh, the Agency had the meddling bitch strangled in her BMW, got *60 Minutes* to help make it look as if she'd been in with the Medellín cartel and gotten burned by them. But by then the damage was done; bleeding hearts were asking questions in Congress. We shut down; we just couldn't handle exposure."

He shook his head. "But you if anybody know what it's like to be afflicted by those who lack vision, Dr. Meadows."

Yes, Mark thought. *And most of them are friends of yours.* He realized, then, that what he very much wanted to do was to kill Dr. Carter Jarnavon.

And here I thought I didn't have any innocence left to lose.

He forced his attention back to the sheaf of computer paper. From the viewpoint of the Card Sharks, the nameless scientist had not gone far enough. From Mark's point of view he or she had gone much too far. Because the researcher had recorded clearly—so clearly even a layman like Casaday could comprehend, never mind Jarnavon—what needed to be done to enhance the virus's lethality.

Ironically, it was to make it *less* lethal, by inhibiting its self-recombinant action. The journal even outlined a possible way to do that: Omit the transposon.

Mark let the printout fall into his lap. Jarnavon gazed at him with shining eyes. Mark met the gaze, even offered a watery smile. Takis-instilled caginess was kicking in.

How good is he? he wondered. His experience of the DEA suggested that they were fully capable of hiring an incompetent to run their mind-control research. They had set nincompoops to pursue him around half the world, after all; why not a half-baked scientist? Certainly they had hooked themselves somebody who showed few signs of having all his marbles.

He can read the journal as well as I can. That means he's not good enough to carry the work forward himself, or Sprout and I would still be in Saigon. For a moment Mark found the inner space actually to be amused at himself, for missing his multiple life in Free Vietnam.

We never know when we're well off. It occurred to him to wonder when the time would arrive at which he looked back at *now* and thought, *Those were the good old days.* He stifled a shudder.

"It's late," he said, glancing at the old-fashioned analog clock—meaning, *with hands*—on the walls. The hands said it was after eight. "I need to knock it off. I've had a tough couple of days."

"Certainly, certainly." Jarnavon bounced to his feet and stuck out his hand like a victorious tennis player. "Until tomorrow, Doctor."

His handshake was cool, dry, and surprisingly strong. *Is he good enough to know if I fake it? Is he good enough to know if I try to recombine the virus into something harmless, or try to poison the whole batch?* Mark had no aptitude for intrigue, though God knew he'd been exposed to it enough since he was driven underground. He would have to do his best to draw the enthusiastic young scientist out, learn just what he might expect to slip by him.

Because, otherwise, Mark Meadows would have to decide between sacrificing his daughter Sprout, or the lives of every wild card on Earth.

The letters crawled before Zoe's eyes, black bugs on a paperback page yellowed by the lamp over her bunk. She had been staring at the same paragraph of *Shell Games* for what seemed like hours, trying not to think.

Visions of the stone catacombs of Jerusalem crept around the edges of the page to haunt her. She couldn't forget the feel of the dead Ukrainian's skin under her hands or the hatred in the New York skinheads' eyes when they brought her father down. She saw the stubby claws on Bjorn's dead feet, naked for any passerby to stare at and cringe. Look, there's a joker man! A dead joker man, whose daughter lay on a narrow bunk in a tiny cabin on a rusty freighter in the Black Sea, playing teamster to the worst abomination humans had managed to invent yet.

In Odessa, someone must be putting the pieces together by now. Any moment, someone would come with guns. Any moment.

But maybe no one had reported the deaths. Maybe no one had looked for the warehouse boss for hours, and hadn't said anything when they found him. Maybe nothing would happen.

She couldn't stand it anymore. Up, across the cabin, back to the bunk, to the door again. If she didn't find something to distract her, she'd go mad. Zoe leaned against the cabin door, thinking—I'll get dressed and find somebody to talk to. Yes.

Who? She couldn't talk to anyone on the ship. Zoe pounded her fist against the door and sat back down on the bunk.

Probably some of the crew spoke English, but she couldn't chat them up. She wasn't Zoe Harris, she was a nameless "wife" of a Turkish entrepreneur and she had to stay in character. She couldn't even talk to Croyd. He was gone, prowling about the ship in the night hours, hanging out in crew quarters or trying to work up a poker game. He didn't sleep and he didn't stay in the cabin much.

Above her, on the deck, heavy footsteps rushed toward the rail. Zoe heard words that had to be curses, unmistakable even though they were Russian curses, full of gutturals she didn't understand. They would come and get her; she knew it. Zoe pulled on a black sweatshirt and a pair of faded jeans. She didn't want to die naked.

Something metallic clanged against the side of the ship.

Who was up there? The Card Sharks, whoever they might turn out to be? The Russian army, hot to recover a stolen and extremely embarrassing nuclear device?

We're dead, Zoe thought. *All of us—the captain who smiles and thinks I'm a mute of some sort; the sailors, who are just working guys trying to get by. All of us. It's an answer of sorts. Let them sink us here, let this hellish bomb sink to pollute the fishes. Let it be over.*

Barefoot, she climbed the ladder that led to the bridge and stopped short at the open doorway that looked out on deck.

Russian sailors were popping up over the side of the ship. Russian sailors with big, ugly guns. She heard the captain's voice, gone oily and smooth, explaining something to a short, thick officer who carried no gun that Zoe could see.

She felt a split second's warmth behind her, someone close. Before she could turn, a hand snaked past her neck and strong fingers clamped themselves over her mouth.

"Shh!" Croyd whispered. Zoe choked back a scream. "Cargo. Fast."

He turned toward the hold. Zoe followed him past the closed doors that led into the four tiny cabins, through the hatch into the cargo space.

"They'll search," Croyd said. He dogged the hatch behind them. "The captain says he's running a Ukrainian ship, not a Russian one. The Russians say they're searching anyway. Something about medical radioactives that got into some crates accidentally." Croyd scooted down the ladder, talking as he went. Zoe came down behind him. "Fuck, Zoe. The Russians know a bomb's missing, and they won't even talk about it to each other."

They would have Geiger counters, then. Zoe looked at the row of irrigation pumps lined up in the ship's hold.

The stocky Russian officer opened the hatch from the deck. He turned and began to climb down the ladder. No gun. He had a black case strung over his neck on a strap. He was facing the bulkhead, not the murky cargo hold. Zoe grabbed the neck of her sweatshirt and tried to tear it.

"Zoe! Are you crazy? They'll see us!"

"I can't help it, I've got to fix the counter or we've had it. Shit! Help me with this, would you?"

Croyd, looking baffled, tugged at the thick fabric.

"*Rip* it!" Zoe hissed.

The neckline tore. The Russian officer had reached the deck and turned at the sound. Croyd dropped the cloth as if it burned his hands. Zoe screamed and swung her open hand at Croyd. It smacked against his face with a satisfying sound.

Someone hit the light switches, probably the captain, who clambered down the ladder behind the Russian. Bare yellow bulbs gave enough light to see pathways through the stacked crates. Zoe sobbed, twisted away from Croyd, and ran across the deck toward the Russian. The sobs were real, generated from sheer, sick terror. Under her bare feet, the rough metal decking made her clumsy, and that made her look even more helpless than she felt. Good. She held the torn sweatshirt across her breasts like a towel. When she got close to the Russian, she reached out for him. The sweatshirt sagged, baring her nipples. Zoe stumbled into the Russian's arms and buried her face against his shoulder. She got a close look at the instrument slung across his chest. It had a screen like an oscilloscope, tiny flashes appearing and fading. The little box ticked like a drunken cricket.

Now, if Croyd would just *think*!

The Russian, gentleman that he was, tightened his arms around her while Croyd shouted something. The Russian replied. Zoe cringed against the man's chest as if to take shelter and tried to imagine the innards of a Russian particle detector. Two Russian sailors climbed down the ladder and took up positions beside the captain. They held their guns at the ready. They were children, Zoe realized, still in their teens.

Croyd held both hands open in what seemed to be exasperation. He came forward slowly, talking nonstop.

Copper wire. There had to be copper wire that led from the battery to power this thing, and there had to be a metal snapper that made the tapping little cricket sound, or a diaphragm of some kind. She didn't know which phosphor was making the little flashes on the screen. Opaque the screen? No, too obvious. Zoe took a deep breath and sobbed it out toward the little box. There. The copper wiring would slowly draw itself thinner, and then coalesce into tiny spheres, beads that would separate and begin to rattle, maybe. So be it.

Croyd began to sound like he was begging her to forgive him. Zoe peeked at him from under the officer's sheltering arm.

"Zoe?" Croyd asked.

Zoe drew away from the Russian. She ran to Croyd, grabbed his face in both hands, and gave him a passionate kiss.

Croyd shrugged. The Russian shrugged. The captain smiled, but the smile faded as the Russian officer began to explore the rows of stacked crates, his gadget in his hand.

It ticked as he walked along, but the ticks were keeping a steady rhythm. He frowned at the screen, shook it, and then continued to walk through the cartons. Zoe hoped she had the timing right. He went past the pumps. Zoe held her breath, but the officer kept walking at a steady pace, his eyes on the instrument's little screen. The officer passed the pump and Zoe sighed. Croyd's arm tightened around her shoulders.

The officer nodded as if he were satisfied, but he barked out a couple of orders in Russian and motioned to his sailors. They began to open crates, an activity that led to protests by the Ukrainian captain. More sailors appeared, called down from the deck. They looked with disinterest at barrels of barley and bales of textiles. They poked at the four irrigation pumps and didn't seem to find them interesting at all. They were more interested in a crate of Japanese VCRs.

Zoe stayed huddled in Croyd's arms, watching the search. A deal was struck. A few of the VCRs got handed up the ladder, and the sailors disappeared.

Croyd nuzzled his nose against Zoe's neck like the fond lover he was supposed to be. He whispered in her ear. "I'll go find out what the captain thinks about all this," he whispered. "Go back to the cabin, okay?"

"I'll be on deck," Zoe said. "Come and *tell* me, damn it!"

The officer smiled in the direction of Zoe's chest as he went by. He hauled himself up the ladder, puffing at the exertion.

Zoe waited until Croyd had time to get to the bridge. She

climbed up the ladder and went to her on-deck retreat, a niche between two pallets of fertilizer sacks, hot and stuffy in the daytime but cool enough, *cold*, in the hazy night. She'd spent a few hours here while the freighter made its way from port to port, abominably slow, business as usual and plenty of time for tea to be sipped and packages to come and go in the hold.

A corner of tarp made a little tent for her. The bow watch probably knew she came there, but the boy never bothered her.

Zoe couldn't see anything that looked like a Russian ship. The sailors seemed to have disappeared into the water.

From the north, a pair of huge helicopters buzzed out of the night. Zoe could see fat guns slung beneath their bellies. She pressed her back against the sacks and huddled under her tarp, holding her torn shirt over her shoulders. The choppers cruised over the deck, bathing it in spotlights that cast crazy shadows as they passed by. They finished their pass and went away, but not far. She could hear them. Damn. Stay here? Go back to the cabin, a metal box where she felt like a trapped rat? Oh, damn. She sat frozen, afraid to move.

The choppers made another pass. In the darkness that followed, Croyd slipped across the deck and ducked under the tarp beside her.

"We're not going to get shoved overboard because our captain is a Moldovan," Croyd said. "Don't ask me to explain how that is, I couldn't quite figure it. The Russians didn't find anything, and the captain of the Russian sub is probably going to report that the whole deal about the medical radioactives was a false alarm. But they might just shoot us out of the water anyway, for practice."

"That's comforting," Zoe said. The choppers buzzed in the distance, circling for another pass.

"Well, the Russian navy will probably keep anybody else from bothering us, at least for a few nights."

"Does our captain have a *clue* about what's going on here?" Zoe asked.

"No," Croyd said. "I came on like I was an offended passenger. I didn't hear a word about anything wrong in Odessa. Somebody must be keeping that little scene real quiet. Figure it, Zoe. The guy we bought this thing from is a crook even to the Ukrainians. The Ukrainians want the Russians to take all the warheads out of the Ukraine, and the Russians don't have the resources to do it. And anyway, Snailfoot said the KGB were the only ones who *ever* had access to the arming devices. So the Ukrainian we bought this thing from had to be part of the KGB, because he promised the Black Dog he could deliver the whole package. The Ukrainians probably figure somebody did them a favor."

Snailfoot's lecture ran in her head, his proper British accent making the words even more terrible. *The Russians won't tell the West, even if they discover that a warhead has been stolen. Why? You don't dismantle a tradition of secrecy that easily. And other warheads are missing, or so we hear. The numbers don't add up, and no one has admitted it yet.*

But don't think about that. It's not part of the plan.

"Searches are routine, the captain says. He says he gets boarded about twice a year. That's why he always carries a few portable goodies to get confiscated. Keeps the sailors happy," Croyd said.

The choppers came in low, buzzing the deck. Their blue-white lights angled across the deck and made it seem to tilt. Croyd squeezed closer to Zoe and slipped his arm behind her back, hugging her in a painful grip. He was trembling, from speed or terror or just because he was wired that way. She hoped it wasn't speed, not yet. The choppers lifted away, leaving the two of them in the dark again.

"I guess they didn't like the brand name on the VCRs," Zoe said.

"I told the captain to stock CD players next time. Are there any of those cookies left? The ones your mom sent?"

"Rugelach," Zoe said. "You ate them all, Croyd."

"That was a nice kiss you gave me back there when the Russian was watching," Croyd said. "Isn't fear supposed to be an aphrodisiac?"

"So they say," Zoe said. Out in the water, a dark tower rose and sank away again: the Russian sub, still nearby.

"I don't get much chance at relationships," Croyd said. "I never know what shape I'll be in when I wake up again. I'd hate to waste this body. It's as close to standard as I seem to get these days."

"What do you mean?"

"Well, I woke up as a lizard once. A lot of women don't think lizards are sexy."

But some women might, Zoe figured from the way he said it. She shivered, her sweatshirt not enough protection from the night's wet air. Croyd pulled her close. He was warm, not at all like a lizard. He was warm and alive, and Zoe found that the lizard part of her brain, the old primitive part of it, was screaming for dominance. *Let me live*, it moaned. *Turn off the horrors and let me live.*

"We could check out the systems," Croyd said.

Check out the systems? How technical! "Croyd! I'm not a test pilot!" Zoe scrambled out from under the tarp. She hurried across the dark deck, down to the enclosed cabin.

It was stuffy. It was lonely. She wasn't sleepy; there was too much adrenaline charging through her system for sleep to be even a remote possibility. She paced the three steps of the cabin's length and back again. She couldn't stop thinking. She couldn't think.

The choppers made another pass, close enough to vibrate the walls, and she ducked. The Russians might have given up and let the Ukrainians know that a warhead was missing, that they had traced it to the Odessa docks. They would never tell the Turks, or anyone in the West, what had happened, but they might sink every ship in the Black Sea before morning, just as a precaution. This might be the last night of her life. She deserved to die. She *wanted* to die, if dying would erase Anne's cancer, her father's death, the horrors in New York that had driven her to an uncertain refuge in the war zone that was Jerusalem.

But the Black Dog intended to keep this bomb from ever being used, and the Escorts could get out of Jerusalem in payment for her help. And she lived, every cell, every breath toned by a respite from terror and ready to keep on living, to *exult* in life.

She *was* horny. Croyd? Well, she was stuck with him for a while. Sex had become a remote possibility in her life. There hadn't been anyone since Turtle. Turtle had been so sweet. Turtle had taught her how to relax. She wished he hadn't disappeared back to the West Coast. She wished he weren't so happy with Danny. But she *liked* Danny. Messing up somebody else's nest wasn't a game Zoe cared to play, thank you. Zoe picked up Turtle's book and paced the cabin again.

Croyd had cut that man's throat without even blinking. Croyd wasn't a nice person at all.

Croyd knew she was an ace. If she animated a few things when she got excited, he wasn't likely to freak out. She couldn't hate him for killing the Mideasterner. It had to be done. She'd killed a man herself, once. And she was aroused; she could feel energies in the air around her. Why *not* Croyd?

She breathed lightly on Turtle's book. *Shell Games* sailed through the air and landed on the bed. It lay on its back and clapped its pages like hands.

Someone tapped at the door. Zoe frowned at the book. It jumped to the floor beside the bunk and quit quivering.

She opened the door for Croyd. He was grinning, and he held a sack behind his back as if it were a surprise birthday present.

"Would you mind some company?" Croyd asked. "I think it's going to be a long night."

"I don't know. This is hardly my idea of a romantic setting." Zoe waved her hand at the crowded cabin. It was painted in institutional green enamel, richly incised with Cyrillic graffiti. The bunk was rock-hard and covered with a scratchy brown army blanket, its surface peppered with random holes from cigarette burns.

Croyd stepped toward the bunk and put his sack down. "I'll see what we can do about the ambience," he said. He pulled out a candle, a saucer to stand it in, a bottle of champagne beaded with condensation, and two thick, brown pottery mugs, slightly chipped.

"Champagne?"

"I bought it from the captain. I said it was to settle your nerves."

"You're supposed to be a good Muslim," Zoe said.

Croyd said something in Turkish.

"What's that supposed to mean?"

"Today, I drink. Tomorrow, Allah forgives."

The thud of the diesels speeded up and the ship began to heave, lumbering through the swells at a faster pace.

"We're running for the Turkish coast. Full speed ahead," Croyd said. He held a match to the bottom of the candle and set it carefully in its saucer. "There."

The choppers buzzed by again, as loud as freight trains. They left relative quiet behind them, the ship silent except for the booming of the diesels.

"The choppers won't come back," Croyd said.

"Do you know that for sure?"

"No." He set the mugs down by the candle. "I'll need some sort of towel to get the cork out of this champagne."

Zoe turned off the overhead light, pulled her torn sweatshirt over her head, and tossed it to Croyd.

The message was terse and grumpy. That in and of itself told Gregg that it had come from Churchill.

Come to 9 Shannon Lane, Lamberg, nine o'clock Friday, rear entrance. A friend's house. You'll be let in. This had better be important.

Lamberg was a small village five miles outside of Belfast. Gregg and Hannah were driven there by the Fists, in the rear of a panel van. Scarlet Will, driving the van, stopped down the street from the rear gates of the house. "We let you two out here," Brian said to Gregg and Hannah. "We'll drive around a bit, then stop down at the next corner, where we can see the gates. When you come out, head this way."

Gregg slid down the rear of the van, with Hannah following. Brian shut the door after them; the van moved away in a puff of blue exhaust. The house was surrounded by a tall fieldstone wall. The street, well away from the village center, was quiet and dark, though there were spotlights up near the wrought-iron gates that broke the wall. "Let's go," Hannah said, and she began walking toward the gates. Gregg followed.

A man in the uniform of the local constabulary was standing behind the gate, his semiautomatic weapon held casually ready. "We're expected," Hannah told him. The guard looked at her, at Gregg, and let the gate swing open. When they were inside, he nodded to Hannah. "Hands out; spread your legs slightly, and turn around, please."

Hannah grimaced, then did as instructed. The guard frisked her carefully, then looked at Gregg. "And you, sir."

"Does it look like I'm hiding anything?"

"Sir?"

Gregg sighed and raised up on his rear feet. The man patted him down efficiently and quickly, then tilted his head to speak into the microphone on his lapel. "They're clean," he said. "I'm sending them up." He pointed through the trees to the house and spoke to them. "Follow the path to the double doors. *He'll* be waiting there."

Gregg saw the familiar silhouette framed against the light as they approached. Churchill was short, round, and wide, and the smoke from his cigar left a fragrant, blue-white trail in the evening. He was dressed as if for a dinner engagement, though the tuxedo's coat had been exchanged for a satin-trimmed smoking jacket. He was balder than Gregg remembered, only a few wisps of white hair remaining on his head. His pudgy face was a landscape of deep wrinkles, the eyes twin dark holes in the white skin. A hand came up as they approached, fingers like short sausages grasping the cigar and pulling the well-gnawed end from his mouth. He looked at Hannah and at Gregg.

"Our reports always said you were a womanizer," Churchill's gruff voice said. "I'm surprised you can still maintain that reputation now."

You arrogant SOB. Once I could have . . . Gregg forced the irritation down. Churchill, like so many of the political leaders of the past three decades, had been a puppet of Gregg's. He could still sense the sour taste of the ancient man, never one of his favorites. But he had no choice now, and no way to pull those strings. "And our reports, Winston, always said you were too old to last much longer. I'm surprised you're still breathing."

Churchill barked a short laugh at that and stepped aside from the door. "You're Hartmann, all right," he said. "Come in." For a man twelve decades old, Churchill moved well. He shuffled like an old man, taking small, careful steps, but Gregg had seen men half Churchill's age do the same. Churchill led them to a small library, where he settled carefully into a plush leather chair, leaning back and wreathing his head in cigar smoke. He gestured to the other chairs in the room. His breath was loud and slow. "Sit, please. Would you like something? I can have the kitchen staff find something for you . . ."

"No, thank you," Hannah said. Gregg just shook his head. He crawled up into one of the chairs, wriggling until he could see comfortably. Churchill took a deep draw on his cigar, letting the smoke dribble out of pursed lips.

"Tell me," he said to Gregg. "What was it I said to you back in 1984, when you came to see me during the WHO tour? I recall there was a moment in private where we talked about your aspirations for the presidency . . ." Churchill didn't look at Gregg; his hoary eyes appraised the smoke curling around the reading light on the smoking stand alongside his chair.

"You told me that I was a 'damned, bloody fool' if I thought that being the head of a country would bring me anything but 'an ulcer, a headache, and an early death.' You also said that kind of power was 'better than Scotch whisky, and more intoxicating.'"

Churchill chuckled, a deep, liquid sound. "Ahh, your message didn't lie then. You *are* Gregg Hartmann, after all. Back from the dead."

"Yes."

Churchill took a long, slow breath. "A pity. I didn't want to believe any of this." Churchill puffed on the cigar, exhaling a thundercloud of blue.

"Those are terrible for your health, you know," Hannah told him.

"At my age, young woman, you indulge in what vices you can," Churchill answered, but he set down his cigar in a bronze holder. "I know the name Hannah Davis, of course," he said to her. "I'll be frank, Miss Davis, when I first heard your tales about the Card Sharks on the news reports a year ago, I thought you were crazed. I thought Gregg crazier for supporting you." Another breath, wheezing like an asthmatic sigh. "Unfortunately, my sources tell me that far too much of what you reported was true. Pan Rudo . . ." Churchill shook his head. "I've never been able to trust a Nazi, reformed or not, so I suppose I'm not surprised. Is it true, he's still alive?"

"Yes," Hannah told him. "In a fine, young, blond Aryan body." Gregg looked at her, then realized that she was playing to Churchill's obvious prejudices and his tolerance of attractive young women. The intelligence reports that had passed Gregg's senatorial desk had also told him about Churchill's numerous affairs. The old man sniffed and cleared his throat.

"And you say that these Card Sharks have developed a virus to kill those infected by the wild card?"

"Yes," Gregg said. He and Hannah gave Churchill a detailed account of the past year, ending with the discovery of the virus and Rudo's escape with the vials. Churchill listened intently, occasionally interjecting a question of his own. He began smoking again. Churchill seemed to draw deeper into his chair as their tale went on, sagging and growing darkly angry with time. "Your note mentioned that at least one of the people around here is a Card Shark," Churchill said at last. "Give me his name."

"General Horvath," Gregg said.

— — —

The change was a subtle thing, but palpable, like going from sunlight to shadow, a warm summer breeze to a cool autumn chill. It was as simple as passing a checkpoint on a road and crossing from the Republic of Ireland to Northern Ireland.

The checkpoint was manned by British soldiers who took their work seriously. Not even Flint's presence granted them a pass. The soldiers examined their papers and inspected the limo before allowing them into Belfast. It was not so much that the landscape itself had changed, but that the touch of man lay heavier on it. There was more barbed wire and armed men than Ray had ever seen in his life. The people they passed seemed pinched and sullen. Belfast was more an armed camp than a peaceful confluence of a third of a million souls. Ray felt as if they'd entered a live war zone. He became fidgety, his mind revved up a notch as if it anticipated action at any moment.

Even Harvest seemed affected. She peered out the window, a slight frown creasing her forehead as she watched Belfast reel by. Only Flint remained aloof, as distant and unreadable as if sculpted from the rock that gave him his nickname.

British HQ was bustling. Men in officers' uniforms were marching to and fro with grim looks on their faces. Even the ordinary guardsmen, normally phlegmatic to the point of stoniness, seemed uptight.

"Is it always like this?" Ray asked.

"Well," Flint rumbled, "Northern Ireland is a difficult place. Very difficult. The sectarian violence between Catholics and Protestants has been going on for decades. Oh, it's not continuous of course. There are periodic bits of calm. You may have heard the recent revelations that Her Majesty's Government has been holding secret talks with both sides—the Irish Republican Army and the Royal Ulster Constabulary. Since the press has seen fit to publicize these tête-à-

têtes, Her Majesty's Government has decided to bring the talks out into the open. Churchill has recently arrived to lead the negotiations. I'm afraid that General Horvath will be more concerned about security for Sir Winston than in tracking down a couple of Americans who dropped into the country illegally."

"God knows we wouldn't want something to happen to him," Ray said. "What's the fate of a hundred-and-eighty-year-old geezer compared to the rest of the world?"

There was the sound of grinding stone as Flint swiveled his neck to look down at Ray. *"Sir Winston holds the fate of all of Ireland in his hands. That is not an inconsiderable burden. And he's only one hundred and twenty."*

"Yeah, whatever. It'd be tragic for his life to be cut so short."

Harvest elbowed him. "Who's General Horvath?"

"The head of the British Expeditionary Force in Northern Ireland," Flint whispered.

"We don't want to keep him from his duties," Harvest said.

"Nonsense," Flint replied. *"He wants to meet you and get a briefing on this Card Shark business."*

"We'll tell him what we can," Ray said. He suddenly saw certain advantages to the scenario as it was shaping up. Let Horvath spend all his time nurse-maiding the ancient politician, guarding him from loonies from both sides of the political spectrum who wanted to blow the old gent back into the middle of the last century. That would leave the way open for Harvest and himself to do a little poking around on their own. After they ditched the walking stiff, of course, who seemingly had been assigned to be their personal watchdog.

The walking stiff led them to an office zealously guarded by an orderly who looked as though he'd been left over from the Crimean War. He spoke quietly into the intercom on his desk, then rose, eyed the three of them with open suspicion, and opened the door to Horvath's private office.

Horvath was coming around his desk to greet them with typical British restraint as they entered the room.

"Foxworthy, good to see you," he mumbled stiffly.

"*And you, Peter.*" Flint performed the introductions. Horvath was perfunctory with Ray, a little more effusive with Harvest, taking her hand and bowing over it.

"Good to see you. Nice to come by and chat. 'Fraid I can't offer you too much time."

"We don't want to take you away from your work," Harvest said.

"No. No. Don't worry. Sit. Here." Horvath pulled out a chair for Harvest and waved Ray to the other. Flint loomed like a cliff behind them, there being no chair in the room solid enough to take his bulk.

Ray sat. For all his clipped brusqueness, he noticed that Horvath placed Harvest where he could get a good look at her silk-clad legs. He didn't blame the general. He looked, too, and he remembered them scissored around his back, pulling him in tightly, as they made long, hard love the night before.

"Now then," Horvath said. He shuffled through some papers on his littered desktop. "Looking for two Americans. Jokers, what?"

"One joker," Harvest said, "one natural. A woman." She seemed to have caught Horvath's propensity for speaking in clipped sentences.

"Ah, yes. Here we are." He scanned one of the papers, looked up with a cocked eyebrow. "A caterpillar? Surely you jest."

Ray shook his head. "No joke." He told them all about Hartmann and Hannah Davis, omitting only the part about the Black Trump. Barnett had said to keep it secret, so he did.

Horvath listened attentively. "Extraordinary. Yellow, you say?"

Ray nodded.

"Well. My men shall be on the lookout."

"About those parachutes your men found?" Harvest prompted.

"Ah, yes." Horvath shuffled more papers. "Here we are." He handed Harvest a slim file. "Not much, I'm afraid. We'll check on it, but can't spare too many men now."

"Ah, yes," Ray said. "The Churchill situation."

Ray heard a sound that might have been Flint clearing his throat, but the phone on Horvath's desk rang, interrupting them.

Horvath's phone manner was as brusque as his personal approach. "Yes," he said. "Of course. The devil you say. Well, then. Certainly. They are not to leave." He hung up the phone, looked at Ray and Harvest, and uttered the longest sentence they'd yet heard him say. "Your yellow caterpillar is now having a brandy with Winston Churchill. I've ordered him detained."

Ray and Harvest looked at each other.

"What're we waiting for?" Ray said.

The breath exploded out of Churchill in a skeptical huff and a burst of cigar smoke. "That's preposterous. I've known the man for years. I *appointed* him to his post here."

"Horvath is definitely one of them," Hannah said. "Gregg and I thought that once Rudo and General MacArthur Johnson escaped with the vials of the Black Trump, they might come here for protection. I've already told you what Rudo looks like now. Johnson—"

"—is a tall, muscular Black man, about forty-five or so, very handsome and striking."

"Yes," Hannah said. "How do you know him?"

Churchill shook his head. "I saw him from a distance, talking with Peter a few days ago. I thought the man looked familiar, but I didn't make the connection until just now." Churchill puffed on the cigar until he seemed to peer through a cloud. "Worse, most of the security men here have been assigned by Peter." Churchill ground out his cigar, stabbing it into the tray and smashing it. "I am afraid that will mean that General Horvath is aware of our meeting. I . . . I need to think about this. There is someone else I want to speak with, and then I'll make my plans. I'll have to move carefully."

"Why?" Hannah asked. "And who are you going to talk to?"

Churchill glared at her, not unkindly. "You seem to have a mistaken impression of my abilities, Miss Davis," he told her. "While I have a certain influence, I also hold no official position. I can't guarantee your safety, especially since you tell me that the person who controls the army is a Shark. Northern Ireland, as you know, has a reputation for violent solutions to its problems. As to whom I am going to speak with—it will be someone I trust, as you have trusted me. That should suffice. I'd offer you the safety of my rooms in Belfast, but I'm afraid that I'm no longer sure that's true. The two of you must have somewhere you'll be safe for a few days, I suppose?"

Gregg looked at Hannah. "I suppose," he said.

"Good. Then you'll come here again in a week, let's say. By then I should know what I can do. Until then, be careful."

"What about you?" Hannah asked.

"I'm one hundred and twenty years old my next birthday," he told her. "And very visible. I don't plan on dying anytime soon. Don't worry." Churchill pulled himself slowly from his chair. As he escorted them from the house, he moved more than ever like an old, old man.

"A good meeting?" the guard asked them when they were back at the gate.

"We hope so," Hannah told him. She smiled, and the man smiled back.

Gregg didn't like the smile. It was a mask, and he had a sudden sense of hidden colors inside the man: tasty colors. Luscious colors. "He's a very impressive man, Mr. Churchill."

"I think so," Hannah answered.

"Hannah," Gregg said. "Let's get moving."

Gregg tugged at the gate. It swung open, and he started through. The guard had moved from the gravel drive as the heavy bars passed, then stepped back. "Mr. Hartmann," he said. "Not yet, I'm afraid."

Gregg heard a metallic click behind him, a sound that was out of place in the night. With frightening clarity, he realized what it was. He turned to see the guard's weapon pointed directly at him, and he knew that he was dead. Gregg was frozen, motionless. He could see the muzzle and waited for the flash that meant death. Gregg first, then Hannah.

Except that Hannah moved. She shoved the gate with a grunt. The heavy iron bars slammed into the guard from the side. He fought for balance, but his feet went out from under him in the loose gravel. He started to turn as he fell, ready to fire anyway.

Hannah kicked him in the side of the head. The sound of shoe against skull was hollow and loud, and the man's head snapped sideways with the impact. He groaned and went limp, his weapon clattering to the gravel. Gregg looked at Hannah. "College soccer," she said. "I was a great forward. Let's go."

They could see the van, parked at the corner. They ran for the vehicle. The back doors opened and Scarlet Will poked his head out. "Get it started!" Gregg yelled to him. He could feel himself just on the edge of uncontrolled adrenaline overdrive from the fright of their close call, and he tried to ignore the growing buzz. Hannah was just in front of him. Scarlet Will held his hand out for Hannah and pulled her into the van as Cara, in the driver's seat, turned over the engine. Scarlet Will leaned down for Gregg, his hand extended. Gregg grasped his hand in his own.

What happened then would be forever a confused welter of images and feelings for Gregg. There was no sound, but suddenly Will's head jerked back, then came more forcibly forward. Will's hand was still clasping Gregg's as a red volcano erupted from the back of his skull, a fine mist of blood and brains splattering the interior of the van as the body, in motion from pulling Gregg, tumbled onto the floor.

And Gregg . . . He *felt* the death. The link was faint, a bare shadow of what it had been with Puppetman, but the unexpectedness of it staggered him. For a moment, he was lost, trying to find the gossamer shreds of the death's emotions, already fading. *Can it be? Oh, God, can it be?*

No. It was gone now. A ghost.

"The *police!*" someone was shouting, and Gregg saw a pair of uniformed men running toward them. "It's a trap!"

"Hartmann!" someone else was yelling. "Get in, man!"

Gregg shook himself. Another shot whined, pinging from the metal door a few inches from him. Gregg leapt and Stand-in pulled the doors shut as the van squealed away from the curb.

In the swaying van, Brian cursed slowly and monotonously as he brushed at the gore that had splattered his clothing. Hannah stared down at Scarlet Will, on his back, his face a ruin of blood and bone.

Gregg stared, too, wondering what he had felt and wondering also whether he wanted it to be true or not.

— — —

Horvath, busy as he was, decided to come along. It showed, Ray thought, how seriously he took his responsibility in providing security for Churchill. It made for a crowded vehicle with Ray, Flint, Harvest, Horvath, and the driver, but it was only a short trip out to the village where Churchill was ensconced.

It was a nice place, ancient and mossy and blazing with light as they drove up. The hullabaloo at the gate immediately told Ray that something had gone wrong.

"Report," Horvath clipped when they reached the checkpoint.

"Sir!" Everyone stood like they had wooden poles rammed up their butts. "The, uh, gentleman and his companion escaped, sir."

"Shots fired?"

"Yes, sir. As per instructions we returned fire only when fired upon."

"This is very distressing." Flint's whisper only hinted at his distress. He clenched his fists, making the sound of rocks grinding together.

Horvath nodded. "Casualties?"

"None on our side, sir. I believe we hit one of the gentleman's party. They were Twisted Fists, sir."

"Very distressing," Flint added.

Horvath nodded again. "You know what that means. Keep alert."

"Yes, sir!" The sentry saluted again, and Horvath signaled the driver to proceed.

Ray and Harvest glanced at each other. "The Twisted Fists are operating in Ireland?"

"Yes," Horvath answered. "Terrorist scum."

"If your men killed one, it'll be five for one."

Flint nodded ponderously. *"The violence spirals higher and higher."*

They parked the car and were ushered into the study where Churchill sat behind a desk, wreathed in cigar smoke. He didn't look too bad, Ray thought, not a day over ninety, anyway. He looked chubby even in his expensively tailored formal wear, topped by a nice maroon smoking jacket. He was mostly bald and totally wrinkled, but his eyes burned with energy and, if Ray was any judge of emotions, anger.

"Come in, come in," he said querulously. "I suppose you heard what happened outside."

"Yes," Horvath said. "Pity, that."

"Yes." Churchill pierced him with his ancient, cunning gaze. After a moment he swept his eyes past Horvath, looking at Ray and Harvest. "You must be the Americans. Come in, sit down."

They did as he bid. Flint introduced Ray and Harvest and remained standing, casting his shadow over the scene and making Ray feel nervous, like someone was reading the paper over his shoulder.

"That gunplay was terrible business, General. It'll make my job here all the more difficult if you rouse the Fists."

"It was, Sir Winston. Pity the Fists started it."

"Yes," Churchill said. "Who knows what goes on in the minds of terrorists?" He seemed to fall into a reverie for a moment, then gathered himself and looked up again. "Pardon an old man's musings," he said, frankly eyeing Harvest. "I'd like to discuss things with you in more detail, but I'm afraid that's going to have to wait. I'm an old man and I need my rest, but first other things must be done. Foxworthy."

"Sir."

"We'll be moving to the Belfast Hilton. Tonight."

"Sir!" Horvath said with as much emotion as Ray had seen him muster. "Do you think that's wise?"

"I do," Churchill growled. "We've already had gunplay here. My security has been compromised." He returned his attention to Flint. "Your men of the Silver Helix will take over security. Organize it."

"*Sir,*" Flint repeated.

"Why replace my men?" Horvath asked stiffly.

"Your men tangled with Twisted Fists tonight, General. If I surround myself with wild card security people, the Fists will be less inclined to include me in their plan for revenge."

"They wouldn't anyway, sir."

"Perhaps not, General. But we'll do things my way."

"As you wish, sir."

Churchill stood. "Indeed, General." He turned his attention back to Ray and Harvest. "Perhaps tomorrow we'll get a chance to chat longer. I'm very interested in your perspective on the Card Shark situation."

"Thank you, sir," Harvest said. "It will be an honor."

"Yes, sir," Ray added.

He knew a dismissal when he heard one. Flint stayed behind to organize things, as Churchill had requested. Horvath returned to Belfast with them and was his usual communicative self. He said nothing; only a brief "Goodbye" when he dropped Ray and Harvest off at the Belfast Hilton, where they were also staying.

The meeting played itself over in Ray's mind as they were driven back to their hotel room.

"You find anything strange about our chat with Churchill?" he asked Harvest at her door.

She shook her head. "He seemed a little preoccupied, but he is a hundred twenty years old and someone may have just tried to kill him."

Ray shook his head. "It wasn't that. It was his attitude. Suspicious. Questioning. I don't know."

Harvest looked at him. "Do you know if you're coming in or not?"

Ray suddenly smiled. "Try to keep me out."

Harvest put a hand on his cheek. "I could. But I think it'd be so much more fun if you just came on in."

Brian looked down at the body of Scarlet Will, laid out on the bed where Hannah had slept the last few nights, the dead joker's head covered with a bloody sheet. Gregg could feel the volcano heat of Brian's emotions as he stared at the corpse, and when he looked up again, the force of his gaze was nearly enough to cause Gregg to stagger backward.

"Five for one," Brian whispered, and the words had edges of torn steel, glimmering with fire-pierced red in Gregg's mind, tasting of dark sweetness. "Five for one, it is. Five nat deaths will pay for Scarlet Will."

"No." That was Hannah, her voice a small, purple welt in the greater darkness of Brian's fury. Her clothes were still stained with Will's blood. "You can't do that. That's no solution—that's just a continuation of this endless violence. More senseless death."

Brian whirled on Hannah. None of the other Fists dared to interrupt. Gregg could feel them, all reflecting Brian's anger and feeding it back into him.

"Shut up, woman," Brian snapped, each word a whiplash. "You have no say in this."

"I sure as hell do," Hannah insisted. "Churchill gave us his word that he'd help. I'm not going to have you ruin that chance."

"We've just *seen* how effective Churchill will be." Brian spat. Gregg reached out mentally, stroking the corona of fire around Brian. *I was right when I first met him*, he marveled. *He's so like Gimli. I remember. I remember . . .*

It tasted good.

"There's how much Churchill can help," Brian raged, his fingertip trembling as he pointed at Scarlet Will. "There's your example of how powerful his influence is. The police don't listen to Churchill; they listen to Horvath. We kill the fuckers—*that's* how you show them."

"Brian—" Hannah persisted.

"Shut up, nat," Brian snapped. He glared at her, up and down. "You're a fine attractive woman, you are. But that means that you don't, you *can't,* understand how it is for us—no matter what you've done."

"This might ruin our chances of finding the Trump virus."

"Don't you listen, woman? This isn't about your bloody virus. It's about *us!*" Brian gestured, tapping his index finger on his chest. He looked at Gregg, and his eyes narrowed. "And it's about you, too," he said. "You want help from the Fists? Then I think it's time you prove your worth, worm. Five for one, and you will help."

Brian's statement sent an odd, undefinable thrill through Gregg. "No," he said, but inside, someone whispered: *Yes!*

As if listening to that voice, Brian hissed the word at the same time. "Yes," he said. "Because if you don't . . ." Brian glanced from Gregg to Hannah and back. "If you don't, we may just make an example of your sensitive nat friend here."

Just before docking, Zoe changed into a Carole Little from last year's season, black georgette printed in thirties ecru florals, almost ankle length, and a headscarf, black silk shot with tiny bronze stripes. She would never get the knack of keeping one on her head.

Limestone villas dotted the rolling hills above the little town of Ordu and formed a backdrop for the silhouette of a ruined basilica. Mountain peaks, some of them still marked with snow, rose in the background. The scene was medieval, more like Switzerland than anything else Zoe might have imagined.

A battered blue school bus, perched on dual sets of huge balloon tires, waited on the pier. Crates and boxes were tied on its roof. Some of its windows were broken and covered with cardboard.

That couldn't be what we're driving, Zoe thought, but then she saw a man in pleated twill harem pants and a turban made of two fat coils of dotted red silk, on watch beside the bus.

Balthazar? He wore mirrorshades to hide his strange eyes. Jan? If she didn't see Jan, if Jan wasn't here and absolutely okay, Zoe planned to run. She didn't know where. She didn't know how, but if Jan wasn't here, this was it.

"Not much longer, Zoe," Croyd said. He vanished into the small shed that was the freighter's bridge. "Wait on the pier."

She went ashore and almost lost her balance. The pier was solid. It wasn't rocking. Zoe tried to remember how to walk while a boy on a motor scooter buzzed past on the shore road spilling Michael Jackson music from the boom box tied behind him.

Jan, a small figure in swirling black skirts, climbed down from the bus. She jumped up and down and danced across the pier. Zoe met her hug.

"Shh," Jan whispered. "Talk later."

Jan wore a black scarf over her hair. She wore two bolero jackets, one bright turquoise, the other maroon cotton. Under her skirts, Zoe caught a glimpse of what looked like pajama trousers, with brown and white stripes. Jan had grown an inch in the past week. She looked happy.

The crew off-loaded the irrigation pump. It swayed in its harness of chains, rocking down to rest on the pier, its green enameled metal bright as neon against the rusted sides of the

Ukrainian freighter. Zoe told herself not to think of it as anything but an irrigation pump, a Rubik's cube of metal and PVC pipe, a plumber's nightmare that looked as if it could suck up half the Euphrates.

The thing was so small. Zoe thought of bombs as ICBMs that lurked in giant silos. Maybe this was all a scam. But then she felt, even from twenty yards away, the horrid silent heat fitted inside this particular pump.

Zoe and Jan, as was proper for women in Turkey, stood aside and watched the men do what men did. Balthazar stood with folded arms, watching the pier, the ship, the bus. At intervals he reached into a sack and brought out date confections the size of hen's eggs and chewed them methodically, like cud. Croyd and the captain appeared on deck and gave each other a bear hug, maybe a result of Croyd's parting gifts. Croyd came ashore with the Turkish customs officer and disappeared into a concrete-block building.

On the freighter, sailors hauled lines and moved around the decks, performing inexplicable tasks that resulted in the freighter's sliding away into the morning haze over the oil-slicked waters of the Black Sea. Zoe wondered if the freighter would make it to the next port. Twice, before dawn, Zoe had seen a sub's conning tower lift from the water, too close to the freighter for comfort.

Zoe's stomach tied itself into a knot. She forced herself not to squeeze Jan's hand, sweaty in hers. If Jan was worried, she didn't let it show. Zoe kept her touch light and expected to see, at any minute, the door burst open, the guards with their rifles pointed at her gut. She didn't want to think about the interior of a Turkish jail.

Croyd was taking so long in there. The haze was beginning to burn off, and she felt sweat trickle down the back of her neck. Her scarf was slipping again. She tied the knot tighter.

Croyd came out grinning. A man in a khaki uniform and a fez followed him, mustache aquiver. The official called out a few quick words, and a bystander ran to the steel door of a nearby building. In short order, a forklift appeared, driven at great speed. Six burly Turks accompanied it. Croyd and the official stood and watched, chattering away. The customs man pointed to the bus. Zoe heard the words "Mercedes," and "diesel," and "the Bronx," while the crew of dockworkers wedged the pump through the opened doors at the rear of the bus. The bus sank a couple of inches on its suspension.

They've blown it, Zoe thought. *This thing will break through the floor, through the pier, and sink. We've had it.*

Croyd's hands drew the curves of a fat, strong woman in the air. The bus accepted the weight. The official laughed. There were bows, and huge smiles, and more bows, and then Croyd turned away.

Balthazar vaulted into the driver's seat of the bus, his hand on the scratched metal knob that shut the swivel doors. The party climbed in. The diesel coughed to life and produced a largish fart of black smoke, and Balthazar eased the bus toward the road that led through the middle of the village and south.

"The customs guy has a cousin in the Bronx. Runs a Greek restaurant," Croyd said.

"He's a Greek?" Zoe asked.

"No. But there wasn't a Greek restaurant in six blocks, so that's what he opened. He says he uses his mama's recipes and New Yorkers can't tell the difference." Croyd's voice seemed normal enough, but there were beads of sweat on his forehead. It wasn't hot, even in the bus. "It's funny how this language thing works. I don't know anything until somebody says something, and then it's like a movie comes on in my head. I could see this customs guy when he was a kid growing up. He had a pet goat, and he pretended it was Trigger."

"Trigger?" Jan asked.

"Trigger was Roy Rogers's horse. He was a palomino. God I'm *old*," Croyd said. He twisted his back against the bench seat, crossed his arms, and stared out the window.

Balthazar eased the bus along that narrow asphalt road. A group of blond men with green eyes sat at the *locanta*, under a porch hung with pots of flowers and crowded with small tables. Their eyes watched the bus, the occupants, the morning. Smells of baking bread, coffee, and tobacco wafted through the air. They cleared the village, working their way past schoolchildren in dark uniforms walking in groups, past cars of all descriptions, many of them new and highly polished. Unperturbed by the traffic, a woman and her baby perched sidesaddle on a donkey led by a scowling man.

"Baksheesh?" Balthazar asked.

"A hundred for customs. Sixty for the forklift," Croyd said. "American."

"Not too bad," Balthazar said. He took off his mirrorshades. Zoe winced. His eyelids were crusted with yellow gunk, swollen so that his eyes were half-closed.

"Balthazar? Your eyes?"

"Turmeric and olive oil, with a sprinkle of cayenne," the joker said. Zoe couldn't make herself focus on the damage, couldn't see past the swelling to look at his strange yellow irises. Balthazar steered around two men on horseback and dodged a green Citroën that seemed to have twenty people in it. His hands were tight on the steering wheel. "People don't stare at pus."

"Do they hurt?" Zoe asked.

"Yes."

"Why don't you just use makeup?" Zoe asked.

"We might get searched," Balthazar said.

Thank you, Zoe thought. *For thirty seconds or so, I had managed to forget that possibility.*

The morning was cool enough to be pleasant. An almond grove cast pools of black shade. Vineyards marched their rows across folded hills. The traffic thinned out.

Zoe tried to settle against the bench seat, one that had been designed to hold schoolchildren. The upholstery was lumpy and something dug at the small of her back.

Balthazar heard her sigh and glanced up at the rearview mirror. "Sorry about the bumps," he said. "The upholstery is stuffed with lead aprons straight from hospital supply catalogs in the good old USA." Balthazar turned his head and spat out the side window.

"It's hot," Zoe said. "I can sense it."

"Yeah. I don't know about the safety margins, so I put the lead in. Can you tell how many rads we're getting, Zoe?"

"No. I can't." Zoe slumped down in her seat, getting as much lead between her and the back of the bus as she could. She felt small prickles at the back of her neck. Croyd tapped his heel on the floor of the bus, twitchy. Speeding already, or just scared.

"I'll pick us up some rad monitors when we get to Suşehri," Balthazar said. Suşehri was a dot on the map. Zoe couldn't imagine it as a source for particle detectors, and couldn't imagine that buying one there wouldn't start gossip. Balthazar knew something she didn't, or maybe he was teasing her. She decided not to take the bait.

Jan, sitting beside her, stared at the joker with utter adoration. Zoe watched the girl watching him. Jan was in love. Jan had just turned fourteen. Balthazar was thirty, or close to it. Zoe felt some mothering instincts rising that she never knew she possessed. Balthazar was a dirty old man! Balthazar, on reflection, probably didn't know Jan had a crush on him.

They had spent two weeks traveling together. Alone!

So? With Balthazar oblivious, what was the harm? They

were companions who had set off together to transport a nuclear device across hostile territory, and if they got caught, a quick death would be the kindest of outcomes. And, hey, Zoe Harris was in this mess, too. This wasn't a movie she was watching from the safe confines of an upholstered seat in a theater in Westchester. Zoe told her mother hen persona to shut up.

The road climbed toward the mountains. Poppy fields looked like carefully tended gardens of nettles. Every passerby seemed to be a scout for the ambush Zoe was certain existed at the next curve in the road.

The tan Chevy Blazer behind them had followed them all the way from Ordu. She could see it in the rearview mirror. She could see Balthazar watching it, glancing up again and again to check its position. The road widened slightly. The Blazer pulled up next to the bus and Balthazar slowed.

The driver, a silver-haired man wearing a polo shirt and a turban, smiled and waved as he passed them.

Zoe sighed.

"This is the easy part," Balthazar said. "Relax while you can."

Relax? Oh, sure. Right, Zoe thought, *relax.* She looked down at her hands, at her fingers pinching tight pleats in the fabric of her skirt. She let go and tried to smooth the creases.

"I'm hungry," Croyd said.

"We'll get lunch in Suşehri," Balthazar said.

Jan scooted closer to Zoe and listened while Croyd talked about foods he had known and loved, menus he had eaten his way through in one sitting, platters of bacon and eggs and stacks of pancakes and waffles and entire trays of Danishes, each described with painstaking attention to detail.

Follow the plan, Zoe remembered. *The plan is we're all so fucking normal here.*

By the time Croyd had finished a description of profiteroles with Grand Marnier chocolate sauce, Balthazar pulled the bus up to a *pidecis*, a roadside stand sheltered under fig trees—the figs were small and green, but an occasional lazy wasp investigated them anyway.

Wailing Turkish music clashed with recorded rap in the bazaar just up the road: a little square sheltered under awnings and hung with rows of kilims. Zoe and Jan stayed in the bus, and Balthazar and Croyd ordered food at the wooden counter. After a time, they brought rounds of flatbread baked with cheese and egg to the bus and handed them inside, and other *pides* covered with spiced ground lamb. And tea. Hot tea in a jar, with a service of tall glasses set in brass holders. Zoe sipped at hers. Balthazar reached into one of his generous pockets and produced a can of Coke for Jan. She smiled at him with adoration. Croyd opened a cardboard carton lined with squares of baklava, offered them around, and then settled himself on the fender of the bus.

"I'll be back real soon now," Balthazar said. He adjusted his mirrorshades and went toward the market. Not far from the bus, a shopkeeper brought out a kilim that looked to be a Konya design, cream with oval central medallions in pink and gray. Maybe a Kayseri.

Zoe stood on the embossed metal step of the bus and looked at the carpet's soft folds. "I'd like to shop a little," Zoe said, "I really would."

"You're still in tourist clothes." Croyd broke off a little square of baklava and fed it to Zoe. His fingers brushed against her lips and she shivered, remembering spending last night on a narrow bunk sheltered in Croyd's strong arms, remembering the pleasures of a lover who never slept.

Well, yes, she was in tourist clothes. But the rug was *gorgeous*.

"It should be okay if you take Jan with you," Croyd said. "Nobody's paying much attention to us."

"You'll watch the bus?" Zoe asked.

"Sure."

Zoe bought the rug. She didn't argue enough about the price, but she wanted it. She bought it with the Fists' money, but she figured it was a business expense. Anything that could distract her enough not to scream was a business expense.

When she turned away from the smiling rug seller, she saw the tourists from Odessa. The same ones. The man wore pink Bermuda shorts that must have been made by Omar the tent-maker. The woman's khaki skirt exposed bare white legs that looked like they belonged on a Victorian piano. The pair wore matching floppy white canvas hats, sunglasses, and cameras. They were caricatures of tourists, they were too perfectly gross, and they raised their cameras toward the bus.

Zoe ducked inside and dropped the rug over the back of the low seat. "Croyd? We're being followed. I saw those people in Odessa!"

Croyd popped another piece of baklava into his mouth and looked at the pair. "Same ones, huh?"

"I think so. They look strange."

"Are you sure?"

"I don't—yes. I'm sure."

"Zoe, when was the last time you were in Atlantic City?" Croyd asked.

"I've never been to Atlantic City."

"Well, then you wouldn't know that all tourists look the same. Settle down. I'll take the glasses back if you're finished with your tea."

"I'm finished," Zoe said.

Balthazar ambled back toward the bus, holding up a wicker cage. He handed it in to Jan and swung into his seat. Croyd climbed back in and Balthazar maneuvered the bus back onto the road.

Two doves huddled inside the cage Jan held in her lap. She cooed at the birds and offered them crumbs of baklava. "Geiger counters," Jan said "*Très* high-tech."

Jan twisted in her seat and found a way to hang the dove cage from the ceiling of the bus. The little birds swayed above the rows of boxes that separated the passengers from the pump, the real cargo.

The road twisted and climbed higher, toward the Euphrates and the disputed borders of Kurdistan, a place the Turks called part of Turkey, filled with people who called themselves Kurds, not Turks. *Even Xenophon had trouble with the Kurds*, Zoe remembered. *That's why we're going there. Borders in dispute are safer places for us than peaceful lands. In turmoil and distrust, maybe we can slip through.*

The Euphrates couldn't be real. It was a river only known in ancient books, a myth. Somewhere in the looming mountains above them was Ararat, where tradition said Noah's ark ran aground after the destruction of the world by an angry deity.

Zoe felt she swayed backward toward the past with every tilt of the bus on the twisting road. It seemed the four of them rushed down corridors of time, corridors that would lead them to the soiled stone altars of Mesopotamia and ancient rites of sacrifice. Gods with the bodies of men and the heads of beasts might appear on the narrow road at any moment. *We've just presented a live offering to the monster that rides with us*, she realized. Would it be accepted? Or burnt?

Eric Fleming's yacht was a thing of beauty; polished wood, gleaming brass, huge canvas sails snapping in the wind. "There's not a bit of plastic on her," Fleming told Peregrine proudly as he stood on the forecastle or the poop deck or whatever it was, leaning on the rail with the blue of the ocean behind him. "She's a genuine antique, last of her kind. Before they went to those tacky twelve-meter J-boats like *Circe* used to race for the America's Cup."

"She's so *fast*," Peregrine said admiringly, in a voice of equal parts honey and velvet, calculated to make any halfway functional male reach for the nearest lubricated condom.

Eric Fleming accepted the compliment with a manly smile. He was a big bull of a man with a windburned face and calluses on his hands. "Beauty and speed, that's what I look for in a yacht," he said, smiling. "And in a woman."

The boat *was* fast. Jay had to admit. Eric-me-hearty had come popping over from his island in jig time once the editor of the *Townsville Drover* had rung him up to report that the world-famous Peregrine herself was there in Queensland, asking for an interview. He'd met them at the Townsville marina, all smiles and rough-hewn Aussie charm as Peri introduced her crew. Finn had the camera, Sascha had the sound equipment, and Jay had his hands in his pockets. "And what do you do?" Fleming had asked him. "Nothing," Jay had replied. "I'm the producer."

Some of the *Circe*'s crew greeted Finn with badly concealed distaste when the centaur trotted up the gangplank with the minicam on his back. One in particular—an older beachcomber type, bare-chested and tanned, with a week's growth of sandy beard that made an odd contrast to his silver-gray hair—stared at Finn with a near-homicidal loathing in his ice-blue eyes.

Yet neither he nor any of the others dared say a word. Fleming could scarcely object to Peri having a joker cameraman; technically, those huge wings made her a joker, too. Jay suspected that Fleming was a lot more interested in Peri's tits than in her pinions. The tastefully understated bulge in the front of his white trousers tended to confirm that analysis, but the only bulges that concerned Jay were the ones under the jackets of some of *Circe*'s crew. He would have welcomed the opportunity to pop a few of them inconspicuously off to, say, the Tombs, but there were too damn many of them.

"We can begin whenever you're ready," Fleming said. "Remember, no questions about my love life. I never kiss and tell."

Peregrine gave a throaty laugh. "We'll save that for a more . . . intimate . . . moment." Then she ran the tip of her tongue along her lip in a way that reminded Jay of Ezili, which was no doubt where Jerry had swiped the gesture. "Ready, boys?" Peri asked her crew.

Finn hoisted the minicam to his shoulder and fumbled for the switch that turned it on. Sascha checked his sound levels and held up the boom mike over Eric Fleming's head. Jay took his hands out of his pockets and said, "Rolling," which sounded like something a producer would say.

Peregrine stepped closer to Eric Fleming and smiled dazzlingly for the camera. Her long dark hair streamed in the wind as the *Circe* raced across the sea. "I'm here on the yacht *Circe* with Australian press mogul Eric Fleming," she said.

"Please, Peri," Fleming said, with an easy laugh, "I'm no mogul, just a fair dinkum Queensland rancher who happens to own a few newspapers."

Sascha's skinny arms were already trembling from the strain of trying to hold the boom over Fleming's head. "Boss, I'm getting a lot of background noise," he said.

Peregrine looked around sharply, her wings fluttering with sudden anxiety, and Jay felt a cold finger trace a path up his spine. That was the little code they had worked out to make use of Sascha's telepathy. So long as Fleming was telling the truth, the sound would be good. If he tried lying, Sascha would report trouble with tape hiss. And background noise meant *danger*.

Jay slid his hands back into his coat pockets and made the right one into a gun. He looked around nonchalantly. The *Circe*'s crew were all around them, watching. "You know, Peri," Jay said, "maybe this boat isn't the best place to do the interview. Too much background noise. The wind and the sails and all."

"You may be right," Peregrine said. She spread her wings wide, as if to take off, but of course the real Peregrine flew by a kind of telekinesis and that was something Jerry Strauss could not mimic.

"I'm heartbroken," Eric Fleming said lightly. "I was really looking forward to our interview. Don't you want to ask me about the Card Sharks?"

Sascha dropped the boom mike to the deck. *"Background noise,"* he said, ripping off his earphones. "It's all around us."

Jay had to admire the way his junior partner rose to the occasion. "What *about* the Card Sharks?" he/she asked with Peregrine's bedroom voice as Jay inconspicuously began to slide his hand out of his pocket. "Do they really exist? Are you one of them? Where is Brandon van Renssaeler?"

"Yes, yes, and right here," said a voice behind Jay. Something hard poked him between the shoulder blades. "And I'd keep that hand right where it is, Mr. Ackroyd."

Gregg was driven across Jokertown in the rear of a rusted panel van, crowded with plumbing supplies and two other jokers: Cara and Stand-in. Brian and Trio sat in front, the latter driving. Hannah was left behind, under guard by others of the cadre. "If they don't hear from me by sunset, they kill your Hannah. You understand, caterpillar?"

Gregg had looked hopelessly at Hannah's bleak face.

Gregg almost hoped they would be stopped by police and searched, but the short trip was uneventful. The van bumped to a stop, and Brian opened the doors. "We're here," he said. "C'mon." Gregg noticed that the jokers were carrying duffel bags that sagged heavily. A burning knot settled deep in Gregg's body.

They moved quickly from the van to an alleyway. Gregg had a bare glimpse of the street: dirty, cobblestoned, with oil-filmed water pooled in the holes where the stones were gone. The houses nearest them seemed to lean toward each other as if needing support in their old age. Jokers moved in the street, most of them studiously ignoring the odd quintet who had appeared in their midst.

The alley ran between buildings for two blocks. A door suddenly opened and something resembling a small toilet brush waved at them. Gregg was escorted into a tiny, dark hall between the door and a screened door leading into a restaurant kitchen. The toilet brush turned out to be the arm of a joker, who was covered everywhere with bristly combs: head, face, chest, legs, and arms—the arms were covered with a fine lather of soapsuds, and from the screen came the clatter of dishes.

"Any other customers?" Brian asked the toilet brush.

"Just the one party you asked about," the brush said. "The *police*."

Brian nodded. "And old Lang?"

"He's out, down at the pub. Won't be back until dinner rush."

Brian grinned. "Perfect. I think it's time you took a break, lad. Take the others with you. G'wan now."

The brush disappeared into the kitchen. A few moments later, he and three other jokers filed out of the kitchen. None of them looked at Brian, Gregg, or the others. The door closed behind them, and Brian gestured toward the kitchen. "In with you, caterpillar. It's time."

Inside, Brian peered through a screen into the dining room, from which Gregg could hear laughter and the music of a guitar, fiddle, and bodhrán. "Good. The captain's in there—it's the wedding party for his deputy's daughter." He looked at Gregg, who felt the knot in his stomach squeeze tighter. "Lang's is next street over from the Town," Brian told him. "A fashionable place for parties, where the nats can be waited on by jokers, who stay nicely in back except when needed, and who don't dare walk the street in front." Brian nodded to the woman. "Cara, Stand-in, you ready?"

They opened the duffel bags. Cara placed a hooded mask over her face. Stand-in—the mismatched joker—groaned as his body began to alter, morphing quickly into the image of a strawberry-headed young nat. Cara and Stand-in both slammed clips into their automatic rifles; Brian and Tripod also armed themselves. "Okay," Brian said. "Trio and I will cover the back. G'wan!" Cara and Stand-in moved quickly through the curtain into the dining room.

Gregg heard screams, china shattering on the floor, and Stand-in's brusque voice. The music came to an abrupt, discordant halt. *"Don't move!* Now, get out of your seats, move over against the wall! That's it; keep the hands where we can see 'em! The door, lassie—lock it." A few seconds later, Cara's voice sounded in Gregg's head; «Caterpillar, come on in.»

"Go on," Brian told him. "Cara will tell you what to do."

"I can't go in there. They'll *see* me—that's why you're staying back here, isn't it? Because you can't disguise yourself?"

"Aye." Brian grinned at him. "No sense in making it easy for Horvath when he comes looking for revenge. But you won't be here after you've gone to the Dog, will you? So *let* them spend their time looking for you."

Gregg went in. Cara and Stand-in had lined the patrons against the back wall of the dining room. The window shutters were pulled, the front door locked. Wedges of sunlight speared through the blinds and across the wall, limning them in harsh illumination: men and women, old and young, child to teen to adult to ancient, the bride in wedding white and lace, the groom in his dress uniform, and all of them nats. They stared at his entrance with frightened eyes. Gregg could smell the fear, like the scent of panicked cattle entering a slaughterhouse. Some of the children were crying, terrified, as they clung to their parents. The faces of the adults ran the gamut from fright to a revulsion that he could almost touch.

Stand-in had his weapon against the captain, a bald-headed, portly man whose pants displayed a spreading stain of urine. Stand-in touched the trigger once; the gun coughed and the officer jerked backward as blood and brains splattered the wall behind him. He slumped to the floor as his wife screamed.

Gregg staggered himself. In the instant of the man's death, he felt . . . something. For a moment, his vision clouded with a brilliant yellow-white, and with the hue came a feeling of . . . pleasure?

"One," Stand-in said. "Four to go."

«Five for one,» Cara echoed in his head. «You choose the rest, caterpillar.»

"I can't," Gregg wailed, looking at the faces of the nats, their eyes. *But you can, can't you? Didn't you feel it, when Stand-in pulled the trigger, didn't you taste it? Remember how good Scarlet Will tasted? Remember?* This would have been a feast for Puppetman, a banquet of misery. The death, the fear, should have been orgasmic, but it couldn't be, shouldn't be. Puppetman was dead, all these many years. And the Gift he'd had for so brief a time had never let him feed, had never allowed him to partake of the emotions. He remembered how it had once felt, but that was only memory. Gregg looked, and he knew he should flee. A sense of temptation flooded him. *This is a test, Greggie. This is your trial.* "You can't make me do this. This is obscene."

Cara's head tilted under her mask. Then her quiet voice rang in his mind once more. «Now, I'm thinking that Brian would remind you that your nat woman is still with us. Choose now, or you've chosen her rather than any of these people. Brian actually fancies Hannah, but that won't stop him, not after what he's said. He's never been someone to confuse sentiment with business. If you force him, she will be one of the five.»

"No."

«Hartmann, you have thirty seconds. We can't stay here. Choose, or Brian will have us shoot three now and kill Hannah when we get back.» Then, gently: «I'm sorry, I know this is cruel, but it's no more cruel than what's been done to us.»

"I can't," Gregg said again, but it was only a whisper this time. He looked at the nats, their faces in soft focus because of his myopia. The captain's wife continued to sob over the body of her husband. *How can I choose? These are children, mothers and fathers, grandparents. They're lovers and friends. They're innocent. How can I choose?*

And the voice inside answered him: *Because it will taste good, Greggie. That's how you coped with the cruelty and the horror. Deal with it the way you've always dealt with it—because it will give you pleasure.*

«Ten seconds,» Cara said.

The children were wailing. One young man, one of the groom's men, had gone to his knees, sobbing. A woman held her infant against her shoulder, glaring at them defiantly as if her hand could shield the infant from the bullets. Gregg looked from face to face; he found he could hate none of them enough.

I never killed total innocents with Puppetman. This is slaughter. This is pure terrorism.

"Mummy, oh Mummy, I'm *scared!*" A young, pretty woman pressed her child against her body while she glanced at them from the side of her eyes. Her fear was bright green, and it pushed against Gregg like a tidal swell. He knew that if he could touch her, he could find the strings to that emotion. He could orchestrate her emotions; he could play her fright like a violin. "Hush, love," the woman whispered, "they're not going to hurt us . . ."

«Choose now, Hartmann!»

Gregg looked at Cara, "I hate you," he told her. "This will just prolong the violence."

«Maybe so, but this will happen, regardless. Choose, or Hannah dies as well.»

You see, Gregg told the contending voices, *I have no choice. This way I save Hannah. This way, I can save more lives than I take.*

Then enjoy it, came the reply. *Touch them as you choose. Take them.*

Gregg glanced back at the nats. "Him," he said, pointing at an old man near the door. He scuttled up to the man, who pressed back against the wall, shaking his head. Gregg reached out with his stubby hand. The shock of the touch was like instant heat. He felt himself responding. The old man's terror was thin—Gregg tugged at the strings and was pleased to see it swell and deepen. The old man moaned and the sound was like golden syrup.

"Him. Her." One by one, he pointed them out, touching each of them in turn, his cartoon voice and his toy fingers a mockery of Death. They were all older, the ones Gregg chose. As far as he could tell, none of them had family here to witness their executions.

Gregg told himself it was the least he could do. He hoped that mattered. He hoped that would ease the pain.

He knew it wouldn't.

«That's three, Hartmann. One more.»

Gregg looked at the groom. The man was trembling, whether from rage or fright or some mixture of both, Gregg couldn't tell. *Him,* the voice whispered. *It would be so tasty, so lovely . . .*

No, Gregg told it. *We've had enough pain here. Enough.* He thought the words, but he found that he could not move. He stood in front of the groom, in front of the weeping bride, and he wasn't able to move.

«Hartmann . . . »

You know you want him . . .

"Him," Gregg said, the word a half-sob as he touched the man. The bride screamed, and the pain in her voice was exquisite. "A lovely choice," Stand-in told him, and he started forward, raising his gun. Gregg turned and scuttled from the room, not wanting to see, not *needing* to see. The strings, the mental connections, came with him. Behind him, he heard the first shots and the screams.

He sighed in the mingled pleasure and self-hatred the sounds gave him.

"That detective school of yours wasn't exactly Harvard, was it?" Dr. Bradley Finn snapped at Jay as a couple of salty nautical types trussed up his forelegs with a length of rope. His hind legs had already been tied up tighter than a Christmas goose.

Jay ignored him. "What are you going to do with us?" he asked Eric Fleming. They'd tied his hands together behind his back so tightly that he couldn't feel them.

Fleming squinted off at the horizon, then turned back to Jay. "In a few hours *Circe* will be out in the deep waters well beyond the reef. That's where we toss you in. You've shown a great interest in sharks, Mr. Ackroyd. Well, I understand there are quite a few in those waters. You'll be able to investigate to your heart's content."

Peregrine moaned, sounding almost like Jerry Strauss for a moment. "Not sharks," she said. "Please, anything but sharks. I must have seen *Jaws* a hundred times. Can't you just shoot us?"

"We're not killers," Brandon van Renssaeler snapped.

"Great moral distinction you got there," Jay observed.

Van Renssaeler looked distinctly uncomfortable. He turned away sharply and went below.

Fleming seemed much less perturbed. "Brand is a rare thing in this day and age," he observed. "A lawyer with a conscience. It does get in the way sometimes. Fortunately, I'm the next best thing to a journalist, and we all know that journalists have no qualms at all." He looked at his crew. "Let's get them below."

The sailors were all done practicing their knots. They hoisted them up one at a time and carried them belowdecks to the owner's cabin. It took eight men to manhandle Finn through the hatchway, and they were none too gentle about it. "Do all your plans work out this well?" the centaur asked Jay as they dropped him with a *thump* on the polished teak decking.

Jay would have shrugged, but shrugging was tough when you can hardly move your shoulders. "Hey, it worked. We found your boy Brandon, didn't we?"

"You shouldn't be too hard on him, Dr. Finn," van Renssaeler commented. "It was really your fault that we caught on to your little subterfuge."

When he spoke to the centaur, his tone was as cold as the

blue in his eyes. Bare-chested and barefoot, his skin dark from the sun, his beard growing out, and his hair uncombed and unkempt, Brandon looked like the island he'd fled was more likely Gilligan's than Manhattan, but those eyes were a dead giveaway. Jay would have kicked himself for not having noticed them sooner, except that his legs were tied together, too.

"*My* fault?" Finn said with indignation. "What did I do?"

"We knew who you were the moment you were described to us," van Renssaeler said. "There are very few palomino-pony centaurs in the world, and only one who recently escaped from protective custody on Governors Island. You see, I've taken a strong interest in you these past few weeks, Dr. Finn. It might have something to do with the fact that you're fucking my daughter."

"I *love* your daughter!" Finn said. "And Clara loves me. We want to get married."

"I don't think this is the best time to ask Daddy for her hand," Jay said, but Finn wasn't listening.

Neither was Brandon. "I'm tempted to say, *over my dead body*, but in point of fact it's more likely to be over your body, if Eric has his way."

"Let's not let Eric have his way," Jay suggested.

Fleming tsked. "On Eric's boat, Eric always gets his way, Mr. Ackroyd. I'm surprised at you, suggesting mutiny like that."

"Understand, we have nothing personal against you or any other wild card," Brandon said. "If anything, I feel sorry for you."

"That's real comforting to know," Jay said.

Brandon ignored him. "None of you asked to get this virus . . . but you did. You and I may think that's tragic, but there it is. You're diseased, Dr. Finn." He looked around the cabin at the other captives, at Jay, at Sascha slumped in his chair with his hair falling across his eyeless face, at their faux Peregrine. "All of you are diseased. You want to wed Clara, you tell me. Imagine if you had a daughter. Now imagine that a man with AIDS came to you and said that he loved her and wanted to many her. How would you feel? What would you say?"

"The wild card isn't AIDS," Finn said. "It's not contagious and it's not necessarily fatal." The centaur tried to stand, struggling against the ropes that held him, but it was hopeless.

"Not one hundred percent of the time, no," Eric Fleming added. "Would that it were. Then there'd be no need for the Card Sharks."

"I hear you're working on that," Jay put in. "The Black Trump, isn't that what you call it? Catchy name."

Fleming and van Renssaeler exchanged a look. "You know about that, then," Fleming put in.

"You think we flew down here to see the wombats, or what?" Jay said sharply. "Yes, we know about it."

Brandon van Renssaeler suddenly looked very unhappy. "I assumed you had come for me. To hunt me down, arrest me, or likely kill me. Isn't that what you people usually do to your enemies?"

Fleming said, "We had nothing to do with the Black Trump project. In any organization with the size and scope of the Card Sharks, differences of opinion are inevitable. I never signed on for genocide."

"Nor I. I opposed Rudo and Faneuil on this scheme since the beginning," Brandon said. His mouth was tight with anger. "They took my own daughter and used her as their tool. I will never forgive them for that."

"Then help us stop them," Bradley Finn pleaded. "Clara says that you're a decent man . . ."

That was a mistake. "Don't you *dare* talk to me about decency. Pan was more than glad to tell me everything . . . everything you did to her, to Clara, you filthy little . . ."

"I didn't *do* anything to Clara," Finn snapped back, furious. "We made love. Together. It was great."

Brandon van Renssaeler strode forward as if he wanted to kick Finn to death right then and there. "Shut up!" he said. "Just shut up, do you hear me?"

"Easy, Brandon," Eric Fleming said. He stood up and put his hand on van Renssaeler's arm, pulling him back.

They were all shark bait unless they got the conversation off Finn's sex life real quick, Jay realized. He was groping for something to say when Jerry Strauss spoke up for the first time since they'd been taken below. "I'm a joker, too, Eric," she said softly, "and you seemed eager enough to make love to me."

Fleming smiled sadly at her. "That's quite different," he said. Jerry was still Peri, and she looked delicious even in bondage. Fleming touched her lightly under the chin, lifting her face toward him. "You are very beautiful, you know. I'm sure I'll go to my grave regretting that your masquerade didn't go a little bit longer. We did seem to have a certain chemistry, don't you think?" He leaned over and kissed her very lightly on the lips.

They still think she's Peregrine! Jay realized with a start. And why not? It made perfect sense. Peri had been part of the campaign against the Card Shark conspiracy almost since the start. Gregg Hartmann had first broken the silence on *Peregrine's Perch*. And if they thought they had Peregrine . . .

"She is beautiful," Jay blurted, vamping wildly. "Too beautiful to die. We're all too beautiful to die, even Sascha. A lot of people like flesh-colored eyes."

"You've given us no choice," Brandon said.

"There's always a choice," Finn said. "Help us stop Rudo. Help us find them before they release the Trump. You can save the world, or you can stand by and watch a million people die, washing your hands like Pontius Pilate and pretending you had nothing to do with it. Clara said—"

Brandon hit him. A hard backhand across the face that snapped Finn's head around. *"Don't mention her name!"* he said. Then he turned and walked out.

Finn had struck home with the Pontius Pilate crack, Jay realized. Too damn close to home. Daddy Brandon had run rather than face up to it.

A long silence filled the cabin. There was only the sound of the ocean outside, the wind sidling in the high canvas.

"Peri, I am deeply sorry," Fleming said at last, with something that sounded like genuine regret. "I wish I could just cut those ropes and watch you fly off into the sunset, but . . ." He sighed. "It really makes very little difference what we do. When Rudo releases the Black Trump, all of you are doomed anyway."

"Hey, if it makes no difference, why bother?" Jay said. "You're no killers, you said so yourself. Let us go. The Black Trump will take care of us anyway, and you won't have nightmares about Peri getting chewed up like some extra in a Spielberg outtake. Look at those legs on her. Do you really want a school of great whites fighting over them like drumsticks?"

"Hammerheads, more likely," Fleming said with a shrug. Clearly he was less prone to qualms than his friend Brandon. He got up and moved toward the cabin door.

If Fleming left, too, they were doomed. They'd sit here trussed and helpless until *Circe* was out past all hope, and then it would be time to play pattycake with the hammerheads. Jay was searching for something to say, some new appeal, anything that might give them a chance, when Sascha lifted his head and said wearily, "Don't bother, boss. The background noise is real bad in here."

Eric Fleming opened the door.

"Eric," Peregrine said. Fleming looked back. "Please," Peri said. Jay was startled to see that there were tears on her face, rolling slowly down her cheek. "Please, Eric, I know you don't dare let us go, but . . . please . . . as a favor . . ."

"If there's anything I can do to make these last hours easier, you have only to ask," Fleming said gallantly. "What was it? Would you like a drink?"

"I . . . please . . ." Like a shy schoolgirl, she averted her eyes. Her voice was so soft it was practically a whisper. "I want you to make love to me, Eric. Please . . . just once, before . . ."

Fleming blinked at her, stunned. Then, slowly, a broad smile crept across his face. "No problems," he said.

The owner's cabin had the biggest bed. Fleming ordered Jay, Sascha, and Bradley Finn lugged back up on deck. As two of his sailors hoisted Jay up on their broad, manly shoulders, Eric-me-hearty was gently untying Peri's ropes and undressing her with his eyes. Jay didn't need Sascha's power to read *his* mind.

Halfway up the steps, one of the salty dogs grinned and said, "Wouldn't I love to have me a peek in *that* porthole."

"You and me both, mate," said Jay.

The pub smelled of death. Ray was used to that, but this was the wrong place for it. This was usually a warm, cozy place, smelling of food and comfortable companionship. The bodies on the floor, lying in congealed pools of blood and brains and shit, were obscene.

Harvest was tight-lipped as she looked at them. Flint marched around the room like a haunted statue.

"Fist vengeance," he said in a sibilant, angry whisper.

"Old men and women," Ray said. He stopped in front of one body. "And the groom?" he asked.

Flint nodded.

This was beyond obscenity. Ray had no word for it. He was a fighter, a fighter and a killer, in fact, but these acts done in cold blood were utterly beyond his understanding and beneath his contempt.

"Fucking cowards," he muttered.

Harvest's blue eyes were as cold as the corpses laying at their feet. "I'll get them for this."

"We both will," Ray promised her.

She looked up at him briefly and then turned away.

"You should hear this, Ray, Harvest," Flint said.

Most of the witnesses had already gone. A few were still waiting in one of the small side rooms to give their statements. One stood in the doorway to the death room, talking to the constables, looking much like death himself.

"I'm tellin' you," he said as Ray came within earshot of his shuddering voice, "it was the bug that chose 'em."

"Bug?" Ray asked.

The man looked at him. He was an older man, much like the ones who had been gunned down, and Ray could see both relief and guilt in his eyes that he'd escaped their fate.

"Aye, sir," he repeated. "All yellow and bug-like, with many pairs of feet and a hideous red bulb of a nose."

Ray looked at Harvest and Flint. "Hartmann! Hartmann picked out the victims!"

"No doubt, then," Flint said. *"He's mixed up with the Twisted Fists."*

Ray couldn't believe it. He'd been Hartmann's bodyguard for years. He'd seen him through personal and public tragedies, he'd almost died for the bastard when he stepped between him and that little fuck Mackie Messer! Now Hartmann was acting as the finger man for a bunch of twisted shits who made war on old people. Hartmann didn't even have the guts to pull the trigger himself. Ray shook his head for the first time feeling really enthused about the idea of going after Hartmann and bringing him back to justice.

He looked at Harvest. It seemed, as she looked at him, that she could almost read his mind.

"You're doomed, you bastard," Ray said aloud. "Your ass is mine."

Jay was propped against a mast and rolling with the motion of the *Circe* when Eric Fleming came back up on deck, bare-chested and whistling "Waltzing Matilda."

The helmsman called down, "So how was she?"

Fleming grinned like a cat who'd just had a big slice of canary pie à la mode. "I'll throw my shrimp on her barbie any day, mate," he said. Not the most fortuitous choice of metaphor. The helmsman looked a shade puzzled.

Fleming swaggered over to Jay. "How you doing, mate?"

"I've been better, all things considered," Jay replied. "I think I saw some fins circling around out there."

Fleming's head turned sharply, his eyes crinkling as they scanned the horizon. "Where? What kind of fins?"

"Tailfins from a '59 Caddy. Pink. It's probably Elvis."

"You're such a wiseacre," Fleming complained. He called over one of his crew. "Get that bloody rope off his legs."

"Sir?" The sailor looked confused.

"You heard me," Fleming snapped.

"No problems," the sailor said, kneeling. He pulled out a knife and deftly cut the rope off Jay's ankles.

Fleming yanked Jay to his feet. "You give me any trouble and you'll be hopping over the side quick as a wallaby. You got that, mate?" He shoved him roughly. Jay stumbled ahead of him, down the steps, as pins and needles pricked his feet with the sudden return of circulation.

. "Enough with the goddamn Aussie talk," Jay hissed when they were safely out of sight. "Christ, Jerry, for a moment there I thought you were going to break into 'Tie Me Kangaroo Down, Sport.'"

"Sorry," Fleming said. He looked behind him anxiously as he opened the door to the owner's cabin, but no one was following. Quickly and quietly, he ushered Jay inside, then bolted the door.

The real Eric Fleming was sprawled across the bed, naked and unmoving, with Peregrine's white silk panties shoved in his mouth and secured by a couple of lengths of tape.

"He's not dead," the other Eric assured him as he untied the ropes around Jay's wrists.

"I didn't think he was. Dead guys don't usually need panties in their mouths to keep them quiet."

"Knickers," Jerry-Eric said nervously. "Down here I think they call them knickers."

"I thought that was England," Jay said. "Hey, what do I know from lingerie? It's all just silky bits you've got to rip off to get to the good stuff underneath." The ropes fell away. Jay massaged his wrist with his numb fingers. His hands hurt. His face hurt, too, a dull throb from the broken nose. He looked over at the Fleming on the bed. "How did you—"

"We had a nude pillow fight. Once I got the pillow over his face, I turned into Arnold. What are we going to do with him?"

"This," Jay said. He pointed a finger at Fleming, dropped the hammer of his thumb. *Pop.* "Now you're the only Eric Fleming aboard *Circe*. Congratulations."

"Won't they notice that Peregrine is missing?"

"They'll just figure the boss is keeping her around for sloppy seconds." Jay grabbed Jerry-Eric by his ears and kissed him on both cheeks. "Remind me to get you an Oscar. *Oooh, Mr. Fleming, please fuck me just once before we die . . .*"

Jerry beamed visibly. "I *was* convincing, wasn't I? I remembered what you said in the van, about always betting on the dick, and I figured it was worth taking a shot."

"You should listen to me more often," Jay told him.

"So what now?" Jerry asked, with an eagerness that sounded a shade too young for Fleming. "Can you pop away the crew?"

"There's got to be forty of them," Jay said. "I don't like those odds. Besides, if I got rid of the crew, who the hell is going to drive the fucking boat? This thing is like the *Titanic* with sails. No, we have to keep up the charade that you're really Eric Fleming. Where's van Renssaeler?"

"In his cabin."

"I'll take care of him," Jay said. "You go up and have Sascha brought down. Say as little as possible. You're the boss; you don't have to explain yourself."

"What about Finn?"

"Let's leave Romeo the Love Pony up on deck," Jay told him as he headed for the cabin door. "The salt air will do him good, and we're fresh out of knickers."

As Jerry-Eric headed back up the steps, Jay checked out the other cabins. Brandon van Renssaeler was behind door number three, which Jay figured was a real good sign that the time had come to play *Let's Make a Deal*. Brandon was stretched out on a narrow bed with a damp washcloth across his eyes. There was a nice little blue-steel automatic on the bedside table.

Jay slipped silently through the door and picked up the gun. Then he gave the bed a little kick. "Up and at 'em."

Brandon rolled over and grabbed for the pistol that was no longer there. "Pretty fast, for a lawyer," Jay said. "This what you looking for?" He dangled the automatic to give Brandon a good look, then opened the porthole and tossed it out. There was a faint, reassuring splash.

Brandon stood up. "Quite dramatic, Mr. Ackroyd, but now we're both unarmed."

"I wouldn't say that." Jay made his hand a gun, pointed his finger at the center of van Renssaeler's chest.

Brandon came along quietly to the owner's cabin. A moment later, Eric the Impostor joined them with Sascha. Jay bolted the door while Eric was cutting Sascha loose from his ropes. Brandon van Renssaeler watched the proceedings curiously. "What's wrong with this picture?" he said at last. "Eric, what are you doing?" When he got no answer, he frowned. "You're not Eric. Who are you?"

"Nobody," Jay told him. He pulled over a chair, sat down in it backward, inches from van Renssaeler. "I could threaten you, I suppose, but you don't look like the kind of man who'd respond well to threats. We came down here looking for you, yes, but only because we need your help. Your daughter thinks you have a conscience. I hope to hell she's right, because we don't have a prayer of stopping the Black Trump without you. So what do you say?"

There was long silence as Brandon van Renssaeler looked deep into Jay Ackroyd's eyes. "He's thinking about it," Sascha put in. "Part of him wants to help, he—"

"I'll speak for myself, thank you," van Renssaeler interrupted sharply. "What did you do with the real Eric Fleming?"

"I popped him off to Freakers, a joker strip bar in Manhattan. He was buck naked with a pair of knickers in his mouth, so I figured he'd fit right in."

Van Renssaeler nodded. "I suppose that was . . . kinder than what he had planned for you."

The faux Fleming shuddered "Sharks . . ."

"All right," van Renssaeler said. "I'll tell you what I know, on these conditions. First, no harm will come to me or anyone else aboard *Circe*."

"If you'll help us bring off the masquerade and get this tub back to Townsville, that shouldn't be a problem."

"Agreed. Second, you and your friends will do nothing to harm my daughter. Whether you stop Rudo or not, Clara's name must be kept out of this. The world must never know about her role in the creation of the Black Trump."

"Part of the world knows already," Jay pointed out. "The rest isn't going to find out from us, I can promise you that much."

"I suppose that will have to do. There's one final condition. You must swear that Dr. Finn will never see my daughter again."

Jay had to think about that one for a moment. He gave a shrug. "I don't know how we do that," he admitted.

Sascha said, "He wants this bad, Jay. If you turn him down, he's thinking we can all just get fucked and die."

"You're a real prick, van Renssaeler."

"I've been quite a successful attorney for a long time, Mr. Ackroyd," Brandon replied crisply. "I'd like an answer, please."

"We don't have to play this game," Jay pointed out. "Sascha is a telepath. So maybe I'll just ask the questions and let him pluck the answers from your head."

"If Sascha was that *good* a telepath, we wouldn't be having this conversation," Brandon said, with a certain smugness.

Sascha looked gloomy. "He's thinking about . . . law. Cases, precedents. All these whereases and wherefores."

"You can't keep that up for long," Jay said.

"You don't have long," van Renssaeler returned. "Rudo is out there right now with the Black Trump."

Jay kicked over his chair in frustration.

Jerry-Eric said, "This guy is starting to remind me of Loophole Latham."

"All lawyers are alike in the dark," Jay said, disgusted. "All right, counselor, you win. If we survive, I'll pop Dr. Finn off to Takis. A hundred light-years, give or take a few. I can't get him any farther away from your precious, darling daughter than that."

"I want it in writing," van Renssaeler said. "I'll draft it myself. If you fail to perform, there will be stringent penalties. I'll take everything you own."

Jay threw up his hands. "Fine, whatever. Jesus. Jerry, find him some paper." He stuck a finger in Brandon's face. "If you think you're going to get it notarized, you're shit out of luck."

At first he thought the lizards had awakened him.

The little pudgy lizards who clung to the outside of the trailer were known locally as *taukte*. It was what the locals thought they were saying. To Mark's ex-Joker Brigade bodyguards back in Nam, they'd been fuck-you lizards, betraying a certain subtle difference between Western and Eastern ears.

And they were out there in the night, saying whatever the hell it was they said. But that wasn't what roused him.

He wasn't alone.

A silhouette against the star gleam diffusing through the cheap curtains of the bedroom window; a deformed shadow in darkness, but still identifiably human.

"Quasiman?" Mark asked, in a voice not unlike the lizards' *taukte*.

Quasiman looked at him. From the way he held his head, he seemed . . . lucid but distracted.

"How'd you find me, man?" Mark asked, struggling to sit

up. He wore a T-shirt and briefs, both of which were soaked with sweat that turned to instant ice in the blast of the air-conditioning.

"You're important. You were more important once." Quasiman looked at him and frowned. "No. No, that isn't right. You've *been* important, but you're going to be more important. I think that's it."

"You've got to help me, man!"

But Quasiman was frowning, and the alert set of his shoulders was melting away. "It's all jumbled up in my head. If only I could get . . . things straight. But time is like—"

He turned toward Mark, held up both his hands. And faded.

Mark lunged at him, as though he might prevent him from teleporting by grabbing him. All he did was bang his chin and give himself a rug burn on the elbows.

Quasiman was gone.

Four

They stopped at a roadside camp on the banks of the Euphrates. There were other campers there, tents and fires against the chill night, smells of wood smoke and roasting lamb. Zoe heard the hum of the road in her ears. Somewhere in the distance, a child laughed. There was food to be cooked—a woman's job in this setting. Were she and Jan expected to pitch the tent, too? Balthazar was unloading stuff from the bus, and the motions his arms made brought back a kinetic memory of the twisting road, the high passes. Zoe closed her eyes and tried not to stagger when she climbed down to solid ground.

"You'll need to change, Zoe," Balthazar said. He handed over a plastic bucket filled with folded clothes.

"Did you pick these out?" Zoe asked.

"I did," Jan said. She finished layering charcoal into a little brazier, handed it to Croyd, and brushed her hands on her skirts. "Let's go wash up."

The river was a dark expanse of hushed water, held quiet by the Kehan dam. Jan tossed a bar of soap toward Zoe and matter-of-factly stripped out of her layers of clothes. Jan's breasts had budded but her hips were still narrow, her thighs thin and childish, pale in the moonlight reflected up from the river.

Balthazar and Croyd tended the fire, both of them pointedly looking in the other direction.

Zoe stripped out of her sedate georgette Carole Little, her Vassarette bra, and the last pair of Hanes Silk Reflections she expected to see in a long time. She knelt and dipped her hand in the river. It was melted ice. "I can't!" Zoe yelped.

Jan laughed and waded in, standing knee-deep in the black river and sluicing up armfuls of water. So Zoe did. The soap smelled good. Zoe scrubbed at her skin until it roughened with goosebumps, and then the air felt warmer than it had and the prospect of getting into those awful clothes didn't seem quite so terrible.

"Aren't they the worst?" Jan asked. "I mean, I'm not into *style,* but these rags are to gag."

Ankle-length cotton trousers printed with roses on white, like antique pajamas. Long black dresses with long sleeves. Zoe's was covered with printed bouquets of some strange flower. She couldn't see the colors well in the moonlight. She figured that was a blessing. Jan climbed back into her plain black cotton skirts and layered her two short boleros over it.

Zoe bundled her clothes and climbed the rocky shore back to camp. Balthazar looked up and smiled. He was turning meat and skewered vegetables on the grill. Zoe pointed to her bare feet. "What about shoes?"

"Sneakers," Balthazar said. "You'll need to wrap your heads, both of you."

"Oh, sorry," Jan said. "I keep forgetting." She pulled a pair of voluminous headscarves out of the bottom of the bucket. "Which one you want, Zoe?"

"Just toss one over," Zoe said. It came sailing, stripes on

black. She tried for the look she'd seen in port, folds of fabric puffed around the face and draped down one shoulder. The scarf was slick. She was never going to get the hang of this.

"What do we do with the clothes I took off?" Zoe asked.

Balthazar held out his hand. Zoe gave him the bundle. She watched meat sizzle on the brazier and tried not to watch while Balthazar folded a rock into the package and used her perfectly good pair of pantyhose to knot it together. He walked away. She heard a splash.

About twenty yards from the bus, Croyd worked on getting a pop-up tent popped up. They were to set watches to make sure no one came near the bus. They were not to sleep in the bus unless they had no choice. It was part of the plan.

Balthazar went inside the bus and rummaged around before he came back to the fire. "Here," Balthazar said. "There's more that goes with your outfits, ladies."

He gave them each a dowry in gold jewelry, his hands spilling over with chains and coins and filigree work, earrings and bracelets and ankle bracelets.

Croyd finished with the tent and helped fasten Zoe into her cache, chain after chain after necklace, his fingers moving skillfully to fasten clasp after tiny clasp, while Balthazar tended the grill.

"It looks nice," Croyd said.

"I feel like a belly dancer," Zoe said. She felt exotic, earthy. Not because the clothes had beauty, for they certainly didn't. She felt costumed for primeval struggles, for feminine mysteries of dignity and power. Jan seemed to change before her eyes. No longer a gawky adolescent, she suddenly moved with the quiet grace of a woman. To keep the gold silent, Zoe realized. She knows instinctively that moving silently might save her life sometime. Poor baby.

They sat around the brazier and ate lamb skewered with

vegetables and seasoned with fresh thyme and scatterings of some hot vinegary sauce that Balthazar pulled out of a hamper, all rolled in rounds of fluffy, thin bread.

Jan stayed close to Balthazar's side. She swung her bracelets at him and he patted her avuncularly on the shoulder. Jan's eyes glowed, at a low intensity, not much more apparent than the simple gloss of young love. Zoe started to chide her for it, but the camp was sheltered between large boulders, out of sight of any other humans, and Croyd walked its perimeter like a nervous bloodhound.

Zoe felt like an intruder. Should she do anything to stop this? Balthazar wouldn't harm the child, but he might have to tell her a definite "No" at some point if he realized what was happening. Zoe dreaded the storm of hurt feelings if that occurred. This group couldn't afford hurt feelings.

Zoe jerked when sleep made her slump forward. And saw, as Croyd led her toward the tent where she would sleep and he would not, Jan bringing the caged doves out of the bus to sleep inside the tent. Beside Balthazar's bedroll, she cast him a longing glance, but he seemed oblivious.

Harvest looked into the mirror, focusing on Ray's image, as he stood behind her. "Not now, Ray," she said flatly.

Ray had kissed the back of her neck, softly, fleetingly, holding her sweep of blond hair cupped in one hand. "What's the matter, babe? You've been sitting and staring into the mirror for over an hour now."

She stared longer. Just when Ray had given up all hope of her speaking, she did. "Did you know my father, Ray? My father or my mother?"

Ray frowned. "I don't think so. Should I have?"

"I should have. But they were killed in 1976 after the Jokertown Riots. They were killed by Twisted Fists avenging joker deaths in the riot. I was six years old. My father and mother had never hurt a joker. They'd never hurt anyone."

Ray didn't know what to say. "I'm sorry."

He didn't know what to do so he kissed the back of her neck again, then again, and again. He felt her shiver as his lips brushed a particularly sensitive spot.

"I can't stop thinking about them."

Ray didn't know if she meant her parents or the people they'd seen slaughtered in the pub.

"It's in the past, babe. You can't change it. Why relive it?"

"Don't you ever think about the past?"

Ray shook his head. "Never. Only in dreams sometimes."

"Can you make me forget?"

He slid a hand down her chest, inside her blouse. Underneath she wore only a silk teddy over her bare breasts. He cupped one. It was firm and warm to his touch. He felt her nipple stiffen as he rubbed it.

She sighed, shifted in her chair. Ray moved his other hand to a silk-clad thigh. She opened her legs, giving him better access. Her head slipped back, she found her mouth with his. Her mouth was as sweet as the rest of her body. She sighed into his mouth, and the doorbell rang.

"Damn," she said, almost biting Ray's tongue. She stood up, pulling away from Ray and straightening her clothes. "Come in," she said aloud.

Damn, Ray thought, wasn't the word for it. He stared narrow-eyed at the door as Flint, stooping to get in under the lintel, ponderously entered the room.

"*Good evening,*" he said in his customary whisper.

"It was going to be," Ray muttered.

"What can we do for you?" Harvest asked, silencing Ray with a glance.

"*Sir Winston has requested Agent Ray's presence for a private interview,*" Flint said.

"Churchill?" Ray asked.

"We don't know any other Sir Winstons," Harvest said impatiently. "What does he want?"

There was a grinding sound as Flint shrugged his massive shoulders. "*I imagine it's private.*"

"I see. All right. If you'll just excuse us for a moment, Captain."

Flint bowed decorously. "*Certainly,*" he said, and navigated through the doorway, pulling the door shut after him.

"What do you think he wants?" Harvest asked.

Ray shrugged. "You're asking me? Maybe he knows something. Maybe he wants to stir things up. Churchill is England's most powerful wild carder. Oh, sure, Flint stomps around looking grim and whispering like a goddamned ghost, but Churchill knows how to get things done."

"Remember what the president said," Harvest reminded him. "Don't mention the Trump."

Ray hesitated. "I don't know. Maybe I should. Everybody's waltzing around like this is some kind of picnic. Well, it's not. Maybe it's time to light fires underneath some butts."

Harvest frowned. "President Barnett said to keep it a secret."

"President Barnett's not here."

"I could order you to keep quiet."

Ray grinned. "You could."

Harvest stared at him. "Okay. Do what you think is best."

"I always do."

"But you better be right on this."

He kissed her, quickly. She seemed unenthusiastic. Ray hoped he could relight the fire under *her* butt after his meeting with the geezer was over. "Ever know me to be wrong?"

"Hmmmmm."

Flint was waiting in the hallway outside. Ray followed him to the elevator where the British ace punched for the top floor. Two men were waiting for them when the elevator finished its trip. One was huge, though not as mountainous as Flint. He stood nearly six foot six and his turban made him look even taller. His chest was deep, his shoulders broad. He had a full, flowing beard and carried a long knife in a jeweled sheath. The other man was taller than Ray, but he looked small in comparison to his companion. He was lean and quiet in a menacing sort of way.

"These are two of my best men from the Silver Helix," Flint said. *"Rangit Singh—the Lion."*

"I have heard of you, of course." Singh spoke with a British accent. "Someday we shall perhaps test each other." He flexed his huge hands and grinned broadly.

"Yeah, sure," Ray said. "When my dance card's not so full."

"And this," Flint said, indicating the other agent, *"is Bond, James Bond."*

Ray looked at him and frowned. "You're kidding?"

"No, he's not bloody kidding." Bond, James Bond seemed aggravated. It seemed to be his habitual state. "So my parents had a bloody sense of humor, didn't they? Could I help that?" he asked aggressively.

Ray shook his head as Flint knocked on the door to Churchill's suite.

"Nope."

"Come," Churchill called.

Ray followed Flint into the room. He turned at the last moment and looked at Bond. "I'll let you know when SPECTRE shows up," he said, then closed the door.

The room was posh, elegant, and dimly lit. It also stank of cigar smoke. Expensive cigar smoke, but stinking cigar smoke nonetheless. Churchill was sitting behind an antique desk, smoking. He wore the same outfit he'd worn the night before. He struggled to his feet as Ray approached, and leaned on a cane as he offered the agent his ancient hand.

It was spotted with age and shrunken down to nothing but bone and sinew, but the oldster still had surprising strength in his grip as he took Ray's hand. Ray was careful not to squeeze, afraid that he would crumble the bones to dust.

Churchill leaned forward aggressively on his black, silver-handled cane, his face wreathed in puffs of cigar smoke.

"Sit down, sir," he rasped at Ray, waving in the general direction of the chair across the desk from him. He waited until Ray had taken the seat, then plumped down with a satisfied "Oooomph" in his own chair. He stuck a finger inside his tight collar and tugged.

"Getting too old for this nonsense."

"Yes, sir."

Churchill's eyes were those of an ancient reptile, cold and unreadable.

"Too old to waste time, entirely too old," he said after a long, uncomfortable silence.

"Yes, sir," Ray replied, wondering what the old fart expected him to say.

"So what's this I hear about a Black Trump?" Churchill barked.

Ray sat back in his chair. Not a cagey person at the best of times, Ray was totally bewildered by the unexpected question.

"Who told you about that?" he blurted.

"Hartmann did when I spoke to him last. Before that nasty business at the gate."

Ray nodded. There was the sound of geologic movement behind him and a huge shadow suddenly engulfed his chair.

"What's this Black Trump?" Flint asked.

"A killer virus, Brigadier, created by the Card Sharks and aimed at killing all wild carders. Gregg Hartmann told me all about it. I was satisfied that he told me the truth." Ray felt Churchill's eyes bore into his and found himself nodding. He didn't know if it was an ace power or simply the force of the politician's will that made him spill the secret. "What exactly do you know about it?"

Ray wet his lips. There was no percentage now, he thought, in holding back. "I saw it. I saw it in action—"

Churchill leaned forward, his eyes fixed on Ray, his face wreathed in smoke.

Ray stopped suddenly and looked around.

"What's that sound?" he asked, and the world exploded around them.

The room's windows shattered in a blast of automatic rifle fire as Ray hurled himself, chair and all, backward. He twisted his head and saw a helicopter hovering outside the ruined window. The blades were muffled, but Ray had nonetheless heard the silenced *whup-whup-whup* of the chopper's approach. In a nice bit of flying, the pilot held the chopper a steady three feet from the blown-out windows, and the man in black who had shattered the panes with a burst of gunfire leapt from the chopper's belly into the room. He hit the carpet, rolled, and came up shooting.

"*Noooooooo!*"

Flint's whisper notched up into an agonized roar as he took a slow-motion step toward Churchill. Before he could get into place Ray lifted and threw his chair, smashing the gunman in the chest and knocking him backward as two others leapt daringly into the room. The door flew open and the Helix agents joined the action.

Ray glanced toward the desk. Churchill was down, out of

sight. Two of the gunmen were shooting fruitlessly at Flint. Their bullets ricocheted off his body, striking sparks. The first gunman was dazed by the impact of Ray's chair. He staggered around the room, toward the British agents.

Flint held up his right hand and snapped his fingers with a sudden, popping sound. One of the gunmen staggered as a blossom of blood sprouted on his chest. He fell as Flint snapped his fingers again. The second gunman collapsed, his right eye gone.

Ray looked out the window. The chopper was still hovering. Ray locked eyes with the pilot.

"Goddamn," he said. It was General MacArthur Johnson. The first gunman lifted his weapon, but he was too close to Singh. The ace roared like a lion—Ray wondered if that was how he'd gotten his name—grabbed the gunman by shoulder and crotch, and hurled him out the window, right at the chopper. The human projectile screamed as he flew through the air and struck the glass bubble of the chopper's canopy. He bounced off, leaving a smear of blood on the canopy, and screamed all the way to the ground. Johnson fought the controls for a moment, then smiled at Ray, gave him the finger, and flew away into the night.

Ray tensed, standing in the shattered window frame, then something told him, *No, don't do it. No chance.* He pulled himself from the edge and turned back into the room.

The other gunmen were dead. Flint had shot them with bits of his own fingers, deadly as any stone arrowhead. Flint was turning back toward Churchill. Ray moved quickly and smoothly around him.

He knelt by the fallen man. Churchill had been stitched across the chest. His beautiful smoking jacket was torn and bloody, as was the flesh under it. His eyes focused on Ray. His lips moved, but Ray couldn't hear what he was trying to say. He gathered the ancient, shattered body into his arms and put his ear close to Churchill's mouth.

"What is it, sir?"

"Ge . . ." Churchill said. "Ge . . . Gen . . . er . . . al."

"I know, sir," Ray nodded. "Try to rest. The doctor—"

Ray put his lips together and frowned. Churchill was gone. Ray looked up at Flint, looming over him. If it were possible for a statue to look stricken, Flint did.

Ray shook his head, all insouciance drained from him. "He's dead."

"What did he say?" Flint asked.

Ray shook his head. "Tried to tell me that General MacArthur Johnson was responsible for the attack. But I'd already recognized the bastard piloting the chopper."

"My God," Flint said heavily. *"What will we all do now?"*

Ray had no answer for the stricken ace.

"Dr. Meadows?" O. K. Casaday's voice called from the lab's far end.

Mark looked up from the workstation, on which he was trying to unravel the intricacies of WordPerfect 6.0. It was lunchtime. Jarnavon and the quietly helpful platoon of lab-coated technicians, Asian and Western, who acted as interface between Mark and the array of still largely mysterious equipment, were nowhere to be seen.

"Take a break," Casaday said. "Give the eye bones a rest."

The CIA man was not in the habit of offering idle invitations. Mark figured that, had he been a *real hero*—like Mel Gibson in those movies he tried not to watch—he'd come zapping back with some cleverly defiant banter. Of course, the *result* would still be the same: Casaday had a gun, an army of heavily armed guerrillas at his beck and call, and Mark's only daughter as hostage; he would get his way. But he'd know what was *what*.

What really *was* what was that Mark was no hero, not without his friends. He was tired, scared, and utterly over his head. He stood up and nodded. "Okay."

They walked outside. The clouds were piling up over the mountains to the east, day by day. Monsoon was coming. But until the rains arrived there was nothing to mitigate the sun, which slammed down on Mark's head like a Stooge's frying pan when he stepped out into its domain.

The camp bustled with its usual activities—soldiers drilling, trucks moving back and forth between the compound and the poppy fields that paid the bills. Nearby an officer was instructing a group of what Mark took to be recruits in the fine points of shooting down government helicopters with American-made Stinger missiles.

"So how's the work coming?" Casaday asked. He strode across the huge camp as if he had a destination in mind. Mark, seeing no alternative to following, saw likewise no point in asking what that destination was. He didn't really care. It wasn't going to be any place he wanted to be.

"Slow, man," he answered. "I'm not real up to speed on all this stuff. Scanning—tunneling microscopes, that kinda thing. All new to me."

But the techs were ready, willing, and able to operate the arcane gimcracks *for* him. All he had to grasp was what uses they could be put to, and the courteous and efficient staff would do the actual dirty work. Damn them anyway.

"Yeah," Casaday said skeptically. They were walking toward a largish hootch, out kind of by itself near the rolled

German razor tape that formed the perimeter. "I still can't believe you don't know how to use a personal computer. I mean, you're supposed to be a trained scientist."

"I got trained a long time ago," Mark said defensively. "I ran a head shop. I never had anything to do with computers."

"How did you keep your accounts, that kind of crap?"

"Somebody did the books for me." That somebody was Susan, one of the pair of surly, brush-cut CUNY students he had hired to help him back in the vanished Cosmic Pumpkin days. He found himself missing his clerks, even though they had despised him, rather as one might miss a pit bull who had wandered into the yard and whom one had adopted out of a combined sense of Good Samaritanism and intimidation.

Casaday snorted. "Yeah. I guess." He looked at Mark sidelong. "You're a smart guy, Meadows. That's why I brought you here. That's why I figure you wouldn't try to bullshit me about kitty-cat crap like that."

From the hut ahead came a scream. Sprout's scream, shrill and desperate.

Mark burst into a run, loose-legged and gangly, scattering the inevitable crows. He went booming in the door of the hootch. Dimness, a flash of movement in his peripheral vision, and then *impact*. He went sailing back out to land on his butt on the hard, red earth.

Casaday sauntered up, looking cool in his linen suit and white straw fedora. "Looks like Layton got a bit overenthusiastic again," he said. "I'm going to have to have *words* with that boy."

He reached a helping hand down, which Mark was not too proud to accept in his frenzy to help his daughter. Ribs aching, he lunged back into the hut.

To one side a grinning Layton held Sprout by the arm. She

wore a T-shirt tied up to bare her midriff and cutoff blue jeans. She struggled helplessly.

On the other side of the single room Lou Inmon sat, bound to a chair.

Gunther Ditmar stood beside him with a butcher's apron on over his mildewed suit. He held some kind of shiny metal implement. Several men in black pajamas stood watchfully by the wall.

The bound joker raised his head and looked at Mark. His great golden eyes were swollen almost shut.

"Sorry, boss," he said. "I thought I could help you, but things don't always work out like we plan, do they?"

"How'd you like my sidekick, Doc?" Layton asked.

Mark bared teeth at him and lunged for his daughter. Layton did a fancy little sidestep between Mark and the girl, grinning. A pair of Black Karens grabbed Mark's arms and hauled him back.

"What's the hell's going on?" Mark demanded, struggling futilely. "Sprout, honey, what's the matter?"

"Oh, Daddy, they were gonna hurt Unca Louie!" she wailed.

"And we still are," said Casaday, strolling in the door. He stopped and looked down at the captive joker. "Some people don't know when they're well off, Doctor, can you imagine that? This poor sucker was set up as president pro temp and in prime position to make it a permanent deal. But he just couldn't let things go."

"What are you *doing*? Why do you have Sprout here?"

"Object lesson," Casaday said.

"Are you out of your mind? She—she's a child, Casaday. What do you expect her to get from an 'object lesson'?"

"Not her," Casaday said. "You."

Mark deflated. It was humiliating to be held immobile by

two guys who didn't come up to his shoulder, but he could not break free. They were *strong*.

He wasn't.

"Okay. Then let her go. Him, too. You've made your point, believe me."

Casaday shook his great round head. "No way, Jose. This—thing—caused us trouble, Doctor. We want you to see what happens to those who make trouble for us. Herr Ditmar, you may proceed."

Ditmar clicked his heels, nodded. He brandished the implement, which proved to be a pair of wire cutters with yellow plastic handles.

"Many times you encounter someone who has an unusually high pain threshold or an unusually strong will," the German said didactically, as if Mark had wandered into the middle of his lecture. "It is common to believe that such people are immune to physical persuasion." A smile. "In fact, such is seldom the case."

He reached down and took the pinkie of Osprey's right claw, raised it. The skin was yellow and lightly scaled, like a bird's. The talon was black. The joker glared at him.

"Casaday," Mark said between teeth clenched so hard he could feel them creak, "get her *out* of here."

Casaday smiled. With the air of a gardener pruning his champion roses, Ditmar reached down and snipped the tip of the finger off at the first joint.

Osprey vented a great eagle-scream of fury and pain. Sprout's terrified shrieks mingled with his as his blood sprayed the yellow teddy bear embroidered on her shirt.

Mark fought like a mad thing. He could not get free of the two compact men hanging on to his arms.

"Don't bother fighting them, Dr. Meadows," Casaday said. "They practice the local martial art, *bando. Boarmen*, they call themselves, because it's boar-style *bando* that they do. No, not as in *Martin* Bormann, Ditmar; don't get a hard-on, here."

Ditmar giggled. He was wiping blood from his glasses with his handkerchief.

"I could take 'em, though," Layton said. "They're not really that tough."

"Layton, shut the fuck up," Casaday said conversationally. Mark vomited on the floor and had the almost-subconscious gratification of seeing the two boar boys hop back.

Casaday covered his nose with his own handkerchief. "Christ," he said in annoyance. "Get him out of here."

The boarmen stepped forward and pitched Mark into the yard. He finished returning his breakfast to Mother Earth. A hand caught him by the hair at the front of his head and hauled him up onto his knees.

Casaday had hold of him. He and Ditmar stood over Mark. Layton held Sprout in the hootch's doorway. She seemed to have passed out and hung limp in his grasp.

"And that is the way to break even the toughest-willed subject," Ditmar continued as if there'd never been a pause in his narration. "You start with the smallest of joints—first fingers, then toes—and work your way upward. The body has a surprising number of joints, Dr. Meadows. Sooner or later, one proves to be the straw that breaks the camel's back."

Mark decided to have the dry heaves for a while. Casaday made a disgusted sound and let him go.

"Finished?" the spook asked when the spasms subsided. Mark nodded miserably. "Get him some water and a fucking towel."

Mark climbed to his feet, reeled. Ditmar was nowhere to be seen. The sun was poking through his eyelids like steel needles, jabbing through his eyes and out the back of his skull. "You sadistic son of a bitch," he choked.

"No, that's Ditmar," Casaday said. "I am a son of a bitch, but a practical one."

As if on cue, another scream shook the walls of the hut behind Casaday.

"What are you *talking* about?" Mark asked through a sudden torrent of tears.

"You're a smart boy, Meadows, like I said before. Obviously you got it doped out that young Carter isn't in your league, as far as this recombinant-DNA bulljive goes. So it might've occurred to you that you could string us along forever, saying you just couldn't figure out a way to make any progress, and we'd never be the wiser. Right?"

Mark glared at him. Layton grabbed Sprout by the left buttock, pinched. She came awake and screamed.

Mark hurled himself at the kickboxer. Casaday stiff-armed him onto his butt. He hit his tailbone on hard ground, making sparks explode behind his eyes, and then the ever-helpful boarmen had his arms again.

"Layton," he said, "you're a dead man."

"Who's gonna kill me, Meadows? Your ace friends? You're jack shit without your drugs, asshole, and we all know it." He put back his ponytailed head and laughed. His teeth were perfect.

"Don't jack me around, Meadows," Casaday said. "You've thought of trying us on for size. Admit it, or I'll see what else Layton can pinch."

Sullenly, Mark nodded.

"Okay. So here's the deal. We're working to a deadline. That means you're on a deadline, too—or, more correctly, your baby girl is. You have three weeks to show us some results in the lab. Results Carter-baby can verify. Otherwise—"

He laughed. "Well, your girl's quite a hot little honey, but I have to admit she isn't my type; not enough vitamins. She *is*

Layton's type. He likes his women white and not-so-bright; hell, your foxy little one's his dream girl. You blow your deadline, I give her to him. But don't worry—you get to watch."

By this point Mark was back in control of himself enough that he didn't give Casaday the satisfaction of watching him struggle in vain. He just stared. His eyes were a blue much paler than the furnace sky, and infinitely colder.

"We are operating at zero tolerance, here, just like your buddies in the DEA. You try to run, I give her to Layton. You try something smart, like sabotaging our main culture of the Trump—same thing. And if you really, truly fuck up, and don't deliver the goods *at all*"—a big old used-car salesman's smile—"I give her to Ditmar. You read me, Doctor?"

A Karen had arrived with a gourd full of water and a coarse towel with VALE OF KASHMIR HOTEL, TEHRAN embroidered on it in green. Mark rinsed his mouth, spat, mopped his face. "I can't promise results, Casaday. You have to know that. I'm not up-to-date on the science. I don't really understand half the equipment you have. What you want may not even be *possible*, man!"

Casaday snorted. "Tough. It's the reality fucking sandwich, Doctor: Bon appétit."

Yet another scream from the hut. Casaday smirked. "Sounds like the colonel's worked his way up to the knuckle," he said. "Your joker pal still has five fingers and two thumbs left. That's what? Twenty-one joints on just the hands? Fuck. I was never any good at math."

"But it's not *fair*!" Mark cried.

The CIA man sneered at him. "Fair's where they give colored ribbons to hogs and pumpkin pies," he said.

A commotion inside the hut, an outburst of trumping, a squeal of surprise and outrage. A moment more and Lou Inmon lunged through the doorway, knocking Layton and

Sprout sprawling to the hard-packed earth. The joker had managed to break the straps that fastened his legs to the legs of the chair.

"Listen, boss," the joker gasped. The feathers of his head were matted scarlet with blood. "I fucked up. Sorry."

Layton jumped up, started for Osprey. Sprout lunged away, scrambling on all fours. Cursing, the kickboxer turned to pursue her.

"Just remember," the joker said. "You ain't been forgot!"

"Fuck," Casaday said. "I'm in a Three fucking Stooges movie." He reached inside his jacket, drew his .45, snapped it out to the full extension of his arm, and fired. The bullet hit Inmon on the right brow ridge. He dropped like a bundle of rags in the doorway.

Casaday turned back to Mark, tucking his pistol into his shoulder holster.

"Now get your ass back in the lab, Meadows, or I'll tell Layton to get out his Kama Sutra Love Oil ahead of fucking schedule."

Croyd woke them before dawn. They traveled the valleys downward and east, past Diyarbakir and east again, heading for the border at Qamishli. Looking like Kurds, or so Croyd said. If there was fighting in the hills, they didn't see it. Villages changed from Turkish to Kurdish control sometimes at gunpoint, but the Turkish government tried to keep news of the rebellions hushed. Turkey is one country, they insisted. Come visit. But not that town, please. Not this season.

Balthazar stopped once at a roadside phone, an incongruous orange intrusion from the twentieth century. He spent a long time there, feeding in coins, and came back to the bus with a grim expression.

"We want to get across this afternoon," he said, answering questions none of them asked. "We'll have more trouble at night. Different set of guards then. We're going to visit our Kurdish cousins about ten miles south of town. We're taking the pump to them and going back home for the summer. That's the story, anyway."

"Give me the names of these cousins," Croyd said.

Balthazar did—a genealogy complete to the oldest uncle and the newest child of a family that had been resettled into Syria, displaced across the border after a battle in Iran.

"I don't think we'll get much hassle from the Turks or the Syrians," Balthazar said. "The Turks don't really care if Kurds cross the border going *out* of the country. The Syrians won't bother us because they think we're going *back*. We don't look rich and we don't look indigent. You can handle it, Croyd."

Croyd's attention seemed to be on the roadside, intent on fields and the clumps of trees. He watched as if he looked for snipers or maybe snakes. He was never still. Always, a finger tapped, a foot. He shifted in his seat with quick, restless motions.

"This gets me to Rudo?" Croyd said. "Tell me that's really going to happen, Balthazar—or whatever your name is."

"This gets you to Rudo, wherever he ends up. Last the Fists heard, it was Europe again. We're after him, Croyd."

"You've *lost* him?" Croyd twisted in his seat, as far away from Balthazar as he could get. He looked as if he might cry. "You bastards. You've lost the trail. I could be looking for him myself. You could be lying to me about this jumper stuff. Maybe I killed him after all and he stayed dead. Why the hell should I believe you?"

"You sound paranoid. What's the matter, man?"

"I do? Yeah, I guess I do. I'm getting sleepy. It's too early. I don't want to get sleepy yet."

The road, barely two lanes if you were imaginative, widened and curved. Squat silver tanks and a maze of fat pipes marked an oil field. Yellow arrows on the road and signs in several languages marked the approach of the border.

"Jan?" Balthazar asked.

She lifted a satchel from the floor, rummaged in it, and handed a muslin sack of rice to Croyd.

"What's this?" he asked.

"In there," Jan said.

Croyd stirred the grains and brought out a ziplock full of rainbow capsules.

"We need you awake," Balthazar said. "Take one of those and get us past the border. We'll talk about this other stuff when we're in Syria."

"I hate speed," Croyd said. He picked an orange and black capsule from the sack and dry-swallowed it. "I never wanted to go to Syria."

"My name really is Balthazar. Always was, even back in Alabama." The joker brought the bus to a stop, its diesel rumbling in idle. Croyd passed the rice sack back to Jan and climbed down to meet the border guards.

There were men with guns. There were papers for Croyd to hand over, questions and answers. Croyd flicked his hand toward the bus and Balthazar got out and stood beside him. The building was a concrete block, its windows barred, its perimeter surrounded with chain-link fence. A board painted with black and white diagonals hung across the road. Zoe stared at it, willing herself not to see the three guards, not to evaluate their strength against that of Croyd and Balthazar, not to think of the photographs of hemorrhagic flesh and staring eyes, the glossy prints the Hound of Hell handed over so casually. Black Trump victims, so he said.

We're stopping that hell with the threat of another, she thought. *We aren't bad people. They won't stop us here. Please.*

When Croyd turned and beckoned for her and Jan, she was able to get up and get out of the bus without shaking too much. She led Jan close to the barrier while two of the guards climbed into the bus.

The third one was still talking to Croyd. If Croyd was sane enough to do his job, they were talking money.

He would manage. He wasn't crazy yet; she had to believe it. Jan squinted into the sun, her eyes, as ever, on Balthazar.

Something clanged against metal in the bus and Jan flinched, a quickly controlled jerk of her shoulders. The guards were moving back and forth in there, looking for whatever, looking at the damned pump. Croyd's guard took a step toward the bus. Balthazar's mirrorshades watched the guard. The sun glanced off his lenses and struck Zoe's eyes as he turned to look back at the road from Turkey. A brown, dusty Ford Bronco chugged up behind the bus and stopped.

Croyd's guard yelled something. The two guards in the bus climbed out again. One flicked his right hand in a quick gesture and Croyd's guard disappeared with Croyd behind the barred door of the border shed. The pair who had rummaged through the bus went back to talk to the couple in the Bronco. Zoe turned toward the gate, too fast, making her skirts whirl, damn it, and sighed a precautionary sigh at the little motor that lifted the barrier.

"What?" Jan whispered.

"Insurance. Let's get in the bus, Jan." For under the floppy white canvas hats, it was the tourists from Odessa who sat in the Escort, sweating in the afternoon heat and staring at the back of the bus without moving a muscle.

Jan reluctantly followed her into the bus, trailed by Balthazar.

Croyd stepped outside the shed door in the middle of a conversation, waving both arms and chattering rapid-fire Turkish. He stopped in midsentence as the barrier lifted and Balthazar rolled the bus forward. Croyd ran for the step and swung inside as they passed the barrier.

Croyd stuck his arm out the window and waved goodbye. One of the guards waved back and then stopped. His attention seemed to be diverted by the sight of the barrier, which lifted and sank, lifted and sank again and again, faster and faster, while the old, blue bus chugged into Syria.

"What the hell did you do that for?" Croyd asked.

"The tourists," Zoe said. Her teeth were chattering. "From Odessa. Didn't you see them?"

"The Odessa Ovoids? No. I didn't see them."

"They pulled up behind us," Balthazar said. "Now y'all hold on, hear? I think we're going to do a little evasive maneuvering about now."

"Read it back to me," Jay Ackroyd said. "I want to make sure you got it right."

"I got it, I got it, I just don't understand it," Peter Pann complained. The overseas connection made his voice sound even smaller and thinner than it did in person. "*KNAVES OF HEARTS*," he read. "That part is all in caps. *Sharks schooling in Asian waters. Fishing should be OK,* and you want just the letters *O* and *K*, not *o-k-a-y. Meet Peninsula Hotel, Hong Kong, asap, or we're all Librarians.* Signed *Your Stud Buddy Finger*."

"That's it," Jay said. "Have them box off the ad so it stands out more. If they can, I want it bordered with suit symbols, you know, hearts, spades, clubs. Heavy on the hearts."

"I always knew you were a romantic. How long do you

want this to run?" Peter's voice was faint and faraway. It was still night back in New York, and he sounded sleepy.

"Three weeks," Jay said. "After that, it won't make any difference. I want it running in *The Washington Post, The New York Times,* the *Jokertown Cry,* the *International Herald Tribune, The Times* and *The Guardian* in England, *USA Today,* the *Los Angeles Tribune,* and any other papers you can think of. Oh, and some magazines. *Soldier of Fortune, Rolling Stone,* and *Variety.*"

"I'll be on it first thing in the morning."

"Be on it right now. It's already morning in some of the places we need to reach. How's Topper doing?"

"They're still holding her out at Governors. I've been keeping an eye on her with a tink. Her old friend Straight Arrow paid her a visit. They yelled at each other some, but when he left he didn't know anything he didn't already know when he arrived."

"Remind me to give Melissa a raise," Jay said.

"Screw Melissa, give *me* a raise," Peter came back. "I never understood why Topper needs a salary anyway. She can reach into that hat and pull out doubloons, silver certificates, bearer bonds, the Hope Diamond, anything her little heart desires. Why work?"

"Damned if I know," Jay admitted. He said his goodbyes, hung up, and checked the coin return for loose money. No such luck. It wasn't his day.

He had stashed the rest of his crack investigative team at a Pizza Hut down the street. He walked back with his hands in his pockets, stopping just long enough to buy Sascha a new pair of shades from a street vendor.

An elderly Aborigine was standing outside the door to the Pizza Hut, rocking on his feet and wearing Eric Fleming's clothes. He was tall and very black, with white hair and wrinkled skin and sad eyes that saw deep into the vanished dream-time. "How's Peter?" he asked as Jay opened the door.

"He said to tell you that he's really enjoying your wine cellar," Jay replied. He went inside. Jerry hurried after. Sascha was in a booth, scarfing down what remained of a large anchovy and green pepper pizza while Finn grazed at the salad bar; the booths were not designed to accommodate centaurs. Every eye in the restaurant was on the two jokers.

Jay slid in across from Sascha and flipped him the sunglasses.

"What's the plan?" Sascha asked, as he put on the glasses over the blank space where his eyes should have been.

Finn clomped up to listen, his rear blocking the aisle between the booths. Jerry was looking at Jay intently. Jay had a headache. His nose was throbbing, the world was about to end, and he was trapped in a Pizza Hut with Larry, Moe, and Mister Ed.

"We know that the Sharks started with three flasks of Clara van Rensselaer's original cultures," Jay said carefully. "Brandon claims that Rudo divided them up. One for him, one for General MacArthur Johnson, one for that spook bastard Casaday."

Jerry heard the venom in his voice when he said that last name. "You sound like you know Casaday."

"Our paths have crossed," Jay admitted. "I only saw him twice, but I remember him real good. He set me up to die. Things like that stick in your memory. Question is, is Casaday a rogue or is the whole fucking CIA compromised? Call me paranoid, but I think the best policy right now is we trust nobody except other wild cards, and I'm not so thrilled about them." Jay scratched his bandage. "This is where we split up."

Sascha and Jerry nodded gravely in unison. Finn said, "Is this another one of your fabulous plans, Ackroyd?" He was in a terrible mood for a guy who had just avoided being eaten by sharks.

"Afraid so," Jay admitted. "So long as we stay together like a giant charm bracelet, we're a little fucking conspicuous." He gestured. "Look around you. These people are all trying so hard not to stare at us that their eyes are crossed."

Jerry turned his head and looked around, nodding.

Sascha's shades stared right at Jay. "I'm seeing Vietnam in your thoughts. Some bar in Saigon."

"Rick's Cafe Americaine," Jay told the telepath. "An old hangout of the Joker Brigade. I spent some time in Saigon after the war, looking for a Joker MIA. Never found him, but I got to know Rick's pretty good. That's where you and Jerry should start. Brandon said Casaday is the CIA sector chief for Nam. If we have half a prayer of picking up his trail, it's going to be there."

Jerry's head whipped back around. "There's a *war* going on in Free Vietnam. Don't you read the papers? They started having coups and countercoups and purges five minutes after Mark Meadows died."

"You bet they did," Jay said. "And that smells of Casaday all the way. Saigon is full of jokers. You two will blend right in. Just keep asking questions. They won't talk, but Sascha can pull the answers out of their minds. Ask about Meadows, too."

"Meadows?" Jerry said. "Why? Do you think Casaday had something to do with his death?"

"Just ask, okay? And if you find out anything about anybody, phone Peter and wait until you hear from me."

His junior partner nodded. "I used to do a great Charlie Chan. What do you think, Warner Oland or Sidney Toler?" He snapped his fingers. "No, Peter Lorre as Mr. Moto, he was great!"

Jay said, "Here's an idea. Try a *real* Asian."

"I need a mirror," Jerry said. He sprang up out of the booth and dashed off to the men's room.

Jay sighed. In the silence that followed, Finn asked quietly, "Where am I going?"

Jay almost said *Takis*, but thought better of it. They'd all agreed not to lay that on him just yet. "Home," he said instead. "At least Sascha can slip into a pair of sunglasses. No offense, Doctor, but you stand out like a horse's ass."

"I know what I look like," Finn said stiffly. "I don't care. I'm in this thing to the end."

"This is the end, so far as you're concerned."

"Do I have to remind you that it's my dad's plane at the airport?" Finn said, like a kid saying *It's my football, I get to play quarterback if I say so.* "Nobody's going anywhere without me."

Jay just shook his head. "We don't dare go back to the Learjet. Fleming's people know about it by now. Doc, you've done everything you can, but right now you're more of a liability than an asset."

"You think you're going to find the Black Trump without me?" Finn challenged. "You could be in the same *room* with it and you wouldn't know what to look for. The three of you don't know a retrovirus from a retrorocket. You think Rudo is going to have the stuff in a big drum with BLACK TRUMP stenciled on the side? Maybe a foaming beaker with a skull and crossbones on it?" The centaur's blond tail was lashing back and forth in anger. "And what do you plan to *do* with it when you find it? Flush it down the toilet?"

Jay had started to shape his hand into a gun to pop Finn back to the safety of Jerry's wine cellar, but now he hesitated.

"There's nothing for me in New York," Finn went on. "If I show my face at the clinic they'll just pick me up again. I can't work or walk the streets or go home. What do you expect me to do, sit around Creighton's watching CNN until I hear that the Black Trump's been released? Fuck that, Ackroyd. You pop me back to New York and I go straight to the authorities. I have a lovely singing voice."

Jay lowered his finger and sighed. "You win. I'm going to Hong Kong. You'll go with me. We'll disguise you somehow. Glasses, maybe. I don't know."

The door to the men's room opened. An old, thin, stooped Vietnamese man came out wearing Eric Fleming's clothes, walked over to the booth, and sat down. "How's this?" he asked.

Jay Ackroyd looked him over. "Ho Chi Minh visits Ho Chi Minh City. Swell. That ought to make *all* the newspapers. Of course, they may wonder why you can't speak Vietnamese . . ."

A mud-walled town, narrow streets, a mosque, stands of fig trees in irrigated fields, a boy herding three goats and four younger siblings, all moving by so fast that they seemed frozen in stop-motion. Four fat geese and a sharp turn around a windowless shade. A steep traverse into a wadi, and a climb back up the other side, fat tires crunching over boulders the size of a child's head. They topped the wadi and came out on a flat plateau, no shelter, no stands of trees, hours of daylight left. The long silver snake of a pipeline led southeast. A road, or at least a well-tended track, ran beside it. Balthazar put the pedal down, and they lumbered toward Damascus at a hearty fifty miles an hour, the bus swaying on its strange suspension and the doves cooing startled protests.

"Eee-hah!" Croyd yelled. "I like this!"

"Don't mind it myself," Balthazar said.

Zoe unfolded her new kilim to tuck over her lap. They reached the Euphrates again and went south along its banks for half the night.

The campsite was a stand of date palms, their fronds rustling in the night wind. The camp was below the roadway, near the level of the river, but the bus couldn't be seen from the road, and a little ridge gave a good view to the east. Zoe helped Balthazar set up the tent, then set his sleeping bag outside.

When she was done, she spotted Croyd pacing the ridge about a hundred yards from the camp. Instead of joining Jan in the tent, she grabbed her sleeping bag and went to intercept him. They sat for a long while, watching the river, the trees, the broken little hills. The stars were very bright.

Croyd talked. He got up at times and paced back and forth, and he never stopped talking.

"Algebra," he said. "Zoe, do you know these people invented algebra?" He waved his hand at the empty landscape. "They even invented the zero. Can you imagine inventing a zero?"

Zoe shook her head, realized Croyd couldn't see the motion because she was sitting by the brazier with her sleeping bag pulled up over her head. "No," she said, a garbled no that was mixed with a yawn.

"Do you think they're lying about Rudo?"

"I don't know. I think the Fists would lie if they thought they needed to."

"That's no answer."

"There's a bomb in the pump. They aren't lying about that."

"How do you know?"

"I can sense molecular structures, Croyd. There's a big heavy dose of fissionable stuff in there. Really."

"Then maybe they'll get Rudo for me. I have to believe that, I guess. Or I could just go to sleep somewhere and try to get back to New York."

"I wouldn't go back," Zoe said. "No way." She yawned again.

"You're tired. Rest. Sleep. I'll be quiet." Croyd fiddled with the last of the coals in the brazier and didn't say anything for a while. Zoe drifted into half-sleep, dreaming of Spanish dancers with castanets. They whirled around and around, and under the black lace of their mantillas their faces were white bone—

"Zoe?" Croyd whispered, his lips close to her ear.

The castanets were palm fronds, clicking in the night's wind. She jumped. "Guess I was drowsing," Zoe said.

Croyd kissed her. It was a hungry kiss, a speedy kiss. It roused her to total alertness. She got her sleeping bag unzipped with one hand and pulled Croyd in with her. It was a single bag. They were a tight fit. She wondered if Croyd had waked Balthazar to stand watch, but the thought wasn't a high priority at the moment. She tried rolling on top. That was fun. The knot on the waist of her trousers was proving difficult, and she giggled, trying to keep her voice quiet.

A bright, orange blossom flared behind the date palms. The shot struck the bus, a sound so loud it was a white gap in her ears. She heard a zinging ricochet.

Croyd's foot kicked at her shoulder as he backed out of the sleeping bag at near-light speed. Zoe embraced the sand beneath her and found she was worming her way toward the tent, flat on her belly.

Had they hit the bomb?

It wouldn't blow up. The Permissive Action circuitry was coming to Jerusalem in a different package, or so Snailfoot had told them. Even if you shot through the metal casing around the damned thing, or cracked it open, all that would happen would be that a few pounds of fissionables would get scattered around.

I'm glad Snailfoot told me that, Zoe thought. Another shot slammed into the bus, this one from the little ridge where she and Croyd had kept watch for a time.

The optical ghost of the first shot hung in front of her eyes, a bright, orange blur that wouldn't blink away. Through it, she saw a man behind a palm tree, a white blur of headdress bent toward the sights of a rifle, aiming across her toward the bus. Sand. Glass. Kill him. Zoe blew at the sand beside her face. It rose, a dust devil made of tiny needles, and whirled toward the rifle barrel.

She heard the diesel grind over. And stop.

"Zoe!" Jan yelled. Zoe rolled and saw Jan in the door of the bus, crouched over a rifle. "This way! Run!"

The diesel coughed again. Jan's gun staccatoed a cluster of shots toward the ridge. A rifleman fell, his cloak deflating around him like a struck tent.

"Shit!" Croyd yelled. "I almost had him!" He was halfway up the ridge, naked, and he fell backward—hurt? No, rolling down the sand of the ridge faster than a man could run. He got his legs under him at the bottom of the slope and scuttled toward the bus.

The starter ground and the diesel coughed and died.

"Get it going, Balthazar!" Croyd yelled. "There's headlights coming! There's more of them!" Croyd leapt the steps and crashed into his seat. "Who were they? Who? Start this bus, man!"

"Shut up! I'm trying!" Balthazar yelled over the whine of the starter.

The engine turned over. Over. It chugged into life. The fat wheels ground sand and crested the ridge.

The world began to move with desperate slowness. From the north, a pair of low headlights came inevitably forward. The biggest, shiniest lorry in the world was headed into the car's path, just *there* all of a sudden, and silent as death. *Its soundtrack is missing*, Zoe thought, but then engine noise blasted her ears, the roar of a huge motor and a wail of abused tires as the lorry twisted off the road, its headlights broadsiding the bus that Balthazar was frantically trying to aim toward some invisible space that would let him miss both the lorry and the car. The lorry fishtailed and skidded over the ridge toward the river, its horns bellowing. Date palms snapped like toothpicks. Balthazar braked the bus to a stop. He threw himself out the door on some mission Zoe couldn't understand, following Croyd. A couple of white-robed men scrambled away from the lorry's path, robes aflutter and rifles blasting every which way. The big truck's cab tipped at the edge of the bank. It balanced and rocked back and forth. The trailer slewed sideways and rolled into the river. In slow motion, it pulled the cab down with it. Jan, seeming utterly calm, sighted on one gunman, pulled the trigger, and swept her sights to the other. "Squeeze. Don't pull," she whispered to herself, and the second rifleman went down. Croyd, still naked, scrambled toward the riverbank, and a brown Ford Bronco pulled off the road and cautiously followed the lorry's path through the trees. The car stopped and two people got out.

Zoe wasn't sure how she got there, but she found she was standing on the bank, watching in total amazement as Ms. Odessa removed her floppy hat and her camera, pulled off her skirt, and made a perfect shallow dive into the river. Mr. Odessa pulled a spare tire out of the Ford and tied it to a length of rope. He whirled it over his head and sailed it into the water.

"Mother will get him out," Mr. Odessa said, while a man's voice yelled, "Put me down." Splutter. "Let go! Bloody hell!"

"Hush!" Ms. Odessa said. "Quit fighting me or I'll be forced to strike you. Silly fellow anyway, showing up in the middle of the road like that. I should let you drown!"

"That's all of them," Croyd said, jogging past. He'd grabbed his pants en route, and he held them in one fist. He had a rifle in the other. Where had the guns been hidden? Zoe didn't really want to know.

Mr. Odessa was reeling in the tire and the pair who clutched it. He grunted, and Zoe grabbed the rope and helped him pull.

"Here you go. We're on solid ground now." Ms. Odessa crouched down and tucked her hands under the armpits of a stocky man in a streaming wet windbreaker and a soggy cap that dripped water over his face. She heaved. The man got to his feet. He coughed and climbed up to the pod of light made by the Bronco's headlights. He had a stogie in his mouth, utterly limp. The man blinked at his rescuers, at the guns that Croyd and Jan held. He turned, looked at the overturned lorry, and threw his soaked black cigar away.

Ms. Odessa climbed into her clothes while Mr. Odessa stowed the tire and the carefully coiled rope in the Bronco. "Well, Mother," he said. "I think we should be on our way. I'm sorry about your truck, young man, but I'm sure these folks will give you a ride."

The lorry driver nodded, looking dazed. Young man? He was forty, at least.

Ms. Odessa fastened the waistband of her skirt and climbed into the Bronco. It backed away.

Mr. Odessa's voice came from the open window. "They'll never believe this in Omaha," he said.

"That fellow isn't a very careful driver," Ms. Odessa said.

The Bronco paused at the edge of the deserted road, signaled a right turn, and drove into the night.

"Bloody hell," the lorry driver said. "Oh, bloody hell." He pulled his soggy Andy Capp hat off, wrung it out, and settled it firmly over his bald spot. "There's no way to get my rig out of the water. There's a roadblock about twenty miles down the road. Some bloke told the Syrians you're carrying a bloody load of heroin in this bloody bus of yours. Now those ruddy do-gooder Yanks will tell them where you are. Oh, bloody hell!"

The man began to trot uphill toward the bus, his boots squishing with every step. "I had a proper winch in the rig. Could have lifted your little item out and stowed it in no time. 'A simple little job,' those bastards said. 'Just go load this hot pump these blokes are carrying and bring it to Jerusalem,' that's what they said."

Zoe followed him, Jan behind her with her rifle. On the ground, beneath broken palm fronds, Zoe saw an array of white bones, a skeletal hand still clutching the stock of a rifle. Its barrel was polished away. So was the arm that had held it. Zoe shuddered and kept going, watching the silent countryside, the empty road.

"Bloody Pakis, shooting up the countryside; bloody Yank tourists out where they shouldn't be," the lorry driver muttered.

Balthazar stood on the bus steps, holding a bulky gun. The lorry driver strode toward the nose of the old Bluebird. Croyd intercepted him, suddenly in position between the man and the bumper. Croyd wove a net in the air with his arms, dancing barefoot like an NBA guard. "Who the hell are you?" Croyd asked.

"John Bruckner. The Highwayman. Put your pants on, whoever the hell *you* are, and open the bonnet so I can see what I'm stuck with driving!" Bruckner shoved Croyd aside.

"I have a gun," Croyd said.

"Yes, but do you have a torch? In case you haven't figured it out, mate, this bloke called the Hound of Hell sent me to get you into Jerusalem. Now, we're not moving until I look at this effing rig of yours, and if we don't move in about five minutes flat, your little tea party is over."

"Torch?" Croyd asked.

"He needs a light," Jan said.

"Do it, Jan!" Balthazar called from the steps of the bus.

Jan flashed her eyes over the "bonnet." Croyd lifted it. The Highwayman examined the engine, his thick hands intimate with hoses and seals. He grunted something, climbed down off the bumper, and slid underneath the bus on his back. Jan followed him. Zoe, dazed, watched the glow from Jan's eyes move toward the rear end of the bus until Bruckner and Jan climbed out from under.

"Well, close her up!" Bruckner barked in Croyd's direction. The stocky man climbed up on the fender, reached for the high end of the exhaust pipe, and passed his fingers across it. He sniffed his fingers and licked them and then climbed down, shaking his head and muttering.

"It will have to do," Bruckner said. "I suppose I can't leave you. Not quite the decent thing, the nobs would say. But I won't have anyone in front with me, d'ye hear? Get your asses aboard. We're rolling."

"Balthazar?" Croyd asked. "Can we trust this guy?"

"He'll get us there if anyone can." Balthazar climbed over the driver's seat and pulled Jan up after him. "Get in, Croyd. Zoe. Just don't look out the window, or if you do, ignore what you see."

The engine caught at the first touch of the starter. It had never sounded quite like it did now. It purred. Zoe pushed Croyd into one of the too-small bench seats and climbed in beside him. She pulled her kilim out of his way and stuffed it behind the seat.

"Headquarters said they couldn't get you here. They said there was some sort of trouble in Ireland," Balthazar said.

"There's always trouble in Ireland." Bruckner babied the bus out to the road. The gleaming silver of the Euphrates rippled past. The Highwayman nursed the diesel toward speeds that seemed impossible. "It's time for a little 'shortcut' now," Bruckner said.

"Croyd?" Balthazar asked. "Why don't you put the gun down and put your pants on? Okay?"

Gregg had often replayed deaths in his mind before, mostly for the pleasure the memories would bring him. But never before had death stalked him, never had it sunk iron talons in his soul and torn him open inside.

Gregg would have cried, but his joker body had no tears. One of the voices inside would have cried with him, but the other . . . The other would have laughed.

For three days after the murders in Belfast, the Fists had holed up in an abandoned mine in the Wicklow Hills, far to the south, near Dublin. The property belonged to a nat whose son, a joker, had died in the riots of '78. The land was gorgeous, hills painted with emerald and jade and perfect cottages of pristine white, like a picture postcard.

And the landscape was haunted. Gregg stood under the eaves of a stand of oak trees, on a hill overlooking a sheep-gnawed pasture and the owner's cottage, but he saw none of it. Another, more visceral, scene filled his vision.

"Oh, God," Gregg breathed. "God."

"Mummy, I'm scared." The child was crying, but then Gregg was no longer standing there before the row of frightened nats. Instead, Gregg was the child huddled against the breast of his mother, and Cara aimed her weapon at him. He tried to reach her with Puppetman, tried to use the power, the Gift, to make her turn away, but Puppetman was locked away somewhere hidden and the Gift was silent, though Puppetman's faint evil voice laughed and mocked Gregg. He pulled away from his mother and tried to run, but his joker body

refused to cooperate. He screamed as the cold steel muzzle pressed against his head, a scream that was echoed from elsewhere in the dining room as Stand-in fired and Gregg waited for his own death to come. He looked up at Cara, ready to plead for his life, but other features rode the blank mirror of Cara's face, appearing one after another after another: Ellen, Sara Morgenstern, Peanut, Misha, Mackie Messer, Succubus, Andrea . . .

And he LOVED it. He felt their pain. He reveled in it, ate it like candy.

"Gregg? Gregg, I'm here . . ."

"Hush, love. They're not going to hurt us," his mother said, but the hands of all his old victims tore him away from her, and she screamed in terror. They were chuckling as they crowded around him, as they pressed the cold steel muzzle to his head, as he closed his eyes and wondered whether he would hear the sound of the shot, whether he would feel any of the pain, and whether the pain would taste good . . .

"Gregg . . ."

Hannah held him, and there was no shot. Slowly, the waking dream began to fade, and Gregg shuddered in her arms as she clutched him. "It's okay," she said. "You're remembering again?"

"Yes," he said. The warmth of her hands was almost painful. He could feel her fingers on his skin, could feel *beyond* them, into Hannah's body. As with the murders in Belfast, he could feel her, could sense her sympathy like a wave of cobalt blue, shot through with a pale white that was her revulsion and the primal scarlet of her caring, that allowed her to overcome that distaste. He could see the emotions, he could taste them, as he once had. *You have a connection . . .* Gregg continued to talk, but his mind was on the sudden merging.

"I killed them, Hannah," Gregg said desperately. *Touch the scarlet . . . See how it builds under your hands, Greggie? See? Tell her what she wants to hear and watch the reaction.* "I pointed at them and they killed them. I keep hearing the screams whenever I fall asleep, Hannah. I can't dream of anything else, and it even hits me when I'm awake. I keep trying to figure out what I could have done to stop it from happening, but I can't think of anything. I keep thinking I should have at least *tried*."

The scarlet surging. The pale white nearly gone. The blue so bright, so sweet . . .

"There was nothing you could do."

"Then why do the dreams keep *coming*?" *Tell her what she wants to hear . . .* "Hannah, I'm useless. Rudo destroyed me when he jumped me; he just didn't have the decency to actually kill me. I don't know what I can do, I don't know how to help, I feel totally useless and I'm just . . . just *scared*." *The red pulses with the word, awakening echoes in her. She knows fear, and the sharing of it makes her one with you. The white is gone, hidden. Yes . . .*

Hannah's arms went tight around him and Gregg relaxed into her embrace. Her skin was warm, deliciously fragrant. She didn't pull away, not this time. Inside her, Gregg would not let her. "I didn't want to do it, Hannah. I didn't have a choice." *Pulsing, rising. Oh, God, I can taste her . . .*

"I know." Softly. "I know. Gregg, you can't torture yourself this way. We did the wrong thing, going to the Fists. Maybe we could have gone public and forced the government to find Rudo and the vials. Now we're relying on a band of joker guerrillas. We've had a taste of the Black Dog's philosophy. They worship death, not life."

"Hannah, they're reacting as they see the world react to them. I think . . . I think I can understand how they feel." Gregg pulled his head back. Hannah was looking down, her dyed hair curtained around her cheeks and a curious expression on her face. She looked very different from the Hannah who had come into his office a year ago: thinner, no makeup, wearing dirty, worn overalls and a dingy T-shirt, her hair stringy and in need of a shampoo. Somehow, she'd never looked more attractive. He caught a glimmer of the revulsion from her again, and pulled a blanket of scarlet over it. It worked. Gloriously, it worked.

Gregg, is this what you want to become, once again? Are you sure . . .

"And you forgive them?" Hannah was asking.

Gregg paused. "I understand them," he answered as softly as the breeze across the meadow. "I don't know about forgiveness." *The things I could tell you about me,* Gregg thought *What would you think if I laid out all of my past for you? I wonder if you could understand them? Could you forgive me? I don't think so . . .*

He'd forgotten the ghosts of the restaurant, reveling in the pleasure of being inside Hannah's emotions. The pleasure had its physical response as well. He could feel the erection growing low on his body. Hannah noticed it also. Her hand, trembling, touched it, just for an instant. In that moment, the scarlet affection paled, and when Gregg tried to bring it back, tried to pull those strings, they snapped. He went tumbling back into himself.

Hannah was looking at him. She still held him, but her caress had gone empty and slack.

"Well, 'tis indeed a pleasant sight, this."

"Goddamn!" Hannah let go of Gregg entirely. "Brian, you're a son of a bitch, you know that?"

The joker gave Hannah a momentary, mocking smile, then his face fell into serious lines. "There's news you need to know. If you're not otherwise occupied."

"What news?" Gregg asked. The odd erection had vanished like a broken rubber band.

"Not here. I'll tell you back at the mine. Come on," Brian said.

The mine was shallow, a mere hole in the side of the hill. Ancient oaken trusses held up the earth; toward the rear, rock glistened where the vain effort to find a vein of fabled Irish gold had ended. Cara and Stand-in busied themselves around the fire in the back, from which the odor of stew wafted.

Brian was watching them when they entered. Hannah scowled at him. "So what's this news?" Gregg asked.

"Don't worry, caterpillar. It's important enough to warrant the interruption." All the sardonic amusement left the tiny joker's face, leaving behind a face emptied of all emotion. "A bulletin just came over the radio a few minutes ago: Churchill's been assassinated. The old man's dead."

"What happened?" Hannah asked. "How?"

"During a meeting with some American ace. The assassins were army officers; they're dead, of course. Horvath is promising a complete investigation."

Gregg stood there, shocked. Brian sniffed, as if in justification. "Churchill couldn't even protect himself," he said.

«A hell of a coincidence, don't you think?» Cara mentally piped in from the rear of the cave. «You two go to see Churchill about Horvath and your Black Trump, and now the man himself is shot to death.»

"Aye," Brian said, "I thought that, too."

Hannah leaned against the wall of the cave. Gregg could sense wild emotions coming from her: shock, grief, sadness, unfocused rage. "Horvath and Johnson must have felt threatened," she said. "That's the only thing that makes sense. Churchill did something that made them feel they were in danger of being exposed." Her voice caught, and Gregg felt the surging purple sorrow. "The poor man. He was so sure he couldn't be harmed . . ."

Churchill dead . . . It seemed that even an immortal could fall prey to a terrorist. Churchill's funeral would draw thousands upon thousands of mourners, and dignitaries from every country in the world would be there to pay homage . . .

Gregg could not breathe. The realization hit him like a hammer blow. *The funeral . . . Johnson . . .*

"It makes too much sense," Gregg said. "My God, it makes all the sense in the world."

"What?" Brian asked him.

Gregg could barely hold his body still. The whole world seemed to vibrate in his myopic eyes. "Brian, there's just been a change of itinerary. We have to get to England."

The lab was dark except for light pools beneath a few hooded lamps and pilot lights glowing like tiny demon eyes. Mark was working late. Again.

When he did retreat to his trailer, it wasn't so much to rest as to escape the lab, and especially the constant, hovering presence of Dr. Jarnavon. The youthful scientist had two modes: worshipful chatter and worshipful silence. After a few days, the second wore on him as much as the first.

It wasn't as if Mark was *sleeping* much. Whenever he closed his eyes he saw faces of the dead. People he'd gotten killed— Osprey going down with a bullet through his great eagle's head—but worse than that, all the wild cards he'd ever known: Doughboy, Peregrine, Jay Ackroyd. *The people I'm condemning to death.*

Nuances in the lab journal abraded him with the suspicion that the nameless researcher was a woman. He hoped that was just some kind of sexist stereotyping on his part, or stress-fueled imaginings: He preferred to think of women as gentle, nurturing. He knew better; he'd seen what Vietnamese village women did to secret-police agents of the former Communist regime who had caused some of their menfolk to disappear. But still . . . Mark chose to cherish some illusions.

Like the one that I'm a hero. That he could recapture the purity and glory of the Radical, the golden revolutionary ace into whom he had turned the first time he tried LSD, in time to save the Lizard King and the kids in People's Park from the National Guard and the Establishment ace, Hardhat. All his subsequent forays into chemically opened reaches of his own mind had sprung from the quest to bring Radical back; the "friends" he had learned to summon had been to his mind pale substitutes, ultimately unsatisfying.

If he really had *been* the Radical. He had long since begun to doubt it. He had a few vague tachistoscope flashes of recollection that might have belonged to the Radical—and might just as easily been cobbled together by his subconscious, out of the few flashes of the People's Park confrontation he'd caught before he reeled into an alley and passed out, and from after-the-fact accounts. Usually he had clear recollections of what his alter egos saw and experienced and thought, just as they were generally aware of what befell the baseline Mark persona.

And although he was denied them, his friends were making their presence felt. At least, JJ Flash and Cosmic Traveler did. Starshine and Moonchild were gone, possibly beyond recall. Aquarius took little notice of anything any landling did. But the remaining two weren't backward about nagging him from the cheap seats of his head.

As if his conscience needed the help. *How can I feel superior to whoever it was who created the Trump?* he wondered bitterly. *I'm making it deadlier . . . to my own kind.*

He had an excuse, of course: He was doing it to save his daughter. *And what demons drove the first researcher?* The printouts gave few clues. Obviously, whoever he or she was, they had compelling reasons, too.

A scrape behind him, lost soul or shoe sole. He spun and saw it was both.

"Dr. Meadows," Quasiman said.

His eyes looked clear. "You've got to help me," Mark said in a rush, trying to pack what he could into whatever window of lucidity the joker ace had. "Do you know what they're doing here?"

A pause that almost stopped Mark's heart, then a nod. "I've . . . been a lot of places, seen . . . a lot of things. I know."

He's still tracking, Mark thought, trying not let the flood of relief distract him, *as much as he ever does.*

"Will you help me?"

A nod.

"I need two things. First, you have to get Sprout out of here. Can you do that? Can you take her with you?"

Quasiman frowned, considering that. Mark dug his fingers into his thighs to keep from grabbing Quasiman and trying to shake loose a reply.

"Yes," Quasiman said. "It hurts. But . . . I can do it."

If he remembers, JJ Flash's voice said in Mark's mind. *He's on a whole 'nother plane than the rest of us, and it spends a lot of time in tailspins.*

"Another thing," Mark said. "I need drugs."

"Drugs?" Quasiman asked. His voice sounded dreamy.

"Drugs. Illegal drugs. Cocaine, speed, LSD, psilocybin— anything, stimulant, narcotic, hallucinogen, whatever. If it's psychoactive, I can use it. Can you get me some?"

Quasiman nodded.

"Please, man. Bring them as quick as you can. A whole lot's riding on this!" He was on his feet now, hands beseeching before his narrow chest.

Quasiman had continued nodding. It was beginning to take on a metronomic quality. "Sure, I'll help you," Quasiman said. "Or did I already?"

"Jesus! Listen to me. Focus, *please* focus! You have not rescued my daughter. You have not brought me drugs. You still have to *do* those things—"

Quasiman's face went slack. A drop of saliva welled over a loose lower lip and ran down his chin. He smiled beatifically. "Glad I could help, Doctor," he said. "If you need anything else—"

He vanished. "Wait!" Mark shouted. "Oh, holy Christ! Wait!"

"Wait for what?" a voice said. "Who are you talking to, Doctor?"

Mark jumped. Jarnavon had come into the lab and was walking right toward him. He felt sweat enfold him like clammy Saran wrap.

Jarnavon walked up crisply, swiveling his head left and right. Green and yellow and red pilot lights danced across the lenses of his horn-rims.

"Hm," he said. "I thought you might be calling to a technician, but I don't see anybody."

He reached up to tip the glasses forward on his nose. "Who were you calling, Doctor?"

Mark collapsed into the swivel chair, feeling like a wrung-out bar rag. "Ghosts," he said.

"Ghosts?" Jarnavon tittered. "Whose ghosts?"

"All the people you want me to murder."

Nothing about the *Mae Lang* particularly recommended the ship, except for the fact that she was owned and captained by one Paddy O'Neal, whose daughter, Gregg learned, was

Cara, the mouthless joker. If Captain O'Neal knew that Cara and her joker friends were Twisted Fists, he gave no indication of it. There were jokers among his crew, and O'Neal treated them no differently than any of the rest. Gregg and Hannah were given a cabin together. Brian had smirked as he'd told them; Hannah shrugged, but she'd also made certain that she and Gregg had no time together, that they were always with someone else. Gregg and Hannah had explored what little there was of the freighter in the first day of the passage. As a cruise ship, the *Mae Lang* was a miserable failure, but Hannah had feigned interest in everything. When they'd finally come back to the cabin, late that night, she'd immediately said how exhausted she was and had fallen asleep in her clothes.

Because you're ugly. Because you're a worm and she's a nat . . .

The voice had laughed all through his dreams.

Hannah wasn't in the cabin when Gregg woke up. For a minute, he lay there, curled up like a cat in the scratchy woolen coverlet at the foot of the bed, taking in the slow roll of the cabin and the briny smell of the sea. Gregg wasn't sure what time it was: early morning, by the slanting, swaying wedge of sunlight drifting across the room. He could see someone standing near the porthole, but his vision seemed worse than normal—he couldn't tell who it was.

"Hannah?" he called softly.

"No," answered a voice that Gregg recognized all too well.

"Quasi," he said. "You show up in the strangest places. What are you doing here?"

"Shopping," the hunchback said.

"Great place for it." Gregg wriggled and stretched, then let his long body droop to the floor of the cabin until he was standing on his lower pair of legs. The rest of him followed, and he paddled over to the hunchback. Gregg looked up at the hunchback, who was staring vacantly into space. "Quasi?" Gregg called again, louder. "Hey, Quasi!"

Quasiman blinked. Otherwise, there was no reaction. His right leg disappeared, and he toppled over as stiff as a marionette, leaning at an angle against the cabin wall.

"Great," Gregg muttered. "Hannah's gone, and Quasi's stuck in neutral." Gregg went over to the door. Hannah hadn't latched it—it opened. As he started out, he heard a *pop* behind him. When he looked back, Quasiman was gone.

The narrow corridor smelled of the cattle crowded into the decks below. Rust bled through most of the riveted seams of the wall, staining white paint gone yellow with age. At the end of the corridor a grimy window in another door showed the bobbing gray sea horizon. Gregg went through it.

Cold wind damp with salt spray hit his clown nose, fragrant with decay and cow dung. The decking was wet and slippery. A steel railing drooped rusty chains along the flank of the ship's superstructure, blurred in Gregg's vision. Gregg sniffed, smelled nothing out of the ordinary. He went right.

Gregg heard the voices before he turned the corner around the stern: Hannah and Brian. Gregg wasn't sure what made him stop there, the words or the harsh tone of Hannah's voice.

". . . back off. Now."

"Now, lass, I saw you with the caterpillar. I can't be less a man than *that.*"

Brian. For a moment, Gregg thought the man's voice sounded like that of Puppetman, oily and sinister in Gregg's head, and a queasy and strangely *jealous* fright settled deep in him. Gregg didn't wait to hear more. He came around the corner to see a blurred Brian pressed close to Hannah, his head no higher than her waist. Brian saw Gregg at the same time—the joker turned toward the intrusion. "Hey—" Gregg began, raising up on his hind legs.

Brian kicked him.

The blow, entirely unexpected, came from an out-of-focus left field. Gregg felt the world snap into slow motion around him as his body jolted backward into overdrive. Six legs pumped wildly and out of control. Gregg went skidding madly up the side of the ship, careened upside down across the metallic overhang and back down one of the supports. Fighting for control, he skittered along the rail like an insane tightrope walker on speed, balanced precariously on the edge of a drop into the rolling, greasy waves of the sea below. He shot past Hannah and Brian ("Mother of God! I've never seen the like of that . . .") and slammed headlong into the next roof support. That dropped Gregg back onto the deck and redoubled his speed. He shot past the two going the other way, bounced off the low bar of the railing, and bulleted along the walkway like a ball down a pinball chute. He hit another support near the forward turn and went tumbling down a set of metal stairs to the deck. He felt none of it; the body simply kept moving, the legs flailing.

He passed Captain O'Neal, out on morning inspection, somewhere on the forward lower deck. The man watched Gregg with wary eyes as he slid into the greasy anchor chain and reversed direction, finally starting to gain some control over his wild retreat. "Do you exercise like this every morning, man?"

Gregg didn't answer. Furious with himself, he turned in the direction of the stairs and headed back toward Hannah. By the time he reached the stern again, he had slowed to normal.

He could also hear Brian screaming.

"Let me go, you crazy woman! Are you insane?" Gregg squinted. Hannah was holding Brian out beyond the railing by the front of his shirt, high above the foaming wake of the *Mae*

Lang, his jacket half off. His legs kicked wildly, and even in Gregg's nearsighted vision, he could see the red veins popping in Brian's emerald face. "Damn you, woman!"

Hannah's anger arced like fire in his head. He could taste it, rich and sweet, and he could also sense the control she had of it, iron wrapping the flames. "You want me to let go, Brian?" Hannah asked all too sweetly. "No problem . . ."

"No!" Brian shrieked, and his fingers dug into Hannah's forearms. "Blood of Christ, bring me in! Bring me in! I can't swim!"

You could take away that control. You could stoke the flames so they melt the iron . . .

"You're going to leave me alone? You're going to behave?"

"Woman . . ."

"Swear it," Hannah said. The wind threw salt spray into Brian's face; the joker sputtered.

Do it now, hissed the voice. *Do it now. She hates the man, hates everything he stands for. It would be so easy, and his death would taste good. And afterward, her guilt for dessert . . .*

"I swear," Brian shouted. "I'll leave you be. Just put me down."

Do it!

No! Gregg shouted back. *I won't listen to you. I don't know you.*

Oh, you know me, Greggie. You could even give me a name, if you weren't so afraid.

No! Gregg forced the voice out of his mind. He sagged, and his link with Hannah suddenly dissolved. He could feel nothing from her; he was only watching.

"All right," Hannah was saying to Brian. She brought the joker back over the railing and set him on the deck. Brian shrugged his jacket back around his shoulders. He glared at

Hannah, at Gregg, watching them. Gregg thought the man was going to say something, but the look on Hannah's face seemed to stop him.

Brian brushed at his shirt where Hannah's fingers had wrinkled it and stalked silently away.

"I guess he wasn't in the mood for a dip," Hannah said. Gregg looked away from Brian's retreat to see Hannah gazing at him. He dropped his gaze.

"Yeah. I noticed," Gregg said, and the exhaustion in his voice surprised him. The adrenaline high was gone, and what energy he had left had gone in the mental battle. The bland, ugly grayness of the morning matched his thoughts.

"Gregg? What's the matter?"

"I'm . . ." *I'm haunted. I'm visited by the ghosts of dead things.* Gregg groped for words, trying to define the boundaries of his feelings. "I used to know what I was there for, what I could do." *Yes, and look at what you did with those powers . . .* It was the softer voice this time. "At least, I thought so. But now . . ."

"Gregg," Hannah said softly, crouching down beside him so that he could see her face, sharply focused against the blurred background of the frothing sea. "You wanted to be my knight in white armor just now? Is that it?"

"No. Well, maybe." Gregg sniffed a loud liquid sound from the clown nose. "If you had needed me, I'd've been a hell of a lot of help, wouldn't I?"

I could have helped. From deep inside. Bitter.

Hannah smiled, and he hated the gentleness of it. "I don't know. You were quite a distraction, actually."

"Hannah—"

"I'm sorry," she said. The smile faded on her lips. "Gregg, I . . . I've always believed that things happen for a purpose. There was a reason I was dragged into this with the church fire; there was a reason that we found out about the Sharks before they could finish the Trump. And there's a reason why you're still alive."

There's a reason why the old power is returning. But Gregg, you have to control it this time. You can't listen to it. You have to be the one in charge . . .

"Even as a joker?" Gregg asked, and he wasn't sure whether he was talking to Hannah or the voice.

"Even as a joker," Hannah answered quietly. Her hand started toward him, hesitated, and finally brushed along his long spine. "You're *alive*, Gregg. You could just as easily be dead. From what you've told me, you should be. And there's a reason. I know it."

"I wish I did," Gregg told her. "I really wish I did."

Mark fanned the STM pictures on the black tabletop like a hand of cards. Dr. Carter Jarnavon leaned over his shoulder to peer at them. The smell of his hair cream was like fingers poking up Mark's nostrils.

Mark had a single straw to cling to, to keep his sense of self afloat. *If only this jerk doesn't see it.*

"We're making progress," he said, tasting bile at the back of his throat. "Cobbling together the BT virus without the transposon is reducing the DNA recombination rate, just the way the lab notes say."

Jarnavon bent close to peer at the images. Mark felt sweat bead along his hairline. "And how are the cultures doing? Is this really leading to more viable strains?"

Mark struggled. "Sometimes." He tapped a computer screen aglow with tables. "Some variants survive as long as seven generations. But it's, like, a crapshoot, man. They're more likely to die out after one or two, or even fail to reproduce; the *average* is two generations. Which isn't what you're looking for."

"No," Jarnavon said, shaking his head gravely. "Mr. Casaday wants no limits at all."

Mark sighed and swiveled his chair to face him. Inside he was just a big bag of wet matted blackness. Since Quasiman's visit to the lab Mark had replayed the ace's parting words over in his mind daily. Hell; *hourly,* more like it, awake or asleep.

And every iteration drove another nail of certainty through his skull: *He's not* coming *back. He thinks he already* has, *thinks he's rescued Sprout, thinks he's brought the drugs so I can whistle up one of my friends and save the day.* By the time Quasiman got his jingle-jangle time-sense squared away, all the world's wild cards were likely to be just another odd historical interlude, like communism, but even briefer.

"Like I've told him," Mark said, not forgetting to whine, "he can just shoot me now, then. It's like the *nature* of this thing to be unstable. An average generation span of six, seven, maybe ten at the way outside is the best we can shoot for."

His lips twisted. "That should give him what he wants, anyway. After seven generations, the only wild cards left will be the ones isolated from the rest of humanity. Out on mountaintops and stuff." Like Fortunato. *Can he avenge us? Will he bother?*

"Or quarantined, of course," Jarnavon said. "As you will be, Doctor."

Mark turned away.

Jarnavon shook his head. Pungent cream slimed down his brief rusty-brown hair, but a cowlick poked stubbornly up in back.

"Doctor, Doctor," he said, "you're a good man. You want to do the right thing. That's one of the things I've always admired about you."

"I guess we admire those who are what we aren't," Mark said.

It was as if a shutter slammed shut before the youthful face, like a navy signal lamp. *You bloody* fool! Trav chimed from the back of Mark's skull. *Don't bait him! He can expose your whole mad scheme! I told you no good would come of this . . .*

The researcher recovered quickly, smiled. One of those hail-fellow-trying-to-be-one-of-the-guys smiles, as of a nerd who doesn't yet realize the reason all the jocks are laughing is that one of them has covertly set his shoestring on fire.

Mark had been there. Only *he* had moved on.

"Heh," Jarnavon said, "heh-heh." He shook his head. "Don't you *see*, Doctor? What we're—what *you're* doing here is right. It's for humanity."

He felt anger rise like lava inside him, fenced it behind his teeth. "Murdering all the jokers and aces in the world is for *humanity*?" he demanded. "Give me a break!"

Behind thick lenses Jarnavon's eyes glowed with apostolic fervor. "But it *is*. In a few generations most of the population of the Earth will be jokers—sad, twisted, tortured souls. Long before that the aces will have taken over. Nats will be nowhere; they'll be slaves, then cattle, and then extinct. I know *you're* not working toward that, Doctor, but overall it's inevitable. It's biology.

"I know what we're doing, what we're asking you to do, seems harsh. But it's necessary to save humanity—the nat majority. You used to be a hippie, Doctor. Remember that old slogan, *power to the people*?"

He raised a hand as if to give Mark a brotherly pat on the shoulder, caught the look in Mark's eye, dropped the hand back to his white-smocked side.

"Think of it," he said, "as the greatest good for the greatest number."

Mark turned away. He had no answer. He had believed that once, too. Experience had shown him with brutal clarity where such false compassion culminated: in long lines marching to the showers, lumps of pumice they had been told was soap clutched in their hands.

Squeaks and rustles as the younger man bobbed in his shiny black shoes. "Speaking just for myself, I'm pleased at the progress you're making. More than pleased—amazed. You really are a genius, Doctor."

Mark swallowed and shut his eyes.

"Mr. Casaday has high expectations," Jarnavon said. "But he also has a great grasp of the realities. I'm glad I'll be able to tell him you're making good progress."

He hesitated, dropped his voice to a near-conspiratorial murmur. "I'd hate to see him give your little girl to Layton or Ditmar, Doctor. Really I would."

Mark's shoulders knotted. For a few moments he listened to Jarnavon breathing heavily behind him, and then the *squeak-squeak-squeak* of the younger man walking away.

When the lab door closed he relaxed in a shuddering exhalation of breath.

Yes! he exulted silently. His pulse became thready with something like triumph. *He didn't more than* glance *at the imaging.* Although he doubted Jarnavon had the skill to read what was truly here, Mark had feared. Profoundly.

Because that was the unwitting favor the Trump creator had done Mark. Along with showing the way to turn the virus into an even greater evil, the unknown researcher had also provided the perfect camouflage for Mark's *other* project, which might save the wild cards—and, incidentally, Mark's vision of himself as a decent human being.

Because there was a way to beat the Black Trump: Overtrump it.

The pictures lying on the back rubberized tabletop showed a strain of the Trump paired to a highly infectious but generally mild flu—a simple process, basically a reprise of work already done. But this was a special species of Black Trump: a scorpion without its sting. To the body's immune system, it *looked* like the Trump.

But it was no more lethal than the common cold.

The Overtrump could be used to create a vaccine. Riskier but quicker would be to release it deliberately as a counter-infection, like fighting a forest blaze with a backfire.

It was an edge-hanging game Mark played. He dared not document his real work; he had to keep everything in his head and concoct a reasonable cover for his Overtrump development. That was just possible by carefully compartmentalizing the tasks he assigned the techs who actually ran the lab's advanced equipment; none of them knew enough to piece together what he was doing or had any reason to question it.

Of course, they might talk among themselves, and some bright boy—his helpers were exclusively male—might make a connection. Or Dr. Carter Jarnavon might have a brainstorm.

The worst danger was that Jarnavon's adulation for the older scientist might overcome his apparent natural laziness, lead him to go systematically over all Mark's work. He *did* know enough to spot that a number of Mark's experiments were apparently superfluous, and he could probably take it from there.

Keeping all the data in his brain, and covering it with reams of hardcopy counterfeit, made Mark's head hurt. The strain of his double game kept the hum of low-level stress constant in his ears. He fought ceaseless blinding headaches, could barely keep down food. He longed for the shelter offered by his old girlfriend Mary Jane, but that was denied him—his opium-growing hosts disapproved of smoking dope.

He even longed for that release that, except for a few weeks after Sprout was taken from him by a New York court, never had much appeal for him: to crawl into a bottle and hide. But while his captors didn't object to booze, and were more than willing to provide him with it—or anything he might ask for, except drugs or freedom—he didn't dare drink. He couldn't afford the mental fog—or the risk of lubricating his lips.

It was a desperate game, a three-cornered bet: his daughter, the wild cards, his own humanity. A slip could lose all three.

And he wasn't even sure the game could be won. Creating the Overtrump was nothing: Jarnavon could have done it. It was much easier than the stable Trump Casaday demanded.

But even if Mark made an Overtrump, he had no idea of what good it might be. In the unlikely event that Casaday failed to kill him as soon as his usefulness was done, the Card Sharks would certainly keep him under wraps until his gene-crafted horror had run its course. How he might release the Overtrump in time he had no clue.

Of course, if Quasiman suddenly gets his act together . . . Savagely he quelled the thought. Futile hope just distracted a mind in need of total focus. Thinking acid-edged thoughts about the only game in town, he began once more to leaf through his stack of images.

The bus was a mouse and the sphinx that loomed before them was a giant cat, a cat the size of a mountain. It watched the bus with blind eyes of crumbling sandstone. Bruckner rammed the old Bluebird straight between its paws. The creature opened its mouth and took them inside. The diesel roared into the wide desert that was the beast's belly, where red stars streaked across a limitless dome of black sky. The twisted starlight sleeted into the back of Zoe's neck in silent pulses or quantum outrage.

"Where are we?" Jan asked.

"On a shortcut," Bruckner said. "We're going from point A, where my truck landed in the sodding river, to point B. Point B is the last stretch of open road from Jordan into Jerusalem."

Croyd seemed calmer than he had been. His muscular tension had changed in subtle ways. The twitchy restlessness of sleep deprivation had been replaced by a purposeful alertness, a sort of myofibrillar hum. "It feels like that was good speed I took," he said. "High-octane speed." He stared out the window, where a row of solemn, massive bulls lumbered past, burdened with garlands of blood-red blossoms. "Good speed doesn't do this. Can these guys get in here, Bruckner?"

"Haven't yet," Bruckner said.

The blossoms opened to show hearts of glass needles. They exploded from the flowers like darts and chattered against the sides of the bus, but that was behind them now.

A blizzard of white salt drifted against the windows. The sweep of the windshield wipers ticked against the beating of Zoe's heart. Out on the endless plain, pyramids of quartz the size of pearls or mountains vanished and appeared, synchronized with her pulse. Not quartz; the pyramids were shiny handfuls of pills that Croyd held, counting out the varieties in a bemused and distant voice. "Black mollies, hexagons, sexamyls, spansules," chuckling as he counted them, but when Zoe looked at his hand it was empty.

"Did you see that statue?" Bruckner asked.

Zoe didn't see a statue. She saw kaleidoscope patterns of silver teeth, biting at the night. "That statue was a giant copy of my award that was. The Order of the Silver Helix," Bruckner said. "Di pinned the medal on me herself, she did after I trucked those chaps to the Falklands. Proudest day of me life, but it didn't cut the alimony payments by one whit, nor the ruddy child support. Child support. Never got it from my dad. Never knew who he was."

A black tornado of a djinn bowed at the waist to let Bruckner pass. Zoe felt something cold at her waist. A tendril of black smoke snaked through a bullet hole in the side of the bus. She yanked her headscarf off and stuffed it in the hole, forcing the djinn back into the void.

Terrible white heat filled the bus, brighter than the sun, hotter than ice, a nanosecond's light where motes of dust circled and one of them cried with Anne's voice. It was a whirlwind, and it sucked them all into its vortex, the dead man from Odessa, Jellyhead, whose soft skull made a tiny, sucking *pop* as it imploded, a lamb with milk-white fleece that turned its huge goat-eyes to Zoe with sad reproach and burst into flames.

Bruckner sent the bus into a screeching turn. Its tires wailed protest. "Behind us! Cover us, Goatboy!" he yelled.

Balthazar twisted toward the rear of the bus, the barrel of his rifle swinging over Jan's head to aim at something back there. "Nothing," Balthazar said. "I see nothing!"

"It was after us. Ohmigod. Spooks and devils and roads made of broken bones, I've never seen the like. Sit tight. I think we can dodge it."

"It?" Zoe asked.

"There are things out here that don't bear thinking about," Bruckner said. He floored the accelerator and locked his hands on the wheel, steering the lumbering bus through an unseen maze with small, measured motions of his hands and shoulders.

Don't think, he'd said. Zoe tried not to.

Between her and Croyd, a man's solid weight shifted the

springs of the seat. Hunchbacked, he smelled of Old Spice and sweat. His sad face seemed so kind.

"You're not Hannah."

"No," Zoe said. She couldn't hear herself speak and wondered if she spoke at all, or if she had entered a dream space where speech was impossible. Her muteness gave her a sudden rush of hope that she might someday, somehow, wake.

"No," she said again. This time her voice was her own, harsh, loud. But the man was still there.

"You'd like Hannah. Everyone likes her." He patted Zoe's hand, his fingers warm and solid.

The man got up and leaned over Bruckner. "Do you have any drugs?"

"Hey, guv'nor!" Bruckner growled. "No hitchhikers now!"

"Sorry," the hunchback said. In moments, he had faded away.

There was nothing outside the bus but sand, endless dunes, and starlight. Zoe wrapped herself in her kilim. Croyd patted the seat of the bus with his palms, drumming out a complex rhythm. After a time, Zoe's heart slowed to something like a normal rhythm.

"I'm so tired." Jan sounded like a fretful toddler. "Needles, I'm hungry, too, but I've been on the street all day and I'm so *tired*. Let me stay. Please?"

Alabaster minarets grew before them, thick as nettles in a field, an impenetrable maze. They crawled through it forever, missing the delicate spires by millimeters, Bruckner cursing as he drove. Days? Months? The sun never rose.

The bus moved slower than the camel plodding along past the window. A square tent decorated with fringes made of shredded bank drafts sat atop the camel. A hand wearing no rings lifted the curtain of the tent. The warehouse manager from Odessa stared at Zoe, his eyes polished spheres of granite.

"Why did you come to Baghdad?" Balthazar asked in wondering tones. He stared at something out the windows on his side of the bus. "I was to meet you in Damascus."

Jan covered his eyes with her palms and crooned to him. Croyd had curled up into a ball, his head sheltered beneath his crossed arms. He chuckled to himself at times.

"Well, we're past Damascus," Bruckner said. "Damascus was those minarets and such like. We're outside Amman now."

They were braking to an intersection, a road cut into the scoured earth of Jordan, a dark night.

"Forty miles to go," Bruckner said. "You'd think the Holy Lands would be a bit *larger*, now wouldn't you?" He jerked the bus around a donkey carrying a cloth-wrapped bundle twice its size. "Ruddy beast should have headlights," Bruckner said.

"Did we make it?" Zoe asked.

"We aren't through the gates yet," Bruckner said.

"Is there another border?" Croyd uncurled and sat up. "I hate borders."

"Not a border. Just the Allenby Bridge," Balthazar said.

A sheikh in silks trotted by on a magnificent chestnut mare. Lean hounds loped beside him, sniffing at the road. A jeep cruised past carrying four soldiers in camo, guns at the ready. The soldiers waved and smiled. *Wherever we were*, Zoe thought, *we're still there*. Humans and beasts streamed up toward Jerusalem, coalescing into a thick stew of bodies and vehicles that crowded toward the Allenby Bridge, ready for morning and a day's business.

Bruckner eased the bus toward the checkpoint, a busy place where the UN flag hung limply over the crowds. He cranked open the window on the driver's side and leaned his head out. "We are residents," he said. "These people are, anyway. Me, mate, I'm a British subject loyal to the Queen, and I'm taking this besotted vehicle in to a *garage* for them. Breakdown, don't you know?"

Brisk, bored soldiers climbed aboard. The guns of the night had vanished somewhere. There was a rustle of papers, frowns, a thorough examination of baggage. One of the soldiers cooed at the dove cage. Jan smiled at her. The sun struck the yellow stones of the city walls and turned them to gold. Going home.

The guards waved them through. Zoe had even forgotten to be frightened, or her level of terror was now peaked at a maximum dull roar and nothing as minor as a bunch of soldiers peering at the pump could bother her anymore. She didn't know which. Her eyelids felt sanded and the bright morning hurt her skin.

Halfway across the bridge, Croyd leapt for the door of the bus. "That's him! Let me out! It's Rudo!" He slammed his elbow against the swivel doors on the bus and jumped out into the crowd.

"What's with that chap?" Bruckner asked.

Croyd dodged through the crowds, heading into the Jewish Quarter, his turbaned head bobbing up and down.

"Pharmaceutical psychosis," Zoe said. Just what we needed. "Let me out, Bruckner! I'll go hit him or something."

"Bring him back, Zoe," Balthazar said. "We have to stay with the bus."

"I know," she yelled, out the doors and trying to keep her eyes on the entrance to the alley where Croyd had disappeared.

Zoe fought her way around a flock of wooly lambs. She felt exposed suddenly, and realized her headscarf was still stuffed in the wall on the bus. No matter.

She jumped into a space in the center of a display of brass teapots, leapt again, and came down poised on one foot, got to the corner in two fast jogs, remembering games of hopscotch in front of the stoop and Bjorn laughing while she played.

Croyd sprinted toward a group of businessmen in dark suits, unremarkable except that all their calfskin attachés seemed to match. Croyd was half a block ahead of Zoe, and the alleyway was filled with awnings, vendors, and morning crowds. Zoe pushed her way toward him. Someone yelled. On tiptoe, she could see an eddy in the crowd, a wave of humanity moving out of the way. An orange peel sailed through the sky and landed on the green-and-white stripes of the awning beside her. Zoe pushed forward, shoving people out of the way. *Yes, Bjorn,* she told her dead father. *I'm being rude.*

Croyd lay stretched on his back, his eyes closed, his breathing deep and slow. A woman knelt beside him, dark hair, power suit in a gorgeous shade of spring green, calfskin attaché with a discreet UN insignia. She was feeling for Croyd's carotid pulse.

"What happened?" Zoe asked. "I'm his friend. What did you see?"

"He slipped on an orange peel. I didn't see him hit his head or anything like that; he fell on his—butt, to be clear about it. Then he just stretched out like this. He's breathing okay, but he doesn't respond to anything. I even slapped him. Gently."

How soon did Croyd start to change after he went into one of his sleeps? Zoe didn't know. She had to get him off the street before he began to metamorphose or whatever it was that he did.

"It's a—seizure disorder. He needs his medicine. Fast. I have to take him to it. Help me with him, would you?" Zoe knelt beside him, trying to figure if she could carry him by herself.

"You can't *move* him!" the woman protested.

But I have to, Zoe thought. She ran her hands down the back of Croyd's neck as if she knew what she was doing. "His neck's okay," Zoe said. "Really. It's safe, and I have to—cool him down. He gets hyperthermic when he's like this."

Sneakers, black cotton skirts, Jan's feet. Next to her, Balthazar stood with Zoe's kilim folded over his arm. Bruckner had inched the bus to the mouth of the alley and a blare of horns and curses announced that he'd stopped it there, traffic or no.

"With four of us, it should be easy to carry him," Balthazar said. He flipped the corners of the rug open and spread it on the street. Jan helped him roll Croyd over on it. "If you'll just take that corner, Miss—?"

"Davidson," the woman said. "Sheila Davidson."

"Miss Davidson. When I count three. One. Two." Sheila Davidson hooked the strap of her attaché over her shoulder and grabbed her corner of the rug. "Three," Balthazar said.

They hauled Croyd to the bus and laid him on one of the bench seats. He put his thumb in his mouth and curled into a fetal ball, smiling.

"He'll be fine," Balthazar said. "There's no need to stay. We'll take care of him."

"Well. I'm late for work as it is," Sheila Davidson said.

"Thank you," Balthazar said.

Bruckner did at least wait until she had both feet on the ground before he rolled the bus forward. In three turns, they were through the gate and in the packed, busy turmoil of the Joker Quarter.

No hurrahs. The guards, impassive, watched them drive in. Balthazar spoke briefly with one of the Fists, and they carried Croyd away somewhere—asleep, to awake changed. Zoe wondered if she would ever see him again. And if she did, who would he be? Bruckner and Balthazar talked briefly and then Bruckner was gone. The bus vanished into a side street and might never have existed. Balthazar and Jan and Zoe stood in the souk, and business swirled around them. Business as usual.

"Now I can go hug Anne," Zoe said. "And I can shower! And I can get out of these *clothes*! Jan? I'll race you home."

"I don't think so," Jan said.

Zoe felt the guard's presence before she saw him next to her, grim, determined, a man with orders and a gun.

"Miss Harris? This way, please."

"No!"

"Tell her, Balthazar," the guard said.

Balthazar sighed. "It's not over, Zoe. The Black Dog wants to see you. Now."

But I don't want to see the Black Dog, Zoe thought. *Never, ever again. Run?* But Balthazar's hand held her right arm just above the elbow and Jan flanked her other side, urging her toward the door in the shadow of the gate, and two of the Fists guards up on the walls turned on some unheard signal, their attention suddenly on Zoe Harris.

What could the bastard want this time? Wasn't one nuke enough for him?

"I'll tell Anne you're back safe," Jan whispered. She darted away with Balthazar, their night-black robes fluttering through the passageways in quick flickers of motion. Images of carrion birds came up from somewhere and faded again. Strobe effect. That was fatigue. Zoe felt as though she'd been taking some of Croyd's speed.

"You did well," the Black Dog said. He sat at a conference table and motioned for her to sit down. There was a chair by the door. Zoe took it, sitting at his insistence but not where he pointed.

"Am I supposed to say 'Thank you'? Fuck that. I want to go home."

"Soon. Soon. We've just moved into a worst-case scenario. The Nur al-Allah has the Black Trump."

"Who?"

"A desert fanatic. A damaged ace who thinks he speaks with the voice of Allah himself."

Snailfoot slithered into the room, a sheaf of printout clutched in his hand. The Black Dog seemed to expect him and offered no greeting. Snailfoot sat down and began to sort papers.

"The Nur hasn't made the news much lately, but he's got followers, he's got funding," the Black Dog said. "Anyone who keeps hatreds alive in the Mideast gets money, and the Nur al-Allah hates the wild card. He will use any weapon he can find to destroy it, even plague. *Jihad,* he's thinking. The holiest of wars."

"He's an ace? Then how does he figure he won't die of the Trump once it's loosed?"

"*If* it's loosed," Snailfoot said. "Please."

"He thinks aces are blessed of Allah and jokers are cursed. He thinks no plague would touch him," the Black Dog said.

"However, er, *skewered,* his grasp of bioscience may be, he knows he needs some Western devil science to multiply enough agent to be useful." Snailfoot's words were for the Black Dog. He ignored Zoe. "Rudo's a psychiatrist, so he can't do the work himself. They've picked up an Afghani virologist, a bent medic from Grenada—they're looking for others."

"Rudo?" Zoe asked. "Does Croyd know about this yet?"

"No," the Black Dog said. "I can't let him know, not until we've found out how to get the Trump away from him. Croyd wouldn't let reason keep him from killing Rudo if he got the chance."

"Go to the UN! Tell them! Surely it's time to do that now!"

"Don't be a fool, Zoe Harris. Tell the UN that a dead ex-official of theirs is working on a genocidal plague? By the time the bureaucracy digested that news, we'd all be dead. We've got a few people in the Nur's camp. I figure he's got a few in ours. In fact, I plan to make sure he does. He needs to find out we've got the bomb, but not until we know we can destroy his stash of Trump."

Snailfoot squared a stack of papers on the desk. "We've prepared a dossier for your new identity, Zoe, plausible reasons for your Western education and your hatred of the wild card. You're the only chemist we have available at the moment." He slipped a paper clip over the stack and slid it across the table in Zoe's direction.

"Oh, no. I'm a *chemist,* not a virologist! I don't know anything about this stuff."

"The Nur won't know that you don't. And Rudo needs help fast. He won't argue. The man's in a hurry," the Black Dog said.

"I *can't!*" Zoe said. "Please. I want a shower. I want to go home."

Azma slipped through the door, soothing plump Azma, concern on her face when she saw Zoe. "You're getting roots," the woman said, her soft touch gentle on Zoe's hair. "We'll have to do a touch-up."

"I want to see Anne," Zoe said.

"Before you leave," Azma crooned. "Of course you will."

Three

Ray looked all around, turning in a circle and shaking his head.

"It's big," he finally said. "It'll be a bitch to keep an eye on everyone when it's crowded."

"I've never heard Westminster Abbey described quite like that," Flint whispered, his words echoing weirdly in the cathedral's cavernous interior. Only Flint, Ray, and Harvest were present, though probably a platoon of spies could have been hidden among the statues, monuments, and screens scattered around the ancient cathedral.

Harvest smiled. "He has the soul of a poet."

Ray grinned himself. "You don't need poets for this business, you need guys like me."

Flint looked down on them gravely. *"It took some serious campaigning on my part before I could get Her Majesty's Government to accept your presence in the security contingent."*

"Well," Ray said, "I could see why you wouldn't want us screwing up Churchill's funeral. You guys did such a swell job guarding him when he was alive."

Flint frowned. *"Enough of that. I got the secretary to agree to your presence by insisting that it was Sir Winston's wish that you be included in anything that might deal with Card Sharks. I did it to have someone on the job I knew I could trust. Don't make me regret my decision."*

"What do you mean, someone to trust?" Harvest asked.

"Sir Winston believed that our security net had been punctured by Card Sharks. He was going to name names at the meeting, but . . . Well, you know what happened. He trusted Ray because he's an outsider and a wild carder. He was going to accept Ray's judgment of you. By the way—I suppose I should make this official. Do you think Agent Harvest is trustworthy?"

Ray looked at her. "Trustworthy?" he asked. He hesitated only a moment. Ray was beginning to suspect that he loved her. He supposed that he trusted her. "Hell, yes!"

She smiled at him.

"Very well. The problem is that I don't know whom to trust among our own people. With representatives from nearly every nation in the world arriving tomorrow for the funeral, we can't allow a successful Card Shark attack."

"It would be a hell of a time to release the Trump," Ray said. "The diplomats would bring it back to their own countries, spreading it around the world in a heartbeat."

Flint nodded creakingly. *"My thoughts exactly. I don't think they'd be daring enough to disrupt the ceremony—but we can't afford to take any chances. You two will be my aces in the hole, my trump for the Trump, so to speak. If Johnson and the Sharks do assay an attack, they must be stopped. The fate of the entire world is in our hands."*

"No shit, Sherlock," Ray said.

The Fists flew her to London. Heathrow was a couple of hours of crowded boredom, questions from oh-so-polite customs officials, and another ramp into a plane, this one to Damascus. Zoe slept through most of the night, wrapped in her kilim, its folds bunched behind her neck to make a pillow. The plane reeked of tobacco, rosewater, and musky sweat.

Zoe Hazziz, an American-born Egyptian whose father had died in the '67 War, took a room in a hotel that had quarters for unattended women. The hotel provided a guide for her: Khaled, a taciturn man, not young, who walked with a limp, so that she could walk the streets with some semblance of dignity. Her scarf had come to seem comforting, its folds at her neck a screen against appraising eyes, but she wasn't in full chador. It wouldn't have fitted her profile—Western-trained, a modern woman.

Khaled led her to the address she had given him, but he stopped at the entrance to the alleyway, narrow and fetid. This was the Street of Doves? A dog's bloated carcass lay belly-up in the sun. The drone of flies feeding on it was louder than the noise of the streets behind them.

"This is not a good place," Khaled said.

"Still, I must go. I am expected." Expected for an interview, a response to a plea for employment, by Allah's mercy, for an orphaned daughter of one of the faithful—the letter drafted by Snailfoot, mailed from London to a merchant in Damascus, a man who was faithful to the Nur.

"This is not the dwelling of a merchant," Khaled said.

The blue door. She was to enter the blue door at midmorning, in the Street of Doves. Zoe settled the straps of her pack on her shoulder, the kilim tied like a bedroll. Wrapped in it were a few toilet articles, a little jewel case that contained— something Snailfoot had given her, something she wasn't supposed to think about. She picked up her skirts and ran. Khaled did not follow her, or if he did, the bedouin standing in the suddenly opened doorway discouraged him from entering.

The bedouin motioned her toward a man in khaki who sat in a rattan chair in the shady room. Above his starched collar, his face was dead white, clean shaven. He needed a beard to disguise that weak chin, Zoe decided. A wooden ceiling fan stirred the air above his head, surprisingly cool. A latticework partition led to another room. It took Zoe a moment to realize that the statue next to the chair was not a statue, it was a giant man, motionless, in a motorized wheelchair. The back of the wheelchair was decorated with red and white satin tassels.

"Miss Hazziz," the man in the wicker chair said. "I am Samir Zahid."

Something was not right with his lower jaw. He didn't hiss, but the skin around his mouth seemed too generous, as if he were missing a lot of teeth. The bedouin sank to the floor beside Zahid, so that the three of them stared up at Zoe in that intent way that still bothered her. She stayed on her feet. She could not sit down until she was invited to do so.

"Your brothers have not been dutiful. They are employed. Why are they not providing for you?"

"They are young men. Married, with children. I would not have their wives denied what my brothers can give them."

"Admirable," Zahid said.

Zoe kept her eyes down. A cockroach explored the gaudy carpet by her feet. New York had bigger roaches; this one looked half-starved.

"Why did you leave New York?" Zahid asked.

Now for the big lie. Remember Bjorn, say this as if you spoke of him. "My father. Abominations like those who killed my father, who now dwells in Paradise, walk the streets without fear. How could I live in such a place?"

"He died a fighter?"

"One of Allah's accursed killed him," Zoe said. That was true. But it wasn't a joker who had killed him, not a wild card victim.

The giant in the wheelchair spoke quickly in Arabic. Zahid nodded.

"It may be that Allah in his mercy has found a task that you might perform to earn your dowry, perhaps even to help avenge your father. It is risky, bringing Westernized women into contact with the virtuous women we shelter in the desert, but—you are trained as a chemist? The work is highly secret. No one must ever know what it is that you will do if you work with us. Do you understand?"

Zoe nodded. The cockroach had wandered to the edge of the carpet.

"She might talk," the giant said.

"There are ways to gain silence, even from a woman. She might serve, Sayyid," Zahid said to the giant beside him.

This was Sayyid, the Nur's war leader? Snailfoot had said he was a giant, yes, but Snailfoot hadn't known if he'd survived that day in the desert when Hartmann had been shot. He'd been crushed by an ace power, Snailfoot had said. Every bone broken. His face was marked with deep lines of pain.

"Take her to Rudo, then," the giant said.

The bedouin rose to his feet.

"Wait! Search her," the giant said.

The bedouin took a step toward Zoe.

"Search me? I have no weapons," Zoe said. She backed toward the door, hoping Khaled hadn't left the alley, left her here.

"Weapons! Do you think we would fear a woman's weapons? No, but we must know that you carry no taint of abomination. We must know that you are not marked by the wild card." The giant clapped his hands.

A woman, veiled except for her eyes, came from behind the lattice.

"Strip," the giant said.

Zoe supposed it was meant to be humiliating. It wasn't. Let those fools see what a good body looked like, for once. She climbed out of her layers of black gauze, almost with a feeling of relief, and walked deliberately to stand in reach of the giant named Sayyid. The veiled woman reached for her as if to hold her back. Her eyes looked frightened.

"Don't fear for me," Zoe said. "These *virtuous* men will do me no harm." She raised her arms over her head, feeling their measuring eyes on her skin. Inches away from the giant, she turned full circle, slowly, and then arched her pubis forward. Nothing hidden. Zahid tapped his fingers against the arm of his wicker chair.

"I am no joker," Zoe said.

The bedouin hissed.

"Get dressed," Sayyid said. "We're leaving. Bring the truck into the alley, Izzat!"

The bedouin rushed for the door as if he were embarrassed.

The woman dropped her eyes and vanished behind the lattice. Zoe got into her clothes and slipped her shoes on.

"Come," Sayyid said. "We're leaving now."

He motored his wheelchair to the door. Zoe squashed the roach under her heel and followed him.

Out in the bright sunlight, a van as tall as a double-decker bus backed into the alley, past the crumpled body of the guide named Khaled, flies already buzzing around the drying pool of blood that seeped out from beneath his belly.

"Our work is secret," Sayyid said.

Izzat hustled to the side of the van and let down a wheelchair lift. Sayyid motioned Zoe into the van. The lift groaned under his weight. The door closed.

– – –

Ray twitched as Harvest's blunt nails skittered down his back. He lay on her stomach, one of his legs thrown between hers, his thigh resting on their juncture. Her hair was tousled, her breath just returning to normal as she stared at the ceiling and idly ran her hand down Ray's muscular back, where the sweat was starting to dry.

"What're you thinking?" Ray asked.

"Hmmmm?" She looked at him. "I'm glad you had your face fixed. The photos in your file make you look like one ugly bastard."

Ray shrugged. "Never meant too much to me. It'll get battered again and I guess when it gets too bad I'll have it fixed again."

She put her hands on Ray's chest and pushed. He turned and flopped on his back, and she straddled him, looking intently at his abdomen and chest.

"Remarkable," Harvest said.

"What?"

She traced a line with one fingernail from his pubic hair, up his flat, hard stomach to his ridged chest. "This is where Mackie Messer opened you up that time in Atlanta, isn't it?"

"Yeah." Ray frowned. It hadn't been his proudest day. The twisted ace with the buzz-saw hands had gutted him like a tuna on the floor of the Democratic National Convention. But Ray had bought enough time for another assassin known as Demise to do the job on the little bastard.

"And not even a scar," Harvest said, drawing him back to the present as she kissed his chest, approximately where Mackie's hand had punctured his stomach.

"I heal good and fast."

Harvest looked up and smiled at him. "You do have remarkable recuperative powers."

Ray nodded.

"Let's hope you'll just need them tonight, not tomorrow."

Ray shrugged. "I'll be ready, no matter what."

"I know you will."

Her tongue licked the spot she'd just kissed and worked its way down.

Ray smiled. He would be ready. No matter what.

The Temple of Ten Thousand Buddhas was in the New Territories, high on a hill at the top of a long, crooked flight of steps that wound up from the Sha Tin Railway Station. The guidebook said there were 400 steps. It lied. There were 431 steps. Jay Ackroyd counted every one of them on the way up. It was a good thing he'd left Finn back at the hotel. He didn't think ponies did real well on steep, narrow steps.

The entrance to the temple was guarded by towering statues of huge, fierce, hideous Chinese gods. They didn't scare Jay. You saw a lot worse walking the streets of Jokertown every day. Inside the temple was dim and cool. The wall above the main altar loomed fifty feet high. It was painted a dark red and divided into a myriad of small niches, like a honeycomb. A miniature gold-and-black Buddha sat in each niche, every one different from its brothers, all of them seemingly looking down on Jay.

"There are actually twelve thousand eight hundred of them," a familiar voice said quietly behind Jay, "but 'the Temple of Twelve Thousand Eight Hundred Buddhas' lacks a certain je ne sais quoi."

Jay turned toward the voice. "You mind telling me why I had to haul my ass out here and climb all those steps? What was wrong with the lobby of the Peninsula Hotel? You got something against comfortable chairs, Belew?"

J. Bob Belew smiled thinly. "Napoleon never let the enemy choose the battleground."

"Napoleon never had to hump all those goddamn steps."

"Prosperity is making you soft, Mr. Ackroyd," Belew observed. He was a compact man, shorter than Jay, but every inch of him was sinew and muscle. He was dressed in khaki-colored pants with a razor crease and a white safari jacket. His hair had started brown and gone gray; he cropped it close to his head, and compensated with an ostentatious walrus mustache.

Belew loved that mustache. He waxed its ends and played with it constantly, especially when dropping bon mots and quoting classical proverbs. Jay discovered that he found this just as irritating now as he had back in 1979, when he and J. Robert had almost died together on an abortive mission to rescue the hostages in Iran. Several other aces *had* died, including a man called the Librarian, who perished of a mortal wound that hadn't been mortal when Jay had popped him back to the medics at Desert One. "So where did you see the ad?" Jay asked.

"Everywhere," J. Bob said. "I hope you don't think you were being clever. You might as well have taken out a notice in the *Card Shark Quarterly*."

"Yeah, well, I would have just phoned you up, but when I looked in the Yellow Pages under *Spies*, you weren't listed."

"A bit out of your depth here, aren't you?" Belew said. *"Love the little trade which you have learned, and be content with it*, Marcus Aurelius. Were you aware that you were being followed from the moment you left your hotel? A man and a woman."

Jay looked around slowly. There was no one in the temple but monks and tourists. "Where?"

Belew stroked the bottom of his mustache with the back of

his hand. "Not here. While they were following you, two of my men were following them. We made sure they missed the ferry. Shall we stroll?" He took Jay by the elbow and drew him out a side door onto the temple grounds. Outside, another flight of steps led farther up the hill. Jay groaned. "Hong Kong is an invigorating city," J. Bob said as they climbed. "So much energy, so much activity . . ."

"So much money," Jay said.

"Precisely. It gives the city a certain ideological purity. Nothing matters here but wealth. Even jokers are welcome, if they have the gelt. At the moment, they are pouring in by the thousands, fleeing the chaos in Saigon." There was a hint of sadness in Belew's voice at that. He stopped and gazed out across the valley. "You can see Amah Rock from here. Over there. The stone that looks like a woman with a baby on her back."

Jay took a look. Amah looked like a big lumpy rock to him, but if J. Bob wanted to say it was a woman, fine. Jay had once been hired to scour Mexico in search of a tortilla that looked like Jesus Christ. He never argued these things.

"Local legend has it that the rock was once a living woman, the wife of a fisherman who put to sea and never returned. She waited for him patiently, faithfully, never tiring, until one day the gods pitied her and turned her to stone."

"That was swell of them," Jay said.

"In a way it was," Belew said, twirling the waxed end of his mustache. "Chinese women go to Amah Rock to pray for patience and faithfulness. In the last decade, a good many jokers have gone there to worship as well."

"Swell," Jay said. "Only I didn't come halfway around the world to admire the hair on your lip and talk about rocks. I need to find our old friend O. K. Casaday."

J. Bob Belew turned back to face Jay. "If Casaday could be

found easily, I would have found him years ago. Emerson said, *Pay every debt as if God wrote the bill.*"

"Imagine thinking up something like that in between making all those refrigerators," Jay said. "Look, I didn't figure Casaday was sharing your flat, but I thought you'd know how to track him down if anyone could."

"I have my resources," Belew admitted. "As does Casaday. At the moment, his are rather more extensive. He is still an operative in good standing with the Central Intelligence Agency, while I am a discredited former minister-without-portfolio of a country that will be a footnote to history in a matter of months. Poor Mark. Asia is hard on the innocents."

"The Card Sharks are a fuck of a lot harder," Jay said. "Mark Meadows is still alive."

For the first time, he saw a spark of interest in Belew's eyes. J. Bob stroked the underside of his mustache thoughtfully and smiled. "You surprise me, Jay. How long have you known?"

"I didn't *know* until just now," Jay said. "I guessed. Talk to me, damn it. Was it Casaday?"

"Yes. One of his better efforts. Casaday has never been noted for the precision of his operations, but this time he outdid himself. He was even thoughtful enough to supply a brace of corpses to pass for Mark and Sprout. A gaunt Western man of undetermined origins and a blond Danish teenager kidnapped from Singapore. I'm still not quite sure how he got them inside the Presidential Palace. They were both alive right up to the instant of the explosion. I blush to admit that had me fooled for a while, but Casaday made one small slip. The Danish girl was four weeks pregnant."

"How do you know that?" Jay asked.

"Let's just say I made certain arrangements and had my own autopsy performed," Belew told him.

"So what did they do with Meadows?"

"I've been trying to determine that," J. Bob said. "Thus far, without success, I'm afraid. Why kidnap him in the first place? The chancellor had enemies, certainly, but it would have been much simpler to kill him than to stage this elaborate subterfuge. When I find that piece of the puzzle, the picture may come clearer."

"It wasn't the chancellor they kidnapped," Jay said. Suddenly he saw it as plain as the mustache on Belew's face. "It wasn't Cap'n Trips, either. It was Mark Meadows, the lab rat they needed. The Sharks must be desperate for guys in white coats who know which end of the Bunsen burner to light. Faneuil and Clara were their big germ warfare gurus and both of them are out of the picture. So who do they have left? Rudo? He's a shrink. Michelle Poynter's a nurse. You need two Nobel Prizes and a note from Dr. Tachyon's mother before you're allowed to mess around with the Black Trump, and they have to brew up a shitload of it."

J. Bob was staring. "Black Trump?" he said, lifting an eyebrow quizzically. "Do tell."

All that long day's drive, they said nothing to her. The van was enclosed and, mercifully, air-conditioned. Zoe could see glimpses of paved roads, trucks, donkeys through the driver's window, but later there were only twisting, rutted tracks where she feared Sayyid's great weight, swaying in his chair, would tip them over. They traveled west, and west, and they kept going and turning after the sun had set.

She found a numb place in her mind, where she finally stopped listing the dead: Bjorn; the skinhead; the warehouse manager; the man who looked so surprised, sitting there with the mark of Croyd's razor across his throat—did Croyd forget people while he slept? The Escorts would get him to Anne, to his corner in the one-room flat.

There is a balm in Gilead, there is a bomb in—

She had made needles of sand, and they had polished away a man's flesh, his life. A dead man lay beside a dog in an alley.

There is a balm in Gilead.

They had passed her a water jug, each of them drinking in turn before they gave it to her. She drank, trying not to taste the traces of their three different chemistries around the lip of the jug. The water was stale.

They stopped, once. The men stretched, and yawned and scratched, and then went to piss into a scrawny acacia before they got back in the van. Sayyid stood up for this and walked a few steps. He wasn't paralyzed, then. Zoe went to the back of the van and pulled up her skirts to empty her bladder on the sand. No one stopped her or seemed to notice.

Now, in the starlight, the van descended a series of hairpin turns and stopped. Sayyid opened the side door, gripped the handles of his wheelchair, and levered himself down. He walked, slowly, toward a tent, followed by Zahid and the driver.

Zoe hauled her pack out of the van and followed them.

The tent loomed high against the stars, its size suggesting that it had been designed to accommodate the giant's height. Zahid stopped at the entrance and turned to Zoe. "Cover your face!" he whispered.

Zoe pulled her scarf over her nose. The voices inside were speaking English. Curiously accented English, and one voice was a whisper, a melodic whisper.

· The whisperer was the Nur, and his light was green, green as an emerald. His skin glowed like a lamp. Sayyid made a laborious bow to him. A blond boy, pale as an angel, a young and beautiful boy, barely a man, folded his arms across his chest and watched the giant make his obeisance.

"Were you successful, my friend?" the Nur asked. His voice was a resonant whisper, a compelling presence of muted sound.

"I have found a chemist," Sayyid said. "Unfortunately, she is a woman." The giant eased himself into a waiting wheelchair.

"A chemist?" the boy asked. "What sort of chemist? What is your training?"

The Nur looked at Zoe. "You may speak," he said.

Speak? If he asked, she would sing, she would talk until morning, tell all the stories that Scheherazade had ever told, and make up more. He was a fountain of wisdom, he was irresistible, this tired man with the scar across his throat, this battered pillar of Allah's will.

This is the enemy, Zoe told herself, *an ace whose power is the charisma of his voice, his beautiful whispering voice. What must it have been like before his sister cut his throat?*

"I have a bachelor's degree in chemistry," Zoe said. "From CCNY."

The boy laughed. "Impossible!" he said to the Nur. "This is the team with which I am to work? A paramedic trained in Grenada who did not pass his examinations? This woman, who perhaps is trained to wash bottles but knows nothing of biochemistry, of virology?"

"You will have the skills of Dr. Samir Zahid," the Nur said. *Of course,* Zoe thought, the great and wonderful skills of Samir Zahid. Why is this boy worried?

"Dr. Samir Zahid, an Afghan trained in Moscow, and we know how strong Russia's science was in her declining years. Yes."

She sensed the increased tension in Zahid but he said nothing.

"And your own skills," the Nur murmured. "Do not discredit them."

So calm, so soothing. This tent was so beautiful, lighted in celadon, emerald, glowing with his power. Zoe wanted the Nur to keep talking, to say anything at all.

"I am a psychiatrist. For long years I treated only diseases of the mind."

Pan Rudo? This boy was Pan Rudo, this innocent angel?

"You have this essence, this 'Black Trump,' and you have the expertise to multiply it. You will do so." The Nur picked up an inhaler, sprayed mist into his throat, and hawked discreetly into a large handkerchief.

"Go," he croaked.

"You have no questions for the woman, Najib?" Sayyid asked.

The Nur made a small motion with his hand. "She may leave with Dr. Rudo."

No questions. Why should there be? The Nur al-Allah would kill her, kill them all—Rudo, the angry Zahid, the failed paramedic from Grenada—once the Trump was readied for use.

Ray wasn't much of a churchgoing man, but even he had to admit that it was a damned impressive sight.

Westminster Abbey was packed. You could have probably squeezed in another mourner or two, but only if everyone took a deep breath and held it. It was not a good situation from a security viewpoint.

Westminster was laid out in the shape of a cross. The main

entrance opened into what Flint had called the nave—a wide aisle that went from the base of the cross to where the arms met. The arms were called transepts. During normal services they would be mostly empty, but this was not a normal service. At the heart of the cross, the interaction of transepts and nave, was the sanctuary and high altar. The upper arm of the cross, the apse, was a maze of chapels with numerous tombs of dead kings and queens.

The nave was packed with mourners, from the entrance where the Unknown Soldier was interred in the floor all the way back to the transepts. Five rows of portable wooden pews ran across each transept. Behind the pews was standing room only, as crowded as Ebbets Field during a pennant race.

The apse was as dark as a medieval abbey usually is, and deserted, except for lurking security men. Ray had the feeling that the trouble would come from there.

He circulated as best he could around the edges of the crowd. Heads of state and other foreign dignitaries sat in the front rows along with the queen and whatever high-society Brit could wangle an invitation. Ray didn't recognize too many of the politicians, but Vice President Zappa was sitting in the front row near the queen. Wild carders sat in the pews behind the politicians—among them Nephi Callendar—though Flint was in the command post coordinating security. If anyone noticed the odd figure in the tight, white fighting suit, they gave no sign. Ray was starting to wish he'd worn his black suit instead of the white. The abbey was a lot dustier than he'd realized.

Gregg looked up at the ornate vaulted roof of the medieval abbey and an image came to him. "All we need is Quasi."

"Wrong church, wrong country," a voice with a heavy East

London accent answered Gregg. The joker's name was Alfred. *Most folks call me Bowler, doncha know,* he'd told them. The reason seemed obvious enough: A fleshy growth on the man's head, neatly blackened with matte paint, was a nearly perfect replica of an English gentleman's bowler hat. Dressed in coat, tie, and gloves, he could pass for gentry—until etiquette demanded that the hat be taken off or tipped, anyway. Alfred was the local contact for the Twisted Fists. "Besides, Westminster Abbey's a much nicer place than Notre Dame. I always sympathized with old Quasimoto, though."

"That's not who—" Gregg started to correct the man but decided it wasn't worth it. He glanced at Hannah, but he had no shoulders with which to shrug. Instead Gregg lifted himself up on his rear legs to get a better view around them.

Far below them, the main expanse of the abbey was a sea of mourners. The space where Churchill's casket would eventually sit was a landscape of bright pointillistic dots of flowers at the juncture of the north and south transepts of the building. A fog of incense was thick in Gregg's nose, and the organ pipes arrayed around them thundered with Mozart's *Requiem,* shaking dust down from the ceiling.

Gregg, Hannah, and Bowler were on a narrow catwalk behind the ranks of pipes, snuggled high above the floor and the galleries. *"Getting a few of us in won't be a problem,"* Bowler had promised them. *"Keys, one of our people, works on the organ—he knows ways security won't check."* Gregg was dubious, but Bowler had been right. Keys—a joker whose only visible sign of jokerhood had been his fingers, which had the too-white luster and stiffness of piano keys—had brought Hannah (blond, again) and Bowler in as his assistants; Gregg had been smuggled in inside a pipe case. Once inside the building, they'd made the long, dirty, and narrow climb to their aerie; Keys had left later that morning, alone.

Outside, in the massive crowds filling Victoria Street, Brian, Cara, Two-Face, and some of the London Fists were scattered, watching for Rudo, Johnson, Horvath, or other known Sharks. As the invited mourners filed inside, Hannah and Bowler scanned their faces with binoculars, also searching.

What they were going to do in case they saw Johnson wasn't entirely clear, even to Gregg. They'd made hazy plans, but no one knew whether Johnson would be there himself or if some unknown local Shark might be used, or how the Trump virus might be released. For that matter, they weren't certain *anything* would happen, but the sour weight in Gregg's gut told him that he was right, that the Sharks would be unable to pass up this opportunity to infect wild carders from all over the globe.

It's what you'd do, after all, if you were one of them. It would be so tasty. Ahh, the glorious agony . . .

If Brian and the others found Johnson before he got into the building, that was their best chance. If Johnson was spotted among the mourners within the abbey, Bowler had lugged in a high-caliber rifle with a scope, but that would be the last resort. They'd tried to contact Popinjay, thinking to pop Johnson out of the crowd to somewhere safe, but no one seemed to know exactly where Ackroyd was. Two Fist sympathizers were down in the congregation itself, one of them—a deuce called Slumber—was hopefully capable of removing Johnson or some other Shark without drawing too much attention to the group.

They'd done what they could do. Gregg had the fear it wasn't going to be enough. He lifted himself so he could peer over the organ pipes again, wishing they could have found a quieter hiding place, and looked down at the congregation. Toward the western entrance, he could see what looked to be a giant statue dressed in a uniform: Captain Flint, heading the security team. Even with Gregg's lousy vision, Flint stood out. Gregg swept his gaze over the congregation, to the flag-draped coffin, to the transepts leading off the main hall . . . "Damn!" he said.

"What, Gregg?" Hannah asked.

"Look over by the right of the sanctuary, near the columns. Tell me what you see."

"What? The guy dressed—" Hannah stopped.

"—all in white," Gregg finished for her in a swirl of breathy organ crescendo. "Yeah. Billy Ray. Even as nearsighted as I am, I can tell. Trust Carnifex to wear his dress whites, even at a funeral."

"It's beginning." Flint's eerie whisper sounded even more ghostly coming from the tiny receiver plugged into Ray's ear.

Ray was stationed at the mouth of the south transept, among those lesser lights standing in Poets' Corner. Ray had a good vantage point leaning against the base of Shakespeare's statue. It was a pretty nice statue. At least Ray had heard of the guy, which was more than he could say for most of the other poetic geniuses whose monuments were all around him. It was a good place to keep an eye on the entrance to the apse, the darkness from which Ray was sure the trouble would come.

He looked around and caught Harvest's eye. She was sitting among the dignitaries, in an aisle seat on the third pew in the north transept. She looked great in black. Ray flashed on an image of her panting under him, her strong legs scissored across his back. He grinned at her and gave a thumbs-up. He saw her smile under her black veil.

"The coffin is coming down the nave," Flint reported, and Ray forgot about Harvest.

He began to breathe harder, smiling, as he felt his pulse speed.

– – –

"Damn. Is he still after *us*?" Hannah's knuckles, gripping the pipe supports, had gone white, and Gregg could smell the sudden fear in her.

"If he is, then we're in real trouble here." Gregg dropped down again. He felt exposed and trapped. "Keep an eye on Ray," Gregg said to Hannah. The coffin was making its slow way down the central aisle. "They're going to try it," Gregg said. "I know they are. Ray's handlers must think something's going to happen here, too, or he wouldn't be here. We just have to figure out *how*." Gregg went back to where Hannah stood. The ceremony was underway, the Archbishop of Canterbury in his robes and miter droning in front of Churchill's casket, his amplified voice reverberating through the airy expanse. Gregg watched, trying to see something they might have missed before, the best way to bring in the Trump. Sending in infected people would work—let them cough slow death into the crowd. That would also kill those who brought the virus in, not that the Sharks would care, and worse, it couldn't guarantee wide-scale infection, any more than having someone in church with the flu meant that you'd catch it, too. No, Rudo and Johnson would want something more comprehensive than that. More certain.

What? What would I do?

Gregg scanned the abbey with squinting eyes, across the blurred faces of the assembly, up the gilded, fluted walls, across the domed ceiling. At the high altar, the ceremony continued. A priest emerged from the gilded doors of the sanctuary, bearing a large crystal decanter and several golden chalices—wine for the Communion.

– – –

The pallbearers deposited the casket draped with the Union Jack in the open area before the high altar and stepped aside, melting into the shadows. An honor guard from every branch of the British military, they were more than just show. From the five-foot-tall Gurkha dressed in khaki to the six-foot-four redcoat with bearskin hat, they were all Flint's trusted agents, but among them, Ray knew, there was probably a Shark or two. The question was, which one did he have to keep an eye on?

Ray didn't dwell on it but marked their positions, ready to treat them as friend or foe as their actions demanded. He looked over the crowd, paying little attention to the priests and their ceremony. He was wired, on edge, ready for thunder and lightning to explode in the gloom of the dark cathedral.

But nothing happened.

The Mass droned on. The atmosphere was close and hot. The clouds of billowing incense didn't help any. Ray's sensitive nose was soon twitching. It seemed as if the Mass were going to last forever. Ray glanced away from the mouth of the apse. Before the high altar, a couple of priests were puttering around with the Communion wine.

That meant that things were winding down. Ray frowned. Maybe he was wrong. He'd felt sure that the Sharks would take advantage of the situation and pull off an outrageous stunt to galvanize their shattered movement. His feeling was rarely wrong. His instincts served him nearly as well as the battle computer that was his mind. He never—

"Sweet fucking Jesus," he whispered in sudden astonishment. It couldn't be!

"What is it, Ray?" Flint, ensconced in the choir loft, had picked up Ray's whisper through the transmitter Ray wore.

To the astonishment of the onlookers, Ray hauled himself

up the face of Shakespeare's statue, put an arm around the playwright's neck, and hung there precariously for a moment.

"It's him," Ray said through clenched teeth. "The priest screwing around with the Communion wine. It's General MacArthur fucking Johnson!"

"What?" Flint exclaimed.

Ray moved, his heart surging with genuine terror.

The priest, Gregg noticed, was a Black man. *Clara said the virus would be soluble in water. Water . . .*

Suddenly, Gregg noticed Ray moving. Moving toward the priest. "Hannah!"

"What, Gregg?"

"That priest. The one with the wine."

Hannah snatched up the binoculars, rolled the focus wheel. "My God," she said. "It's him, Johnson." Gregg could feel the shock hit her, a wave of nauseous yellow, and, following it, the surging orange-red of fear as the realization hit her. "The wine . . ."

"I can take him out," Bowler said. "Here, move . . ."

Bowler started forward, adjusting the scope on his rifle. But Gregg saw the flash of white at the same time. Billy Ray had seen Johnson, too, and he was moving. Gregg wasn't sure how Ray had gotten there, but somehow he'd climbed up on a statue of Shakespeare, and now he leapt like Tarzan. Already there were shouts of protest, and Johnson looked up.

"Come on," Gregg said. "We have to get down there. All we need is for Ray to knock over the decanter in the middle of a fight . . ."

— — —

Ray knew that the Black Trump was in the crystal decanter of wine that Johnson was patiently waiting to add to the large chalice. Ray knew he had to get to it before Johnson knew what was happening and just dumped it. Spilling it wouldn't be nearly as effective as having everyone drink the shit, but it would probably get the job done.

Ray's mind seemed to slow down as he swung into action. He knew that he was moving faster than any man could, but time was like liquid amber, and he was an insect moving through it, seeing everything around him with total clarity and precision.

He jumped from old Will Shakespeare's statue to the next, barely hanging on. People were just starting to look up at him, but he moved on before they could finish pointing at him.

He flung himself off the next statue and he could see April Harvest stand and reach for the .38 that she carried holstered in the sweet hollow of her back and he almost shouted, "No! There's no shot!" because there were at least half a dozen priests between Harvest and Johnson, but he clamped his mouth shut because he didn't dare alert the Shark that they were on to him.

Flint was a screaming whisper in Ray's ear, but he ignored him. There were no more statues to jump on, and his path to the high altar was still blocked by mourners.

He looked, figured vectors and velocity in his subconscious, then flung himself off his perch. He caught a bug-eyed bronze bust set high in a niche, prayed it would take his weight, noted the inscription WILLIAM BLAKE, then pushed off, extending desperately like a diver angling for the water.

Somehow he cleared the last rank of mourners. He crashed loudly onto the cathedral's flagstone floor. Everyone looked at him, including the Archbishop of Canterbury—including General MacArthur Johnson—and then he was on the move again. Harvest's pistol cracked. Everyone panicked and started screaming, but Ray was already in the clear area before the sanctuary. He sprinted past Churchill's bier and went up the stairs to the high altar.

Johnson lifted the decanter high to smash it down on the flagstone floor and Ray's mind went blank with panic. He dove desperately. His brain flipped back twenty years, reverting to simpler days. He wasn't a government agent anymore. He wasn't Carnifex, the name the Mechanic had hung on him during his first government mission all those years ago. He was just Billy Ray, a kid playing football for the University of Michigan, and he had to get the ball, he had to catch the pass or there'd be a disaster of epic proportions. If he didn't get it, they'd lose the game. There'd be no victory. There'd be no Rose Bowl, no pro contract. Hell, there'd probably be no bed full of cheerleaders after the game.

He hurled his body lengthwise, jaw clenched, joints aching as he stretched every possible millimeter.

The decanter crashed into his hands. A crazed light danced in Ray's eyes. He had good hands. The coach had always told him that. Real soft, good hands. They cradled the decanter and instinctively Ray curled into a ball as he crashed against the floor. It was a jarring collision, but he tucked the decanter against his stomach as he skidded, bounced down the stairs, and slammed against the base of Churchill's bier.

Jesus Christ, Ray thought. *That had to be the best catch of my career.*

He looked up. The pallbearer in the red jacket and bearskin hat was towering over him. Ray blinked sudden sweat from his eyes, and the redcoat stabbed down with the bayonet he'd had up his sleeve. He ran Ray completely through, blunting the bayonet's point on the flagstone on which Ray lay.

– – –

They hit the first security man coming out of the tiny stairwell leading to the second-story gallery. Gregg saw him first, radiating in the infrared as he stood in the shadows. The man seemed occupied by voices in his ears and the obvious ruckus on the main floor. "Hey—" Gregg said loudly, and began to run the other way. The man stared open-mouthed for a moment, then started to pursue.

He ran directly into Bowler's rifle butt, coming around the corner of the stairwell, and went down hard as blood sprayed from his broken nose.

Bowler *tskked* once and fished in the unconscious man's jacket, pulling out a small handgun from a shoulder holster. He held it to the guard's head.

Hannah jerked Bowler's hand away. "No," she said.

Bowler looked annoyed. "If we don't, he'll wake up and report us. No one will hear the shot, not with the organ's racket."

"Forget it," Hannah repeated, her hand still on Bowler's wrist. "He didn't do anything to us."

"Bloody right. I knocked him cold."

"Then leave him that way."

Bowler snatched his hand away from Hannah. "You with your girlfriend on this?" he asked Hartmann.

Gregg started. He'd been watching the confrontation with an odd horror. *Choose,* the memory of Cara's voice whispered in his mind. *Choose who will die.*

Let him do it, whispered the other voice. *Taste it, feel it.*

Gregg shuddered. He reached out with the stubby hand and touched the unconscious guard. He could feel the strings. He could touch them.

Gregg pulled his hand away again.

"We're not Fists," he told Bowler. "We do things differently."

"Brian was right," Bowler muttered. "The two of you are looney. Here, then," he said, reversing the handgun and giving it to Hannah. "You make your own damn decision when to use it, then. If you can."

"You point with this end, right?" Hannah said in mock innocence.

Bowler frowned under the growth on his head. He took a small walkie-talkie from the man's suit pocket and stepped on it. Plastic crackled under his heel. "That'll have to do, I suppose," he said. "Lead on, caterpillar."

Fool, whispered the voice. *Fool.*

Ray screamed, pain and outrage combined. "Fucking Card Shark!"

His attacker looked down, somewhat appalled. He suddenly knew that he'd made a mistake. If he'd stabbed Ray through the heart he'd have killed him instantly. Even Ray's unnatural vitality couldn't have overcome a wound like that. A gut wound, painful as it was, just pissed him off.

Ray was on his feet before the Shark could jerk the bayonet free. Ray glared at him as blood ran down his legs, the bayonet poking through him like he was a beef kabob.

He wanted to rip the son of a bitch apart with his bare hands, but his mind screamed at him to hang on to the decanter. His dilemma was solved when someone grabbed the guard from behind and jerked his head up to look at the vaulted ceiling. A strong brown hand slipped a curved knife against the guardsman's throat and blood fountained upon the abbey's floor. The Shark dropped twitching to the flagstones.

The Gurkha pallbearer was grinning at Ray. He gestured at him with his bloodstained kukri. "You one tough son of a bitch."

"You bet," Ray grunted. He grabbed the bayonet and pulled it out through the wound, catching his breath as it came free.

He looked around, shaking his head. It was panic and chaos combined and squared as the mourners ran around and screamed, knocking down wooden pews and trampling one another. Before the high altar the archbishop and the other priests were staring at him, appalled by the blood and death that had entered the sacred space of their abbey, and perhaps even more frightened by the mask of pain and hate that was Ray's face.

But Ray broke into a grin. He couldn't believe his good luck. That bastard General MacArthur Johnson was still standing near the high altar, watching. Ray turned to the Gurkha and shoved the decanter at him.

"Take this! Guard it with your life."

The Gurkha saluted and took the crystal. Ray started to turn toward the dais, but someone slammed him, hard, in the back. Ray hit Churchill's bier and the coffin shifted. There were renewed screams and moans of anguish from the onlookers as someone landed on Ray's back and a muscular arm encircled his throat. *Johnson, goddamnit,* Ray thought. He couldn't breathe. He stood up, bearing Johnson's weight on his back.

"I've got you now, motherfucker," the Shark whispered in Ray's ear. His arm squeezed Ray's throat with the strength of a twenty-foot anaconda. The pain in Ray's stomach was excruciating, and he couldn't breathe.

He growled wordlessly, reaching backward, but he couldn't get a grip on Johnson. He tore the priest's robe from the man's back, but he couldn't tear the man from his own.

He started to stagger. He knew that if he fell he'd never get up.

— — —

They emerged from St. Faith's chapel into the south transept, down the stairs from which monks had once gone from their dormitories to the choir for night offices. The massive Rose Window, filling the upper southern wall, threw fractured, multicolored light down on a scene of chaos. On the high altar, Ray was fighting with Johnson; Gregg saw Harvest, the woman agent who'd been with Ray in New York, trying to push her way to the altar.

She was a salmon swimming upstream in a human flood. Half the people were scrambling over a tangled landscape of chairs, trying to get away from the commotion in the center of the abbey, while others stood and stared, or shoved back at the mourners trying to get through. Other fights had erupted around the floor—security people tried vainly to regain control of the situation. From the balcony, Gregg caught a glimpse of Brian, and the leprechaun let loose a burst of automatic gunfire that sent people diving for the floor. Gregg couldn't tell what the joker was firing at, but chunks of masonry flew from the railing in front of the Fist, and Brian ducked away. The roar of voices echoed as the choir stuttered to a halt and the organ abruptly choked off mid-chord.

Gregg and Hannah seemed to have lost Bowler in the rush.

Gregg could hardly see as they moved into the loud confusion. The floor was a forest of black-clad legs. He hopped up and down, trying to get a clear view. "What's going on?" he screamed at Hannah over the din. "Can you see that decanter?"

"No!" Hannah shouted back. She pushed away a panicked lady in a hat that looked like Klaatu's ship. Gregg had given up hope of trying to fight the exiting crowd; he stayed in the lee of a statue. Across the hall, he could swear that he saw Quasiman perched on top of some unknown statesman's head. Gregg squinted, but people kept jostling him and he couldn't get a good look. "Isn't that Quasi?"

"Where?"

"Over . . . Damn, never mind, he's gone." If Quasi had been there, he'd vanished already. "We really have a great bunch of allies."

"I thought . . . Oh, shit!"

"What?" Gregg asked.

"Horvath," Hannah said. "I'm certain I just saw him, coming down from the altar and moving this way, but I've lost him again. Ray's fighting Johnson on the altar." Hannah righted one of the chairs, jumping up on it to see above the people spilling past them. "There's Horvath! Some short guy in a weird uniform had the decanter, and he just gave it to Horvath. He's on the other side of the transept, staying near the wall." Hannah leapt down again. "Gregg, Horvath's carrying that decanter like it's the damn Holy Grail. It's got to be the virus."

She started after Horvath, pushing into the crowd. A man yelled at her, pushing back, and Hannah went sprawling onto the floor in front of Gregg. Gregg could feel her confusion as she scrambled out of the way of the fleeing crowd and got to her feet again. "Got to get him, get the virus . . ." she said, preparing to throw herself back into the whirl of people. Gunfire went off again, on the other side of the church. People started screaming and pushing harder for the exits.

"Kick me," Gregg said.

"What?"

"Kick me."

Hannah looked at him, then grinned. "Oh," she said, and brought her foot back.

Ray's mind was no longer functioning on a conscious level when he shuffled backward and slammed Johnson against

Churchill's casket. He heard Johnson grunt with pain. He staggered away from the bier, then slammed into it again. The pressure around his throat lessened and his lungs sucked in a molecule or two of oxygen. It was all he needed. He slammed Johnson against the casket once again, breaking the Shark's hold. There were screams and moans from what was left of the onlookers as the coffin slid, tilted, and fell off the bier.

It crashed to the flagstones with a resounding boom. The lid popped open and Churchill rolled out. Ray, down on one knee and gasping for breath, looked at his waxy face. "This is one hell of a funeral," he told the remains.

Johnson had apparently decided on the better part of valor. He was heading for the darkness of the apse, holding his side like he'd cracked a rib. Ray hoped he'd cracked his fucking back. Johnson was fast, strong, and agile, but Ray, even with a bayonet-sized hole through his gut, was an ace. He was up on his feet, running after him.

They passed history that Ray never even noticed—the tomb of Henry the Seventh; the massive blue-and-red stained glass window dedicated to the heroes of the Battle of Britain; the shrine of Saint Edward the Confessor, the last Saxon king and the man who had the church rebuilt in 1065; and the tombs of the cousins Mary and Elizabeth, queens both.

Ray knew they were heading toward the south transept. He lost sight of Johnson, and when he went around a corner and found himself in Poets' Corner again, he skidded to a halt.

"Goddammit," he said.

Johnson had blundered into Harvest, or perhaps vice versa. But Johnson clearly had the upper hand. He had Harvest around the throat, her gun pointed at her head.

"Stop right there, Ray, or she gets it."

"You've got more lives than a fucking cat."

"More'n you can take care of, anyway."

They were backing up, heading for the screened-off chapel that was the back wall of the south transept. Ray started to follow, but Johnson squeezed her throat harder.

"I'll kill her."

"You do and you've got nothing to bargain with. I'll be all over your ass."

"Don't worry about me," Harvest said. "The Black Trump!"

"What the hell about it?"

She pointed as best she could. "The goddamn caterpillar's after it."

Ray whirled to see Hartmann chasing Horvath. What the hell was Hartmann doing here? By the time Ray turned back, Harvest and Johnson had disappeared through a door in the chapel's back wall. Ray was indecisive. "She can take care of herself," he finally said and started after Horvath, the caterpillar, and the decanter of virus-tainted wine. "I hope."

Hannah's kick, harder than Gregg expected, catapulted him into overdrive. For the first several seconds, he had no control at all over his direction. He slammed into the wall, scrambled up the stone front of some statesman's statue, and hurtled from the head to the fluted columns of the wall. Below him, the crowd had snapped into slow motion. As Gregg finally gained some control over his hyperactivity, he saw Horvath several yards away, heading for a small door to the right of the entrance to St. Faith's chapel. Near Poets' Corner, Billy Ray saw Gregg and pointed.

Someone had knocked over Churchill's casket; the old man's body was spilling out of the coffin, one pudgy arm flung wide as if inviting someone to join him.

Gregg leapt off the column, landing on the shoulders of a matronly woman in black dress and veil, and jumping from her shoulders to the top of a middle-aged man's head. He skidded—knocking the man's toupee awry—and leapfrogged toward Horvath across the heaving sea of heads as people reacted belatedly to his presence. Horvath, moving as if immersed in water, turned slowly to see what was causing the new uproar. He saw Gregg and began running toward the door, slipping through it as Gregg hopped down into the clear space near the far wall. Gregg managed to slither through the opening before the door shut.

The sounds of panic faded. Gregg was standing at the top of a flight of steps leading down; Horvath had turned a corner ahead of him, doubling back under St. Faith's chapel. The Hannah-given adrenaline rush was fading; Horvath seemed to be moving at normal speed now, and Gregg hurried after him. Gregg's nostrils were full of the scent of rage, and he could hear Horvath's shoes clattering on stone flags as the man reached the bottom of the steps. Gregg half-ran, half-slid down the last flight of stairs on the evaporating edge of overdrive, and saw Horvath's back twenty-five yards ahead. The man had stopped and was staring at something ahead of him in the corridor. Staring at someone. Gregg saw a blurry figure step out of the shadows ahead of Horvath.

"Hannah Davis," Horvath said. He glanced over his shoulder and saw Gregg. "And Gregg Hartmann, too. I should have had you killed back in Belfast."

"Too late," Hannah told him—she must have come down from a stairway on the other side of the chapel. Gregg could see the gleam of metal in her hands: the handgun Bowler had given her. "Put down the decanter."

Horvath held it up, instead, swirling the dark red liquid inside. "So you know what this is," he said. He backed up a step.

"Horvath—"

"Shoot me, and I'll drop it. Shoot me and the virus spills right here. Then what do you do?"

"What happens? Then I shoot you, just for being obstinate. I'm a *nat*, Horvath. The virus won't hurt me.

"It'll kill Hartmann."

Hannah's gaze flicked over to Gregg, and he saw an azure affection there, and the muted gray of regret. "Yes. And I'd trade one life for the millions we'd save. That's a trade I'd make any day. Any time."

"I don't believe you."

Hannah smiled, and it was the coldest expression Gregg had ever seen on her face. "Then that's another mistake on your part, General. It's your move."

For long seconds, Horvath stared at Hannah. The virus swirled under the cut glass. Then he slowly set it down on the flags. "Gregg—" Hannah said. Gregg scurried forward and retrieved the decanter. Holding its slow death in his hand, he made certain to brush against Horvath as he passed. The eddying emotions around the man strengthened as he made the contact, letting him follow the welling emotions back to their source. His link made, Gregg moved back.

"Now what?" Horvath asked.

Hannah sniffed. "Now you tell us where Rudo is. That's not all the virus. There were three vials. My guess is that you got one. Where's Rudo? Where are the other two vials of Trump?"

"You think I'm going to tell you, just because you're holding a gun? You don't know me. You don't know me at all."

Gregg reveled in the confrontation, feeling the wild anger from the two of them. Hannah, he could tell, was beginning to waver, not certain what to do next. He found the strings to her anger, to all the resentment over what the Sharks had done to her over the last year, to the underlying rage over the death and pain they'd caused over the decades. He opened the channels to that fury, let it pulse and surge until it pushed aside the pale yellow. Hannah suddenly moved the muzzle of the gun; her finger convulsed on the trigger. The sound of the shot was deafening, and Horvath went sprawling, clutching at his right knee. Blood trickled from between his fingers.

"You don't know me, either," Hannah told him. "Rudo destroyed my life, murdered my friends, and tried to kill me. Now you're trying to kill everyone infected by the wild card. You people want to play God. Well, I told you before; I'll trade one life for several anytime, and if it's yours, I don't mind playing God myself. Now, where's Rudo?"

"I won't tell you," Horvath muttered through gritted teeth. He moaned. "I can't tell you because I don't know. Jesus, my knee . . ."

Gregg reveled in the pain and at the same time yanked the strings of Hannah's rage once more. Hannah's finger moved, the gun barked, and Horvath rolled on the floor, smearing blood from a shoulder wound. "The next time, it's your balls," Hannah told him. "Rudo—where is he?"

"In Syria," Horvath said, nearly a scream. "With the Nur." Hannah stepped forward until she was standing over the man, pointing the blackened muzzle between his legs. The smell of gunpowder was almost overpowering, but there was another smell—Horvath had pissed his pants. "It's the truth, I swear it. Oh God, please . . ."

"Does Rudo have the other vials?"

"One, yes." Horvath's eyes were wide, fixed on Hannah's weapon. Gregg could feel the pale tendrils of shock dimming the hues of his panic.

Gregg let go of the strings, his eyes closed as the orgasmic pleasure of the pain washed through him. *You see, it's as good as you remember. So wonderful, so tasty* . . . Hannah blinked; she backed away from Horvath, the gun suddenly trembling in her hand, and she looked down at the wounded man, aghast.

It wasn't for the pleasure, Gregg told the voice. *He's told us where Rudo is. That was the reason. I did it so we would know.*

Sure you did, Greggie. Sure you did. Doing the wrong things for all the right reasons . . .

Hannah took a deep breath. Gregg felt her push the rising guilt back, but he knew it would be there later: a snack. "All right," Hannah said. "Gregg, get the virus. We have to get out of here."

"What about me?" Horvath wailed. "I'm bleeding."

"We'll make sure someone finds you," Hannah said.

Gregg, his stubby hands wrapped around the decanter, stopped. He could sense someone else watching. Someone whose emotional matrix was very familiar.

"That won't be necessary," Billy Ray said, stepping out of the shadows behind Hannah. "Someone already knows."

The woman with the gun blanched when Ray stepped out of the shadows. His fighting suit was stained with blood and dust, his face was smeared with the same. Hartmann had the decanter full of death clutched in his clumsy-looking hands. Ray advanced slowly toward him and the woman with the gun. What was her name?

"Saw you at the airport, Senator, but you didn't stay to chat. When was the last time we had a chance to talk about things? Not since I spilled my guts for you in Atlanta, back in eighty-eight."

"Uh—" Hartmann started to back away, edging closer to the woman. She clearly didn't know what was going on. She waved the gun in Ray's direction, but he ignored her.

"You've got something I want, Senator. Something I've chased halfway across the world."

Ray advanced past Horvath, who was groveling on the floor with knee and shoulder wounds. Fucking Shark. He realized now that Churchill had probably been trying to warn him about Horvath when he'd thought the old man was telling him about Johnson.

"You just wait," Ray told him in passing. "You're next." Ray focused on Hartmann and the bimbo with the gun. "Give me the decanter, Senator."

"I—I can't, Billy. It's dangerous."

Ray felt something inside him explode. "Of course it's dangerous, you fucking idiot! It's full of the Black Trump!"

"I know! I know!" Hartmann said, his ridiculous head bobbing up and down. "But it's safe in our hands. Trust me. We'll take care of it."

Ray laughed. "Trust *you*? I wouldn't trust you as far as I can fucking spit, Senator. I saw your handiwork in the pub."

". . . I saw your handiwork in the pub."

Ray was talking to Gregg, but it was Hannah who answered. "We all make mistakes," she said. She swung around to face Ray, the gun held in both of her hands, the muzzle pointed at Ray's chest. The front of Ray's fighting suit was torn and covered with blood, but Ray seemed more amused than concerned. "Let's not make another one right now," Hannah continued. "We could use a little help."

"You act like you have room to bargain," Ray answered. "One part of my job was to find you two and bring you back to the States. I always do my job. Don't I, Senator? Even when I get no thanks and no recognition. Even when I get chopped to pieces protecting someone."

The violet resentment literally poured from the man, and Gregg plucked the familiar strings of Billy Ray's psyche. It was like fondling a favored, much-handled instrument. There was a brilliant fury there, very recent, Gregg suspected, from the extent of it that Ray's fight with Johnson had not gone as well as it could have. *That's good. Ray will want to redeem himself.*

Underneath the violet, Gregg could still feel a deeply hidden small core of blue: respect for what Gregg once had been. Ray had enjoyed his years as Gregg's bodyguard. He'd loved the power and prestige the position gave him. That was still there, covered over now by years apart and Gregg's shabby treatment of Ray after the convention. Gregg set himself to repairing the damage, to fusing the strings once more and shoveling aside the neglect.

"Billy," Gregg said as soothingly as he could, cursing the thin voice of his joker body. "Hannah's right. We're on the same side here."

"That's not the way I understand it."

"Here," Gregg said. He lifted the decanter. "This is what Horvath and Johnson were trying to release. Here's the Black Trump." Ray looked at it, and the hue of Ray's anger changed subtly. "You know that Hannah and I have been telling the truth, don't you? You know what the Black Trump is."

"I've *seen* what it does," Ray said tersely.

"There were three vials," Gregg continued. "I don't think you know that. This is one. Horvath's told us that Rudo has one of the other two. And we know where he is."

With the words, Gregg yanked the strings, pulling hard. Ray seemed to sway for a moment with it, but then the thing inside Gregg pulled back at the strings. *No, that's not the way. Ray's dangerous, remember? He's already tried to kill you. This isn't the way. It won't work.* The coldness returned to Ray's voice. "What are you offering, Hartmann?"

"This," Gregg said. "As I said, we're on the same side, really. I think we stand a better chance if we join forces. I want to trade Rudo's location for our freedom—and a ride to where Rudo is." Ray wasn't listening. Not anymore. It didn't matter. Gregg found that he didn't really want Ray's cooperation. There was something else that would be . . . tastier.

"Not a chance," Ray said. "I don't cut deals with assholes and murderers."

"Hey!" Hannah said, and at the same time, Gregg yanked at the strings of her emotions, hard. Her black-red intense anger was still there, and twin spots of color flared high on her cheeks at Ray's accusation. "Fuck you."

"Sure." Ray grinned nastily at her. "Any time you like, darlin'. Right before I take you both in." Still grinning, he started forward, and Gregg could feel his certainty that Hannah wouldn't fire, that she wouldn't pull the trigger.

So easy. So tasty . . .

The gun jumped in Hannah's hand, the flash from the muzzle making Gregg blink. Ray gave a surprised *"Hunh?"* and staggered backward, crimson spreading out on the blood-dappled white uniform from a stomach wound. Hannah pulled the trigger again, and again, and again, as Ray went to his knees and then collapsed on the floor, as Gregg tugged at the strings and sucked at the sweet, joyous pain in Ray's mind. He let go of the connection to Hannah, let her emotions drop back to normal.

Hannah dropped the gun, suddenly. She looked at Ray, at the moaning Horvath, at Gregg. "My God," she breathed. "Oh, my God."

"Come on," Gregg told her, relishing Hannah's guilt—a dessert after the twin feasts of Horvath and Ray. "We have to get out of here."

Two

The guidebook said that Jerusalem was a city of a thousand names, and proceeded to name a few of them: Shalem, Yerushalem, Yir'eh, Tsiyon, Jebus, Ir David. Gregg decided that one of them must translate as "City of Contradictions."

In their first day in the Holy City, Gregg and Hannah saw more suffering and poverty than either of them had ever glimpsed in the States; they also saw more riches and wealth than they might have thought possible—vast, gilded temples and palatial estates. The poor, if nothing else, were more numerous. They were of all races and religions, heads covered against the sun, their bodies dusted with dirt that had once clogged the pores and caked the heels of prophets, pilgrims, and conquerors.

But one couldn't eat history, couldn't take shelter in antiquity.

Gregg could taste the complex emotions of the city. The strands of violence and rage, of love and hope, of despair and sorrow, faith and devotion—they swirled in the heated winds off the fig-dotted hills, snaked around the pale stone buildings and twined in the narrow, winding streets. The seductive tendrils, so full of delicious hues and shades, pulled at Gregg. He wanted to call out to the driver of their taxi to stop, to let him out so that he could follow the emotions back to their source, so that he could make the connection that would let him play with the colors of Jerusalem's soul.

Given what they'd seen on their taxi tour of the city, they hadn't expected the Joker Quarter to be anything less than squalid. Their taxi driver would not drive past the gates of the quarter—maybe it was the armed joker guards obviously on watch there, maybe it was simple fear of jokers: Gregg couldn't tell from the emotions wafting from the man.

"This is gonna be just great," Hannah said as she paid the driver. She tugged at the robe she wore. "Even Mr. Greasy Hair here won't go in. Lovely." She glanced at the silent Fist guards with ill-disguised contempt. They watched as Gregg and Hannah walked into the quarter.

They expected squalor. They were surprised. Certainly the buildings were old and run-down, certainly there was abject poverty here, misery and starvation, but there was also an ill-defined sense of order that had been missing outside. The streets were mostly clean, and people went about their business without seeming to worry about the others passing them on the street. They saw women and children moving about unescorted, something the taxi driver had mentioned as unusual in Jerusalem. Hannah was stared at more than Gregg. There were scowls directed at her, and an elderly woman—her fluttering veil revealing large tufts of hair protruding from her nostrils—hissed "Nat bitch" in passing.

Gregg decided that the hues of the quarter were as appetizing as those of Jokertown had been. *Yes,* the voice echoed. *A lovely place. We must get to know it better.*

They checked in to a hostel near the Gate, taking what they were told was the only room available, on the first floor. The joker at the desk, his skin dappled with orange spots and blue stripes like some gaudy tropical fish, ignored Hannah and would only speak to Gregg. When Hannah asked for an extra key, he slid it across the counter to Gregg. He asked about luggage and sneered when told that they had none. "Enjoy your stay, sir," he said as they left the lobby. Gregg let himself savor Hannah's irritation as they made their way down the dark corridor to the room.

"Now what?" Hannah asked. There was only one bed; neither of them commented on the arrangement. She prodded the mattress with one hand, then bounced on it experimentally a few times. "No TV. Probably just as well. Brian said that he'd send word to the Dog that we're coming. Do we wait for him or do we go looking?"

. . . must get to know it better . . .

"I think it'd be best if I go out alone," Gregg told her. "We've already seen how nats are treated here. Stay here and rest—try to take care of the jet lag. I'll see if I can make contact with the Dog." With the words, he slathered blue weariness over her unease. Hannah nodded.

"Be careful out there," she said. She leaned back and closed her eyes. "Maybe it's just because of the Fists, but I have the feeling that the violence is never quite buried here, that if you just scratch the surface of the city, it'll all come leaping out."

Gregg smiled. "I think you're right," he said.

A few minutes later, outside, he blinked in the fierce sunlight. He could see jokers wandering past the entrance to the hostel, his enhanced sense of smell could scent a thousand odors hanging in the still air, but he was searching with other senses.

There . . . You feel it? Anger, laced with worry. Over this way . . .

I don't have to do this, he told the voice firmly. *I don't.*

I know, came the soothing reply. *That was the old Gregg, addicted to the power. But this time you can control it. Still, you need to use it, need to remember how it works. You'll need the power to find the virus and destroy it. That's the reason. That's the only reason.*

Gregg hopped down from the worn steps of the hostel, turned left, and wriggled down a narrow side street, following the invisible trail. Here, the houses leaned out over the street toward their neighbors as if for support. Quickly, the sun was eclipsed behind ancient façades and laundry drying on lines, sending the occasional errant shaft down to expire on granite cobbles. Jokers loitered in the doorways, staying in the cool shadows and out of the midday heat. The city smelled of spice and a hundred noontime meals, of perfume and raw sewage. Through it, Gregg hunted the unseen radiance of frayed emotions. He ducked into an alleyway between two nondescript buildings, avoiding the fly-infested garbage cans. *Yes. It's very close . . .*

Gregg looked up. Through open windows a story above him, he could hear faint voices arguing heatedly in rapid-fire Arabic. The deeper, male voice held the same hues as the trail he'd followed—dark and richly red, like fine, raw meat; the shrill female voice that answered him was marbled with frustration and laced with fear: an old argument, then, one that had led the two into a physical confrontation before. As Gregg stood there, listening, the voice tugged at him.

Go on . . .

There's no connection. I can't feel him, can't control him without that.

Then we'll create the link.

It's dangerous. Stupid. I don't need this. I don't have to do it . . .

The voice seemed to sigh. *The side door's open. Go up the stairs. Knock on the door. Say you're looking for someone, apologize for interrupting, and shake hands with the man before you go. That's all. You'd have him. He'll taste good. I promise.*

As Gregg stood there in indecision, he heard the scrape of leather on stone.

"Gregg Hartmann?"

Gregg started guiltily at the voice, his small body lurching upright in a defensive posture. A boy was standing in the dappled shadow at the alleyway's opening—a man-child, no more than fifteen, and the hands that dangled at his side were tipped with razor-like, gleaming claws. Like the city, he was a dichotomy: an innocent face underlaid with implied violence. There was a delicious torment in the child, a chaotic turbulence that Gregg suddenly wanted to touch. The sound of voices above was suddenly only sound. The hues and shades wrapped around them vanished, but he could see fresh colors around the boy, sharp and bright. He wanted to touch them.

"Who are you?" he asked.

"I'm Needles," the boy said. He lifted his hands; the claws rasped with the motion. The voice held the accent of New York City. "I . . . I was told you'd be here. I've come to take you and the woman to the Black Dog."

"You're with the Fists? You're American?"

A nod. The mingled colors swirled with the motion.

Gregg sniffed suspiciously. "I was told the Dog was difficult to see. Kind of strange that we're not here an hour before we get an invitation."

"He's been expecting you. He said to tell you that he knows about Westminster and the Trump." The boy shrugged, scuffed at a loose cobblestone. He looked sidewise at Gregg, brown eyes behind a ragged thicket of hair. "From what I've seen, it's not exactly politically correct to turn down an invitation from the Black Dog."

"Then I guess I'm glad you came to fetch me, Needles." Gregg held out his tiny hand. After a moment's hesitation, Needles's claws brushed Gregg's skin. Gregg snatched at the tendrils of emotion that clung to the boy, following them back, letting his mind run along the path of the youth's mind and set the linkages.

Yes . . . We have him . . .

Needles's hand dropped. Claws clashed like a tray of flatware. "Come on," Gregg told him. "Let's get Hannah."

"I'll, pant, get, *pant,* I'll get you, *pant,* for this," Bradley Finn gasped back at him around the seventh or eighth mile, as the rickshaw jounced along through Hong Kong's teeming streets.

"Is it my fault you're out of shape?" Jay said, looking up from the map spread across his knees. "You ought to pay me for the workout. Besides, with the cost of malpractice insurance and all, you never know when you're going to need another trade."

Finn looked back over his shoulder and his broad hindquarters to where Jay lounged in the seat. "How come, *pant,* I have to, *pant,* pull, *pant,* and you, *pant,* get to ride?" Sweat had left rings under the arms of the centaur's baggy shirt and plastered his hair to his forehead in damp strands beneath the wide straw hat. A liquid tendril of brown was creeping slowly down one check.

"I told you," Jay told him, again. "Joker rickshaw boys pulling tourists around are a dime a dozen. This way, you blend right in; nobody looks at you twice. Just part of the local color. By the way, your disguise is running."

Finn took a hand off the right pole and wiped away the trickle of dyed sweat. His cheek was a kind of greenish brown where the dye had run. "You *had* to, *pant,* to get the, *pant,* cheapest brand." Finn was a palomino no longer; now he was more a muddy brown, with black patches, and a few red highlights. He looked like a mess, actually, but the bathtub in their hotel suite looked a lot worse.

Jay shrugged. "Hey, I was buying in bulk, the guy cut me a deal," he said. They crested a hill and began to plunge downward, accelerating rapidly. "He even threw in that swell coolie hat for free. Listen, after you drop me off, find a pay phone and check in with Peter. Have him tell Jerry and Sascha to stand by for new orders. If Belew's turned up a lead, we may need— Jesus, *slow down!*" A gaggle of camera-laden tourists was crossing the street ahead. Middle-aged American women scattered, shrieking, in all directions. They were all wearing T-shirts covered with ideograms. Probably Chinese for *I'm a stupid tourist and I paid way too much for this ugly shirt.*

A pothole the size of Cleveland gaped in front of the rickshaw. With unseemly malice, Finn guided the right wheel into it, bouncing Jay down and up again and leaving him with his kidney somewhere near his tonsils.

"Real good," Jay said through clenched teeth. The map flapped against his thighs. He smoothed it out, turned it around, and frowned, glancing back up at the passing scenery for the street Belew's message had specified. The Chinese ideograms on the signs were impossible to decipher in the first place, and the bumpy ride didn't make it any easier. "Turn right at that corner and look for a shop with ducks in the window."

"*All* the shops have ducks in the window," Finn bitched, but he turned right, taking the corner on one wheel so that Jay had to hang on for dear life. The map went sailing away and plastered itself across the windshield of a huge antique Rolls-Royce, whose chauffeur honked at them. Finn shot him the finger.

"Cut that out," Jay said. "You're supposed to be a humble joker rickshaw boy, not a New York City cabbie."

Finn was too busy panting to answer. The street veered up-hill again, and finally Finn began to slow. They climbed up and up and up some more, and finally Jay saw ducks. *"Ducks,"* he shouted. "Ducks at nine o'clock. Stop!"

Finn stopped, his mane leaking brown fingers all over the back of his shirt, his chest heaving. Jay climbed out of the rick-shaw on wobbly legs. "I hope you don't expect a tip," he told Finn. He walked off before the centaur could gather the breath for a reply.

Inside the duck shop was dim and quiet, and full of deli-cious smells. The food in Hong Kong was fabulous, Jay had discovered, but it was better not to ask what it was that tasted so good as you were scarfing it down. It usually turned out to be fried tripe or crispy goose bills or sweet-and-sour panda testicles, and then you had to taste it again as it came back up.

An elderly Chinese man emerged from behind a bamboo curtain, took one look at Jay, and nodded silently. Jay nodded silently in reply and went through the curtain, down a narrow flight of steps, to a cool basement vault where J. Bob Belew was smoking a pipe of opium with a monkey the size of Orson Welles.

The monkey took a deep drag from the long pipe, and said, "And this is the famous Popinjay. Often I have wished to meet you, Mr. Ackroyd. You would have been a great success in my profession." The monkey spoke English with an Oxford ac-cent, but the effect was somewhat spoiled by his tail, which swayed sinuously behind him in rhythm with his words.

"What profession would that be?" Jay asked, looking around for a chair. The basement was crammed with fakey lacquer screens, Ming vases, and life-sized funerary soldiers, cheap Hong Kong knockoffs of priceless Chinese antiquities.

"Lord Tung is a smuggler," Belew said.

"Smuggling is such a harsh word," the monkey demurred.

He offered the pipe to Belew, who accepted it gravely. "I am only a trader and, in my own small way, one who fights for economic freedom for all. What a man wishes to buy, I sell to him. What a man wishes to sell, I buy." He smiled at Jay and bowed his head.

Jay took another look around. Okay, so maybe the stuff *wasn't* cheap, fakey Hong Kong knockoffs. He was a detective, not a museum curator. What the hell did he know? "I'm real happy for you," he told the fat monkey-man with the sleepy eyes, "but maybe we could get to the point? The meter's running in my rickshaw."

J. Bob Belew took a pull from the opium pipe and held it for a long moment. Smoke curled up from his nostrils when he finally exhaled. He looked completely at ease here, but then, Belew *always* looked completely at ease, no matter where he was or who he was with. "Lord Tung has some information for us," J. Bob said calmly, like they had all the time in the world.

"My house supplies advanced Western laboratory equipment to a number of pharmaceutical manufacturers throughout Asia," Lord Tung said. "Of late, one such concern has been making a number of rather eccentric purchases."

"A scanning-tunneling microscope is well beyond the needs of most Golden Triangle drug cartels," Belew put in.

"I am prepared to supply full details," Lord Tung said.

"Real good," Jay said. "Inquiring minds want to know." He reached back for his wallet. "How much?"

"Please, Mr. Ackroyd, put your billfold away," Lord Tung said. "I have no need of your money. We are all friends here, are we not?" He smiled at Jay and offered the opium pipe.

Jay glanced at Belew. J. Bob gave him an almost imperceptible nod. Jay took the pipe. He didn't know quite what to do with it. "Friends," he said. "Right. Whatever you say." Lord Tung was watching him. Jay put the stem in his mouth. The pipe was almost as long as his arm. He felt like an idiot. He sucked in, got a lungful of sweet smoke, and coughed violently. "*Smooth,*" he choked out, between gasps. What the hell were you supposed to say? Jay didn't know the etiquette of opium dens. *Maybe it was like wine tastings,* he thought. "A nice mellow bouquet, with just a hint of presumption," he tried. "Yum yum."

Lord Tung laughed like a child. An especially large and hairy child, but a child nonetheless. "I like you, Mr. Ackroyd."

"And I want to marry you and have your children, Mr. Tung," Jay returned. He passed the pipe off to Belew quickly, before they made him take another puff.

"*Lord* Tung," Lord Tung corrected, with a hint of steel in the high, dreamy voice.

"Whatever," Jay said.

The huge monkey-joker folded his hands over his belly like a big, hairy Buddha and smiled, yellow eyes blinking slowly.

J. Robert Belew spoke up. "It is pleasant to know I have had some small part in bringing such good men together, and to witness the beginning of this great friendship. *A new friend is as new wine; when it is old, thou shall drink it with pleasure.*"

Jay was still trying to work that through and see if it came out as a compliment when Lord Tung said, "I would never think of taking money for the information I have to share with you. It is ever a great joy for a friend to help a friend."

That one didn't take much working through. Jay was getting the idea.

"Yeah, I love that, too," he said. He tried to look helpful. "Anything I can do for you, Lord Tung?"

"Perhaps . . . no . . . I hesitate to ask . . . it would be a crime to sully the serenity of this golden moment by imposing on your kindness and goodwill."

"I know Jay would think it no imposition, Lord Tung,"

J. Robert Belew said. "Nothing gives our Popinjay more delight than being of service to a friend."

"Boy, howdy," Jay said in a flat voice. "Fiddle dee dum, fiddle dee dee, helping pals is all for me."

"Why, then," Lord Tung said, "I will ask for only the smallest of favors, as a token of your esteem and affection. I would never wish you to inconvenience yourself on my behalf, but this is such a little thing, you need only to lift a single finger . . ."

Jay got his drift. He lifted the single finger in question. "This little piggy went to market," he said. "I don't know if J. Bob here clued you in, but I can only pop things to places I've been. I need to picture the destination in my head."

"I am fully aware of the extent and limits of your power, my friend," Lord Tung said smoothly. "I have, oh, many good friends in New York who would be pleased to accept delivery at any location you would deem appropriate. Your offices, say, or your apartment in Manhattan."

"My offices," Jay said firmly. His wife was used to strange items popping up in the apartment, but the arrival of a midnight moving crew from Chinatown would probably throw even Hastet. He glanced around at all the lacquered screens, the Ming vases, the funerary soldiers. "So what do you want popped?"

"Why, all of it," Lord Tung said, with a huge smile that revealed a mouth full of yellow teeth. Then he laughed and laughed and laughed.

Gregg wasn't certain what he expected the Black Dog to look like, but somehow the reality wasn't a disappointment. Nothing about the Hound of Hell was ordinary. Part of it was the atmosphere of the catacombs, this silent maze buried unguessed, beneath the tempestuous, quarreling warrens of Jerusalem. Part of it was the Dog himself. He radiated presence, something beyond the image brought by the black robe and mask, the tall muscular presence. His charisma was tangible, pulsing and hypnotic and undeniable. Dangerous.

As dangerous as I was. Once.

No, replied the voice. *As dangerous as you are NOW.*

Gregg didn't answer. Even in the old days, at the full height of his power, he'd been afraid of aces and those whose power he didn't know. The Black Dog had *something*, and that made Gregg uneasy.

"Gregg Hartmann," the Black Dog said. His English had a trace of some accent Gregg could not place, and a smirk rode in the words. He gestured to the chairs set around the wooden table in the room. An enameled decanter of strong coffee sat in the center, under siege by empty china cups and pinned in the glare of a spotlight. Gregg thought the decanter looked good enough to eat.

"So good to meet you at last, Senator, even under these circumstances." The Black Dog turned to Hannah, and the eyes behind the mask regarded her with an intensity that had been missing when he looked at Gregg. "Ms. Davis. Even Arabic garb can't hide your beauty."

Gregg could have told the Dog that tactic was a mistake. He felt the arc of Hannah's irritation jab from under her surface colors.

Hannah looked at Gregg and sighed. "We don't have time for this polite shit," Hannah said, turning back to the Black Dog. Her voice sounded harsh against the mellifluous, deep tones of the Fists' leader; it brought Gregg's puppet-like head around, startled. If Hannah felt the pull of the Dog's presence, then his unwanted compliment—after the events of the past weeks—had shredded its power. "You've been told what almost happened in England—it could *still* happen. Do you understand the importance of this? If you do, then we need your help. We must find the other two vials of Black Trump, or even your little subterranean stronghold won't save you."

The Black Dog almost sounded amused. "You have a lot to learn about this society," he told her. "There are certain ways that things must be said before they are heard."

"In other words, I'm just a woman and a nat, so shut the fuck up?"

The voice acquired an edging of frost. "I'm only saying that this is not the States, and that someone with your intelligence will realize that she cannot act as if it was."

"And I'm sure that the Black Dog has the intelligence to realize that we *are* from the States," Gregg said before Hannah could speak, "and will understand our directness and forgive it."

The Black Dog sniffed behind the mask. "That was almost smooth, Senator. I see that you didn't lose your political instincts when you became a joker." The Dog glanced at the silent woman behind him, then back to Hannah and Gregg. "I understand more of the importance of recent events than the two of you believe or know. Unfortunately, your arrival here was a bit . . . late, even if your presence in England turned out to be fortuitous. You see, my sources are very good, in nearly every country of the world, and I've known about the Sharks and the vials for some time."

"Then why haven't you done anything about them?" Hannah asked. "That's the most criminal thing the Fists have ever done."

The Dog glared at her. "I've done what I needed to do, and what I could do," he told them. "We always suspected that Jerusalem was one place they would try to release the virus, and we were certain the Nur was a Shark. However, we weren't sure where Rudo was. Your information tells me that he managed to slip through our intelligence net and get to the Nur finally, and *I know* where the Nur is. So the puzzle pieces have fallen in place, and now we *can* act."

"Where is the Nur?" Gregg asked.

The Black Dog only raised his hand, but the gesture was sufficient to make Gregg go silent, as if rebuked. "I have already made my plans," the Black Dog said. "I know what to do to get the rest of the information we need. And I know what to do once I have that information."

"I'll bet it has something to do with lots of people losing their lives," Hannah said. "That seems to be about the only thing the Fists are good at."

The Black Dog almost seemed amused. "Perhaps. Actually, what I have in mind doesn't involve violence, only a threat of it. We believe that the Nur and Rudo are planning to release the Black Trump virus in Jerusalem. We also believe that the Nur's reverence for the Holy City would make it impossible for him to damage a single stone of its streets. If the Nur is going to threaten jokers, then *we* will threaten to destroy the Dome of the Rock."

"The Nur has a whole damn *army* to protect the Dome. All he has to do is say the word."

The Black Dog shrugged under his robe. "An army means nothing. You see, the Twisted Fists have a nuclear device."

He said the words the way Gregg might have said *I have a loaf of bread.*

"*What?*" Gregg's voice broke in a screech. Alongside him, he could sense Hannah's speechless outrage.

"I think what I said was clear enough," the Black Dog answered.

"That's total insanity. What is this, the ultimate five-for-one nonsense?" Gregg continued. "A nuke set off in Jerusalem will

kill millions, not to mention destroying some of the most sacred relics of Western religion."

"Certainly, that's a worst-case scenario," the Black Dog replied patiently. Calmly. "Senator, we don't intend to set off the
bomb—not here, anyway."

"Of course not," Hannah said. "You just *borrowed* it."

The Black Dog turned to Hannah, and his voice was all at
once swift, cold steel. "Ms. Davis, you seem to think that the
Twisted Fists are nothing but thugs and murderers."

"Judging by what I've seen so far," Hannah answered defiantly, "that's an excellent description. I'd love to be proved
wrong."

The Black Dog inclined his head slightly to her. "I don't
think the Fists have anything to prove to you, to Senator Hartmann, or to Father Squid and your other friends. I answer to
my own conscience and no one else's." For a moment, the tension held in the room, then the Black Dog let go a breath, and
it eased.

"Let me try to explain. This is what we've learned in the last
few days. The Nur has set up a portable lab for Dr. Rudo. It
could be located in any of Nur al-Allah's nomadic camps in
Syria, and we suspect we know which one. Once we locate it,
then we can destroy the Trump by"—the Black Dog paused,
and seemed to smile under the mask—"more conventional
methods."

"What about the bomb?" Gregg persisted.

The Black Dog shrugged. "Senator, as much as I appreciate
your concern, I think you can see why we need the nuke until
the Trump is destroyed—it will be a very effective tool for co-
ercing the Nur to cooperate. If for any reason the Nur decides
to call our bluff, or if we are unsuccessful in destroying the
virus in the desert, well"—the Dog shrugged—"then an effective and powerful backup system is necessary."

"Couldn't you think of anything except a fucking nuke?"

"God knows I tried," the Black Dog said. He almost seemed to smile. "And now for your part. Our nuke is useless unless the Nur knows that we have it. *You* know the Nur. You've met him, and you know his power. I think you and Ms. Davis would make good messengers, don't you?"

"Burma," Jay Ackroyd bitched as he followed J. Bob Belew up the stairs from the empty vault in the basement. "Fucking terrific."

"If we move fast and take them unawares, we have a chance," Belew said. "Casaday was always too impressed with his own cleverness. It makes him sloppy."

"That warms the cockles of my heart," Jay said.

Belew pushed through the bamboo curtain, with Jay right behind him. The old Chinese man was puttering around the shop. Belew stopped at the counter, gestured at the long row of hanging ducks, and said, "Two, please."

The little Chinese man bowed his head, climbed on a stool, unhooked two ducks, and began wrapping them in crisp white butcher paper cut from a roll. "What's that for?" Jay asked, baffled.

Belew brushed his mustache with his thumb. "Lunch." He accepted the package, bowed to the old man, and walked out into the sunlight. Jay came after him. The rickshaw was still sitting in front of the duck shop, but Finn was gone. Jay looked up and down the street. "Lose something?" Belew asked.

"Finn," Jay said. "I told him to find a pay phone and check in with my man in New York. I hope he didn't get lost."

"You would do well to lose the doctor permanently," Belew said. "Amateurs have no business in an operation like this."

"According to you, we're all amateurs," Jay said.

Belew smiled thinly. "True, but you and the rest of your operatives are amateurs with ace powers. Dr. Finn is not. He has no useful skills, he's conspicuous, he's too emotionally involved, and he argues when he should be taking orders."

Belew was right, but there was something about the way he made his pronouncements that pissed Jay off. "He's a doctor. We may need medical expertise somewhere along the line." He changed the subject quickly, before Belew could frame a reply. "Listen, how the hell are we going to do this? Casaday is going to have a small army guarding the camp, right?"

"Most likely," Belew admitted. "Give me forty-eight hours to contact certain persons in Yangon, and we can go in with a regiment of Burmese paratroops. It's not the way I normally do things, but under these circumstances I don't think we have much choice."

"Wrong," Jay said. "We go in there, guns blazing, with a bunch of your numbnuts, and Casaday whacks Mark before you can get to him. We'll do this my way. I'll get Creighton and Starfin back from Nam, tell Peter to hop a plane, and we'll sneak in before Casaday even knows we're there. All aces. Once we find Mark and his daughter, I can pop everyone else out and—"

"*Those who cannot remember the past are condemned to repeat it.* Santayana. We tried that plan fifteen years ago in Iran. You will recall how that ended. And you're forgetting something. This is not a rescue mission. Our task is to destroy Casaday's supply of the Black Trump. If we fail in that, the fate of Mark Meadows and his daughter becomes largely irrelevant."

"Spare me the *Soldier of Fortune* shit, Belew," Jay said. "I don't buy a word of it. You risked your own life to get me out of Iran in one piece, and you don't even *like* me. Meadows was your friend. There's no way you're going to abandon him."

"Iran was a different circumstance. Genocide was not in the

cards. Don't delude yourself, Ackroyd. I like Mark Meadows, I even admire him in a way, but I *will* sacrifice him, if that's what the mission requires . . . as I would sacrifice you, and Dr. Finn, and even Sprout, poor child. I have seen friends die before."

Jay looked at Belew. "Jesus, you're a cold bastard."

"I'm a professional. If it makes you feel any better, I'd risk my own life just as readily."

"Swell," Jay said sourly. He would have said a lot more—including a few things he might have regretted—but suddenly he heard the sound of hoofbeats. He looked back over his shoulder and there was Bradley Finn, galloping up the steep hill like Man o' War driving down the backstretch.

J. Bob stroked the underside of his mustache with the back of his hand. "A brilliant disguise," he said dryly. "I would never have recognized Dr. Finn. Unless I was looking for a centaur."

Finn came panting to a stop in front of them, chest heaving, all sweaty and lathered, his shirt stuck to his skin. "They, *pant*, they found him, *pant*."

Jay exchanged a look with Belew.

"Perhaps you could you clarify that, Doctor?" Belew said.

Finn was almost hyperventilating. Jay put a hand on his shoulder. "Take it easy. Catch your breath first."

The centaur took a couple of deep breaths. "Jerry and Sascha. Found Casaday. Reading minds. Followed leads. Told Peter. The Black Trump. In Burma. Drug lab. Sascha saw it." He tapped his forehead. "In the mountains. Peter told me." He fumbled a damp paper out of his shirt pocket with fingers stained brown from wiping away cheap dye. "Here," he said, thrusting the paper at Jay.

Jay glanced at it, shrugged, and handed it to Belew. "Same latitude and longitude. Jackpot. Looks like I didn't need to play pattycake with the monkey after all. Jerry is turning out to be an honest-to-God detective." He grinned at J. Bob. "Hey, why not, I taught him everything he knows. We need to work out a rendezvous and plan our—"

Finn interrupted, shaking his head wildly. "No. No. You don't understand. Peter told Jerry to wait, but Jerry wouldn't listen, he said he and Sascha could handle it, he had a plan, they were going in, no time to waste. By now they're in Burma."

For a moment, Jay could not believe what he was hearing. "You're kidding right? You've got to be kidding. Tell me he wouldn't do anything so stupid."

"Why not?" Belew said. "You taught him everything he knows."

"Shit." Jay sat down in the back of the rickshaw and cradled his head in his hands. "Shit shit shit shit shit," he repeated in a furious burst of eloquence.

He felt sick.

Belew crumpled up the paper and said crisply, "Well, that's done. Casaday will kill them both, most likely."

"If he doesn't, I'll kill them myself," Jay promised in a bleak voice. "We have to get to Burma."

"We will," Belew promised grimly. "We may even arrive soon enough to identify the bodies." He climbed into the rickshaw beside Jay. "Doctor, the airport, double quick, if you'd be so kind."

Monsoon season was past, but rain had returned to the mountains, as if to remind the human inhabitants of the power of the storm and keep them duly humble. At first Mark thought the sounds from outside, breaking through the white-noise roar of rain on his trailer to kick him out of sleep, were thunder.

But thunder didn't stutter with that knuckle-rapping cadence of Kalashnikov-series assault rifles, which had become so drearily familiar during the liberation of Vietnam.

His first reaction was to sit bolt upright in bed, crying, "Sprout!" Belatedly the combat self-preservation reflexes J. Bob had dinned into him kicked in. Realizing that the thin-gauge metal walls around him wouldn't even slow metal-jacketed small-arms rounds, he rolled out of bed onto the floor.

Curiosity got him next. He belly-crawled to the window, elbows and hips dragging sheet-wound legs in a weird lamia slither. He *knew* the thing to do was to lie as flat as humanly possible and then some, and think thoughts of oneness with the rough, puke-colored carpet. But the fear was beginning to bubble within him, along with a clamor of voices.

Slowly—as if that made any difference to a stray bullet—he raised his head. Pushing flimsy curtains up with his forehead, he peered over the sill.

The night was black, the rain dense. Random muzzle-flashes lit the downpour like lightning. Mark couldn't tell if the fire was incoming or outgoing, but a lot was going somewhere.

"*Sprout!*" he screamed, and stumbled to his feet. Time for more gratitude to Belew, who had also insisted on teaching Sprout to hug the floor when she heard gunfire. She'd be as safe as possible.

For a while. The only reason Mark could conceive of for the sudden noisy outburst of nocturnal emissions, on his bare-legged scramble through the trailer, banging knees on furniture and scraping elbow on the walls, was that government troops were attacking the opium-army camp. Nothing he had heard about the forces of the socialist military junta in Yangon suggested they'd bother distinguishing between the Black Karens and their captives. He recalled talk about the games the army liked to play with captured rebel women, and his throat filled with sour bile as he slapped frantically for the front-door knob.

A grenade crunched off somewhere as he yanked the door open. He didn't see the flash. Water hit him in the face as if a frat rat had been lurking in wait with a bucket.

This high in the mountains, rain was *cold* at night. Mark ran in a wild, high-stepping splashing dash toward Sprout's barred hootch, elbows pumping. To his left a muzzle flare danced. Bullets went past his head with a sound like a giant sheet tearing. He realized he made an ideal target: a great capering pale scarecrow, wearing white briefs that almost glowed in the dark.

He kept running. He had no room inside for fear for himself. All that mattered was his daughter.

No lights shone from Sprout's hootch. A broad lumpish figure stood before the door. It turned as Mark came splashing up.

It was Ditmar, wearing a black East German Army leather greatcoat. The legs of his pajamas had penguins on them. A Makarov pistol glinted in one chubby fist.

A smile spread across the torturer's face. "Ah, *Herr Doktor*. It seems both of our first thoughts were for your daughter."

A pale oval in the barred window. *"Daddy!"* Sprout cried.

"Baby, *get down!*" Mark exclaimed, gesturing frantically. He turned to Ditmar. "Get away from her, you perverted son of a bitch."

Ditmar shook his head and clucked reprovingly. "Ah, Doctor. Certainly it is imprudent to speak so to a man with a gun."

Mark gathered himself to leap on the German. The little Mak didn't have much stopping power, and Ditmar wasn't Layton; if Mark didn't take more than a round or two, he might be able to break the torturer's neck before he dropped. The odds weren't good, but then, once he was dead all decisions would be made, and the Sharks could no longer compel him to destroy his own kind . . .

"Steady, there, Meadows," a voice rasped. O. K. Casaday came stilting out of the rain, white suit translucent and molded to his gaunt frame, what hair he had plastered to his great round Charlie Brown head. He had a government Colt .45 in hand.

Mark let a long breath out through bared teeth. The moment had passed. The fight had fled him.

Casaday turned to Ditmar. "All right, Fatso, shove off. I got this under control."

Ditmar blinked moist frog eyes. *"Bitte?"* His single black eyebrow hunched in the middle, like a cramping caterpillar. "Your voice—is something wrong?"

It was occurring about then to Mark that Casaday didn't sound at all like himself. The CIA spook turned his head and coughed into his hand.

"Gotta cold. Laryngitis. Just hit me. Now shag ass. Don't you know there's a battle on?"

The German stuck his side arm in a pocket and bustled off. Night and rain swallowed him in one wet gulp. Keeping his pistol pointed at Mark, Casaday went to the hootch door and pounded on it.

"Open up," he yelled. "It's Casaday." Mark heard metallic fumbling sounds familiar to any former New York dweller.

Casaday turned his head toward Mark and caught his eye. Then he winked.

The door opened. The round, brown face of Sprout's Black Karen duenna peered uncertainly forth.

"The girl," Casaday demanded. The woman expostulated in her own language. *"Now."*

The woman vanished. A moment later she came back, herding Sprout like a sheepdog, trying to twitch a pink terry cloth bathrobe closed over her T-shirt and panties.

"Daddy!" the girl exclaimed. She hurled herself at Mark and caught him with a stranglehold around the neck. Her pink Gund bear dangled from one hand.

"Baby, baby, it's okay," Mark said, feeling like a lying shit. Casaday gestured with the gun.

"Let's get a move on."

"Come on, honey." Mark disentangled himself as delicately as he could, caught her by the biceps, and urged her into motion.

The firing seemed to be dying down. Mark had the impression that most of it was now outbound from the compound, which might or might not be a good sign. If it was a government raid, it seemed to have been repulsed.

"Where are we going?" Mark asked.

The spook showed him an odd lopsided smile. It was an expression Mark had never seen out of Casaday before, and not one he would have thought him capable of. "Out of here, with any luck, Dr. Meadows."

They were among parked vehicles, the rain making tiny explosions on the hunched dark backs of the cars. "Got to be one with the keys in it somewhere," Casaday murmured. "Be a real pain to have to hot-wire one."

Mark stared at him. "What's going on here, man?"

Casaday chuckled. "There's more here than meets the eye, Doc," he said. "Here we go." He pulled open the door of a Jeep Cherokee and shoved Sprout in.

A spotlight nailed them from the concertina-wire perimeter like a Network death-beam. "Uh-oh," the CIA man said under his breath.

A squad of Black Karens approached at the trot, rifles at port arms. Casaday stood up straighter and stepped forward. "What the hell's going on here?" he demanded.

"I was just about to ask that frigging question," a voice said from behind the advancing Karens. O. K. Casaday's voice, and no mistake.

The black-clad soldiers fanned out around the Cherokee, trying to point their rifles at Mark without aiming them at Casaday. Mark froze.

The tall figure of O. K. Casaday resolved out of the glare of the spotlight to stand confronting O. K. Casaday.

"All right. Meadows," the new Casaday said, "what the fuck kind of shenanigans are these?"

The Black Karens were gaping from one Casaday to the other. All Mark could do was the same.

"It's a fucking impostor," Mark's Casaday said. "Achoo! Shoot the son of a bitch and stand back."

The Karens muttered at each other, then stepped back to cover all four white people impartially. "You know," the new Casaday said conversationally, "if these dinks get too confused, they're just gonna shoot us all and let Buddha sort us out."

"This is bullshit," the other said. He coughed consumptively. "*Fuck* this cold."

The newcomer cawed a laugh. "No shit. The question is, who's trying to bullshit which bullshitter?"

"Boss"—Layton appeared with more rifle-toting Karens in tow—"we caught this motherfucker . . ."

He stopped. His head swiveled from left to right. His ponytail swung like a drowned mink. His eyes bulged.

"Don't throw your neck out, Layton," the new Casaday said. "What've you got?"

"We, uh, we caught this shithead sneakin' around outside

the wire." A pair of Karens dragged an obvious Westerner forward. He wore a waterlogged white tropical suit like the ones on the Casadays. The right sleeve was stained dark from the upper biceps down.

The wounded man moaned, lifted his head a fraction. He had a pencil-thin mustache and no eyes.

Mark recognized Sascha, who used to work in the Crystal Palace when Chrysalis was still alive. The new Cassaday's lip curled. "A fucking joker. What *is* this, Meadows?"

Mark licked lips that were already as wet as they were likely to get. "I don't know," he said. "I swear to God."

"We got some kind of ace asshole playing cute tricks on us, Layton," the first Casaday said, sounding more like the real thing. He jutted his lantern jaw at the other. "Shoot that puke and let's get out of the rain before we melt."

Layton's hand started inside his camouflaged bush jacket. "Don't be a bigger jagoff than usual, Layton," the second Casaday said.

The kickboxer stopped, let his hand slide back into the open. "Boss," he said, eyes flicking from one Casaday to the other. "Uh—how do I know which *is* the boss?"

"Don't be stupid, Layton," Mark's Casaday said. "Shoot."

"You got a good knockout punch, Layton," the intruding Casaday said.

"Take your best shot. Coldcock us both and see what the fuck we turn into."

Layton was nothing if not obedient. He glanced from one Casaday to the other, then took a skipping step sideways, whipped his stiffened right leg back and around and *up* in a spinning reverse roundhouse kick to the jack-o'-lantern head of the Casaday who had just spoken. He flew out from under his hat and landed on his ass in a bow wave of brown water.

Even for a kickboxer, a move like that took time. The Casaday of the first part took advantage. As the kick was getting underway he was diving into the driver's seat of the Cherokee and cranking the key.

The engine caught like a pool of spilled gasoline. Wheels spun, flinging a rooster tail of mud that drenched Layton as he turned with a shout and dove for the Jeep. Outreached fingertips grazed the rear bumper, and Layton went facedown in red muck.

The Black Karens were watching these weird round-eye antics with undisguised fascination. The satellite dish never pulled in anything as entertaining as *this*.

Layton hauled his face out of the mud, spat some out, and screamed, "Don't just stand there, you fucking little monkeys! *Shoot the asshole!*"

"No! Wait!" Mark jumped before their guns, capering and waving his hands as the angle-cut muzzle brakes came up, hoping they'd think *he* was the asshole. The Black Karens scowled at him and danced around trying to get a clear shot as the Cherokee busted the perimeter wire with a musical twang.

The second Casaday had picked himself up. He now wore a two-tone suit, red in front, white in back. He held a handkerchief to a blood-drooling mouth.

"I should have said, punch one of us, and bust the one you *didn't* pick," he said. "You're such a dumb fuck, Layton. It was inevitable you'd whack out the wrong one first."

"I'm *not* dumb!" Layton said. For some reason he looked to Mark as if for support. "I'm not dumb."

Casaday shook his head. He was working his tongue around inside his mouth as if trying to dislodge a piece of food stuck between his teeth. He spat a broken tooth into his handkerchief, stared briefly at it, and threw tooth and handkerchief into a puddle.

From the night beyond the wire, a gout of yellow flame,

outlining black brush. The *whoomp* of a gasoline explosion compressed their eardrums a second later.

"*Sprout!*" Mark screamed. He ran for the breach in the wire, not caring that he was inviting a burst in the back.

"Keep up with him, you jagoffs!" Casaday shouted. Layton and the Black Karens raced in pursuit.

The hurtling Cherokee had gouged a flattened half-tunnel down a brushy hillside. Mark went vaulting and slipping and sliding through, and if adrenaline didn't lend his lanky frame grace, it gave him the wherewithal to make it through more or less upright.

The Cherokee had nosed into a little gully that now ran with chocolate-colored water, runoff from the camp clearing. It was fully involved in a fire that didn't give a good goddamn for the torrent. Mark stopped dead, and was just wishing that God would stop his heart and get it the hell *over* with when he saw Sprout sprawled on the ground beside the wreck.

He slid on his knees in the mud, like a figure skater bringing home his routine, gathering his daughter in his arms. She was wet and hysterical, but unharmed. Her bear was gone.

They were on their knees, clinging to each other like clumps of seaweed and sobbing uncontrollably, when a Black Karen stepped up behind Mark and slammed the back of his head with the heavy wooden stock of his AKM.

Mark didn't fuzz out right away. He lay on his back blinking at rain that kept trying to get in his eyes, while a torrent of voices poured through his head. He couldn't make out what they were saying, and drew a vague comfort from that. *Then* he went away.

Ray slept.

Despite his torn flesh, ruptured organs, and smashed bones,

despite his pain and anger and grief, Ray slept. He dreamt of his childhood, of the countless roadhouses his mother dragged him to. He dreamt of the hundreds of cheap motels, the dozens of men, some kind, some angry, most indifferent, whom his mother lived with from time to time. They never abused Ray, not seriously, unless indifference could be called abuse. He dreamt of the doctors who diagnosed him as hyperactive and the drugs his mother was too scatterbrained to administer effectively.

When he dreamt of the first time he picked up a football, the dreams changed. He was no longer nobody. He was the first player to go from the Busted Butte Central High six-man football team to a major college, where he led the University of Michigan to the Rose Bowl in his freshman year, broke his leg in three places in the first half and his ace turned and he tried to get back into the game and people realized there was something strange about the boy nicknamed Kid Wolverine.

So it was government service rather than a pro-football career, and his first mission was the botched attempt to rescue the Iranian-held hostages. There Ray learned about the taste of blood and earned his second nickname, Carnifex, given him by the Mechanic, an ace agent with a classical bent, and God, was that almost twenty years ago?

Ray kicked ass for the government, never questioning, never thinking, just doing. He killed more than he could remember, and came close to death himself half a dozen times—at the claws of the werewolf clan in that not-so-sleepy little New Mexican town, at the buzz-saw hands of Mackie Messer, under the waters of New York Bay during the Battle for the Rox.

But there he learned that action itself wasn't enough. He needed something else. He needed meaning in his life. He needed, he now knew, April Harvest. He had never needed anyone, not even when he was a child. Not his mother, not that son of a bitch, Hartmann. No one. Never.

But now he knew he needed April. He would find her. Nothing would stop him.

Ray woke, his dreams over.

Captain Flint was standing in front of his hospital bed. He looked concerned, if a stone statue can possibly look concerned. Next to him, looking dwarfed and harried, was Nephi Callendar.

"We thought you were going to die," Flint whispered in his sepulchral voice. He sounded like a disappointed Grim Reaper.

"Me?" Ray asked with a grin that was only partly forced. "From a couple of bullet wounds?"

"You took seven rounds," Flint intoned. *"Two pulped your liver. One shattered your right humerus. Two perforated your small intestine. One bisected your spleen. One lodged in your chest near your heart. I won't even mention the bayonet wound."*

"Is that all?" Ray said. He sat up. "How long have I been out?"

"Only three days," Callendar said. "That's not very long, even for you." Ray looked at the tubes feeding into his left inner elbow and pulled them loose. He swung his feet over the side of his bed.

"What about April?" he asked Callendar.

The agent sighed. "Johnson still has her . . . we think. At least we haven't found a body."

"Hartmann and his bimbo?"

Flint and Callendar glanced at each other. Finally Flint reluctantly whispered, *"They seem to have disappeared during the confusion."*

Ray shook his head. "Jesus Christ. Great job, Flint. You and your boys deserve a big round of applause." He stood. Nausea punched him in the gut.

"Easy, Ray," Callendar said. "You've taken some bad wounds and lost a lot of blood."

"Fuck you," Ray snapped. He ripped his hospital gown off with one hand and tossed it on the bed. He examined his body. The entry wounds had all closed, but the puckered scars still looked angry and raw. He knew that everything hadn't quite knitted together inside. Still, he could move, he thought. He took a tentative step, felt his stomach surge into his throat, and swallowed. "Get me some clothes," he told Callendar.

"Well, if you're feeling up to it," Callendar said. He looked at Flint, who looked back silently. "There's something we need you to do."

Ray was about to tell Callendar to take the mission and shove it up his ass, but something stopped him, some new-found sense of restraint and cunning.

"What?" he asked.

"The Black Dog has a nuclear bomb. He's got it in Jerusalem and he's threatened to use it."

"What, and blow up the whole city? Himself included? He's fucking crazy."

"He may very well be," Flint whispered. *"Apparently he feels his back's against the wall. He's caught between the Nur and the Card Sharks."*

"Jerusalem, huh?" Ray remembered Horvath's words to Hartmann and that bitch who'd gunned him down.

"One other thing," Callendar added. "There've been indications that Johnson's in the city and that he knows about the bomb and is trying to get it, either for the Sharks to use or simply to take it away from the Fists."

"Well, *that* would be a relief," Ray said. "I told you before, Nehi. Get me some clothes."

Callendar sighed. "That's *Nephi*. All right. But remember

your mission. Forget about Hartmann for now. Recover that nuke at all costs. And arrest or terminate the Black Dog."

"Terminate. Jesus Christ, Nephi, you're starting to sound like one of those fucking bureaucrats. You mean kill, don't you?"

"Well, yes."

Ray nodded. But for once death and destruction weren't on his mind. He was thinking of April Harvest, of the heat of her body and the sweetness of her mouth, and he knew that he was in love.

"Just what the *hell* went on back there, man?" Mark asked the eyeless man, almost shouting to be heard over the hum of the C-130's four big turboprop engines.

Sascha Starfin raised the Styrofoam cup two-handed to his mouth, snatched another convulsive gulp of the water Mark had given him when he woke up a few minutes before. A few drops of blood dotted a bandage wound around Sascha's upper arm. The round that hit him had punched a clean hole through muscle, missing bone. His eyeless face was bruised and puffy, and dried blood was caked on a split lower lip. Layton had worked on him, Mark guessed.

Nylon netting pinned crates holding notes, equipment, and the Black Trump cultures—including Mark's secret Overtrump—in the rear of the aircraft. The squat black-painted Hercules had dropped out of the rising sun's red eye to touch down on what looked like a wide stretch of road like a hippo ballerina coming down from a grand jeté. The Black Karens loaded it like ants on meth, and the plane took off without even cutting its engines.

"We were trying to rescue you," Sascha said dully. "Me and

my, uh, partner." He took another hit of water, shook his head. "What the hell am I being cagey for? Me and Creighton. It's not like I didn't tell *them* everything."

"Don't worry about it, man," Mark said earnestly. "Anybody would have done the same thing. Once *they* start in on you, you're gonna talk one way or another." He nodded toward the front of the cavernous cargo compartment, where Casaday, Layton, and a couple of Western goons Mark hadn't seen before sat on the bench that ran down both sides. Dr. Carter Jarnavon snoozed near them with his head on a rolled-up lab coat, drooling. Colonel Ditmar noticed their attention and gave them a fat smile that glistened like oil in the dim light.

Mark remembered Osprey tied to a chair, the awful *snick* of bolt cutters, blood spurting, Osprey screaming . . . and that exact same smile. He felt sick.

He glanced down at his daughter, filled with the irrational need to be reassured that she was—however momentarily—safe. She slept on the floor by his feet, wrapped in olive drab blankets.

Another wave of pain crashed through his gut. Sprout was acting strange. She was very stiff around her father, cool almost, pushing him gently but definitely away when he tried to enfold and reassure her. That evoked his greatest secret fear, that he had lived with since she was born: that one day she would awaken to the fact that he was a failure as a father and reject him.

Has it happened? Is she rejecting me? The fear was given additional torque by the realization that it was selfish, and emphasized his unworthiness all the more. He imagined the hand of God following the Herc across a map of Asia, pointing, and accompanying it the legend glowing in mile-high letters: MARK MEADOWS, FAILED FATHER.

Oh: AND GENOCIDE. Can't leave *that* out.

Sascha was talking again. "Sorry, man. My mind drifted."

The joker nodded accommodatingly. "I was saying my boss is an old friend of yours. Jay Ackroyd."

"Jay? He's looking for me? Why? I'm supposed to be dead. It was on CNN."

"Well, *he* wasn't. Not exactly. He's hunting one of the Black Trump containers. One trail led through Saigon. He sent me and Creighton to follow up. He asked questions and I read minds, so it didn't matter if they answered or not."

Mark blinked. Then he remembered what Sascha was. Cap'n Trips had never passed much time in the old Crystal Palace, but he'd been there.

"Anyway, we did some detective work. Some people down on the riverfront saw some pretty suspicious cargo being loaded on a sampan the night of the blast. No, they didn't say anything to us about it." A slight smile. "They didn't have to."

"I . . . guess not."

Sascha rubbed soft, white hands together, interlacing the fingers as if scrubbing them. Mark thought he was still trying to wash away the guilt of spilling his guts. Then he stamped the thought back down where the skimming telepath wouldn't catch it.

You're being a liberal weenie again, JJ Flash told him from the cheap seats of his skull. *Can you really afford to be that sensitive right now? You got better things to do with your mental energies.*

Sascha was looking at him with those blank flesh patches over his eye sockets. Mark realized he was politely waiting for Mark's internal dialogue to get over.

Hey, Sascha, JJ thought, *my man! How's it hangin'?*

"Been better, JJ, I got to tell you," Sascha said. "How's by you?"

Same old same-old. Trying to get over.

Mark squeezed his eyes shut and kind of vibrated his head. Attention drew JJ Flash like sunlight draws a growing plant. *He* was old pals with Sascha; he had frequented a lot of places Mark stayed away from, including the palace.

Okay, guys, Mark thought, *cool it. I'm not gonna be odd man out of a conversation with my own multiple personality disorder.*

Wrong again! a shrill thought came. *True multiple personality disorders are prohibitively rare. You just don't want to admit that we're real people, trapped by your own irresponsible indulgence in drugs inside your—*

Traveler, Mark thought pointedly, *shut the fuck up.*

"*Anyway,*" Sascha said, turning his eyeless gaze away from Mark, "we hired some local talent and came for you. And I guess you know the rest of the story."

Yeah, but do you*? Do you know what it might have cost me?* Mark abruptly filled his mind with a giant image of a section of DNA twist.

"Good idea," Sascha said in a hoarse whisper. "Don't think anything around me you don't want *them* to find out."

Mark nodded, keeping his mind full of different-colored CATG balls, webbed together, DNA, ad infinitum. Deep down, he felt shocks of dread that Quasiman would lose track of him, not knowing where to bring the drugs . . . if he even remembered them.

"Yeah," he said hoarsely. "So, uh, who was this partner of yours?"

"Guy named Creighton. He can make himself look like anybody he wants. I'm glad he made it out, anyway." After the downpour had washed away any tracks, the Jeep fire had died down enough for the Black Karens to discover there was no body in it. The shapeshifting ace and his hirelings had gotten away clean.

Mark tried hard to sit on bitter thoughts about a man who

would scuttle off and leave Sprout captive. Sascha sighed and cast another Zen glance toward Casaday and company.

He stiffened. Mark looked up to see Casaday himself striding back toward them.

"So how's our new guest doing?" the CIA man asked. "Accommodations to your liking?"

"Well, I like it lots better now that that trained monkey of yours isn't beating on me anymore."

Casaday laughed. "Better not let him hear you say that," he said. "I suppose you're both wondering why we're bothering to take Mr. Starfin along with us, instead of leaving him back on the Salween Plateau with a bullet in his head. Of course, it *could* be for the pleasure of rolling him out at about thirty-five thousand feet, which is our current cruising altitude, by the way."

He gave a Shark's smile to Sascha. The eyeless joker got paler.

"But relax. We got a much better use in mind for you."

Sascha gasped. Casaday nodded. "That's right. The good doctor here might need a guinea pig to test out that extended-virulence Trump he's been putting together for us. We don't want to let all his good work go to waste, now, do we?"

Sascha turned an eyeless glare of accusation. "Meadows, you're not—oh, you son of a bitch!"

Mark buried his face in his hands.

Ray's plane landed at Ben Gurion International Airport near the Mediterranean coast, about thirty miles west of Jerusalem. The plane was largely empty, though a few businessmen and tourists were still daring enough to visit the city that was so important to three of the world's great religions.

Ray blended into the crowd, sparse at it was, catching the

first bus to Jerusalem. It was hot, but it was a dry heat. Some-how, though, that failed to make Ray feel any better. The bus was air-conditioned, but Ray was sweating and still more than a little shaky from the wounds he'd received in the Westmin-ster Abbey imbroglio.

Callendar had sent him after the Dog, but Callendar wasn't pulling his strings anymore. No one was. His prime objective was to find Harvest. If she was still alive. No, he wouldn't even think about that. She was alive. She had to be. Then there was the matter of Hartmann and the bimbo with the automatic. Je-rusalem, especially the Walled City where the wild carders hung out, was not a big city. Ray was sure to run into Hart-mann and the woman. Sure to run into the Dog, too, and if it came to it he wouldn't be averse to a little animal training. But Harvest came first. Harvest and Johnson.

The bus passed through brown desert, several times skirt-ing the crazy-quilt Palestine border, and reached the suburbs of the New City almost before Ray realized it. Access to the New City was relatively easy. Wall-less, borderless, mostly Jewish, New Jerusalem was three hundred thousand strong and constantly growing. It was much more security conscious than the average American city. Soldiers and policemen were everywhere. But Ray's business wasn't in the New City.

He disembarked with the others but bypassed the modern, multistoried tourist hotel that was the bus's destination. He went to the cab stand, told the driver "Old City," and got in. He was sweating profusely and already felt washed out.

The Old City was still encompassed by Jerusalem's medi-eval walls. Part of it belonged to Israel, part of it to Palestine, but it really belonged to the people who lived there, fought there, and died there for it every day. Traditionally it'd been divided into Christian, Muslim, Jewish, and Armenian quar-ters. When the wild carders arrived, they'd pushed out the least numerous, least powerful group and took that quarter for themselves. The Armenians had either been absorbed by the others or else disappeared into the dustbin of history; no one really knew.

People had been fighting and dying for their part of Jerusalem for the last fifty years, but it was just another city to Ray, maybe a little more crowded, dry, and dirty than most. The cab dropped him off at the New Gate, which was guarded by Israeli soldiers. They didn't really care much, since he was going in rather than going out, so he was only waved through the metal detector. He stepped through and entered another century.

The streets were twisty, the buildings crowded together, the smells foreign, somehow ancient. The first thing Ray did was find a small hotel off the main streets whose proprietor took cash and didn't ask questions.

The hotel room was so dirty that it made Ray's skin crawl. The walls were peeling and filthy with finger marks and handprints. The unwashed carpet was worn clear through in several spots and stained almost everywhere else. It smelled of urine and vomit. Ray didn't look too closely at the bed.

But it was dark, quiet, and out of the way, which was what Ray needed. Time was obviously of the essence. He didn't have the time for a careful investigation, even if that was his style. He had to find Harvest fast.

There was only one way he could think of to do it. There was a war going on, and when there was a war you always needed soldiers. The easiest way to track down Johnson and find Harvest would be to join the Sharks, but there were problems with that. For one, he was pretty well known among them and, for two, Ray was sure that you couldn't just join up. They didn't exactly have recruitment offices on every street corner.

The alternative, Ray thought, was to go with the Twisted Fists. Not that they were the Rotarians, either. Normally it was difficult to join them, but the dossier Callendar had given him said that lately there'd been confusion in the organization. Now would be the time to join.

Of course, there were two little problems. The Fist leaders probably knew him. Even though he wasn't that famous and his face had changed half a dozen times over the years, there was no doubt that he'd be better off with a new face if he wanted to join the Twisted Fists. And he also had to be a joker.

He looked at his face in the rust-spotted mirror over the room's stained porcelain sink. He rubbed his jaw and grimaced. This was not going to be pretty. He sighed, took a deep breath, and closed his eyes.

He smashed himself in the nose.

Involuntary tears of pain started from Ray's eyes as he felt cartilage break. He looked back in the mirror. His nose was flat, just how he wanted it. But the job wasn't done. He took the straight razor from his shaving kit and looked at it, grimacing.

"The face first," he said aloud. "Then the hands."

Before long he was crying again, but he didn't stop cutting. The tears ran down his slashed cheeks, diluting the blood that dripped freely into the sink below. When he was done with his face he started on his hands. Soon the razor was slippery with blood.

When he'd finished, he bandaged his face and hands as best he could, then he lay down on the bed. He'd already put in a supply of water, fruit juice, and vitamins, and had straws to drink them through.

Twenty-four hours later he left the hotel.

— — —

Mark stood alone in a pool of light. The five petri dishes arranged in a neat line on the tin lab table told their story in a silent shout.

The Sharks' new hideout seemed to be a combination of bomb shelter and emergency command post for the provincial Communist Party brass—Guangdong, way southern China, across the line from Hong Kong, at least until 1997, when the line would magically go away. The People's Republic of China was paranoid enough to still be testing thermonuclear weapons—if that was truly *paranoid* for a country trying to keep a lid on a numerous and vigorously oppressed Muslim minority—but with the collapse of the nation the Chinese leadership had always considered its true enemy, the USSR, the Guangdong CP evidently felt safe enough to let the facility out for rent.

The lab was on a lower level, possibly the lowest, and seemed to have been set up for medical treatment rather than research. That didn't matter. The Sharks had brought everything Mark needed to complete his betrayal of the wild cards.

"Dr. Meadows."

At the sound of that hated voice Mark felt a wild urge to sweep the flat round jars off the table onto the floor. *Go for it,* JJ Flash's voice urged from the back of his skull. *They'll never let us go anyway. Why not cop a quick exit?*

But he didn't. He just held himself there, braced at the apex of the triangle of his arms like an asthmatic struggling to breathe.

Then Jarnavon was standing next to him, blinking down at the petri dishes through his thick horn-rimmed glasses. "These are the wild-card positive tissue cultures you introduced the tenth-generation Trump variant to, aren't they?" he asked in tones of cathedral reverence.

Mark's jaw muscles trembled. His teeth creaked. He nodded once, convulsively.

Jarnavon raised a hand as if to clap Mark on the shoulder. It hesitated in midair, hovered, and then the younger man shook hands with himself in an I'm-the-champ gesture.

"It works." The words came out of his narrow nose in a sort of giggling snort. "It works! Oh, Dr. Meadows, you've done it! Humanity will remember your genius forever!"

"Yeah," Mark rasped. "That's what I'm afraid of."

Gregg decided that if Jerusalem was the Disney World of religion, then the Temple Mount was the Magic Kingdom. All they needed were street vendors hawking Crucifix ice cream bars, Yahweh's All-Kosher wieners, or "I'm A Dome-Head" hats. The city was littered with ancient holy sites, the detritus left behind as one group after another had occupied the area in the centuries-long tidal swell of war and conquest. The ground was watered with martyrs' blood, there wasn't a stone left that hadn't been part of some temple or shrine or church at one point or another. A miasma of holiness threaded through the streets like a glowing fog. You breathed sanctity and exhaled history. You could not escape it: The legacy of this city became part of your blood and heart and soul.

And the Black Dog was willing to blow it into atoms—or so he claimed.

Gregg and Hannah were at the Western Wall, the Wailing Wall, watching the supplicants. Two rails partitioned the great Herodian limestone blocks of the lowest course into a section for men, a (smaller) area for women, and a (much, much smaller) area for jokers. All three areas were busy, the knot of people waiting longest, not surprisingly, at the joker section. Behind these ruins of the long-destroyed Second Temple—the edge of the Temple Mount and perhaps Judaism's most sacred site—loomed the gilded presence of the Dome of the Rock, called Qubbat as-Sakhra in Arabic, the third most holy place in all of Islam. The rock enclosed by the Dome, the bared summit of Mount Moriah, was said by the Muslims to be one of the stones from the Garden of Eden, and was the place from which Muhammad ascended into heaven. Those of the Jewish faith believed that this was the rock taken from underneath God's throne and thrown into the void, from which the very Earth was created. The Temple Mount was somewhat less sacred to Christians (though the Golden Gate behind the Dome was reputed to be where Jesus entered the Temple Mount after his descent from the Mount of Olives on Palm Sunday), but only a thousand or so feet to the west was the Church of the Holy Sepulchre, containing within its walls Calvary, where Jesus was crucified, and the tomb into which his body had been placed.

A nuke wasn't going to leave much to worship but radioactive waste.

But would the Black Dog really push the button on all this if the Nur calls his bluff? Gregg wondered. *Or is the nuke really for the Nur?*

You'll find out, the voice answered him. *That's your job.*

"What's he doing?" Hannah asked. She gestured toward a man dressed in Hasidic black, who at their distance was just a blur to Gregg. Hannah realized it a moment later. "I'm sorry—you can't see that far, can you? The man's stuffing a little folded piece of paper into a crack between the blocks of the Wall. Why?"

"You put your prayer on a slip of paper," Gregg told her. "Sticking it into a crack here is making sure that God reads it directly. At least that's what I've been told."

"What's your brand of religion, Gregg? You've never mentioned anything about it."

"I was raised Catholic. I . . ." Gregg stopped. "I kind of lost my faith somewhere along the line." *Around the time I found Puppetman,* he wanted to say, but didn't. *Puppetman was my God, my own dark deity.*

"Did you ever get it back after you lost it?"

Gregg shuddered, involuntarily. *What's the matter, Greggie?* the voice asked. *Answer her.* "No. Though being here makes you think about things like that. What about you?"

"Methodist. I still believe, I guess, though I don't go to services regularly. And you're right, there's a feeling here." Hannah crouched alongside Gregg, her arm around his body, uncaring that people stared at them as they passed. A discreet distance away, openly watching them, was Needles. Needles was supposedly their guide while in Jerusalem; Gregg knew the boy was more guard than guide, making certain that the two of them did nothing to harm the Twisted Fists and reporting what they did back to the Black Dog. Sightseeing while they talked over the Black Dog's requests was relatively safe; contacting any of the authorities would probably get them killed. "Gregg, what the hell are we going to do? I can't believe that the Black Dog would ask you and me to go into the desert and talk to the Nur. Delivering his ultimatum to the Nur is only going to get us killed—maybe that's what the Black Dog wants. It certainly isn't going to get the virus destroyed; the Nur won't fall for that bluff."

But seeing the Nur is what you want, too, isn't it, Greggie? When you heard the Dog say the words, you knew you wanted to go. The power . . . the Nur . . . "I don't know. I really don't know. He said he'd arrange for us to be under a flag of truce—we deliver the message, and we leave." The sun was hot on his back and sent shimmering highlights dancing from the Dome. *And we take the Nur's strings with us.*

"I don't think the Dog was bluffing, Gregg. You don't go to the trouble of buying a nuke unless you're planning to use it.

It's a lousy conversation piece. He'll use it—if not against the Dome, then against the Nur."

"I agree."

"We can't let him do that."

Gregg glanced away from the Wall and the Dome, up toward Hannah's earnest face. "Do you have any ideas on how we can stop him?" His thin, high voice sounded more annoyed than he wished, and Hannah stood up abruptly without saying anything. Needles scowled in their direction.

"Hey!" he called. "What you two talking about?" He took a few steps toward them. Gregg noticed that tourists were giving the three of them a wide berth.

"We're talking about stupidity," he told Needles. "The radioactive kind."

The kid blushed. Gregg could see the green-purple of embarrassment wash over his mind like a bruise. "Just shut up about that," Needles said. "The Black Dog knows what he's doing."

"That's exactly what we're afraid of," Hannah told him, and Needles's face reddened further.

"We need that nuke," Needles insisted. "Zoe wouldn't have helped him if it wasn't important." The voice was strong, but Gregg could see the pale yellow underpinnings of uncertainty in his aura.

"Important for what?" Hannah continued. "Has the Black Dog decided that five for one is too low a ratio? Is he going for five thousand for one? Look, you're just a kid. I've seen this five-for-one revenge crap. I've seen it up close."

As Hannah spoke, he could see something change in Needles's face, in his odor, in his colors. "You have, too," Gregg broke in abruptly. "Haven't you?"

"Yes," Needles admitted. He shuffled his feet, looked across at the Dome as if eye contact would burn him. "But I . . . I . . ."

"You didn't like it, either, did you?" *A tug at the strings . . . Oh, yes, this is delightful.* Needles's guilt filled Gregg like a fine meal, satisfying a hunger he hadn't known he felt. *Yes . . . So hungry, after so long . . .*

"It was necessary. We had to do it, to teach the nats not to fuck with jokers like us."

"Sure, that's what they told you. Just like with this god-damn nuke. But what did you feel?" Gregg persisted, enjoying the taste of the youth's discomfiture. Needles looked at his shoes, like a kid being scolded by a parent. "Did you enjoy it, Needles? Did you like feeling the pain? Did this guy scream nicely for you?"

That brought the youth's eyes up, angry. "What kind of monster do you think I am?" he said. "I'm not some sick creep. I don't enjoy hurting people."

The voice laughed and Gregg shuddered. *I'm not, either,* he told it. *I know I was, once. But not now. Not now.*

"Right." Hannah sniffed her disapproval. "That's why you joined the Fists. So you wouldn't have to hurt people."

"I joined so that the people I love wouldn't get hurt," Needles told her, sweeping his hair back from his eyes. A child, still, Gregg realized. "So I could protect them. That's all. I joined because I thought they would help us: me and Zoe and the others."

"Who's Zoe?" Hannah asked, but Needles just shrugged. Gregg could feel a sadness settle around him like a veil. Just because he could, he deepened the colors, and was pleased to see tears well in his eyes. The youth blinked hard, suddenly looking away toward the Western Wall, to the supplicants placing their prayers in the cracks between the stones, his eyes bright, his mouth shut with his lips tight, and his hands clenched. Gregg knew what he was thinking by the colors of deepest aquamarine drifting around him.

Sudden bright white blossomed in the center of the sapphire melancholy. It tasted of anise to Gregg. "All right," Needles said. "So maybe I don't like the Fists much, either, and I wish the Dog weren't keeping no fucking nuke in the catacombs. There ain't much we can do about it, is there?"

"I don't know," Hannah told Needles. "You have a piece of paper on you?" The boy plunged his hands into his pockets, pulling out a bedraggled slip that looked like a receipt. "That'll do," Hannah said.

"What are you going to do?" Needles asked.

"I'm going to borrow a pencil, and then we're going to take a walk," Hannah told him, pointing at the Wall and the line of supplicants. "I'm going to stick the paper in there and ask *Him* what the hell we should do—ask for a sign. Anyone got a better idea?"

"Not really," Gregg told her. But down inside, the voice grumbled. *Yes, you do,* the voice told him. *With me, you can make things right. All you have to do is use me, Greggie . . .*

"Come on, you two," Hannah said, interrupting his internal reverie. "We're in the Holy City; we may as well pray."

They wound their way through the crowds toward the joker section. As Gregg brushed against people, he caught snippets of their emotions. As they approached the back of the line, he was frowning. There was a hostile atmosphere in the area, one that made the voice inside perk up. "Hannah, why don't we head back for the quarter?" Gregg said uneasily.

"What's the matter?"

"I don't know. It's just—"

Afterward, Gregg was never really sure how it started.

Suddenly there was shouting and a quick flurry of activity. Then screams, and the cough of a handgun.

People pushed against them. Needles unshouldered his rifle and sent an ear-shattering burst into the air. That earned them a brief clear spot as everyone in the vicinity dove for the ground or fled. All around the open area near the Wall, people were running, and the narrow lanes between the stalls were clogged. The scent of gunpowder was nearly overpowering. Hannah started forward, stopped; Gregg, trying to stay with her, bumped into her legs.

It was worse than Westminster. There was no focus to anything, and he couldn't see.

In the Joker Quarter, Ray felt eyes on him wherever he went. He prowled the streets, familiarizing himself with their sights and sounds and smells. He went from market to café to bazaar. He stopped at a dozen cafés, using a straw to sip heavily sugared tea through what was left of his mouth. He inspected the goods in half a hundred shops, buying things here and there, listening and watching without seeming to.

By the end of the day he knew about the silent, black-clad guards who watched over the quarter's streets. He also knew the streets themselves as well as he ever could, and he was starting to get edgy even in his newfound patience. He considered half a dozen plans, all of which he knew would end in disaster, but, damn it, he had to do something; he just couldn't wander the streets from sunrise to sunset, watching, listening, and hoping.

He was considering going up to one of the Fist guards and doing something foolish when the sound of gunfire, echoing weirdly off the ancient stone buildings, sounded from a couple of streets away.

He smiled, though you couldn't tell it from what was left of his face, and hustled down a slop-filled alley toward the ratcheting gunfire. He stopped a moment to orient himself, went down another alley, crossed a street, cut through a small square filled with the carts of fruit vendors, and suddenly found himself on the edge of a large square that was packed with frightened, screaming people. Most of them had hit the ground. Some were desperately crawling for the pitiful cover afforded by a dozen or so food and souvenir stands scattered throughout the square. Some weren't moving or screaming at all, their blood staining the ancient cobblestones.

It was easy to tell the two sides apart. The Sharks were dressed in khaki spruced up with odds and ends of paramilitary geegaws—though, Ray noted, they didn't have the fruity berets favored by the last bunch he'd run across. The Fists were easy to pick out, too. They were the ugly-looking ones, and they were losing.

Thirty or more bodies lay in bloody pools on the pavement. Most were obviously bystanders caught in the crossfire, from the look of their clothes Conservative or Orthodox Jews. But some of the bodies were Fists, their black uniforms spattered red with blood.

As Ray watched, one of the Fists was blown out from behind a fruit cart he'd been using as cover. There were four or five of the jokers left, facing twice that number of Sharks. Most of the Fists seemed to be trapped against a tall wall that formed one end of the square. They had no cover except for the cowering bystanders trying to squash themselves flat against the pavement.

Ray moved in to change the odds.

The first couple were easy. Their backs were to Ray and they were concentrating on the Fists in front of them. Ray wasted no time. He swooped down on them and smashed them with his clubbed hands before they even knew he was there. Unable to contain his frustration or anger and without a hint of pity for his targets, Ray's killing blows left the Sharks in crumpled heaps at his feet.

— — —

For a minute or more, there was little they could do but try to avoid the fighting, trying to stay in the lee of the action. There were more gunshots, screams. Gregg could feel Hannah's panic and Needles's growing anger.

A new fight broke out not far to their right when they were nearly to the edge of the square. Through the moving screen of the crowd, Gregg saw two men grab a joker whose head looked like it had been hit with a shovel and then frozen, the nose flat and his mouth welded almost entirely shut with scar tissue. Gregg saw the joker's hands come up, and the fingers were fused together like the mouth. Still, the Sharks had made a mistake in their choice of opponent; the joker took one in each hand and slammed their heads together with a sound like coconuts. When he let them go, both men dropped like rag dolls, blood streaming from their noses and mouths.

"Assholes," the joker mumbled in an American accent, and the stitched mouth grinned in seeming satisfaction. "That was hardly worth the effort." The grin and the words sent a cold chill through Gregg. He knew that lopsided smile, even with the changed and altered face. *Jesus!* the voice shrilled in his head. *It's him!* For a moment, the riot around them vanished. The world disappeared, focusing down to a universe that consisted only of the joker's face. Gregg could hear nothing, could see nothing else but those eyes and the hatred in them. The presence within him cowered, even as it searched for the strings to that fury. *Ray! It's fucking Billy Ray! He's come after us!* The strings burned in Gregg's mind, and he let them go, knowing he couldn't handle them.

"Come on!" Gregg shouted to Needles and Hannah. "Now!" With the word, he tugged hard at their strings. They followed, infected by his panic.

"Gregg?" Hannah asked as they pushed through the chaos,

heading downhill toward the quarter. Behind them, they could hear screams and wails and the sound of sirens approaching. The entire square was an unfocused mêlée, with more people rushing in toward the scene. Gregg, on all sixes, weaved through running legs. "Where are you going?" Hannah asked, trying to keep up with him. Needles panted alongside her.

"Anywhere that's out of Jerusalem," he shouted back over the din. "Looks like we got the answer to that prayer of yours."

Ray had them flanked. He took one of the dead Sharks' rifles in his clumsy hands, pointed it in the general direction of the other Sharks, and triggered a long burst. It got their attention even though it only splattered the sandstone wall above their heads. Attacked from front and side, the Sharks chose discretion over valor and slipped back into the surrounding alleys.

For a moment there was stillness broken only by the frightened or pained weeping of the bystanders. The Fists checked their shot-up comrades, who were mostly ready for the grave. One of the jokers headed toward Ray with a peculiar, sliding sort of gait. He wore a black cotton cape and cowl and was built oddly, kind of roundly. As he approached, Ray could see that his body ended in a snail-like foot that left a broad smear of mucus in his wake.

"Well, chum," he said from behind his mask with an incongruous, cultured British accent, "you certainly saved our bums. Now just who the bloody hell are you?"

"They call me Mumbles," Ray said.

"What?"

"Mumbles. I said 'Mumbles.' "

"How apropos," the joker said.

The joker looked long and hard at Ray, but Ray had no

doubt that he could pass inspection. His nose was smashed almost flat. He had slashed his face with the razor, then held his lips pressed together until they'd fused, except for one small spot in the right corner of his mouth where he could shove in tiny bits of food and drink liquid through a straw. He'd sliced his hands the same way, cutting deep into the sides of his fingers and holding them pressed together so that the flesh grew into living mittens. It made his hands clumsy as hell, but that was something he could live with, though he didn't look forward to eventually correcting the problem.

"They call me Snailfoot, though my name is Reginald."

Ray didn't take the hint.

"Well," Snailfoot said after a minute, "been long in our fair city?"

Ray shook his head. "No. Not long. I've come to join."

"Join?" Snailfoot asked.

"The Black Dog. The Twisted Fists. I've come to fight."

There was a long moment's silence, then Snailfoot said, "Well, my friend Mumbles, you've certainly come to the right place. Come along—and mind the slime. It's damn slippery."

The other Fists had long since recovered their casualties and disappeared. No one in the crowd was inclined to stop Ray and Snailfoot, nor could Ray blame them. As they were heading toward an alley, a flash of color suddenly caught Ray's eye and he stopped and stared.

"What is it?" Snailfoot asked.

Ray shook his head. "Nothing," he said. "Just a caterpillar. A three-foot-long, yellow caterpillar."

"Stay here long enough, mate, and you get used to sights like that."

Ray nodded. He watched Hartmann and the bimbo mill around with the rest of the crowd. The Old City was a small place. They'd run into each other again. Ray knew they would.

– – –

Mark came awake in blackness, bolt upright, his body slimed with sweat quickly chilled by the overactive AC. His nostrils were dilated to the staleness of recycled air, and he felt the soft, incessant machines that kept the underground complex alive buzzing in his bones, like fluorescent-light shimmer made tangible.

He sensed a presence. Human nearness seemed to press against his damp, chilled skin.

"Who?" he demanded groggily. "Who's there?"

"Me," a voice said. A great hunched shadow sidled forward to let the soft, yellow glow of a night-light illuminate one trouser leg.

"Quasiman?"

The off-center head nodded.

"How'd you find me?"

"This was where you were," the joker said. "All places are . . ." His voice drifted. Mark sensed powerful hands making vague circles in the air.

"Don't go drifty on me, man!" he said sharply, then, plaintive: "Please."

"All places are pretty much the same to me, Doctor. I'm sorry; my mind was wandering there. Sometimes it goes a place, and then it's a little while before my body follows."

"I've noticed that. Did you, like, bring the drugs?" He could barely bring himself to ask the question.

"Drugs?"

The uncomprehending reply hit Mark as if the superhumanly powerful joker had palm-smacked him on the forehead "Nooo!" he moaned. "You're not tracking me continuously, are you?"

"No, Dr. Meadows. That's not . . . not the way . . . my mind works."

Mark jumped off the lumpy bed, threw on a light, grabbed a pad and felt-tip pen from the nightstand. Takis-ingrained reflex made him tear off the top sheet and put it on the bare tabletop before he started to write: no point leaving neat little impressions of everything he wrote on the sheets beneath. He had searched his little apartment, in his inexpert way, and had turned up no bugs. From what little he knew of them, the Communist Chinese were pretty low-tech, and less totally obsessive about security than the Soviets, so he thought there was a good chance they hadn't built AV surveillance into the room.

And if they have, he thought grimly as he scribbled, *I'm screwed right this second anyway.*

"Here!" he said, practically throwing the sheet of paper at Quasiman.

The joker frowned at the sheet. A general slackening of posture, the way the hand that held the paper floated downward toward the lumpy waist, told Mark he was losing his audience again.

"Listen," he said, hissing because he was afraid to shout, longing to grab the man by his thick biceps but uncertain what might happen if he were in contact with Quasiman when he phased out. "I gave you a list of the stuff I need. They're psychoactives, illegal as hell. Is that a problem?"

"Problem?" A drop of drool slid over the joker's lower lip and started rappelling from his chin. He held the paper up to his face, a handbreadth before his eyes, like a child pretending to read.

"Psil-o-cybin," he read, picking over the syllables laboriously, as if he were trying to sort them in the palm of one hand. "Di-hy-droxy-ace-tone. Complete sentences. Laws aren't a problem for somebody who . . . can come. And go."

He went. Mark collapsed to his knees on the floor and beat

his palms on thin orange carpet that smelled of strange Asian disinfectants.

I don't talk to you much, God, he thought, *and I don't really even believe in you. But if you're there, man—please get him back here with the drugs before I have to choose between killing my daughter and playing Martin Bormann.*

A satellite scanning this part of the desert would see black goat-hair tents, a nomadic camp whose appearance would not have seemed unusual to the eyes of Suleiman the Magnificent. There was nothing remarkable here, only a smallish herd of goats, the jumbled stonework of an ancient well. The goats were tended by walking tents that were women in chadors— timeless, even to the water jugs on their shoulders.

The tents sheltered bubble domes made of translucent poly- mer. The groans of the camels tethered outside mingled with the sighs of compressors, the chug of buried generators, the clink of lab glassware.

Zoe worked, not in chador, but in a clean suit, double gloves, and a full-face hood with a transparent mask. A chador would have been cooler, even in the refrigerated domes, where work went on at all hours and odd hours. The dome was empty at the moment, her bosses napping in the midday heat. No one got enough sleep; their schedules were ruled by the time needed for viral generations, not for human sleep cycles.

Zoe yawned. Washing flasks. Setting racks in the autoclave. Taking them out again. Her tasks were simple and boring.

She worked under Zahid's orders and tried to stay away from Paolo, the blond Brazilian medic, who seemed unnatu- rally horny. She was getting to be an expert at shifting her hips out of his way. Her work was boring, but the clock kept ticking and every hour, every cell replication, made the possibility of the Trump's release closer. These bastards were going to get the Trump ready before she figured out how to stop them, and damn it, how was she ever going to find out anything from Rudo if she couldn't get him to talk to her!

Rudo was here, yes, an uncanny presence, his controlled gestures and formal, almost military posture not quite in synchrony with his youthful face, his fine-textured creamy skin with its faint dusting of freckles. He was *The* Card Shark, Snailfoot had told her. He was an old man in a young man's body. He had been a powerful figure in the UN, a scholar in the service of world health with a twisted sense of eugenics.

Rudo worked with grim determination and spoke only with Zahid. Dr. Pan Rudo seemed impatient, hurried, but he kept his impatience in check and kept the motley crew hard at work with the skills of a trained diplomat—which he was.

Or had been.

"Don't kill Rudo," the Black Dog had told Zoe. "Rudo has the Trump with him, but we don't know how much he has, or if he's split his stash. Stay with him until you learn what he knows. Then get out. We'll take it from there."

She had the pocket locator the Twisted Fists had given her, a little marvel that gave geographic coordinates at the touch of a button. All she had to do was memorize the location of the camp and learn the location of every drop of the virus.

"Then what?" Zoe had asked, back in the echoing stone warrens of Jerusalem's catacombs.

"Find some way to make it seem as though you have sprained your left wrist. Wrap it in a bandage—a visible bandage. We will have someone in the camp who will know this signal and get you out."

She had tried to argue. But Jan had watched with pleading eyes, and Needles waited for her to fail, to betray his trust in her. And Anne? Anne knew only that she'd been asked to do something important.

"I still don't like the black hair bit," Anne had said.

"It's just a phase I'm going through," Zoe had told her. *Right, Ma. This little interlude of murder and terrorism is just one of those things. I'll come back and pull my shifts at Subtle Scents and we'll go shopping. Sure.*

Zoe checked the temperature settings on the incubators, heated against the dome's air-conditioning that protected the humans from the scorching heat outside. Inside the incubators, bathed in warm moist air, murky flasks of cell cultures waited to be infected. Dissolve the glass containers, diddle the incubator controls to flash-fry every nanogram of solution into sterile dust? Yes, certainly, she could do that.

But she didn't know if the flasks held all of the Trump, or if they held any Trump at all. There might be other flasks stored somewhere in fuming liquid nitrogen, waiting to release Hell itself on the world.

Zoe washed another Erlenmeyer flask and set it on the rack to drain.

She looked up as a hunchbacked joker materialized above the sink, his feet almost touching a rack of clean glassware.

"Watch out!" Zoe yelled.

He jerked sideways in the air and missed the counter. Zoe thought she saw one of his feet detach and find its way to the end of his leg when he moved, but surely not. She blinked, and he stood beside her, his large hands held out as if to beg alms.

"How did you get here? Oh, never mind. Hello."

"I need things. For Mark."

"Mark? Who the hell is Mark?" He wasn't masked or gowned. All the cultures were stored, but she handed him a mask anyway.

"I have a paper." He pulled a scrap of waxy paper out of his pocket. "Mark needs these. To help him kill the Black Trump."

Dihydroxyacetone, metal salts, phenol, a few organic acids—simple compounds, mostly. Why would anyone need this stuff? You could order it at any chemical supply house. Organic acids. Oh.

"Mark wants to trip out and forget about the Black Trump, it looks to me," Zoe said.

"He's locked up. They are hurting his little girl. Help him, Zoe."

The joker pleaded with his eyes, and she didn't know why, but she believed him. Somebody was hurting his kid? She'd had her absolute fill of that. Whoever this Mark was, if all he needed was a few chemicals, what the heck? She didn't mind stealing from Rudo and his gang. As fast as things were going here, it was unlikely that the thefts would be noticed.

"Can you—?" read, she almost asked. There was no reason to believe this man was illiterate. "Can you carry a sack when you do your teleportation bit?"

"Sure I can."

"Good." She grabbed a wastebasket liner and some small ziplocks. "Help me, okay?" She handed him a bottle and grabbed a felt-tip marker off the counter. "You fill, I'll mark. Hurry! Somebody could come in."

The hunchback worked as fast as he could, his clumsy-looking fingers skillful with the flexible sacks, the closures. They worked their way down the alphabetical rows of dark glass bottles, filling and stashing while Zoe listened for the hiss of the airlock door. The guards didn't come in here, ever, but Rudo did, and the rest of the science crew.

T is for tyrosine, V for vanadium powder—what the hell would this Mark person do with vanadium? He had some weird catalysis going, she figured. She portioned out some in a baggie. Air whooshed at the doorway.

"You've got to leave," Zoe whispered. She threw the vanadium in the plastic sack and shoved it at his shoulder.

"We don't have it all," he said in a perfectly normal tone of voice that seemed to come from a loudspeaker.

"I don't have any xanthine anyway! Get!" Zoe hissed.

"I have to help Mark! It's *important!*"

How did you shove someone into dematerialization? The inner door was half-open. She saw a plastic hood, behind it a shock of blond hair—oh, please, not Rudo.

"Please, go poof or die!" She turned to get between the hunchback and the doorway, trying to hide him. The cluttered counters stood between him and the intruder, but the joker was taller than Zoe was by a head.

Paolo stumbled through the door and giggled as it closed. He staggered toward her with a canteen in his gloved hand. "Jus' checking the supplies," he said. "Who ees your visitor, Egypt?"

He was heading for the five-liter jug of lab alcohol.

"What visitor?" Zoe asked.

The hunchback was gone.

"I thought I saw—Egypt, help me fill thees little jug, hokay? I am no Muslim, and sleeping is so hard here."

The Brazilian paramedic couldn't sleep? Maybe he had a shred or two of conscience left. Zoe helped Paolo fill his canteen and shooed him back out the door. Let Rudo find him drunk. She would like that.

"So how are you doing, honey?" Mark asked gently.

His daughter sat beside him on the bed, her blue-jean-clad

hip not quite touching his. She wore a baggy GUESS sweat-shirt. Her hair hung loose down her back, brushed to golden radiance. Sitting there with her hands clasped between her knees, her head tipped forward so that her face was all but hidden by her hair, she looked heart-achingly beautiful. Another man would likely have found her incredibly attractive. But to Mark her appearance was nothing but the mirror for what she was inside, innocent, pure, and beautiful of spirit. When he looked at her, he saw her as she really was: perpetually four.

"Fine," she said in a subdued voice. She coughed into her hand.

He glanced around. This was his reward, his thirty pieces of silver; Casaday was so pleased with him that he'd given him a few moments with Sprout. "You like the room?" Mark asked.

"It's okay."

He felt as if his soul were draining away through the soles of his athletic shoes. He cast around, picked up a stuffed bunny. It was white and turquoise, with an ear that went off in a random direction and a scuff on its nose; a replacement for the Gund bear she'd loved so much, left behind in Burma.

"You like the bunny, sweetheart?" He dandled the animal on his lap. "I know you miss your pink bear. But this is a pretty cute bunny."

She brushed hair from her face, turned, accepted the animal, gave him a wan smile. "Yes, Daddy," she said. "It's a cute bunny." She hugged it to her breasts.

She sounds so grown up, Mark thought. Suddenly he was overcome. He gathered her into his great gangly arms, pressed her against his ribs, pressed his cheek to her hair.

"Oh, baby, baby," he moaned, petting her, feeling her hair go damp and matted from his tears. "I'm so sorry I got you into this. I'd do anything to get you out."

She squirmed in his arms. He clung the tighter. "I know I

haven't been much of a daddy to you," he sobbed. "But I'll find a way to make it up to you. Somehow—"

With surprising strength, she eeled out of his grip. He sat, staring at her in shock, and then his long face crumpled. He began to cry with the great gasping, bawling cries of a baby, face a red fist, tears pouring down like water from a backed-up pipe.

"Baby, baby, please don't turn away from me," he begged, reaching blind hands toward her.

She caught his hands, clung to them until the first volcanic upwelling of grief was gone. Then she pushed his hands back onto his thighs, firmly yet gently.

"There, Daddy," she said. "It's okay. Please don't cry. I . . . I still love you, Daddy."

He sniffled, looking at her through a gauze of tears. That catch in her voice had snagged his soul and torn it. "Do you really?" he asked, knowing he was whining.

Blue eyes big and child-solemn, she nodded. "We'll be okay, Daddy," she said. "Really. We'll be fine."

He sniffed loudly. "You really think so?" he asked, knowing it couldn't be, hating himself for the weakness of seeking reassurance from a child.

But she nodded again. "Oh, yes," she said, sounding too wise for her lisping child's voice. "Something is bound to turn up."

"Nefertiti had not a more beautiful profile."

Zoe jumped. She hadn't heard Rudo over the clink of the glassware. The bastard moved like a ghost. Zoe grabbed a bottle brush and scrubbed at a gelatinous scrap of dried serum in the bottom of a beaker.

"You do not respond to my compliment," Rudo said. "I am

a pariah here, it seems. None of the women will even look at me."

"In the Koran, the most abhorrent feature of the examiners— the angels who judge—is their blue eyes," Zoe said. Rudo's eyes were so pale they were almost colorless.

"Ah. So that is it. I am ugly."

"No," Zoe said. "You are not ugly." Thinking, *You are anathema. You are a demon who plans to kill my people. You are my ticket to freedom, if you will tell me what you know. Talk to me.* But Rudo was turning to leave.

"Dr. Rudo? I—"

"Yes? Haste, haste, we are busy here."

"I am so lonely here. I don't speak the language the women use. Thank you for speaking to me." Zoe looked at the flask she held. It would make such a satisfying noise if she broke it over this monster's head.

Rudo smiled. "Pack those flasks carefully once they are dry. We are moving the camp when darkness falls."

Zoe nodded. She caught a glimpse of what Rudo had been; his authority, his sense of command, permeated this young body he wore.

"Perhaps you would share my accommodations in the Land Rover," Rudo said. "Unless you prefer to ride in the bed of the truck with the other women, of course."

"Thank you," Zoe said.

"Such a tense little Egyptian," Rudo said. He put his hands on her shoulders and turned her to face him. "But so lovely."

She kept her eyes downcast. Azma's lectures had taught her not to make eye contact with men, and this time it made sense. Maybe he wouldn't see that she really wanted to spit in his face. The hood made that idea impractical, anyway.

Rudo frowned at her. "You're off duty. Get some sleep. We will all be busy tonight."

Get some sleep, right. Zoe went to the stifling confinement of the women's tent and stretched out on her kilim in the close, fly-buzzing heat. Beads of sweat formed under her breasts and rolled down her sides. They felt like ants walking on her skin. She sat up, picked up her water jug, and poured it over her hair, letting the water soak into the black cotton robe that was her required off-duty garb.

It helped. The brown-black shade of the tent became a moonscape and, dreaming, she flew between ivory minarets that sang with the clear, soprano voices of a boys' choir. They chanted the Fauré *Requiem*, unspeakable sorrow.

Jay Ackroyd shoved the bear under his jacket and peered around the back of the empty hutch. A detachment of small brown men with big black guns was crossing the open square in the center of the camp. The field was a sea of brown muck, and the men made sucking sounds with their boots as they marched. Jay pulled his head back, held his breath, and tried not to drown in his own perspiration. He waited until the Karens were past, took another quick peek, and slid quietly back into the bush.

Beyond the camp was nothing but roots and rocks and stinging flies and a hell of a lot more mud. Every step plunged him ankle deep in thick sucking muck that squished between his bare toes. He'd lost his right shoe near the perimeter going in, with no way to retrieve it except by hand—a process about as attractive as bobbing for turds, and likely to attract the attention of the Black Karens. It made more sense to abandon the other shoe, so he had.

More small brown men with more big black guns were patrolling the narrow rutted track that passed for a road. Jay managed to sneak past the first sentry, who was taking a dump behind the burnt-out shell of an overturned jeep. He never saw the second until a rifle was shoved in his face and the man started screaming at him in Burmese. He popped him off in mid-scream. By then the first guy was pulling up his pants and reaching for his gun, so Jay had to pop him away, too. "Shit," he groused, shaking his head as he jogged down the road. He was getting rusty at this stuff.

The cave was a good mile and a half from the Black Karen camp. Two more small brown men with guns were outside, but these two were Belew's small brown men. Cambodians. "Hey, didn't I see you guys in *The Killing Fields*?" Jay had asked when Belew had first produced them. The Cambodians had just looked at him with flat, hard eyes, the same way they looked at him now as he came staggering out of the bush with his legs caked in mud halfway to the knee.

Finn was inside the cave, wearing a flak jacket and a Kevlar horse blanket that Belew had had made up for him. Where J. Bob got these things Jay would never know. Finn's dye job had aged badly, turning his mane a splotchy green. Against the back wall, three Black Karen captives had been neatly trussed and gagged and propped up against the rock.

Wordlessly, Finn handed Jay a canteen. Jay took a long swallow of lukewarm water, wiped his mouth with the back of his hand, and said, "Jesus, it's so fucking hot out there, even the bugs are sweating." He gestured toward the three captives in the back of the cave. "Our guests give you any trouble?"

Finn shook his head. "The first one screamed a bit. The other two were pretty docile. I tied them up as soon as they appeared. You get into the laboratory okay?"

"Piece of cake. Skulking was my major in detective school." Jay sat on a rock to scrape mud out from between his toes. "I'm getting sloppy, though. Too much desk work. They kept spotting me. It was embarrassing. The Karens are going to come up about a dozen short when they do roll call tonight. Aside from Moe, Larry, and Curly here, I popped them all to Freakers. Waived the cover charge and everything, they ought to be grateful. Where's Belew?"

"One of his Cambodians found something," Finn said. "He went to take a look. Did you find anything in the lab?"

"Lab stuff," Jay said. "Computers, test tubes, little brown guys in white coats. No Meadows and no Casaday, but they were here, all right. I looked for steel drums labeled BLACK TRUMP and revealing notebooks full of plans for genocide and world domination, but I couldn't find any. I was looking for that scanning tunneling microscope, too, until I realized that I wouldn't know a scanning tunneling microscope from a Cuisinart."

"Then how do you know that Meadows was here?" Finn asked.

"I found this in an empty hutch." Jay pulled the bear out and handed it to Finn. It was pink plush, with button eyes: a child's stuffed toy.

The centaur physician looked at the plush toy in confusion. "What is this supposed to mean?"

"It means that Sprout Meadows was here until very recently, Doctor," J. Bob Belew said. Neither Jay nor Finn had heard him enter the cave, but there he was, looking impossibly crisp and cool in starched khaki, high leather boots, and a photojournalist's vest, like he'd just stepped out of the centerfold in *Soldier of Fortune*. Jay had to repress a sudden urge to shove him down in the mud.

Belew took the bear from Finn, and for a moment there was genuine emotion in those cool, gray eyes. Then he blinked, and just like that he was all business again. "Undoubtedly they moved out in some haste and certain nonessentials were left behind."

"Yeah, that's how I figured it," Jay said. "Where were you?"

"We found a body," Belew said. "A joker."

His words hit Jay like a physical blow. There had been no word from Jerry or Sascha since they'd decided to go off and play Rambo. Jay half-rose from the rock where he was seated. Finn threw him a glance and shuffled his feet anxiously. Jay tried to find the question, but his throat had gone very dry. "Was it . . ."

"Not one of your friends, Ackroyd," Belew said. "One of mine. His name was Lou Inmon."

"Black Trump?" Finn's voice was anxious.

"No, Doctor. The instruments of death were more traditional. He was tortured. *Greater love hath no man than this, that a man lay down his life for his friends.* Another debt to Casaday's account." Belew's eyes went to the captives in the back of the cave. "What do we have here?"

"Two lab technicians and a cook," Jay said. "I figured maybe they could be persuaded to tell us where Casaday moved his circus."

Belew looked them over thoughtfully, playing with his mustache. Finally he said, "Remove the gags."

Finn trotted back to the Karens and pulled the cloth from their mouths, one, two, three. Belew stood in front of them. "Do any of you speak English?" Moe looked at the dirt. Larry shook his head. Curly pretended not to hear. Belew tried French. Nothing. Belew said something curt and cold in a language Jay did not recognize. The three men stared at him sullenly.

"Swell," Jay said. "We got See-No-Sharks, Hear-No-Sharks, and Speak-No-Sharks." He thought for a moment. "J. Bob, tell them that if they cooperate, they'll win a free trip to New York City. Times Square, Yankee Stadium, the Empire State Building. They'll all be eating hot dogs and driving cabs inside three weeks."

"Is that a bribe or a threat?" Finn wanted to know.

Belew ignored the exchange. "Doctor, ask the guards to step inside for a moment."

Finn looked at Jay, who shrugged, went out of the cave, and came back a moment later with the two Cambodians. The captives stared at them anxiously. Belew rattled off a long speech in Burmese or Chinese or Vietnamese or some such language. The only part of it that Jay recognized was *Khmer Rouge*, but the Black Karens seemed to understand well enough. Their faces grew anxious.

Then Belew snapped an order and the Cambodians took a step toward the captives, and Moe looked over wildly at Jay and said, "New York New York. Tell everything."

Jay grinned and made a gun with his fingers. "We're listening."

"Green card?" Moe added hopefully.

"Don't push it," Belew said sternly, and the cook began to sing.

The voices in her dream turned to howling winds. She woke choking, the air in the tent thick with powdery ocher dust. Zoe wrapped her hood around her face and helped strike the tent in the spring's first real sandstorm.

"The simoom!" a voice called out. Camels screamed outrage and tried to stay curled up on the sand. Goats bleated, unhappy about the wind and even more unhappy about being driven anywhere in it. Zoe fought her way toward an empty space the wind scoured in the air. She saw a woman's hand in deft motion, tying a Styrofoam cooler to a camel's back.

"Can I help?" Zoe asked.

The woman kept working and did not answer.

"Over here, Egypt!" Rudo appeared, a white-skinned ghost wearing a white suit and a totally out-of-place pith helmet swathed in what looked like mosquito netting. He grabbed Zoe and pulled her toward the lee side of a bulky Land Rover. Zoe dragged her pack behind her, the kilim wrapped around her clean suit, her gold jewelry, and the precious locator under the seam of a red leather jewelry case. She tossed the pack through the opened door and climbed in after it.

The driver, a turbaned man Zoe hadn't seen before, nodded to Rudo and closed the partition between his seat and the passenger section of the car, leaving Rudo and Zoe in an enclosure of leather and burled wood—unexpected luxury. The driver gunned the motor and eased the heavy vehicle out into the swirling sand.

"This storm is good," Rudo said. "We will leave no tracks, and our change of location will be hidden from the satellite eyes. Until the wind dies down only, but the camp that appears in the morning will not look like the camp we are now leaving."

If only she could get him to tell her what she needed to know, she could be out of here, back in Jerusalem. She had to get him to talk. He'd said he was lonely. His young body would have needs. Hateful though he was, she had to charm him. "I understand so little of—our work here," she said.

"Knowledge can be dangerous. No matter. You would not be here if your hatred of the wild card had not driven you to seek us out."

That, in a twisted way, was true. Zoe tried to look like an admiring junior on her first date with a football hero. He *was* a pretty boy.

"This, ah, *cleansing agent* whose replication I am trying to oversee, against all odds in these primitive conditions, is my hope that humanity can become free of the suffering caused by this hideous alien disease—and I have been a prisoner of my obsession for years. Granted, Jerusalem's small, pathetic Joker-town is not where the agent should be released," Rudo said. "So, well, I will have faith in the epidemiology of world travel. And even here, my goal will be accomplished."

"The righteous overcome adversity," Zoe said. She looked down at her hands, tightly folded in her lap, and prayed that what she had just said was true. But who was righteous?

He frowned, and the frown was a terrible thing, a disapproval that made her tremble. A man with the authority lent by many years of power looked at her through a youth's pale eyes. Zoe wondered if the vacated body Rudo wore still had memories, hopes, a capacity for outrage. No. The boy who had lived behind those eyes was gone forever.

"You grew up in New York," Pan Rudo said. "You are a twentieth-century woman. Why do you quote platitudes?"

"When in Rome . . ."

"Ah. But in this little space, so safe from prying eyes, you do not need to do that, Zoe."

Oddly enough, she did feel some of the tension leaving her shoulders. "Thank you. I really mean that. It's difficult, acting like a nonperson. I miss—New York."

"I miss access to a good research laboratory. I am not a virologist. Zahid works, but he is a frail reed, his knowledge barely adequate. This is such a tricky business, he tells me, working with this fragile virus. It resists multiplication to quantities that will be sufficient to the task."

"So that's what you're doing," Zoe said. "I really know so little about virology." Yikes, did that sound stupid! "I wanted to go on with my studies—biochem, virology. But my brothers' schooling took precedence." Her mythical brothers. Two?

Three? She didn't remember how many she was supposed to have. Not a good direction to let this conversation drift, no.

Rudo smiled and patted her hand. "I have become a student in the field. Would you like to hear me recite my lessons? There is no pleasure greater than an interested listener. And we will be on this journey until nearly dawn."

The driver fought the wheel of the Land Rover, and they lurched steeply down some unseen dune. The wind ground sand against the doors.

"Your—obsession—is to relieve suffering?"

"Ah. Yes."

"But the Black Trump will kill whoever gets it. At least that's what the lab workers say."

"They talk too much. The Black Trump will kill, yes, but there is no other answer. You think of the dying, but that is the softness of women. I do not hold it against you. Zoe, I have studied the workings of the human psyche for years. The healthy have courage. Ask any healthy human, like yourself, whether they would sacrifice themselves to avoid spreading a hideous plague to their loved ones, and they will say 'Yes!' With courage, with conviction! But with illness, with contamination, the psyche changes. The organism loses its higher functions, its courage, in a drive toward survival. The sick are sheep, animals who bleat and follow any leader."

And once a confused and frightened people had meekly marched into cattle cars, shocked and dazed by the unthinkable, trusting in the rules of civilization. They had believed in law, in decency. Never again. Since that time, no one could ever truly believe in law, or decency. Never again.

"At such times, the courageous must act for them. It is my destiny to be one of the courageous."

They had found a smooth track of some sort and the vehicle sped up, heading for the new camp in the night. In the murky darkness of the rocking jeep, Rudo almost glowed with purpose.

Well, the wild card virus *had* spread untold suffering. Some of its victims had suicided, from pain or self-loathing, or because they couldn't live with the changes in people who had once loved them. If all the jokers and aces in the world just went to sleep, painlessly—would that be so terrible? Had it happened in the fifties, Zoe Harris would never have been born, would never have lived to become a murderer, a woman manipulated by love into a theft that could kill millions. Would Rudo's solution be so terrible? No child would fear the wild card, ever again, if he succeeded.

"You are thinking of painful deaths, I tell you, Zoe, that need not happen. For normal humans, only a minor respiratory illness. With lots of sneezing, lots of dispersal potential, isn't that a nice touch? Once the disease is established to be universally fatal to those who are infested with the Takisian virus, then the suffering of the afflicted can be eased without guilt. I will work very hard to see that it is so."

Cyanide and morphine? How gentle, how *reasonable*. Zoe *wanted* to believe him. He looked so innocent, so clean, a white acolyte dedicated to purity, to peace, to health. Nat or no, he had charisma.

"How soon? When will this happen?"

"Don't be impatient, Egypt. Do you wish to leave our company so soon? Does not the Nur pay you well?"

Did he? Her salary didn't come to her, a mere woman. It went to her designated guardian, a fictional brother in Alexandria.

"I am a stranger here. I—don't like the food much."

"Mutton! My tongue is coated with the taste of mutton! And that dusty-tasting spice!"

"Cumin. It's in everything."

"I would give much for a good stein of dark beer."

"It's spring. In Manhattan, there will be places serving wild strawberries. The tiny ones, red as rubies."

Rudo licked his lips. His tongue was pointed and very pink. "With cream and a glass of May wine. Are you a gourmet, Zoe?"

"Sometimes." As if she watched a movie, she saw a never-again Zoe from years past, her hair loose in the wind. She hustled toward an afternoon class, her tongue busy with strands of rich, dripping mozzarella on a slice of New York's finest pizza, hot enough to burn her fingers.

"We must console ourselves." Rudo reached into a pocket of his white safari suit and came out with a silver flask. Monogrammed.

"I—I'm supposed to be a good Muslim. From Manhattan."

"This is very good brandy." He looked almost hurt that she might refuse. "Tonight we drink. Tomorrow, Allah forgives."

Croyd had said that.

"Perhaps—" Perhaps she would throw up if she touched something this man's lips had touched. Remember the boy. Do this for the boy whose body this man inhabits. Do it for Jan, for Needles. Rudo unscrewed the cap, a heavy silver shot glass lined with gold.

"A taste." *Let's get you drunk,* Zoe thought. *Let's find out if this young body you're wearing can hold its liquor. Let's hope not.* "To success." Zoe took a sip of the aromatic stuff, smooth and good, and passed the cup back to Rudo.

He tossed down the brandy and refilled the cap.

Zoe sipped at her portion and frowned.

"You don't like it?" Rudo asked.

"A hint of bitterness. Perhaps it's the silver I taste."

"Let me see." He took a good mouthful and rolled it on his

tongue, and swallowed. "It's fine." He finished the second shot.

"Could I have some more?" Zoe asked.

For answer, Rudo reached forward and found a knob in the buried wood of the partition. He opened a compartment, a portable bar, complete with cut-crystal highball glasses and a selection of goodies.

"Oh, look!" Zoe reached for a tin of salted nuts. *Let's make you thirsty, yes.* She pulled the tab on the nuts.

"Here!" She fed him a salted almond and let her fingers linger on his soft lips. Again. And more cognac.

For herself, too, and she cooed at Rudo and hoped the flask was full enough. After the third shot, his cheeks went pink.

The Land Rover roared on through the night. His skin was perfect, an infant's silky skin, so fair. She remembered the boy who had lived in it, and tried to offer him what comfort she could.

As she stroked him, nuzzled him, made love to him, part of her screamed with outrage, and another part accepted, even craved, the humiliation.

This is what you deserve, slut. She heard the words so clearly. The sand was talking to her. *You sleep with every man you meet. Why worry about one more?*

I need to make this man talk, she told the voice. *There are millions of lives at risk here! What's wrong with using sex as a weapon?*

That explains Rudo. And I guess Turtle was part of your education. What about Croyd?

Croyd—was fun! Just plain fun, okay! Stop it, she told the voice in her head, knowing it for hallucination, and welcoming this evidence of madness, thinking, *How wonderful. As soon as I can, I'll go completely mad. But not now, voice. I have to listen to Rudo. Don't bother me.*

Rudo talked.

Then, his head lolling against the padded leather seat, and his flushed face slack-jawed with sleep and satiation, it seemed the ride would never end. Zoe rummaged in her pack and found a white scarf. She wrapped it tightly around her left wrist and hoped to hell the driver was a Fists agent.

The white mouse kicked furiously against the restraint of Mark's rubber-gloved fingers. Mark glanced over his shoulder. Carter Jarnavon sat perched on a stool by a wall of the lab, watching with rapt attention. They were at the stage of mass-culturing the Trump, preparatory to suspending it and loading it into pressurized canisters. The younger scientist was on hand to watch and make sure Mark didn't try any last-minute sabotage.

Feeling almost giddy, Mark kissed the mouse on its pink nose. He was continually taking samples from the main Trump culture, monitoring it to make sure it stayed viable. As far as Jarnavon knew, the mouse was a control.

It wasn't. Some of Sascha's Xenovirus Takis-A-positive tissue—taken under anesthetic, to Mark's surprised relief—had been implanted in it. It had then been injected with Black Trump II.

That was over twenty-four hours ago. The Overtrump worked.

And that wasn't all.

Mark held the mouse up, looked into its tiny red eyes. *You and me, little guy,* he thought. *We have a secret.*

Maybe I don't have to be Hitler after all.

Mark replaced the mouse gently in its cage. He started toward the mass culture vat.

"Tsk-tsk, Doctor." Jarnavon wagged his finger. "Mustn't get too close. I'd hate to have to call a guard."

Mark turned away barely in time to mask his grin. *He doesn't have a clue. He thinks I'm going to try to kill off the Trump.*

If he only knew.

Mainly to distract himself from Cosmic Traveler's answering yammer of panic, he wandered to the incubator where the latest set of BT-II infected human-tissue cultures were. There were five petri dishes. The sixth was non–wild card positive tissue that had been infected as a control.

Mark glanced at it. His heart lurched. He turned to Jarnavon, face ashen.

"Get Casaday," he said. *"Now."*

Ray heard the messenger coming down the hallway leading to his room. Ray had changed hotels, moving into the Joker Quarter to be closer to his new chums, as Snailfoot put it. He actually found the inn by the Zion Gate to be rather to his liking. The room was small but neat. It was relatively quiet for a room over a bar. Jerusalem jokers, it seemed, were peaceful drinkers.

There was a soft knocking at Ray's door and he called, "Come in," as clearly as he could.

The door opened to reveal a boy standing in the hallway outside. He was a teenager, thin and ratty-looking, with a handful of what looked like downy feathers around his ears.

"Snailfoot sent me," he said with the voice of a teen trying to be tough.

Ray nodded and got up from the bed where he'd been dreaming of Harvest.

The boy was as tall as Ray, but thinner. His eyes had a desperate sort of toughness about them and Ray knew that he was someone who didn't belong here, someone caught in the killing who would have been better off going to some nice high school, doing homework and dating cheerleaders and maybe playing basketball or something. But here he'd turned into a killer, and it didn't sit well with him.

Lucky, Ray thought, *I never had that problem.*

"You're new," the kid said.

Ray nodded. "That's right," he slurred from his mutilated mouth.

"My name's Owl."

Ray's face twitched into what his mouth allowed him of a smile. "Call me Mumbles."

"All right." The kid flashed a smile, man to man, happy maybe, to run into someone with a worse mutation than his own. He looked desperately young. "Snailfoot wants us."

They went out into the hall, down the stairs, and through the common room of the inn. Ray waved at his host, a blubbery blob of a joker who always had a smile on his moonlike face. But then the guy never moved very far from the beer tap, so maybe that was why he was always smiling.

"What's up?" Ray asked as they hit the street.

"Something pretty big, I think," Owl answered. He was excited and afraid, but tried to sound cool and unaffected. He almost succeeded. He lowered his voice. "I think we're going to hit the Sharks this afternoon. Take the fight to them."

Ray grunted. "Good."

They headed northwest, toward the Christian Quarter.

"Via Dolorosa," Ray read from the street sign. "Weird name."

Owl glanced at him. "It's The Way of Sorrow," he said. "You never heard of it?"

Ray shrugged. "Lots of things I never heard of, kid."

"Well," Owl said, "it's a pretty famous street."

"Is it?"

"Sure. It's, you know, the street Jesus Christ carried his cross up when he was condemned to death. He was crucified there. The Church of the Holy Sepulchre was built on the spot." Owl pointed to a building on the left.

"No kidding?" Ray asked.

Owl shrugged. "That's what they say."

"You believe it?"

Owl shrugged again.

They were well into the Christian Quarter. The streets were crowded with people of all apparent religious persuasions. There were obvious tourists draped in cameras and polyester, Muslims in their robes accompanied by dark-eyed veiled women, and Jews of every type, from modern-dressing Sabras to Hasidim in their black suits and snappy hats.

The Church of the Sepulchre didn't look like much. It was squarish, with a small dome over the middle of its roof. It was made from the same brownish sandstone that the entire Old City seemed to be built of. There were a lot of people crowded around it, apparently waiting their turn to enter.

Christ died there, Ray thought, *if the stories were true.* Ray wasn't sure they were. He didn't have any particular reason not to believe, but he'd never really thought about it. He'd never really thought about a lot of things, until recently.

He glanced at the kid walking determinedly at his side. Odds were that the boy wasn't going to get out of this alive. He practically had a bull's-eye painted right between his eyes. For a moment Ray wondered about his own odds of leaving Jerusalem alive. Then he realized with a start that he'd never thought like that before. He'd never worried about odds. He'd just acted. He frowned, wondering if this was the first crack in the mental armor that had kept him alive through so many adventures on so many killing grounds.

He felt something tug at his sleeve and he whirled, hand high and ready to strike. He stopped barely in time as he saw Owl flinch back.

"Jesus, Mumbles, take it the fuck easy. What's wrong with you?"

"Sorry," Ray mumbled.

"Well, pay attention." Owl sniffed and looked at Ray with a new sort of caution in his eyes. "You move fast, man," he said in a wondering tone.

Ray smiled, because he knew that the way it looked made people uneasy. "I hit hard, too."

"Well, don't be hitting me, man. We're on the same side. Anyway, we're here."

They were in front of another church, smaller, less kept-up, and a lot less of a tourist destination than the Church of the Holy Sepulchre. The sign on its wooden double entrance doors told why.

OUR LADY OF THE SPASM, CHURCH OF JESUS CHRIST, JOKER, it read in five languages.

Owl said, "Used to be Armenian Catholic. I guess we got the church when we got rid of the Armenians. Come on."

They went up the stone steps and through the double doors. Inside it was dim and cool. It had been a long time since Ray had been in a church—not counting Westminster Abbey—and it made him feel vaguely uncomfortable. There were a number of worshippers. Most were jokers, though a few tourists had wandered into the place.

"This way," Owl said in a whisper. The church seemed to affect him as well. He led the way down the pews, ignoring the supplicants praying there or simply resting out of the heat. A priest went by. He had a face like a wet, wrinkled mushroom, hair like just-watered moss. He ignored them as they went by the altar with its depiction of the two-headed Jesus Christ, Joker, nailed to the Helix.

"You know where you're going?" Ray asked a little louder than he intended.

Owl shot him a look of pure teen scorn. "Sure I do. The crypt is this way."

There was a niche in the wall behind the altar, with a stone staircase winding down. It was poorly lit and the stairs were worn by centuries of foot traffic.

"Careful," Owl cautioned.

They went down. The air became cooler, mustier. Infrequent naked bulbs of dim wattage lit their way. After a few moments the staircase bottomed out before a wooden door black with age.

"The crypt," Owl said by way of explanation as he opened the door and went in. Ray followed cautiously. His last underground experience had been somewhat unsatisfactory and he wasn't eager to duplicate it, but curiosity was starting to get to him. What the hell was going on, anyway?

The crypt was virtually empty. There was a stone altar that looked ancient even to Ray's unpracticed eye. A couple of long, thin candles burned atop the altar, illuminating the mosaic before it. Owl gestured as they passed.

"That's pretty old," he explained. "It's supposed to mark the spot where Jesus met Mary as he carried his cross to Calvary. It's one of the Stations of the Cross. I forget which one."

"No kidding?" Ray said.

Owl nodded. "This is what we want."

He went behind the altar. There was a grated metal door set in the floor, heavily padlocked. Owl produced a key. It scraped in the lock, turning with a rasp of metal on metal.

"Give me a hand. The door's damn heavy."

Ray hunkered down next to him, grabbed the bar, and heaved. It came up with a loud screech. Owl looked at him appraisingly.

"Say, you're pretty strong, too."

"I work out a lot and watch what I eat."

Owl nodded. "You first. I have to lock up. Here, take this."

He handed Ray a small flashlight. He shined it down another staircase descending into darkness. Water dripped from the walls, echoing eerily.

"It's damp."

"Yeah. Snail says we're below the water table here." Owl pulled the grille shut after them and locked it again. "Come on. Be careful."

Old Jerusalem, Ray soon discovered, was a city underground almost as much as it was aboveground. It was lousy with caves, grottoes, and catacombs connected by passages and galleys and crawlways, only some of which were natural and most of which had been in use, off and on, longer than many of the structures above the ground. The Twisted Fists had apparently appropriated their share of underground Jerusalem. Ray got hopelessly confused after just a few twists and turns.

"Hope you know where you're going," he told Owl.

The kid flashed him a smile. "No problem." He checked his wristwatch. "We're right on time."

"For what?"

Owl stopped, gestured ahead of him.

"For that."

There were a dozen jokers, tough-looking, battle-hardened veterans, armed to the teeth and looking more than ready to kick ass. Snailfoot was among them. He smiled.

"We're paying a little visit on the Card Sharks, chum. Welcome to the party."

Ray smiled a smile that took even his new friends aback. "Great," he said. "That's just what I wanted to hear."

"Look at it, damn you," Mark shouted. For emphasis he slammed his hand on the tabletop beside the petri dish. "Even you should be able to see what's going on."

Lip curled, Casaday inclined his big round head ever so slightly over the dish. "So it's a dark splotch. What the fuck, over?"

"This was the control," Mark said.

"So?"

"So it *died*, Casaday. The new Trump strain killed it, just like the others."

"This late news flash may come as a complete surprise to you, Meadows," Casaday said, "but that's the fucking *point* of this whole Chinese fire drill."

"But this was the nat tissue culture, Casaday. The new Trump doesn't kill just aces and jokers. It kills *everybody*."

Casaday looked at him hard. Then he laughed. "Nice try, Meadows. But bullshit. Won't work."

Mark grabbed his arm. "Don't you see, man? This thing'll wipe out half the planet!"

Layton moved forward, peeled Mark's hand away from Casaday, and twisted it up behind his back in a painful lock. "Hands off the merchandise, Doc," Casaday said. He nodded to the kickboxer. Layton pushed Mark away and sneered at him.

In desperation, Mark turned to Jarnavon. "Tell him what it means, Doctor. *Tell* him."

The younger scientist walked over to glance down at the petri dish. Then he took off his glasses and polished them on his tie. "Clearly the culture was contaminated somehow," he said, looking everywhere but at Mark. "It happens all the time." He put his glasses back on. "It hasn't got any real significance, Mr. Casaday," he said. "No significance at all."

"Are you *crazy*?" Mark yelled. He hurled himself at the younger man. A pair of Westerners—mail-order mercs or CIA cowboys who shared security duties with the local talent—caught him by the arms and held him back. "Have you been doing mission research so long you've forgotten what real science is? You're condemning a billion people to death, Jarnavon! Not just a few thousand jokers and aces. *This thing'll kill anything human!*"

"It doesn't do to disappoint the patrons, Doctor," Jarnavon said. "Maybe you should have stayed in research long enough to learn that."

"Enough of this happy horseshit," Casaday said. "Get your ass back in the lab and start loading the canisters, Meadows. We go as fucking planned."

He stalked toward the door, Jarnavon trotting like a lapdog behind. "Wait!" Mark screamed. "Please, you have to believe me. *Don't do it!*"

At the door, Casaday turned to show him a goblin smile. "You lose, Meadows," he said. "This ain't rock and roll. This is genocide."

The Twisted Fist raiding party slipped through the underground passages like worms in the earth. Ray felt his excitement grow, pushing aside the unwelcome introspection that had haunted him of late. Snailfoot was in the lead; Ray was bunched in the middle with Owl next to him. The kid looked grimly determined. He glanced up once when he felt Ray's eyes on him and looked away immediately. Ray wiped the smile from his face. No sense in bothering the kid any more than necessary.

They traveled through the connecting subterranean system for a quarter of an hour or so, which was enough to take them virtually anywhere below the Old City. They stopped in a grotto that, judging by the smoke stains on the ceilings and the skeletons bunched in wall niches, had seen a lot of use during the last couple of centuries.

Snailfoot gestured with his electric lantern, and one of the jokers scurried forward. He was a small, wizened creature, vaguely rodent-like in his lack of chin and length of teeth. His skin was pale, his hair thin, his eyes small and blinking. He looked like he spent a lot of time underground—and preferred the darkness to the sunlight.

"Take the point, Tarek," Snailfoot said. He turned to the others. "Move quietly, gents. We're above enemy territory."

Skulking wasn't Ray's specialty, but he could move quietly if he had to. Some of the Fists, however, weren't exactly skilled in the skulking department. Ray winced at every misstep and stumble. He hoped that none of the Sharks kept an ear on the floor.

Tarek, at least, was a pro. He had tiny, quick feet that carried him silently down the corridors, and a sharp, sniffing nose that led him right to a cul-de-sac where he stopped and pointed at a dressed sandstone wall, hopping from foot to foot with suppressed eagerness.

Snailfoot motioned him back to the group. They gathered in a tight knot. "The Sharks," Snailfoot said in a low voice, "are on the other side of that wall. Our only problem is breaking it down quickly enough so that surprise stays on our side."

"Explosives?" Ray asked.

Snailfoot looked at him, as if surprised that he'd spoken. He shook his head. "No. We can't risk it. This part of the catacombs is especially delicate. An explosion, no matter how carefully shaped, might bring down the whole section."

Ray snorted. Amateurs. He'd worked with explosive experts who could blow a particular cabinet in a china shop and not even chip any of the other teacups. Of course, he couldn't tell them that.

He left the group, went quietly to the wall.

"Mumbles!" Snailfoot hissed. "What're you doing?"

Ray ignored him. He flattened against the wall, arms outspread, feet braced, and pushed. He grinned into the stone. He was no fucking Golden Weenie, but he wasn't exactly a weakling, either.

"*Mumbles!*" Snailfoot hissed somewhat desperately.

Ray started to push. He could feel the wall shift under his misshapen hands. He turned back to look at the others who were staring at him with varying degrees of astonishment and disbelief.

"Grab your guns, boys," he said. He was grinning like a maniac, but he couldn't help it. "The wall's going down."

"Mumbles!"

Ray heaved with all his strength. He felt ligaments strain and tendons pull. Something groaned—either him or the stone wall. Rock shifted, scraping loudly across other rocks and then there came again the groaning sound and this time Ray knew it was the wall. He heaved again, spots of color dancing against the blackness of his closed eyes, and then it fell.

Stone blocks crashed down from above. One smashed his shoulder and bounced off, one hit him directly on his back as he leaned forward, off balance from the wall's sudden collapse. He breathed a lungful of dust from the clouds swirling around him, and he knew how Samson must have felt when he threw down the temple.

He laughed aloud.

Someone behind him said in a small voice, "Oh, my gosh."

Several someones in front of him looked up from their meal, speechless. They were Sharks, all right. Ray could recognize their paramilitary outfits anywhere.

"Aaaaaaaahhhhh!" Ray said.

And charged into the room.

He didn't know how many Sharks there were. He didn't care.

He didn't know if the Fists followed him. He didn't care.

His eyes darted around the room, registering targets without realizing it, looking for one particular face. General MacArthur Johnson.

The room was a combined dining/bivouac area, sensible in the limited space within the Old City. The room's center was taken up by two long plank tables at which half a dozen Sharks were sitting, eating. Another half dozen were sitting or lying on their cots, cleaning weapons, reading magazines, or catching z's.

Ray roared into the room screaming like a demented soul, shirt torn, bleeding from where he'd been struck by the falling blocks, gray dust ghosting his hair like a specter, mutilated face grinning like a half-skull.

He reached the first Shark, who was seated at the dining table with nothing more lethal than a chicken leg in his hand. Ray threw him an elbow, catching him in the mouth, crashing lips and smashing teeth, knocking him off the bench. Ray pivoted, took two running steps, and scooped the second Shark off the cot where he sat cleaning his rifle. He slammed the Shark against the wall and pushed his grinning, scarred face against his.

"Where's Johnson?" Ray gritted through his fused lips, his eyes shining madly.

"Wha'—wha' you say, man?"

"Johnson!" Ray spat. He could feel the blood rush to his face. He could feel the veins pounding madly in his neck and forehead and he knew he was dancing close to the edge. But he made no effort to pull himself back.

The Shark finally understood. He shook his head wildly. "I don't know."

Ray headbutted him and let his unconscious form flow down the wall and puddle back on the cot.

The Sharks were shaking off their astonished paralysis and were reaching for weapons. Out of the corner of his eyes he saw his Fist comrades peeking through the hole he'd shoved in the wall.

One of these mothers must know where Johnson was. It was only a question of finding the right one, but Ray's smile twisted into a grimace as he realized he wouldn't have time to question them all before they'd get to their weapons. All right. He could deal with that.

The third Shark was standing up from the table as Ray reached him. He clenched one of his damaged hands tighter and smashed it into the Shark's solar plexus. The Shark turned green, puked up his lunch, and collapsed. Ray hurdled him and landed on a Shark who was trying to scrabble away. Ray grabbed a fistful of hair, slammed the Shark's head on the table, and turned before his victim slipped unconscious to the floor.

A Shark was standing by his cot, pistol out and pointing at Ray. He fired twice as Ray closed the distance between them. The first bullet just missed, the second punched through the taut muscle above Ray's collarbone, and then Ray hit the Shark at full speed, picked him up, and smashed him against the wall.

As the Shark slid limply down the wall, Ray heard a voice shout, "No automatic weapons! You'll hit Mumbles!"

It was Owl's voice. *The kid's got a brain,* Ray thought, then he bent, picked up one of the cots, and swatted two Sharks who were rushing him. They went down in a tangle of limbs and Ray tossed the cot away and leapt on them.

One had a knife, a shiny, ugly thing that looked sharp enough to slice steel like cheddar cheese. Ray took it from him, like candy from a disoriented baby. Out of the corner of his eye he saw that at last the other Fists had entered the fray. He had time now.

He kneeled on one of the Sharks. The Shark thrashed about like a live insect on a pinning board, but Ray ignored him. He held the other down with one clubbed hand and dangled the knife in front of his face.

"Where's Johnson?" he asked.

The Shark surged against him but couldn't break away. "I don't know," he spat sullenly, but there was something in his eyes that suggested to Ray that he was lying. A scene from one of Ray's favorite movies flashed into his mind and he inserted the tip of the knife in the man's left nostril.

"Say again?"

"I don't know!"

Ray flicked the knife and cut the Shark's nose open. He moved the tip of the knife to the other nostril.

"Care for a matched set?" he asked above the Shark's screeching.

"He's a got a place near the Seventh Station! By the Judgment Gate!"

Ray looked exasperatedly at the Shark he was kneeling on and brought the knife butt down, hard, on his forehead. He quit struggling.

"You shitting me?" he asked the other Shark.

The Shark shook his head wildly.

"If you are, I'll find you again and take the rest of your nose."

"I'm telling the truth!"

Ray nodded judiciously and clocked him on the side of the head with the knife butt.

He looked up again to find the room a shambles. The Fists were slightly outnumbered, but they had their weapons to hand, which gave them an advantage over the surprised and disoriented Sharks. In the heat of battle some of the Fists had forgotten Owl's instructions and the *rat-a-tat-a-tat* of automatic weapon fire echoed loudly through the room.

That was sure to bring more Sharks on the run. Ray looked around. The Fists had done all right. Most of the Sharks were down. One or two had run away. The others were lying in bloody heaps. Owl, Ray saw, had a look on his face somewhere between revulsion and exultation, leaning more toward revulsion. Snailfoot was helping Tarek up. The rodent-like joker was bleeding profusely from the stomach. It didn't look good.

One of the other jokers started after the fleeing Sharks, but Ray stopped him with a barked command. "Let them go!"

The joker stopped, looked at Ray, then glanced at Snailfoot who was still trying to help Tarek stand.

"Are you in charge, Mumbles?" Snailfoot asked.

Ray shook his head. "Just good sense. We did what we came to do. Hurt them bad."

Snailfoot nodded slowly. "I see your point. Yes." He looked at the others. "All right, let's go."

They gathered together. No one was seriously hurt, except for Tarek. Owl looked proud and scared at the same time.

"Man," he said to Ray, "I never seen anyone move like that."

Ray shrugged it off. "We'll talk about it later. Let's go."

"Right," Snailfoot said. He gestured at the unconscious bodies Ray had left littered over the floor. "Finish them."

"They're unconscious," Ray said.

Snailfoot looked at him. "So?"

Two of the other Fists were supporting Tarek. Ray came face-to-face with the Fist leader. His chest was awash with blood from the bullet wound that was even now starting to knit. More blood had splashed on his face from the Shark's cut nose. He held the knife lightly in his hand and said mildly to Snailfoot, "I say leave them."

"So they can kill another time, my dear chum—"

"I'm not your fucking chum," Ray said. "They come against us again, we kill them any way you want. For now, leave them."

"They can follow us through the tunnels—"

"They're strangers. This is your home territory. They'd be nuts to go after us. Besides, post hidden sentries and blast them to hell if you want. But for now, leave them."

Snailfoot looked at Ray coldly, then said in a dead voice, "Very well." He looked at the other Fists. "We leave them. This time."

Someone started to say something, but Owl broke in, "We have to get Tarek to a doctor, fast."

"Right-o," Snailfoot said, his usual jaunty self again. "Let's go. Ali and Nyugen, take Tarek." He turned to Ray. "Mumbles, since it was your idea, you and Owl will serve as rear guard. If any Sharks show, I sincerely hope you'll be able to overcome your scruples and kill them."

Ray grinned. "Bet your ass on it, chum. If you have an ass."

Coming into the Nur's encampment, even under a flag of truce, made Gregg's stomach churn with memories. The last time he'd met the Nur—seven years ago, now—Gregg had overreached himself. Prodded by the addictive need inside him, haunted by the personality that rode his soul, the visit had been a disaster only narrowly averted when he'd forced Kahina, the Nur's seeress-sister, into slitting the ace's throat.

Gregg himself had been shot in the chaos, an event that would destroy his political aspirations a year later. The Nur had become a watershed from which his life had careened downhill, losing him along the way his career, his mistress, his wife, his secrets, and—at last—his power.

The Nur's fault, all of it, the voice told him, tasting his thoughts.

Sand whipped around the Land Rover Needles drove. They'd followed the directions of the taciturn, djellaba-clad, and bearded man who was their guide—met as planned in Damascus—driving across the vast Syrian desert, skirting the mountains of Jabal Duriz and onto the arid plateau where only hawthorns and a few stubborn scrub brushes grew. The sky was a furnace overhead; jerry cans of gasoline gurgled in the back of the Rover, a white flag fluttered from the aerial.

As they bounced over the lip of a rocky hill, the wind was suddenly fragrant with camel musk. A crowd of parti-color tents huddled around the stone walls of a small village spread out below them. Their guide stood up on the seat and waved to two guards that none of them had noticed, crouching behind boulders on either side of them. There was a long, chattering exchange in Arabic, then they were waved forward. Gregg could feel the apprehension rising like a cold ocean current from Hannah and Needles as they maneuvered downslope to where a crowd was suddenly gathering. "Gregg? I don't like this," Hannah said. "Look, over there by the building on the center square."

Gregg looked where she pointed, squinting. Blurrily, he

could see a human form swinging from a gibbet high up on the side, a cloud of flies buzzing around it. The body was a joker's, the legs fused into a flipper-like tail—a cruel joke of the virus: a mermaid in the desert. Seeing the corpse displayed this way brought back memories; the Nur had presented him with a similar display the last time they'd met. "Oh, man," Needles moaned. His hands twitched, and claws rattled.

"Don't react," Gregg told them. "That's what he wants. Needles?"

Needles was peering through the gathering darkness at the crowd watching their approach, and Gregg could sense a flash of recognition from the boy as he saw a veiled and robed woman with a bandage wrapped around one wrist. "Who's that?" Gregg asked.

"No one," Needles said quickly. Gregg could tell by the muddy orange of the words that Needles was lying. Gregg wondered at that, but there didn't seem to be any point in pushing it. Not here. Not now.

Their guide had leapt out of the Rover as they pulled into the clearing in the middle of the village, talking and gesticulating furiously with an elderly mullah. Finally, the guide waved at them. "This way," he grunted in his accented English. "The Nur will see you."

As they entered the building, flanked by guards with Uzis, Gregg realized it was a small but ornate mosque, the walls and floor inlaid with tile in intricate patterns of lapis lazuli and gold, lamps throwing long-legged shadows from the pillars. On the dais of the minbar, the pulpit, a giant sat in a wheelchair. With a shock, Gregg recognized the crippled giant: Sayyid, the Nur's general. The scene before him was—eerily—nearly a mirror of the one seven years before. The power squirmed like a maggot inside him. "Oh, no," Gregg whispered, involuntarily.

"Yes, I remember, too," said a voice, and a man in white robes strode out from behind a curtain on the dais.

Seven years had done little to touch the Nur. His raven hair was now shot through with gray and he'd added a paunch to his once-athletic body, but his skin still glowed emerald in the dusk, and the eyes were still coal-black and piercing in the handsome face. One thing only had changed—the Nur al-Allah's throat was crossed by an ugly, twisting scar that was a darkness on the lambent skin, the legacy of a knife wielded by Kahina, his sister—a knife that Gregg's will had guided. There was a faint smile on the Nur al-Allah's face as he approached the edge of the dais and looked down at the trio. Gregg was cold: a coldness deeper than the approaching night chill. His body trembled on the edge of overdrive; he wanted to run. The Nur stared at them: a joker with talons for hands, a blond nat woman uncomfortably dressed in chador, and Gregg: something only barely humanoid.

The Nur al-Allah threw back his head and laughed.

The sound was like a ringing of chimes, like a chorus. The amusement touched each of them. The guards around him chuckled with the Nur; Needles looked around sheepishly, a half-smile pulling at his own lips, and Hannah smiled uncertainly, caught in the Nur's magic laugh. It caught Gregg, too, a need to please this charismatic man, to share his laughter. Down below, where the old strings were attached, a voice railed, cursing.

"Marhaban," the Nur said: *Greetings.* "So this is what has become of the great Gregg Hartmann. Inshallah, after all, and I see that He has given you a body to match your mind. You are cursed of Allah, infidel; He has finally made it visible."

The Nur's voice: Gregg remembered that glorious instrument, that cello of a voice that rang and reverberated, gleaming with power as vivid as that of the ace's glowing skin.

Kahina's knife had shaved some of the power, had carved the purity from the tones and left the instrument scratchy and uneven. Still, Gregg could feel the power behind it—damaged the voice might be, but not powerless. Not at all. Hannah's smile had wavered and disappeared with the words. When she spoke, her voice sounded weak and puny alongside that of the Nur. "Neither Gregg nor Needles is 'cursed of Allah,'" she told the Nur. "They are just victims of a virus, as are you."

The Nur smiled at her and spread his hands wide. He gleamed in the lamplit dimness of the mosque, like a luminescent emerald. His eyes gleamed, depthless. "Do I seem a victim?" he asked, and the voice dripped reasonableness, it begged agreement. "Young woman, I sense your faith, and Allah has protected you for it. The two of us might call our God by different names, but He is the same. You pray to God because you believe that His will can accomplish anything. I agree; Allah is supreme; and knowing that, you must also know that there are no 'victims.' Not the slightest grain of sand stirs without Allah's knowledge and consent, and even the desert wind is Allah's tool. This sickness of yours is no different—it is but another weapon in Allah's hands. Those who are worthy, Allah rewards, those who are not . . ." The Nur stopped, and his gesture took in Gregg and Needles. Needles hung his head under the influence of the Nur's admonishment; Gregg lowered himself to all sixes.

"You once dangled people from the spiderweb fingers in your mind, Gregg Hartmann," the Nur continued. "My sister was one of them. Tell me, Gregg Hartmann—is my Kahina still alive?"

The Nur stared at him, as did Sayyid. *Kahina: the Nur's prophetess sister, and Sayyid's wife. I let Mackie Messer slice open her living body in front of Chrysalis and Digger Downs, and I gorged myself on her dying agony . . .* "No," Gregg answered, because he found that he could not lie into the Nur's gaze. "She's not."

The Nur nodded; Sayyid seemed to sink heavier into the seat of the wheelchair. "I knew she was gone," the Nur said. "Allah told me, and I have already mourned her loss and forgiven what she did to me. If only her faith had been stronger . . ." The sadness in the prophet's voice throbbed. Gregg could see tears in Hannah's eyes, a reflection of the Nur's pain, and Gregg found himself wanting to confess, to shout out his guilt and cast himself down before the Nur and await his judgment. *I'm sorry. It wasn't me, not really. It was Puppetman, and I've rid myself of him. I control the power now. I'm using it for the right things, finally . . .*

But the Nur shook away the memories of Kahina. "And now Gregg Hartmann is only a messenger boy for the dog-faced jackal howling in the Holy City." His voice was a lash, and they all cowered before it. "That is the only reason why your presence is tolerated—because you are not even worth our contempt. Give me the Dog's message, and I'll give you the reply of the Prophet."

Gregg struggled against the voice. Hannah's face was flushed under the black cowl of her clothing, as if the words she wanted to speak were trapped; Needles stared at the glowing Nur with his mouth open, his claws dangling at his side. *The strings are still there, the ones you set long ago,* the voice whispered.

But he knows! Gregg wailed. *He felt it when we touched him, all those years ago. He felt it and he laughed. Remember?*

The strings . . .

The Nur waited, seemingly patient. Sayyid stirred in his wheelchair, and even without the link, Gregg could sense the eternal pain of the giant, his body crumpled under the anvil of Hiram Worchester's ace. Sayyid's mind was wrapped in the fog of the pain, the brilliant tactical instrument blunted by its internal torment. "Nur al-Allah," Sayyid said, though his eyes were on Gregg. "We waste time with the abominations. Destroy them as they deserve. There is no dealing with fanatics like the Twisted Fists."

The Nur raised his hand. "I know I allowed them to come here against your wishes, my brother," he said, his voice soothing honey. "Let us hear them. Even Muhammad listened to the petitions of his enemies." The Nur turned back to them. "Say what you have come to say."

Gregg glanced at Hannah; she seemed in a trance, lost in the Nur's influence, her defiance exhausted with her first protest. Needles stared at the floor, not even able to lift his head. "We know about Pan Rudo," Gregg said, his voice sounding weaker and thinner than ever against the rich texture of the Nur's words. "We know about the Black Trump."

Sayyid's head turned sharply in surprise, but the Nur only folded his glowing arms over his chest. An ephemeral smile tugged at his lips and vanished. "It is the task of the faithful to aid the work of Allah," the Nur said. "I don't deny that we would cleanse the world of the defiled."

The strings . . . The voice nudged Gregg, insistent, and he opened his mind, let the power drift outward until it found the old channels into the Nur. The link pulsed with the Nur's energy, and Gregg hardly dared to touch them, but the power, hungry, urged him forward. Gregg touched, and though the strings burned in his mind, the Nur did not seem to notice. *Yes* . . . the voice sighed. *Yes* . . .

Hannah had stirred, shaking her head as if to clear the mists of a waking dream. "You don't understand," she told the Nur, her voice like that of a whining child. "The Black Trump will kill you and Sayyid as well as the jokers. It will kill those who haven't even manifested the virus."

"The Black Trump will only kill jokers," the Nur told them soothingly, and Gregg could now feel the hard emerald certainty in the man's mind. "All others are protected by Allah."

"No. That's not true," Hannah insisted, her voice shrill, and the Nur smiled down on her like an indulgent parent.

"I speak the truth, daughter. You still don't understand. Those Allah has gifted, even those whose eyes are blind to Allah's pleasure in them, are protected. I have seen this. I myself have been exposed to this virus to demonstrate this to my people, and I lived while the jokers who were given the same virus died. It is true."

"No," Hannah said again, weaker this time. "Nur al-Allah, Pan Rudo doesn't share your beliefs—none of the Card Sharks do. He hates all wild carders, jokers and aces alike. Rudo could easily fake a demonstration like that. A placebo . . ."

"Your faith is weak," the Nur told her. "That is all." Gregg listened, nibbling at the Nur's bright faith. *But look . . .* the voice told him, and Gregg saw it, too. Inside the crystalline fortress of the Nur's belief, Hannah's words sparked against a flaw, a crack in an emerald facet. *He says the words, and he makes you believe him, but the same thought has occurred to him. He wonders. Far down below, even the Nur wonders. Widen the crack . . .*

No! Gregg cried. *We don't dare . . .*

Hannah had bowed her head again, acknowledging the Nur's scolding. When she spoke again, it was to the floor. "The Nur may be right," she said. "I pray that he is. But that's not the message we've been told to deliver. There's more. The Black Dog has a nuclear weapon," Hannah told him, and her words seemed empty and silly. "We have been asked to say that unless you destroy the Black Trump, the Twisted Fists will use their weapon to destroy the Dome of the Rock in Jerusalem."

The declaration brought Sayyid half out of his chair. "You

would dare threaten Qubbat as-Sakhra? You would defile the rock of Muhammad?" Sayyid's hands trembled on the grips of the chair, the cords in his neck standing out with the effort. He fell back with a cry. "*Aiiee!* Our people said that the Fists had brought something into Jerusalem from the north. Now we know their full deception."

"This is true?" the Nur asked, turning to Gregg, and the colors of his soul deepened, shattered by an eruption of brilliant orange and seething black-red.

"Yes," Gregg answered. "It's true. He says he would do it, and I believe him."

"Then I will send back an answer to the Black Dog," the Nur said, nodding grimly. "And I think that to give the Dog the answer he deserves, your heads will be a sufficient reply."

"Nobody's coming," Owl said in a voice that revealed his relief.

"Of course not," Ray said. He'd bandaged his bullet wound and cleaned the Shark's blood from his face as best he could. His shirt was a total loss, but he'd found one to replace it before leaving the Shark bivouac. He looked nearly normal, for a joker, but a dangerous light still danced in his eyes. He was still jazzed. He still wanted Johnson's ass.

They waited by a bend in the tunnel for half an hour to make sure, but the Sharks weren't about to follow the Fists into their subterranean domain. They'd been burned badly enough already.

But the day wasn't over yet.

"Where's the Seventh Station, Owl?" Ray asked.

"Where Via Dolorosa meets Souk Khan al-Zeit."

"The Shark said it was called the Judgment Gate."

Owl nodded. "According to tradition the gate that was

there during the time of Jesus led to the city's execution ground."

Ray smiled again and Owl looked away.

"Sounds appropriate," Ray said. "Let's go."

"Go?" Owl asked. "Go where?"

"To this Seventh Station. I have to meet a guy there."

"Mumbles," Owl said as he followed Ray through the tunnel, "what're you talking about? What guy?"

"He took something. I want it back." Ray stopped and looked at Owl. "Look, kid, the less you know the better. Here. You're the one who knows the territory. You lead the way."

Owl looked at him for a moment, then nodded. "Okay."

They took a tunnel that led into a different system of catacombs. At least they looked different to Ray. After a few minutes they came to a set of rusted metal rungs hammered into the tunnel wall, leading up to what looked like a manhole cover in the street above their head.

Owl pointed up. "Souk Khan al-Zeit is right above. Can't miss where it comes together with the Via Dolorosa."

"Okay, Owl. Thanks. Now beat it."

"Hey," Owl said, "I'm going with you."

Ray, looking up at the rusty metal rungs, shook his head. "Not this time."

Owl pulled back, anger on his face. "What's the matter? You think I'm not good enough?"

Ray looked back at him. "You're plenty good. But this doesn't concern you. This is personal." He left it at that. There was no sense in telling the kid that he didn't want him splattered by violence any more than he had to be. The kid wasn't a killer by choice, like he was. He was a killer by circumstance, and there was no sense in piling up the body count in his psyche if circumstances didn't warrant it.

"Personal?" Owl asked.

Ray nodded.

"Well, okay."

Ray nodded again, turned, and started up the ladder.

"Mumbles?"

Ray turned, looked down at Owl.

"I never seen anyone who could fight like you."

Ray looked at him a moment. "I was born with it, kid. That's all. Some people are, some aren't. I just was."

Owl nodded, and waved as Ray went up the ladder.

The Nur al-Allah gestured, and the guards around them came forward.

Needles swung at them, his daggered hands flailing wildly and catching in the sleeve of one of them. The man cried out in pain, but Needles's hand was trapped in the folds of cloth, and others grabbed his arms and bore him down to the ground. To Gregg's right, Hannah kicked at the first man to approach her, who went down howling and clutching his shin. Two more guards were on her before she could run.

Gregg felt hands clutching at his stubby top arms, and he pulled away. The men hung on heavily, and the pain sent a pulse of brilliant white through him. The world slowed down, and he was in overdrive, the adrenaline buzzing in his ears. Gregg twisted impossibly fast in the guard's grasp, tearing himself loose. Four legs skittered on tile; like a dog on a linoleum floor, he went busily nowhere for aching moments before he found some traction and shot wildly away across the mosque. He found himself scrambling pell-mell directly into a pillar. Gregg tried to turn, couldn't, and slammed into the unyielding stone. Groggily, he could hear someone shouting. Stone chipped from the pillar just above his head, followed instantly by the report of a weapon.

Gregg ducked and went blindly forward. He rammed Sayyid's wheelchair. The giant spun the wheels in slow motion, trying to move away from Gregg, and chrome glittered in Gregg's eyes. A sudden desperate idea took him. Gregg focused on the chrome, on the delightful metal.

He vomited.

Sayyid, wheeling away from the mad joker, suddenly tilted over as one wheel of his chair turned to metallic goo. The giant toppled with a cry, sprawling on the dais. Gregg hopped on top of the stricken, moaning ace, his head above Sayyid's. "Let us go, or I do the same to Sayyid," Gregg shouted to the Nur. "I'll melt your general's head like a fucking snowball."

The bluff worked. Gregg knew that, if he followed through, nothing would happen to Sayyid beyond a nasty, smelly mess on his head, but the Nur's guards stopped, looking to their leader for direction, and the Nur glared at Gregg. "Back away, abomination!"

The command was stentorian and, to his ears, impossibly deep. Gregg stood stock-still, quivering against the fury and compulsion in the Nur's voice. Under him, Sayyid whimpered like a child, helpless to move his own weight. "I command you with Allah's voice, Gregg Hartmann," the Nur continued. "You will back away from Sayyid now."

Gregg tried to force his body to remain still. He took a step, but it was slow and alone. He sobbed with the effort. "Back away!" The Nur's voice cracked with the word.

The strings, Greggie . . .

Gregg felt it then. With the break in the Nur's voice, a nodule of brown rot showed itself in the gleaming emerald power of the Nur. *You see, the Nur is not certain of his own power anymore. His voice has weakened, and he's not sure he can force you.*

"I don't want to do this," Gregg told the Nur, and he pulled at the strings of the Nur's mind at the same time. "We have heard the Nur al-Allah's words, and we know how powerful they are, and how the truth shines in them. But the Nur must know that there is also truth in our words. The Black Trump is a thing of man: of Pan Rudo, not of Allah. Like a nuclear weapon, is it something that you can use safely? Are you really certain that it won't destroy you as well as your enemy?" *Yes, that crack again, that flaw. Wedge it open, pull at it . . .* "I don't want to hurt Sayyid, any more than I want the Black Dog to use that damn nuke. The Black Dog doesn't want you to use the Black Trump; I don't want you to kill Hannah or Needles or me."

Gregg could feel the Nur's power fighting him now. The crack began to close, despite all his efforts. Inside the voice wailed. *Hurry! Now!* "We have twin standoffs, Nur al-Allah: you and the Black Dog, and us right now. Let us go, and you win this one. We're just messengers, as you said. Less than nothing. We're not worth wasting Sayyid's life on. Give us the word of the Nur al-Allah to take back to the Black Dog, and we will leave, trembling. Don't all the books of the Qur'an begin with the phrase: 'In the name of Allah, the Compassionate, the Merciful'? Be merciful now."

The Nur's mind seethed under Gregg's manipulations, and the strings tore at Gregg's mind, burning. But the Nur grimaced and gestured to his men. "Let them go," he said, then nodded to Gregg. "Back away," he said softly, and his voice pushed at him like a hand, the strings tearing away. Gregg stepped off Sayyid mutely. As Hannah and Needles came over to him, the Nur bent down and touched the cheek of his fallen brother-in-law gently. "I'm sorry I didn't listen to you," he told the ace. "You were right, as you always are." He gestured to his guards, who came forward and helped the groaning Sayyid to a sitting position. Then the Nur frowned at Gregg again.

"You will tell the Black Dog that the Nur al-Allah does not

bow before any abomination. You will tell him that those of Allah will come down upon him, a mountain sent to crush an insect, if he dares scratch the smallest stone of Qubbat as-Sakhra. Tell him that the Nur al-Allah is guided only by the Lord, and that I fear nothing, not his threats or his Twisted Fists or his bomb, because Allah protects me. As for the Black Trump, I will ask Allah again for His guidance, but know that if I choose to use it, the Black Dog's threats will mean less than the whining of some cur slinking around my tent. Now go," the Nur roared, and his voice cracked with the words. "Go! I give you back your lives."

No one said anything until they were back in the Rover and away from the Nur's encampment, their Muslim guide driving once more. Hannah finally seemed to shake off the Nur's presence as they careened over the rock-strewn hillside and the village was hidden from sight. "I thought we were dead," she breathed. "I really thought this was it. Gregg, I don't know how you talked him out of it, but thanks." Her gratitude was like a bath of warm light. Gregg reveled in the nourishing glow, and the voice triumphed inside.

You see! I'm back, Greggie. I'm back, and you need me. You NEED me . . .

The manhole opened in the center of a dead-end street with no traffic and few pedestrians. No one paid much attention as Ray emerged from the labyrinth, replaced the cover, and joined the foot traffic heading up Souk Khan al-Zeit. He whistled as he walked, as best he could through his nearly nonexistent mouth. Things were coming together. The center would hold. Soon he would see April Harvest again. It would work out. It had to.

The Via Dolorosa was just ahead. He scanned the buildings

closely and stopped to look at a plaque set in one. The sign was written in five languages in three alphabets. In English it said: THE JUDGMENT GATE. ON THIS SPOT ONCE STOOD THE GATE THROUGH WHICH JESUS OF NAZARETH CARRIED HIS CROSS ON HIS WAY TO CALVARY.

He stopped, considered. This had to be the place.

Deciding upon a covert rather than a frontal assault, Ray went to the alley siding the building. There was a stout wooden gate set in the sandstone wall. Near the gate was a buzzer. Ray studied it for a moment, then pushed it, twice.

There was a short silence and then Ray heard approaching footsteps. A bolt was thrown, and the wooden gate creaked open. A man stood there in khakis and polished boots. He had an assault rifle, slung. Ray smiled.

"What is it?" the Shark asked, irritated.

"Delivery," Ray said.

"Delivery of what?" the Shark asked, even more irritated.

"This." Ray smashed him in the face. The Shark jerked back, fell. Ray stepped over him and shut and locked the door. This was definitely the right place.

He stood in a beautifully kept garden. It was the greenest spot he had ever seen in Jerusalem. The grass was as green as an emerald. Flowers and fruit trees were in full bloom. There was even an ancient water fountain, the stone Cupid atop it softened by rain, greened by algae. And sitting in a lawn chair by the fountain, reading a book, was the end of his quest, the answer to his dreams.

"April!"

She looked up, startled. It took a second, but Ray realized that she probably didn't recognize him. "It's me, Ray."

She stood, her puzzled look giving way to astonishment. "Ray?"

He nodded, heading toward her.

"*Ray!*" she called, warning in her voice.

He jumped instinctively, rolling and diving. The fusillade missed but tore the potted palm next to him to shreds. The knife he'd liberated from the Shark earlier in the day wasn't exactly made for throwing, but Ray stood, threw, and dodged all in one continuous motion.

A second burst of gunfire was suddenly cut off and Ray picked himself off the ground. A Shark was slumped over a waist-high hedge, Ray's knife protruding from his throat.

"Jeez," Ray said aloud. "Almost missed."

He recovered the knife, cleaned it on the dead Shark's shirt, and stuck it back in his waistband. He liberated the Shark's rifle and turned to Harvest, who had come up behind him. He grinned at her.

"Jesus Christ, Ray. What happened?" She looked incredulous and horror-struck, all at once.

Ray put a hand up to his face. "Oh, this. Don't worry. It's not permanent. I'll fix things once we've wrapped up this little affair."

She shook her head in disbelief. "What *are* you doing here?"

"I came after you," he explained. "I knew Johnson still had you. At least I hoped he did. I hoped you were all right. You are okay?"

She nodded, still somewhat dazed.

"Well, let's get the hell out of here. I'll fill you in later."

"Ray!" she said, pointing again, this time at the wall surrounding the garden. Peeking over it was a head. Ray waved.

"It's okay. He's a friend." Ray tossed Harvest the rifle. "Hang on to this while I open the door." Ray unbarred the gate. It swung open. Owl stood in the doorway. Behind him was a pack of Fists. "What the hell are you doing here?" Ray asked, but he was grinning.

"Thought you might need some help."

Ray shook his head. "Not so far—"

Owl, looking past Ray, suddenly opened his eyes wide. "Look out!"

Ray whirled. Harvest had the rifle up and pointing. General MacArthur Johnson had entered the garden. He was looking around, bewildered.

"Got you now, you son of a bitch!" Ray said.

He started toward Johnson with a grin on his face, but before he could reach him Harvest swung the rifle in Johnson's direction and triggered a blast. It stitched across his chest and he danced jerkily with the multiple impacts, then sagged to the ground. He was dead by the time Ray reached him. There was still a bewildered look on his face.

Ray looked at Harvest. "You didn't have to do that," he said.

She nodded grimly. "Oh yes I did."

Ray looked down at Johnson's body. "Well," he said, "I suppose you were entitled."

"We're out of our league with this."

Hannah's voice spoke softly in the darkness. They'd stopped for the night, the Rover pulled over to one side of the dirt track that served for a road. The sky was dusty with bright stars; a few dozen yards in front of their vehicle, their Syrian escort had started a small fire of twigs and brush. The flames crackled and hissed, sending their own brief stars twirling upward into darkness. Needles was outside, sitting to one side of the fire; Hannah and Gregg had stayed in the Rover, huddled in the back seat with a blanket wrapped around them.

"We did what the Dog wanted. We got the Nur's answer."

"Fanatics in front, fanatics in back—you know, if you closed your eyes and just *listened* to the Nur and the Black Dog, you'd have trouble telling them apart."

Gregg shrugged. Their conversation seemed to take place somewhere far off. Much louder, much more insistent, was the conversation in his head.

You OWE me, Greggie. I got you out from the Nur with your precious, ugly little skin still attached, and you owe me. I'm hungry. Give her to me. Let's take her—we'll BOTH like it.

No, Gregg answered angrily. *You don't understand. You never understood. She loves me WITHOUT you. You'll just destroy that, make her affection into something sick and perverted. It won't be real.*

The voice only snorted in derision. *Listen to yourself. You're pitiful. C'mon, Greggie, you've already used me with her, remember? Back in Ireland; you'd have had her beating you off if that snot-ass of a leprechaun hadn't interrupted.*

You don't know that. I knew it was wrong. I wanted to stop; I might have. And I never tried again, did I? I tell you now—she's mine and we're leaving her alone.

Be a fool, then. We both know how she feels about you, don't we? You're no man, not anymore, Greggie, and she's not ever going to love you the way she did before, not without me. But have it your way. I'm still hungry, and you still owe me. Give me the other one, the voice purred. *Can't you feel the dark one, the Syrian? You don't mind something happening to him, do you?*

Gregg could sense the pulsing emotions as soon as the voice mentioned them. He'd opened the Syrian almost as a reflex, the first day out from Damascus. The man was like a rotten pomegranate. His hatred of the three of them boiled just below the surface tangle of his thoughts. He said very little, but Gregg could tell that he hated jokers with all the intensity of the Nur himself. The only reason their guide hadn't left them stranded in the desert was his sense of duty. The dark shapes of his thoughts swirled around the campfire like smoke.

He'd be so easy, and you don't need him, not anymore. You know how to get back to Damascus from here.

". . . don't you think so, Gregg? Gregg?"

Gregg realized that he'd missed what Hannah was saying. He nodded. "Yes," he said and didn't know who he was answering. "Of course you're right."

Hannah leaned back in her seat with a sigh. She stared up at the stars, lost in her own thoughts while Gregg rode the power toward the campfire beyond the windshield. *This is almost too easy.* The voice laughed. *Feel it. Feel the way he looks at Needles. He's the only one of you the Syrian's afraid of.* Gregg could sense the hue of the man's thoughts. The man was brooding, hunched with knees to chest as he watched the flames. The hatred in him was pus-yellow, and it filled his soul, underlying everything else. This was a man who would have come to the Nur because of the bitterness and gall that was already in him. The Nur's revulsion toward jokers was a twisted perversion of his faith; this man's loathing was more personal and rooted deep in his memories. Only two things held it back: his obedience to the Nur, and a small node of fear for the claws of Needles's hands. There was nothing in him that feared Gregg, and as for Hannah . . .

Easy. Tasty.

Gregg released his ace. The power sped from him like a beast suddenly uncaged, leaping with a roar toward the Syrian man's mind. Dampening the man's caution toward Needles was but the work of a moment. More difficult were the bonds of the man's obedience toward the Nur. Carefully, Gregg pushed down the bars of iron-red faith, while at the same time easing that hatred forward, caressing the sour folds, tugging at the links.

Through the windshield, Gregg saw the man suddenly get

to his feet. He stared up at the stars, then down at Needles, who glanced at the man in surprise. The Syrian spat on the ground, then said something to Needles that Gregg couldn't hear. He didn't need to—he could taste the venom: sweet and fulfilling, an appetizer for the hunger inside. Gregg felt the hatred swell like lava, felt the swell of responsive anger spark in Needles.

Now . . . Needles said something in return. There was another exchange of unheard words, while Gregg felt the Syrian's bile change slowly from pale yellow to burning orange-red, while Gregg used the power to send adrenaline surging through Needles. Alongside him, Hannah suddenly noticed the burgeoning confrontation, sitting up in her seat with a gasp. "Gregg—" she began.

Too late. Razor-edged steel glinted in firelight, sand kicked from under the man's feet. Needles hurtled to his feet at the same time as the man attacked. The youth's hands, fingers spread wide, slashed quicker than the Syrian's knife—a rake across the abdomen, another across the throat. In Gregg's mind, the hatred dissolved in the shock of delicious white agony from the man. Gregg could feel the triumph inside Needles, and he pumped it, jacked it high. Needles grimaced, his hand came back. Even as the Syrian toppled, Needles plunged his hand deep into the man's stomach, curling his fingers so that the blades of his hand ripped and gouged and tore. The man fell backward, a hand scattering glowing coals.

A thin shriek followed sparks into the black sky.

The thing inside Gregg ate the Syrian's death like candy. Even Gregg could feel the orgasmic pleasure of the man's pain, the slow spiral into oblivion. Then it was over. The power inside him sighed and dropped the strings.

"Needles!" Hannah screamed, running from the Land

Rover. Her voice echoed in the darkness, rebounding from the stones. "Oh, God . . ."

The boy turned to them. The tight grimace on his face dissolved into a frown, a sob.

"He just came at me," Needles said. Blood dripped from the curved talons of his fingers, a slow, thick rain on the arid earth. "I had to defend myself."

Needles's eyes begged their understanding, their forgiveness. "I had to," he said again.

"I understand," Gregg told him. "You're right. You had to."

Inside, Puppetman—sated—laughed.

And so did you, Greggie, it told him. *So did you.*

Mark stood in the lab watching the technicians pump the suspended virus into the fourth and final canister. Three had already been trundled out on dollies to be loaded into a panel van acquired by the Guangdong Party brass the same way they got their Rolls-Royces and Mercedes: They bought it off a street gang that swiped it off a Hong Kong street. Hot cars were Guangdong's number one import.

The canisters were almost sinister in their nondescriptness, aside from the fact that they were enameled this weird, unearthly shade of vibro-electric blue with a touch of green that struck the eyeballs and made them ring like a bell. The enamel was well dinged and flaking, as if they'd enjoyed long and useful lives already. Mark hoped they were sound.

He was wandering a drunkard's-walk path through the lab, taking last-minute note of this and that on a clipboard. The Chinese technicians and the Western guard sitting in a corner with an MP5 on his lap paid him no attention. He was a crazy American scientific genius, so nobody bothered trying to figure out what he was up to at any given moment. And if he went nuts and tried to sabotage the tanks at this late date, the guard would shoot him, and Casaday would give his beautiful, feebleminded daughter to the German who looked like a smoothed-off and Vaselined toad. His *good behavior*, in short, was pretty much taken for granted at this point.

No one, therefore, noticed when he wandered near the humming compressor pumping megadeath mist into the electric blue tank. The mechanical pencil he was tapping on the metal clip of his clipboard took a bad rebound and jumped out of his stork-leg fingers and rolled under the cylinder.

Mark was instantly on his knees with his slat-lean butt in the air, making a long arm beneath the rack that held the blue canister. The guard said, "Sheit," and stood up.

"No, man, it's cool," Mark said, transferring his weight to the elbow so he could wave the hand that wasn't under the rack reassuringly. "Just retrieving my pen. Give me a sec and I'm out of here."

The guard stood frowning at him. For whatever reason, Mark was still valuable to the Sharks, or he'd be dead. Casaday being Casaday, the guard was doubtless well primed with knowledge of the obscene and ghastly penalties that would be his if he shot Mark without a damned good reason. Similar horrors awaited him, on the other hand, if he allowed Mark to monkey-wrench anything. He did what most people did when caught in dilemma's vise grips: dithered and hoped for the best.

The process seemed to take a while even for a geek science wonk who was by definition all thumbs. The guard was beginning to shift his weight and play with the safety, and the techs were complaining in blue jay Cantonese when Mark reeled his arm back and stood up. He brandished his pencil high.

"See? Everything's cool." The guard nodded and sat down. The technicians went back to monitoring their gauges.

Mark went back to packing and tapping. Pacing and tapping.

The lab door opened. Layton came stomping in, looking pissed off. That was rest state for him, but Mark's heart tried to jump out his mouth like a frightened squirrel anyway.

He saw Mark, stopped, and fired his finger at him like a nine-millimeter round. "*You!* Bring your ass with me."

Mark just stared at the kickboxer. Layton smiled. "Or do I gotta encourage you?" he asked.

He didn't. Mark stumbled forward like a beef steer with a hot date with a hammer.

"Guangzhou," J. Bob Belew announced.

"Gesundheit," Jay said. He had to shout to be heard over the *whap-whap-whap* sound of the chopper's huge rotors.

Belew shook his head. "Canton to you, Mr. Ackroyd." He spread the map out on his knees, and Jay and Finn leaned in closer to look. Belew's Cambodian friends were strapped in behind them, giving the fish eye to Belew's Hong Kong Chinese friends while the jungles of Thailand flashed by below and everybody fingered automatic weapons.

"The complex was originally constructed as an underground bomb shelter for Guangdong Communist Party officials in the event of a nuclear war," Belew was saying. "Given the age of most high-level Red Chinese, they wisely included a hospital wing and medical research facility, specializing in geriatric medicine. State of the art, at least as the art is practiced in China."

"Oh, real good," Jay said. "It wasn't enough we had to deal

with the Sharks and the CIA, now we've got a few billion Red Chinese to fuck with us, too."

Finn was studying Belew's map. "The Sharks have got to be targeting Hong Kong." He pointed. "Look how close it is."

"Agreed," Belew said. "Hong Kong and Saigon have the only two significant joker populations in this part of Asia. The facility in Guangzhou is a bare hundred kilometers from the New Territories, where most of Hong Kong's jokers live. You couldn't ask for a better staging area."

"And Hong Kong is a center of world trade," Finn said. "The airport . . . God, if the Black Trump gets loose there, it will spread all over the world in a matter of hours . . ."

"Is there any way we can convince the authorities to shut down the Hong Kong airport?" Jay asked Belew.

"It would take more convincing than we have time for," J. Bob replied. "Aristophanes said you cannot teach a crab to walk straight, but I'd sooner try that than attempt to convince the Crown Colony to cut off trade for as much as ten minutes."

"So we need to make sure the stuff never gets to Hong Kong," Jay yelled. His stomach did a lurch as the huge helicopter hit a patch of turbulence. It was an old CH-46 Chinook, shaped like a big green banana with rotors at both ends, designed to belch platoons of paratroopers out on top of bad guys, although Jay figured Lord Tung had used it for other purposes. He kept wondering what kind of repair a war surplus chopper owned by a big monkey was likely to be in, until he decided that even if the rotors all fell off, it was no big deal. The Black Trump would probably kill them all anyway.

"Dr. Finn," Belew asked the centaur, "assuming the virus was ready to go, what would be your optimal method of delivery?"

"Aerial," Finn replied, without a moment's hesitation. "Provided you had a large enough supply in droplet form. Spray it from crop dusters, cover the whole city, infect as large a population as possible. The one thing we've got going for us is that the virus is only fatal for the first three or four generations. So the Sharks have no choice but to try to maximize the initial dispersal, to create as many vectors as they can."

"So all we have to do is cut off all air traffic between Canton and Hong Kong," Jay said. "It would help if we had somebody who could fly. Where the hell is Jetboy when you really need him?"

"I've sent some men to cover Guangzhou's airports. Dr. Finn, I'd like you to go with them."

"Why?" Finn said, suspiciously.

Belew was patient. "My men know Mark by sight, and they have descriptions of Casaday, but we'll need you to watch for Ackroyd's two operatives. Besides, a joker would be rather conspicuous where Jay and I are going. We need to get into the complex and destroy the virus before they can move it."

Jay's brain was running in circles, like a hamster on a wheel. "I hope you know the secret password, Belew, 'cause I sure as hell don't. A place like this is going to have security out the wazoo."

Belew gave him a cool, ironic smile. "Didn't that famous detective school of yours teach you how to penetrate top secret enemy installations, Mr. Ackroyd?"

"You know, they covered it, but I slept late that day. Maybe we could dress up in Domino's uniforms and go in with a pizza. Other than that I'm fresh out of plans."

"You're not far off the mark," J. Bob said, stroking his mustache. "That's more or less precisely what we are going to do."

Jay blinked and Finn looked up in sudden alarm. *"Excuse me?"* they said in unison.

- - -

It was a medical examination room. Sitting in an old-fashioned wooden chair, nude but for boxer shorts, his arms and legs secured to the chair's arms and legs with wire, was Sascha Starfin. A goon, local or at least ethnic Chinese, stood behind him with folded arms and shuttered face. A technician in a white smock stood by a counter on which sat a rack of tiny stoppered vials, each labeled with a lot number scrawled on a piece of tape. Beside it a hypodermic syringe rested on a scratched but gleaming stainless-steel tray.

The joker turned his eyeless face to Mark. "Don't do it," he said.

Mark stared around like a cat caught in a blind alley by a pair of pit bulls. Casaday was there, smiling his cool Halloween-pumpkin smile. Dr. Carter Jarnavon was on hand, too, looking truculent and dubious by turns.

"What the hell *is* this?" Mark demanded. His voice cracked like a Ming vase dropped on cement steps. He already knew what it had to be.

"Your good friend and mine, Dr. Jarnavon here, reminded me that you're a resourceful son of a bitch, not necessarily the stumbling geek you act like most of the time," the spook said. "It occurred to my nasty, suspicious mind that you might get the notion of playing *cute tricks*."

Mark swayed. *Busted!* His head felt like a helium balloon. His knees felt like well-boiled samples of the pasta that Marco Polo had *not*, as a matter of fact, introduced to Italy from China.

Tumult in his head: Traveler, *I told you so!* JJ Flash, *They can't know* anything. *If they did, they'd already be pruning Sprout like a shrub to punish you* . . .

Mary had a little lamb, little lamb, little lamb. He tried to fill his forebrain with noise. Sascha was utterly panicked. He'd babble anything he could to save himself. *Oh, God. Sprout, baby.*

"You know my respect for you is all but limitless, Doctor," Jarnavon said. "But, sadly, I'm all too aware that your heart hasn't really been *in* the work you've been doing for us, great and necessary though it was."

He took off his glasses and polished them on the tail of his smock. "You demonstrated the extended virulence of the new BT strain by using it to kill xenovirus-positive human tissue cultures. But then it struck me: Might you have secretly introduced some foreign agent, a toxin or even an unknown pathogen, in order to kill the cultures and mask the fact that the tenth-generation Trump strain *wasn't* really virulent?"

"No, man. I didn't do anything like that." *You slimy little shit.* "Think about what you're saying. You have my little girl."

"Your problem is, Meadows, you think too much," Casaday said. "First off, you think too much about what a terrible thing it is you're helping to do to all the twisted wild card freaks and monsters in the world. And you think you're smarter than the rest of us. You might even think it was worthwhile sacrificing your little honey to save the jokers. Or you might think you could get away clean."

"You've got to *believe* me," Mark wailed.

"I'll tell you what I believe," Casaday said. "I believe that you're gonna stick that needle in this ugly fucker's arm and drive it home. And if he doesn't bubble up and die pretty fucking pronto, I believe I'm gonna give your golden-haired little girl to *Herr Oberstleutnant* Ditmar. Are we getting to be on the same page, here, Doctor?"

"Hey!" Layton yelped. "You said I could have her."

"Don't get your underwear in a bunch, dipstick," Casaday said. "He's gonna give in. We got him by the teeny-tiny balls, and he knows it."

Mark held up beseeching hands. "Just don't make me do it, man. I *can't.*"

Jarnavon shook his head, tut-tutting to himself. "I can administer the injection, Mr. Casaday."

A grin was making its slow evil way across Casaday's face. "No," he said. "He does it himself. Or Ditmar starts carving his initials in the girl's ass."

Mark turned as if he were immersed to the waist in half-set concrete, picked up the syringe and a vial from the rack. He kept his mind filled with Jimi Hendrix playing "The Star-Spangled Banner."

"Sascha," he said, poking the needle through the rubber cap and pulling back the plunger, "please forgive me, man. I don't have any choice."

The eyeless joker began to scream.

It seemed that Needles, not Gregg or Hannah, had been the key player in the visit to the Nur.

"You saw her?" the Black Dog asked. "You're certain."

Needles nodded. They were in the Black Dog's quarters deep in the catacombs. Snailfoot stood like robed and cowled Death near the door; everyone else was sitting on ornately brocaded pillows, Gregg curled on one like a house cat. And, like a cat, he found that he was sensitive to motion around him. He kept expecting Billy Ray to appear from hiding at any moment. He didn't like the feeling. The paranoia made it difficult to concentrate on what was being said around him.

"It was Zoe," Needles was saying. His emotions leaked out from his head like a sieve, confused and bewildered. "I noticed her as soon as we entered the Nur's encampment. She had the bandage around her arm. She saw me, and nodded."

Puppetman yammered for the boy. Gregg ignored the insistent voice. *Okay, Greggie. Play it your way. I'm not hungry now. But I will be. Very soon.* Gregg forced the creature down into the

mind cage he'd constructed so long ago, the bars battered and
bent from years of the power's hammering and scorched from
Tachyon's probing so many years ago. Gregg wondered if the
bars would hold. *They have to. They're all I have.*

Puppetman giggled to itself.

In contrast to Needles, the mind-hues of the Black Dog were
sharp-edged and bright. "Hartmann and Davis have given us
the Nur's answer—which is basically 'fuck you.' Well, I have
an answer to that."

"What are you going to do?" Hannah asked. "This isn't
about the Nur and the Fists, not anymore. Everyone's in danger. Every last wild carder—"

The Black Dog chuckled under his mask. "Your concern is
very touching, but out of place, I'm afraid."

"What are you planning to do?"

"Whatever I need to do," the Black Dog replied. He laughed
harshly at his own retort and left the room with Snailfoot in
tow, cutting off Hannah's protest.

"Damn it!" Hannah said. The catacombs echoed with the
sound of her anger. She looked at Gregg, helpless, her fists
knotted at her side. Needles's fingers twitched, the talons
clashing. "What do *we* do now?" Hannah asked.

Hungry . . .

"I don't know," Gregg answered.

Harvest was uncommunicative and subdued. Ray could
understand why. He didn't ask her what Johnson had done to
her. He figured it would come out someday, and if not, that
was fine, too. Ray watched her as they slept in the same bed,
eager to awake her with his kisses, but understanding also
why she'd be reluctant to make love to him in his present condition. That, too, would change when he'd get his face fixed.

Early the next morning there was a knock on their door. It was Owl. The Black Dog wanted to see them. Ray himself was eager to meet the almost-legendary joker. Now that he had Harvest back it was time to start thinking about that nuke.

Owl took Ray and Harvest underground again. They twisted and turned as usual, then Owl stopped. He turned and looked at Ray, holding out a couple of blindfolds. "You have to put these on," Owl said.

Ray rolled his eyes. "Oh, please."

"No, really," Owl said. "It's orders."

He could see the pleading in the kid's eyes. He looked at Harvest and shrugged. "Well, if it's orders . . ."

He and Harvest stood quietly while Owl blindfolded them. "Put your hands on my shoulder," Owl told the two. "I'll guide you."

They complied. Ray could have counted the steps and the turns but didn't think it worth it.

They finally stopped and Owl removed their masks. Ray blinked and looked around. They were in a small, squarish room that was furnished largely by carpets and throw pillows on the floor. A man was sitting on one of the pillows. He wore a mask that was the face of a black dog.

"Come in," he said. "Sit down." He dismissed Owl with an imperious gesture.

Ray sat on one of the pillows, feeling a little silly. "What do you want?" he asked.

The Black Dog regarded them steadily from underneath his mask. "I should ask the same of you two." He turned so that he was looking directly at Harvest. "You're the missing American special agent, April Harvest."

"You have a good intelligence department."

The Dog waved a depreciating hand. "We try. You'd be surprised how deeply some of our sources are placed." He turned his attention to Ray. "You, I don't recognize. But, from the presence of Miss Harvest and the glowing reports I've received of your fighting ability—and the not-so-glowing reports about your attitude—you must be Carnifex."

Ray grinned, half-pleased at the recognition. "So who are you under the mask, Sherlock Holmes?"

The Dog shook his head. "We won't discuss that. You're after the Black Trump, of course."

"No shit, Sherlock," Ray said.

"Pan Rudo is working with the Nur, trying to culture enough of the Trump to spread it around the world," the Dog said. "We know where their laboratory is."

Ray said, "Well, let's go after them!" He jumped to his feet, eager to get going, to destroy the last vestige of the Black Trump as soon as possible. "What are we waiting for? Let's get going."

"We?" the Dog asked. "How did this become 'we' all of a sudden?"

Ray squatted down so that his scarred face was inches from the Dog's. "It became 'we' five weeks ago, when I saw what the Black Trump does, Dog Man. You going to keep me from going after it?"

"Ray's right," Harvest said pulling him backward to thump butt-first on the floor next to her. "There's no sense fighting over this. I suggest we call a truce until the Trump is destroyed, and work together toward that end."

The Black Dog nodded slowly. "I'd like to keep my people away from the Trump, but I could care less about you aces and nats. I'll give you a day. Destroy the Trump and rescue our agent in the Nur's camp, an ace named Zoe Harris. If you fail, we have another way to deal with it."

"What do you mean?" Harvest asked.

The Black Dog seemed to smile again. "I'm sure you heard about a certain commodity we've recently acquired."

"You mean the bomb?" Ray asked.

The Dog shrugged. "To come to the point, yes. We'll give you a day to get the Trump, and Zoe Harris, out of the Nur's camp. If you fail, we'll nuke it."

"Well, that's better than blowing up Jerusalem," Ray said, "but do you really know what you're doing? How're you going to deliver it—"

"I suggest," the Doc said, "that you leave the details to us. You worry about the Trump and Ms. Harris."

Harvest looked at him narrowly. "Then we have a truce until the Trump is destroyed?"

The Dog inclined his head. "A truce."

"Great!" Ray said. He jumped up again.

The Dog said, "Don't worry about transportation. I think you'll find our travel accommodations most satisfactory."

The Chinese medical tech took the thermometer from Sascha's mouth and held it to the light with rubber-gloved fingers. Sascha let his head drop to the side and moaned. His skin was ashen, his face flecked with sweat. Standing slumped against one wall with Layton right beside him like a Siamese twin, Mark stared at him in nauseated fascination.

"Thirty-ni' point fo' degree," the tech announced with a cheery smile.

"Thirty-nine degrees?" Casaday exclaimed. "Fuck *me*. What does this virus shit do, freeze the motherfucks to death?"

"That's in Celsius, Mr. Casaday," Jarnavon said.

"What is that in white man measure, God damn it?"

"One hundred and three."

Casaday sucked in a deep breath, let it out through distended nostrils. "I thought the puke would go into convulsions, fall over, maybe his head would turn purple and explode. Instead he's getting a temperature and a runny nose."

"This isn't the wild card itself, Mr. Casaday," Jarnavon said. "It's not going to have such a rapid effect. The symptoms the subject is displaying are entirely appropriate."

"'The subject,'" Mark echoed dully. "You got a way with words, Jarnavon. He's not a subject, he's a human being. It's guys like you who make all scientists look like soulless robots."

Casaday laughed harshly. "Listen to the Last Hippie, here. He's about to be the biggest name in genocide since Martin Bormann, and he gets all hot and bothered over the fate of one crummy monster."

Mark covered his face with his hands. "If nothing else," Jarnavon said, as chipper as a Mormon cheerleader, "we have our proof that the Trump is still virulent. Dr. Meadows hasn't played us false."

He rubbed his hands together. Mark stared at him with peeled-onion eyes. *He thinks he's giving me a compliment.*

Casaday scowled, then bobbed his huge head toward the door. "All right then. Get him the fuck out of my sight."

"I want to be with Sprout," Mark said.

"When I say so," Casaday said. He looked at Layton. "Take him back to the lab and lock him in. Let him stew in his juices surrounded by reminders of the real good turn he's done all his little ace and joker buddies around the world."

"Wait a minute," Ray said. "This fucking camel has eight legs!"

The camel turned calmly and looked at Ray. "You don't look so great yourself, pal."

Owl suppressed a giggle as he saddled the beast. "I want you to meet a friend of mine," he said. "This is Croyd Crenson."

"The Sleeper!" Ray and Harvest said in unison.

"What are you doing here?" Ray added.

"Right now, eating hay. Then I'm going to drink a lot of water, because that desert is going to be a bitch to cross. Then, when we get to the Nur's camp, I'm going to kill Pan Rudo, though right now I'm not too sure how. Maybe I'll stomp him to death. Maybe I'll bite him to death." He grinned, exposing big, ugly camel teeth. "What do you think?"

"I think this is insane," Harvest said.

"Look," Croyd said, "I'm not too happy looking like a walking cigarette commercial myself. I just woke up yesterday, after a blessedly short sleep, looking like this. Worse, smelling like this. And the only thing I can eat is hay!"

Ray pulled at his lip thoughtfully. "Could be worse, I suppose."

"Damn right," Croyd said. "I could have woken up as a giant penguin or something. At least this body will be useful. All right. So much for the hay." He turned to a big tub of water and started to slurp it up. He stopped, looked at Owl. "I don't suppose you have anything fresher. This water is kind of green."

Owl shook his head. "Sorry."

"Oh well." Croyd went back to drinking. He drank a long time and a lot of water. He finally looked up, water drooling from his pendulous lips. "All right. Mount up."

Ray looked at Harvest. "This is never going to work."

"Oh, just shut up and get on my back. Have some faith for a change."

Ray and Harvest exchanged looks. "Well," Harvest said. "All right."

Ray got on first. Harvest followed gingerly, sitting behind Ray and wrapping her arms around his waist. Croyd lurched to his feet. Ray grabbed the saddle pommel and clutched Croyd's side tightly with his knees.

"Don't forget these," Owl said. He handed Ray and Harvest a pair of burnooses complete with scarves to shield their faces. He tied a pack of equipment to the saddle rack. "Good luck."

"Thanks," Ray said.

"Hold on," Croyd said, and started to trot.

They were already on the outskirts of the city, having been driven there by Owl to meet Croyd. Croyd simply headed out into the desert.

"I hope you know where you're going," Ray called out.

"Don't worry," Croyd said. "I have a perfect sense of direction."

He put on some speed. Then more. And more. Soon his feet were a blur on the desert sand and they were going as fast as Ray had ever gone in a car. Faster.

Ray was thankful for the burnoose and scarf. He was even more thankful for the woman clasping him from behind. But as they raced into the desert, fear was pulling at the corners of his consciousness with icy fingers. He was going to have to face the Black Trump again.

And that frightened him more than he cared to admit.

One

A scrape of shoe leather on linoleum. Mark's heart jumped around in his chest like a coked-up frog. He spun away from the computer monitor, which was blossoming with silent screen-saver fireworks. *What's happening to Sascha spooked them, they decided to listen to me, they came back—*

Quasiman stood behind his swivel chair, gazing down on him in near darkness, with the flicker from the monitor illuminating a gaze of benign intelligence. He held something in a large, misshapen hand.

"Thank *God*, man!" Mark whispered hoarsely. He unfolded himself from the chair like a drunken sandhill crane from its nest. "We're running out of time. The Black Trump has mutated; it's become lethal to anybody human, not just wild card positives. And they're going to release it anyway. They think it's a trick."

Quasiman nodded. "I remember." He dropped a packet into Mark's outstretched palm.

Mark glanced at it, feeling as if his head had become a helium-filled balloon. It was a wastebasket liner, jammed with glassine packets of powders, mostly white. Relief was as intense as an orgasm, as intense as when the dentist's drill finds the nerve . . .

Catch a grip, here, JJ Flash warned him. In his own persona he thought, *I'll have to test these. Can't risk turning into Monster with Sprout around—*

"There's something you have to do, man," he said in an urgent whisper. "They have four canisters they're going to release over Hong Kong. One of them—"

"Hey! What the fuck!"

The huge joker put his hand to Mark's breastbone and pushed. It was a gentle gesture, but Mark went sprawling into his chair as if he'd taken a shotgun blast to the chest and slid back across the linoleum to bang into his desk and begin to topple over.

The head-squashing stuttering report of a machine pistol in an enclosed space followed the shout from the lab door. Quasiman phased out as bullets cracked through the space he and Mark had occupied seconds before. Mark yelped and dove the rest of the way to the floor. The computer monitor gave up the ghost with a flicker and imploding *pop,* and test tubes in ranks shattered into crystal snow. Mark flattened himself and held his hands over his head.

Over the ringing in his ears—he'd always thought "a shot rang out" was a sly cliché until he'd been fired at a few times in Nam—he heard O. K. Casaday's outraged shout: "Knock that shit *off,* you dickless wonder! You don't know what's fucking *in* here!"

Mark slid the packet of drugs out of sight beneath the desk and risked a peek at the door. Nobody was paying him any attention. Casaday was just knocking up the arm of one of his CIA cowboys. The arm in question had a handgun-sized Micro Uzi in it, which snarled the rest of its magazine into the dropped ceiling. Casaday dropped the man with an overhand right as shredded acoustic tile fell on his shoulders like snow.

"*Fuck!*" Casaday shouted, holding his wrist and shaking his fingers. "My hand!"

The inevitable Layton stood blinking behind him. "Why didn't you let me hit him? It's my job."

"Because I was closer," Casaday snarled. "Besides, you were just standing there with your prick in your hand, you stupid son of a bitch."

Layton frowned. "Don't call me stupid," he said.

Reasonably confident no more large-particulate lead pollution was about to be emitted, Mark was picking himself up like a handful of broken crockery. Casaday gave up wringing his wrist and strode forward.

"Just what in the name of fuck do you think you're doing?" He slapped Mark stingingly across the face before Mark could reply. "You were talking to some kind of freak ace, weren't you?"

Casaday grabbed Mark by the front of his shirt. "You were trying some *funny business*, weren't you, Meadows?" he said, slapping him back and forth to emphasize his words. "You thought you were gonna be *smart*. Well, I *warned* you what would happen if you came smart with *me*. Didn't I?" *Slap.* "*Didn't I?*"

He shoved Mark away. Goons seized his arms and clamped him in place as Casaday turned. "Tell that Kraut fuck to haul his fat ass down here on the double," the renegade commanded. "Bring the little blond snatch, too. And get that little weasel in the lab coat in here. *Now!*"

Minions went flying. Layton reached into a back pocket of his Bugle Boys, took out a pair of fingerless black punching gloves, flexed his fists, and looked expectantly at Casaday. "Can I thunder on him some, boss?"

"Shut the fuck up," Casaday said. He had his butt propped against a lab counter and was whistling a voiceless tune.

"What are you going to do?" Mark asked.

"Nothing good," Casaday said.

In short order the cast Casaday had demanded was assembled. Sprout writhed and squealed when she saw her father, but a grinning Layton twisted her arm up behind her back. "People," Casaday said in his grating voice. "We have a problem. This *fuck* here's been in contact with some kind of teleporting freak." He backhanded Mark savagely across the face. His big knuckles hit Mark's cheekbones like pebbles.

Casaday winced, rubbed his hand again. "How's the eyeless puke doing?"

Dr. Carter Jarnavon blinked through his horn-rims and smiled. "Very well, Mr. Casaday. He's convulsing and vomiting. I don't think he can last much longer."

"Then we're good to go. Let's get the cylinders loaded. We can't take a chance that this shitheel hasn't blown the whistle on us."

"But the plane," Layton said. "It won't be ready until tomorrow—"

"Screw the plane." Casaday checked the Rolex strapped to his hairy, knobbed wrist. "At eight o'clock the airship *Harmony* leaves the Canton airport to take a load of limp-dick tourists back to HK. It's gonna have some unexpected cargo on board."

Jarnavon stood there with a little smile imprinted on his face. "I mean you, chisel-dick," Casaday snapped. "Move!"

Jarnavon turned to Mark, performed a comic opera bow. "Doctor," he said. "It's been a tremendous pleasure." He left.

"And now," Casaday said, turning to Mark with a huge smile carving its way across his face, "the time has come wherein you learn the truth of the old saying, 'Payback's a motherfucker.' Ditmar!"

The German actually clicked his heels. *"Mein Herr!"*

Casaday walked up to Sprout. The girl cringed away as he raised a hand to stroke her cheek.

"Take her," he told the German. "She's yours. *All* yours."

"*No!*" Mark yelled.

Layton had his lower lip stuck out in a pout. "You said *I'd* get her if he acted up, boss," he said plaintively. "You said that."

"No, I said that was an option. It wasn't like an exclusive offer or anything. Besides, we got work to do, remember?"

"But you said I could have her."

"Okay. So I lied. Who gives a puppy fuck?" Casaday reached out and grabbed a pinch of Layton's cheek. "Listen up, lunch-meat. There's a billion fucking people in China, and all of 'em work cheaper than you do. And this is where all that Mickey Mouse chop-socky bullshit of yours got its start anyway, am I right? Yeah. So catch the latest news flash: You can fucking be *replaced*. Do you read me?"

The kickboxer nodded sullenly, still hanging on to Sprout like a child ordered to relinquish a favorite toy. Mark struggled wildly, but the men holding him might have been statues from that frothing psychopath Emperor Shih Wangdi's funerary army.

"Okay, then," Casaday said, striding toward the door. "Let's get cracking. We got places to see and people to do."

"What has happened to your hand?" Rudo asked.

He hadn't noticed the bandage yesterday. A jeep with a white rag tied to its antenna had come into camp and Zoe's heart had soared when she saw Needles, but she had not dared approach him. There had been some sort of uproar in the Nur's tent, and a joker that looked like a yellow bug had gone in and come out again—alive. There had been shouts, and Zoe tried to make sure Needles and the buggy joker saw her, but the jeep had driven away, leaving only rumors, no rescue.

The rumors said that the Black Dog planned to nuke the camp, but the Nur's followers hadn't moved it. Why hadn't Needles picked her up? Why not?

Rudo seemed to have forgotten that he'd asked her a question. He kept his attention on the morning camp and its bustling activity. The Nur's tent was empty, for a helicopter had picked up the Nur and Sayyid at dawn, gone on some mission or another—someone had said that they were headed for Jerusalem, to lead a war against the Black Dog.

Really? A green man and a crippled giant, alone against the Fists? Whatever. The Nur was gone, and his followers seemed convinced that they were safe, that Allah would protect them against a nuclear attack—but guards watched the empty horizon, and the sky.

Zoe let a breeze slip through the loose arms of her black cotton robe and watched women trot to a water truck and fill their jars.

Rudo frowned at the truck. The limitations posed by hauled water would make work in the lab difficult. They had set up camp near a low range of purple cliffs. There was enough moisture here to feed some scrubby vegetation, but there was no well.

"Your hand!" Rudo sounded exasperated.

"Nothing. A little sprain," Zoe said. She cradled her bandaged left wrist in her right hand.

"While we made love? I am sorry. Let me check it for you." Rudo reached for her wrist. Zoe twisted away from him before she could stop herself. She smiled, trying to hide her revulsion.

"Really. It's nothing."

"At least let me see if we can prepare a proper splint for you."

Zoe let him lift her hand. Where would be a good place for it to hurt? She picked an area on the pinky side of her wrist and winced when he probed there, his fingers gentle.

"Ah. Do you feel anything in your fingers when I push here?"

Should she? She shook her head. "No."

"Good. The ulnar nerve is not compromised. See? All these years since anatomy class and yet some things are imprinted! A splint, a splint. Come with me."

She followed him to a tent that hadn't been at the last camp, more brown than black, and smaller than the others. It stood by itself under the scant shade of a cliff, well away from the other tents, out of sight of the main camp.

It was a sort of infirmary. As her eyes adjusted to the sudden shade, Zoe saw cabinets of stainless steel on large wheels, their doors opened on arrays of autoclaved instruments in sealed white packages. There were four cots, their corners made up with military precision, each one—

Occupied by the lumpy bodies of jokers who lay on their backs with their hands behind their heads. Jokers, yes, with oddly shaped bodies, mismatched faces. One poor devil was covered with a pelt of fur that looked like mink and was drenched with sweat and streaks of salt—a deformity that must be near fatal in this arid country. The furred man moved and Zoe saw a gleam of metal at his wrists.

The jokers were handcuffed to the cots. They were silent. Dead? No, a woman's third eye blinked; a white-furred boy took a deep, quiet breath. Two of the jokers had IVs connected to veins in their arms. The fluid was bright yellow.

Rudo rummaged through the instruments. "Always what I

look for is in the last cabinet," Rudo said. "Here!" He found a foam and aluminum splint wrapped in blue plastic. "This will maintain a slight dorsiflexion, a proper anatomic position. And you will be able to work in it. That's good, yes?"

He unwrapped the splint and she let him fit it to her wrist. She stared at the jokers, not even trying to hide the horror she felt. Rudo looked up at her.

"Our patients are not in the best of health," Rudo said. "Paolo is correcting malnutrition, infections, dehydration. Jokers are not treated well in the desert."

"What's . . . What's in the IVs that makes them yellow?"

"Vitamins," Rudo said. He put his hand behind her elbow and guided her out into the bright sunlight. When they were out of earshot of the tent, he said, "These four brought us here, you might say. The opportunity presented by their capture seemed to override the inconvenience of having to haul in water for our work. You see, for our tests to be effective, we need to have a healthy, premorbid substrate. You *do* understand."

"My work," Zoe said. "I must return to my work." The sand near her feet came suddenly into sharp focus, every grain highlighted with utter clarity. It was innocent, pure stone. It had never lived. She envied it.

The sleeve of her robe had slipped down over her splint. She rolled it up.

"Work. Yes," Rudo said.

Zoe ran from him, seeing the desolate cliffs, the empty landscape, aware that thirst and death waited behind every dune. It was time to get *out* of here, damn it. How?

The Land Rover and the flatbed truck that had been at the last camp had been driven away before dawn. The water truck was the only thing with wheels left in the camp. There were no telephones, no communication setups of any kind. Zoe had looked hard for them. This camp was as isolated as anything in the twentieth century could be.

The camp was far enough from water that it had to be trucked in, and that meant it was a long way from humans, probably a long way from roads. She couldn't walk out and live.

She felt Rudo's eyes on her back. Slowing, she walked into the laboratory tent. She scrubbed her hands, her face. She rinsed her mouth and spat.

Where was the Black Dog's goddamned rescue? *Where?*

Sprout lay staring at Ditmar with wide blue eyes as he stripped off jacket, tie, and shirt with surprising alacrity.

"Ah, *liebchen*," he said, unfastening his trousers and sliding them down his saggy butt. "You are so very lovely. Normally I like the loveplay first—" He nodded toward a scuffed black valise by the wall. "But you have got me so excited, *liebchen*, I don't think I can wait. No, not at all."

"You sick son of a bitch," Mark said. The words rang hollow in his ears. Not that they weren't meant, but that they were so utterly futile. But with each bony wrist handcuffed to a leg of the sturdy metal chair he sat in, he couldn't do much more than talk.

Ditmar turned him a wet smile. "Perhaps I am, Doctor," he admitted, "because I find myself even more excited at the prospect of violating such a beautiful innocent while her own father watches."

Mark squealed wordless outrage and tried to hurl himself at the torturer. His legs got tangled up with the legs of the chair, and he fell heavily on his side on the floor, nearly wrenching his arms from their sockets.

He had, it seemed, achieved the theoretical maximum for

failure. His drugs were under a desk in the lab, he had created a virus that might wipe out all of humanity, and now he was about to watch his daughter be raped and tortured to death. After all that, anything Ditmar did to him would be child's play.

He had created the Overtrump, of course, and seemed to have succeeded in arranging to have the Card Sharks themselves release it. But that was a victory so hollow as to accentuate defeat: He didn't know a whole lot about the rates at which epidemics spread, and couldn't have said whether the fact that there were three cylinders of Black Trump to one of Overtrump suggested that the lethal virus would spread three times as fast. But he was morally certain that before the day was over, he would have murdered millions more people than he had saved.

Ditmar had his trousers pooled around his ankles and one foot lifted off the floor as he fumbled with his shoe. He had a certain grace despite his bulk. At least he managed to stay balanced.

"Later," he said to Mark, wrenching one shoe off and tossing it aside, "later I will play. And then, who knows? I may find myself once again in the mood for love."

Mark glared at him from the floor. He pulled off the other shoe. "You could try to run, you know," he said to Sprout. "You're an athletic girl, despite your mental condition; you look fit and strong and so lithe. You might even get past me."

He dropped the shoe and stepped out of his trousers. "Of course, you'd be caught. And then I would have to hurt you. But that's the *fun*."

"Leave her alone," Mark begged, "please. I'll give you anything."

Ditmar stopped with hands on hips, looking comical and sinister in a gray-green undershirt, boxer shorts, and black socks held up by garters. *"Ach, so?* And what have you, a bound prisoner, to give me? Nothing except your daughter's lovely body. And I am about to have *that* anyway."

He chuckled at his own wit. "No, *Herr Doktor,* the best thing you can give me now is your undivided attention." He turned back to Sprout. She lay there in an artless sprawl, jeans-clad legs wide, T-shirt hiked up to bare her flat belly. He clucked and shook his head. "Ah, but you do not comprehend what lies in store, do you, child?"

He advanced toward the bed. His thighs were bluish-white in the fluorescent light, with a translucent sheen like dough. Sprout backed away till her head hit the wall, then wriggled into a sitting position as Ditmar knelt on the bed astride her legs.

Mark was baying like a dog, yelling at the German to leave her alone. Ditmar gave him a smirk over his shoulder, then clasped the front of Sprout's T-shirt with pale sausage fingers and wrenched. The thin fabric tore away from the collar. Beneath it she wore a simple white bra.

The torturer watched her warily, in case she tried for his eyes. But she just stared at him and tried to squirm away; little mewing sounds came from her mouth. He liked that; the front of his boxer shorts was tented out visibly.

Ditmar held up his right hand, pressed a button on a flat oblong object he'd been holding concealed. A blade snapped into place.

"Get away from her!" Mark screamed hoarsely. Sprout froze, started to raise her right hand.

"No, *liebchen,"* the German breathed. "Do not be afraid. I will not hurt you. Yet."

He put the tip of the knife against her sternum and brought it sharply up. The reinforced elastic holding the cups of the bra together gave way. The bra fell away. Her breasts tumbled free, large and pink-nippled.

"*Ach*," Ditmar breathed reverently. "*Wie schön, wie schön.*"

He ran the knife tip down her flat belly. Her flesh shrank from the steel caress. When he reached the hem of her white cotton panties he dug in the point, not quite hard enough to pierce the skin. She uttered a squeak of pain and terror.

"Still, *liebchen*," Ditmar said huskily. "Remain very still."

He cut through the elastic-reinforced hem at the waist. Methodical as a surgeon, he cut the panties down the side, then sliced through the elastic around her thigh. She held almost comically still, like a child playing a game of freeze tag.

He ripped the panties open, stared down a moment at her as if transfixed, then cut open the other side. Mark was too hoarse to make any more noise. He could only lie on his side, blowing like a marathon runner and wishing he could make himself not watch.

The German pressed his stiletto under Sprout's short ribs and buried his face between her breasts. She screamed. He pressed the knife in harder and began to move his face side to side, slavering sticky-slimy saliva all over her breasts with a tongue like a swatch of wet motel carpet.

Sprout put her head back and closed her eyes. Her fingers clutched at Ditmar's fat back. Mark's eyes bugged out as his daughter ground her pelvis into the German and moaned, "Fuck me! Ooh, fuck me *hard!*"

Ditmar reared back like a startled horse. Then he whinnied "*Himmel! Herr Gott sei Dank!*" and buried his face at the base of her neck, dry-humping madly away.

Sprout wrapped her right arm around him, pinning him to her as she writhed beneath him. Her left hand was free. Mark watched in disbelief that turned to horror as the forefinger extended, straightened—and *grew,* morphing like a computer-generated movie effect into a six-inch needle of bone.

So this is it, Mark thought, clear thought stream among the rushing turbulence of voices in his skull. *This is madness.*

Sprout grabbed the thinning hair at the back of Ditmar's skull, tugged. He raised his head. *"Ja, liebchen?"* he said. His mustache was matted with spit.

She drove the bone needle into his right ear.

As he convulsed, she eeled from under him and jumped off the bed. "Jesus, that's gross," she said. She looked down at droplets of blood on her breasts, while she shook gore and brain bits from her finger, which had resumed its normal dimensions. "I'm glad he kept his damn drawers on."

Mark had drawn his head into his shirt collar as far as it would go, like a gaunt, ungainly turtle seeking shelter. His first thought was that Sprout had somehow turned up her own ace and been transformed into some kind of bizarre shape-shifting killer slut. Now he didn't know what to think. "What the hell are you?" he choked as soon as he could form words.

"Oh, nobody, really," "Sprout" said. She turned and walked to a mirror hung over the dresser. "When you last saw me, I was O. K. Casaday. You can call me Creighton."

Mark stared. In spite of lifelong efforts to avoid doing anything that might be called *inappropriate,* he had seen his daughter naked. She had a young child's dislike for the restraints imposed by clothing, and while patient explanation had gotten her to be more modest around strangers, sometimes when they were alone together she would forget herself and come popping out of her room wearing only one sock, or her T-shirt, or her pink fuzzy bunny slippers.

This was not Mark's daughter, as if any doubt remained. Her body was built even leaner, and her skin had a glossier, harder look to it than Sprout's. The breasts were high, conical, and suspiciously firm. She looked, he realized, like Barbie with a bush.

"Sprout doesn't look like an exotic dancer with augments," Mark said accusingly. "You got an unenlightened view of women, man."

"Oh, yeah?" "Sprout" was frowning into the mirror. "If you're so pure, how come you know what a stripper with a boob job looks like, hmmm?"

She glanced back at the dead German. Mark gasped; the outlines of Sprout's face had become grotesquely puffy, as though she had the mumps.

"Where's my daughter?"

"Back in California by now." Creighton walked over to kneel by the body and peer at its face.

"What are you talking about? California? How?"

Creighton stood. He had already begun to resemble the corpse more than Mark's daughter. The swollen head looked horrific atop the lithe, naked female body. He returned to the mirror. "We had it all set up to rescue you guys, back in Burma, so when we crashed the wire in the Cherokee all I had to do was hand her over to our friendly elves. That ex-NVA topkick we hired to straw-boss the local talent seemed the sort who'd be too damned proud to do anything other than what he said he'd do. And anyway, I already promised him a boatload of money if he helped us get you or your daughter back safe."

A bomb burst behind Mark's eyes. The shrapnel was flower petals, like something from the Summer of Love. *Sprout. Is safe.*

"Thank God," Mark breathed. Then, "So that was you all the time?" He started feeling queasy all over again.

Creighton's eyes rose to the mirror and caught his on the bounce. "Yeah. And don't start making faces. Think about how I felt, with you all the time trying to slobber on me. Not to mention *him*." A feminine hand waved at the body.

"So that's why Sprout was so cold to me!" Mark said with a smile.

"Well, yeah."

"Why did you go back?"

"If you were there, you were working on the fucking Black Trump. I wanted to stay as close as possible and hope I got a break." He shrugged. "I didn't, till now."

He turned back to the body for a final inspection. To Mark he was already indistinguishable from the dead man . . . from the neck up.

He looked at Mark with Ditmar's frog eyes. "I heard some guards laughing about what you did to Sascha. I guess I should feel grateful, since you did it to save me, even if you didn't know it was me. Still . . ."

Mark's face split into a huge, manic grin. "But I saved Sascha, too! I made, like, an Overtrump, right under that evil little weasel Jarnavon's pointy nose. I injected him with a *counter* to the Black Trump, not the Trump."

"From what they said, Sascha's pretty sick," Creighton said doubtfully.

"Yeah. It's like the original vaccination, man, what Jenner did way back before Pasteur was even born. I gave him a dose of the same flu I hooked the Trump to. Only he won't die of this strain. And when he gets over it, he'll have antibodies to keep him from getting the real thing."

Creighton blinked, grinned. "Good one, Doctor. Maybe we haven't lost all the wild cards."

Mark bit his lip. He didn't have the heart to tell the strange ace that the stakes had gotten a *little higher*. "They're gonna hijack a blimp at the airport and release the Trump over Hong Kong," Mark said. "We better hurry."

Creighton-Ditmar nodded, glanced down at Sprout's bare

breasts. "Time for the rest of the process, Doc," he said. "You might, uh, want to turn your head."

The wind whistled like an invisible chorus, kicking up clouds of sand that swirled like gritty fog as Croyd came to a screeching halt in front of a tall, ridged sand dune.

"We're here," Croyd announced.

"Jesus, my butt hurts," Ray said as he slid to the ground. He helped Harvest off and they both walked around a bit, stretching and groaning.

"The camp is right over that dune," Croyd said, pointing with his snout. "I'm going to get that bastard Rudo."

"You and what other circus animal?" Ray asked. "Look, if it's that damned important, I'll bring him to you trussed up like a Thanksgiving turkey. *After* we find and destroy the Trump."

Croyd seemed mollified, but it was difficult to tell with a camel. "All right," he said.

The darkness and the sandstorm made their job easier, providing them with cover, masking the noise made by their approach, and keeping most of the Nur's people in their tents. They hunkered down behind a low dune, Ray peering through eyes shaded against the blowing grit.

"Well, there it is," he said. "Anything look unusual, out of place?"

Harvest looked at him. "How would I know? I'm from Manhattan."

"Damn," Ray said. "We should have brought along some locals. Well, why don't we start with the big tent? It looks important."

"All right," Harvest said. "That's as likely a candidate as any."

Ray went first, scuttling low like a crab across the floor of some waterless primordial sea. Harvest followed. They skirted the camp, keeping to the shadows and shifting dunes, moving silently. Once they saw a lurking guard, but he was more interested in keeping out of the blowing sand than guarding anything. They left him huddled, miserably trying to find some shelter in the lee of a tent. When they reached the big tent near the middle of the camp, they stopped to catch their breaths.

"I'll go in first," Ray said in a low voice. He hesitated a moment. "How about a kiss for luck?"

Harvest shook her head. "Not until you get your face fixed."

Ray grinned. "I'll hold you to that. And a lot more."

There was no way he could get into the tent quietly, so he did it quickly. He dove in, banging the door open, hit the ground, rolled, and came up to see a young man, a boy really, sitting on a pile of cushions and writing in a notebook. He looked up, surprised and irritated at Ray's unexpected entrance.

"Who are you?" he asked with a frown.

"I'll ask the questions, dork," Ray said. "Who the hell are you?"

"I'm Rudo. Dr. Pan Rudo."

Ray grinned. "No, you're not. You're busted."

He heard Harvest come through the door.

"We've got the Shark bastard," he told her.

And something exploded against the back of his head, and Ray thudded to the floor, unconscious.

Rudo had left the lab last night, carrying a little inhaler in his hand. He'd drafted two of the older women for infirmary duty. They hadn't come out yet.

The sandstorm had returned, the simoom, whose name

meant "forty," for it always *felt* forty days long, or so they said in Jerusalem. The storm hissed through the camp like a maddened dervish, and Zoe blessed it for the cover it might give her.

Paolo was confined to the infirmary tent with the jokers. Rudo hadn't left the infirmary all day—he was still inside. Near the entrance to the infirmary, a tarp had been stretched over a table. Two basins waited there, and stacks of green gowns, gloves, and masks.

Zoe stayed in the shelter of the women's tent until she saw Zahid leave the lab and stagger to his tent, his arms raised over his face to protect it from the stinging sand. Zoe went toward the empty lab tent as if she had night work to do there. The guard outside huddled with his back to the wind. He didn't ask why she carried her pack with her. She was one of those Western devil scientists, after all.

Zoe opened the airlock seals and stepped into the lab. The mask she grabbed felt comforting on her face. She pulled on gloves but no clean suit. The fans on the negative pressure hood were shut down, all dangerous materials stowed for now, or so she hoped.

In the Coleman refrigerator, inhalers of Black Trump waited, right where Rudo had told her they would be. Fourteen inhalers, in a box with places for sixteen. This was all Rudo and Zahid had managed to make? It couldn't be, not after all the work they'd done—

Rudo had said sixteen—he'd *sworn* that was all there was. *"It's such a tricky little virus, so fragile,"* Rudo had told her. *"But if carefully used, it will be enough. Each victim creates the next, isn't that lovely?"* During that drunken ride across the dunes he'd talked about the Nur's promise to send infected volunteers on commercial flights—and then even a small quantity could blanket the world, for the virus multiplied easily in human hosts.

Zoe grabbed the little box and counted the inhalers again. *Fourteen!* Rudo had taken one to the joker tent. Someone else had the fifteenth vial.

Her hands shook. She almost dropped one of the bottles. One at a time, she set them in the autoclave, sealed its door, and punched the controls for the longest cycle of killing heat the machine could produce.

Time to go. Whether or not Rudo had lied to her about the quantity of virus, she could feel pretty sure that no other lab worked on this horrid project. The desert camp had all the Trump that existed; she had to believe that. Get home, tell the Dog to destroy every living thing in this place—beg him to use his goddamned nuke?

See, Zoe? What you have become? You are going to beg the Black Dog to use a nuclear device on this camp, and you know there are innocents here.

Like the guard outside. I know it. Shut up, voice.

She had to have water if she was going to walk the desert. There were calculations for water loss that varied with exertion and heat, but Zoe didn't know them. She rummaged in the supply cabinet and taped four rectangular plastic IV bags of sterile water around her middle, two bags on each thigh. She sloshed when she walked, but the bags didn't show under her robe.

Now. Get out of the bubble dome without collapsing it. Zoe picked up a scalpel and walked to the back of the enclosure, tasting freedom beyond the plastic barrier. She breathed on the sharp blade, instructing it. It cut smoothly through the tough plastic. Zoe slipped under the edge of the dome and pulled her pack through the opening. The dome sealed itself behind her. One stroke of her little blade sliced through the goat-hair tent that concealed the dome.

"Good timing, Zoe," a voice whispered. A camel stuck his head through the slit in the tent. "I was looking for you."

When Ray came to, he found himself wrapped in chains like some kind of fucking mummy.

"What the hell?" he said groggily. He squinted, trying to focus his eyes.

Harvest and Rudo were sitting side by side on a pile of cushions, drinking from teacups.

"He's awake," Rudo said.

Harvest shook her head. "His skull must be harder than I thought."

"April? What the hell is going on?"

She sighed and rolled her eyes. "God, Ray, do I really have to explain it to you?"

Ray felt like he'd been smashed in the head again; pounded flat by Crypt Kicker, and gutted by Mackie Messer, all at the same time.

"You're a Shark," he said in a sick voice. "You're a fucking Shark."

"Oooo. Give the man a prize for deductive reasoning."

Rudo snorted.

Ray surged against his chains, but he couldn't break them. His ankles were bound together, his arms were wrapped from elbow to wrist behind his back. He couldn't bring any traction or leverage to bear. He flopped around like a gaffed fish, then stopped, panting for breath, when he realized that Harvest was laughing at him.

"Have you ever tested the Trump on an ace, Dr. Rudo?" Harvest asked.

"Well," Rudo said. "There was Crypt Kicker. Of course, he

was already dead when we exposed him to it. And I never did get a chance to observe the final results."

"Well, here we have the perfect specimen." She picked up a small device from Rudo's desk. It looked like a nasal sprayer. She squatted down in front of Ray and smiled. "Well, lover, I guess it's goodbye. You know, I did kind of enjoy our time together. The fact that I knew I was going to kill you soon did add a certain poignancy to our lovemaking."

"Bitch," Ray spat.

Harvest shook her head. "You're really not very bright, are you?" she said, and sprayed him right in the face.

Rudo checked his watch, scribbled in his book. "This should be interesting."

"I'll kill you both," Ray promised through gritted teeth.

"Sure you will." Harvest turned to Rudo. "Shall I take care of that fucking camel for you before I go?"

Rudo nodded. "No need. He'll make an interesting test subject. A pity about Zoe, though. You can't trust anyone these days." He sighed. "Hafaz will give you the keys to the water truck. Drive safely, now. No sense taking unnecessary risks at this late stage of the game. In a week or so there should be no more wild carders."

Harvest smiled. "It's been an honor working with you, Doctor."

Rudo kissed her on the cheek. "Me too, dear. I hope we meet again very soon."

"I do, too." She stopped, looked down at Ray. "Bye, lover. I'm off to spread cheer across the city of Jerusalem. I'd kiss you goodbye, but I'm afraid you're just too damn ugly now."

"I'll see you again," Ray promised.

Harvest laughed. "Right." She opened the door and disappeared into the night.

"Lovely girl," Rudo said as she left.

— — —

It was definitely a camel. It looked like a camel. It smelled like a camel. It talked.

Zoe looked up from where she crouched in the narrow space between the plastic dome and the tent wall. This apparition wasn't her newfound inner voice speaking. So it had to be—"Croyd?" Zoe asked.

"Yeah."

"Are you alone?"

"I am now. I brought Carnifex and April Harvest in to bust up the camp. I was supposed to come in and get them out, but April took off in the water truck and I can't find Billy Ray anywhere."

"The *water truck*? That's all the water there *is* here."

"So they'll dry up. They aren't on our side, Zoe. Where's Rudo? As soon as I kill him, we can leave."

"You're taking me out of here?"

"Yeah. Where is he?"

Zoe shoved her pack through the slit in the tent and crawled out behind it. Even seen through the dense murk of blowing sand, Croyd was a disaster. He was as tall as your average camel, but most camels had four legs. Croyd had eight, and no hands.

"Shhh!" Zoe hissed. "There are guards out here. Are you crazy?"

"I'm not crazy. I'm not exactly happy being a camel, either. But don't worry about yelling. Nobody can hear a damned thing in this wind." He brayed like a camel, and the camels tied in their temporary pen didn't bray back. "Where's Rudo?"

"We can't wait to kill Rudo. We've got to get *out* of here. Let the Black Dog do this!"

"Let the Black Dog do what? Kill Rudo? No way."

"I've destroyed most of Rudo's stash of Trump, but I can't

find it all," Zoe said. "Croyd, I don't know where all of it is! We've got to let the Black Dog burn this camp to the ground and everyone in it. Is this April Harvest on our side?"

"I think so. I thought so."

He had a camel's way of working his jaw back and forth. She wondered if his new physiology equipped him to eat grass and chew his cud.

"If you're not sure— We've got to get back to Jerusalem. Fast."

"As soon as I find the bastard. Which tent?" Croyd asked. He took off at a lope, apparently unworried about guards with guns. Who would believe they saw an eight-legged camel in a sandstorm, anyway? Still, they might shoot first and decide they were seeing things afterward. Zoe lost sight of Croyd in the storm. She ran, and hoped no dedicated guard would shoot her.

Where would he go first?

She caught up with him as he reached the table in front of the infirmary tent. He was pushing his nose, er, muzzle against the tent flap when she tackled a pair of his legs. Croyd kicked. Zoe went sprawling. One of the basins tipped over, splattering water in all directions. A stack of clean gowns and masks fell to the sand. Camel Croyd backed up and nosed at a plastic jug of chlorine bleach.

"Smells bad," Croyd whispered. "Why did you try to trip me, Zoe?"

"You could die in there. At least put a mask on," Zoe hissed. She reached for one and waved it at him.

He lowered his long neck. Zoe pulled the elastic band over the back of his head and fitted his snout into the mask.

But he couldn't open the tent flap without her help.

"Let me in there," he pleaded. "Please, Zoe. Help me."

Help him get them both killed? But he was her only way

out, and he wasn't going to budge until he'd found Rudo or made a good hard try. Zoe pulled the tent flap aside. Light spilled out into the clouds of wind-borne dust. Zoe heard nothing inside, not a sound. The camel shifted his bulk and nudged his way into the tent.

"Oh, God!" Croyd said. "Oh, God."

Zoe struggled into a gown and a mask. She pulled on a pair of gloves, stretching the left one over her aluminum and white flannel splint, and followed Croyd.

Croyd stood just inside the gloomy space. He blinked constantly, as if he were trying to clear his vision. The yellow light cast by a Coleman lantern was too bright, terrible, merciless. No detail was hidden.

They were all dead, and they had died horribly. Something in the Black Trump caused a breakdown in the clotting system. The cots were soaked with thin blood. The jokers had bled from every orifice, even from their tear ducts. Dry streaks of brownish red tracked the matted fur on the face of the mink-man. He had died with his eyes open, staring at eternity.

The walls of the tent billowed, pushed by the wind outside. Runnels of sand made their way across the tarps that had been spread for flooring.

On it, two dark heaps lay—the two women from Zoe's tent, drafted as nurses by the *kind* Dr. Rudo. She took a cautious step toward them, knowing even before she really looked. They had pulled aside their veils, forgetting modesty in a struggle for air to fill their bubbling lungs. Their faces had been beautiful, Zoe realized, before the Trump had sucked away the fluids from their skins and left only these sagging, skeletal masks behind it.

They were dead.

Rudo hadn't told them to mask or gown. They weren't trained nurses, and they were nats. It would be like him to let them catch the Trump. To see how they reacted. After all, nats were supposed to only get a mild case of the flu . . .

"He's not here," Croyd said.

"It kills nats," Zoe whispered. "The fucking Black Trump kills nats."

"Out uff der vay, svinehunds!"

A pair of technicians looked up with frightened eyes at the bizarre pair approaching: the tall skinny American with his hands cuffed behind his back, the dumpy German brandishing a Makarov. They scooted away down the cement-walled hallway and were gone.

"Piece of cake," Creighton whispered.

"Jesus, man, that's like the worst German accent *ever*. You sound like the bad guy in some old Republic serial."

"It worked on them," Creighton said smugly.

"Yeah, but they're Chinese."

"Shudt upp," Creighton said in his ghastly Katzenjammer Kids accent. "Ve're dere."

Mark rolled his eyes. "Ditmar" reached past him to open the door to the examining room.

Sascha lay on his back on a metal examining table, shackled to it by one wrist. He moaned softly. He wore only his boxer shorts, and his pallid body was coated in sweat. Despite a heavy smell of disinfectant, the room stank; he had soiled himself.

A Chinese med-tech and a Western goon sat around reading Asian porn mags from Hong Kong. They looked up in surprise.

"Out!" "Ditmar" bellowed. "Go! I will tage ofer now!" He said, gesturing toward the door with the pistol. The pair went rabbiting out of it. "See?" Creighton's voice asked. "They went for my accent, too."

"They went for that gun you were waving around," Mark said. He let go of the unlocked handcuffs, which he had been holding almost closed around his wrists, and tossed them into a wastebasket.

"Meadows?" Sascha asked, turning his head left and right as though looking for his partner. *"Jerry!"* he said.

"In the flesh. That fat sadist's flesh, at the moment. I'm not going to have to worry anymore about forgetting myself and trying to take a pee standing up."

"You stupid son of a *bitch*, Meadows!" Sascha screamed, spittle flying from his mouth. "You give me that hoodoo bug, I spend three hours in absolute hell, and I don't even die! What the hell kind of mad scientist *are* you?"

"Reluctant," Creighton said, casting around the examining room. "Sounds as if you're feeling better now, anyway, old man. Where are the keys to those cuffs?"

"In the pocket of the guy you chased out," Sascha said sourly.

"Well, okay." Creighton held up the Makarov and jacked the slide. A gleaming golden cartridge came flipping out the side and bounced ringing on the floor.

"Shit," Creighton said, "that never happens when they do it in the movies."

"It already had a round in the chamber, you ninny."

"'Ninny'?" Creighton echoed. "You sure don't have much touch for invective, Doc. At least get with the nineties and call me a dickweed, or something."

He extended the pistol, closed one eye, and took aim at the handcuffs that bound Sascha to the table.

"Give me that," Mark said, and astonished himself by

reaching out and snatching the pistol out of Creighton's pudgy hand.

"Hey!" Creighton yelped, grabbing at the weapon.

"What were you planning to do with that, anyway?" Mark asked, fending him off with a long arm.

"Shoot the cuffs off him."

Mark slipped on the safety and stuck the Mak in a back jeans pocket. "No way."

"How are we going to get him loose? We don't have much time."

"You're the detective," Mark said. "Pick the lock or something."

Muttering seditiously, Ditmar bent down to examine the handcuffs.

The door opened and Layton walked in.

Mark hastily put his hands together behind his back. Layton stopped and blinked at him.

"Hey! What's he doin' here?" He glared at Ditmar, who straightened, dusting invisible lint from his shirtfront. "Aren't you supposed to be fucking his daughter?"

"*Ja, ja,*" "Ditmar" said, waddling forward with his fat face wreathed in a comradely smile. "But I'm all done. Und I felt zo bad you got cheated I vas just comink to look for you."

He laid a hand on the kickboxer's shoulder. "It's your turn now."

Layton made a face. "Shit! I don't want her if she's all cut up and shit."

"No, no. I *zaved* dot. Ve do it later, maybe togezzer?" He was urging Layton toward the door. As he did, his forefinger stretched, narrowed, hardened.

Layton turned a suspicious frown back at him. "Say, you don't sound like—"

The fast-motion growth of the finger caught the corner of

his eye. "Shit!" he exclaimed. He lashed out with a back kick that launched "Ditmar" across the room and against the wall.

Mark, who had expected this turn of events, had slipped a hand down into his back pocket. Now he whipped out the Makarov.

He had always doubted he could bring himself to shoot a firearm at another human being. That was an odd scruple, he knew, given that as JJ Flash he had *incinerated* people. But he didn't like guns.

But now he had no problem. He pointed that stubby little Soviet handgun at the kickboxer and blazed away.

Unfortunately, he wasn't too clear on aiming. Layton dropped. The nine-millimeter bullets blew craters in the white-washed cement wall and ricocheted around the room, whining like lost souls. Sascha yipped and rolled off the table, almost wrenching his arm out of the socket.

With frightening speed Layton rolled forward, swept Mark's feet out from under him with a long leg. Mark bounced off a chair and landed badly but kept his grip on the Makarov. He tried to point it at Layton, but the kickboxer was already on his feet again. He skipped forward as Mark's hand came on-line, snapped the weapon from his hand with a crescent kick.

Layton grinned down at Mark. "Now we get to play," he said.

"Ditmar's" bulk landed square in the middle of his back. "But first, you valtz mit me!" Creighton shrilled in his hideous accent.

Without hesitation, Layton gave Creighton an elbow in the eye. The shapeshifting ace squawked and fell on Ditmar's broad bum.

The momentary distraction was all Mark needed. He was on his feet and out the door, running for the lab with elbows pumping and all the speed in his long gangling legs.

"Jesus, Meadows, don't run out on us!" he heard Creighton yell. The cry was punctuated by a nasty *thump* and a groan.

Mark just ran. *Gotta get to the lab*, he thought. *Got to get my drugs.*

It would seem Lord Tung's associates gave good paper.

Good enough to get them past Chinese customs at Guangzhou airport. Good enough to get the delivery truck waved through the chain-link fence that enclosed the perimeter. Good enough to convince the bored and inattentive guard at the loading dock to admit them to the complex.

And then, just when Jay was starting to figure maybe this was going to be a piece of rice cake, they'd come up against some asshole who actually gave a shit.

The Chinese lieutenant sat behind the security desk going over their documents with a fine-tooth comb. He didn't look the least bit inscrutable to Jay. In fact, he looked hostile, verging on angry, and the way he kept holding up every requisition form and bill of lading to the light was making Jay squirm. The collar of Jay's lab coat was damp with sweat, and his horn-rimmed geek glasses kept slipping down his nose, spoiling the effect of his wonderful disguise. It wasn't as snazzy as a Domino's uniform, but it had gotten them this far—that and the paper and the computer monitors in cartons on the dollies behind him.

The Chinese lieutenant handed a bill of lading to the sergeant beside him, who began to check it against the numbers on his clipboard, running a thick finger down a column of figures. Jay would have loved to pop the suspicious son of a bitch off to some tollbooth on the Jersey Turnpike, only there were two privates with guns across the room watching their every move, and behind them a heavy steel door that looked extremely locked. The red eye of a security camera stared down from the ceiling.

The sergeant gave the bill of lading back to the lieutenant. The lieutenant asked Belew a rude question in Cantonese. Belew answered brusquely in the same language. Jay wished he understood what they were saying. His command of Chinese was limited to *no tickee, no washee* and that was probably Mandarin anyway. The lieutenant waved the paper in Belew's face and rattled off more Cantonese. Belew shouted something back.

The lieutenant stood up, waved his arms, and shouted louder.

Jay pushed the horn-rims back up with the index finger of his right hand, just to get ready.

The lieutenant snapped an order. Orders sound the same in any language. One of the privates crossed the room and started to rip open the computer cartons. The lieutenant sat back down and picked up the telephone on the desk. "Casaday," he said.

Jay didn't need a translator for that. He dropped his finger. The lieutenant vanished with a pop. Before the phone hit the desk, Jay was whirling. The private by the door blinked out as he was bringing up his gun. The private by the cartons started to shout until two of Lord Tung's thugs grabbed him. Then he got very docile very fast. The sergeant kicked over his chair and fumbled for his pistol. Belew knocked the gun from his hand and slammed him back against the wall.

Jay saw the sergeant's eyes. He stepped closer and shoved his popping finger up into the sarge's right nostril. "Translate this," he told Belew. *"Open the door, or else."*

J. Bob did the honors, and all of a sudden the room smelled like an outhouse. As ace powers went, Jay's was almost harmless, but it often terrified those unfamiliar with it. When you see people suddenly cease to exist and you don't know that they have simultaneously reappeared on the pitcher's mound at Ebbets Field, it does tend to loosen the sphincter. The Chinese sergeant gibbered at Belew wildly. "He says only the lieutenant knew the combination."

"You believe him?"

"I can smell his sincerity. The bowels don't lie."

Alarm klaxons went off suddenly all around them. Jay jumped a foot. "Swell," he said, looking at Belew. "What's Cantonese for *The shit has hit the fan*?"

"Break out the guns," Belew ordered over the scream of the klaxons. One of Lord Tung's boys shoved the private to the floor. The others started opening cartons and smashing computer monitors. Glass flew everywhere.

Belew released the sergeant and crossed the room. He ripped the cover off the keypad beside the door. Then he put his pinky into his mouth and bit it off at the second knuckle. He spat the finger onto the floor and shoved the bloody stump into the wiring. Electricity arced and Jay caught a whiff of burning flesh. He felt his stomach lurch. Locks whirred, clicked, disengaged; the steel door slid open.

Behind them, Lord Tung's boys were pulling machine pistols out of the computer casings. Jay popped their captives to Times Square while Belew removed his bloody finger from the keypad. One of his associates tossed him a gun. He caught it in the air, checked the action, and looked at Jay.

"Jay, do you want—"

"No," Jay said sharply. He'd been over this ground with Belew before. "My finger never jams, I don't have to reload it, and it's a lot quieter than your toys."

"I don't think quiet is an issue at this point, but suit yourself." Belew stepped through the door. Jay was right behind him. Corridors stretched off in three directions, and there was an elevator door to their left. There were no guards yet, but lots of guys in lab coats were peering out doors looking alarmed. Belew fired a burst into the ceiling and they looked a lot more alarmed and closed the doors. "There's no way to know where Casaday stashed the Black Trump," Belew shouted over the klaxons. "We'll have to split up, search room by room. I'll take this level. Mr. Ackroyd, down one." He yelled orders to Lord Tung's boys in crisp Cantonese.

Jay took the stairs two at a time. The klaxons were still hooting. They sounded a lot like the klaxons on Governors Island. He tried not to think about that, considering how well that had come out. Two guards were running toward him when he burst out on the lower level. They raised their guns, but Jay raised his finger faster. He started jogging down the corridor, opening doors. He peeked into toilets, storerooms, laboratories, libraries, and lounges. Every time he saw a face, he popped it off to this little noodle place he knew on Mott Street. The more people he got rid of, the fewer would be left to sneak up on him from behind. Besides, the noodle place needed the business.

Halfway down the corridor, he heard shouting from around the corner. *English* shouting. Hard on its heels came a staccato burst of gunfire. Jay ran.

Down the echoing cement hall to the lab. Somewhere a klaxon began its mechanical goose honk of distress. Mark yanked open the door and practically fell into the lab, wheezing, looking as if he were trying to take bites of badly needed air with his big horse teeth.

Made it, he thought, bracing arms on a table for support. His lungs were fire, his legs water. *Just let me catch my breath and everything'll be all right . . .*

A flicker in his peripheral vision, and something rang the side of his head like a bell.

Mark reeled. Or maybe the world was spinning around him. Blackness seemed to flash in his skull, and his vision contracted to a point. The warning horns had somehow gotten into his skull . . .

Focus widened like a ripple from a stone dropped in a pool. The surrounding blue gave way to Layton, standing light on his feet in the lab, grinning at him.

"You tried to run out on me, Doc," the young man said with a big grin. "You didn't think I'd waste time farting with those two numbnuts back there, did you? The guards can take care of them."

Lithe as a figure skater, he spun. Stiffened, his right leg swept *back* and *up* and *around*. The heel slammed into the side of Mark's neck and sent him sprawling, with great purple afterimage balloons exploding behind his eyes, as if somebody had popped a photoflash in his face.

The best part of that particular kick was that he never felt the impact when he hit the floor, light as a feather . . .

He rolled over and began to crawl doggedly toward his workstation at the rear of the lab. The whole right side of his face was Novocain numb. He only noticed his nose was bleeding when he paused a moment to rest—so hard to move!—and noticed the red drops falling to the floor from his upper lip.

He felt himself lifted by the back of his work shirt. As if he were a child, Layton hoisted him onto his feet, let him sway a moment while he transferred his grip to the front of Mark's shirt. Then he drove a short black-gloved punch in under Mark's ribs.

Mark doubled. All the air exploded out of him. His eyes bugged out with the urgency of expelling more air than he had in him. It was the pulmonary equivalent of the dry heaves.

Layton straightened him right up with a rising elbow-smash to the face. "You know, Doctor," the kickboxer said, "I was real disappointed when Casaday ripped me off about that little girl of yours."

He gut-punched him again, this time keeping a grip so Mark couldn't fold or fall to the floor. "I don't do disappointment *real well,* Doctor. I used to be fucking light-heavyweight champion. I get what I *want*." For punctuation he slammed a backfist into Mark's temple and sent him flying.

Mark tried to gather himself. Some reptile-brain tropism made him turn and crawl, as by blind instinct, toward the back of the lab, toward his drugs. If they hadn't found them yet.

A flurry of footsteps, a thundering impact in the side, a spear of pain as Layton's kick broke ribs. Mark curled, moaning about himself.

Move, damn you! JJ Flash urged from the depths of him. *Don't give up!*

Don't listen to him! came Cosmic Traveler's panicky rebuttal. *You tried it your way, and now see what you've done! Give in—tell him about the Overtrump, everything. It's our only chance—*

That did it. Mark made himself straighten out, though it felt as if his body was encased in ice interpenetrated with his own nerve endings, so that when he moved and broke his brittle coating, he felt the pain of that, too. He got onto elbows and knees and crawled.

From some Olympian height he heard Layton's laugh. "That's it, Doc. Crawl like a fuckin' bug." He grabbed Mark's shirt, dragged him upright again.

"You look like a big old daddy longlegs," Layton said. "I used to pull the legs off those little fuckers for fun, when I was a kid."

He hit him then, both hands alternating, maybe half a dozen times *bam-bam-bam,* a machine-gun burst of blows to the face. Mark staggered back. Layton did a little skip, side-kicked Mark in the chest. Mark backpedaled, slammed against the desk. He put his hand down for support, felt pain from his palm—a minor pain but penetrating, slicing through the raw red throb of agony that was his whole existence.

He looked down. For a moment his vision refused to focus. When it did he saw he had dropped his hand amid glass fragments from an imploded computer monitor.

Layton came and placed himself before Mark. He smiled at him, then jumped straight into the air. His right foot lashed out in a high kick that snapped Mark's teeth together and his head back and made sparks fly from his brain like an anvil.

Mark dropped. One arm flopped lifelessly beneath the desk.

And the fingertips encountered cool smoothness.

By enormous effort he turned the hand over, felt. Something firm yet giving, like flour. Felt through plastic. Further exploration suggested composite lumpinesses.

Layton stood above him admiring his handiwork. "Well," he said, "it's been real, Doc. But I think I'm going to finish beating you to death, and then find out just what happened to that hot-pants daughter of yours. Looks like her date with that creepy Kraut slob didn't work out . . ."

Mark burrowed under the desk. He grabbed the plastic bag, tore at it with fingers that seemed to be swollen like balloon animals and have too many joints.

What are you doing now? Trav wailed. *You haven't had a chance to test it! You don't even know what's there, much less if it's pure—*

He had gotten a bad batch of chemicals before. The result had been Monster, a horned horror seven stories tall, who sported a six-foot hard-on for the world and squeezed lightnings from his fists. Monster's sole purpose for existence was to spread the true gospel of Main Pain.

But then, Sprout was away, and safe. Creighton and Sascha, if they were still alive, would have to look out for themselves.

And beyond that, it was only Mark and the bad guys.

"Come on out, Doc," Layton said. "You can't get away that easy." He grabbed Mark by the belt and started hauling him out.

Mark smiled a ghastly red-rimmed smile. Then he tore open the pouches and crammed random powders into his mouth.

The first thing they teach you in detective school is never, never, *never* go running blindly into rooms where people are screaming in pain. Jay poked his head through the door cautiously, his finger ready.

A young blond guy with black gloves and a ponytail was hauling a broken scarecrow out from under a steel desk. The scarecrow was licking something off his fingers. His mouth was bloody and crusted with white powder. The guy with the ponytail had him by the leg.

Jay would have known the scarecrow anywhere.

"Mark," he said, stepping into the room, and hoping that Ponytail would let go of Mark's leg so Jay could pop him off. Big mistake. Big, big mistake.

Ponytail let go of Mark Meadows all right, but he moved too fast for Jay to get a bead, in a whirling, leaping spin that ended when he planted a foot deep in Jay's solar plexus. The breath went out of him in a rush and Jay doubled over, trying to point. Ponytail screamed and leapt again, and this time Jay got a knee in the face. Right on his bandaged, broken nose. The world became a red wash of pain; Jay went down hard.

The lab seemed to be spinning. There was a rushing sound, a roaring of vast winds. Jay closed his eyes, opened them again. Light was flashing all around him, strobing painfully. Either he'd died and gone to disco hell or Ponytail had hit him *really hard*, Jay thought as he tried to roll under a lab bench.

Then he heard Ponytail mutter, "What the fuck?" Jay blinked and tried to focus through the pain. That was when he realized there was a tornado in the lab.

It was black as the twister that had swept Dorothy off to Oz, alive with strange lightnings, howling, sweeping up papers and cigarette butts and small items of glassware. Overhead, the fluorescent lights started to blow up, one by one, until only the ragged strobe of the lightning remained to light the darkness. Petri dishes and test tubes were cracking to pieces, and a computer monitor imploded with a crunch. Ponytail spun at every sound. The darkness seemed to shiver. The world became a negative of itself. The tornado was a shrieking white wind full of dark splotches. Ponytail grabbed on to a lab table.

In the eye of the storm stood a tall man, glowing black, alive with energy. He raised his arms and threw his head back as the lightnings stabbed at him, feeding him. For a second Jay thought it was Mark Meadows, but the face was younger, smoother, beardless. The man's skin was translucent, and Jay could see the bones inside him glowing like neon, and the ghostly play of muscles. Sparks danced through his long hair. He was laughing.

One of Mark's friends, Jay thought wildly, *but which one?* Something wasn't right here. He'd seen Mark transform on Takis, but it had never been anything like *this*.

The laughing man seemed to drink the storm. The winds died and all of a sudden the world and Jay's stomach turned right side out again. White was white, black was black, the wind was gone, the room was dark, and Jay's face hurt like a son of a bitch. He grabbed the edge of the lab bench and tried to pull himself to his feet. "Mark?" he said uncertainly.

"Mark is gone," an unfamiliar voice replied.

A shining youth stepped into the light, graceful and golden. He was as tall as Mark Meadows, and as blond, but there the resemblance ended. He was young, no more than nineteen, clean shaven and bare-chested, as slender and smoothly muscular as a Greek statue. Long, straight hair fell down past his shoulders. He wore sandals and faded jeans cut off just below the knee, and around his neck hung a heavy golden peace symbol on a leather thong. Jay had never seen him before. "Are you one of Mark's friends?"

"The first and the last," the golden youth replied. His smile was brilliant. He had deep blue eyes that had never known defeat or disappointment. Charisma seemed to come off him in waves.

Ponytail stepped out of the darkness. "The last is right, you hippie freak." He was tall and blond, too, but somehow he looked like a bad copy of the other, the golden one. "So who are you, Surfer Jesus?"

"Last time I made the scene, they called me the Radical."

"I think I'll call you Pansy Boy," Ponytail said.

"From a fascist cocksucker like you, that's a compliment."

Ponytail put his hands on his hips. "So what do you do? Walk through walls? Fly? Shoot fire out your dick?"

"You sure you want to find out?" Radical asked softly.

Ponytail vaulted a lab table and landed right in front of him. He raised gloved fists into some kind of kung fu ready stance. "Try me, you ace freak."

"Are you some kind of fucking *moron*?" Jay interjected. They both ignored him.

"You're just a nat," Radical told Ponytail. "What do you think you're going to do to me?"

"This," Ponytail said. He slammed his right shin against Radical's left thigh in a savage kick. Radical grunted and dropped to one knee. Ponytail spun and kicked him in the chest. Radical went sprawling. Ponytail stood back and laughed. "How do you like me now, baby?"

Radical sat up, wiping blood from the corner of his mouth, but still smiling. "Dead," he said.

"Ooooh, I'm *scared*," Ponytail said. He circled around his prey, savoring the moment.

Jay shaped a shaky hand into a gun. "Enough," he said.

Radical waved him off. "Let him have his fun."

"Get up, pussy," Ponytail told him.

Radical got up.

Jay had had enough of this bullshit; he was practically suffocating on the testosterone fumes in here. He pointed to pop Ponytail off to Bellevue where he belonged . . .

. . . and missed. Ponytail was moving.

He leapt, spinning, a high kick that would snap Radical's neck like a rotten stick. His foot slammed into the side of the youth's smiling face . . . and went right through it. Off balance, Ponytail went down hard, hitting the floor with a thud.

Jay tried to pop him again, but Ponytail rolled. A lab bench behind him vanished instead. Ponytail arched his body backward and popped upright like a jack-in-the-box as Radical charged. Radical's left fist snapped out in a jab that flashed past the kickboxer's guard, hit him in the face with a sickening crunch. Ponytail somersaulted backward, away from him. Jay moved his hand, dropped his thumb, missed again. "Hold still, damn it," he said.

Ponytail came up behind a lab table with his jaw hanging loose from his face and blood dripping from his mouth. He didn't look like he was having fun anymore. One hand went behind his back. It came out holding a chunky black machine pistol.

The peace-sign amulet was in Radical's left hand. He spun it once around his head and released it as Ponytail aimed his piece. The amulet struck the handgun and shattered it.

Jay had a bead on Ponytail, but suddenly Radical was between them. He flew over the lab table, seized Ponytail by the throat, and lifted him off the ground with one hand. The kick-boxer recovered sufficiently to drive a knee into the short ribs on Radical's right side. Radical grunted in pain. "That hurt."

Ponytail kicked him again. Radical's fingers were still locked around his throat, digging deep into his flesh. The kick was weaker this time. Ponytail's face was darkening.

"Drop him," Jay shouted at Radical. "Let me pop him off, damn it." No one paid the slightest bit of attention.

Ponytail clawed at Radical's eyes and kicked him again, feebly.

"Third strike," Radical said. "I guess you're out."

His hand burst into flame. Ponytail screamed. The fire streamed up Radical's fingers, and the kickboxer's throat began to blacken and char. An instant later his hair caught fire.

"Mark, *no*," Jay screamed. *"Let him go!"*

"I'm not Mark," the Radical replied, but he did let him go. The kickboxer's whole head was wreathed in flame as Radical flung him away, contemptuously. Ponytail flew across the lab and struck the wall with a sound like a cement truck hitting a German shepherd. For a moment he hung there, crucified sans nails, staring at Radical until his eyes melted and ran down his cheeks. The laboratory was bright as day, its shadows lit with the light of the burning man. The sprinklers came on suddenly.

"Jesus Christ," Jay said softly. His mouth tasted of blood. Water ran down his face like a cold rain, stinging his eyes.

For a moment Radical just stood and breathed. When the body peeled off the wall and fell heavily to the tiled floor, he turned to Jay. "What time is it?" he asked softly.

"Seven thirty-four," came the answer, crisp and certain. J. Bob Belew stood in the door, outlined against the light from the corridor. "So Mark really was the Radical," he said, bemused.

The Radical made a V shape with his fingers. "Peace, man," he said. The water from the sprinklers plastered his long hair to his face, but his eyes were as hot and blue as the Summer of Love.

"Right, you're a regular fucking Gandhi," Jay snapped.

The Radical gave a shrug. "He was a genocidal fascist," he said as Arnold Schwarzenegger entered the lab, supporting a battered, bloody Sascha Starfin.

"Jerry!" Jay moved to his junior partner, dizzy from pain. "You're alive." He blinked. "What kind of asshole stunt did you think you were trying to pull? You're fired, both of you."

"You can't fire me, I'm your partner," Arnold rumbled in a bad Austrian accent. "Besides, we're all going to die. Casaday is on his way to the airport with enough Black Trump to kill every wild card in Hong Kong."

Jay groaned. He felt like lying down someplace for a long time, but forever was a shade too long. "I can't believe we went through all this shit just to *lose*!"

The Radical was smiling. "Keep the faith, Jay. We shall overcome, man. Sascha knows."

The telepath raised his eyeless face. "Meadows came up with a cure for the Black Trump. He thinks of it as the Overtrump."

"Straight dope," agreed the Radical. "Only one problem. Casaday took that, too."

Ray jerked and pulled against the chains, but they wouldn't give. He had to do something, he couldn't just lie there and die. The revelation of Harvest's real nature and feelings gnawed at him more deeply than the knowledge that he'd taken a dose of the Black Trump right in the face. But Ray responded to her betrayal like he did to all the great fears and disappointments in his life. He got angry, then he got angrier. He pulled against his chains until he was soaked with sweat, but they didn't break.

He was held fast. He was going to die on the floor of this fucking tent, murdered by the woman he loved.

Rudo suddenly straightened up at his desk. "Does it feel a little warm in here?" he asked. Ray looked at him and stopped struggling. He laughed aloud. "What's so funny?" Rudo asked.

"I may be going to die," Ray said, "but you won't live to see it."

"What do you mean?"

"You're sweating, Doc. You're sweating blood."

Rudo put a hand to his forehead, then looked at his palm. "Oh, my God," he said in a small, quiet voice. "Oh, my God."

Ray laughed again. He pulled at his chains like a mad dog and a searing pain ran through his right arm as he felt bones snap. He yanked at the chains, catching his breath as his broken arm twisted, creating enough slack so that he was able to pull his arms free.

The broken arm dangled limply. Pain danced through it like fire, but he ignored it. He could use his good arm, now, to help supply leverage, and there was nothing, nothing by God, that could tie him down. His body bent like a bow, the chains the bowstring he pulled taut, and something was going to snap, either his spine or the chains. It proved to be the chains, though when Ray heard the *crack* he wasn't sure. He lay panting on the floor and realized that the longer he stayed there, the more likely he was to die.

He opened his eyes. Rudo was sitting at his desk with a stricken expression, but he held a gun pointed right at Ray.

"You'll stay right there, Mr. Ray, and we'll die together. Or move, and you'll die first."

– – –

Camel Croyd wheeled on his eight legs and took off into the sandstorm at a rate of speed that was unreal. Rudo should have been in the infirmary tent. He wasn't there, and it looked like Croyd would check every tent in the camp.

Zoe trotted off in the direction she thought he'd taken, grateful for the mask she wore. It kept some of the dust out of her lungs, but her eyes watered like crazy. She couldn't wipe the tears away; her gloves might have picked up some of the virus.

Rudo's voice stopped her cold at the entrance to the Nur's tent.

". . . or move and you'll die first," Rudo said. His quiet tones sent chills down her spine.

Zoe ripped aside the curtains.

Rudo, pale, sweaty, and terribly ill, lay slumped against a pile of cushions, facing Zoe. He held a gun aimed at the man who lay on the floor in front of him—a muscular joker with fused fingers, a horrid face, and something very wrong in the way one of his fists fitted on his arm.

His arm was broken. The joker lay in a loose tangle of chains.

A camel appeared beside her, a camel wearing a surgical mask. Croyd stopped short at the sight of Rudo's gun.

Rudo smiled through bloodstained teeth. "One should see angels when one is dying, not camels. Always, the clerics lie."

"I'm Croyd. Remember me?"

Rudo's smile faded. He seemed to find some reserves of strength, enough to lift his gun in both hands and aim it at Croyd's head.

Zoe saw only the gun, the possibilities of it. *Get the gun. Kill the gun. This is no time to die. Kill the gun, how?* There were two aluminum bars inside the flannel of her splint—*Yes!* She kept her eyes on the gun and raised her arms slowly, hoping Rudo would think she was making a gesture of surrender. She breathed on the splint as she raised her arm, reworking the blunt metal into sharp points and instructing them with a hunger for arterial blood.

They ripped free of the flannel and buried themselves in the pumping arteries of Pan Rudo's right wrist.

The gun flew into the air and the joker twisted onto his back and caught the gun in his fused mitten of a hand. Croyd shoved his way past Zoe and leaned his long neck down, his muzzle within an inch of Rudo's throat.

"Don't *touch* him!" Zoe shouted. What had Croyd planned to do? Bite out Rudo's throat? Struggling in her sterile gown, never meant to fit over a heavy robe, she moved closer to the heap of dissolving flesh that had been Pan Rudo.

Rudo's eyes were vacant, distant. He smiled up at Croyd's mask.

"Where's the rest of the Trump?" Zoe yelled. "Where is it?"

He looked up at her masked face, through it, beyond it. "There's plenty. I lied to you, telling you there was only the pittance in the inhalers. The Black Trump is in the water truck. Enough to fill it."

He took in a shuddering breath and then his face went slack, his eyes staring, motionless, at some hell Zoe hoped she would never see.

"*Bang,*" Croyd whispered. "You're dead."

The wind shrieked and the walls of the tent billowed. Above it, the ugly joker's breath sounded labored, as if he wasn't getting enough air.

Croyd shook his long neck, and he made a frustrated *whuffing* sound.

The joker got to his feet. "Now that we've had our moment of silence," the joker said, "let's get our butts in gear. That bitch

Harvest is probably halfway to Jerusalem by now." He tried to make a fist with his broken arm, and his twisted face distorted even more. He lowered the arm back down to his side, carefully. "Give us a ride, Croyd; we're outta here."

Croyd was already at the doorway, a pair of his legs drumming impatiently against the sand.

"The *hell* we are!" Zoe yelled. "You're both covered with virus, idiots! Nobody's going anywhere until you're scrubbed down, and I'm not even sure . . ." The joker named Billy Ray was probably dead already. His voice sounded muffled, as if he had the beginnings of a cold.

"Yeah. Okay. We'll wash up first," Billy Ray said.

"There's some stuff in the lab tent," Zoe said. A shower head for chemical accidents, and chlorine bleach in quantity. She hoped there was a water reserve connected to the shower, that it wasn't just for show. "Follow me."

She ran out into the hell of blowing sand, Croyd and Billy Ray behind her. A guard loomed up in front of her, his rifle aimed at her belly, a startling apparition in the swirls of yellow dust. She threw herself flat on the sand. A muffled *crack* sounded behind her. The guard fell. Zoe scrambled to her feet. Billy Ray trotted past her and scooped up the guard's rifle. Zoe followed him, thinking, *We'll have to wash the stock on the damned thing.*

She opened the airlock. Croyd squeezed through it. She shooed him toward the shower head.

She handed Billy Ray a mask.

He took it with his good arm and put it on. "We're gonna wash him down?" he asked.

"Yeah. Him first, then you, then me." The idiot was holding the rifle with his broken arm. "Sheesh!" Zoe said. "Don't you have any pain receptors at all?"

"I heal fast."

Zoe grabbed a gallon of chlorine bleach and a mop and handed them to the ugly joker. "For the camel. Start at his head and work back."

Bleach reacted with camel smell and released a truly remarkable stench, even filtered through Zoe's mask.

"That stings!" Croyd protested.

Zoe scrubbed at the inside of one of his eight legs. "Sorry," she said. "Lift your foot. Not *that* one!"

"I've never smelled anything this bad in my life," Billy Ray said.

"Just a little harder, right there behind my fifth knee," Croyd said. "Ahhhh." He arched his hump like a satisfied cat.

"Shut up, camel." Billy Ray scrubbed harder.

"We've got to *hurry*," Zoe said. "Somebody's going to find that guard."

"How many guns in camp, Zoe?" Billy Ray asked.

"I don't know. I've never seen more than half a dozen guards at the perimeter. Sayyid would have kept close track on the guns, I guess."

"I'm going outside. If I see any guards, I'll take 'em out." Billy Ray picked up his newly washed rifle and left.

Zoe swabbed Croyd's short tail. "Can he do it?" she asked.

"He's good," Croyd said. He snaked his neck around and looked at her. "Can you wash this stuff off yet?"

"The shower is designed to clean up chemical spills," Zoe said. "If I pull the chain, it's on until the tank is empty. We'll have to wait for this guy to get back."

"He's fast," Croyd said. He peered up at the shower head with longing.

Ray went outside the tent.

The wind howled, the sand blew like a scouring pad. Ray

tore his clothes off and let the wind blow up him for half a minute until he felt clean. He knew that he wasn't, but at least he felt clean.

He huddled down, turning his face away from the wind. This was the tricky part. His hands were clumsy. The one attached to his broken arm was entirely useless. He had to be careful now, damn careful.

The Black Trump was the only thing in his life that had ever scared Ray shitless, and he'd decided that if he was going to face it again he'd have some kind of protection. He'd mashed his nose flat, all the better to hide and hold nasal filters. He'd closed off most of his mouth for the same reason.

He'd known earlier that night that he'd have to face the Trump again, so he'd put the biological filters in his nostrils and stuffed another in the corner of his mouth. He was so surprised and angered by Harvest's betrayal that he'd almost forgotten to use them, but instinct had taken over at the last second and his tongue had slipped them into place.

He extracted the filters and dropped them on the sand. He stood for a moment, naked in the clean desert wind. He needed clothes, a splint for his arm, and a way back to Jerusalem. First, though, he had to get sterile, if there was any bleach left over from washing the camel.

He went back into the tent and grinned at Zoe Harris. She was pretty good looking. "I'll wash your back," he said, "if you wash mine."

Camel Croyd, dripping with bleach, backed away from Billy Ray.

Billy Ray wasn't masked—

"Don't *breathe*!" Zoe yelled. Billy Ray nodded, reached up for the stack of masks by the door, and put one on.

"What's next?" he asked.

"Shower," Zoe said. The Joker's broken arm hung limp by his side. "Wait! Let me splint that arm first!"

Billy Ray put the rifle on a lab counter and held out his wrist.

"Oh, damn," Zoe said. "My splint's ruined." Its metal braces were buried in Rudo's arm. She tore the Velcro straps away from the soft splint, held it in front of her mask, breathed, and wrapped the splint on Billy's wrist.

"What good's that going to—uurgh!" Billy Ray said, as the splint went rigid on his arm. He grabbed the edge of the lab counter with both hands and looked a little pale.

"Thanks, lady," Billy Ray said. "Don't slow us down, Zoe. Where's the bleach?"

It was a pity his face was so ugly. The rest of him wasn't, Zoe observed, as she stripped out of her surgical gown, her gloves, and her sweaty cotton robes. Billy Ray swabbed bleach over her back. She returned the favor.

"You always wear water bottles?" Billy Ray asked.

"I thought I'd have to run for it," Zoe said.

"Keep them," Billy Ray said. "We haven't made it out of this damned desert yet."

Zoe reached up and yanked the shower chain, and the three of them spluttered in a deluge of clean, tepid water.

"Outside!" Zoe said. She grabbed her robe. "We get dressed *outside*!"

Starkers, they ran out into the storm. Sand drove against Zoe's wet hair and coated it in gritty mud.

"We've got to catch April," Billy Ray said.

"We *have* to make sure nobody leaves this camp," Zoe said.

"They can't walk out. Croyd can get us to April's truck, and then he can run to Jerusalem in no time flat." Billy Ray fastened his belt and picked up his guns.

"What is he, a supersonic camel?" Zoe asked.

"Yeah."

"The camels. The people here could leave on the camels."

"I can turn the critters loose," Croyd said. "They'll follow me."

Billy Ray and Croyd started around the back side of the tent, on their way to the camel herd. Zoe followed, grabbing her pack out of the sand as they passed it.

"We'll be stopped!" She couldn't hide the quaver in her voice. "If that water truck makes it to Jerusalem before we do—"

Billy Ray untied the camels. They snorted at the sight of Croyd but they got to their feet in the sand and crowded around him.

"That's all of them," Billy Ray said. "Sit down, Croyd, and we'll climb on." Zoe climbed on Croyd's hump and grabbed a double handful of muddy camel hair. Billy Ray clambered on behind her. "Giddyap," he said.

Canton airport lay on the city's outskirts, on land built up from the rich, moist soil of the great Xinjiang delta. Flying low above the paddies Radical saw a modern-looking multilane road leading to a terminal building and hangars. Held down by guy lines out in the middle of the runway, looking like the Macy's float for the song "Och, Johnny, We Hardly Knew Ye," lay the airship *Harmony*.

The runway looked deserted in the slanting yellow sunset light. No baggage and fuel carts roaming around, nobody standing by the blimp. There was an Airbus parked off on the right wing of the terminal, with a skyway ramp hooked up to it, but he couldn't see any activity around it. That might mean much or little; in the distance Canton looked like a pretty big city, and he would have expected more traffic.

"Well," he said into the heavy humid breeze of his passage, "let's try the direct approach." As peasants shin-deep in reeking water raised up their conical hats and pointed, he flew toward the terminal building. He was relishing the sense of *liberation* after so many years, and he wasn't as alert as he could have been despite the situation. He saw flashes like pale highway flares from several points on the roof, then heard nasty sharp cracks in the air nearby.

Somebody was shooting at him. He heard the full-auto reports as he swooped toward the front of the two-story terminal. He frowned. He was guilty of poor discipline; he had known he was flying into danger. He had let himself get carried away . . .

The front of the terminal was glass. Or had been. Most of it lay in glittering shard snow on the sidewalk and street. He heard more gunshots as he touched down lightly on the sidewalk, saw muzzle flashes in the gloom.

Small arms fire didn't concern him too much. Bullets hurt like hell, and bruised, and if people concentrated enough fire on him he would certainly go down from the sheer battering. But he was Radical, and he was free. Standing upright, he walked through the vacant windows into the building.

Cold air hit him like a bucket of water. The air-conditioning was still blowing, keeping the muggy air at bay. In front of him rose an escalator. To the left were ticket counters; to the right a couple of baggage carousels. It looked surprisingly like an airport back in the States.

Except, of course, for the party of raggedy-ass South China Sea piratical types who were blazing away from the ticketing area at guys in khaki uniforms with red stars on their caps hunkered down beside the carousels. More guys with guns crouched at the top of the escalator, but Radical didn't get a great look at them.

The pirates and the locals didn't notice the newcomer. There's something about somebody firing an automatic weapon at you from sixty feet away that tends to concentrate your attention. Radical slipped off his peace medallion, began to swing it in circles on its chain.

Gunfire erupted from the top of the escalator. Whoever was up there had been engrossed watching the shootout on the lower floor, but now Radical's arrival had been noticed. More bullets shattered the air by his head. He smiled. By this time his medallion was a spinning blur.

He let it go. The heavy peace symbol flashed through the air and split the skull of a Chinese gunman. He dropped, anointing his comrades with his blood and brains.

The others turned around and cut loose on Radical with everything they had. Their bullets passed through the smiling blond apparition. So did the bullets from the men on the second floor.

A few serene paces and Radical was in among the uniformed troops. He held out his hand. His medallion leapt from the floor by the wall and flew into it.

He grinned more widely at the astonished troops. "Okay, boys," he told them, "time to show you what a *real* communist party is all about."

He began to whirl the medallion around his head. Steel gun barrels sparked and parted when it struck them. Heads and limbs didn't spark but parted just the same.

The official Chinese party line opposed belief in the supernatural. That worked as well as anti-superstition campaigns had everywhere else. Which is to say, the loyal soldiers of the People's Liberation Army knew there were no such things as evil spirits. Except, of course, when one appeared in their midst.

They ran.

Radical swung his medallion a couple times more to clear various clinging bits of stuff from it. Then he swayed and sat down on the lip of the carousel. Going insubstantial had really drained him. It surprised him. He knew that he partook of the powers of Mark's other alter egos but, unlike them, he didn't have substantial memories of an earlier life. The world had started for him in that battle at People's Park, and all the time intervening had been spent in a state below semiconsciousness, trapped in the depths of Mark's psyche.

A bandy-legged little bearded guy with a red rag tied around his head and a patch over one eye came up. "You one of Belew's boys?" Radical asked him.

"Bell You," he agreed happily, touching his chest. "Lu."

"Lu," Radical repeated. "We need to get up that escalator pronto."

Lu's one eye moved nervously. "No can. Too many on top, too many guns. We try, all die. You lose."

"You have a way with words, Lu," Radical said, smiling. He stood up. He felt better already, and losing was the farthest thing from his mind. "The solution is simple."

"What that?" Lu asked, squinting suspiciously.

"Follow me." He turned and strode for the escalator.

The men up there reacted quickly, loosing gales of small arms fire. A pair of bullets struck him in the chest, but they were nine-millimeter rounds from an Uzi, with nowhere near the punch even of the short 7.62 bullets the Kalashnikovs fired. They stung, and rocked him back, but they didn't *hurt* him.

He laughed and answered fire with fire—JJ Flash's plasma flame. A gunman standing square at the escalator's top caught the brunt of the blast and fell in flames, but he was well dead before his central nervous system could register pain. Two others crouching behind the housings where the flexible handrail fed back down into the mechanism weren't so lucky and caught air superheated by the plasma jet. One came hurtling downward past Radical to find the hard ground floor for anesthetic. The other tottered back, shrieking and waving his arms in his terrified comrades' faces like a flame-feathered bird. It was rough, but Radical wanted it to be. The fear of burning is fundamental to the human organism. It would make the others quail, or at least stand back—he sent another blast, a generalized dragon-belch without specific target, ahead to keep the way clear.

He gathered his legs—twice as powerful as a nat's—beneath him and sprang. He landed at the top, legs spread, grinning hugely. He held up a flame-wreathed fist in a revolutionary salute. "All right, you imperialist lackeys," he declared. "Who wants some?"

All of them, apparently. There were at least twenty armed Westerners on the second floor, leavened with a few PLA security troops. Every one of them leveled his weapon at the apparition and held down the trigger.

At least a score of bullets struck the center of Radical's glorious bare chest at once. The impact knocked his glorious ass right back down the unmoving escalator steps.

Sascha Starfin sneezed, spraying snot all over the interior of the rattling flatbed truck.

"Real good," Jay told him. "I feel a lot safer now."

Behind the wheel, J. Bob Belew gave off a sand-in-the-gearbox chuckle. They were riding in a rickety, farting stake bed truck liberated from the underground facility, down a road whose pavement seemed to crumble away beneath their tires. Ahead, the airport appeared across flooded rice paddies, where straw-hatted peasants worked to the timeless rhythms of Chinese show tunes playing from tinny sixties-vintage Japanese transistor radios.

Jay was mashed in the cab between Sascha and J. Bob. He jumped every time Belew reached to work the floor-mounted stick shift, which was jutting up between the detective's knees.

"Are we there yet?" Sascha asked, his voice thick and congested. If he'd had eyes, they would have been running.

"The terminal is the building that looks like a baleen whale smiling at us," Belew said. "And there's the good ship *Harmony* beyond it." A white roundness swelled like a tumor from behind the terminal. "They're due to take off for Hong Kong at sunset."

"How fast is that damn thing?" Jay asked.

"She's good for upward of sixty knots," J. Bob said, "but it'll take her a while to get up to speed, largely due to air resistance. Be a long trip there—hour and a half, maybe—but once they're on the scene you couldn't ask for a better vehicle to disperse the virus."

A face appeared at Belew's window. It was a handsome, round Asian face with deep, soulful eyes.

"Jesus!" Jay sputtered. "Can't you pick a face and stick with it? Who the hell are you now?"

"Chow Yun Fat," the face said. "The Cary Grant of the Orient. He stars in all those John Woo action flicks."

"Real good," Jay said. "Maybe the Card Sharks will all want your autograph."

"Chow Yun Fat is like a god in Asia. They'll never shoot at him." Chow Yun Fat showed them a suave smile.

"What's that sound?" Sascha asked.

As if for emphasis, the truck backfired juicily. "It's our wonderful conveyance," Jay said. "The Chinese have figured out how to make the damn things run on pinto beans."

"No, not that," the joker said snuffling. *"That."*

Jay listened. He heard it, too. "Either Casaday is making up a bunch of popcorn, or Radical started the party without us."

"The terminal," Belew said. A quarter-mile ahead they could see the tall windows lit in pulses from within, as if pranksters were flicking lights on and off at random. "That's a firefight in progress," the mercenary said. "Looks as if Dr. Finn and Tung's men are having a difference of opinion with the local security forces."

Jay moaned and sank down in his seat. "Whose bright idea was it to send Bradley to the airport?"

"We're all at risk, Mr. Ackroyd," Belew said. "A bullet in the head may be a kinder fate than the Black Trump."

"A Bullet in the Head!" Chow Fat Jerry exclaimed. "That's one of the movies Chow Yun Fat made with John Woo."

"I wouldn't know," Jay said gloomily.

"Hang on," Belew warned them. He spun the wheel hard right and mashed the accelerator down. The truck departed the road, rolled across a shallow ditch with the engine grinding and groaning protest. It struck the steel-mesh security fence and plowed through with a scream of anguished metal. Broken wire ends scraped along the doors like fingernails on a blackboard.

"Are you out of your fucking mind, Belew?" Jay screamed, as the truck bounded onto the cement apron, in among hangars.

J. Bob was grinning beneath his mustache as if this were the greatest game of all time. "If you don't like action movies," J. Bob said serenely, "you're really going to hate *this*."

— — —

Radical lay for a moment at the foot of the steps. From above came a shrill rebel yell of triumph.

Lu's face floated upside down above his. "Not dead?" the man said, wonder in his voice. He poked a thin brown finger at Radical's wounds, touching them to make sure they were real.

Radical glanced down at himself. His chest glowed with a lot of little pink circles, as if someone had been beating on him with a ball-peen hammer. He was going to do serious bruising. "I'm fine," he said, managing not to croak it—although it felt as if somebody had been trying to resculpt his ribs with a cold chisel. He snapped himself up onto his feet like a gymnast. And he laughed. Despite the pain, despite the danger, he felt *great*. He was free, after so many years chafing in captivity.

Enjoy it while it lasts, came a voice from deep inside his skull.

For an instant he frowned. It felt disorienting to have the thoughts of such a dangerous reactionary rattling around in his own skull. Like having a traitor within.

I don't plan on going back to being that poor bourgeois fool Meadows in an hour, he thought haughtily.

None of us does, Harpo, JJ thought back. *None of us does.*

He shook the doubts off like drops of water in his wavy surfer-dude hair. He wondered what time it was. Then he decided he had no time to wonder.

"Let's try that again," Radical said. He flew up the steps—literally, a handspan above the rubber handrails. A pair of gunmen had crept up to the head of the escalator. Each was trying to outwait the other, fearful of getting a faceful of flame. When they caught sight of Radical shooting up at them they started to rise, trying to bring MP5 machine pistols to bear. Radical spread his arms, swept both of them up, and bore them right into the faces of their comrades.

Goons went everywhere. Radical got his feet beneath him, planted far apart, and began to swing his peace symbol above his head. Then he just waded into his opponents, giving them no clearance to use their firepower.

"All I'm saying, guys," he said in a ringing, sarcastic voice, "is give peace a chance." The golden medallion hummed round and round, splitting limbs and heads like a circular saw, surrounding the ace with a wave of blood like the splash from a boulder falling into a lake. Some brave soul grabbed his left wrist—then shrieked soprano as flame flared up Radical's arm.

Radical grinned at the man as he staggered back, staring at the charred nub his hand had become. "What's the matter, comrade? Too hot for you?"

A Chinese soldier popped up to his left, shouldering a Type 56. Radical phased out as the soldier fired an ear-roasting burst. Goons screamed and fell as the bullets scythed through them.

The man lowered his weapon, gaping. Radical phased back in, swayed slightly—*shit, that takes it out of me!*—and turned the weapon to a yellow-glowing ingot in the man's hands.

He turned around, grinning into the faces of his terrified antagonists. "I'd love to stay and rap," he said, "but I've got a blimp waiting. Peace."

He turned. Flame flashed from his hands. The high windows looking out on the runway shimmered like mirages and vanished, puffing into incandescent gas.

Radical flew out where the windows had been, soaring up to let the rays of the setting sun, angling up over the terminal building, strike him fully. Energy filled him—energy, confidence, purpose. He felt the sun's heat inside him. *Nova* heat.

Nothing could stop him now.

— — —

Belew brought the flatbed screeching around a corner. Automatic weapons fire chased them across the field. Lord Tung's boys were returning fire from the back of the truck. Jay half turned in his seat and saw one of their men take a hit and tumble off the back, but Belew only accelerated, swerving.

In the shadow of the terminal building, J. Bob slammed on the brakes hard. The flatbed skewed around and came to a screaming halt beside a ring of baggage trailers that had been driven together to form a makeshift breastwork. Behind the piles of tourist luggage stood a ragged handful of Belew's South China Sea pirates, and Bradley Finn, MD.

Tung's boys were leaping off the truck even before they were stopped, scrambling for shelter behind the wall of Samsonite. Chow Yun Jerry sauntered after them. Belew moved around the truck, snapping orders in Cantonese. Jay tumbled out and helped Sascha down from the cab. "This way," he said, taking the blind joker by the arm. As they ran for the luggage, a burst of automatic gunfire punched into the planks surrounding the truck bed.

Finn and the pirates laid down covering fire until they were safe behind the suitcases. "You all right, Doc?" Jay asked him.

"No thanks to you guys," the centaur said. He had his hair tied back with a red bandana, and he was wearing his flak jacket and his Kevlar horse blanket. The bandana was soaked with sweat; he looked like Rambo with a tail and dyed green hair. "You took your own sweet time getting here. When Casaday showed up with the Black Trump, we figured you were all dead." He squinted at Jay. "Your face looks even worse than before."

"You should see the other guy," Jay said.

The airship *Harmony* was grounded about fifty yards from

the terminal, held down against a slight eastern breeze by cables tied to trucks. There were figures crouched behind the trucks, and more lying outside the terminal with rifles pointed at their luggage. Desultory fire punched holes in Guccis, American Touristers, and cardboard valises alike.

"I can't tell our guys from their guys," Jay said.

"The ones shooting at us are their guys," Belew said. "It appears we have more than the Sharks to deal with." He gestured across the tarmac toward some little brown men in uniforms with red stars on their hats.

"Tell me about it," Finn said. "We were doing okay when it was just Sharks, but then those guys showed up and started shooting at us, too."

"People's Liberation Army," Belew informed them. "Security. No such thing as a purely civilian airfield in the People's Republic. There's probably a few truckloads of militia headed this way to back them up."

"Swell," said Jay. "I was just thinking how this was much too easy, might as well make it interesting."

Chow Yun Jerry joined them. "Where's Casaday?"

"In the terminal, with the Black Trump and about a hundred hostages," Finn told them.

"Hostages?" asked Jerry. "What hostages?"

"The paying customers waiting for their blimp ride."

"Chinese standoff," Belew said, stroking his mustache.

Jerry flashed them a boyish grin. "Wrong director," he said. "That's John Carpenter." He stood upright behind a particularly large mound of baggage, hands on hips, looking cool. Even Lord Tung's pirates were shooting him admiring glances and muttering among themselves.

From the terminal came an angry crackle of gunfire. "We need to secure the blimp before Casaday can load the virus," Belew said.

"Great plan, J. Bob," Jay said. He was hunkered down, trying to peer through cracks between suitcases. "Tell it to the guys hiding behind those trucks. See what they think."

"Let me handle them," announced Chow Yun Jerry. He stood upright, straightened his clothes, and strode around the end of the barricade onto the open field.

"Get back here!" Jay screamed at him.

Jerry held up a hand, waved, smiled, strolled casually toward the blimp. The incoming fire ceased. "Chow Yun Fat!" the defenders exclaimed in unison.

Then they all raised their rifles and cut loose for all they were worth.

Jerry dropped as if he'd been shot. Jay thought he had, until he came shinnying like a monkey up the front of the baggage barricade and tumbled over with bullets snapping past his ears. The elbows of his shirt were blown out from his high-speed belly-crawl.

"Of course," Belew said conversationally, "John Woo is the most outspokenly anti-Communist filmmaker in Asia, and the local boys may have figured they could reap some Brownie points by dusting off his pet star, cultural icon or no."

"Shut the fuck up," said Jerry, batting away Sascha's hands, which were feeling for bullet holes.

"You got to start watching a better class of movies," Jay told his junior partner. A man who looked suspiciously like a Card Shark made a dash for the blimp. Jay popped him off a split second before several bullets whined off the empty tarmac where he had been. No one was safe out there.

"Uh-oh," Belew said.

"Uh-oh?" Jay repeated. "Who the fuck said that? Confucius? Pericles? Harpo Marx? What, *uh-oh*?"

Belew nodded toward the terminal. A wave of tourists in T-shirts and Mao suits and sundresses were being herded from one of the gates out across the field. Jay could hear a woman crying, even at this distance. The tourists edged out onto the tarmac slowly, frightened and unwilling, but there were Shark gunmen among them, giving them no choice. "Uh-oh," said Jay.

One of Tung's men raised his rifle. Finn grabbed his arm and wrenched it down. "No shooting! Those are civilians, damn it!" The man stared at him blankly until J. Bob roared at them in Cantonese.

The passengers were heading for the blimp's boarding ramp, decked with red and yellow ribbons. In the midst of all that frightened humanity Jay glimpsed the pumpkin head of O. K. Casaday, bobbing along surrounded by hostages. Then it was gone again.

"They're rolling the canisters to the blimp," Sascha called. "I can see it in their minds. They've got them on dollies."

"Casaday, you evil motherfucker," J. Bob said. Jay looked at him; Belew said *motherfucker* about as often as Mother Teresa did.

Casaday had a wall of sweating hostages pressed all around him and his cannisters. No way for Belew or Tung's pirates to fire without mowing down the innocents.

Belew studied the moving clot of humanity, weighing them with his eyes, his face emotionless. He dropped the banana magazine from his gun, slammed home a fresh one, and barked out a rapid series of commands in Cantonese. Lord Tung's boys and the South China pirates swung their weapons on the shuffling throng, and Sascha moaned, clutching Belew by the arm. "You can't. There are women and kids."

Jay whirled to face Belew. "You *son of a bitch*."

Belew's voice was almost sad. "A hundred innocent lives against a world. We have no choice, Jay."

"*No!* Tell them to hold their fire," Jay said. "Let me pop the hostages away first . . ."

"There are too many of them," Belew said. "There's no time."

There was a roar of flame behind them, as the terminal windows blew out in a huge gout of white fire and shattered glass. Jay whirled. One of the pirates began to shout in fear. Out on the field, the crowd of hostages shattered into a hundred terrified individuals. Some of them dropped to the tarmac, hands over their heads; others screamed and broke for safety. Jay saw a Shark swing his gun toward a running woman with a child in her arms. His finger was faster. The Shark was gone before he could squeeze the trigger, off to a nice little cave in Burma.

A human figure rose up out of the fireball, bare-chested, golden, alive with light. His long hair whipped behind him like a banner as he streaked across the sky.

Suddenly no one was shooting at them anymore. All the guns were pointing upward, pouring lead into the sky.

"Is he ours?" Finn asked Jay. "Who is he?"

"The Radical," Jay told him.

Finn gave him a baffled look. "What's a Radical?"

Belew stroked his mustache. "*All is ephemeral—fame and the famous as well.* Marcus Aurelius. People's Park, Dr. Finn. 1970."

The centaur shrugged. "Before my time."

"It's Mark Meadows," Jay said. "Leastwise he used to be Mark Meadows. Now . . ." He flew like Starshine, Jay realized. Starshine who had died in the night of space, back on Takis. He drank the sun's power like Starshine, too, and beams of light played from his fingers. He was as quick as Moonchild, with Starshine's light powers and the fire of Jumpin' Jack Flash, and back at the lab he'd gone insubstantial, one of Cosmic Traveler's tricks. He was *all* of Mark's friends rolled into one. For some reason, that thought chilled Jay to the bone.

"Forget the soldiers," J. Bob Belew muttered under his breath. "Disable the blimp."

Radical held his hands out before him. Sunbeams lanced from them, blinding-bright. Jay had to shield his eyes. Away across the field a fuel truck exploded into a pool of red and yellow flame and black smoke. "The *blimp*," J. Bob repeated, with iron in his voice.

Up on the terminal roof, a Chinese soldier tracked the flying man with his machine gun. Bullets zipped around him. Radical banked and swooped. The sunbeam flared again. The prone soldier became a spark and vanished in a wisp of greasy smoke.

"Jesus," Jay said.

Other defenders blazed merrily away, but Radical was too quick for them. He streaked away to the east, curved around, and came whipping back low. Sunbeams flared from either hand. Men blazed up and died before they could scream.

Jay turned to Sascha, feeling ill. "You're lucky you can't see this," he told the eyeless joker.

"I hear them screaming in my head," Sascha replied grimly.

Across the field, a Chinese soldier tossed away his gun and tried to run. Light stabbed down from above, and he flared up like a moth caught in a torch-flame and vanished.

Chow Yun Jerry shuddered. "I'm glad he's on our side."

"Are you?" Jay said flatly. He wasn't so sure.

"*The blimp, you stupid motherfucker!*" Belew swore.

Twice in one day, Jay thought; *now Mother Theresa would* never *catch up*. Suddenly Jay had a clear view of a young white guy in a flapping lab coat, pushing a dolly ahead of him as he raced toward the airship. There were two canisters on the dolly, and Jay had a clear shot. He pointed . . . and froze.

One of the four canisters was the Overtrump. If he popped that one away . . . But even as he weighed his choices, he lost sight of the dolly behind a dozen hostages running for freedom.

"*Fuck,*" Jay snarled. He'd blown it.

It was all up to the Radical now.

Radical laughed, flew forward. The sunbeams stabbed out from him in all directions, and at each touch of radiance someone puffed into vapor and died. Casaday and company were running now, the guards urging the hostages to follow with bursts of gunfire at their feet, and into the bodies of stragglers.

"Be my guest," Radical said. "I can fly faster than you can run."

He was almost over their heads when he saw white smoke blossom from the distance, way off to his left. *Shoulder-fired missile,* he knew; Mark had seen enough of them going off, waging counterrevolution in Vietnam.

He loosed a beam from his left hand, swept it left to right. He was rewarded by the flash of an explosion; evidently the rocketeer had been carrying some reloads.

And then, somehow, he saw the missile. A dot of blackness against the graying sky. A dot that grew larger rapidly without showing any apparent motion.

Which meant it was headed straight for him.

Radical aimed both hands at the approaching projectile. As he willed forth a sunbeam, he also willed himself insubstantial, just in case.

Neither thing happened. Flying, flashing, and phasing out was just too much for the system. Instead of becoming invincible, and blasting the rocket out of existence, Radical began to fall.

The rocket was based on the Soviet RPG-7V, an antitank weapon whose straightened-sperm shape was almost as famous to millions of CNN viewers as the AK-47. In this case its warhead was a high-explosive charge, meant to attack people, which meant its blast was less focused but wider spread. Radical had been almost exactly twenty-three hundred feet distant when the rocket was launched. That meant it hummed through the space he'd occupied—and an internal fuse burned down, detonating the warhead not ten feet away from him.

Radical saw a flash. Then black.

Jay watched helplessly from behind the luggage as Radical plummeted seventy feet to the tarmac. Jerry moaned. Sascha pressed hands over ears as if that would block out their pain.

The golden youth hit with a loud wet smack, the sound a butcher would make slapping a piece of meat down on a tabletop. J. Bob Belew squeezed his eyes briefly shut. *"How dieth the wise man?"* he quoted. *"As the fool. Ave atque vale,* Mark."

The dollies were just disappearing into the *Harmony*'s sleek carbon-fiber gondola. Jay saw the man in the lab coat, boyish and plump, standing at the top of the ramp as the gunmen herded the last of the passengers to either side of him. He looked over the field through horn-rimmed glasses. "Put down your guns," he shouted out. "You can't stop us now! You've lost!"

With a loud clack J. Bob switched his rifle to single-shot. He brought the weapon to his shoulder, aimed, fired in one smooth motion. At the same instant a matronly Chinese woman in high heels turned an ankle on the gangplank and jostled the man in the lab coat. He turned his head a few degrees.

The bullet struck his right cheekbone and blew it out the side of his face in a spray of blood and white fragments. He windmilled his arms and fell, and was instantly dragged aboard by goons while others knelt to rake the luggage barricade with fire. Jay and the others hunkered down as suitcases and knapsacks thudded to the impact of hit after hit. A hard-shell gray Samsonite took a round and exploded, showering them with T-shirts and underwear. J. Bob shook his head. "Some days it doesn't pay to get out of bed."

This wasn't going real well, Jay decided; worse, the fucking Sharks had other vials of Black Trump. "Sascha, I'm sending you back to New York. Jokertown. Sneeze on people, it may be our last chance." Sascha didn't have time to argue. You could scarcely hear the *pop* over the gunfire.

"They're casting off," Finn said in disgust. He prodded Jay on the shoulder with the barrel of a gun. He had a machine pistol in one hand and an automatic in the other. "Tell Clara I love her. Tell her I'm doing this for her."

"Doing *what*?" Jay said suspiciously. "I don't want you doing anything, just stay—"

Finn darted around the blunt nose of a baggage cart and took off for the blimp at a gallop, firing with both hands as he ran, his shots ringing out wildly in all directions.

"Finn, damn it, *no*, you moron," Jay swore, racing after him. Lead fingers reached out to touch them from everywhere: from the terminal, from the hangars beyond, from the trucks where crewmen were scurrying to cast off the guy lines. Jay yelped, reversed direction, and dove back toward cover.

Finn galloped straight ahead, bullets kicking up around his hooves, running like Secretariat on a good day. Two Shark goons knelt on the ramp, blazing away at the approaching cen-taur. A shot slammed into his withers. The Kevlar stopped the round, but Finn staggered under the impact. A second shot knocked him down.

"*Cover him!*" Belew shouted, and repeated it in Cantonese. Tung's boys began to blast away. Jerry joined in. Jay popped off one of the goons on the ramp. The other wasn't so lucky. He did a crazy dance as the stream of bullets hammered him sideways and went tumbling to the ground.

Belew barked a command and three of his South China pirates went tearing after Finn, screaming like banshees and firing on the run. Behind the trucks, automatic weapons began to chatter. The pirates flopped like rag dolls, one two three, the last man cut almost in half by Shark fire. Not one of them got ten yards.

Every time one of the bad guys raised his head, Jay popped him off to that swell cave in the mountains of Burma. Problem was, most of them were keeping their heads down. The damned trucks made a much better barricade than a bunch of baggage.

"I wonder," Jay muttered, suddenly thoughtful. He'd never tried anything anywhere near that big before, but . . . "Might as well, can't dance." He took a deep breath and pointed, his right hand a gun, his left tight around his right wrist to steady his aim. He dropped a thumb.

The nearest truck vanished with a *clap* of inrushing air that was audible clear across the field.

Several Shark gunmen vanished with it. The rest found themselves standing out on the tarmac in plain view with rather dumbfounded looks on their faces. They weren't standing long; Belew was just as surprised as they were, but a lot faster on the uptake. Tung's boys and the pirates cut loose a few seconds behind J. Bob, and by then Jay had popped off the other cable trucks, one after the other. His head was throbbing so hard he could scarcely see.

Finn was back on his feet and running again. "He'll never make it," Jerry said. The airship's engines whined up through the sound spectrum as power was applied. Hydraulics began to fold the ramp up toward the blimp's smooth, white belly. Jay steadied himself with a hand on Belew's shoulder.

"Don't you have an aphorism handy?"

"Come on, Dover," Belew roared, *"move your bloomin' arse!"*

The ramp was off the ground, halfway retracted. Without breaking stride Finn jumped. He landed on the ramp, began to slide back. He scrabbled his hooves wildly and futilely for purchase, dropped one of his guns, began to slide back.

And the ramp hoisted him up into the gondola.

The airship *Harmony* lifted into the sky, blocking out the sunset as it rose. The airfield grew strangely quiet. The only sound was the whine of the *Harmony*'s engines. The supporting cast, native and import, had either turned to puffs of incandescent gas and floated away on the breeze or were lying dead on the tarmac. For almost a minute, no one was shooting at anyone.

Belew had his big, blocky handgun out, working the slide to check the load. He stuffed it back in its holster at the small of his back, sang out orders to Tung's pirates, who passed him a handful of magazines for the Chinese assault rifles.

"I'm going to secure that helicopter and go after them," he said, stuffing the spare magazines into his pocket. "If I don't make it, you know what to do, Jay—and may God go with you." He squeezed Jay's shoulder and scuttled out from behind the luggage-cart barricade. Four of Tung's boys went sprinting after him.

"Helicopter? What helicopter?" Jay shouted after him. The only aircraft on the field was the Airbus parked at a terminal gate.

"There it is," Jerry told him. "It was behind the blimp."

Jay looked at where he was pointing. Sure enough, a little bubble-front chopper sat with rotors spinning at the edge of the field. It was almost lost in the huge shadow of the blimp. "Fuck the helicopter," Jay said. He had a better idea. A brilliant idea. His success with the trucks had left him feeling weak as a kitten but wildly confident. He shaped his hand into a gun and pointed up, at the huge white bulk of the *Harmony*, outlined against the setting sun. He'd send the fucking thing to the south pole on Takis, he decided. He dropped his thumb.

Nothing happened.

His finger had never jammed before. He tried it again. Again. The airship began to move away, untouched and serene. "Okay," he said, "so I don't do blimps."

J. Bob Belew was racing across the field, Tung's boys a few steps behind him. They were halfway to the chopper when a flickering fire bloomed within a dark hangar. Jay could see J. Bob's body jerk as the machine-gun burst hit him. The stream of bullets swept back and forth, mowing down the pirates.

Jay caught a quick glimpse of a rumpled white suit and an oversized balding head. *Casaday.* The fucker hadn't gone with the blimp. Before he could react, Casaday shot him a finger and ducked back around the corner of the hangar. He was carrying some kind of machine gun with a big drum magazine. Jay found himself loathing guns more and more with every passing moment.

"We have to do something," Jerry said. His voice had changed.

Jay was startled to see Sly Stallone standing beside him, assault rifle in hands. He looked at what remained of their stalwart crew. Him, Rambo Jerry, and a half-dozen pirates. "Any of you guys fly a helicopter?" The pirates looked at him blandly. "A chopper," Jay said, "you know." He spun a hand over his head and went, *"Whoop whoop whoop."* It didn't seem to help much.

"I don't think they speak English," Rambo Jerry said.

"Real good," Jay said. "Shit. I guess it's up to me."

Jerry said, *"You* can pilot a helicopter?"

Jay shrugged. "How hard can it be?" He thought a moment.

"I'll go for the chopper, you guys take out Casaday." He made gestures at the pirates, pantomiming. "Run. Shoot, *Ra-tatatatata*." More blank looks. "This is working swell. Maybe we have to lead them by example."

Jerry took a deep breath. "Yo," he said. "When?"

"Now," Jay said. He ran. Jerry fired a burst toward the distant hangar, then came pelting after him, shooting on the run.

Every step felt like someone was probing Jay's nose with a dental drill. After about five feet he figured the pirates were a little slow on the uptake; after ten he knew they weren't coming.

Their dash took them past the spot where Radical had fallen. The ace looked like a cat who'd been run over by a cement truck. But even in the thickening doom there was no mistaking it: the lung exposed in the shattered rib cage was unmistakably pumping. Jay leapt over him and went on; he had problems of his own.

"Wait, he's alive," he heard Jerry call out behind him. He glanced back and saw his junior partner kneeling beside the body. There was no time to go back and argue; Jay kept running.

A sudden burst of machine-gun fire spurred him on. Whether it was O. K. Casady shooting at Jay or Jerry shooting at Casaday or the pirates finally pitching in with covering fire, Jay had no idea. Someone was shooting; that was enough for him. He lowered his head and sprinted. His footfalls drove spikes through his head, and the wind off the chopper's rotors buffeted him as he got close. He was so blind from pain he almost ran right into the blades, but somehow he managed to reach the cockpit and pull himself inside. The pilot was still in his seat. "Follow that blimp," he told him, panting.

There was no reply. Jay looked over. A neat little hole had been punched through the canopy, and half the pilot's head was gone. Blood was drying on what remained of his face, and fat Chinese flies were crawling across his brain. Jay's stomach turned over.

The *Harmony* was far to the southeast, picking up speed. Jay shoved the body out onto the tarmac and slid over into the pilot's seat, still wet with the blood of its last occupant. He looked at the dials and gauges and sticks. The blades were already spinning; Jay figured that meant he was halfway there.

"Ackroyd!"

At first he thought he was hearing things. Then the shout came again, high and thin over the *whap* of the rotors and the chatter of automatic weapons. J. Bob Belew was pulling himself across the tarmac on hands and knees, leaving a trail of blood. *"Ackroyd!"*

Swearing under his breath, Jay jumped out of the helicopter and scrambled toward Belew. "I thought you were dead," he said as he knelt down beside him.

"Sorry to disappoint you," Belew said between clenched teeth. His handlebar mustache was sticky with blood, and more blood bubbled out between his lips when he spoke. "Help me up."

"Can you fly a helicopter?" Jay asked, like an idiot. What was he saying? Does the pope shit in the woods? The Mechanic could *be* a helicopter.

Belew's face was white as bone, drained of all color. Jay got an arm under him and helped him to his feet. Belew moaned and closed his eyes. For an instant Jay thought J. Bob had fainted on him, or maybe died, but then his eyes opened again. "Hurry," he whispered. Jay supported him as they staggered back toward the chopper. Bullets whined around them.

The *Harmony* was well to the south now, dwindling visibly as dusk settled around them.

As they limped past the chopper's tail, Belew thrust his hand into the spinning rotor. There was a wet meaty sound. Blood spurted. Fingers and bits of bone scattered like jacks. Jay shuddered. "I *hate* it when you do that," he said fervently.

Belew pulled his ruined hand close to his chest and tried to stanch the bleeding with his good one. "... *get* ... *me* ... *on* ... *board* ..." he said. Jay could barely make out what he was saying, but Belew's eyes were wide open, feverish.

Somehow Jay managed to shove him into the chopper, lifting him over the pilot's body. J. Bob ripped off a panel with his good hand and shoved his bloody stump into the wiring beneath. Bone and blood and muscle became one with steel and aluminum and plastic; the Mechanic's soul entered the machine.

The copter began to lift, leaving Jay standing flat-footed on the field. "Hey, *wait a minute!*" he yelled.

And then he saw him.

Rising from the weeds beyond the field, not ten feet away, grinning his jack-o'-lantern grin, rumpled and evil, O. K. Casaday raised the snout of his machine gun. "Belew, you hoary old fuck," he screamed over the rotors, "where do you think *you're* going?" Laughing, he hosed down the front of the chopper with a stream of fire. The glass canopy exploded in a million pieces, and Jay could see Belew's body shudder under the impact of the bullets.

The chopper's tail angled up, the nose fell, and for a second Jay thought it was all over. A second was all it took. Instead of crashing, the copter lurched forward, right at Casaday. Bullets sparked wildly on steel. There was just enough time for O. K. Casaday's laughter to turn into a scream before the main rotor took his head off. The blades angled down a shade more and cut him clean in half before the body had even begun to fall.

Jay ran and jumped, pulling himself up and in as the chopper went screaming into the sky. "Jesus, Belew, I thought you were dead for sure that time," he shouted.

Then he realized that Belew was past listening. J. Bob was slumped against the controls, his warm blood leaking from a dozen bullet holes to mingle with the hot hydraulic fluids leaking from the chopper. Whatever life and strength he had left in him was going into the helicopter now. The Mechanic had become the machine.

The airfield fell away below them. The *Harmony* was miles ahead, lost in the gloom to the south.

The sun had set, Jay realized. On Canton and maybe the world.

Croyd was fast, all right. They sped over the dunes with a stampede of racing camels behind them, but the herd fell farther and farther behind.

"They can't keep up," Croyd said.

"They're falling behind, all right. Damn it, Croyd, they'll circle back to camp if they lose sight of you. You'll have to slow down," Zoe said.

Croyd braked, a tilting and scary procedure all by itself. Zoe held on for dear life, glad of Billy Ray's strength, for he managed to keep both of them attached to Croyd.

Croyd wheeled around and looked back at the herd. "You're right. They'll go where they think the closest water is. I'm thirsty myself." He knelt on the sand. "Now what?"

"Beats me," Billy Ray said.

Zoe slid off Croyd's back, pulling her rolled kilim with her. Her knees felt shaky.

"I guess it's time for a magic carpet." Croyd picked up the kilim with his big teeth and shook it.

"Oh, fuck," Zoe said.

If antigravity were a force, it was one she had no idea how to engineer. Wool, sand, wind. Zoe knelt on the spread kilim and held a corner of it in her mouth, tasting the structure of coils in the soft wool, traces of ammonia from sheep urine, and the simple bitterness of aniline dyes. Carbon strands, ammonia. Cadmium? *Cadmium is supposed to be a no-no,* Zoe remembered. *No more yellow paint for artists.*

Cadmium made such a good catalyst. Hydrogen. Hydrogen from water, cadmium-drive catalysis, hydrogen cells to push against the wind and provide some lift. A strong alignment was needed, a perfect directional twist on the cells honeycombed from the structure of the wool. *We may burn up, the carbon will melt—melt into diamond, if need be. Needs be. Waffled diamond for insulation, Croyd, here we go.*

Wondering, as she breathed the changes into the hand-woven twists of wool, if Croyd could still function sexually when he was this far gone into craziness. Wondering if Turtle was making love to Danny, laughing on old sheets washed to the texture of silk, sunny and cool in the Venice apartment. Wondering if the boy Pan Rudo had been was now at peace, his silky skin and delicate touches bringing unspeakable pleasures to an alternate woman in an alternate, benevolent universe. She hoped so.

The kilim writhed, expanded, went rigid as sheet metal.

Zoe ripped two of the water packs away from her waist and dropped them beside Croyd. "Here's a bribe for your friends." She handed two of the bags to Billy Ray. "Get on behind me," she said. "And pour. This may be a bumpy ride."

Gregg was glad for Needles's company as he walked around the quarter; if Ray showed up again, he'd use Needles to make damn sure that this time the ace stayed dead.

Guilt tasted of licorice, fear of anise, and anger was as sweet as sugar. "You know what the Black Dog has planned, don't you?" Gregg asked Needles. They stood in front of an orange seller's stall. The odor of citrus wasn't nearly as strong as the scent of Needles's confusion. "No," he said loudly and fast, and the lie was distressingly obvious in his face. Needles knew it; the boy became far too interested in the orange he held in his clawed hand. "I'll take this one," he said to the joker behind the stall, whose skin was as pulpy as the orange. "How much?"

"Needles," Gregg persisted. "You've heard rumors or you've heard the Black Dog say it outright. What's he planning?"

"I . . . I can't tell you."

"That's a little different than 'I don't know,' isn't it?"

Needles colored nicely, like a teenager caught necking in the car. Gregg sipped at the taste, sampling its sweetness, and he yanked on the strings: pulling here, pushing back there. "Look—" Needles dropped the orange back onto the pile as the seller yelled at him in Arabic. "Let's walk. Too many people listening."

They left the quarter, moving into the souk just beyond the gate. Needles didn't speak as they moved through the crowds of mingled nats and jokers. Gregg didn't push, letting him walk and enjoying the taste of the internal battle going on inside him. "Damn it," Needles breathed. "I shouldn't . . ."

"You have to go with what your heart says," Gregg told him, and as he said the words, he pulled aside the doubt in Needles's mind. With the power, he strengthened the underpinnings of old lessons, brought up the memory of how horrible Needles had felt when he'd first killed. He conducted the orchestra of the youth's mind, playing a symphony whose ending he alone knew. "Listen to your feelings, and you'll know whether to tell us or not. Hannah and I want to help you, Needles. We want to do what's *right*, that's all."

Tugging, making him dance to our tune . . .

Needles stopped and looked down at Gregg as the crowds moved around them. "I'll tell you," he said, and started walking again. As they moved through the souk, Needles began to speak, haltingly at first.

And in the silence of Gregg's mind, Puppetman laughed in delight.

Radical came back to awareness in a plenum of pain.

For a time he lay there, feeling semi-regular jolts slam through the throbbing wound that was his body like Richter eight earthquakes. Nowhere in his various lives had he or Mark or anybody gotten a clue that this much pain existed. Even the death of Starshine—a suddenly vivid memory, passing like a train bound the other way—hadn't hurt this much.

He opened his eyes. The full moon had begun to rise. The light fell between the upright stakes that surrounded the truck bed in bars, striping his body. When it entered his eyes, it hit him like a drug.

Moonchild, he thought, as the pain receded like the ebb tide. She had the power of healing herself, and moonlight augmented her powers, as the light of the sun fueled Starshine's. *The moonlight's healing me.*

He stirred, and it was like being broken on the wheel all over again. Moonchild's gift was healing his hurts, but it and the moon had their work cut out for him.

He looked around. It was full dark. The truck was jouncing toward the light-dome of a huge city, with Sly Stallone behind the wheel. Creighton.

And it hit him, like the RPG warhead going off all over again: *I've been here more than an hour.*

I'm free. Really free.

Inside, he felt a clamor of voices. And panic, rearing and swelling like an angry king cobra: *the blimp!* Had it reached Hong Kong by now? Was the very breeze become a messenger of death, infecting all it touched with cool fingers?

He laughed, though it seemed to tear tissue from the inside of his throat in handfuls and made his lips feel as if they were being sliced with razors.

"I'm alive," he said. "And I'm back to stay. No way do I lose. No *way*."

He coiled himself and leapt through pain into the sky.

"So you know what they have planned," Hannah said to Needles. They were walking in the crowded bazaar near the gates to the Joker Quarter, isolated in the midst of the afternoon throngs and the calls from the sellers in the stalls. The quarter was noisy and oblivious to the plot being launched underneath its streets. The teeming colors of the people brought Puppetman crawling to the edge of the cage, peering out hungrily; Gregg pushed him back.

"Yeah," Needles said. "Most of it, anyway. The Black Dog's had the nuke altered since Zoe brought it back—they rigged a timing device and mounted the whole thing on a truck bed. The plan is to have that Highwayman guy drive it in—he's got some old truck, about the same size as that one." Needles indicated a battered, dusty water truck sitting on the other side of the open square. "They'll off-load the bomb, set the timer, and get the hell out. By the time anyone figures out what's going on, Bruckner's gone, and *Boom!*"

Needles made a mushroom cloud with his daggered hands.

The driver had climbed up on the roof of the water truck across the way. Gregg could see her through gaps in the crowd: a tall woman with her hair tucked under a military-style cap. In the sunlight, sweat gleamed from her fair skin. Gregg looked again, squinting. The woman wore a gauze mask over her mouth. She was holding something in her hands—a long hose that trailed back to the rear of the water truck. Given the sandy dust coating the stainless-steel cylinder, Gregg wasn't surprised that the driver would want to wash down the truck, though why she would do so in the middle of a crowded square escaped him. Hannah had noticed her, too; she was staring at the woman.

"All this garbage just means we can't wait any longer," Gregg said, still watching the woman. "You were right, Hannah. We have to get word to someone as soon as we can. Maybe even Ray . . . Hannah?"

She didn't answer. The hues of her mind weren't even directed toward him. They flared outward, the colors strange. Gregg looked up at Hannah. She, too, was staring at the driver on the cab of the water truck. Water gushed out from the nozzle of the hose. The woman directed the fine spray out into the crowd around the truck, turning to douse everyone in range. There was a sudden eruption of shouts and curses and laughter. Several joker children screeched in delight and began frolicking in the mist and mud.

"Did you hear me, Hannah?"

"That woman," Hannah said. "What in the hell is she doing?"

Gregg squinted again. "I don't know. Needles, what is this? Do they bring out the water trucks to cool things down, keep the dust settled?"

Needles shook his head. "Never heard of it."

The woman continued to spray. Gregg noticed something

else. There were armed guards around the truck. Several of them—stern-faced nats, each one.

"Except for the kids, no one looks to be enjoying it very much. And she still has her mask on . . ." Hannah was frowning, and her colors went a sudden alarming purple. "Jesus! Gregg, that's the woman who's working with Billy Ray: April Harvest. We have to get out of here," Hannah said urgently, suddenly. "Needles, come on . . ."

"Hannah?"

"I don't have time to explain," she said. "Just trust me. *Come on!*"

Hannah hurried them back into the Fist compound at a run, pushing through the throngs around the souk, not stopping until they passed the startled guards and passed back into the catacombs. "Get the Black Dog!" she snapped at Needles. "And tell them to keep the damn doors closed. Don't let anyone else in who's still outside. Not until everyone here is wearing masks, gloves, and filters."

"What's going on?" Gregg managed to ask her. Puppetman howled inside him, a sound of animal fear, and Gregg suddenly knew. "Oh, Jesus," he said. "You're wrong. You have to be wrong."

"I hope like hell I'm wrong," Hannah said, and shades of purple and red wrapped around her like an unseen veil. "We have to get to the Black Dog. They've got to stop that truck . . ."

Zero

The *Harmony* swelled ahead of them, a white whale shimmering in the moonlight. "Slow down," Jay told Belew, shouting to be heard over the rotors. "You want to match speeds. Bring us in alongside the gondola, close as you can get, and I'll jump across."

Even as the words were leaving his mouth, Jay wondered what the hell he was saying. He'd *jump across?* He looked down, at the ghost moon shimmering on the dark waters below. It was very pretty. If Jay slipped while he was jumping across, he'd have a long time to admire it on the way down.

The *Harmony* filled the world. "Not so fast," Jay cautioned Belew. "You can slow down now." He could see pale tourist faces pressed to the windows of the gondola, watching their approach. "Any time," Jay said. The huge envelope of the airship loomed over them like the face of a cliff. "Now," Jay said, "now would be a good time to slow." The cliff was about to fall on them. The tourist faces were screaming. *"Veer off!"* Jay shouted.

They plowed into the side of the gondola in an explosion of glass and metal. Something slammed Jay in the face, hard, and the bolt of pain that went through him was so bad that he lost consciousness for a moment, or two, or ten.

When he opened his eyes again, he could hear the shriek of the wind and the sound of people screaming. His head was ringing. There were two Belews in the seat beside him, spinning around each other. Both of them seemed to be unconscious or sleeping or dead.

Jay crawled out of the helicopter on his hands and knees, through a tangle of twisted metal and broken glass. He dropped a couple of feet, slammed into an unsteady floor, and blacked out again. Then there was a blaze of pain. He opened his eyes to find a pair of hunchbacks crouched over him, shaking him. Their eyes looked down at him soulfully. "You can't die yet," they said in chorus, shaking him. "You can't die yet."

The two hunchbacks became one. "Quasiman," Jay muttered. The cavalry had arrived, drooling, "What are you doing here?"

"I always come here," Quasiman said, perplexed. "I have to do something." He frowned, trying to remember. "There was a paper. I need to get drugs for Mark."

"I think you did that already," Jay told him. The hunchback looked lost. "Help me up," Jay urged.

"Hold on to me," Quasiman said. Jay draped an arm around his neck. Quasiman pulled him erect. Blood was running down his face and soaking through his bandage. The floor slanted under his feet. The tourists were as far away as they could get, clinging to the walls and hiding under the furniture. Jay looked behind him and saw the wreckage of the helicopter where it had punched right through into the cabin. He reeled unsteady, blinking. He felt as if he were trapped in a dream. There was something strangely familiar about all this. He could not remember what it was, but the sense of déjà vu was overwhelming.

There was a sharp *crack* and something whistled past his ear. Quasiman vanished as suddenly as he had appeared.

Somebody was shooting at him, Jay realized dreamily. "Freeze, or the pony gets it!" a shrill voice screamed.

Across the cabin, a man with half a face stood with a gun in one hand and a spray nozzle in the other. The gun was pressed to Finn's head. The spray nozzle was pointed at Jay. It was fed from a long hose that led back to a bulky metal cannister on the man's back. Jay didn't need three guesses to figure out what was in the canister. There were other canisters on the floor behind Finn.

"I'm sorry, Jay," Finn said mournfully. "I blew it."

Jay realized blearily that there were bodies littering the deck; Shark gunmen, four of them at least, and a fifth wounded and moaning in the corner. The little centaur hadn't done badly at all, from the looks of it. Half Face looked to be the only guy still standing.

Half Face pressed the barrel of the gun against Finn's temple and shouted, "I mean it! One move and the joker's dead." The right side of his head was a mask of blood, and the shoulder of his white lab coat was stained a deep red. He waved the spray nozzle around threateningly.

"You release that shit and the joker is dead anyway," Jay told him, playing for time. "Along with me, you, and the rest of the world. What would you say if I told you your precious Black Trump kills nats, too?"

Half Face giggled crazily. "I'd say, *Liar, liar, pants on fire.* You can't fool me. I'm a trained scientist."

Finn gaped at Jay. "Nats, too? Everyone? *Clara?*"

Jay nodded.

Finn lifted a forefoot and slammed a hoof down hard on the instep of the man with half a face. Jay heard a *crunch* as bones snapped. Half Face screamed. Finn ducked, kneed him in the groin, and wrenched the pistol out of his fingers.

By then Jay was moving. By then it was too late.

As Finn wrestled with him for the spray nozzle, Half Face clenched his trigger finger. A fine mist sprayed out. It felt like a soft drizzle as it touched Jay's face. Half Face giggled. "Ooops," he said. "Sorry, you're dead."

Finn wrenched the nozzle away and gave him a backhand slap, hard across the cheek. Half Face went down like a sack of potatoes. Finn slumped helplessly. "I'm sorry," he said. He sounded so tired. "I tried, but . . . Oh, God . . . Clara . . ."

Jay bent over Half Face to examine the tank on his back. *One chance in four,* he thought, thinking of Hastet. And there it was: a mark on the bottom of the cannister.

The world spun dizzily. "We can't die yet," Jay said. "We haven't seen *The Jolson Story.*"

Quasiman materialized out of nowhere. "Don't drink the wine!" he shouted in alarm. "They put it in the wine."

Jay didn't know what the fuck the hunchback was talking about, but he had an idea. He took the spray nozzle from Finn and gave him a quick spritz. Then he hosed down Quasiman.

"What are you *doing*?" Finn said, horrified.

"Saving the world," Jay said, yanking Half Face's arms out from the straps that held the tank to his back. Half Face groaned in protest. "Quasiman, come over here." The hunchback stepped close. Jay hefted the bulky tank onto his twisted back and helped him tighten the straps. "This is Mark's Overtrump," he told him. "Do you know what you have to do?"

"I remember now," Quasiman said. "I have to take it . . ."

"Everywhere," Jay finished for him. "Hong Kong, Saigon, Jerusalem, New York, Paris, everywhere there are aces and jokers. Spray Hannah and Father Squid and Peregrine and everyone else you know, no matter where they are. Spray Squisher's Basement and Aces High and the Louvre and the Kremlin and the Taj Mahal. Spray O'Hare and Tomlin and Heathrow, all the big airports you can find. Keep moving. Don't waste it all in one spot. This is all we have, and there's a whole world out there to dose. Do you understand?"

The hunchback nodded. "What if I forget?"

"You won't," Jay told him, praying that he was right. "You won't forget."

"I won't," Quasiman said, vanishing.

Finn was staring at the place he had been. "Overtrump," he said. "You mean . . . a cure . . . a vaccine . . . My God, you entrusted our only hope to a, a, a . . ."

"A joker," Jay said. Finn shut up.

There were still three canisters to take care of. The Black Trump, the *real* Black Trump. If this stuff got loose, it would be a horserace between the two viruses. Win, place, and die. Jay shaped stiff fingers into a gun. A canister vanished with a soft *pop*. Then a second one . . .

He was pointing toward the third when the tourists began to scream. The floor was tilting under him. Jay looked over his shoulder, just in time to see the wreckage of the helicopter shudder and slide backward and fall away, leaving a jagged hole in the gondola. A sudden gust of wind plucked at him with cold fingers. Finn clutched for a handrail. Jay clutched at Finn. Tourists grabbed furniture and children. Souvenir booklets and maps and postcards skittered across the floor and were sucked out through the jagged hole into the night. A Chinese woman followed, screaming.

"*The Trump!*" Finn shouted.

The last cannister of Black Trump was rolling across the gondola, toward the darkness. Jay lurched for it as it went by, missed, and hung on to Finn for dear life.

The tank bounced across the deck and slammed into Half Face where he lay. He clutched it to him, embracing it like a lover. "*Mine!*" he screamed. He hooked a leg around a railing as his plump hands fumbled greedily with the valve.

Jay let go of Finn.

The wind took him. He flew across the cabin. Half Face saw him coming. He lifted the cannister with both hands and smashed Jay full in the face with it. The pain was blinding, and Jay heard bones crunch in his cheek, but somehow he managed to get one hand on the tank and the other one in Half Face's hair.

They rolled over and over, and went out the hole together, into the empty, moonlit sky.

The night air several hundred feet up was cool, not the usual Southeast Asian twenty-two-degrees-of-latitude furnace blast. The lights of the New Territories appeared below him like pinpricks in the mantle over Hell. Radical flew on, upheld solely by the light of the moon and his own long-chained will to struggle.

His mind phased in and out of consciousness. Sometimes he almost lost track of who he was; sometimes he seemed to be JJ Flash, or dour Aquarius, or Cosmic Traveler, or even Mark. Sometimes he had flashes of Moonchild and once or twice even dead Starshine.

The moonlight was energizing him. But his body was trying to use all that energy to repair the terrible damage the missile warhead had done. It took constant application of willpower to hold himself in the sky—and when he would begin to fade again, the borders of his personality blurring, he would find himself dropping at an alarming rate.

Focus wandering . . . *a small boy on a stove-hot sidewalk, under blinding Southern California sun. A little girl on a tricycle, with black hair in pigtails and lavender eyes* . . .

He was falling again. The cool rush of air saved him, caught him, returned him to himself. He shook his head, and he reveled in the agony-waves that motion sent crashing through his body; they returned him to Now.

Ahead, a half-ellipsoid shimmer of light. The lights of Hong Kong, reflected on the underbelly of the airship *Harmony*.

He sped up. The effort felt as if it were tearing his mind like a sheet of rotten cloth. He forced his arms out straight in front of him, fists clenched, and drove onward.

The airship swelled in his vision. He saw the air around his outthrust fists shimmer and turn red as subconsciously he summoned a JJ Flash fire blast. His body dipped toward the hungry water.

No, he reminded himself. *I can't burn the blimp down. I can't be sure of getting the Black Trump that way* . . .

From the gondola, an object detached itself, dropping toward the choppy waters of the harbor below. On raptor instinct alone Radical dove, using gravity's insistent pull to gather speed.

The wind shrieked and the stars pinwheeled around them as they fell, tumbling, locked together tighter than honeymooners, arms and legs entwined around the cannister.

Half Face was screaming, *"Let go! Let go! It's mine,"* and hitting him in the face, over and over. Every punch felt like an icepick up his nose, but Jay wouldn't let go.

He tightened his legs around the canister, dug his fingers into Half Face's hair, and began to slam his forehead into the valve. Half Face shrieked and kicked at him. The moon was below them, then the water, then the moon. Half Face screamed as a handful of hair and scalp ripped off in Jay's fingers. *"We're going to die!"* he yelled.

"Might as well," Jay said. "Can't dance." The moon spun around them dizzily.

Then the sky came lurching to a sudden halt.

Arm locked around Jay's waist, Radical fought to level off. He knew how an eagle felt, trying to lift a hare.

Jarnavon clung to the canister, blood-masked half-face distorted with emotion beyond the point of madness. Ackroyd likewise clutched the metal container, like Sprout with a favored teddy bear.

"*No!*" the scientist screamed at Radical's face. His legs flailed night air, pants cuffs hiked well up over his brown shoes. "*You can't!* All I've worked for—the brave new order—"

"Ackroyd," Radical said in the hoarse, wind-torn whisper that was all he could force out still-blistered lips. "Just let go."

From a handspan away the detective's eyes stared into his without comprehension. Then he said, "Oh," and relaxed his death grip on the metal cylinder.

Jarnavon fell away beneath them. A bony hand feverishly turned a stopcock. "You'll see!" he cried. "I'll release it anyway! I've still won, you fools!"

Radical let himself and Jay fall free. He flung his arm down, hand outstretched. "No," he rasped. "You lose."

And a wash of plasma fire jetted forth. Jarnavon shrieked as flame vaporized him and the canister.

Zoe and Billy Ray rode the winds, leaving Croyd and his camels far behind. Sand ground against the carpet and needled the faces of its riders. Billy Ray dripped water on the carpet; molecular hydrogen hissed energy to drive them south. Zoe breathed instructions to the carpet and it found a place in synchrony with the wind, a calm place where its energies grew incrementally, an asymptotic curve on the graph of improbability.

They could ride this current into Jerusalem, this peaceful nexus between energies. They sat on the carpet as if it were a bobsled. Billy Ray had his knees locked around her waist. She leaned back against him, wanting to cringe from his ugliness but grateful for his warmth. The air was cold up here.

A woman named April Harvest drove death toward Jerusalem. Zoe looked for any sign of a truck, for any fresh tracks made by anything, but the scouring sand hid all traces of roads and nothing moved across the dunes but the wind. *This is the way the world ends,* she chanted to herself. *Not with a bang but a sneeze.*

Stars broke through the clouds of sand and winked away again. One of the clouds rolled over and smiled at her. It wore the face of the dead skinhead who had killed Bjorn. The Russian entrepreneur stood up behind him and tried to hand-roll a cigarette, but the wind kept blowing the tobacco away, each of the shreds a drop of brownish blood.

At least she wasn't hearing voices again.

"I'm muddy," Billy Ray said. "I hate being dirty."

"I'll never get the sand out of my hair," Zoe said.

The man behind her was in superb physical shape, his muscles taut as plates of steel. She guessed he worked out as a sort of defense against his ugliness.

"How long until we get there?" Billy Ray asked.

Zoe looked at the little pocket locator. "Half an hour," she said.

"We can't go faster?"

"No."

The joker behind her shifted his posture. "Damn," he said. She could feel the tension in him, a rage that seemed personal rather than righteous. But he wasn't the kind to talk much, it seemed.

Zoe watched for roads, for trucks, for people who might shoot at them. *We're dead, Daddy,* she told Bjorn. *I don't think I can get Mommy out of this, or the kids, or me. I'm sorry.*

You aren't dead yet, honey. Bjorn spoke to her, his voice a voice of wilderness, so that she tasted fresh-caught salmon tossed on spring riverbanks and nosed for honey in the tickling dust of dead trees.

She was hearing voices, yes, but at least she wasn't hearing the voices of strangers, or of sand.

"Don't fall asleep," Billy Ray said.

"Sleep? Sleep would be so nice, but I won't sleep. I'll be good. Sorry, Daddy," Zoe said.

Billy Ray shook her. "Stop that! Don't flip out, okay?"

My world is dying and I can't stop it. We're all going to die, but this man says don't flip out. He's crazy, Daddy. "Okay," Zoe said.

A hunchbacked man sat on the air beside them. He had something like a scuba tank strapped on his back. "Billy Ray," the man said. "I know you."

"*Quasi?* What the hell are you doing here?" Billy Ray said.

"I have to go. Everywhere he said. Spray them all. I have to remember. Be careful." He fumbled for something attached to the tank on his back, but before he reached it, Quasiman dissolved into the air.

"Yeah, right, Quas." Billy Ray shrugged and stared at the landscape. Dawn showed roads below them now, and scrubby fields, and the earthen ramparts and barbed wire fences that marked a land in turmoil.

"Zoe? That's Jerusalem, up ahead," Billy Ray said. "Maybe you'd better bring this thing down."

She smelled smoke. Something was very, very wrong. The popcorn sound of gunfire rose toward them from the huddle of yellow stone, the maze of streets where people rushed back and forth like ants fleeing a kicked anthill. The streets were filled with cars and donkeys and camels and trucks, but none of them were water trucks.

She had to get Anne, get the Escorts, get them out!

The city was on fire. Zoe spiraled the carpet down toward Jerusalem.

Ray was worried about the attention they might attract as they approached the city on the flying carpet, but he soon saw that Jerusalem had other things to worry about. As they swooped down over the Walled City they saw smoke, street fights, and bodies lying everywhere.

"Jesus," Ray said. "It's a madhouse down there."

They landed on the flat roof of an apartment building avoiding the gates that were heavily guarded from the outside.

"I've got to find my mother and the kids," Zoe said. "What are you going to do?"

What was he going to do? He didn't know. He had to find Harvest and stop her, although it looked like they might be too late for that. He hated her. He should hate her. But he realized that he didn't. She'd betrayed him.

Betrayed, hell, she'd tried to kill him in a particularly excruciating manner. But he could only think of her beauty, her cockiness, her coolness under pressure, her near-insatiable desire. She was everything he ever wanted in a woman, and by God he loved her still. He would always love her. Shit. What was he going to do? He gave Zoe the only answer he could.

"Kick ass."

Ray inserted clean filters in his nose and put one of Zoe's extra surgical masks over his mouth. He felt feverish and light-headed. It could be an army of microbes working on him, whittling down his defenses until he collapsed in a pile of red goo. Or it could be the fact that he'd lost his woman, broken his arm, and hadn't eaten for twelve hours. Whatever, it wouldn't hurt to be a little cautious, what with the Black Trump raging through the city.

"So long, Ray," Zoe said.

"So long. And good luck."

They opened the hatchway on the roof and went downstairs. It was a death house. An entire family—kids, parents, and grandparents—had perished in their own blood. He and Zoe parted at the door. She went to seek her own family.

Ray went to look for April Harvest.

"They've found the truck!" Needles burst into the room where Gregg and Hannah waited. "It's near the Wailing Wall. Come on—the Black Dog's already gone after it."

Puppetman shrieked inside. *No! We can't go out there!* Hannah was already up. Her face grim as she pulled her filter mask down, her hands covered in a double pair of rubber gloves, she took the Uzi that Needles offered her. "Hannah," Gregg began, "we don't know if masks and filters are going to stop the Trump. We can't—"

"We have to," Hannah said. Her voice was muffled but her conviction was clear to the power inside Gregg. He could barely see the core of doubt inside it. "I'm not going to stay here. If you can't, fine. But I'm going."

"But I don't . . ." Gregg stopped. He wore a mask, too, one jury-rigged to fit him as best they could, and his feet were swathed in wrappings of plastic that made it difficult for him to grasp anything. *If I get out there and one part of this garbage doesn't work, I'm dead!* he wanted to cry, and he knew the power inside him was shouting the same words. But Hannah was already heading out the door behind Needles, and he didn't want to be alone.

Not here. Not now.

"Wait!" he called. "I'm coming with you."

Together, they went from the catacombs out into the streets of Jerusalem.

In the hours since Hannah and Gregg had seen the water truck, the Black Trump had begun its terrible reign in the Joker Quarter. For those infected, the first symptom was a raging headache, followed quickly by a fever that would not break. Still, this was no worse than a bad sinus infection. "A few days' bed rest, some decongestants . . ." That was the doctor's reply to the first calls from the parents of the joker children sprayed by Harvest.

In another few hours, those same parents called again, in fear and panic this time.

The virus attacked the bloodstream, tearing apart the red blood cells and at the same time sending a series of disastrous clots throughout the body. The skin became a network of bruises, and the thinning soft skin tore open with the slightest provocation—the bleeding, once begun, would not stop. Purple lesions were visible within six hours, and the victims bled from every available orifice: the mouth, the nose, the anus, the eyes, from the ripped skin. That blood was laden with the virus, and a touch was enough to infect someone. Coughing, the victims sprayed poison into the air. Later, the victims would vomit immense quantities of black fluid: clotted blood and bile.

As the clots rippled through the body, strokes were common. Victim's faces became rigid, masklike, expressionless. Like a zombie, they might lie unresponsive or their personality might change: rage and acute paranoia were common. Bleeding, dying, some fought those trying to care for them, breaking away with desperate strength and escaping out into the city.

In every case, those infected would die. There was no reprieve.

The Black Trump was the Black Queen done slowly. It was the rot of the grave inflicted on a living, aware host. It was agony and torture and anguish, and death was the only release from its grasp.

The evening breeze scattered the seeds of terror, and they grew.

Gregg and Hannah entered into a scene of carnage. Fires were burning in several of the houses—whether set by the infected themselves or by terrified neighbors, they'd never know. The strobes of police and fire vehicles bounced from the walls.

Gregg could sense the quick rise of fright in Needles. The boy's face was drawn and pale. He cradled his Uzi in his hands, twisting them around the short, ugly barrel, his claws clattering against the vented steel. Gregg could see his fear, coiling green around him. Puppetman hollered and fought— *Stop it! Goddamn you, stop it!*—but the bars held. "I wish I knew where Zoe was," Needles said as they came to the gate out of the quarter. "Jellyhead, Angelfish, Anna. I wish I knew they were okay."

Hannah glanced at Gregg. *Don't let him go!* "Go on," Hannah said. "We know how to get to the Wall. One person more or less isn't going to make any difference. Not now. Go on."

Needles hesitated. Then he nodded. As Puppetman shrilled curses, Needles took off running back into the quarter. The strings to the youth pulled taut, thinning with distance, and then Gregg could no longer feel him. Hannah sighed, and Gregg saw the tears behind the glass ports of her mask.

What the hell. There's a thousand more out here tonight . . .

He had no idea how long it took to move through the nightmare streets to the Wailing Wall. Crowds raced through the narrow streets, screaming and raging, breaking windows of the shops, looting, attacking people blindly. Twice, Hannah had to fire her weapon in the air to frighten off attackers. There were bodies everywhere, and it was difficult to tell if they'd been killed in the rioting or by the Black Trump. Gregg didn't bother to look closely enough to tell. Puppetman screamed the whole time, shaking the walls of Gregg's mind in terror, afraid that with each ragged inhalation, Gregg was breathing in their eventual death.

As they approached the square before the Wall, they could smell smoke and see firelight bouncing from the fronts of the stalls. "Shit," Hannah breathed, and ran.

The water truck was burning, the smoke black and full of the smell of burning rubber, gasoline, and flesh. There were bodies scattered around the truck; some Fists, but most of them in the uniform of the Sharks. "I don't see Harvest, or the Dog," Hannah said. She leaned down, peering at the nearest body, and Gregg saw her pull back as red terror shot from her mind. Puppetman moaned. "Christ!" Hannah said. She backed away.

"What?" Gregg asked. "Who is it?"

"A Shark. A nat," Hannah answered. "But look—" She pointed, and her finger trembled. Gregg sidled forward on all sixes, ready to retreat and feeling his body trembling. In the light of the burning truck, he could see the man's face.

Dark blood was still pulsing from his mouth, from his nose, from his wide-open eyes. His arms were covered with purple bruises, and they leaked blood as well. He smelled of corruption.

"Yes," someone said harshly to their right. The voice was familiar. "Humorous, isn't it?" The speaker came around the corner of one of the stalls, using an automatic weapon for a crutch, and Gregg saw the mask: a hound's face. A bullet had shattered the man's right leg; Gregg could see the blood and the fragments of white bone in the gaping wound. The Dog had wrapped a tourniquet about the leg just below the knee.

"What's humorous?" Gregg asked.

"The Black Trump kills nats, too. Don't you find that funny? I do. It's the funniest damn thing I've ever heard."

The Black Dog laughed, a sound dark as the blood.

It's a war, Zoe told herself, *it's a war and people are dying, but it can't be the Black Trump. It* can't *be!*

Billy Ray led her into a room where her last shreds of hope lay dead, where huddled corpses lay in heaps. The simoom howled outside and the Black Trump was loose in Jerusalem.

"Come on, Zoe!" Billy Ray shoved through the doorway of the tiny rooftop room. Zoe scanned the huddled corpses as she went past them, looking for Anne, or Owl, but these were strangers. They weren't *hers*, thank God. She followed Billy Ray out, down ancient stairs whose steps were smooth curves, the stone worn away by generations of human feet.

Billy Ray vanished in the crowd on the street. A joker appeared out of the haze and snatched at the pink snout of Zoe's surgical mask. Zoe straight-armed the poor devil out of the way. Damn, if only she'd thought to carry the carton of masks out of the lab! Too late, too late. She pulled the kilim over her head to hide the mask and kept running.

Got to get Anne. Got to get the kids. The Trump is loose and they might die, but I know enough isolation technique so we won't spread it to each other—so does Jellyhead, she's had some medical training; she can take care of the others if I die.

Gunfire broke out where two alleys intersected. Zoe caught

a glimpse of the black robes of Fist guards battling nats in green-and-brown camo. She dodged into a twisting alley, away from the guns and the screams.

No go. The alley dead-ended in a pile of burning mattresses. Clouds of black smoke that reeked of kerosene rolled toward her. Zoe ducked under an awning and jerked a table out from beneath it, scattering cucumbers and lemons into the street. She hoisted herself onto the awning and climbed the wall.

Others had taken to the rooftops, trying to avoid the crush of the streets. Zoe saw a rifle aimed in her direction, dropped and rolled, and ran for home. Someone screamed behind her. In the alleys below, coughs and pleas rose from the swirling crowds. A few robed figures crawled toward the city gates or lay against the walls, no longer able to crawl.

But Zoe was running the other way, into the quarter.

She reached her own roof, dropped onto the tiny stoop, and pounded on the door.

"Mama! Mama, let me *in*!"

"Zoe!" An adolescent's voice cracked on the shouted word; Owl? Angelfish? The door opened and Zoe faced a rifle barrel, Angelfish above it. Anne sat on a chair, her hands behind her. Both of them were masked in doubled bandanas, but they *were* masked.

"Don't touch me!" Zoe slid inside the door and braced her back against the wall, her hands behind her. A newscaster's rapid patter came from Needles's boom box in the corner. "Where's everybody? We've got to get *out* of here!"

"Jellyhead's out with Jan and Balthazar, setting up quarantine shelters where they can," Anne said. "Angel tied me to this chair when I tried to leave with them."

"I had to," Angel said. "I'm sorry, Zoe, but—"

The stripes on Angel's face pulsed with color; he was nervous about Zoe's reaction. "Good for you, Angel." Food, some water, the rifle Angel held should keep people from coughing in their faces. Zoe grabbed a clean garbage bag and pulled food and a plastic jug of cold water out of the tiny fridge. *Were the waterlines contaminated? We'll boil it before we drink it.*

"They say it's a biologic weapon that kills jokers. We have to fight it, Zoe. Let me help them. I'm going to die anyway," Anne said.

"Ma! Listen to me! There are dead nats on the streets out there! This plague kills everyone who gets it! The Black Dog has a nuclear bomb, and if the Black Trump doesn't kill us, he'll set it off, or the UN will use one of theirs to do the job! We can try to live through this or we can get blasted into atoms!"

"We can't leave," Anne said. Even perched on a kitchen chair with her hands tied behind her, she spoke with sweet reason. "The UN has set up roadblocks. So if you'll just have Angel untie me, we can get to work. While we have our strength, we'll do what we can."

". . . repeat, do not try to leave Jerusalem. If you feel ill, please report to the medical stations in your neighborhood, where UN workers will assist you. Do not pan—"

The announcer's voice stopped abruptly, replaced by static.

"Angel?" Zoe tied the plastic sack of food and water to the belt of her robe and signaled Angelfish with a look. He untied Anne's bonds. She blinked at the smoke outside and started down the stairs.

"No, Ma," Zoe said. "Up on the roof."

"What?"

"There's transportation there," Zoe said. She leapt and scrambled up, Angel beside her with his rifle.

"Hold up your arms, Ma," Zoe said.

"Oh, for pity's sake," Anne said, but she lifted her arms, they hauled, and Anne made it over the parapet and onto the roof.

Zoe puffed her carpet back to life, settled Anne in the middle, and climbed into steering position. "Get on behind us, Angel," she yelled. "Pour when I say!"

Angel dripped water onto the carpet's tail, Zoe shouted, and they lifted off into the smoke.

"Shit, Zoelady!" Angel yelled "This is seriously righteous!"

"Can we pick up Jan and Needles?" Anne asked.

"I'm looking, Mama." Zoe aimed the carpet for the shortest route over the walls. "The three of us barely fit on this thing; no, Ma, I can't get them."

Up, up, over street fires and screams. The red streaks of tracer bullets dotted the smoky air. Zoe cleared the wall and aimed for high, for south. She could see the Zion Gate, the road to Bethlehem. On it, Israeli and Palestinian soldiers in gas masks and goggles stood back-to-back, ready to shoot anyone trying to come in or out of the tortured city.

Zoe pushed the carpet into a steep climb.

A cluster of bright blossoms flared up from the Allenby Bridge. She stared at it in fascination. It was pretty, and so far away.

The carpet lurched.

"Zoe, I'm hit!" Angel yelled.

Anne twisted around and got hold of the boy, pulling him toward her with a mother's strength. The carpet bucked and Zoe fought for control. Back. Back into that hell.

She circled the carpet toward the walls and down into the city, aiming for any refuge, dodging bullets she couldn't see, looking for the thickest smoke, the greatest confusion. Among the buildings now, skimming the tops of the crowded, narrow streets.

Anne's voice screamed something she couldn't understand, a distraction Zoe didn't need; around this corner was a straight stretch of street where she could set this baby down.

Bruckner, Bjorn's voice said.

He isn't here, Daddy. Zoe skidded the carpet to a halt in the crowded street. The crowd was fleeing something she couldn't see.

"Nuke!" she heard. "They're going to blow us to hell!"

In wedge formation, a dozen black-robed jokers with rifles fought their way through the smoke-hazed crowd. Zoe got her arms beneath Angel's armpits and heaved him toward the scant shelter of a doorway, out of the line of traffic. Anne threw herself over Angel, shielding him with her body.

Open mouths, screams, chatter of automatic fire, the cracks of rifle stocks and fists, Zoe took an elbow in the ribs and stumbled against the wall, kicking out at the black robe in front of her.

The joker grabbed her and pulled her away from Anne and Angel.

"Mama!" Zoe screamed. "Let me go!" She struggled with the joker who held her and tried to fight her way back toward Anne. He slapped her, a blow that made her gasp. Above his mask, strange yellow eyes—

"Balthazar!"

"*Hurry,* Zoe!" the goat man yelled.

Ray had never seen a city gone mad before. People were fighting with nothing to fight for, running with nowhere to run. They were looting and stealing even as they sweated blood.

He looked all over the city for Harvest. He saw her handiwork everywhere. Darkness had fallen by the time he reached the Wailing Wall. He heard the sound a block away; when he entered the square, a thousand candles were burning. A great mass of people knelt at the Wall, praying with all their hearts, men and women and jokers intermixed; in their fear and grief, no one was trying to enforce the age-old segregations.

They'd finally realized that God doesn't give a rat's ass whether you're man, woman, or joker, Ray thought, *and it's too damn late for most of them.*

He was about to continue his hopeless quest to track down Harvest when an apparition, an answer to the wailing prayers of the multitude, appeared suddenly in the darkness. Quasiman.

He still had the tank strapped to his back. A hose ran from the tank. He started spraying the crowd. Candles began to flicker out.

At first most of the faithful didn't realize he was there, but a soaking from a power nozzle gets your attention pretty quickly. Someone else remembered that the Black Trump had been brought to Jerusalem as liquid sprayed over a crowd. And they went crazy. They deserted the Wall with a single, outraged roar.

Ray didn't know what the hunchback was doing, but he remembered his cryptic warning. *Don't drink the wine . . .* It seemed clear to him that Quasi would never hurt anyone.

Not that the maddened crowd would see it that way.

Ray raced to Quasiman's side, flinging jokers aside as he bulled through. He planted himself firmly in front of the hunchback. Quasi had materialized in front of a hummus stand; the crowd could only come from the front and sides. "Back off!" Ray roared.

The crowd came at them with fear-maddened features and clawed hands, screaming and cursing in half a dozen languages while Quasiman looked on, blank-eyed. "No," the hunchback said. "I remember . . . It's to help . . ." Ray had said that he was going to kick ass. Well, here were a shitload of asses to kick. He launched into a series of lightning attacks. He didn't have time to be careful. He felt bones snap and crunch as half a dozen of the mob went down in the first second. Some were trampled under and hurt a lot worse than by Ray's fists, feet, or elbows.

Ray's broken arm hadn't fully knit. It hurt like a son of a bitch when he connected with it. The pain was turning to a deep nausea and he didn't know how long he'd be able to hold out; he was beginning to think that this hadn't been such a good idea.

Then the joker let fly with the sprayer he carried on his back. The mob went mad. Suddenly it no longer wanted to be near the carrier of death. The rioters in the front rank suddenly went into reverse. Those in the rear peeled off and the mob parted in front of them like the Red Sea in front of Moses.

Ray hunkered down and took a deep breath, letting his tingling arm dangle limply. "Jesus," he said aloud, "I need a vacation." He turned to Quasiman. "Well, now that I've saved your ass, tell me what the hell you've got there."

For once, Quasiman seemed to be relatively in one piece. "The Overtrump," he said. "Jay said to spray them all, all over the world . . . To keep them safe . . ."

Ray felt as if a crushing weight had been lifted from his shoulders. "Well, Christ, Quasi. Give me a squirt."

He took off his face mask and popped the filters out of his nose and Quasiman sprayed him in the face.

"Who made it?" Ray asked after Quasiman had hosed him down.

"Mark Meadows," Quasiman said.

"The hippie?" Ray asked. Jesus, who knows what was in something cooked up by Mark Meadows? Still, the guy was supposed to know his shit. "Well, how did he—never mind. Explanations later. Right now we have to get you to the authorities."

Quasiman nodded decisively. "I remember. Let's go."

Hannah turned to Gregg. Her face was lined, drawn. She brushed limp hair back from her face. "I . . ." Hannah started to speak. She grimaced. Her hands fluttered up and fell again to her lap. "Gregg, this is it, isn't it? The Card Sharks got what they wanted, and more. Unless the Trump gets wiped out now, it's going to spread, and one hell of a lot of people are going to die. Everywhere. Everyone."

Gregg took a breath. He could smell the smoke, the death all around him, and he knew that if he could smell it, it could kill him. Fires lit the night sky. His body wanted to run, wanted to flee. Hannah had gone to the wounded Black Dog, helping the Fist leader. "Yeah. We lost—I thought we had a chance, but we lost."

"We can end it," Hannah said, "if we want to."

Puppetman howled, shaking the bars of his cage. "Hannah—"

"You know it's the only way, Gregg. There's no choice, not anymore."

"Hannah, do you realize what you're saying? That means—"

"Yes," she said. She brushed hair back from her forehead, as if what she were saying was simple small talk. "It means all of us here die. One way or the other. What the hell. We can die sitting here until the virus kills us. Or we die when the bomb goes off."

"What are you saying?" the Black Dog asked. His breathing was labored, and he hung on to Hannah. The Fist had lost a great deal of blood, and Gregg could feel him fighting against shock and pain—a table laid out for the feast. Puppetman hungered.

"Your nuke," Hannah told him. She swept her free arm out, taking in the square and the city beyond. "Look at this. The virus is out there, killing. The panic's already spreading. People are going to get into cars, into boats, into airplanes. They'll flee—and some of them will be carrying the virus. Where they go—Damascus, Tel Aviv, Cairo, Athens, Tokyo, Hong Kong, Rome, London, New York—they'll bring the virus there. Unless we stop it. Now."

No! shouted Puppetman in reply. *I won't let you! I'm BACK, damn it! I'm not going to die now, not again!* The mind-creature hurled himself at the bars inside Gregg's head, and Gregg staggered with the impact. *Fuck you!* it shrieked. *Goddamn it, let me OUT!*

For a moment, the power was free, and Puppetman went tearing madly at the strings to Hannah. Gregg caught him, dragged the thing back while it tore and scraped at him with mental claws and fangs, spitting and hissing. *You idiot! You fool! She wants to KILL us!*

You can't touch her. I told you. I won't allow it.

She doesn't goddamn LOVE you, Greggie. You've seen the rotten shit inside her; you've seen the way she really feels.

You're wrong. Anyway, she's right—this is what we have to do.

And you're suddenly a moral paragon? You're a saint? I KNOW you, you shit. We always wanted the same things, down inside. You wanted it all the same way I did. And you know what? YOU brought me back. You brought me back. You brought me back because you missed it.

Liar! The rage allowed Gregg to grasp the power and hurl it back into darkness, slamming the bars in place once again. *Liar!* He breathed hard, raggedly, allowing himself to see the world around him again. While he'd been away, wrestling with Puppetman, the Black Dog had come to his own decision.

"I thought we were on opposite sides," the Black Dog said to Hannah.

"Are we still?"

"I guess sides don't much matter anymore," the Black Dog told her. "We need to hurry."

"Gregg?" Hannah had turned to him. He could feel the fire of her gaze.

Noooooo! "Yes," Gregg told her. "I'll help. It's the only way we can end this."

I'm not going to let it happen, Greggie. The voice snarled deep down in its cage. *I tell you now: I'm not going to let you kill us.*

Limping, hobbling, the three of them made their way down streets bright with fire through the maddened, terrified city.

"There," the Black Dog grunted at last. He pointed down a cul-de-sac. Centuries-old buildings hemmed in the narrow entrance. "Damn!"

Gregg looked. An ancient, slat-sided truck was rumbling as someone revved the engine, gunning it again and again. Twisted Fists were off-loading something from the rear into a garage behind the truck. They looked up as Gregg, Hannah, and the Black Dog approached.

"What the hell are you doing?" the Black Dog snapped. "Who told you to unload the nuke, Bruckner?"

A florid-faced man in an Andy Capp hat leaned out from the driver's window. "My decision, mate," he said in a thick, lower-class British accent. His headlights speared out into the night. "I'm getting the hell out of here. Anybody that wants to go with me, they're welcome."

"You can't do that," Hannah shouted over the thunder of the truck. She looked at the jokers milling around the truck, clambering over the side into the back. Even with Gregg's nearsighted eyes, he could see the bruises on some of their arms; he could see jokers helping fevered, unconscious brethren onto the truck. "Some of them are infected. You'll just spread the virus."

"Get out of my way, lady," Bruckner snarled in return. "You're in my way."

"You can't!"

"I can. I will. And I'll run you the hell over if you try to stop me."

The Black Dog had thrown off Hannah's support. Now he reached for the Uzi still strapped around him, bringing the weapon to bear on Bruckner and the truck. "I give the orders here," the Black Dog said. "And I say—"

A single shot echoed, cutting off the statement. The Black Dog grunted and his body twisted around violently, the Uzi flying out of his weak grasp. As the Black Dog crumpled, Bruckner gunned the truck and jammed it into gear. Hannah and Gregg pressed against the walls as the truck went by in a wave of exhaust and sandy dust, the headlights blinding them as it passed. Hannah ran to the Black Dog as Bruckner and his load of jokers careened around the corner and out of sight. The Black Dog grimaced as she lifted him up, and Gregg saw the red wetness spreading across his abdomen.

"Goddamn!" the Fist said. "Goddamn! My own people . . ."

"The nuke," Hannah said.

"In there." The Black Dog pointed to the open doors of the garage. The Black Dog tried to rise, couldn't. Hannah bent down, facing away from him. "Arms around my neck," she said. "Hold on." With the Black Dog on her back, she managed to stagger into the garage and shut the doors while Gregg examined the machinery inside.

The nuke had been partially disassembled, the metal shell

removed to show wiring and the packs of conventional explosives arranged carefully around the inner core. "It looks complicated," Gregg said.

"It's actually three bombs," the Black Dog answered. "A nuclear device is two atomic weapons of subcritical mass, surrounded by another conventional bomb. That one's really the key; it's a carefully shaped explosion which will force the two sections together into one supercritical mass. A nuke is a dance of death. The conventional explosive—attached to the timer—must go off at the exact moment the two radioactive sections are released. Otherwise . . ." The Black Dog grimaced and slumped down to a sitting position, his back to the wall near the doors. "So tired," he said. "It hurts."

"What do we do?" Hannah asked.

Behind the mask, the Black Dog's eyes had closed. Now they opened again. "Balthazar did some rewiring," the Black Dog said. His breath rattled, liquid. "The timer's there, on top. All you have to do is press a damn button, and the sequence starts: ten minutes, and boom!" The Black Dog started a laugh that turned into a bloody cough. He wiped at his mouth and smeared blood over the mask. "Just one thing," he said when he'd recovered. "Once you start it, you can't stop it."

"What do you mean?" Gregg asked. "That's the stupidest—"

"We were going to drop it off for the Nur, remember?" the Black Dog said. "Balthazar rigged it so that if you tamper with it, or pull the wires, you set off the conventional explosive."

The timing device hung on a tangle of wires over the front of the mess, incomprehensible Cyrillic characters inscribed on the black steel. Hannah crouched alongside Gregg, and the closeness of her caused Puppetman to slam against the walls of Gregg's brain. The device had been simplified: a large red button, protected by a plastic shield, had been set in the center. The Black Dog had wanted to make it simple for Bruckner to set the timer and make his escape.

That would make it easy for them now.

No! **Puppetman shrilled** insistently inside Gregg. *You can't!*

This time, as Gregg tried to push the power back down, Puppetman slithered desperately from his grasp. For a moment, the tints around Hannah deepened. He could feel the desperation that drove Hannah, and within it the sliver of doubt that he knew must be there.

Take her! he heard Puppetman whispering. *The woman's mad, and she's about to kill thousands upon thousands of innocent people. You think the guilt of a few deaths is going to compare to that? How stained will your soul be if you allow this to happen?*

Leave me alone! Gregg screamed, and he pulled back at the power, trying to drag it back into himself. *This is what I want. This way I pay back all my sins!*

This isn't about you, Greggie. It's me.

You ARE me! Gregg cried. *We're the same!*

Puppetman laughed, and for a moment, it ignored the strings, forgot about Hannah. *You finally admit that?* it asked. *After all these years . . .*

Gregg placed mental arms around the power, using its momentary lapse to take it off balance and pull it back inside. For long seconds they struggled, wrestling inside Gregg. When he finally managed to throw Puppetman down, to place the cage around it once more, Gregg was exhausted. He came back to reality slowly, as if he'd been gone hours.

It had been only a moment. Hannah shook her head as if

ridding herself of the shreds of a bad dream and pulled aside the shield on the timer.

"Any last reservations?" she asked, her forefinger poised above the button.

The Black Dog coughed and didn't answer. "Gregg?" Hannah asked.

"Do it," he told her, ignoring the shrill denial inside him.

Hannah pressed down. There was a soft click, then the timer on the bomb hummed, the numbers flickering on the LED display:

10:00

9:59

9:58

As Ray had wandered through the Old City looking for Harvest, he'd noticed medical stations flying the UN flag. He took Quasiman to the nearest one. They had to be careful not to step on any of the dead or dying patients lying on stretchers or the pavement, stacked up around the building that had once been a church.

Ray pushed through to a man in a once-white coat wearing a UN armband and carrying a clipboard. "He's got a vaccine for the Trump!" Ray announced, pushing Quasiman forward. "Some kind of counter-virus or something . . ."

"Really." The doctor looked unspeakably weary. "And who are you?"

Ray drew himself up straight. "My name is Billy Ray. I'm a Special Agent for the US government."

"Go away," the doctor said, "we're very busy here."

Ray grabbed the doctor's arm. He put steel in the grip and in his voice. "Listen, moron, Quasiman here came from halfway around the world to save our asses. Give him a chance! Tell him what you've got, Quasi."

The hunchback turned blank eyes on Ray. "What do I have?"

"Oh, Jesus, don't space out on me now!"

The doctor would have looked panicky if he'd had the strength. He tried without much energy and no success to pull away from Ray. "Young man—"

A woman approached, interrupting them. "What's going on here?" She, too, looked tired and feverish.

"This man is insane, Sheila. He's babbling about a cure for the Black Trump." She peered at him blearily. And suddenly Ray knew her . . .

"I'm a government agent," Ray said desperately. "I met you in Atlanta, at the Democratic convention in '88. Some reception for Hartmann delegates . . . asked you out. You turned me down. Remember?"

"Ray . . . Billy Ray." The name seemed to suddenly stick in her conscious. "Yes, I remember." She looked closely at him. "What happened to your face?"

Ray waved it aside. "I screwed it up so that I could go underground and join the Twisted Fists. Listen! Quasiman has a cure for the Black Trump. Well, not a cure, really, a vaccine or something. He brought it from Mark Meadows."

"Meadows? Mark Meadows?" She seemed to be having problems following Ray's story.

"Yes. Mark. Meadows. The biochemist. Got it?"

Davidson nodded. "Yes. Yes, I think I do."

"This is nonsense," the doctor said. "Even if this man is who he says he is, why, we don't know what that, that other fellow has. We have to test it, double-blind—"

"Test my ass!" Ray roared. "What the fuck difference does it make? Everyone here is dead, anyway! What could it hurt?"

Davidson seemed to shake off her lethargy. "Yes, he's right. Meadows is a brilliant biochemist. If he's succeeded, we'll soon know. If he hasn't . . . Well . . ." Her voice trailed off, hopelessly. "We'll administer the serum."

"I won't allow this . . . this *travesty*!" the doctor said. "I'll—"

"You'll *what*?" Ray said, picking him up one-handed and slamming him against a wall. The doctor fell silent. Ray dropped him.

Quasiman seemed to rouse himself as Ray unstrapped the canister from his back. "Hannah," he said distinctly. "Don't!" And he vanished.

Ray was left holding the canister of the Overtrump.

"Don't what?" Sheila Davidson asked.

Ray turned to her. He noticed for the first time that her perspiration was tinged with blood. "Uh . . . don't waste time. Spray everyone. Listen, why don't you take some of this stuff yourself? It couldn't hurt."

She smiled at him, but it was a pained, wan smile. "No. I don't suppose it could . . ."

Hannah sank down, sitting with her back to the ugly device. She seemed empty. There were no colors around her at all.

"We've got company," the Black Dog said from alongside the door. They could all hear it: muffled shouts, and hammering on the warehouse doors. The doors bowed, and they could glimpse torchlight between them and the front rank of a crowd. There were angry faces there, joker and nat alike, and their fury swelled like a red wave, threatening to tear down the doors all by itself. Gregg shivered with the power of the crowd-emotions. "The locks aren't going to hold."

"Stay back!" Hannah shouted at them, her voice small

against the growing roar outside. Something hard rammed the doors, bending them. "There's a bomb in here! Get away!" Hannah glanced at Gregg. *She's mine! Mine!* "They could still stop us," she said. "I wish the damn thing would hurry *up*!" Then she laughed, almost hysterically. "Listen to me," she said. "Rooting for a damn nuclear explosion."

Gregg looked around the room; the curved steel plates that had once covered the nuke were leaning against the walls of the room. Gregg went to one of them and sniffed its delightful sheen. "Hannah," he said. "Grab these. Put them in front of the door. That's it—jam them in tight. Here, take this bar and stick it on like a brace . . ." Gregg directed the building of a loose barrier of metal around the door. In a few minutes, they had an impressive heap in front of the door.

"That's not going to keep anyone out," Hannah said. "None of it's attached to anything."

"Give me a second . . ."

Gregg scrambled up until he stood on top of the heap. He looked at the metal, let its delicious tang fill him.

And he vomited, carefully, again and again, as he moved around the mess. In a few moments, the metal began to sag and fuse, the plates melting into each other, the bars and braces fusing into the adjoining pieces. The biological welds created a massive unit of steel: plates, bars, hinges, and locks, all lumped around the wood and effectively sealing them in.

"There," Gregg told Hannah and Puppetman. "Now it's over. Forever. No way out, no way in." *And there's nothing you can do about it*, he told Puppetman. *Nothing.*

Inside, Puppetman fumed. Gregg huddled by Hannah and wondered what death would feel like. He snuck a glance at the LEDs.

6:00

5:59

For four minutes now, they'd had time to contemplate their lives, and their deaths. There was nothing to say. None of them spoke. Gregg wondered if there was silence in Hannah or the Black Dog's minds. There certainly was none inside his.

There's still time to stop it! Still time!

All of Gregg's strength went to keeping Puppetman down. He had nothing left for anything else.

"Hannah?"

The voice startled all of them. Hannah scrambled to her feet, trying to bring the Black Dog's Uzi to bear. Gregg skittered reflexively back several feet until he bumped into the wheel of the bomb trailer. Hannah fumbled with the safety, then laughed. "Quasi!" she shouted, dropping the Uzi and hugging the joker. Then the laughter died. "Oh, Quasi, you have to leave here. Now."

"Hell, yes," Gregg said excitedly. Optimism suddenly flooded through him.

We're going to get out of this! We're going to LIVE! "And he can take us with him." Inside, Puppetman suddenly yammered in hope.

"One at a time. That's all I can do."

"Hey," Gregg told the hunchback, and a voice echoed him from inside. *He's got to take you first. Chances are he'll take Hannah somewhere else and then totally forget what he's doing. He'll never make it back in time. You first . . . US first . . .* "No problem. One at a time, then."

"Gregg," Hannah said. She waved a hand at the bomb, at the timing mechanism. "Remember this?"

"So what?" Gregg told her. "It's all set. *We're* not infected, Hannah. There's no reason we *have* to die here. Not now. The bomb will go off on its own. Let it do it while we're somewhere else."

"No," Quasi said.

I'll goddamn MAKE you . . . Puppetman seethed. *Let me have him, Greggie.* Almost, Gregg let the power loose, but he held it back another moment. "Quasi, we don't exactly have a lot of time for discussion here."

"Someone has to stay. I've seen it."

"Why, Quasi?" Hannah asked far more gently than Gregg would have. "Why does someone have to stay?"

"The Overtrump," Quasiman answered. "I brought the . . ." He seemed to forget the word, then his face brightened. ". . . stuff. From Mark." Quasiman stopped. His left hand disappeared and his gaze went vacant. A thin line of drool trickled from one side of his mouth.

Hannah took Quasiman's head in her hands, forcing him to look at her and causing a surge of irrational jealousy in Gregg. "Quasi, please. What are you trying to say?"

For long seconds, there was no answer. "Quasi . . ." Hannah said again, and the joker shook himself. He smiled at her, and Gregg could feel again the outwelling colors of his love for Hannah. "A cold," he told her. "Complete sentences. The Overtrump is the cure . . . Like a cold . . . only then you don't get the Black Trump . . ."

"Oh, God." Hannah let her hands drop. She looked at Quasiman as if he were an accusation. "You're not joking? It works?"

"Works," Quasi nodded. "Working already. You need to stop . . ." For a second, Quasiman's entire upper body winked out of existence, returning eerily a moment later. "I . . ." he said. "I need to take Hannah with me. I . . . can't hold it together any longer. It's getting too hard. I'll . . . forget." The agony in his voice was exquisite. Puppetman howled.

"Going now," Quasiman said. "Hannah . . ." He opened his arms. Hannah looked back at Gregg.

"Quasi, I . . ." Gregg could see the hesitation in her, the

guilt. Puppetman screamed to be released. *She doesn't want to be the one to go. Look at the fear, the guilt, the uncertainty. This is EASY, I tell you. Let me loose and I can make her refuse Quasiman. I can make her say "Take him. Take Gregg." She loves you. She thinks life's dealt you an unfair hand and just a push will make her willing to exchange her life for yours. Just a push . . .*

"I can't leave Gregg," Hannah finished. "Don't you see?" Hannah cried. "We *can't* stop the nuke. It's already too late for Jerusalem." Her face had gone pale, and the colors of guilt and shame surged around her like a wild surf. "God, I've killed all those innocent people . . ."

"It's not too late," the Black Dog husked out. "Remember what I said about the dance, how everything has to go off at just the right time? Set off the conventionals too early, and you'll get a dandy explosion and scatter bits of radioactive material around, but you *won't* get a nuclear explosion."

"How do we do that?"

"Yank the wires. That's the simplest way."

Let me out! I can save US now. To hell with Hannah, let her deal with this.

Quasi won't take me, Gregg told the voice.

Quasi'll do whatever Hannah asks him to do. You know that. Let me OUT!

She'll die if we do that.

So fucking what? WE'LL live.

Puppetman shook the bars. They bent under the pressure, creaking. Gregg's head felt as if it was about to crack, and all the poison inside would come pouring out, all the pain and death he'd accumulated over the years, pouring out like a vile river, pulsing and hot as lava. *OUT!* Puppetman screamed, and the power burst from Gregg's hold. He could see it, a physical presence, a smoky, wraithlike creature that rode the strings connecting Gregg to the others. *Fuck you, Greggie! You never controlled me. Never!* Puppetman flew toward Hannah, already pulling the strings to her mind, and Gregg leapt after it. His stubby arms reached out, and the puppet's mittens of hands clenched at the power's body. He caught hold, and Puppetman wrenched in his grasp, turning and twisting as it tried to escape.

Goddamn you! You can't do this to her. You can't.

You can't stop me, Greggie!

"Gregg, what's the matter with you? What the hell's going on?" Hannah cried out as Gregg, his body contorted from the effort of holding Puppetman, went caroming around the room. "Gregg!" He caught a glimpse of Quasi's face, mouth gaping wide in surprise.

"He's gone crazy," the Black Dog said, levering himself onto his feet. Blood soaked his fingers and his clothes. "He's fighting *himself.*"

Puppetman scrabbled for Hannah, its ebon fingers clutching her strings desperately. Gregg pulled it back, slamming Puppetman against the bomb's truck bed. With each blow, its face changed, an endless parade of faces, each of them someone he'd taken as a puppet: Peanut, Kahina, Hiram Worchester . . . *Stop! You're hurting me!* each of them screamed, but Gregg continued. "Quasi!" Gregg shouted over his shoulder. "Take her! Go!"

Quasi shook his head as if lost, then reached out with powerful hands and pulled Hannah to him. "Go *on!*" Gregg shouted again.

"Gregg, we can't—" Hannah began.

If the initial explosion isn't shaped exactly the right way, or if it goes off early or late, then . . . Puppetman heard Gregg's thought also, and the power redoubled its efforts to get free. *You can't do that! I won't let you toss away my life like that. You want to do something a little good here, fine. You want to kill as few people as possible, great. Let HER do it—we can make her, we can twist her around until she fucking BEGS you to go . . .*

"Damn it, don't you understand? We can do something right. We can finally, really, do something right," Gregg answered, without realizing that he spoke aloud. Puppetman struck at him with ghostly fists. The power writhed, changing shape: Now it was Ellen's tormented shape before him, holding in her hands their dead child, and Gregg wailed. "No!"

"Gregg—"

"Get out of here!"

Gregg found the strings that led from Puppetman to Hannah. He began to tear them loose of the power, bloodily, his hands digging into the creature's death-cold entrails. Puppetman wailed as they tore loose. *You can't do this!*

In Quasiman's arms, Hannah looked back at Gregg, her eyes wide with uncertainty and guilt, and both he and Puppetman felt her decision crystallize in the midst of the shades even as he pulled free the last of the strings. "Gregg, I lo—" Hannah stopped.

"I know," he told her, panting, holding the power back even as it twisted and clawed, as it attempted to stuff the strings back into itself. He could hear the screaming: in the voice of Mackie Messer, of Andrea, of Succubus, of Chrysalis and Gimli and Sara Morgenstern. It screamed in Gregg's voice, the voice Gregg had once had. "I've always known. Now please go. Quickly."

And then she and Quasiman were gone. The only sound was the Black Dog's labored breathing and the silent screaming of Puppetman, inside.

Ray headed for the nearest manhole cover, pulled it up, and climbed down. Inside the tunnel it was dark and cool, almost restful. He was tempted to close his eyes for a moment, but he knew that if he closed them now he never would open them again.

Don't. Quasiman had said . . . and somehow Ray had known.

He plunged into the tunnel, cursing the Fists and their crazy leader. The bastard must be planning to use the nuke to sterilize the city, to bomb the Black Trump out of existence. Him and Hartmann and that bimbo Hannah Davis. Who the hell had appointed them God?

As he ran he passed others in the tunnels. Some were running, too. Others' running days were over. He stopped some, demanding to be led to the bomb, demanding to see the Black Dog, but they either didn't know or were too far gone in disease or panic to help him.

He was past desperation—desperation would have been peace of mind compared to the state he was in—when he finally ran into the familiar face he was praying for.

"Owl! Owl! It's me, Mumbles. Billy Ray!"

The teenager looked up from where he was slumped in a niche in the corridor. At first Ray thought the kid was sick or delirious, but when he grabbed him and looked close he saw that Owl had just been crying.

"Owl, snap out of it! I need help!"

"I . . . I can't find *anyone*," he sobbed. "I can't find Needles or Zoe. Jellyhead is gone and Jan and Angel. I don't want to die alone!"

"It's all right, kid." For a second he crushed Owl to him, holding him in a fierce hug that surprised even himself. "It's okay to be scared. Jesus, you're just a kid. But listen, you're not going to die. Okay?"

He held Owl at arm's length. Owl sniffled. "Really?"

"We've got a shot at it, kid. There's an Overtrump. It's being distributed now. But tell me, is the Dog going to blow the nuke?"

Owl nodded, wiping the snot that was running out of his nose. "He said he had to blow the city to save the world."

"Well, he doesn't know shit. The world's been saved." *I hope*, Ray said quietly to himself. "Do you know where the bomb is?"

Owl nodded.

"Take me there. *Fast!*"

Owl sniffed again and wiped his nose on his sleeve. They moved off together under the Old City.

Balthazar held Zoe with an iron grip and forced his way into the crowd. Nats, jokers, their differences seemed small in the pervading terror. Zoe twisted, fighting to get back to Anne, to Angel. Zoe managed to get a quick look behind her; Angel was on his feet, and *Jan!* Jan supported him on one side, Anne on the other, the three of them in the center of the phalanx of Fists behind Balthazar.

Ahead of them, a battered truck labored toward the Zion Gate, a truck that threatened to collapse under the weight of what seemed to be a thousand people who fought one another in an effort to cling to the battered boards on its sides. Balthazar struggled toward it.

"Bruckner!" Balthazar yelled.

Shortcut. My God, we can get out of here—

The Fists clubbed people out of their way to make a path toward the tailgate of the truck. Someone reached a three-fingered hand down to Zoe and pulled her aboard.

Angel, Jan, and Anne tumbled in beside her. The truck stank of chickenshit. An occasional white feather floated free and out into the street.

Zoe tried to get farther forward, tried to make space for Balthazar, who clung to one of the slats on the truck's side and aimed his rifle at the crowd that followed the truck. The truck's gears ground against each other in agony.

"Only chance," Balthazar panted. "Countdown's running!"

The nuke! The Black Dog was setting off the nuke?

Anne held Angelfish on her lap and sheltered him as best she could with her shoulders, Michelangelo's *Pieta*—Jan pressed a wad of her skirt against the wound on Angel's side; bright blood seeped around the girl's fingers. The truck side-swiped a Mercedes and slewed the other way, its tires screeching. Bruckner was getting up some speed, but they were still within the city walls.

Balthazar slammed the butt of his rifle, once, twice, on a pair of hands that clung to the tailgate. He was crying, and he kicked at another joker who tried to climb aboard.

Zoe understood his pain, the necessity of what he was doing; Bruckner had to get the truck out the gate and up to speed or they couldn't get gone, couldn't save even the few who had managed to fight their way onto this ark. Jan, Mama, Angelfish, if he lived, the three-fingered joker who had helped pull Zoe aboard, the others who whimpered and clung to one another in the crowded truck. All of them might survive, if Bruckner could do his trick with distance.

"Zoe!" Balthazar yelled. "Can you help Bruckner?"

He motioned toward the cab.

Zoe nodded. "I can *try!*" she yelled.

Hands pushed her to her feet. Jan looked up from where she huddled by Angelfish, Jan's eyes glowing bright with terror and hope in the smoky, sand-filled air.

Get Jan out! Save her!

Bjorn's voice bellowed louder than the roar of the truck's laboring engine.

Save these few, not the whole world, but they are dear and precious; yes, Daddy, I'll try.

Jokers shifted out of Zoe's way, pushed her, lifted her over their bodies and forward toward the cab.

Help Bruckner? If she could, she would animate the whole damned truck, give it wings, fly it over the Zion Gate.

The three-fingered joker smiled at Zoe as she was handed over him. He smiled, and coughed, and covered his face with his hand. He stared, puzzled, at the bloody mucus in his palm.

Zoe tumbled through the window of the cab and over the lap of a rifle-wielding Fist before the realization struck her.

The joker was dying. *We carry the Black Trump. Can't leave. Can't take the Black Trump out of the City. Can't.*

"You, is it?" Bruckner's massive arms fought the rust-stained wheel of the rickety truck.

"Yeah. Zoe." She sat wedged between Bruckner and a Fist with a rifle who peppered the crowd with bullets to try to clear a way for the roaring truck.

The truck crashed through a barrier of sellers' carts, old chairs, scrap wood. They flew aside, revealing a more substantial barricade made of parked cars. Bruckner geared the truck down and bulldozed his way through, while metal screeched and glass shattered. The gate was not a hundred yards away. Beyond it, Zoe caught a glimpse of the UN flag, whipping in the yellow gusts of the simoom.

We carry the Black Trump in a rusty truck and all of them will die, nats, babies, murderers, and innocents. She stared at the rusty steering wheel.

Rust. Aluminum. Thermite!

I'm sorry, Bruckner, but we can't leave. We die here. I'm sorry, Anne.

Zoe leaned forward and blew, gently, at the rust on the steering column, at the set of aluminum keys that dangled from the dashboard. Ferrous oxide, aluminum oxide. She turned her head and kissed the rifle barrel beside her, magnesium for a catalyst—

"Bloody hell!" Bruckner screamed. He lifted his scorched hands away from the red heat of the steering wheel as the reaction catalyzed every bit of steel in the truck into glowing heat, as the engine froze, as the wheels fused into solid masses of angry, reactive metal.

The truck stopped dead with its front bumper crumpled into the ramparts of the Zion Gate.

Smoke, wails of terror, blasts of rifle fire, Zoe could see only Bruckner's fist, as large as a country ham. The fist seemed to expand as it drove toward her jaw.

She heard the smack as it connected.

The world turned red and then went black.

"Up there," Owl said, "at the end of the cul-de-sac. They've stashed the bomb in the garage."

"All right." Ray took Owl by the shoulders. "They're distributing the Overtrump at a UN medical station in the old church on Chabad Street. Know where that is?"

Owl nodded. "What about the bomb?"

"Don't worry about that. I'll take care of it."

Owl nodded again. "I—"

"Owl, it was great working with you, but if you don't get going, neither of us is ever going to pull another caper again."

Owl flashed a smile that made him look like a real kid. "Okay. Thanks, Mumbles. Good luck."

"Good luck," Ray said, already climbing up the rungs of the ladder to the street above.

This part of the Old City looked like a ghost town. Ray went up to the garage doors and shoved. They were locked. He thought about knocking for a second, then figured, *Screw it.* He put his good shoulder to the door and pushed. It gave a little but was locked from the inside. He looked at the door. The wood was thick but old. He backed up, gave a running start, and smashed into it, shoulder first. There was groaning and complaining and some wood even splintered off the door. Ray backed up again, charged it, smashed into it, and it started to sag inward.

Cursing his aching shoulder, he got his hands around one of the door panels and yanked. The lock pad yielded, pulling out of the wooden door, and the panel collapsed.

With Hannah gone, Gregg let go of Puppetman. Near him, the LED glowed, the numbers of its face changing inexorably.

1:00

0:59

Puppetman lay still, beaten. Strings trailed from his fingers, the ends frayed. *Why did you do that?* it asked him. *Why? We could have* lived.

I've lived that way before, Gregg told it. *And I ended up living your life, not mine.*

Someone was hammering on the doors, and Gregg could sense a familiar presence close by. "There's no way to disable the nuke other than setting off the explosives early?" he asked the Black Dog again. "You're sure?" The Black Dog just nodded, his mask hardly moving. The leader of the Fists was fighting to remain conscious, the blood loss from his wounds terrible. For a moment, he thought of using Puppetman, of forcing the Black Dog to yank the wires while Gregg fled, but the Black Dog was too weak. There was no strength left in him.

I don't have a choice.

As Puppetman watched, sullen, defeated, Gregg went to the timing mechanism. Yellow hands, his joker hands, grasped the knot of wires trailing from it to the bomb. "It's time for me to do something for myself," he said. As he spoke, the doors to the garage screeched as they were forced open by superhuman strength. Billy Ray stood in the doorway.

"Hey!" Billy Ray yelled. He paused, seeing Gregg with his hands on the timer.

"I never said thanks, Billy, and I'm sorry," Gregg called out to Ray. "And I'm sorry for this, too."

Gregg yanked the wires free of the timer.

Damnation roared around Ray and he closed his eyes. Something wet and squishy slapped him in the face and chest and he opened his eyes, blinking.

He wasn't dead. He wasn't atomized or blown into green glowing bits. He was, however, bleeding. He put his hand to his face and brought it away covered with some kind of green goo. He suddenly realized that it wasn't blood, even, but stuff from the inside of the caterpillar that had been blasted all over the inside of the garage.

Caterpillar parts were everywhere. An abdominal segment with three pairs of attached legs was running in circles around the floor. As Ray watched, it keeled over, kicked a few times, and was still.

"Jesus, Hartmann . . ." The garage groaned and began to collapse. One of the walls looked as if it could come down any second.

Ray walked to where the Black Dog lay in the puddle. The Fist leader was unconscious. He'd caught some shrapnel. For once Ray had been lucky. He'd only been hit by caterpillar parts. He wondered what had happened, then realized that

Hartmann must have pulled the plug on the nuclear explosion but couldn't stop the conventional triggering mechanism from going off. He looked at the bits of caterpillar scattered all over the room.

"Jesus, Hartmann, I guess you were a hero after all."

The Dog moaned. Ray pulled him out from under the rubble and checked him over quickly.

"Goddamn," Ray said aloud. He'd accomplished his mission. He'd prevented the nuke from going off and he'd captured the Black Dog himself. "Goddamn," he repeated.

There was only one more thing he had to do.

Epilogue

April Harvest sat behind her desk, read-
ing *The Washington Times* and shaking her head. She couldn't
understand how it had happened, but the Sharks had failed
again. Obviously, there was some kind of cover-up going on;
what she read in the paper just didn't make sense. There was,
for example, this nonsense about the Trump also proving fatal
to nats. Obvious blather, designed to make the Sharks look bad
in the eyes of the world.

She closed the paper with a sigh.

At least she'd avoided detection. Perhaps Pan Rudo was
still alive. There'd been no mention of him in the paper, but
that was to be expected. He'd get in touch, probably, as soon as
he could.

It was too bad she'd had to kill Johnson, but she couldn't
risk him spilling everything to Ray. Ray . . . He was a fool,
but . . .

Someone knocked sharply on her office door and she
looked up.

"Come in."

"Hello, lover."

The blood washed out of her face like it'd been sucked away
by a vacuum cleaner. She opened her mouth to speak, but no

words came out as Ray sauntered into her office and perched jauntily on the edge of her desk.

"Surprised to see me?"

"I—I—I—"

"I bet you are." He grinned his usual boyish grin. His normal face was back, looking, in fact, even better than when she'd first met him. He held himself a little stiffly, as if he still hurt somewhere, but then, as long as she'd known him, Billy Ray had hurt somewhere.

"How—"

Ray held up his hand, shaking his head. "We don't have much time and I've got some stuff I have to say." He sighed. "You are beautiful, you know, and I love you. I do. It's too bad you're such a murderous bitch."

Harvest didn't know what was more stunning, Ray's sudden appearance or his incredible confession. "Billy, I—"

"Stow it," Ray said. "I can forgive you for trying to kill me. What the hell, I'll bet a lot of people would like to have the guts to try it themselves. Maybe I can even forgive you for being a Shark and doing what you did to all those innocent people. I don't know. But my forgiveness is sort of beside the point. There's a lot of people you have to answer to, April. And you're going to."

She stood up. "What do you mean, Billy?"

"I stopped by Nephi's office before coming here. He was really surprised to see me, seeing as how you'd said I'd been killed at Rudo's lab and all. But he caught on quick when I told him the real story. He should be here any second to arrest you. I asked him for a minute or two with you so we could talk over some things."

Harvest's mind was in a whirl. She collapsed again in her desk chair. "If you love me—"

"What? I'd let you walk?" Ray shook his head. "I may not

be very bright, but I'm not a chump. Not your chump, not any-one's."

They locked eyes for what seemed like a long time. Ray had left the door to her office open and both heard hurried foot-steps coming down the hall.

"There's a gun in the desk drawer," Ray said. "You could go for it."

Harvest smiled. It was a cold, brittle smile that almost cracked but didn't. "As it turns out," she said, "you're too fast for me."

"Yeah. I guess I am."

Nephi Callendar stood at the door. He announced in a florid, dramatic voice, "Agent Harvest, I'm here to arrest you for murder, attempted murder, assault, conspiracy to commit murder—"

"She knows, Nehi," Ray said, without taking his eyes off her.

She stood. "I know," she said and held her hands up, wrists exposed and ready for the cuffs Ray had taken out of his pocket.

He walked along the beach with the sunset sea breeze ruf-fling his tawny hair. He looked like any other surfer dude in Southern California, with his bare, muscular golden-tanned chest and faded dungarees, except perhaps for the combat boots crunching the wet sand.

He was Radical, and he was a free man. There were still fed-eral warrants outstanding for Mark Meadows and his known aliases, which was to say, his "friends." But while the authori-ties might well have had certain questions as to why and how the notorious revolutionary ace Radical had suddenly turned up, a quarter century after his sole known appearance at People's Park and looking not a day older, they had no grounds for asking them. Nor had they any way of linking him to the furtive Mark, not any inkling of such a connection.

So Radical could walk the SoCal beach as he pleased, without looking over his shoulder for the feds. However interested in him they might have been, the authorities had to tread warily. Because, after all, he had saved the world.

He laughed aloud, startling some seagulls standing shin-deep in surf into complaining flight. "This old world is gonna see some *changes* made," he promised the birds, glowing pale orange in the sunset.

Approaching through the mauve gloom he saw two tall figures, one slim and female, one male and almost gaunt, with a brush of hair white as the gulls' wings. As they grew closer, it was apparent that the man held himself rigidly upright against years whose weight was evident in the way he walked.

They stopped, facing each other a few feet apart: Radical on one side, Mark's father and daughter on the other. Sprout clung to her grandfather, who wore shorts and a Hawaiian shirt that would have been colorful in daylight. It seemed inappropriate to the military spareness of his frame. He was like some antique weapon, a government Colt pistol or Mustang fighter, worn but still functional, possessed of nothing nonessential.

"Where's Mark?" General Meadows asked. His voice grated. Throat cancer, recently diagnosed, would likely kill him in a few months, though he was scheduled for surgery.

Looking into the old man's eyes, blue as the sky where he had spent his adult life, Radical touched fingertips to his sternum. "In here," he said.

The old man shook his head. "I don't understand any of this," he said. "Mark never talked to me about any of this ace business. I saw on the news that he could turn into other people, somehow. But I still don't *understand*." He looked down at the sand, looked up again. "The others went away in an hour," he said, more huskily than before. "Why are you still here instead of my son?"

Because I was the one who was always meant to be, I am strongest. I am Destiny. But somehow he could not say these things to this proud, erect, doomed old man.

"I don't know," he said, and that was truth, too. "I don't know how to get Mark back. For now"—he spread his hands—"I'm the one who's here."

He turned to the girl, who had her arms around the old general and looked at Radical with huge eyes.

"Sprout," he said, holding out his arms, "come give me a hug, honey."

She detached herself from her grandfather reluctantly, so that contact between them was broken like something physical, a twig or the surface of a bubble. She stared at Radical with huge, uncertain eyes. The lights of a distant pier reflected in them in strange constellations.

"You're one of Daddy's friends?" she asked in a hesitant, little girl voice. Without waiting she flew to him, threw her arms around his neck, hugged him fiercely.

He took her in arms twice as strong as the strongest man's. "I'm your daddy," he said, stroking her hair.

She burst into tears.

On a cool, pleasant autumn day, the site of the mass grave that held the victims of the Black Trump was a pleasant place, high and quiet. Vineyards and bright green fields marched down the valleys. In the distance, the quiet purple hills of the Holy Land looked serene and peaceful.

Jan clung to Needles's hand. Jan was quieter these days,

and she'd always been a sort of quiet kid. She wasn't always in tears anymore; she hadn't cried for almost a week.

It was mean of Zoe to bring her here, Needles thought, but he hadn't tried to argue with Zoe about it, and Jan had wanted to come.

Zoe hadn't said a single word for weeks after the UN had brought the Overtrump into the quarter. Then she'd pulled a chair up to her workstation in the tiny apartment and asked Jan how school was going, just like nothing had happened. Zoe stayed in the net most of the time, the light from the computer screen reflecting on her thin face in the dark hours of the night, a haunted, driven woman researching some project she wouldn't talk about.

Personally, Needles figured she was seriously tweaked in the head. Seriously gone.

Zoe walked around the perimeter of the square of raw earth, her attention on the plantings of rose of Sharon. Jan brought out the jug she'd carried and watered one of the shrubs—it was a new tradition in Jerusalem, to carry water here and tend the flowers.

Jan got up, brushed dust from the knees of her skirt, and walked to a trench cut deep and square in the dry yellow rock of the hills.

"Next week they'll set up the marble helix," Jan said.

Zoe had finished her lonely tour. Dressed in black, as she always was now, she came up to the pit in the earth and stared into it.

"It won't be like the Vietnam memorial. The names won't be carved in it. Anne Harris. Balthazar Delacourt. James Kilburn. James Russo. The thousand others, bits of bone that came out of the crematoriums after they burned the infected bodies, skulls that no one could identify. Nobody will remember them. Nobody cares. It's last week's news."

Jimmy and Jimmy were Owl and Angelfish, Needles thought, *no matter what Zoe calls them now, and I care. I'll always care.*

We'll never know exactly how they died—most of them.

I remember too much, Zoe. I remember running for home when Hannah and Hartmann sent me away, and how it felt when there was nobody there. I looked for you, for Anne, for Angel.

I saw Balthazar die. People boiled out of that rickety stalled truck. The UN started yelling through a loudspeaker when we tried to rush the gates, and Balthazar heard what they said, that there was a cure. Some joker shot him because they thought he was trying to keep us inside to die.

Angel didn't die of Trump. Angel bled to death. The medics got us to line up and sniff Overtrump, but Anne was coughing by then. Owl—the Trump killed him.

"There's a lot to be learned from last week's news. From history. I have names, places, actions that people recorded on film, in writing. Addresses."

Zoe stood at the edge of the empty pit, her fists clenched so tight at her sides that her arms shook.

"Jack Braun. Thomas Tudbury. Nephi Callendar. A lot of names. The ones who weren't here. The ones who didn't help us, and some of the ones who *thought* they knew what was best for us."

"Like Tachyon?" Jan asked.

"*Tachyon!*" Zoe spit the word. "He's in a category all of his own!"

"What do you plan to do?" Needles asked.

"Kill them."

Zoe turned her back on the memorial and started downhill toward Jerusalem, her long black skirts lashing at her ankles.

— — —

"Why did they give *you* the key to the city?" Jerry Strauss complained as the hostess led them to the big booth in back where Peter Pann was waiting. "I did just as much as you."

"They gave the key to the city to the *agency*," Jay said. "I just accepted it, that's all. What are you complaining about? You got to meet John Woo, didn't you?" He slid into the booth.

Peter looked up from the menu. "Look at these fucking prices. This better be a business lunch." A tink was buzzing around his head, as usual. He swatted at it with the menu, missed, swore.

Jay sighed. "It's great to be home."

Bradley Finn looked over the seating and sighed. "They don't design restaurant booths to accommodate people like me."

"So stand in the aisle the way you usually do," Jay said. "It always makes the waiters so happy." He opened his menu. His face was still mostly black and green and purple, and the bandages made him look like the Mummy's abused child, but he was bound and determined to get some solid food. He'd been living on fruit juice and painkillers all the way from China.

Jerry was still grousing. "I was the one who took out Eric Fleming. That should have been worth the key to the city. And Sascha and I found Mark Meadows before you did. I was the one who rescued Sprout."

"You were the one who got caught and wound up with your tits in a wringer," Jay reminded him. "Actually, they were Sprout's tits, but never mind."

The menu was black and glossy and speckled with stars, like the ceiling overhead. STARFIELDS, it said, and under that, FOOD THAT'S OUT OF THIS WORLD. Jay looked down at the lunch selections and wondered why he bothered. He couldn't pronounce the Takisian words and he knew the cuisine by heart.

He'd been forced to sample every dish when Hastet was fine-tuning her menu.

Finn was looking over the selections curiously. "What do you recommend? I've never had Takisian food before."

"Better get used to it," Jay said.

"Pardon?" Finn said with a puzzled look.

Jerry leaned over and pointed out some items. "Here, these are all very good. Little pastries full of spiced meats and nuts and these crunchy little sprouts, very delicate."

Peter said, "You missed it, Finn. On Thursday they serve bales of hay in this *divine* hot oat sauce." He took out a long black cigar, lit up, grinned.

Finn lowered his menu. "This is the smoke-free section. And I warned you about the horse jokes, Pan."

"*Pahn*," Peter said. "It's Dutch." He blew a smoke ring across the table at Finn and smiled.

Finn raised his hands slowly and began to clap.

Peter sat up, frowning. "Cut that out," he said. A second tink winked into existence and began to flit around his head. Finn kept on clapping. "I mean it," Peter said. A third tink appeared, then a fourth. "You mangy son of a fucking mare," Peter swore. "Here, fuck you, you win, Seabiscuit." He ground out his cigar, but Finn just clapped faster, smiling.

"Oh, applause, applause, did someone do something *wonderful*?" their waiter asked as he came over to the table. He was a tall, slender young man with a gorgeous tumble of blond hair spilling out from beneath his plumed white cavalier's hat.

"Clap if you want a big tip," Finn told him.

The waiter began to applaud enthusiastically, chanting, "Oh, I *do* believe in fairies, I *do*, I *do*."

"*Stop it*, you shits," Peter yelled, swatting at tinks with his menu. He bopped Jerry on the head.

Finn looked around at the lunch crowd. "Clap if you want a

free meal," he shouted out. The whole restaurant burst into thunderous applause. In seconds there were so many tinks buzzing around that Jay could hardly see Peter's face. "I'll get you for this," Peter promised Finn, as he leapt out of his seat. "You're Alpo, I swear." He fled the restaurant at a dead run, cursing a blue streak, a cloud of tinks trailing after him.

"Well, wasn't *that* refreshing," the waiter said when the clapping had died down. He wore purple pantaloons, a gold lamé waistcoat over a red silk shirt, a long white scarf, and matching boots in a suede soft as butter. All the waiters at Starfields dressed like Dr. Tachyon. It was part of the Takisian ambience.

"Very refreshing," Jay agreed. He nodded over at Finn. "All the free meals go on his tab."

"It was worth it," Finn said.

"I'm Rex, and I'll be your waiter today," the waiter said.

"Real good," Jay returned. "I'm Jay and this is Bradley and this other guy is nobody. We'll be your customers."

"What happened to your face?" Rex asked cheerfully.

"If you were really a psi lord, you'd know," Jay pointed out. "I'll have a patty melt. Double onions."

Rex looked hurt. "Oooh, I'm afraid we don't have a patty melt, Jay," he said, with sincere distress.

"You're new here, aren't you?" Jay said. "Tell Hastet to fry the onions until they turn black and scream for mercy."

"I'll have the Ilkazam pie," Jerry said. "No anchovies."

Finn pointed at something on the menu. "This."

Rex collected their drink orders and left. "It doesn't feel right, sitting here ordering lunch when so many people are dead," Finn said after he had gone.

"We saved the world," Jay said. "We deserve lunch. Someday I'm going to die, and millions of people are going to eat patty melts anyway. I'm just returning the favor. In advance."

"Be serious for once," Finn said. "How are we going to get Clara and all the others out of prison?"

"I've got three cunning plans, depending on what powers we want to use," Jay said. He ticked them off. "One, we stage a raid on Governors Island and I pop everybody out."

"You tried that," Finn protested.

"I knew it seemed familiar," Jay agreed. "Two, Jerry here turns into Clara and takes her place."

Finn looked puzzled. "What about Dutton and Father Squid and the rest? And your agent, what's her name, Topper? And if Jerry takes Clara's place, how do we get *him* out?"

"Hey, did I say these plans were perfect?" Jay shrugged. "Three, we fly to Washington, take that White House tour, and Jerry turns into President Barnett and pardons everybody."

To Jay's horror, Jerry rubbed his chin thoughtfully. "Barnett," he mused. "Well, I . . ."

Jay cut him off quickly. "Or we could use lawyers. The arrests were illegal, and Dutton is even richer than you are. So we hire Alan Dershowitz or Dr. Praetorius and turn them loose." Jay toyed with his fork, tapping it gently against his water glass. The crystal rang softly. "No one committed any crimes except Topper, and she's cute, and we did save the world. The feds will deal."

"What if they don't?" Jerry wanted to know.

"Then we bake Melissa a cake with a top hat inside."

The unmistakable scent of burnt onions filled the air. Hastet dropped a patty melt on the table in front of him. "Here, I hope we kept it under the flamethrower long enough."

"My little *wanei*," Jay said, chucking her under the chin.

"Do I know you?" She smiled for Jerry and Finn. "Gentles, your meals will be served momentarily. Real food requires more than scorching." Even in her soiled whites, with her soft, brown hair pinned up under a chef's hat, Hastet looked really good to him.

So did the patty melt. Jay took a big bite, licked grease off his fingers, and nodded. "Not bad." He made the introductions while he chewed. "Dr. Finn, my wife, Hastet benasari Julali Ackroyd, the best Takisian cook on Earth. Honey, this is Bradley Finn, from the Jokertown Clinic. He used to work with Dr. Tachyon."

"I'll try not to hold that against him," Hastet said, looking Finn over carefully. "Are you always that splotchy green color or are you sick?" She turned on Jay before the startled centaur could reply. "I thought you were dead."

"Us?" Jay said. "No way. We're trained professional detectives. We hardly ever die. You got a bottle of ketchup?"

"You're very close to death right at this moment," Hastet warned him. "Your hunchback was here last week. He sprayed half my customers and the food critic from *Manhattan* magazine. Would you care to explain that?"

"Not especially," Jay admitted. "Jerry, how about you?"

Jerry Strauss cleared his throat. "Well, ah, actually," he began. Then something that looked like a ferret in drag popped up from behind Hastet's shoulder and *hissed* at him, all feathers and fangs. Jerry jumped a foot. "Get it away!" he screeched. The only thing that unnerved Jay's junior partner more than Jay's Takisian wife was Jay's Takisian wife's pet.

"Sorry," Hastet said. She crooned at the creature, soothing its blood-red feathers.

Finn was fascinated. "What is it?" he asked.

"A *wanei*," Jay said. "You like it? I'll bet Tacky can get you one of your own. You and Tachyon were really close, weren't you?"

"Not really. I admired him as a doctor. He taught me a lot. I can't say we ever socialized very much." Finn wrinkled up his face. "What's all this about Tachyon?"

"A little wrinkle on the case that I forgot to mention," Jay said. "You know, Doc, you strike me as the kind of guy who's always wanted to travel."

"I'm sick of traveling," Finn said. "I've been to Burma, Red China, Hong Kong, Australia, and jail. Right now, I just want to give Clara a kiss and get back to work at the clinic."

"You're not making this easy," Jay complained.

Finn stared at Jay as if he thought he was deranged. "Are you all right? Head injuries can be funny things. Maybe you should let me take some more X-rays."

"You don't have the time," Jay assured him. "Hastet, sweet, eighty-six that lunch order, will you? Dr. Finn won't be eating."

"I won't?"

"Course not," Jay said, shaping his right hand into a gun. "It's not even lunch time on Takis."

Finn's eyes grew huge. "Wait!" he began, *popping*.

Jerry was looking at him accusingly. "You really did it."

"I had to," Jay said. "The shamus code. I gave my word. There's honor among dicks, too."

"There is?"

"It's in all the movies," Jay assured him. "Don't look at me that way. It's not like they don't have spaceships. I sent him to Tachyon's bedroom, he'll be back before you can say . . . Well, he'll be back, anyway."

Hastet looked very annoyed. "Jay, I cannot believe you did that. You sent him to *Takis*! And without consulting me. You *know* how many spices I need." She stalked away angrily.

Jerry was chuckling. Jay glared at him. "What's so funny?"

"All those free meals," Jerry reminded him. "Finn stuck you with the check."

– – –

"Hannah? You're crying—did I forget something? I don't remember . . ."

Hannah straightened and sniffed. "Quasi," she said. "No, you didn't forget anything."

"Are you sure?" the hunchback asked desperately. "There was so much . . . Chemicals . . ."

"No," Hannah repeated. "No, darling. You did everything. Everything that could be done."

"You're crying for *him,* aren't you?" Quasiman said.

Hannah didn't answer. Her eyes filled again with tears and she wiped them away with her sleeve.

She sat on a hillside looking across to Jerusalem and the Temple Mount. The dawn splashed light across the white buildings of the city. The Dome of the Rock gave back a glittering, mocking answer, as if in defiance of the dark rubble set in the midst of the quarters sprawled below the mount. Jerusalem's New Temple: That's what some were already calling it— a monument to stupidity and hatred, a memorial to the several thousand who had died from the Black Trump before the Overtrump could be delivered to them.

"You loved him?"

Hannah nodded silently. "I think . . ." she said, and had to stop. "I don't know," she admitted after a moment. "I really don't know."

"It's my fault," Quasiman said. "If I could have *remembered* . . ." The hunchback stood with fisted hands tapping an uneven rhythm on his thighs.

Hannah took the hunchback's hands in her own, holding him. She stared into the joker's anguished eyes. "Stop it," she said. "You are not to blame. You did all you could do, and that was more than any of the rest of us could manage, except for Gregg . . ." She took him in her arms, pulling him to her and hugging him fiercely. She was crying again, helplessly, her tears falling on the hunchback's head as she stroked his hair, as she held on to him desperately. Slowly, his arms came around her, his embrace strangely gentle and tentative.

"Damn it!" she said, sobbing into his muscular shoulder. "Goddamn it!" Through the tears, through her grief, she could feel the joker go still and silent. Sniffing, she pulled back. When Hannah glanced at Quasiman, she saw that he'd slipped into a fugue. She put her arms around him again, watching as the sun rose over Jerusalem, as the last call to morning prayer echoed from the towers of the city's mosques, as the city awakened from night.

She wished she could wake herself. She should have left the city days ago. She wanted to. But something held her, made her stop each time she'd started to make the arrangements.

The sun slid over the shoulder of the Temple Mount, casting fingered shadows of Jerusalem's churches and temples that cupped the dark wound in the ancient city's heart. The emptiness there mocked her. "I wanted to love you," she whispered into its accusing silence. "It was my failure, not yours. All the rhetoric, all the talk and denial, but I couldn't love you the way I did once. I couldn't even say it."

"Who?" Quasiman stirred. "Hannah? Have I forgotten again?"

"Just someone I knew once," she answered, still watching the city, watching the slow light touch the lip of the crater.

"If you loved him, then he was a good person," Quasiman said. His hand touched her cheek. "And at least . . ."

"At least?" she asked.

"At least *you* can always remember," Quasiman told her. "If you can do that, you can always keep him alive." He tapped his temple with a forefinger. "Up here."

Hannah took his hand, cradled it against her face, and kissed the palm without answering. In the city, the ruined, tumbled stones were in full daylight now, and Hannah turned away from the reminder. She sighed holding Quasiman's hand.

"Let's go home," she said.

Closing Credits

STARRING	CREATED AND WRITTEN BY
Gregg Hartmann	Stephen Leigh
Jay (Popinjay) Ackroyd	George R. R. Martin
Mark (Cap'n Trips) Meadows	Victor Milan
Billy (Carnifex) Ray	John J. Miller
Zoe Harris	Sage Walker

CO-STARRING	CREATED BY
Quasiman	Arthur Byron Cover
Jerry (Mr. Nobody) Strauss	Walton Simons
Dr. Bradley Finn	Melinda M. Snodgrass
Hannah Davis	Stephen Leigh
April Harvest	John J. Miller
Croyd (the Sleeper) Crenson	Roger Zelazny
J. Robert (the Mechanic) Belew	Victor Milan
Needles, Jan, and Owl	Sage Walker

FEATURING	CREATED BY
Pan Rudo	Roger Zelazny
General MacArthur Johnson	Bob Wayne
O. K. Casaday	Victor Milan

Peter Pann	George R. R. Martin
Sascha Starfin	John J. Miller
Melissa (Topper) Blackwood	George R. R. Martin
Brigadier Sir Kenneth Foxworthy, aka Captain Flint	Kevin Andrew Murphy
The Black Dog	George R. R. Martin
Bobby Joe (Crypt Kicker) Puckett	Royce Wideman
John (the Highwayman) Bruckner	George R. R. Martin
Brandon van Renssaeler	Laura J. Mixon
Dr. Carter Jarnavon	Victor Milan
Balthazar Delacourt	Sage Walker

WITH	CREATED BY
Ditmar and Layton	Victor Milan
The Reflector (Snotman)	Walter Jon Williams
Charles Dutton	Walton Simons
Nur al-Allah	Stephen Leigh
President Leo Barnett	Arthur Byron Cover
Gary Bushorn	Stephen Leigh
Mick and Rick	John J. Miller
The Oddity	Stephen Leigh
Nephi (Straight Arrow) Callendar	Walter Jon Williams
Charon	Stephen Leigh
Lord Tung	George R. R. Martin
Eric Fleming	Laura J. Mixon
Lou (Osprey) Inmon	Victor Milan

About the Editor

George R. R. Martin is the #1 *New York Times* bestselling author of many novels, including those of the acclaimed series A Song of Ice and Fire—*A Game of Thrones, A Clash of Kings, A Storm of Swords, A Feast for Crows,* and *A Dance with Dragons*—as well as related works such as *Fire & Blood, A Knight of the Seven Kingdoms, The World of Ice & Fire,* and *Rise of the Dragon* (the last two with Elio M. García, Jr., and Linda Antonsson). Other novels and collections include *Tuf Voyaging, Fevre Dream, The Armageddon Rag, Dying of the Light, Windhaven* (with Lisa Tuttle), and *Dreamsongs Volumes I* and *II.* As a writer-producer, he has worked on *The Twilight Zone, Beauty and the Beast,* and various feature films and pilots that were never made. He lives with his lovely wife, Parris, in Santa Fe, New Mexico.

georgerrmartin.com
Facebook.com/GeorgeRRMartinofficial
X: @GRRMspeaking

About the Type

This book was set in Palatino, a typeface designed by the German typographer Hermann Zapf (b. 1918). It was named after the Renaissance calligrapher Giovanbattista Palatino. Zapf designed it between 1948 and 1952, and it was his first typeface to be introduced in America. It is a face of unusual elegance.